Virgil

Works - into English Prose

as near the original as the different idioms of the Latin and English languages will allow; with the Latin text and order of construction on the same page - Vol. 1

Virgil

Works - into English Prose
as near the original as the different idioms of the Latin and English languages will allow; with the Latin text and order of construction on the same page - Vol. 1

ISBN/EAN: 9783337367992

Printed in Europe, USA, Canada, Australia, Japan

Cover: Foto ©Andreas Hilbeck / pixelio.de

More available books at **www.hansebooks.com**

THE

WORKS

OF

VIRGIL

TRANSLATED INTO

ENGLISH PROSE,

As near the ORIGINAL as the different Idioms of the LATIN and ENGLISH LANGUAGES will allow.

WITH

The LATIN TEXT and ORDER of CONSTRUCTION on the same Page; and CRITICAL, HISTORICAL, GEOGRAPHICAL, and CLASSICAL NOTES, in ENGLISH, from the best COMMENTATORS both Ancient and Modern, beside a very great Number of Notes entirely New.

For the Use of SCHOOLS, as well as of PRIVATE GENTLEMEN.

IN TWO-VOLUMES.

A NEW EDITION.

VOL. I.

LONDON:

Printed by Assignment, from JOSEPH DAVIDSON,

For W. STRAHAN, J. F. and C. RIVINGTON, T. LONGMAN, B. LAW, C. DILLY, J. JOHNSON, G. G. J. and J. ROBINSON, R. BALDWIN, T. EVANS, J. BEW, T. VERNOR, S. HAYES, D. OGILVY, W. LOWNDES, and W. BENT.

MDCCLXXXV.

TO THE

GENTLEMEN

Who have the immediate Care of

EDUCATION.

GENTLEMEN,

AS the following Work was chiefly designed for the Use of Youth, it naturally claims your Patronage. It is generally allowed, that no *Latin* Author has a juster Title to be read in the Schools than *Virgil*. Other Poets have their Merit, and may be safely studied by Youth while they are under the Care of you, their faithful Guides, who, no doubt, will, in whatever Author you teach, guard your Pupils against the Influence of any Thing that has a Tendency to corrupt their Principles or Morals. But it must be owned, to the immortal Honour of *Virgil*, that his Style is so strictly pure and chaste, that the most raw and unexperienced might be left to steer their Course through the whole of his Works, without meeting with those Rocks and Quicksands, on which unpractised Virtue runs no small Hazard of being shipwrecked. Sure no Poet better deserves a Place than *Virgil* in his own *Elysium* among the *Pii Vates, Phœboque digna locuti*: For at the same Time that he is the just Standard for the Purity of the *Latin* Tongue, and universally admired for the sublimest Poetry, he is capable of inspiring the warmest Sentiments of Virtue. There is a peculiar Tenderneſs and Humanity diffuſed through all his Writings, which never fails to make the Heart better, and ſends away every well-diſpoſed Mind from the reading of him, equally pleaſed and improved. He animates the Soul to the Love of Virtue, by ſetting before us the moſt noble Examples; corrects the Paſſions, by ſhewing their fatal Effects, when indulged to Exceſs, or when directed to improper Objects; makes us feel the Peace and Serenity they bring, when conducted by Reaſon, and regulated within the Bounds of Prudence and Moderation. From him we learn the Force of Piety, and what powerful Incentives to Fortitude, and every heroic Virtue, ariſe from the Belief of a Deity, and a Providence ſupremely wiſe and good. In a word, every Image, every Deſcription, every Character he exhibits; his Fables, his Allegories, his Epiſodes, all are calculated not only to pleaſe the Fancy, but to inſtruct the Judgment, and form the Heart. The Peruſal of ſuch an Author, is like travelling through ſome delightful Country, not only diverſified with a Multiplicity of Scenes and Landſcapes, and whatever can charm the Senſe and Imagination; but where every Object conſpires to nouriſh Health and exhilarate the Spirits: No Enemies, no Beaſts of Prey lurk in ſecret Ambuſh to betray; no Fear of Robbers to aſſault with open Violence: The very Air we breathe in is pure, ſerene, and healthful; the People hoſpitable, honeſt, and humane. 'Tis hoped, therefore, that the following Attempt to facilitate the Study of ſo uſeful an Author, will be well received, Gentlemen, by you, who are Truſtees for the Public, in the important, and truly ſacred Work of Education.

It was far from being the Intention of this Work to encourage Idleneſs, or take away from Youth any Spur to their own Induſtry and Application; but to ſave them the Trouble of poring on Dictionaries, turning over many a heavy Volume of Commentaries, and wading through thorny unpleaſant Tracts to the Knowledge of mere Words. So that, if it ſaves their Time and Pains in one Way, it is only that they may be applied in another, that will be both more pleaſant and profitable to them. If it gives you ſome Relief from the more diſagreeable and burdenſome Part of your Work, it is only to leave you freer and more diſengaged in the Execution of what is the principal Buſineſs of Education. To teach Boys to underſtand an Author's Language, is, you know, but the leaſt Part of your Duty. To acquaint them with his Spirit and virtuous Deſign, to form their Taſte aright, that they may be able to correct his Faults and reliſh his Beauties, feel the Force of his pious or humane Sentiments, and learn to copy out his heroic Characters, and imitate his generous Examples; in a word, to teach them to be ſound Critics on Life and Manners, and to diſtinguiſh the True from the Falſe, *quid verum atque decens, quid pulchrum, quid turpe, quid utile, quid non*; this is your honourable Province, and the chief Deſign of Education. It was ſo in all the Schools of ancient *Athens*, where *Horace* was accompliſhed in the Study of that true Philoſophy, which is the Soul of all his Writings:

Adjecere bonæ paulo plus artis Athenæ:
Scilicet ut poſſem curvo dignoſcere rectum,
Atque inter ſilvas Academi quærere verum.

And it will be ſo in every well-regulated Seminary of Learning.

I would not willingly give Offence, nor ſay any Thing but what is agreeable to the Rules of ſtrict Decorum, and what the Occaſion itſelf naturally ſuggeſts: But if I ſhould appear animated with a more than ordinary Zeal in the Cauſe of Virtue, which is ſo nearly concerned in the right Education of Youth, it is what the preſent melancholy State of this Nation might well juſtify. I hope I may be allowed to ſay, without throwing the leaſt Reflection on any Man, far leſs on that Body of Men, moſt of whom belong to an Order for which I have a very ſincere Veneration; that there never was more urgent Neceſſity than at preſent for you to exert yourſelves with the greateſt Ardour and Fidelity in the Diſcharge of your important Truſt. You, by your very Profeſſion, are ſolemnly engaged to teach and exemplify Goodneſs to Mankind, at a Time of Life when they are moſt capable of being taught, when their docile Minds may eaſily be moulded to every Shape of Goodneſs, and are ſuſceptible of the moſt durable Impreſſions. From you, therefore, it may naturally be expected, that the general Reformation of the Age ſhould begin. Men of mere Speculation may wiſh well to Virtue, and recommend her Cauſe by their Writings; the witty Author may ridicule, or point his keen Satire againſt the reigning Vices of the Age; the Legiſlature may enact, and the Magiſtrate may execute ſalutary Laws; but what will all avail, unleſs the Foundations of National Virtue be laid in the right forming of the Heart at firſt? If the Fountains be foul and impure, all the Art of Man will not make the Streams run pure and unpolluted. The Scripture tells us, that the Tree muſt firſt be made good, and then its Fruits will be good alſo; but if the Tree be corrupt, the Fruit likewiſe will partake of the Corruption. The Seeds and Principles of Virtue are, by the Author of Nature, implanted in the Mind of every Man, and they only need due Culture to make them take deep Root, ſpring up, and flouriſh in the Soul, and ripen into all thoſe beautiful Fruits of Action, that are ornamental to human Nature and beneficial to Society. Indeed, Experience ſhews us, that the beſt Education is not of itſelf ſufficient to eſtabliſh the Mind in an habitual uniform Courſe of Integrity; yet the ſame Experience evinces, that nothing is of ſo much

Importance

Importance towards effecting this great End, as to give the Mind an early Turn and Bias to the right Side; and that, without this, all other Means, humanly ſpeaking, will have but a weak and tranſient Influence.

I doubt not but you are before hand with me in making Reflections of this Sort, and that your own Concern for the public Welfare has, long ere now, inſpired you with noble Reſolutions to improve the Opportunity you have of doing ſo much Good to your native Country. Go on, therefore, Gentlemen, in the Execution of ſo generous and laudable a Deſign; nurſe up thoſe Plants that are under your immediate Culture; oh! take care their tender Virtues be not nipped in the Bud. The Froſts of a few Winters will kill thoſe Weeds that poiſon and oppreſs the Soil; the barren Trees, that are an Incumbrance to the Ground, will wither with Age and ſoon be cut down; but on you, in a great Meaſure, depend our Hopes for many ſucceeding Years and Generations. If the Buds of the Spring be blaſted, or ſuffered to periſh, our joyful Proſpects, not only for that Seaſon, but for the whole Year, are loſt; and one Year propagates its malignant or happy Influence to another, in a perpetual Succeſſion.

If the following humble Performance be of uſe to ſhorten your Way in the Proſecution of ſo laudable a Deſign, particularly in inſpiring young Minds with thoſe pure, refined, and heroic Sentiments of Virtue and Honour, with which *Virgil* every where abounds; I ſhall reckon my Labour richly compenſated, and rejoice in your partaking of thoſe Rewards with which Virtue never fails to crown her honeſt Sons.

THE

L I F E

OF

V I R G I L.

VIRGIL was born at *Mantua*, in the firſt Conſulſhip of *Pompey* the Great, and *Licinius Craſſus*, in the Year of *Rome* DCLXXXIV. ſixty-nine Years before the Birth of our Saviour, on the fifteenth of *October*, which the *Latin* Poets obſerved annually in Commemoration of his Birth. His Father *Maro*, was but a mean Perſon of no Extraction; but his Mother, whoſe Name was *Maia*, was nearly related to *Quintilius Varus*, who was of an illuſtrious Family.

He paſſed the firſt ſeven Years of his Life at *Mantua*; thence he went to *Cremona*, where he lived to his ſeventeenth Year; at which Age, as is uſual among the *Romans*, he put on the *Toga Virilis*, *Pompey* and *Craſſus* happening that Year to be, a ſecond Time, Conſuls.

From *Cremona* he went to *Naples*, where he ſtudied the *Greek* and *Latin* Languages with the utmoſt Application and Aſſiduity: After that, he applied himſelf cloſely to the Study of Phyſic and the Mathematics, in which he made a very great Proficiency.

After he had ſpent ſome Years at *Naples*, he went from thence to *Rome*, where he was ſoon taken notice of by ſome of the great Men at Court, who ſhowed the high Eſteem they had of him by introducing him to *Auguſtus*. But whether *Virgil* did not like the Hurry and Buſtle of a Court a Court Life, or the Air of *Rome* did not agree with his ſickly Conſtitution, is uncertain; however, he retired again to *Naples*, where he ſet about writing his *Bucolics*, chiefly with a Deſign to celebrate the Praiſes of *Pollio*, *Varius*, and *Gallus*, who recommended him to *Mæcenas*, by whoſe Intereſt he was particularly exempted from the common Calamity of the poor *Mantuans*; whoſe Lands, as a Reward to the Veterans for their Bravery at the Battle of *Philippi*, were divided among them, *Virgil*'s only excepted, as appears by the firſt Eclogue, wherein he expreſſes the utmoſt Gratitude for ſo ſingular a Favour, in ſuch a Manner as ingratiated him more and more to *Auguſtus*. It is ſaid he ſpent three Years in writing his Eclogues; and had he ſpent as many more, the Time would have been well employed, that produced the fineſt Paſtorals in the *Roman*, or perhaps any other Language.

Italy being now reduced to the utmoſt Extremity, the Grounds lying uncultivated, and the People in Want of the very Neceſſaries of Life, the fatal but natural Conſequences of a Civil War, in ſo much that the State ſeemed to be in Danger, the People throwing all the Blame on *Auguſtus*; *Mæcenas*, ſenſible of the great Parts and unbounded Knowledge of *Virgil*, ſet him about writing the *Georgics* for the Improvement of Huſbandry, the only Mean left to ſave *Italy* from utter Ruin; in which *Virgil* ſucceeded ſo well, that after their Publication, *Italy* began to put on a new Face, and every Thing went well: For the *Georgics* are not only the moſt perfect of all *Virgil*'s Works, but the Rules for the Improvement of Huſbandry are ſo juſt, and at the ſame time ſo general, that they not only ſuited the Climate for which he wrote them, but have been found of ſuch extenſive Uſe, that the greateſt Part of them are put in Practice in moſt Places of the World at this very Day. *Virgil* was now thirty-four Years of Age; having ſpent ſeven of the prime of his Years in

compoſing

composing this inimitable Poem, which has been, and ever will be, admired as the most finished and complete Piece that ever Man wrote: For here indeed he shines in his Meridian Glory.

Having now finished his *Georgics*; after a few Years Respite, he set about the *Æneid*, when turned of forty; though it is generally believed he laid the Foundation of that great and arduous Work more early, to which he seems to allude in his sixth Pastoral:

Cum canerem reges & prœlia, Cynthius aurem
Vellit, & admonuit, pastorem, Tityre, pingues
Pascere oportet oves, deductum dicere carmen.

But when I try'd her tender Voice, too young,
And fighting Kings and bloody Battles sung,
Apollo check'd my Pride; and bid me feed
My fat'ning Flocks, nor dare beyond the Reed.

Virgil's Design of writing the *Æneid*, taking Air, the Expectations of the *Romans* were raised so high with the Thoughts of it, that *Sextus Propertius* did not scruple to prophesy,

Cedite Romani scriptores, cedite Graii,
Nescio quid majus nascitur Iliade!

And had *Virgil* designed the *Æneid* only as an Encomium on *Augustus*, he might surely have wrote short Panegyrics on his Prince, as *Horace* has done, at several Times, and on proper Occasions, at a far less Expence of Time and Labour than the *Æneid* must of Necessity have cost him: For he has not only given *Augustus*'s Character under that of *Æneas*, but has wrought into his Work the whole Compass of the *Roman* History, with that of the several Nations, from the earliest Times down to his own; and that with such Exactness as to deserve the Title of *The Roman Historian*,

Historian, much better than *Homer* did that of *Writer of the Trojan War:* Most *Romans*, in any controverted Point, submitting rather to his Authority than to the most learned Historian's.

The *Æneid* is an Epic Poem, which being the noblest Composition in Poetry, requires an exact Judgment, a fruitful Invention, a lively Imagination, and an universal Knowledge, all centering in one and the same Person, as they did in *Virgil*, whose prodigious Genius has been the Admiration of all Mankind, and will be so, while Learning and Good sense have a Place in the World. *Virgil* spent about seven Years in writing the first six Books of this admirable Poem, some part of which *Augustus* and *Octavia* longed to hear him rehearse, and hardly prevailed with him, after many Intreaties. *Virgil* to this Purpose pitches on the Sixth, which, not without Reason, he thought would affect them most; as in it he had, with his usual Dexterity, inserted the Funeral Panegyric of young *Marcellus* (who died a little before that), whom *Augustus* designed for his Successor, and was the Darling of his Mother *Octavia*, and of all the *Romans*; and as the Poet imagined, so it happened: For after he had raised their Passions by reciting these inimitable Lines,

O nate, ingentem luctum ne quære tuorum:
Ostendent terris hunc tantum fata, neque ultra
Esse sinent. Nimium vobis Romana propago
Visa potens, superi, propria hæc si dona fuissent.
Quantos ille virûm magnum Mavortis ad urbem
Campus aget gemitus! vel quæ, Tyberine, videbis
Funera, cum tumulum præterlabere recentem!
Nec puer Iliacâ quisquam de gente Latinos
In tantum spe tollet avos: nec Romula quondam
Ullo se tantum tellus jactabit alumno.
Heu pietas! heu prisca fides! invictaque bello
Dextera! non illi quisquam se impune tulisset

Obvius armato: ſeu cum pedes iret in hoſtem,
Seu ſpumantis equi foderet calcaribus armos.

He at laſt ſurprizes them with

Heu miſerande puer! ſi qua fata aſpera rumpas,
Tu Marcellus eris.

At which affecting Words the Emperor and *Octavia* burſt both into Tears, and *Octavia* fell into a Swoon. Upon her Recovery ſhe ordered the Poet ten Seſterces for every Line, each Seſterce making about ſeventy eight Pounds in our Money. A round Sum for the whole! but they were *Virgil*'s Verſes.

In about four Years more he finiſhed the *Æneid*, and then ſet out for *Greece*, where he deſigned to reviſe it as a Bye-work at his Leiſure; propoſing to devote the chief of the remaining Part of his Days to Philoſophy, which had been always his darling Study, as he himſelf informs us in theſe charming Lines;

Me vero primum dulces ante omnia Muſæ,
Quarum ſacra fero ingenti percuſſus amore,
Accipiant, cœlique vias & ſidera monſtrent;
Defectus ſolis, varios lunæque labores;
Unde tremor terris; qua vi maria alta tumeſcunt
Obicibus ruptis, rurſuſque in ſeipſa reſidunt.
Quid tantum Oceano properent ſe tingere ſolis
Hiberni, vel quæ tardis mora noctibus obſtet.

Ye ſacred Muſes, with whoſe Beauty fir'd,
My Soul is raviſh'd and my Brain inſpir'd,
Whoſe Prieſt I am, whoſe holy Fillets wear,
Wou'd you your Poet's firſt Petition hear:
Give me the Ways of wand'ring Stars to know,
The Depths of Heaven above and Hell below;
Teach me the various Labours of the Moon,
And whence proceed th' Eclipſes of the Sun;
Why flowing Tides prevail upon the Main,
And in what dark Receſs they ſhrink again;

What ſhakes the ſolid Earth, what Cauſe delays
The Summer-Nights, and ſhortens Winter-Days.

But he had not been long in *Greece*, before he was ſeized with a lingering Diſtemper. *Auguſtus* returning about this Time from his Eaſtern Expedition, *Virgil* was willing to accompany him home; but he no ſooner reached *Brunduſium* than he died there, in the Year of *Rome* DCCXXXV. and in the fifty-firſt Year of his Age, and was buried at *Naples*, where his Tomb is ſhewn to this Day.

He was tall and of a ſwarthy Complexion, very careleſs of his Dreſs, extremely temperate, but of a ſickly Conſtitution, being often troubled with a Pain in his Head and Stomach: He was baſhful to a Fault, and had a Heſitation in his Speech, as often happens to great Men, it being a rarely found that a very fluent Elocution and Depth of Judgment meet in the ſame Perſon.

He was one of the beſt and wiſeſt Men of his Time; and in ſuch popular *Eſteem*, that *one hundred thouſand Romans* roſe up when he came into the Theatre, ſhewing him the ſame Reſpect they did *Cæſar* himſelf: And as he was beloved in his Life, he was univerſally lamented at his Death. He went out of the World with that Calmneſs of Mind that became ſo great and good a Man, leaving *Auguſtus* his Executor, who committed the Care of publiſhing the *Æneid* to *Tucca* and *Varius*, ſtrictly charging them, neither to cancel, nor add one Word, nor ſo much as fill up the Breaks or Half Verſes.

A little before his Death, it is ſaid, he wrote this Inſcription for his Monument, which does him the more Honour, as it ſavours not in the leaſt of Oſtentation:

Mantua me genuit; Calabri rapuere; tenet nunc
Parthenope: Cecini paſcua, rura, duces.

I ſung, Flocks, Tillage, Heroes; *Mantua* gave
Me Life, *Brunduſium* Death, *Naples* a Grave.

PREFACE

TO THE

PASTORALS.

VIRGIL is univerſally allowed to have excelled all the *Roman* Poets in every kind of Poetry he attempted; and his Poems, which are juſtly eſteemed the moſt finiſhed Pieces of all Antiquity, ſhow how thoroughly he underſtood the human Paſſions, the Laws of Nations, the different Properties of Animals, the Secrets of Arts and Sciences, and of Nature itſelf. How many Proofs has he given in his *Paſtorals*, and other Poems, of his great Skill in the *Epicurean* Philoſophy, which he has almoſt intirely comprehended in his ſixth *Eclogue?* What a prodigious Knowledge muſt he have had of Huſbandry and Agriculture to give ſuch exact Precepts for them in his *Georgicks*, as not only ſuit *Italy*, but moſt Places in the World? How well was he verſed in all the Myſteries and Ceremonies of the *Pagan* Religion? What a complete Maſter muſt he have been of the *Roman* Hiſtory, to interweave the moſt material Parts of it into his *Æneid?* In ſhort, his Knowledge ſeems to have had no other Bounds than thoſe of univerſal Nature. But to be more particular:

Virgil may be ſaid to be the firſt who introduced PASTORALS among the *Romans*, which he copied after that great Maſter of *Greece*, *Theocritus*. This Kind of Poetry is of very great Antiquity, being practiſed by Men in the firſt Ages of the World, while they tended their Flocks: Then it was Nature taught them to amuſe

themſelves

themſelves with Pipes and Songs. They wanted not to hear the chirping of Birds in order to ſing; as the Zephyrs, whoſe Breath ſeems to animate Reeds and make them ſpeak, occaſioned their contriving the like Inſtruments, which were perfected by Uſe and Art. For there is no need to fetch from Mythology and uncertain Hiſtories, the Origin of a Thing which may be found in Nature; and the moſt learned Writers who looked for it out of Nature have not been ſatisfied with their Enquiries. The Paſtoral Life of ſome Nations produced Aſtronomical Obſervations, and placed in the Heavens ſome of thoſe Animals which grazed in the Fields. It has alſo occaſioned the Myſteries of judicial Aſtrology. But becauſe it generally produced Rural Songs, the Poets, who only mind what may pleaſe, pitched upon thoſe imperfect Eſſays, and improved them. They thought, not without Reaſon, that if they repreſented plain and harmleſs Shepherds in ſome ſhort dramatic Pieces, ſinging their Happineſs, or expreſſing their Trouble; ſuch Performances could not fail of having a good Succeſs. And indeed this Sort of Poetry is extremely pleaſant and more charming than any other: It does not contain dreadful Images of War and Battles; it does not ſtir ſad Paſſions by terrifying Objects, nor excites the natural Malignity of Men by ſatirical Expreſſions or ſtudied Imitation of Ridicule; but brings into their Thoughts the Happineſs of a quiet Life, which they are ſo far from enjoying. In one Word, nothing can be more proper to remove their Cares and calm the Uneaſineſſes of their Minds, becauſe nothing can have a greater Affinity with that Condition of Life that can make them happy.

And if it be aſked, why *Virgil*, in that remarkable Paſſage of the *Georgics*, wherein he deſcribes the Happineſs of a Country Life, ſays nothing of the Songs that take up the idle Hours of Shepherds; which Queſtion appears

appears the more natural as *Homer* never ſpeaks of the Country without mentioning rural Muſic; I anſwer, with a great Critic, that if *Homer* acted the Part of a good Poet in this Reſpect, deſcribing Things that had no Exiſtence but in his Imagination, *Virgil* did wiſely avoid a Fault which a mean Poet would have been guilty of; for the *Georgics* being a Work founded upon Truth, *Virgil* could not praiſe a Country Life on account of a Thing whoſe Charms are only in the Imagination of the Poets. On the contrary; becauſe he deſcribes that Life ſuch as it really is, attended with good Nature and Innocence; his Deſcription, adorned with all the Graces of Poetry, makes it ſo charming and agreeable, that thoſe who read his excellent Verſes with any Taſte, may ſo far forget themſelves as to think *Virgil* is to blame in preferring to it the Happineſs of a conſummate Philoſopher. It had been, therefore, an improper Thing for him to repreſent that State of Life otherwiſe. And, ſince he reckoned the Chaſtity of married People among the Advantages that attend a Country Life, *Caſta Pudicitiam ſervat Domus*, he was far from finding any Hapneſs in Love and Jealouſy, which afford the moſt agreeable Songs of Bucolic Poetry. Nor were the ancient Shepherds vulgar illiterate Perſons; but on the contrary, they were rich, powerful, and learned: Even Princes themſelves did not think it below them to tend Flocks, and mind Country Affairs; as appears from many Inſtances in ſacred Hiſtory, as *Jacob*, *David*, &c. and alſo from ſeveral Paſſages of our Author, as in *Eclogue* II.

Quem fugis, ah! demens? habitarunt Dii quoque Sylvas,
Dardaniuſque Paris.

Ah, cruel Creature, whom doſt thou deſpiſe?
The Gods to live in Woods have left the Skies.
And God-like *Paris*, in th' *Idean* Grove,
To *Priam*'s Wealth preferr'd *Oenone*'s Love. DRYDEN.

And

And in *Eclogue* X. beſide ſeveral other Places:

Stant & oves circum, noſtri nec pœnitet illas;
Nec te pœniteat pecoris, divine poëta;
Et formoſus oves ad flumina pavit Adonis.

The Sheep ſurround their Shepherd as he lies:
Bluſh not, ſweet Poet, nor the Name deſpiſe:
Along the Streams his Flocks *Adonis* fed,
And yet the Queen of Beauty bleſt his Bed. DRYDEN.

So that they cenſure *Virgil* without Ground, who blame him for introducing Philoſophy, and even ſomething of the Sublime into his Paſtorals; *a Paſtoral being the Imitation of a Shepherd conſidered in that Character:* And it may well be preſumed that ſuch Shepherds as have been mentioned, were both great Scholars and Philoſophers.

In a true Paſtoral, there muſt be an Air of Piety kept up through the Whole; the Characters ſhould repreſent the Innocence and Plainneſs of the ancient Shepherds: There muſt be alſo ſome little Plot. And the Scene, which is always, or at leaſt generally, a rural Landſkip, ought to take in Woods, Meadows, the Banks of Rivers and Fountains, and even ſometimes the Sea Shore. And as, in order to form a Landſkip, to pleaſe the Sight, a Painter takes particular Care to chuſe the moſt beautiful Productions of Nature, according to the Character he deſigns to draw; ſo a Paſtoral Poet ought to pitch upon a Scene ſuitable to his Subject; and what Scene more proper for Shepherds than to be ſeated on the matted Graſs amidſt beautiful Trees, blooming Shrubs, and purling Streams? Every Object ſo charming, that, when touched by ſo ſkilful a Hand as our Author, one is at a Loſs whether to lay down on the ſoft Graſs, pull the fragrant Blooms of the Shrubs, or quench his Thirſt in the clear Stream.

The

The Scene of a Paſtoral may alſo be charaſterized and embelliſhed, as our Author has done in theſe Verſes;

— — — — *Jamque Sepulchrum*
Incipit apparere Bianoris — — — —

which offers an ancient Sepulchre to the Sight, and produces a noble Effect in the Landſkip. The Sentences muſt not only be ſhort and lively, but the whole Piece ſo.

And, laſtly, there muſt be a Diverſity of Subjects, that the Paſtoral, like a beautiful Proſpect, may charm by its Variety: But, as in Plays, the Decorations of the Stage ought, in ſome Meaſure, to make Part of the Piece that is repreſented, by its Affinity with the Subject; ſo in a Paſtoral, the Scene, and what is ſaid by the Shepherds, ought to be united by a Kind of Uniformity, that Cheerfulneſs may not appear in a ſad Place, nor Melancholy and Deſpair in a ſmiling and pleaſant Scene.

Virgil obſerves all theſe Rules exactly, and far ſurpaſſes *Theocritus*, eſpecially where Judgment and Contrivance have the principal Part. How cloſe he keeps to all theſe Points, is particularly remarkable in the firſt *Eclogue*, which, as a modern Author juſtly obſerves, is a Standard for all Paſtorals. A beautiful Landſkip preſents itſelf to our View, a Shepherd, with his Flock around him, reſting ſecurely under a ſpreading Beach, which furniſhed the firſt Food to our Anceſtors. Another Shepherd in a quite different Situation of Mind and Circumſtances, the Sun ſetting, the Hoſpitality of the more fortunate Shepherd, *&c.*

All his Paſtorals are indeed admirable; but the fourth is the moſt remarkable, as it is a manifeſt Prophecy of our Bleſſed Saviour, uttered undeſignedly by *Virgil:* For it is evident, that from the *Sibylline* Verſes, then in great Repute at *Rome*, our Author applies to the Son of *Pollio* thoſe Predictions which are evidently meant of our Saviour. The ſixth is alſo well worth our particular Notice, in which

which he introduces *Silenus* singing, but rather too full of Inspiration, which is meant by the Ebriety, who relates the Mythology of near two thousand Years in fifty Lines; the Brevity of which is no less admirable than the Poet's great Skill in keeping up the Characters with the utmost Decency. The eighth and tenth are also very remarkable for the curious Descriptions the Poet gives of the Passion of Love: For what can be more natural than that in the eight Pastoral:

Sepibus in nostris parvam te roscida mala
(Dux ego vester eram) vidi cum matre legentem:
Alter ab undecimo tum nec jam ceperat annus,
Jam fragiles poteram à terra contingere ramos:
Ut vidi, ut perii, ut me malus abstulit error.

Thee, with thy Mother, in our Meads I saw
Gath'ring fresh Apples; I myself your Guide;
Then thou wert little; I, just then advanc'd
To my twelfth Year, could barely from the Ground
Touch with my reaching Hand the tender Boughs;
How did I look! how gaze my Soul away! TRAPP.

And never sure was sincere Love expressed in such moving Terms as those of *Gallus* to *Lycoris* in the tenth:

Hic gelidi fontes, hic mollia prata, Lycori,
Hic nemus, hic ipso tecum consumerer ævo.
Nunc insanus amor duri me Martis in armis
Tela inter media, atque adversos detinet hostes.
Tu procul à patria (nec sit mihi credere) tantum.
Alpinas, ah dura! nives, & frigora Rheni
Me sine sola vides. Ah te ne frigora lædant!
Ah tibi ne teneras glacies secet aspera plantas!

Come, see what Pleasures in our Plains abound;
The Woods, the Fountains, and the flow'ry Ground.
As you are beauteous, were you half so true,
Here could I live and love, and die with only you.

Now I to fighting Fields am ſent afar,
And ſtrive in Winter Camps with Toils of War;
While you, (alas, that I ſhould find it ſo!)
To ſhun my Sight, your native Soil forego,
And climb the frozen *Alps*, and tread th' eternal Snow.
Ye Froſts and Snows her tender Body ſpare,
Thoſe are not Limbs for Icicles to tear. DRYDEN.

Nor was a deſpairing Lover ever painted in ſuch lively Colours as in theſe beautiful Lines in the ſame Paſtoral:

Ibo, & Chalcidico quæ ſunt mihi condita verſu
Carmina, paſtoris Siculi modulabor avena.
Certum eſt in ſylvis, inter ſpelæa ferarum
Malle pati; teneriſque meos incidere amores
Arboribus: creſcent illæ; creſcetis amores.

For me, the Wilds and Deſerts are my Choice;
The Muſes, once my Care, my once harmonious Voice.
There will I ſing, forſaken and alone;
The Rocks and hollow Caves ſhall echo to my Moan.
The Rind of ev'ry Plant her Name ſhall know;
Add as the Rind extends, the Love ſhall grow.

And again,

Omnia vincit amor; & nos cedamus amori.

Love conquers all; and we muſt yield to Love.
DRYDEN.

Theſe are but a few of the Beauties of theſe inimitable Paſtorals; for it would be endleſs to enumerate all of them.

PREFACE

PREFACE

TO THE

GEORGICS.

VIRGIL in his Georgics imitates *Heſiod*; but it is generally agreed that he far exceeds him in every Reſpect. Some indeed have objected, that the *Georgics* are wrote in too ſublime a Style to be of Uſe to Huſbandmen, who are, generally ſpeaking, Men of little or no Literature: But they did not conſider, that *Virgil* wrote for a People whoſe Chief Magiſtrates had been Huſbandmen themſelves: *Lucius Cincinnatus* was found at the Plough when he was called to be Dictator; and *Fabricius*, *Curius*, and *Camillus*, were no leſs ſkilled in the Science of Huſbandry than they were in the Art of War.

In ſuch Eſteem were Huſbandmen among the *Romans*, that they highly reſented the leaſt Affront offered to any of them, of which we have an Inſtance in *Scipio Naſica*, Candidate for the Place of *Curule Edile*, who, meeting a plain Countryman, took him by the Hand, and aſked him his Vote; but finding his Hand very hard, *Prithee, Friend*, ſays he, *do you walk upon your Hands?* which ſo chagrined the Countryman, that he complained of the Affront, by which *Scipio* loſt the Edileſhip. *Virgil* could not therefore employ his fine Parts on a Subject more acceptable to the *Romans*, nor more uſeful to his Country, almoſt become waſte by the Civil Wars; he therefore ſuits himſelf to his Readers, inſtructing them while he entertains them, by making Choice of ſuch Precepts of this extenſive Science as give Opportunity for thoſe beautiful Deſcriptions and Images which are the very Spirit and Life of Poetry. And he ſhews no leſs Art in treating of theſe Precepts; for while we read them, we can ſcarcely help imagining ourſelves among the Fields and Woods, viewing agreeable Landſkips.

He begins his *Firſt Book* with giving us the Subject of each *Georgic*, which he comprehends in four Lines; and after a ſolemn Invocation of all the Gods who were any way related to his Subject, he makes this noble Compliment to *Auguſtus*, whom he addreſſes as a God:

Tuque adeo, quem mox quæ ſint habitura Deorum
Concilia, incertum eſt; urbiſne inviſere Cæſar,
Terrarumque velis curam; & te maximus orbis
Auctorem frugum, tempeſtatumque potentem
Accipiat, cingens maternâ tempora myrto:

— — — — — — — —

Da facilem curſum, atque audacibus annue cæptis:
Ignaroſque viæ mecum miſeratus agreſtes,
Ingredere, & votis jam nunc aſſueſce vocari.

And chiefly Thou, whoſe future Seat on high,
In what bright Council of the ſtarry Sky
Uncertain is; whether, great *Cæſar*, Thou
Wilt chuſe to watch o'er Cities here below,
Or on the Fields thy gracious Looks beſtow:
Parent of Fruits, and pow'rful of the Storm,
Mankind to thee ſhall ſacred Rites perform;
Throughout the mighty Orb the Empire own,
And with thy Mother's Boughs thy Temples crown.

— — — — — — — —

Thee

Thee I invoke: Do thou aſſiſt my Courſe,
And to the bold Attempt give equal Force;
Pity with me th' unſkilful Peaſant's Cares,
Begin your Reign, and hear ev'n now our Pray'rs.

Then he enters upon his Work, and ſhews the ſeveral Kinds of Tillage proper for each Soil, gives a Schedule of the Huſbandman's Tools, deſcribes the Changes of the Weather, and the Signs that forebode them: Then points out to the Huſbandman the Work proper for each Seaſon of the Year; when mentioning Autumn he takes Occaſion to give us that inimitable Deſcription of the Thunder-Storm:

— — — *Ruit arduus æther,*
Et pluviâ ingenti ſata læta, boumque labores
Diluit; implentur foſſæ, & cava flumina creſcunt
Cum ſonitu, fervetque fretis ſpirantibus æquor.
Ipſe Pater, media nimborum in nocte, coruſcâ
Fulmina molitur dextrâ: quo maxima motu
Terra tremit: fugere feræ, & mortalia corda
Per gentes humilis ſtravit pavor: ille flagranti
Aut Atho, aut Rhodopen, aut alta Ceraunia telo
Dejicit: ingeminant Auſtri, & denſiſſimus imber:
Nunc nemora ingenti vento, nunc litora plangunt.

Down ruſh the Skies, and with impetuous Rain,
Waſh out the Ox's Toil, and ſweep away the Grain:
The Dikes are fill'd: No Bounds the Torrents keep:
And with the boiling Surges boils the Deep:
Amidſt a Night of Clouds his glittering Fire,
And rattling Thunder hurls th' Eternal Sire:
Far ſhakes the Earth: Beaſts fly, and mortal Hearts
Pale Fear dejects; he with refulgent Darts,
Or *Rhodope*, or *Athos*' lofty Crown,
Or ſteep *Ceraunia*'s Cliffs ſtrikes headlong down:

The Rains condense: more furious *Auster* roars:
Now with vast Winds the Woods, now lashes he the Shores.

He then instances many of the Prodigies that happened near the Time of *Julius Cæsar*'s Death, and shuts up all with a Supplication to the Gods for the Safety of *Augustus*, and the Preservation of *Rome* in these charming Lines:

Di patrii Indigetes, & Romule, Vestaque mater,
Quæ Tuscum Tiberim & Romana palatia servas,
Hunc saltem everso juvenem succurrere seclo
Ne probibete: satis jam pridem sanguine nostro
Laomedonteæ luimus perjuria Trojæ.
Jam pridem nobis cæli te regia, Cæsar,
Invidet, atque hominum queritur curare triumphos.
Quippe ubi fas versum atque nefas, tot bella per orbem;
Tam multæ scelerum facies: non ullus aratro
Dignus honos: squallent abductis arva colonis,
Et curvæ rigidum falces conflantur in ensem.
Hinc movet Euphrates, illinc Germania bellum:
Vicinæ ruptis inter se legibus urbes
Arma ferunt: sævit toto Mars impius orbe.
Ut cum carceribus sese effudere quadrigæ,
Addunt se in spatia; & frustra retinacula tendens
Fertur equis auriga, neque audit currus habenas.

Ye home-born Deities, of mortal Birth!
Thou Father *Romulus*, and Mother *Earth*,
Goddess unmov'd! whose Guardian Arms extend
O'er *Tuscan Tiber*'s Course, and *Roman* Tow'rs defend;
With youthful *Cæsar* your joint Pow'rs engage,
Nor hinder him to save the sinking Age.
O! let the Blood already spilt, atone
For the past Crimes of curs'd *Laomedon*!
Heav'n wants thee there; and long the Gods, we [know,
Have grudg'd thee, *Cæsar*, to the World below:

Where

Where Fraud and Rapine, Right and Wrong confound,
Where impious Arms from every Part resound,
And monstrous Crimes in ev'ry Shape are crown'd.
The peaceful Peasant to the War is prest;
The Fields lie fallow in inglorious Rest:
The Plain no Pasture to the Flock affords,
The crooked Schythes are streigthen'd into Swords:
And there *Euphrates* her soft Offspring arms,
And here the *Rhine* rebellows with Alarms;
The neigh'bring Cities range on several Sides,
Perfidious *Mars* long-plighted Leagues divides,
And o'er the wasted World in Triumph rides.
So four fierce Coursers starting to the Race,
Scow'r thro' the Plain, and lengthen ev'ry Pace,
Nor Reins, nor Curbs, nor threat'ning Cries they fear,
But force along the trembling Charioteer. DRYDEN.

In the *Second Book* he shows the different Methods of raising Trees, to which he ascribes Oblivion, Ignorance, Wonder, Desire, and the like human Passions, which makes his Precepts very entertaining: Then he points out the Soils in which the several Plants thrive best: And thence takes occasion to run out into the Praises of *Italy*, in these admirable Words:

Sed neque Medorum silvæ, ditissima terra,
Nec pulcher Ganges, atque auro turbidus Hermus,
Laudibus Italiæ certent: non Bactra, neque Indi,
Totaque thuriferis Panchaïa pinguis arenis.
Hæc loca non tauri spirantes naribus ignem
Invertere, satis immanis dentibus hydri:
Nec galeis, densisque virûm seges horruit hastis:
Sed gravidæ fruges, & Bacchi Massicus humor
Implevere: tenent oleæque, armentaque læta.
Hinc bellator equus campo sese arduus infert:

Hinc

Hinc albi, Clitumne, greges; & maxima taurus
Victima sæpe tuo perfusi flumine sacro,
Romanos ad templa Deûm duxêre triumphos.
Hic ver assiduum, atque alienis mensibus æstas:
Bis gravidæ pecudes, bis pomis utilis arbos.
At rabidæ tigres absunt, & seva leonum
Semina: nec miseros fallunt aconita legentes:
Nec rapit immensos orbes per humum, neque tanto
Squameus in spiram tractu se colligit anguis.
Adde tot egregias urbes, operumque laborem:
Tot congesta manu præruptis oppida saxis:
Fluminaque antiquos subter labentia muros.
An mare, quod supra, memorem, quodque alluit infra?
Anne lacus tantos? te, Lari maxime; teque
Fluctibus & fremitu assurgens, Benace, marino?
An memorem portus, Lucrinoque addita claustra?
Atque indignatum magnis stridoribus æquor,
Julia qua ponto longe sonat unda refuso,
Tyrrhenusque fretis immittitur æstus Avernis?
Hæc eadem argenti rivos, ærisque metalla
Ostendit venis, atque auro plurima fluxit.
Hæc genus acre virûm, Marsos, pubemque Sabellam,
Assuetumque malo Ligurem, Volcosque verutos
Extulit: hæc Decios, Marios, magnosque Camillos,
Scipiadas duros bello; & te, maxime Cæsar,
Qui nunc extremis Asiæ jam victor in oris,
Imbellem avertis Romanis arcibus Indum.
Salve, magna parens frugum, Saturnia tellus:
Magna virûm: tibi res antiquæ laudis & artis
Ingredior, sanctos ausus recludere fontes:
Ascræumque cano Romana per oppida carmen.

But neither *Median* Woods, nor fertile Soil,
Nor pleasant *Ganges*, *Hermus*' Streams, which toil
Through Beds of Gold, nor *India*'s fragrant Lands,
Bactra, nor th' *Arab*'s Incense-bearing Sands;

All

All cannot, though all boaſt of ſomething rare,
With the juſt Praiſe of *Italy* compare.
Fire-breathing Bulls her Furrows never plough'd,
Nor ſown with Dragon's Teeth, from whence a Brood
Of infant Warriors ſtain'd with Brothers Blood.
Her Meads fair Cattle, Wheat o'erloads her Soil,
And ev'ry where ſhe ſtreams with Wine and Oil:
Her warlike Courſers beat the ſounding Earth,
And tread in Triumph her who gave them Birth:
Thou, gay *Clitumnus*, where thy Currents glide,
There bleating Flocks thy flow'ry Borders hide;
There Snow-white Bulls, the greateſt Sacrifice
Deſign'd for *Jove*, who rules the Deities,
Firſt waſh'd and ſprinkled with thy ſacred Flood,
Pay for the *Roman* Triumphs with their Blood;
Eternal Spring and Summer part her Year,
Her Ewes lamb twice, her Trees twice bloſſom bear:
No ſpotted Tygers in her Foreſts ſtray,
Nor roaring Lions on her Cattle prey,
Nor pois'nous Herbs the Gath'rer's Hand betray:
No noiſome Serpents, with collected Tail,
Wreath on the Ground, or ſpiral Volumes trail.
To works of Nature joins the Works of Man,
To ſhew, by Art improv'd, what Nature can;
Thoſe ſtately Towns from Marble Quarries torn,
Whoſe ancient Ramparts Chryſtal Streams adorn.
Or ſhall my Muſe the *Adrian*'s Praiſes ſhow,
Or *Tyrrhene* Seas which round her Harbours flow?
Shall I great *Larius* or *Benacus* ſing,
Thoſe Sea-like Lakes from whence great Rivers ſpring;
Or ſing the Harbours of the *Locrine* Bay,
Whoſe Moles oppoſe the raging of the Sea?
Which from the Waves the *Julian* Port confin'd,
When *Tyrrhene* Billows Lake *Avernus* join'd.

These Bleſſings are expos'd to ev'ry Eye;
But ſhe has Treaſures in her Entrails lie,
Which Veins of Silver and of Copper hold;
Her Hills are fruitful Caſks of ſhining Gold.
She many warlike Nations has brought forth;
She gave the *Marſians* and *Sabellians* Birth;
Ligurians, us'd to toil in Peace and War,
And the brave *Volſcians* arm'd with Dart and Spear.
From her the *Decii* and *Camilli* came,
With all the Worthies of the *Marian* Name,
The *Scipio's* too renown'd for martial Fame.
And laſt, Great *Cæſar*, great above the reſt,
Who bears victorious Eagles through the Eaſt,
Who all his bold Attempts with Conqueſt crowns,
And lazy *Indians* drives from *Roman* Towns!
Hail, Source of Wine and Corn, *Saturnian* Soil!
For whoſe dear Sake I undertook this Toil!
Eternal Lays of hid myſterious Things,
From ancient Art and Labour's ſecret Springs,
My Muſe, on *Heſiod's* Lyre, through *Roman* Cities ſings.

LAUDERDALE.

This Book is alſo remarkable for that beautiful Deſcription near the End of it, which the Poet gives us of the Pleaſures of a Country Life in theſe inimitable Lines:

O fortunatos nimium, ſua ſi bona nôrint,
Agricolas! quibus ipſa, procul diſcordibus armis,
Fundit humo facilem victum juſtiſſima tellus.
Si non ingentem foribus domus alta ſuperbis
Mane ſalutantum totis vomit ædibus undam;
Nec varios inhiant pulchra teſtudine poſtes,
Illuſaſque auro veſtes, Ephyreïaque æra;
Alba neque Aſſyrio fucatur lana veneno,
Nec caſiâ liquidi corrumpitur uſus olivi:

At

At ſecura quies, & neſcia fallere vita,
Dives opum variarum; at latis otia fundis,
Speluncæ, vivique lacus; at frigida Tempe,
Mugituſque boum, molleſque ſub arbore ſomni
Non abſunt. Illic ſaltus, ac luſtra ferarum,
Et patiens operum, parvoque aſſueta juventus,
Sacra Deûm, ſanctique patres: extrema per illos
Juſtitia excedens terris veſtigia fecit.

O! happy Swains! did they their Bliſs but know!
To whom the Earth releas'd from all the Woe
Of civil Broils, gives with a lib'ral Hand
An eaſy Plenty at their juſt Demand.
What if no lofty Pile, with haughty Tow'rs
A waving Throng, through ev'ry Paſſage pours
Of humble Waiters in the Morning Hours:
What if no Tortoiſe-ſcales incruſting Wood,
Nor *Corinth*'s Braſs amaze the gaping Crowd?
If no brocaded Hangings dreſs the Room?
Nor *Tyrian* Purple ſtain the Milk-white Loom?
Nor *Caſſia* taint pure Oil with ſtrong Perfume?
Yet fraudleſs Innocence, and peaceful Reſt,
Unbounded Plains, with endleſs Riches bleſt;
Yet Caves and living Springs, and airy Glades,
And the ſoft Lowe of Kine, and ſleepy Shades,
Are never wanting: There wild Herds abound,
And Youth inur'd to Toil and Thrift are found,
And aged Sires rever'd, and Altars crown'd:
There Juſtice left, when ſhe forſook Mankind,
The laſt Impreſſions of her Steps behind. B.

In the *Third Book*, after invoking ſome rural Deities, he raiſes a TEMPLE to the Honour of *Auguſtus*, more laſting than the Pyramids of *Egypt*.

Primus ego in patriam mecum, modo vita superſit,
Aonio rediens deducam vertice Muſas:
Primus Idumæas referam tibi, Mantua, palmas:
Et viridi in campo Templum *de marmore ponam*
Propter aquam, tardis ingens ubi flexibus errat
Mincius, & tenerâ prætexit arundine ripas.
In medio mihi Cæſar *erit, Templumque tenebit.*
Illi victor ego, & Tyrio conſpectus in oſtro,
Centum quadrijugos agitabo ad flumina currus.
Cuncta mihi, Alpheum linquens, lucoſque Molorchi,
Curſibus, & crudo decernet Græcia cæſtu.
Ipſe caput tonſæ foliis ornatus olivæ
Dona feram. Jam nunc ſolennes ducere pompas
Ad delubra juvat, cæſoſque videre juvencos:
Vel ſcena ut verſis diſcedat frontibus; utque
Purpurea intexti tollant aulæa Britanni.
In foribus pugnam ex auro ſolidoque elephanto
Gangaridum faciam, victoriſque arma Quirini:
Atque hic undantem bello, magnumque fluentem
Nilum, ac navali ſurgentes ære columnas.
Addam urbes Aſiæ domitas, pulſumque Niphatem,
Fidentemque fugâ Parthum, verſiſque ſagittis;
Et duo rapta manu diverſo ex hoſte trophæa,
Biſque triumphatas utroque ab littore gentes.
Stabunt & Parii lapides, ſpirantia ſigna,
Aſſaraci proles, demiſſæque ab Jove gentis
Nomina, Troſque parens, & Trojæ Cynthius auctor.
Invidia infelix furias amnemque ſeverum
Cocyti metuet, tortoſque Ixionis angues,
Immanemque rotam, & non exſuperabile ſaxum.

I firſt of *Romans* ſhall in Triumph come
From conquer'd *Greece*, and bring her Trophies home:

With

With foreign Spoils adorn my native Place;
And with *Idume*'s Palms my *Mantua* grace.
Of *Parian* Stone a TEMPLE will I raise,
Where the slow *Mincius* through the Valley strays;
Where cooling Streams invite the Flocks to drink;
And Reeds defend the winding Water's Brink.
Full in the Midst shall mighty CÆSAR stand,
Hold the chief Honours, and the Dome command.
Then I, conspicuous in my *Tyrian* Gown
(Submitting to his Godhead my Renown),
A hundred Coursers from the Goal will drive;
The Rival Chariots in the Race shall strive.
All *Greece* shall flock from far, my Games to see;
The Whorlbat, and the rapid Race shall be
Reserv'd for *Cæsar*, and ordained by me.
Myself, with Olive crown'd, the Gifts will bear:
Ev'n now, methinks, the public Shouts I hear;
The passing Pageants, and the Pomps appear.
I, to the *Temple* will conduct the Crew;
The Sacrifice and Sacrificers view:
From thence return, attended with my Train,
Where the proud Theatres disclose the Scene;
Which interwoven *Britains* seem to raise,
And shew the Triumph which their Shame displays.
High o'er the Gate, in Ivory and Gold,
The Crowd shall *Cæsar*'s *Indian* War behold;
The *Nile* shall flow beneath, and on the Side
His shatter'd Ships on brazen Pillars ride.
Next him *Niphates* with inverted Urn,
And dropping Sedge, shall his *Armenia* mourn;
And *Asian* Cities in our Triumph born.
With backward Bows the *Parthians* shall be there,
And, spurring from the Fight confess their Fear.
A double Wreath shall crown our *Cæsar*'s Brows;
Two differing Trophies from two different Foes.

Europe

Europe with *Afric* in his Fame ſhall join;
But neither Shore his Conqueſt ſhall confine.
The *Parian* Marble, there, ſhall ſeem to move
In breathing Statues, not unworthy *Jove*;
Reſembling Heroes, whoſe etherial Root
Is *Jove* himſelf, and *Cæſar* is the Fruit.
Tros and his Race the Sculptor ſhall employ;
And he, the God, who built the Walls of *Troy*.
Envy herſelf, at laſt, grown pale and dumb
(By *Cæſar* combated and overcome),
Shall give her Hands; and Fear the curling Snakes
Of laſhing Furies, and the burning Lakes:
The Pains of famiſh'd *Tantalus* ſhall feel;
And *Syſiphus* that labours up the Hill
The rolling Stone in vain, and curs'd *Ixion*'s Wheel.

DRYDEN.

He then addreſſes himſelf to *Mæcenas*, and enters upon his Subject, in which he lays down Rules for the Choice and Breeding of all Sorts of Cattle, Oxen, Horſes, &c. whence he takes Occaſion to give this inimitable Deſcription of that noble Animal the Horſe:

Continuò pecoris generoſi pullis in arvis
Altius ingreditur, & mollia crura reponit:
Primus & ire viam, & fluvios tentare minaces
Audet, & ignoto ſeſe committere ponti:
Nec vanos horret ſtrepitus. Illi ardua cervix,
Argutumque caput, brevis alvus, obeſaque terga:
Luxuriatque toris animoſum pectus: honeſti
Spadices, glaucique; color deterrimus albis,
Et gilvo. Tum, ſiqua ſonum procul arma dedere,
Stare loco neſcit; micat auribus, & tremit artus;
Collectumque premens volvit ſub naribus ignem:
Denſa juba, & dextro jactata recumbit in armo.
At duplex agitur per lumbos ſpina, cavatque
Tellurem, & ſolido graviter ſonat ungula cornu.

The

The Colt that for a Sire is design'd;
By sure Presages shows his generous Kind
Of able Body, sound of Limb and Wind.
Upwards he walks, on Pasterns firm and straight;
His Motions easy; prancing in his Gait.
The first to lead the Way, to tempt the Flood;
To pass the Bridge unknown, nor fear the trembling Wood.
Dauntless at empty Noises; lofty neck'd;
Slender his Head, his Belly round, broad back'd.
Brawny his Chest and deep, his Colour grey;
For Beauty dappled, or the brightest Bay:
Faint White and Dun will scarce the Rearing pay.
The fiery Courser, when he hears afar,
The sprightly Trumpets and the Shouts of War,
Pricks up his Ears; and trembling with Delight,
Shifts Place, and paws, and hopes the promis'd Fight.
On his right Shoulder his thick Main reclin'd,
Ruffles at Speed, and dances in the Wind.
His horny Hoofs are jetty black and round;
His Chine is double: Starting with a Bound
He turns the Turf, and shakes the solid Ground.
Fire from his Eyes, Clouds from his Nostrils flow:
He bears his Rider headlong on the Foe. DRYDEN.

Nor has the Poet shown less Skill in that curious Description of the Chariot Race.

Nonne vides? cum præcipiti certamine campum
Corripuere, ruuntque effusi carcere currus;
Cum spes arrectæ juvenum, exsultantiaque haurit
Cordia pavor pulsans: illi instant verbere torto,
Et proni dant lora: volat vi fervidus axis.
Jamque humiles, jamque elati sublime videntur
Aëra per vacuum ferri, atque assurgere in auras.

Nec mora, nec requies: at fulvæ nimbus arenæ
Tollitur: humescunt spumis, flatuque sequentum:
Tantus amor laudum, tantæ est victoria curæ.

Hast thou beheld, when from the Goal they start,
The youthful Charioteers with heaving Heart
Rush to the Race; and panting, scarcely bear
Th' Extremes of fev'rish Hope, and chilling Fear;
Stoop to the Reins, and lash with all their Force;
The flying Chariot kindles in the Course:
And now a-low; and now aloft they fly,
As born thro' Air, and seem to touch the Sky.
No Stop, no Stay, but Clouds of Sand arise,
Spurn'd, and cast backward on the Followers Eyes;
The hindmost blows the Foam upon the first:
Such is the Love of Praise, an honourable Thirst.

DRYDEN.

The Force of Love is represented in Words most expressive, and yet so modest as not to offend the chastest Ear. The Battle of the Bulls too is painted in most lively Colours, in these beautiful Lines:

Illi alternantes multâ vi prælia miscent
Vulneribus crebris: lavit ater corpora sanguis,
Versaque in obnixos urgentur cornua vasto
Cum gemitu: reboant sylvæque & magnus Olympus.
Nec mos bellantes una stabulare: sed alter
Victus abit, longeque ignotus exsulat oris:
Multa gemens ignominiam, plagasque superbi
Victoris; tum quos amisit inultus amores:
Et stabula aspectans regnis excessit avitis.
Ergo omni curâ vires exercet, et inter
Dura jacet pernox instrato saxa cubili,
Frondibus hirsutis, & carice pastus acutâ:

Et

Et tentat sese, atque irasci in cornua discit
Arboris obnixus trunco, ventosque lacessit
Ictibus, & sparsâ ad pugnam proludit arenâ,
Post, ubi collectum robur, viresque receptæ,
Signa movet, præcepsque oblitum fertur in hostem:
Fluctus ut, in medio cœpit cum albescere ponto,
Longius ex altoque sinum trahit: utque volutus
Ad terras, immane sonat per saxa, nec ipso
Monte minor procumbit: at ima exæstuat unda
Verticibus, nigramque altè subjectat arenam.

A beauteous Heifer in the Wood is bred;
The stooping Warriors, aiming Head to Head,
Engage their clashing Horns; with dreadful Sound
The Forest rattles, and the Rocks rebound.
They fence, they push, and pushing loudly roar;
Their Dewlaps and their Sides are bath'd in Gore;
Nor when the War is over, is it Peace;
Nor will the vanquish'd Bull his Claim release:
But feeding in his Breast his ancient Fires,
And cursing Fate, from his proud Foe retires.
Driv'n from his native Land, to foreign Grounds,
He with a gen'rous Rage resents his Wounds:
His ignominious Flight, the Victor's Boast,
And more than both, the Loves, which unreveng'd he lost.
Often he turns his Eyes, and, with a Groan,
Surveys the pleasing Kingdoms, once his own.
And therefore, to repair his Strength he tries:
Hard'ning his Limbs with painful Exercise;
And rough upon the flinty Rock he lies.
On prickly Leaves, and on sharp Herbs he feeds,
Then to the Prelude of a War proceeds.
His Horns, yet sore, he tries against a Tree:
And meditates his absent Enemy.

He ſnuffs the Wind, his Heels the Sand excite:
But, when he ſtands collected in his Might,
He roars, and promiſes a more ſucceſsful Fight.
Then to redeem his Honour at a Blow,
He moves his Camp, to meet his careleſs Foe.
Not with more Madneſs, rolling from afar,
The ſpumy Waves proclaim the wat'ry War,
And, mounting upwards with a mighty Roar,
March onwards, and inſult the rocky Shore.
They mete the middle Region with their Height;
And fall no leſs, than with a Mountain's Weight:
The Waters boil, and, belching from below,
Black Sands, as from a forceful Engine, throw.

DRYDEN.

But who can read the admirable Deſcription of the *Scythian* Winter Piece without ſhivering?

At non, Scythiæ gentes, Mæoticaque unda,
Turbidus & torquens flaventes Iſter arenas:
Quaque redit medium Rhodope porrecta ſub axem:
Illic clauſa tenent ſtabulis armenta; neque ullæ
Aut herbæ campo apparent, aut arbore frondes:
Sed jacet aggeribus niveis informis, & alto
Terra gelu late, ſeptemque aſſurgit in ulnas.
Semper heyms, ſemper ſpirantes frigora Cauri.
Tum Sol pallentes haud unquam diſcutit umbras:
Nec cum invectus equis altum petit æthera; nec cum
Præcipitem Oceani rubro lavit æquore currum.
Concreſcunt ſubitæ currenti in flumine cruſtæ:
Undaque jam tergo ſerratos ſuſtinet orbes,
Puppibus illa prius patulis, nunc hoſpita plauſtris.
Æraque diſſiliunt vulgo, veſteſque rigeſcunt
Inditæ, cæduntque ſecuribus humida vina,
Et totæ ſolidam in glaciem vertere lacunæ,
Stiriaque impexis induruit horrida barbis.

Interea

Interea toto non ſecius aëre ningit:
Intereunt pecudes: ſtant circumfuſa pruinis
Corpora magna boum: confertoque agmine cervi
Torpent mole novâ, & ſummis vix cornibus exſtant.
Hos non immiſſis canibus, non caſſibus ullis,
Puniceæve agitant pavidos formidine pennæ:
Sed fruſtra oppoſitum trudentes pectore montem,
Cominus obtruncant ferro; graviterque rudentes
Cædunt; & magno læti clamore reportant.
Ipſi in defoſſis ſpecubus, ſecura ſub altâ
Otia agunt terrâ, congeſtaque robora, totaſque
Advolvere focis ulmos, ignique dedere:
Hic noctem ludo ducunt, & pocula læti
Fermento, atque acidis imitantur vitea ſorbis.
Talis Hyperboreo ſeptem ſubjecta trioni
Gens effrena virûm Riphæo tunditur Euro:
Et pecudum fulvis velantur corpora ſetis.

Not ſo the *Scythian* Shepherd tends his Fold;
Nor he who bears in *Thrace* the bitter Cold:
Nor he who treads the bleak *Meotian* Strand;
Or where proud *Iſter* rolls his yellow Sand.
Early they ſtall their Flocks and Herds; for there
No Graſs the Fields, no Leaves the Foreſts wear:
The frozen Earth lies bury'd there, below
A hilly Heap, ſeven Cubits deep in Snow;
And all the Weſt Allies of ſtormy *Boreas* blow:
The Sun from far peeps with a ſickly Face;
Too weak the Clouds, and mighty Fogs to chace;
When up the Skies he ſhoots his roſy Head;
Or in the ruddy Ocean ſeeks his Bed,
Swift Rivers are with ſudden Ice conſtrain'd;
And ſtudded Wheels are on its Back ſuſtain'd.
An Hoſtry now for Waggons, which before
Tall Ships of Burden on its Boſom bore.

The brazen Cauldrons, with the Froſt are flaw'd;
The Garment, ſtiff with Ice, at Hearths is thaw'd;
With Axes firſt they cleave the Wine, and thence
By Weight, the ſolid Portions they diſpenſe.
From Locks uncomb'd, and from the frozen Beard,
Long Icicles depend, and crackling Sounds are heard.
  Meantime perpetual Sleet, and driving Snow,
Obſcure the Skies, and hang on Herds below;
The ſtarving Cattle periſh in their Stalls,
Huge Oxen ſtand inclos'd in wint'ry Walls
Of Snow congeal'd; whole Herds are bury'd there
Of mighty Stags, and ſcarce their Horns appear.
The dex'trous Huntſman wounds not theſe afar,
With Shafts, or Darts, or makes a diſtant War
With Dogs, or pitches Toils to ſtop their Flight;
But cloſe engages in unequal Fight.
And while they ſtrive in vain to make their Way
Through Hills of Snow, and pitifully bray,
Aſſaults with Dint of Sword, or pointed Spears;
And homeward on his Back, the joyful Burden bears.
The Men to ſubterranean Caves retire;
Secure from Cold, and crowd the cheerful Fire:
With Trunks of Elms and Oaks the Hearth they load,
Nor tempt th' Inclemency of Heaven abroad;
Their jovial Nights in Frolicks and in Play
They paſs, to drive the tedious Hours away;
And their cold Stomachs with crown'd Goblets cheer,
Of windy Cyder, and of barmy Beer.
Such are the cold *Riphean* Race; and ſuch
The Savage *Scythian*, and unwarlike *Dutch*.
Where Skins of Beaſts the rude Barbarians wear,
The Spoils of Foxes, and the furry Bear.

DRYDEN.

The

The Murrain that raged among the Cattle on the *Alps*, with which he concludes this Book, is likewise represented in most sublime Expressions, and can never be enough admired.

But of all the Books of the *Georgics*, *Virgil* seems to have exerted his Skill more especially on the *Fourth:* Nor, had he ransacked all Nature, could he possibly have made Choice of a Subject more curious, or more adapted to his Purpose than that of the Bees, if, as an ingenious Author observes, he had it in his View to recommend to the *Romans* Obedience to the Prince, and Submission to the Laws both to Prince and People, by the Example of these wonderful Creatures; neither could any Subject promise fairer to have a due Influence on the *Romans*, as they had a religious Veneration for Bees, and looked upon them as peculiarly consecrated to *Jupiter*. Indeed the Polity and Government of the Bees is vastly surprising, nor are there any other Creatures in the World, Men excepted, that have any such Thing.

Solæ communes natos, consortia tecta
Urbis habent, magnisque agitant sub legibus ævum:
Et patriam solæ, & certos novere penates.

Of all the Race of Animals alone,
The Bees have common Cities of their own,
And common Sons, they're rul'd by mighty Laws,
Their Country and their Gods the common Cause.

And what Obedience the *Romans* were to pay to *Augustus*, *Virgil* shews them by that of the Bees to their King, who do not think even their Lives too dear for him.

Pretærea regem non sic Ægyptus, & ingens
Lydia, nec populi Parthorum, aut Medus Hydaspes,
Observant. Rege incolumi, mens omnibus una est;
Ille operum custos, illum admirantur, & omnes
Circumstant fremitu denso, stipantque frequentes,

Et ſæpe attollunt humeris, & corpora bello
Objectant, pulchramque petunt per vulnera mortem.

Beſides, nor *Egypt*, nor the boundleſs Space
Of *Lydia*'s Empire, nor the *Parthian* Race,
Nor whom *Hydaſpes* cools with *Median* Springs,
Pay ſuch ſincere Obedience to their Kings;
While he is ſafe, in Concord and Content
The Commons live, by no Diviſions rent.
He rules their Works, all him admire alone,
And ſtrut around him with a humming Tone.
They raiſe him on their Shoulders with a Shout:
And when their Sovereign's Quarrel calls them out,
His Foes to mortal Combat they defy,
And think it Honour at his Feet to die.

Nor did ever the Armies of *Æneas* and *Turnus* make a more ſolemn Preparation for Battle than they: For, if a Difference happens between two Kings, they hum a hoarſe Alarm, reſembling the broken Sound of a Trumpet, upon which they aſſemble together, prepare their Wings, whet their Stings, and ſharpen their Claws, then repair to their King's Pavilion, and attend him to the Field of Battle. On Sight of their Enemies, they challenge them by making a loud Noiſe, and engage with the greateſt Courage and Bravery, reſolved to conquer or die; of which *Virgil* has given this moſt beatiful Deſcription:

Sin autem ad pugnam exierent (nam ſæpe duobus
Regibus inceſſit magno diſcordia motu)
Continuoque animos vulgi, & trepidantia bello
Corda licet longe præſciſcere: namque morantes
Martius ille æris rauci rancor increpat; & vox
Auditur, fractos ſonitus imitata tubarum.
Tum trepidæ inter ſe coëunt, penniſque coruſcant,
Spiculaque exacuunt roſtris, aptantque lacertos;

Et

Et circa regem atque ipſa ad prætoria denſæ
Miſcentur, magniſque vocant clamoribus hoſtem.
Ergo ubi ver nactæ ſudum, campoſque patentes,
Erumpunt portis; concurritur: æthere in alto
Fit ſonitus: magnum miſtæ glomerantur in orbem,
Præcipiteſque cadunt: non denſior aëre grando,
Nec de concuſſa tantum pluit ilice glandis.
Ipſi per medias acies, inſignibus alis,
Ingentes animos anguſto in pectore verſant:
Uſque adeo obnixi non cedere, dum gravis, aut hos,
Aut hos, verſa fugâ victor dare terga ſubegit.

But if to Battle jarring Swarms draw out,
For oft two mighty Kings their Rights diſpute,
Which ſoon inflames both Nations to the War,
You'll hear them chide the lazy from afar;
And warlike Noiſes thro' their Camps rebound,
Like the hoarſe Clangor of the Trumpet's Sound:
They run to Arms, and ruſtle with their Wings,
They ply their nimble Joints, and whet their Stings;
Their King and royal Tent arm'd Crowds incloſe,
And with loud Cries provoke the ling'ring Foes:
A Day for Battle when both Armies find,
Serene from Clouds, and undiſturb'd by Wind;
Then from their Camps they ruſh high in the Air,
And the ſhrill ſounding Charge is heard afar;
They glow with Anger, and with Fury ſhine,
They charge, both Bodies in one Cluſter join:
Thick fall the Dead as Acorns, thick as Hail,
Both Sides each other with ſuch Rage aſſail;
The glitt'ring Kings both Armies Courage fire,
Their little Bodies mighty Minds inſpire:
So bent to conquer, and ſo loath to yield,
Till one has beat the other from the Field.

LAUDERDALE.

Virgil

Virgil then lays down two Rules to hinder the Bees from wandering and leaving their Homes. The first is to clip their King's Wings; and the next to plant Orchards near them, and Gardens well stocked with all manner of Herbs and Flowers; whence he takes Occasion to give us a beautiful Platform of a little Garden, and instances the vast Advantage an old *Corycian*'s Bees had over those of his Neighbours, and the great Benefit that accrued to himself, by the singular Care he took of his Garden, whereby his Bees yielded him great Plenty of fine Honey, more early than any in the Country.

Atque equidem, extremo ni jam sub fine laborum
Vela traham, & terris festinem advertere proram;
Forsitan & pingues hortos quæ cura colendi
Ornaret, canerem, biferique rosaria Pæsti:
Quoque modo potis gauderent intyba rivis,
Et virides apio ripæ, tortusque per herbam
Cresceret in ventrem cucumis: nec sera comantem
Narcissum, aut flexi tacuissem vimen acanthi,
Pallentesque ederas, & amantes litora myrtos.
Namque sub Oebaliæ memini me turribus altis,
Qua niger humectat flaventia culta Galesus,
Corycium vidisse senem: cui pauca relicti
Jugera ruris erant; nec fertilis illa juvencis,
Nec pecori opportuna seges, nec commoda Baccho.
Hic rarum tamen in dumis olus, albaque circum
Lilia, verbenasque premens, vescumque papaver,
Regum æquabat opes animis: seráque revertens
Nocte domum, dapibus mensas onerabat inemtis.
Primus vere rosam, atque autumno carpere poma;
Et cum tristis hyems etiam nunc frigore saxa
Rumperet, & glacie cursus frænaret aquarum;
Ille comam mollis jam tum tondebat acanthi,

Æstatem

Æstatem increpitans seram, Zephyrosque morantes.
Ergo apibus fœtis idem atque examine multo
Primus abundare; & spumantia cogere pressis
Mella favis: illi tiliæ, atque uberrima pinus:
Quotque in flore novo pomis se fertilis arbos
Induerat, totidem autumno matura tenebat.
Ille etiam seras in versum distulit ulmos,
Eduramque pyrum, & spinos jam pruna ferentes
Jamque ministrantem platanum potantibus umbras.

But that my rural Labour's near an End,
Since to the Port with falling Sails I tend;
I would *Pomona* and her Treasure sing,
And how bright *Flora* beautifies the Spring;
How twice a Year the fam'd *Lucanian* Rose,
Near *Pæstum* blooms; how creeping Parsley grows,
And Succory, which wat'ry Banks inclose.
To raise Acanthus and the Daffodil,
How bending Cucumbers their Bellies fill;
How Ivy Twigs the Trunks of Trees surround,
And *Venus'* Myrtles on the Shore abound.
For once I knew an old *Corycian* Swain,
Where deep *Galesus* wets *Tarentum*'s Plain,
Heir to few Acres of a barren Field,
Which neither Wine, nor Corn, nor Grass did yield;
He Coleworts planted, Vervain, Poppy sow'd;
Where Thorns once grew, his Beds of Lillies stood:
When he return'd at Night, with Plenty stor'd,
His unbought Dishes heap'd his homely Board,
Nor envy'd he the Wealth which royal Courts afford.
First in the Spring he blushing Roses sees,
In Autumn first unloads his fruitful Trees;
When Winter cleaves the Rocks, and Nature pains,
And Rivers languish under icy Chains,
He gathers Cotton from th' *Egyptian* Thorn,
Chiding the ling'ring Spring, and *Phœbus'* slow Return.

His Grounds with Pines and fragrant Limes are fill'd,
His Bees, the firſt of all the flow'ry Field,
Produce their young, the firſt their Honey yield.
And all the Bloſſoms which his Orchards bear,
Rip'n into Fruit, when Harveſt crowns the Year:
He plants his Pear-trees and his Elms in Rows;
The Damaſk Plum on Thorns ingrafted grows;
His ſpreading Planes their pleaſant Shade extend,
Where he enjoys his Bottle and his Friend.

LAUDERDALE.

He then proceeds to ſhew the great Oeconomy of the Bees, their unwearied Induſtry, and the Way to come at their Honey without deſtroying them quite: but if they ſhould happen to be all deſtroyed, he ſhows the Method how to reſtore their Kind, in the charming Epiſode of *Ariſtæus* recovering his Bees, with which he concludes theſe admirable Poems.

Theſe and innumerable other Beauties, obvious to every judicious Reader, have gained the GEORGICS the Eſteem and Admiration of all Ages, as the moſt finiſhed Pieces of all Antiquity: For who can help being charmed with the agreeable Manner in which the Poet lays down his Precepts, the Juſtneſs of his Sentiments, the Delicacy of his Thoughts, the Sublimity of his Expreſſion, and the inexpreſſible Beauty of his Deſcriptions? So that we may well ſay in the Poet's own Words,

Tale tuum carmen nobis, divine Poëta
Quale ſopor feſſis in gramine; quale per æſtum
Dulcis aquæ ſaliente ſitim reſtinguere rivo.
Nam neque me tantum venientis ſibilus Auſtri,
Nec percuſſa juvant fluctu tam litora, nec quæ
Saxoſas inter decurrunt flumina valles.

O heav'nly Poet! ſuch thy Verſe appears,
So ſweet, ſo charming to my raviſh'd Ears,

As

As to the weary Swain, with Cares opprest,
Beneath the sylvan Shade, refreshing Rest:
As to the fev'rish Traveller, when first
He finds a crystal Stream to quench his Thirst.
The cool soft Zephyrs don't delight me more,
Nor murm'ring Billows on the sounding Shore;
Nor winding Streams that through the Valley glide;
And the scarce cover'd Pebbles gently chide.

DRYDEN.

Æ N E I D.

THE ÆNEID, in which *Virgil* imitates *Homer*, is a Poem of a nobler Kind, as it is an *Epic* or *Heroic Poem, which*, as Mr. *Rapin* has obſerved, *is the greateſt Work the Soul of Man is capable of performing*: For of it may be juſtly ſaid, what *Scaliger* ſays of *Buchanan*,

Namque ad ſupremum perducta poëtica culmen
In te ſtat; nec quo progrediatur habet.

Nature's great Efforts can no further tend,
Here fix'd her Pillars, all her Labours end.

As, under the Allegory of one Heroic Action, its Deſign is to form our Morals, and inflame our Mind with the Love of Virtue: And this indeed is the chief and principal Deſign of all Poetry, as plainly appears by this and every other Species of it. For the *Lyric* celebrates the Virtues of great Men for our Imitation; *Tragedy* regulates our Pity and Fears; *Comedy* and *Satire* correct our Vices; *Elegy* ſets Bounds to our Sorrow; and the *Eclogue* or *Paſtoral* ſings the innocent Pleaſures of a Country Life: So that all of them have a Tendency to make us wiſer and better. This was the Deſign *Homer* and *Virgil* had in View in their Poems, thoſe Maſterpieces of human Wit, which have been ſo juſtly and highly admired in all Ages. This appears by the very Plan

Plan of their Works. In the *Iliad*, *Achilles* quarre with *Agamemnon*, ſhuts himſelf up in his Tent, and refuſes to fight. Upon which the *Greeks*, who had hitherto been victorious, are beat every Day, and reduced to the laſt Extremity; nor could they recover their former Glory, but by the Reconciliation of theſe two Princes; by which *Homer* teaches us, *That the Safety and Welfare of a Nation depend on the Harmony of its Rulers.* In the *Odyſſey*, *Ulyſſes* being neceſſarily abſent from his Family, and at a great Diſtance from his Country, neighbouring Princes take the advantage of his Abſence, make Encroachments on his Eſtate, lay Snares for his Son, and commit Outrages of all Sorts: But no ſooner does *Ulyſſes* return than he reſtores his Kingdom and Family to their former Peace and Quiet. By which *Homer* would teach us, *That the Preſence and Vigilance of a Maſter and Prince are abſolutely neceſſary to keep good Order in a Family or Kingdom.* *Homer*'s Deſign in theſe two Poems, is plainly to eſtabliſh National and Family Happineſs; nor could a more noble Thought enter the Mind of Man.

Virgil again, out of Love to his Country, and Gratitude to his Prince, who had loaded him with Favours, forms the Plan of the *Æneis*, with a View to eſtabliſh the Authority of *Auguſtus*, and the Happineſs of the *Romans*; and to this End chuſes for the Hero of his Poem, a Man whom the Gods order to found a Kingdom in *Italy*; to obſtruct which *Juno* uſes all her Authority and all her Art, and exerts herſelf the more to prevent its Accompliſhment, that *Æneas* was at the Head of it, to whom ſhe bore an inveterate Enmity, as he was a *Trojan*, and the Son of *Venus*, her great Enemy and Rival. She applies to *Æolus* the God of the Winds to ſink his Fleet; uſes all the Policy ſhe was Miſtreſs of to detain him at *Carthage*; and deſtroys Part of his Fleet in *Sicily*: But in ſpite of all her Oppoſition, he arrives in *Italy* and founds the *Roman* State. By all which *Virgil* ſhews us this great Truth, *That when it is the Will of Heaven to ſet a Prince over a People, their plain Duty is humbly to ſubmit to his Authority.* Theſe are the excellent Morals of thoſe three ineſtimable Poems. But to confine ourſelves to *Virgil*: If from his general Inſtructions, which are the Structure of his Poem, we deſcend to particular Leſſons which are of great Uſe in the Conduct of Life, how innumerable are they! Nor has he delivered theſe Inſtructions in dogmatical Precepts and Maxims, but exhibits them to us in the Perſon of his Hero, to whom he aſſigns a conſtant Piety, the Height of filial Affection, in running ſo many Riſks of his Life to ſave his Parents, and a ready Obedience to the Command of Heaven, in forſaking a Queen for whom he had the greateſt Affection wherewith Love and Gratitude could inſpire the Heart of Man. Nor does he only take this modeſt Way of conveying theſe important Leſſons to us by a third Perſon, but to make us in Love with them, he inſinuates himſelf into our Hearts, by ſpreading Charms over every Thing he touches, and enriches his Poem with curious Deſcriptions, fine Epiſodes, beautiful Allegories, lofty Expreſſions, and Numbers ſo very harmonious, as muſt charm the Ear of every Reader. But, as it would be endleſs to recite Examples of all the Beauties of this inimitable Poem, I ſhall inſtance only a few of them: And firſt, what a beautiful Deſcription does our Author give us of a *Storm at Sea* in the *Firſt Book*, in theſe expreſſive Words:

Hæc ubi dicta, cavum converſâ cuſpide montem
Impulit in latus; ac venti, velut agmine facto,
Quà data porta, ruunt, & terras turbine perflant.
Incubuere mari, totumque à ſedibus imis
Una Euruſque Notuſque ruunt, creberque procellis
Africus, & vaſtos volvunt ad littora fluctus.
Inſequitur clamorque virûm, ſtridorque rudentum.
Eripiunt ſubito nubes, cœlumque, diemque

Teucrorum

Teucrorum ex oculis: ponto nox incubat atra.
Intonuere poli, & crebris micat ignibus æther:
Præsentemque viris intentant omnia mortem.
Extemplo Ænēæ solvuntur frigore membra.
Ingemit, & duplices tendens ad sidera palmas,
Talia voce refert: O terque quaterque beati,
Queis ante ora patrum, Trojæ sub mœnibus altis,
Contigit oppetere! ô Danaûm fortissime gentis
Tydide, mene Iliacis occumbere campis
Non potuisse, tuaque animam hanc effundere dextrâ?
Sævus ubi Æacidæ telo jacet Hector, ubi ingens
Sarpedon: ubi tot Simoïs correpta sub undis
Scuta virûm, galeasque & fortia corpora volvit.
Talia jactanti, stridens Aquilone procella
Velum adversa ferit, fluctusque ad sidera tollit.
Franguntur remi: tum prora avertit, & undis
Dat latus: insequitur cumulo præruptus aquæ mons.
Hi summo in fluctu pendent; his unda dehiscens
Terram inter fluctus aperit: furit æstus arenis.
Tres Notus abreptas in saxa latentia torquet;
Saxa vocant Itali, mediis quæ in fluctibus, Aras;
Dorsum immane mari summo. Tres Eurus ab alto
In brevia & Syrtes urget, (miserabile visu)
Illiditque vadis, atque aggere cingit arenæ.
Unam quæ Lycios fidumque vehebat Orontem,
Ipsius ante oculos ingens à vertice pontus
In puppim ferit: excutitur pronusque magister
Volvitur in caput: ast illam ter fluctus ibidem
Torquet agens circum, & rapidus vorat æquore vertex.
Apparent rari nantes in gurgite vasto:
Arma virûm, tabulæque & Troïa gaza per undas.
Jam validam Ilionei navem, jam fortis Achatæ;
Et qua vectus Abas, & qua grandævus Alethes,
Vicit hiems: laxis laterum compagibus omnes
Accipiunt inimicum imbrem, rimisque fatiscunt.

He

He ſaid, and hurl'd againſt the Mountain Side
His quiv'ring Spear, and all the God apply'd.
The raging Winds ruſh through the hollow Wound,
And dance aloft in Air, and ſkim along the Ground:
Then ſettling on the Sea, the Surges ſweep;
Raiſe liquid Mountains, and diſcloſe the Deep.
South, Eaſt, and Weſt, with mix'd Confuſion roar,
And roll the foaming Billows to the Shore.
The Cables crack, the Sailors' fearful Cries
Aſcend; and ſable Night involves the Skies;
And Heaven itſelf is raviſh'd from their Eyes.
Loud Peals of Thunder from the Poles enſue,
Then flaſhing Fires the tranſient Light renew;
The Face of Things a frightful Image bears,
And preſent Death in various Forms appears.
Struck with unuſual Fright, the *Trojan* Chief,
With lifted Hands and Eyes, implores Relief.
And thrice, and four times happy thoſe, he cry'd,
That under *Ilian* Walls before their Parents dy'd.
Tydides, braveſt of the *Græcian* Train,
Why could not I by that ſtrong Arm be ſlain,
And lie by noble *Hector* on the Plain;
Or great *Sarpedon*, in thoſe bloody Fields,
Where *Simois* rolls the Bodies and the Shields
Of Heroes, whoſe diſmember'd Hands yet bear
The Dart aloft, and clench the pointed Spear?
Thus while the pious Prince his Fate bewails,
Fierce *Boreas* drove againſt his flying Sails,
And rent the Sheets: The raging Billows riſe,
And mount the toſſing Veſſel to the Skies:
Nor can the ſhiv'ring Oars ſuſtain the Blow:
The Galley gives her Side, and turns her Prow:
While thoſe aſtern deſcending down the Steep,
Through gaping Waves behold the boiling Deep.

Three

Three Ships were hurry'd by the southern Blaſt,
And on the ſecret Shelves with Fury caſt.
Thoſe hidden Rocks, th' *Auſonian* Sailors knew,
They call'd them Altars, when they roſe in View,
And ſhow'd their ſpacious Backs above the Flood.
Three more, fierce *Eurus* in his angry Mood
Daſh'd on the Shallows of the moving Sand,
And in mid Ocean left them moor'd a-land.
Orontes' Bark that bore the *Lycian* Crew,
(A horrid Sight)! even in the Hero's View,
From Stem to Stern, by Waves was overborne:
The trembling Pilot, from his Rudder torn,
Was headlong hurl'd; thrice round, the Ship was toſt
Then bulg'd at once, and in the Deep was loſt.
And here and there above the Waves were ſeen,
Arms, Pictures, precious Goods, and floating Men.
The ſtouteſt Veſſel to the Storm gave Way,
And ſuck'd, thro' looſen'd Planks, the ruſhing Sea;
Ilioneus was her Chief: *Alethes* old,
Achates faithful, *Abas* young and bold
Endur'd not leſs: Their Ships, with gaping Seams,
Admit the Deluge of the briny Streams. DRYDEN.

What a moving Scene is that in the *Second Book*, where *Æneas*, after going through Fire and Sword to look after the Safety of his Father and Family, finds the old Gentleman reſolute on continuing in *Troy*, and ſharing the ſame Fate with it, maugre all the Arguments he could uſe to the contrary, nay, though he, *Creuſa*, and *Aſcanius*, with Tears in their Eyes, begged of him to conſult his own Safety by leaving *Troy*. What filial Affection and Duty does *Æneas* expreſs in that moving Speech:

Mene efferre pedem, genitor, te poſſe relicto
Speraſti? tantumque nefas patrio excidit ore?
Si nihil ex tanta Superis placet urbe relinqui,

Et ſedet hoc animo, perituræque addere Trojæ
Teque tuoſque juvat : patet iſti janua letho.
Jamque aderit multo Priami de ſanguine Pyrrhus,
Natum ante ora patris, patrem qui obtruncat ad aras.
Hoc erat, alma parens, quod me, per tela, per ignes,
Eripis? ut mediis hoſtem in penetralibus, utque
Aſcaniumque, patremque meum, juxtaque Creüſam,
Alterum in alterius mactatos ſanguine cernam?
Arma, viri, ferte arma : vocat lux ultima victos.
Reddite me Danais : ſinite inſtaurata reviſam
Prælia : nunquam omnes hodie moriemur inulti.

To fly the Foe, and leave your Age alone,
Could ſuch a Sire propoſe to ſuch a Son?
If 'tis by yours and Heav'n's high Will decreed
That you and all with hapleſs *Troy* muſt bleed;
If not her leaſt Remains you deign to ſave;
Behold! the Door lies open to the Grave;
Pyrrhus will ſoon be here, all cover'd o'er,
And red from *Priam*'s venerable Gore;
Who ſtabb'd the Son before the Father's View,
Then at the Shrine the royal Father ſlew.
Why! heav'nly Mother, did thy guardian Care
Snatch me from Fires, and ſhield me in the War?
Within theſe Walls to ſee the *Grecians* roam,
And purple Slaughter ſtride around the Dome;
To ſee my murder'd Conſort, Son, and Sire,
Steep'd in each other's Blood, on Heaps expire!
Arms! Arms! my Friends, with Speed my Arms
ſupply,
'Tis our laſt Hour, and ſummons us to die;
My Arms!—in vain you hold me,—let me go!
Give, give me back this Moment to the Foe.
'Tis well,—we will not tamely periſh all,
But die reveng'd, and triumph in our Fall. PITT.

But when *Æneas* (finding his Father ſtill obſtinate) put on his Armour, and offers to ruſh out at the Door, chuſing rather to die by the Hand of the Enemy, than ſee his Father, Wife, and Son butchered before his Eyes, who can read what follows without falling into Tears?

Ecce autem complexa pedes in limine conjux
Hærebat, parvumque patri tendebat Iülum.
Si periturus abis, & nos rape in omnia tecum:
Sin aliquam expertus ſumtis ſpem ponis in armis,
Hanc primum tutare domum: cui parvus Iülus,
Cui pater, & conjux quondam tua dicta relinquo?

When, at the Door, my weeping Spouſe I meet,
The fair *Creuſa*, who embrac'd my Feet,
And clinging round them, with Diſtraction wild,
Reach'd to my Arms my dear unhappy Child:
And oh! ſhe cries, if bent on Death thou run,
Take, take with thee, thy wretched Wife and Son;
Or, if one glimmering Hope from Arms appear,
Defend theſe Walls, and try thy Valour here:
Ah, who ſhall guard thy Sire, when thou art ſlain,
Thy Child, or me thy Cònſort once in vain?
Thus while ſhe raves, the vaulted Dome replies
To her loud Shrieks, and agonizing Cries. PITT.

And when the good old Man was at laſt perſuaded there was no Way to ſave himſelf and Family but by leaving his beloved *Troy*, what Compaſſion and Tenderneſs does *Æneas* ſhow to his aged helpleſs Father? How ſoft are theſe words?

Ergo age, chare pater, cervici imponere noſtræ:
Ipſe ſubibo humeris: nec me labor iſte gravabit.
Quo res cunque cadent, unum & commune periclum,
Una ſalus ambobus erit: mihi parvus Iülus

Sit comes, & longe servet vestigia conjux.
Vos famuli, quæ dicam, animis advertite vestris.
Est urbe egressis tumulus, templumque vetustum
Desertæ Cereris: juxtaque antiqua cupressus,
Religione patrum multos servata per annos.
Hanc ex diverso sedem veniemus in unam.
Tu, genitor, cape sacra manu, patriosque Penates:
Me, bello è tanto digressum & cæde recenti,
Attrectare nefas; donec me flumine vivo
Abluero.

Haste, my dear Father ('tis no Time to wait),
And load my Shoulders with a willing Freight.
Whate'er befals, your Life shall be my Care;
One Death, and one Deliv'rance we will share.
My Hand shall lead our little Son; and you,
My faithful Consort, shall our Steps pursue.
Next, you my Servants, heed my strict Commands:
Without the Walls a ruin'd Temple stands,
To *Ceres* hallow'd once; a Cypress nigh,
Shoots up her venerable Head on high;
By long Religion kept: There tend your Feet;
And in divided Parties let us meet.
Our Country Gods, the Relics, and the Bands,
Hold you, my Father, in your guiltless Hands:
In me 'tis impious holy Things to bear,
Red as I am with Slaughter, new from War:
'Till in some living Stream I cleanse the Guilt
Of dire Debate, and Blood in Battle spilt. DRYDEN.

Virgil, in all his Poems, shows he thoroughly understood the human Passions; but he has painted none of them in such strong and lively Colours, as that of Love, in the Passion of *Dido* for *Æneas* in his *Fourth Book:* But to point out all the Beauties of this Book would be to transcribe almost the whole of it: Wherefore I shall

ſhall mention ónly two; the one is that beautiful Deſcription the Poet gives of *Dido* and *Æneas* going a hunting; in which how charming is the Compariſon of *Æneas* to *Apollo?*

Oceanum interea ſurgens Aurora reliquit.
It portis jubare extorto delecta juventus:
Retia rara, plagæ, lato venabula ferro,
Maſſylique ruunt equites, & odora canum vis.
Reginam thalamo cunctantem ad limina primi
Pœnorum exſpectant: oſtroque inſignis & auro
Stat ſonipes, ac frena ferox ſpumantia mandit.
Tandem progreditur, magnâ ſtipante catervâ,
Sidoniam picto chlamydem circumdata limbo:
Cui pharetra ex auro, crines nodantur in aurum,
Aurea purpuream ſubnectit fibula veſtem.
Necnon & Phrygii comites, & lætus Iülus,
Incedunt: ipſe ante alios pulcherrimus omnes
Infert ſe ſocium Æneas, atque agmina jungit.
Qualis, ubi hibernam Lyciam, Xanthique fluenta
Deſerit, ac Delum maternam inviſit Apollo,
Inſtauratque choros: miſtique altaria circum
Creteſque Dryopeſque fremunt, pictique Agathyrſi:
Ipſe jugis Cynthi graditur, molleque fluentem
Fronde premit crinem fingens, atque implicat auro:
Tela ſonant humeris. Haud illo ſegnior ibat
Æneas: tantum egregio decus enitet ore.

Scarce had *Aurora* left her Orient Bed,
And rear'd above the Waves her radiant Head,
When, pouring through the Gates, the Train appear,
Maſſylian Hunters with the ſteely Spear,
Sagacious Hounds, and Toils, and all the ſylvan War.
The Queen engag'd in Dreſs, with Reverence wait
The *Tyrian* Peers before the Regal Gate.

Her

Her Steed, with Gold and Purple cover'd round,
Neighs, champs the Bit, and foaming paws the Ground.
At length ſhe comes, magnificently dreſt
(Her Guards attending) in a *Tyrian* Veſt.
Back in a golden Caul here Locks are ty'd;
A golden Quiver rattles at her Side;
A golden Claſp her purple Garment binds,
And Robes, that flew redundant in the Winds.
Next, with the youthful *Trojans*, to the Sport,
The fair *Aſcanius* iſſues from the Court.
But far the faireſt, and ſupremely tall,
Tow'rs great *Æneas*, and outſhines them all.
As when from *Lycia*, bound in wintry Froſt,
Where *Xanthus*' Streams enrich the ſmiling Coaſt;
The beauteous *Phœbus* in high Pomp retires,
And hears in *Delos* the triumphant Quires;
The *Cretan* Crowds and Dryopes advance,
And painted *Scythians* round his Altar dance;
Fair Wreaths of vivid Bays his Head infold,
His Locks bound backward, and adorn'd with Gold;
The God majeſtic moves o'er *Cynthus*' Brows,
His golden Quiver rattling as it goes:
So mov'd *Æneas*; ſuch his charming Grace;
So glow'd the purple Bloom, that fluſh'd his godlike Face.

PITT.

The other is that inimitable Deſcription of Fame, which a great Critic ſays, ought to be conſidered as one of the greateſt Ornaments of the *Ænied*:

Extemplo Libyæ magnas it Fama per urbes:
Fama, malum quo non aliud velocius ullum:
Mobilitate viget, vireſque acquirit eundo:
Parva metu primo; mox ſeſe attollit in auras,
Ingrediturque ſolo, & caput inter nubila condit.
Illam Terra parens, irâ irritata Deorum,

Extremam

Extremam (ut perhibent) Cœo Enceladoque ſororem
Progenuit, pedibus celerem & pernicibus alis:
Monſtrum horrendum, ingens: cui quot ſunt corpore plumæ,
Tot vigiles oculi ſubter (mirabile dictu!)
Tot linguæ, totidem ora ſonant, tot ſubrigit aures.
Nocte volat cœli medio, terræque per umbram
Stridens, nec dulci declinat lumina ſomno:
Luce ſedet cuſtos, aut ſummi culmine tecti,
Turribus aut altis, & magnas territat urbes:
Tam ficti pravique tenax, quam nuncia veri.

Now Fame, tremendous Fiend! without Delay,
Through *Lybian* Cities took her rapid Way.
Fame, the ſwift Plague, that every Moment grows,
And gains new Strength and Vigour as ſhe goes.
Firſt ſmall with Fear, ſhe ſwells to wond'rous Size,
And ſtalks on Earth, and tow'rs above the Skies;
Whom, in her Wrath, to Heav'n, the teeming Earth,
Produc'd the laſt of her gigantic Birth;
A Monſter huge, and dreadful to the Eye,
With rapid Feet to run, or Wings to fly.
Beneath her Plumes the various Fury bears
A thouſand piercing Eyes and liſt'ning Ears;
And with a thouſand Mouths and babbling Tongues appears.
Thund'ring by Night, through Heav'n and Earth ſhe flies,
No golden Slumbers ſeal her watchful Eyes;
On Tow'rs or Battlements ſhe ſits by Day,
And ſhakes whole Towns with Terror and Diſmay;
Alarms the World around; and, perch'd on high,
Reports a Truth, or publiſhes a Lie. PITT.

How remarkably curious is the Deſcription in the *Sixth Book*, of *Æneas*'s Deſcent into Hell, where the Sybil, after explaining to him the various Scenes of the infernal Regions, conducts him to *Anchiſes*, who inſtructs him in thoſe ſublime Subjects, the Immortality of the Soul, and the Happineſs and Miſery of a future State, and ſhows him the glorious Race of Heroes that were to deſcend from him and his Poſterity, and cloſes this noble Account with the Character of their Genius; then concludes all with the Character of the elder *Marcellus*, in order to introduce that noble heroic Elegy on the Death of the younger *Marcellus*, who was the Darling of *Auguſtus*, *Octavia*, and of all the *Romans*.

Atque hic Æneas (una namque ire videbat
Egregium formâ juvenem & fulgentibus armis;
Sed frons læta parum, & dejecto lumina vultu)
Quis, pater, ille virum qui ſic comitatur euntem?
Filius? anne aliquis magna de ſtirpe nepotum?
Quis ſtrepitus circa comitum? quantum inſtar in ipſo eſt!
Sed nox atra caput triſti circumvolat umbra.
Tum pater Anchiſes lacrymis ingreſſus obortis:
O nate, ingentem luctum ne quære tuorum:
Oſtendunt terris hunc tantum fata, neque ultra
Eſſe ſinent. Nimium vobis Romana propago
Viſa potens, ſuperi, propria hæc ſi dona fuiſſent.
Quantos ille virûm magnam Mavortis ad urbem
Campus aget gemitus! vel quæ, Tyberine, videbis
Funera, cum tumulum præterlabere recentem!
Nec puer Iliaca quiſquam de gente Latinos
In tantum ſpe tollet avos: nec Romula quondam
Ullo ſe tantum tellus jactabit alumno.
Heu pietas! heu priſca fides! invictaque bello
Dextera! non illi quiſquam ſe impune tuliſſet
Obvius armato: ſeu cum pedes iret in hoſtem,
Seu ſpumantis equi foderet calcaribus armos.
Heu, miſerande puer: ſi qua fata aſpera rumpas,
Tu Marcellus eris. Manibus date lilia plenis:
Purpureos ſpargam flores, animamque nepotis
His ſaltem accumulem donis, et fungar inani
Munere.

Say,

Say, who that Youth (he cries) o'ercaſt with Grief;
The Youth who follows that victorious Chief;
His Son? or one of his victorious Line?
What Numbers crowd, and ſhout around the Form divine!
His Port how noble! how auguſt his Fame!
How like the former! and how near the ſame!
But gloomy Shades his penſive Brows o'erſpread,
And a dark Cloud involves his beauteous Head.
Seek not, my Son, replies the Sire, to know
(And, as he ſpoke, the guſhing Sorrows flow)
What Woes the Gods to thy Deſcendants doom,
What endleſs Grief to every Son of *Rome!*
This Youth on Earth the Fates but juſt diſplay,
And ſoon, too ſoon, they ſnatch the Gift away!
Had *Rome* for ever held the glorious Prize,
Her Bliſs had rais'd the Envy of the Skies!
Oh! from the martial Field what Cries ſhall come!
What Groans ſhall echo thro' the Streets of *Rome!*
How ſhall old *Tyber*, from his oozy Bed,
In that ſad Moment rear his reverend Head;
The length'ning Pomp, and Fun'ral to ſurvey,
When by the mighty Tomb he takes his mournful Way!
A Youth of nobler Hopes ſhall never riſe,
Nor glad, like him, the *Latian* Fathers Eyes.
And *Rome*, proud *Rome* ſhall boaſt, ſhe never bore,
From Age to Age, ſo brave a Son before!
Honour and Fame, alas! and ancient Truth,
Revive and die with that illuſtrious Youth!
In vain embattled Troops his Arms oppoſe:
In every Field he tames his Country's Foes,
Whether on Foot he marches in his Might,
Or ſpurs his fiery Courſer to the Fight.
Poor pitied Youth! the Glory of the State!
Oh! could'ſt thou ſhun the dreaful Stroke of Fate,
Rome ſhou'd in thee behold, with raviſh'd Eyes,
Her Pride, her Darling, her *Marcellus* riſe!

Bring fragrant Flow'rs, the whiteſt Lilies bring,
With all the purple Beauties of the Spring;
Theſe Gifts at leaſt, theſe Honours ſhall be paid
To the dear Youth, to pleaſe his penſive Shade. PITT.

In the *Ninth Book*, what a noble Deſcription does the Poet give of true Friendſhip in that famous Epiſode of *Niſus* and *Euryalus*, which, conſiſting of 474 Lines, is of too great a Length to inſert here, I ſhall therefore only take Notice of ſome of the principal Parts of it. However, it will be neceſſary to premiſe what gave Occaſion to this noble Epiſode, which was this: *Æneas* having gone in Perſon to beg Auxiliaries of *Evander* againſt *Turnus*, who was at War with him on account of *Lavinia*; *Turnus* takes the Advantage of his Abſence, and beſieges the City in which his Troops were garriſoned. The *Trojans*, in the utmoſt Diſtreſs for want of *Æneas*, and *Niſus* and *Euryalus*, two dear Friends, then ſtanding Centinels in their Turn, and obſerving the *Rutulians* ſunk in Wine and Sleep, perſuaded themſelves they could make their Way to *Æneas*, *Niſus* makes the Propoſal to *Euryalus*.

Niſus ait: Dîne hunc ardorem mentibus addunt,
Euryale? an ſua cuique Deus fit dira cupido?
Aut pugnam, aut aliquid jamdudum invadere magnum,
Mens agitat mihi; nec placidâ contenta quiete eſt.
Cernis, quæ Rutulos habeat fiducia rerum:
Lumina rara micant: ſomno vinoque ſoluti
Procubuere: ſilent late loca. Percipe porro
Quid dubitem, & quæ nunc animo ſententia ſurgat.
Ænean acciri omnes, populuſque, patreſque,
Expoſcunt: mittique viros, qui certa reportent.
Si tibi, quæ poſco, promittunt (nam mihi facti
Fama ſat eſt) tumulo videor reperire ſub illo
Poſſe viam ad muros & mœnia Pallantea.

Has Heav'n (cry'd *Niſus* firſt) this Warmth beſtow'd?
Heav'n? or a Thought that prompts me like a God?

This

This glorious Warmth, my Friend, that breaks my Rest?
Some high Exploit lies throbbing at my Breast.
My glowing Mind, what generous Ardors raise,
And set my mounting Spirits on a Blaze!
See the loose Discipline of yonder Train,
The Lights, grown thin, scarce glimmer from the Plain:
The Guards in Slumber and Debauch are drown'd;
And mark!—a general Silence reigns around:
Then take my Thought; the People, Fathers, all,
Join in one Wish, our Leader to recall.
Now, would they give to thee the Prize I claim,
(For I cou'd rest contented with the Fame—)
An easy Road, methinks, I can survey
Beneath yon' Summit to direct my Way. PITT.

To whom young *Euryalus* makes this charming Answer, in which he shows he is resolved to run all Risques with his Friend, and takes it amiss he should once think of leaving him behind:

Obstupuit magno laudum perculsus amore
Euryalus: simul his ardentem affatur amicum:
Mene igitur socium summis adjungere rebus,
Nise, fugis? solum te in tanta pericula mittam?
Non ita me genitor bellis assuetus Opheltes
Argolicum terrorem inter Trojæque labores
Sublatum erudiit: nec tecum talia gessi,
Magnanimum Ænean & fata extrema secutus.
Est hic, est animus lucis contemptor; & istum
Qui vitâ bene credat emi, quo tendis, honorem.

The brave *Euryalus*, with martial Pride,
Fir'd with the Charms of Glory, thus reply'd:
And will my *Nisus* then his Friend disclaim?
Deny'd his Share of Glory and of Fame?
And can thy dear *Euryalus* expose
Thy Life, alone, unguarded to the Foes?
Not so my Father taught his generous Boy,
Born, train'd, and season'd in the Wars of *Troy*.

And where the great *Æneas* led the Way,
I brav'd all Dangers of the Land and Sea.
Thou too canst witness that my Worth is try'd;
We march'd, we fought, we conquer'd Side by Side.
Like thine, this Bosom glows with martial Flame,
Burns with a Scorn of Life, and Love of Fame,
And thinks, if endless Glory can be sought
On such low Terms, the Prize is cheaply bought. PITT.

To which *Nisus* makes this moving and affectionate Reply:

Nisus ad hæc: Equidem de te nil tale verebar,
Nec fas: non: ita me referat tibi magnus ovantem
Jupiter, aut quicunque oculis hæc aspicit æquis.
Sed si quis (quæ multa vides discrimine tali)
Si quis in adversum rapiat casusve Deusve,
Te superesse velim: tua vitâ dignior ætas.
Sit, qui me raptum pugnâ, pretiove redemptum,
Mandet humo solita; aut, si qua id fortuna vetabit,
Absenti ferat inferias, decoretque sepulcro.
Neu matri miseræ tanti sim causa doloris:
Quæ te sola, puer, multis è matribus ausa
Prosequitur; magni nec mœnia curat Acestæ.

Let no such jealous Fears alarm thy Breast,
Thy Worth and Valour stand to all confest;
But let the Danger fall (he cries) on me;
For this Exploit, I durst not think on thee!
No—as I hope the blest Etherial Train
May bring me glorious to thy Arms again!
But should the Gods deny me to succeed,
Should I—(which Heav'n avert!) but should I bleed;
Live thou;—in Death some Pleasure that will give;
Live for thy *Nisus*' Sake; I charge thee, live.
Thy blooming Youth a longer Term demands;—
Live, to redeem my Corse from hostile Hands;
And decent to the silent Grave commend
The poor Remains of him who was thy Friend:

Or raiſe, at leaſt, by kind Remembrance led,
A vacant Tomb in Honour of the Dead.
Why ſhould I cauſe thy Mother's Soul to know
Such Heart-felt Pangs? unutterable Woe!
Thy dear, fond Mother, who, for Love of thee,
Dar'd every Danger of the Land and Sea!
She left *Aceſtes'* Walls, and ſhe alone,
To follow thee, her only, darling Son! PITT.

But all *Niſus*'s Reaſons and Remonſtrances are in vain; wherefore they wait on their Generals, who were then holding a Council of War, and having received their Inſtructions they ſet out. Having paſſed the Enemy's Trenches ſafely, they find them faſt aſleep after a Debauch of Wine, among whom they made great Slaughter; but Day approaching, they reſolve to retire. *Euryalus*, like moſt young Warriors, taken with the glittering Spoils of the killed and wounded, ſeizes, among other Things, *Meſſapus*'s creſted Helmet, and puts it on his own Head; which inconſiderate Action proved fatal to both him and his Friend *Niſus*; for by it *Volſcens*, at the Head of a Party of Horſe, eſpies them in their Retreat, upon which they fly to a neighbouring Wood for Safety, where *Euryalus* loſes his Way, nor does *Niſus* miſs him till he was got a great Way off; but how great is his Surprize, when, boldly returning in queſt of him, he ſees him in the Hands of the Enemy? Reſolved to reſcue his Friend, he throws two Lances unobſerved, and kills two of their Men, which ſo enraged *Volſcens*, that he reſolves to revenge their Deaths on *Euryalus*, and drawing his Sword makes up to him; then cries out *Niſus* in theſe beautiful Words, which admirably expreſs the Confuſion he was in, and at the ſame time the great Power of true Friendſhip:

Me, me; adſum qui feci; in me convertite ferrum,
O Rutuli: mea fraus omnis: nihil iſte, nec auſus,

Nec

Nec potuit: cœlum hoc, & conscia sidera testor:
Tantum infelicem nimium dilexit amicum.

Me, me, to me alone, your Rage confine;
Here sheath your Javelins; all the Guilt was mine.
By yon bright Stars, by each immortal God,
His Hands, his Thoughts are innocent of Blood!
Nor cou'd nor durst the Boy the Deed intend
His only Crime (and oh! can that offend?)
Was too much Love to his unhappy Friend! PITT.

This did not hinder *Volscens* from giving the fatal Wound to *Euryalus*, whose Death, and *Nisus*'s brave Revenge of it on *Volscens*, are painted to Admiration in the following Words:

Talia dicta dabat: sed viribus ensis adactus
Transabiit costas, & pectora candida rumpit.
Volvitur Euryalus letho, pulchrosque per artus
It cruor, inque humeros cervix collapsa recumbit.
Purpureus veluti cum flos succisus aratro
Languescit moriens; lassove papavera collo
Demisere caput, pluvia cum forte gravantur.
At Nisus ruit in medios, solumque per omnes
Volscentem petit; in solo Volscente moratur:
Quem circum glomerati hostes, hinc cominus atque hinc
Proturbant: instat non secius, ac rotat ensem
Fulmineum: donec Rutuli clamantis in ore
Condidit adverso, & moriens animam abstulit hosti.
Tum super exanimum sese projecit amicum
Confossus, placidâque ibi demum morte quievit.

In vain he spoke, for ah! the Sword, addrest
With ruthless Rage, had pierc'd his lovely Breast.
With Blood his snowy Limbs are purpled o'er,
And, pale in Death, he welters in his Gore.
As a gay Flow'r, with blooming Beauties crown'd,
Cut by the Share, lies languid on the Ground;

Or

Or ſome tall Poppy, that, o'ercharg'd with Rain,
Bends the faint Head, and ſinks upon the Plain;
So fair, ſo languiſhingly ſweet he lies,
His Head declin'd and drooping, as he dies!
Now midſt the Foe diſtracted *Niſus* flew;
Volſcens, and him alone he kept in View.
The gathering Train the furious Youth ſurround;
Dart follows Dart, and Wound ſucceeds to Wound;
All, all, unfelt, he ſeeks their guilty Lord;
In fiery Circles flies his thundering Sword;
Nor ceas'd, but found at length the diſtant Way;
And, buried in his Mouth, the Faulchion lay.
Thus, cover'd o'er with Wounds on every Side,
Brave *Niſus* flew the Murtherer as he dy'd;
Then, on the dear *Euryalus*'s Breaſt,
Sunk down, and ſlumber'd in eternal Reſt. PITT.

Thus even Death itſelf could not ſeparate theſe two ſincere Friends, to whom *Virgil* gives this noble Elogy:

Fortunati ambo! ſi quid mea carmina poſſunt,
Nulla dies unquam memori vos eximet ævo;
Dum domus Æneæ Capitoli immobile ſaxum
Accolet, imperiumque Pater Romanus habebit.

Hail, happy Pair! if Fame our Verſe can give,
From Age to Age, your Memory ſhall live;
Long as th' Imperial Capitol ſhall ſtand,
Or *Rome*'s majeſtic Lord the conquer'd World command.
PITT.

It would be endleſs to point out all the Beauties of the *Æneid*, but there is one Thing ſo very remarkable, not only in this, but in all *Virgil*'s Poems, that it would be unpardonable to omit it; I mean the great Art and Dexterity *Virgil* ſhows in making the Sound of his Verſe expreſſive of its Senſe; of which I ſhall give a few Inſtances from each of his Poems.

How

How admirably does the Sound of this Line expreſs the warbling of the Pipe:

Formoſam reſonare doces Amaryllida ſylvas. Ecl. i. 5.

And the Sound of this, a ſorrowful Parting,

Et, longum formoſe vale, vale, inquit, Iola. Ecl. iii. 79.

How ſlow does the Waggon move in this Line,

Tardaque Eleuſinæ matris volventia plauſtra. G. i. 163.

One can ſcarcely help thinking he hears the Sheep bleating while he reads this Verſe,

Balantumque gregem fluvio merſare ſalubri. G. i. 272.

Theſe Lines ſeem to heave, in which *Virgil* deſcribes the Giants laying Mountain upon Mountain,

Ter ſunt conati imponere Pelio Oſſam
Scilicet, atque Oſſæ frondoſum involvere Olympum. G. i. 281.

There never was a Crab-tree rougher than this Verſe deſcribing the ingrafting a Filberd on a Crab-ſtock,

Inſeritur vero ex fœtu nucis arbutus horrida. G. ii. 69.

How expreſſive is this Line of the Swiftneſs of Time,

Sed fugit interea, fugit irreparabile tempus. G. iii. 284.

And this, of the Fury of the Storm?

Una Eurusque Notuſque ruunt, creberque procellis. Æ. i. 89.

How ſoft and expreſſive of filial Love and Affection are theſe Words of *Æneas* to his Father,

Ergo, age, care Pater, cervici imponere noſtræ. Æ. ii. 707.

And how harſh does this Line read, expreſſing the frightful Figure *Polyphemus* made,

Monſtrum horrendum, informe, ingens, cui lumen ademtum. Æ. iii. 658.

In reading the following Verſe one would think he hears the Bound the bulky Body of the Ox makes when it falls on the Ground,

Sternitur, exanimiſque tremens procumbit humi bos.
Æ. v. 481.

How admirably does this Line expreſs not only the Swiftneſs of the Horſe, but the Sound of his Feet,

Quadrupedante putrem ſonitu quatit ungula campum.
Æ. viii. 596.

Nor is the Sound of the Trumpet itſelf more ſhrill than the Sound of this Verſe,

At Tuba terribilem ſonitum procul ære canoro. Æ. ix. 503.

With ſuch Charms does *Virgil*'s Poetry every where abound, more than that of any Poet whatever. Who, therefore, as the learned Dr. *Trapp* obſerves, can help being enamoured with the unaffected Beauty of his *Paſtorals*, the finiſhed and chaſte Elegance of his *Georgics*, their entertaining Deſcriptions, their uſeful Precepts in Huſbandry, and their noble Excurſions upon every proper Occaſion, into Subjects of a more ſublime Nature?

But who can read the divine *Æneid*, without being tranſported, and as it were loſt in a Mixture of Pleaſure and Admiration? Who can help being aſtoniſhed at that Force of Imagination, tempered with ſo cool a Judgment? In what human Compoſition is there ſo exact a Harmony, and ſo much Beauty in all its Parts? It would be endleſs to enumerate the many different Images of Heroes, and the Variety of Manners that appear up and down in it; the Conflict of Paſſions and almoſt every Object of the Imagination beautifully deſcribed, all Nature unfolded, the great Events, the ſurpriſing Revolutions, the Incentives to Virtue, the moſt finiſhed Eloquence in the ſeveral Speeches, the ſublimeſt Majeſty in the Thoughts and Expreſſions, in ſhort, the moſt conſummate Art by which all theſe Things are brought into one uniform and perfect

Wherefore we may juſtly ſay of the Poet, what his great Modeſty would not allow him to ſay of himſelf:

Exegit monumentum ære perennius,
Regalique ſitu Pyramidum altius;
Quod non Imber Edax, non Aquilo impotens
Poſſit diruere, aut innumerabilis
Annorum ſeries, & fuga temporum.

He has rais'd a Monument will ſurpaſs
The Age of thoſe that ſtand in ſolid Braſs;
That, eminently tow'ring to the Skies,
In Height the Royal Pyramids outvies:
The Force of boiſt'rous Winds and mould'ring Rain,
Years after Years an everlaſting Train,
Shall ne'er deſtroy the Glory of his Name,
Still ſhall he ſhine in Verſe and live in Fame.

As to this Translation of VIRGIL, though there have been many in Verſe, ſome of which are of great Merit; yet, as the Tranſlators have confined themſelves to Meaſure and Numbers, none of them have expreſſed the Author's Meaning ſo fully and exactly as may be done by a Tranſlator in Proſe. For the Poet is often neceſſitated, for the Sake of his Meaſures, to add, retrench, or otherwiſe deviate from the preciſe Meaning of his Author, eſpecially if he be ſhackled and hemmed in by Rhymes. Beſides, as this Work was chiefly intended for the Uſe of Schools, and of thoſe who have made but ſmall Proficiency in the Knowledge of the *Latin* Tongue, it was judged neceſſary to be much more literal and exact than a Poetical Tranſlation can well bear.

When I call this Tranſlation literal, I do not mean, that I have rendered *Virgil's Latin* Word for Word into *Engliſh*; for this the different Idioms of the two Languages will not admit of; but, that Care has been taken all along, to preſerve the full Senſe of the Author, and to adhere as cloſely to the Letter as was conſiſtent with

Spirit, Elegance, and Propriety of Style; above all, to present to the Reader the same Ideas in *English*, which the Author does in *Latin*, and carefully to affix the precise determinate Meaning to every one of his Words, distinguishing them from others commonly reckoned synonymous, or that nearly resemble them in Sense, however different in Sound. And herein, if I am not mistaken, will be found to lie the precise Difference between this and the Interpretation of *Ruæus* and others, which, in Numbers of Places, have not so much given the strict and proper Sense of their Author, as something like it; that is, they substitute one Idea for another, which is the more apt to mislead the Reader, as it bears a near Resemblance to that of the Author, without being exactly the same. And though this might happen in translating some Authors without doing them much Injury, yet in so judicious and correct an Author as *Virgil*, whose Sentiments on every Subject are so just, every little Deviation from the Ideas of the Original becomes considerable; for if we alter them at all it must be for the worse.

I have only this further to add with regard to the Translation, that though Prose seemed better adapted than Verse to my Design of being almost quite literal; yet the nervous comprehensive Style of the Original obliged me frequently to adopt the Language of Poetry, setting aside the Numbers. For which Purpose, I not only consulted the best of our Poetical Versions, but borrowed Aid from the Works of our celebrated Poets, who have made *Virgil* their Standard, and happily imitated his Manner.

Nor will this Work be useful only to Boys at School, or mere Novices in the *Latin*, but may without Vanity promise to be of some Service even to greater Proficients. Many, even of those who think themselves pretty much Masters of *Virgil*, will find, upon Reflection, that they have but a confused, or at best, but a very superficial and general Knowledge of his Meaning. To such it may

possibly

poſſibly be no unprofitable Labour to beſtow ſome Time and Attention, even on ſtudying the Words of an Author, whoſe Choice is ſo nice and delicate: Eſpecially, if they will take the Trouble to conſult the Notes ſubjoined to the Tranſlation, which are extracted from the beſt Commentators ancient and modern, interſperſed with ſeveral that occured to the Tranſlator himſelf, and which ſeemed neceſſary, either to ſupply the Defects of others, or to ſupport the Senſe of the Tranſlation, where it differs from the commonly received Explication. As theſe Notes are not calculated to make a vain Parade and Oſtentation of Learning, but merely to explain and illuſtrate the Author, they are generally ſhort and conciſe, except where the clearing up of more remarkable Difficulties, or the ſolving ſome curious Queſtions, required a longer Diſcuſſion. What I found of chief Uſe in compiling them, was to make *Virgil* his own Interpreter, and illuſtrate one Paſſage by comparing it with others that are parallel. This often proved the only Reſource in Difficulties which were either intirely overlooked by Commentators, or where they diſagreed among themſelves.

As to the *Latin* Text, no Pains have been ſpared to preſent it to the Reader in its genuine Purity and Correctneſs: For I all along compared the moſt celebrated Editions, namely, thoſe of *H. Stephen*, *Heinſius*, *Emmeneſſius*, *Maſvicius*, *Servius*, and *La Cerda*. And for the Satisfaction of the Curious, I have alſo taken Notice of the moſt material of the various Readings from *Pierius*, *Servius*, *Stephen*, and others.

And that nothing might be wanting to render this Work complete, the Pointing, which in moſt Editions is exceeding erroneous, I have altered throughout, and endeavoured to ſet it to rights: Conſiderable Inſtances of this the Reader will find in *Geor*. iv. 241. *Æn*. vii. 390. and *Æn*. ix. 140.

P. VIR-

P. VIRGILII MARONIS

BUCOLICA.

ECLOGA I.

MELIBOEUS, TITYRUS.

MEL. TITYRE, tu, patulæ recubans sub tegmine fagi,
Silvestrem tenui Musam meditaris avenâ:
Nos patriæ fines, et dulcia linquimus arva;
Nos patriam fugimus: tu, Tityre, lentus in umbrâ,
Formosam resonare doces Amaryllida silvas.

ORDO.

Mel. *Tityre, tu, recubans sub tegmine patulæ fagi, meditaris silvestrem Musam tenui avenâ: Nos linquimus fines patriæ, et dulcia arva; nos fugimus patriam: tu, Tityre, lentus in umbrâ, doces silvas resonare formosam Amaryllida.*

TRANSLATION.

MEL. YOU, Tityrus, lying all along under the Covert of *that* full-spread Beech, practise your woodland Lays on a slender oaten Pipe: We *are forced to* leave the Bounds of our Country, and our pleasant Fields; we fly our Country, *while* you, Tityrus, in the Shade at Ease teach the Woods to re-echo fair Amaryllis.

NOTES.

The Occasion of the first Pastoral was this: When *Augustus* had settled himself in the *Roman* Empire, that he might reward his veteran Troops for their past Service, he distributed among them all the Lands that lay about *Mantua* and *Cremona*, turning out the right Owners for having sided with his Enemies. *Virgil*, or his Father, was a Sufferer among the rest; but afterwards recovered his Estate by the Intercession of *Mecænas*, *Pollio*, and *Varus*. *Virgil*, as an Instance of his Gratitude, composed the following Pastoral; where he sets out his Father's good Fortune in the Person of *Tityrus*, and the Calamities of his *Mantuan* Neighbours in the Character of *Melibœus*. To this Piece of History *Martial* refers in the following Lines:

Sint Mecænates, non deerunt, Flacce, Marones,
Virgiliumque tibi vel tua rura dabunt.
Jugera perdiderat miseræ vicina Cremonæ,
Flebat et abductas Tityrus æger oves.
Risit Thuscus eques, paupertatemque malignam
Reppulit, ut celeri jussit abire fuga.
Accipe divitias, et vatum maximus esto,
Tu licet, et nostrum dixit Alexin ames.

1. *Fagi.* We commonly make the *Fagus* the same Tree as the *Esculus*: But *Ovid* plainly distinguishes them. Metam. Book 10. Lines 91 and 92.

2. *Silvestrem. Musam*, i. e. *Rusticum carmen*, *Lucretius*, Lib. II.

Fistula silvestrem ne cesset fundere Musam.

2. *Meditaris.* i. e. *Exerces*, as in *Plautus*, Stich. II. 1. 34. *Ad cursum meditabor me.* And Cic. 1. *de Orat.* 62. *Demosthenes perfecit meditando, ut nemo planius eo locutus putaretur.*

2. *Avenâ.* For *fistula avenacea.*

5. *Amaryllida.* By *Amaryllis* some understand *Rome*, and *Virgil's* Friends at *Rome*: But there is no Occasion for such Refinement: The Pastoral will appear more beautiful by considering *Amaryllis* simply as the Shepherd's Mistress, whose Praises he sings at his Ease. See *Theocritus*, Idyll. III.

Tit. *O Melibœe, Deus fecit hæc otia nobis; namque ille erit semper Deus mihi: sæpe tener agnus, ab nostris ovilibus, imbuet aram illius. Ille permisit meas boves errare, ut cernis, et* me *ipsum ludere quæ* carmina *vellem, agresti calamo.* Mel. *Equidem non invideo* tibi; *miror magis: turbatur usque adeò totis agris undique. En* ego *ipse æger ago* meas *capellas protenùs: Tityre, etiam vix duco hanc: namque modò connixa gemellos, spem gregis, hìc inter densas corylos, ah! reliquit eos in nudâ silice. Memini quercus, tactas de cœlo, sæpe prædicere hoc malum nobis, si mens non fuisset læva: sæpe sinistra cornix prædixit* hoc *ab cavâ ilice. Sed tamen, Tityre, da nobis, qui iste Deus sit?* Tit. *Melibœe, ego stultus putavi urbem, quam dicunt Romam, similem huic nostræ Mantuæ, quò* nos *pastores sæpe solemus depellere teneros fetus ovium. Sic nôram catulos similes canibus, sic nôram hœdos* similes *matribus; sic solebam componere magna parvis. Verùm hæc* Roma *extulit caput inter alias urbes, tantum quantum cupressi solent inter lenta viburna.*

TIT. O Melibœe, Deus nobis hæc otia fecit;
Namque erit ille mihi semper Deus: illius aram
Sæpe tener nostris ab ovilibus imbuet agnus.
Ille meas errare boves, ut cernis, et ipsum
Ludere, quæ vellem, calamo permisit agresti.
MEL. Non equidem invideo; miror magis; undique totis
Usque adeò turbatur agris. En ipse capellas
Protenùs æger ago: hanc etiam vix, Tityre, duco:
Hìc inter densas corylos modò namque gemellos,
Spem gregis, ah! silice in nudâ connixa reliquit.
Sæpe malum hoc nobis, si mens non læva fuisset,
De cœlo tactas memini prædicere quercus:
Sæpe sinistra cavâ prædixit ab ilice cornix.
Sed tamen, iste Deus qui sit, da, Tityre, nobis?
TIT. Urbem, quam dicunt Romam, Melibœe, putavi
Stultus ego huic nostræ similem, quò sæpe solemus
Pastores ovium teneros depellere fetus.
Sic canibus catulos similes, sic matribus hœdos
Nôram; sic parvis componere magna solebam.
Verùm hæc tantum alias inter caput extulit urbes,
Quantum lenta solent inter viburna cupressi.

TRANSLATION.

TIT. A God, O Melibœus, hath vouchsafed us this Tranquillity; for to me he shall always be a God: A tender Lambkin from our Folds shall often stain his Altar *with its Blood.* 'Tis he hath licensed my Heifers to feed at large, as you see, and myself to play what *Tunes* I pleased on my rural Reed.

MEL. Truly I envy you not; *but* rather am amaz'd *at your good Fortune*; *now that* all around there are such Confusions in the Country. Lo myself, sick *as I am,* drive far hence my tender Goats: This too, O Tityrus, I drag along with much ado: For here just now among the thick Hazles having yeaned Twins, the Hope of my Flock, she left them, alas! on the naked flinty Rock. This Calamity, I remember, my Oaks struck *with Lightning* from Heaven often presaged to me, had not my Mind been under Infatuation: Often the ill-boding Crow from an *old* hollow Oak presaged *it.* But tell me, Tityrus, who is this God of yours?

TIT. The City, Melibœus, which they call Rome, I foolishly imagined to be like this our *Mantua,* whither we Shepherds oft-times are wont to drive the tender Offspring of our Ewes. So I had known Whelps like Dogs, so Kids like their Dams; thus was I wont to compare great things with small. But that City hath raised its Head as far above others as the Cypresses use *to do* above the limber Shrubs.

NOTES.

19. *Iste.* Is the true Reading: *Hic*, *iste*, and *ille*, being thus distinguished: *Hic Deus*, is *this God of mine, or whom I mentioned*; *iste Deus*, is *that God of yours*; and *ille Deus*, *that God of his, of theirs, or of any third Person.*

23. *Sic.* He thought it only different in Magnitude, not in Kind; But, when he came to see *Rome*, he then not only found it distinguished in Degree, but even in Species: It was a quite other Sort of City, just as the Cypress differs in Species from a Shrub.

MEL. Et quæ tanta fuit Romam tibi causa videndi?
TIT. Libertas, quæ sera, tamen respexit inertem;
Candidior postquam tondenti barba cadebat:
Respexit tamen, et longo post tempore venit:
Postquam nos Amaryllis habet, Galatea reliquit.
Namque (fatebor enim) dum me Galatea tenebat,
Nec spes libertatis erat, nec cura peculî.
Quamvis multa meis exiret victima septis,
Pinguis et ingratæ premeretur caseus urbi;
Non unquam gravis ære domum mihi dextra redibat.
MEL. Mirabar, quid mœsta Deos, Amarylli, vocares;
Cui pendere suâ patereris in arbore poma.
Tityrus hinc aberat: ipsæ te, Tityre, pinus,
Ipsi te fontes, ipsa hæc arbusta vocabant.
TIT. Quid facerem? neque servitio me exire licebat,
Nec tam præsentes alibi cognoscere Divos.
Hìc illum vidi juvenem, Melibœe, quotannis
Bis senos cui nostra dies altaria fumant.
Hìc mihi responsum primus dedit ille petenti:

Mel. *Et quæ fuit tibi tanta causa videndi Romam?* Tit. *Libertas: quæ* licet *sera, tamen respexit* me *inertem; postquam candidior barba cadebat* mihi *tondenti: tamen respexit, et venit longo tempore post; postquam Amaryllis habet* nos, *et Galatea reliquit* nos. *Namque, dum Galatea tenebat me (enim fatebor) erat* mihi *nec spes libertatis, nec cura peculî. Quamvis multa victima exiret meis septis, et pinguis caseus premeretur* nostræ *ingratæ urbi* Mantuæ; *dextra non unquam redibat mihi domum gravis ære.* Mel. *Amarylli, mirabar quid tu mœsta vocares Deos: cui patereris poma pendere in suâ arbore. Tityrus aberat hinc: Tityre, pinus ipsæ* vocabant *te, fontes ipsi, hæc arbusta ipsa vocabant te.* Tit. *Quid facerem? neque licebat me exire servitio, nec cognoscere tam præsentes Divos alibi. Melibœe, hìc vidi illum juvenem, cui nostra altaria fumant bis senos dies quotannis. Hìc ille primus dedit responsum, mihi petenti* ab illo; ait, *Pueri,*

TRANSLATION.

MEL. And what important Cause had you to visit Rome?

TIT. Liberty, which, *tho'* late, yet cast an Eye upon me *in my* inactive *Time of Life*: after that my Beard began to fall off a grizzled Colour when I shaved: Yet on me she cast her Eye, and after a long Period of Slavery came *at last*: Ever since that Amaryllis sways me, *and* Galatea hath cast me off. For I will not disown it, while Galatea ruled me, I had neither Hopes of Liberty, nor Concern about my Stock. Tho' many a Victim went from my Folds, and *many a* fat Cheese was pressed by me for the ungrateful City, I never returned Home with my Hands full of Money.

MEL. I admired, Amaryllis, why disconsolate you was *still* invoking the Gods; for whom you suffered the Apples to hang on their *native* Tree. *Now I see the Cause.* Your Tityrus from hence was absent. The very Pines, O Tityrus, the Fountains, these very Groves invited thee *to return*.

TIT. What could I do? It was neither in my Power, *while here I staid*, to rid me of my Thraldom, nor elsewhere could I experience Gods so propitious. Here, Melibœus, I saw that *divine* Youth, to whom for twice six Days our Altars yearly smoke *with Incense*. Here first he gave this *gracious* Answer to me

NOTES.

28. *Libertas.* Not that *Virgil* or his Father were really Slaves: But he speaks of the Oppressions he sustained at home in his own Country as a Kind of Slavery.

33. *Peculi.* Peculium is properly the private Stock of a Slave; in which Sense it is fitly applied to *Tityrus*, who personates the Character of a Slave.

36. *Non unquam, &c.* Literally, *My Right-hand never returned Home loaded with Money.*

paſcite boves ut antè, et ſubmittite tauros jugo. Mel. *Fortunate ſenex, ergo tua rura manebunt, et magna ſatìs tibi: quamvis nudus lapis, paluſque obducat omnia tua paſcua limoſo junco: inſueta pabula non tentabunt tuas graves fetas oves: nec mala contagia vicini pecoris lædent eas. Fortunate ſenex, hìc inter nota flumina, et ſacros fontes, captabis opacum frigus. Hinc ſepes, quæ, ab vicino limite, ſemper depaſta quoad florem ſalicti ab Hyblæis apibus, ſæpe ſuadebit tibi inire ſomnum levi ſuſurro. Hinc frondator canet ad auras ſub altâ rupe. Tamen interea nec raucæ palumbes, tua cura, nec turtur ceſſabit gemere ab aëriâ ulmo.* Tit. *Antè, ergo leves cervi paſcentur in æthere, et freta deſtituent piſces nudos in litore; antè, aut Par-*

"Paſcite, ut antè, boves, pueri, ſubmittite tauros."
Mel. Fortunate ſenex, ergo tua rura manebunt;
Et tibi magna ſatìs: quamvis lapis omnia nudus,
Limoſoque palus obducat paſcua junco;
Non inſueta graves tentabunt pabula fetas;
Nec mala vicini pecoris contagia lædent.
Fortunate ſenex, hìc inter flumina nota,
Et fontes ſacros, frigus captabis opacum.
Hinc tibi, quæ ſemper vicino ab limite ſepes
Hyblæis apibus florem depaſta ſalicti,
Sæpe levi ſomnum ſuadebit inire ſuſurro.
Hinc altâ ſub rupe canet frondator ad auras:
Nec tamen interea raucæ, tua cura, palumbes,
Nec gemere aëriâ ceſſabit turtur ab ulmo.
Tit. Antè leves ergo paſcentur in æthere cervi,
Et freta deſtituent nudos in litore piſces;
Ante, pererratis amborum finibus, exſul

TRANSLATION.

his Suppliant: "Swains, feed your Heifers as formerly, yoke your Steers."

Mel. Happy old Man, your Lands ſhall then remain *ſtill in your Poſſeſſion*, and large enough for you: Though naked Stones and Marſh with ſlimy Ruſhes overſpread all the Paſture-grounds; *yet* no unaccuſtomed Fodder ſhall taint thy pregnant Ewes; nor noxious Diſeaſes of the neighbouring Flocks ſhall hurt them. Happy old Man, here between the well known Streams, and ſacred Fountains, you ſhall enjoy the cool Shades. On the one Hand a Hedge planted on the neighbouring Marſh, whoſe ſallow Blooms are ever fed on by Hyblæan Bees, ſhall often court you by its gentle Hummings to indulge Repoſe. On the other Hand, the Wood-lopper beneath a lofty Rock ſhall ſing aloud to Heaven: Nor mean while ſhall either the hoarſe Wood-pigeons, thy Delight, or the Turtle from his airy Elm, ceaſe to cooe.

Tit. Sooner therefore ſhall fleet Stags feed in the Air, and the Seas leave Fiſhes naked on the Shore; ſooner, each others Bounds being *mutually* traverſed,

NOTES.

46. *Pueri.* Puer has three Significations. 1. *A Slave.* 2. *A Boy in Oppoſition to a Girl.* 3. *Puerilis ætas.*

50. *Graves fetas,* i. e. *Prægnantes: Nam feta ſine addito, et de gravida, et de puerpera dicitur.* In the firſt Senſe it occurs, Æn. VIII. 630.

Fecerat et viridi fetam *Mavortis in antro*
Procubuiſſe lupam.

52. *Inter flumina.* The *Mincio* and the *Po.*

53. *Frigus opacum.* Literally, *the ſhady Coolneſs.*

54. *Ab vicino limite.* The ſame as *in*, &c.

55. *Florem depaſta ſalicti.* A Greciſm, the ſame as *habens florem ſalicti depaſtum.*

55. *Hyblæis apibus.* i. e. *Bees ſuch as theſe of* Hybla, a Mountain in *Sicily*, productive of the fineſt Honey.

57. *Frondator.* Servius gives it three Significations. 1. The Woodman in general. 2. The Vine-dreſſer, who clears away the Vine-leaves when they are too thick, and lays the Grapes more open to the Sun. 3. Any Bird that ſings among the Boughs; whence ſome render it the Nightingale.

57. *Ad auras.* In die, ſays *Servius:* But I rather think it means *aloud*, ſo as to pierce the Skies, as the Phraſe is uſed elſewhere.

63. *Parthus.*

Aut Ararim Parthus bibet, aut Germania Tigrim,
Quàm noſtro illius labatur pectore vultus.
MEL. At nos hinc, alii ſitientes ibimus Afros:
Pars Scythiam, et rapidum Cretæ veniemus Oaxem,
Et penitùs toto diviſos orbe Britannos.
En unquàm patrios longo poſt tempore fines,
Pauperis et tugurî congeſtum ceſpite culmen,
Poſt aliquot, mea regna, videns mirabor ariſtas?
Impius hæc tam culta novalia miles habebit?
Barbarus has ſegetes? en quò diſcordia cives
Perduxit miſeros! en queis conſevimus agros!
Inſere, nunc, Melibœe, pyros: pone ordine vites.
Ite meæ, felix quondam pecus, ite capellæ:
Non ego vos poſthàc, viridi projectus in antro,
Dumoſâ pendere procul de rupe videbo.
Carmina nulla canam; non, me paſcente, capellæ,
Florentem cytiſum, et ſalices carpetis amaras.
TIT. Hìc tamen hanc mecum poteris requieſcere noctem
Fronde ſuper viridi. Sunt nobis mitia poma,

ibus exul bibet fluvium Ararim, aut Germania bibet fluvium Tigrim, finibus amborum populorum pererratis, quàm vultus illius juvenis *labatur noſtro pectore.* Mel. *At nos pulſi hinc, alii ibimus* ad *ſitientes Afros: pars veniemus Scythiam et rapidum Oaxem* fluvium *Cretæ, et Britannos penitùs diviſos toto orbe. En unquam* ego *videns mirabor patrios fines longo tempore poſt, et culmen pauperis tugurî congeſtum ceſpite, poſt aliquot ariſtas mea regna?* An *impius miles habebit hæc tam culta novalia?* An *Barbarus habebit has ſegetes? En quo diſcordia perduxit miſeros cives! en, queis conſevimus agros! Melibœe, nunc inſere pyros: pone vites ordine. Ite, ite meæ capellæ, quondam felix pecus. Ego, projectus in viridi antro, non videbo vos poſthac pendere procul de dumoſâ rupe. Canam nulla carmina;* vos *capellæ non carpetis florentem cytiſum et amaras ſalices, me paſcente* vos. Tit. *Hìc tamen poteris requieſcere hanc noctem mecum ſuper viridi fronde. Sunt nobis mitia poma,*

TRANSLATION.

ſhall the Parthian Exile drink the Soane, or Germany the Tigris, than his *lovely* Image be effaced from my Breaſt.

MEL. But we muſt go hence, ſome to the parched Africans; ſome of us ſhall viſit Scythia, and Oaxes the rapid River of Crete, and the Britons quite disjoined from all the World *beſides*. Say, ſhall I ever, after a Length of Time, with Wonder ſee my native Territories, and the Roof of my poor Cot covered over with Turf, *ſtanding* behind ſome Ears of Corn, my Kingdom, *my All?* Shall *then* a Ruffian Soldier poſſeſs theſe ſo well cultivated Lands *of mine?* A Barbarian theſe my Fields of ſtanding Corn? See to what Extremity *civil* Diſcord hath reduced us, wretched Citizens! See for whom we have ſowed our Fields! Now, Melibœus, graft your Pear-trees, in order range your Vines. Begone, my Goats, begone, once a happy Flock: No more ſhall I, extended in my verdant Grot, henceforth behold you hanging far above me from a Rock with Buſhes overgrown. No Carols ſhall I ſing; no more, my Goats, tended by me, ſhall you browze the flowery Cytiſus and bitter Sallows.

TIT. Yet here this Night you may take up your Reſt with me on *a Bed of* green Leaves. We have mellow Apples, Cheſnuts ſoft *and ripe*, and Plenty of

NOTES.

63. *Parthus.* Is not here to be taken for a particular Native of *Parthia*, but for the *Parthian* Nation in general; as *Germania* in the other Part of the Verſe ſignifies *the* Germans *all in a Body*. So that the Meaning is, *That theſe two Nations ſhall ſooner exchange Countries with one another, than, &c.* Had the Critics attended to this, it might have ſaved them a great deal of needleſs Trouble.

70. *Aliquot ariſtas.* Some Years, [illegible] to ſome, as Claudian ſays, *decimus em*[illegible] But this agrees not with *longo poſt te*[illegible] one implying a long, and the other [illegible] ration; or at beſt it would be an [illegible]

molles castaneæ, et copia pressi lactis. Et jam summa culmina villarum procul fumant, majoresque umbræ cadunt de altis montibus.

Castaneæ molles, et pressi copia lactis.
Et jam summa procul villarum culmina fumant,
Majoresque cadunt altis de montibus umbræ.

TRANSLATION.

Curds and Cream. And now the high Tops of the Villages at Distance smoke, and larger Shadows fall from the lofty Mountains.

NOTES.

tition of the same Idea. Therefore by *Aristas* it seems better to understand *thin Fields of Corn*, where are but a few Ears to be seen; which also suits best with *mea regna*, which in the natural Order of Construction must refer to *aliquot aristas*, not to *culmen pauperis tuguri*.

82. *Castaneæ molles.* Molles either signifies ripe, or *such Chesnuts as were called soft, in Opposition to the* hirsutæ, Ecl. VII. 53. the one being smooth in the Husk, the other rough and jagged.

ECLOGA II.

ALEXIS.

ORDO.

Pastor Corydon ardebat formosum Alexin, delicias domini; nec habebat quid speraret. Tantùm veniebat assiduè inter densas fagos habentes *umbrosa cacumina: ibi solus jactabat hæc incondita* carmina *montibus et silvis inani studio.*

FOrmosum pastor Corydon ardebat Alexin,
Delicias domini; nec, quid speraret, habebat.
Tantùm inter densas, umbrosa cacumina, fagos
Assiduè veniebat: ibi hæc incondita solus
Montibus, et silvis studio jactabat inani.

TRANSLATION.

THE Shepherd Corydon burned for fair Alexis, the Darling of his Master; nor had he any Hope *of Success*. Only among the thick Beeches, with high embowering Tops, he continually resorted: There, all alone, with unavailing Fondness he threw away to the Mountains and the Woods these indigested Complaints.

NOTES.

By *Corydon* here some would have us to understand *Virgil* himself, and by *Alexis* a young Slave of *Mecænas* for whom *Virgil* had conceived a violent Affection, and solicited his Patron to make him a Present of the Boy: To which *Martial* is thought to allude to the Verses above quoted, Ecl. I. Be that as it will, *Corydon* is here represented making Love to this beautiful Youth. His Way of Courtship is wholly pastoral: He complains of the Boy's Coyness; recommends himself for his Beauty and Skill in Piping; invites the Youth into the Country, where he promises him the Diversions of the Place, with a suitable Present of Nuts and Apples: But, when he finds nothing will prevail, he resolves to quit his troublesome Amour, and betake himself again to his former Business.

There is certainly something more intended in this Pastoral than a Description of Friendship or *Platonic* Love; the Sentiments, tho' chaste, are too warm and passionate for a mere *Plato-*

nic

O crudelis Alexi, nihil mea carmina curas;
Nil nostri miserere; mori me denique coges.
Nunc etiam pecudes umbras et frigora captant;
Nunc virides etiam occultant spineta lacertos;
Thestylis et rapido fessis messoribus æstu
Allia serpyllumque herbas contundit olentes:
At mecum raucis, tua dum vestigia lustro,
Sole sub ardenti resonant arbusta cicadis.
Nonne fuit satiùs, tristes Amaryllidis iras,
Atque superba pati fastidia? nonne Menalcan?
Quamvis ille niger, quamvis tu candidus esses.
O formose puer, nimiùm ne crede colori.
Alba ligustra cadunt, vaccinia nigra leguntur.
Despectus tibi sum, nec qui sim quæris, Alexi;
Quàm dives pecoris nivei, quàm lactis abundans.
Mille meæ Siculis errant in montibus agnæ.
Lac mihi non æstate, novum non frigore desit.
Canto, quæ solitus; si quando armenta vocabat,

O crudelis Alexi, curas mea carmina nihil; miserere nostri nil; denique coges me mori. Nunc etiam pecudes captant umbras et frigora; nunc etiam spineta occultant virides lacertos; et famula *Thestylis contundit allia serpyllumque, olentes herbas, messoribus fessis rapido æstu. At, dum lustro tua vestigia, ô Alexi, arbusta resonant raucis cicadis mecum sub ardenti sole. Nonne fuit satiùs pati tristes iras Amaryllidis, atque* ejus *superba fastidia?* nonne fuit satiùs pati *Menalcan? quamvis ille* esset *niger, quamvis tu esses candidus. O formose puer, ne crede nimiùm* tuo *colori. Alba ligustra cadunt, nigra vaccinia leguntur. Sum despectus tibi, Alexi, nec quæris qui sim; quàm dives nivei pecori, quàm abundans lactis. Meæ mille agnæ errant in Siculis montibus. Novum lac desit mihi non æstate, non frigore* hyemis. *Canto* hæc carmina,

TRANSLATION.

Ah cruel Alexis, to my Songs thou hast no Regard; on me thou hast no Pity; thou wilt surely be my Death at last. Even the Cattle now *in this Noon-tide Heat* pant after Shades and cool Retreats; now the thorny Brakes shelter *the vilest Reptiles*, even the green Lizards; and Thestylis pounds the Garlic and wild Thyme, strong scented Herbs, for the Reapers spent with violent Heat. But to the hoarse Grasshoppers and me the Groves resound, while under the scorching Sun I trace thy Steps. Was it not better to endure the rueful Spite and proud Disdain of Amaryllis? Had it not been better to endure Menalcas, though he was black, though thou art fair? Ah comely Boy, trust not too much to a Complexion. White Privets fall *neglected*, the purple Hyacinths are gathered. By thee, Alexis, I am neglected; nor once enquire you who I am; how rich in snowy Flocks, how abounding in Milk. A thousand Ewes of mine stray on the Mountains of Sicily. I want not New-milk in Summer, nor in the Cold *of Winter*. I warble the same Airs which Theban Amphion was wont *to practise*, what Time

NOTES.

nic Lover. But there is no Reason to charge *Virgil* on that Account with the unnatural Love of Boys; a Poet may shew his Talent in describing a Passion which he by no means approves. "The Passion for Boys, Mr. *Bayle* "observes, was as common in Pagan Times as "that for Girls; a Writer of Eclogues there-"fore might make his Shepherds talk accord-"ing to that abominable Passion, as we at "present make the Heroes and Heroines of "Romances talk, without approving the Pas-"sions therein mentioned."

18. *Vaccinia.* Some will have this to be Bilberries: *Servius* makes it the Violet; but from that *Virgil* himself plainly distinguishes it, Ecl. X. 39.

Et nigræ violæ, sunt et vaccinia nigra.

Salmasius and others explain it of the Hyacinth, chiefly because *vaccinium* answers to ὑακινθος in that Line of *Theocritus*, which *Virgil* here not only imitates, but almost literally translates:

Και το ιον μελαν εντι και ἁ γραπτα ὑακινθος.

24. *Amphion.*

quæ Dircæus Amphion erat solitus cantare *in Actæo Aracyntho, si quando vocabat armenta. Nec sum adeò informis: nuper stans in litore vidi me, cùm mare staret placidum ventis. Ego non metuam Daphnin, te judice, si imago nunquam fallat. O tantùm libeat tibi habitare, mecum, rura sordida, atque humiles casas, et figere cervos, compellereque gregem hœdorum* cum *viridi hibisco! Imitabere Pana canendo unà mecum in silvis. Pan primus instituit conjungere plures calamos cerâ: Pan curat oves, magistrosque ovium. Nec pœniteat te,* Alexi, *trivisse labellum calamo. Quid Amyntas non faciebat, ut sciret hæc eadem a* me*? Est mihi fistula, compacta septem disparibus cicutis, quam* fistulam *Damœtas olim dedit mihi dono, et moriens dixit* mihi: *Nunc ista* fistula *habet te secundum* dominum. *Damœtas dixit* hoc; *stultus Amyntas invidit* mihi. *Præterea duo capreoli reperti mihi nec tutâ valle,*

Amphion Dircæus in Actæo Aracyntho.
Nec sum adeò informis: nuper me in litore vidi,
Cum placidum ventis staret mare. Non ego Daphnin,
Judice te, metuam, si nunquam fallat imago.
O tantùm libeat mecum tibi sordida rura,
Atque humiles habitare casas, et figere cervos,
Hœdorumque gregem viridi compellere hibisco!
Mecum unà in silvis imitabere Pana canendo.
Pan primus calamos cerâ conjungere plures
Instituit: Pan curat oves, oviumque magistros.
Nec te pœniteat calamo trivisse labellum.
Hæc eadem ut sciret, quid non faciebat Amyntas?
Est mihi disparibus septem compacta cicutis
Fistula: Damœtas dono mihi quam dedit olim;
Et dixit moriens: Te nunc habet ista secundum.
Dixit Damœtas: Invidit stultus Amyntas.
Præterea duo, nec tutâ mihi valle reperti

TRANSLATION.

on Attic Aracynthus he called his Herds together. Nor am I so deformed *as to be the Object of your Disdain:* Upon the Shore I lately viewed myself, when the Sea stood unruffled by the Winds. I will not fear *to compare even with* Daphnis, thyself being Judge, if the Image does not deceive me. O wouldst thou but vouchsafe to inhabit with me our mean rural Retreats, and humble Cots, to pierce the Deer, and with a Bundle of green Twigs to drive together a Flock of Kids! In the Woods along with me thou shalt rival *even* Pan *himself* in Singing. Pan first taught *us* to join together several Reeds with Wax: Pan guards the Sheep and Shepherds both. Nor be thou averse to wear thy Lip with a Shepherd's Reed. What *Pains* did not Amyntas *take* to learn this same *Art of mine?* A Pipe I have of seven unequal Reeds compactly joined, of which Damœtas some time ago made me a Present; and *in his* dying *Moments* said: Thou art now its second Master. Damœtas said: *Me* the foolish Amyntas envied, besides, *I have*

NOTES.

24. *Amphion.* The famous King of *Thebes* who built the Walls of that City: The Stones whereof he is said to have made to dance into their Places by the Music of his Lyre. He is called *Dircæus,* either from *Dirce* his Stepmother, whom he put to Death for the Injuries she had done to his Mother *Antiope*; or from a Fountain in *Beotia* of that Name.

24. *Aracyntho.* Aracynthus was a Town on the Confines of *Attica* and *Beotia,* where was the Fountain *Dirce:* It is called *Actæo, Attice,* from *Acta* or *Acte,* the Country about *Attica,* Ovid. Met. Lib. II. 720. *Sic super Actæas agilis Cyllenius arces inclinat cursus.*

28. *Tibi sordida rura.* Servius, and all the Commentators after him, join *tibi* with *sordida,* the Country which gives you such Disgust. But that Construction seems not so natural; and therefore we have joined *tibi* with *libeat.* As for *sordida,* it is a proper enough Epithet to Cottages and rural Villages, which are but mean and poorly furnished. Or he speaks in the Character of a Lover, who thinks nothing good enough for his beloved Object.

30. *Hibisco.* A slender Twig or Rush; as appears from Ecl. X. 71.

Dum sedet, et gracili fiscellam texit hibisco.

36. *Cicutis.* Hemlock, here used for any hollow Reeds.

38. *Te nunc, &c.* Literally, *Now it has you its second Master.*

Capreoli, ſparſis etiam nunc pellibus albo,
Bina die ſiccant bovis ubera: quos tibi ſervo.
Jampridem à me illos abducere Theſtylis orat:
Et faciat: quoniam ſordent tibi munera noſtra.
Hùc ades, ô formoſe puer: tibi lilia plenis
Ecce ferunt nymphæ calathis: tibi candida Nais,
Pallentes violas et ſumma papavera carpens,
Narciſſum et florem jungit benè olentis anethi.
Tum caſiâ, atque aliis intexens ſuavibus herbis,
Mollia luteolâ pingit vaccinia calthâ.
Ipſe ego cana legam tenerâ lanugine mala,
Caſtaneaſque nuces, mea quas Amaryllis amabat.
Addam cerea pruna: honos erit huic quoque pomo:
Et vos, ô lauri, carpam, et te, proxima myrte:
Sic poſitæ quoniam ſuaves miſcetis odores.
Ruſticus es, Corydon; nec munera curat Alexis:
Nec, ſi muneribus certes, concedat Iolas.
Eheu, quid volui miſero mihi? floribus Auſtrum
Perditus, et liquidis immiſi fontibus apros.

etiam nunc pellibus ſparſis albo, ſiccant bina ubera ovis die: quos capreolos ego ſervo tibi. Jampridem Theſtylis orat abducere illos à me: et faciat: quoniam noſtra munera ſordent tibi. Ades huc, ô formoſe puer: ecce Nymphæ ferunt lilia tibi plenis calathis: candida Nais, carpens pallentes violas et ſumma papavera tibi, jungit Narciſſum et florem benè olentis anethi. Tum intexens illos flores *caſiâ atque aliis ſuavibus herbis, pingit mollia vaccinia luteolâ calthâ. Ego ipſe legam cana mala tenerâ lanugine, caſtaneaſque nuces, quas mea Amaryllis amabat. Addam cerea pruna: et honos erit huic pomo quoque: et carpam vos, ô lauri, et te, myrte proxima* lauris: *quoniam vos ſic poſitæ miſcetis ſuaves odores. Corydon, es ruſticus, nec Alexis curat* tua *munera: nec Iolas concedat* tibi, *ſi certes muneribus. Eheu, quid volui mihi miſero?* ego *perditus immiſi Auſtrum floribus, et apros liquidis fontibus.*

TRANSLATION.

two young He-goats, which I found in a Valley not without Danger, whoſe Skins even now are flecked with white, each Day they drain both the Udders of a Ewe: Theſe I reſerve for thee. Long Theſtylis has begged to have them from me; and let her have them; ſince my Preſents are diſdained by you.

Come hither, O lovely Boy: Behold the Nymphs bring thee Lilies in full Baſkets: For thee, fair Nais, cropping the pale Violets and Heads of Poppies, joins the Narciſſus and Flower of ſweet-ſmelling Aniſe. Then, interweaving them with Caſſia and other fragrant Herbs, ſets off the ſoft Hyacinths with Saffron Marygold. Myſelf will gather for thee Quinces whitening with tender Down, and Cheſnuts which my Amaryllis loved. Plums I will add of waxen Hue: On this Fruit too ſhall Honour be conferred: And you, ye Laurels, I will crop, and thee, O Myrtle, next *in Dignity to the Laurel:* For thus arranged you mingle ſweet Perfumes.

Ah Corydon, thou art a *ſilly* Clown *thus to flatter thyſelf.* Alexis neither minds thy Preſents: Nor, if by Preſents thou ſhouldſt ſtrive *to win him,* would Iolas, *thy richer Rival,* yield. Alas, what was in my wretched Mind? Undone, undone, I have let the South-wind looſe among my Flowers, and the Boars *to pollute*

NOTES.

51. *Mala.* We have tranſlated it *Quinces,* with *Servius,* and all the Commentators; whereof the white are the beſt and moſt fragrant. See *Pliny,* XXI. 6. But the Deſcription here given ſeems rather to agree to the Peach, as Mr. *Dryden* renders it.

53. *Cerea.* Of a beautiful Colour as Wax. See *La Cerda.* The *et* is wanting in all the ancient Manuſcripts: It ſeems to have been added by ſome Tranſcriber, who had fancied the Verſe would be deficient without it; but the Aſpiration *h* coming after the *a* ſupports it.

57. *Iolas.* Thoſe who think *Corydon* perſonates *Virgil,* and *Alexis* the Slave of *Mecænas* whom he loved, by *Iolas* here of courſe underſtand *Mecænas.*

58. *Floribus Auſtrum immiſi.* A proverbial Expreſſion, applicable to thoſe who wiſh for

Ah, demens! quem fugis? Dî quoque Dardaniusque Paris habitârunt silvas. Pallas ipsa colat arces quas condidit: silvæ placeant nobis ante omnia. Torva leæna sequitur lupum, lupus ipse sequitur capellam; lasciva capella sequitur florentem cytisum; Corydon sequitur te, ô Alexi. Sua voluptas trahit quemque. Aspice, juvenci referunt aratra suspensa jugo, et sol decedens duplicat crescentes umbras: tamen amor urit me. Enim quis modus adsit amori? Ah, Corydon, Corydon, quæ dementia cepit te! Est tibi semiputata vitis in frondosâ ulmo. Quin tu potiùs paras detexere aliquid saltem, quorum usus indiget, viminibus mollique junco? invenies alium Alexin, si hic Alexis *fastidit te.*

Quem fugis, ah, demens! habitârunt Dî quoque silvas,
Dardaniusque Paris. Pallas, quas condidit, arces
Ipsa colat: nobis placeant ante omnia silvæ.
Torva leæna lupum sequitur, lupus ipse capellam;
Florentem cytisum sequitur lasciva capella;
Te, Corydon, ô Alexi. Trahit sua quemque voluptas.
Aspice, aratra jugo referunt suspensa juvenci;
Et sol crescentes decedens duplicat umbras:
Me tamen urit amor. Quis enim modus adsit amori?
Ah. Corydon, Corydon; quæ te dementia cepit!
Semiputata tibi frondosâ vitis in ulmo est.
Quin tu aliquid saltem, potiùs quorum indiget usus,
Viminibus, mollique paras detexere junco?
Invenies alium, si te hic fastidit, Alexin.

TRANSLATION.

my crystal Springs. Ah, witless *Boy*, whom dost thou fly? The Gods themselves have dwelt in Woods, and *there* the Trojan Paris dwelt. Let Pallas inhabit Palaces of which she is the Foundress: Let us in Woods above all Things delight. The grim Lioness pursues the Wolf, the Wolf himself the Goat; the wanton Goat pursues the flowery Cytisus; *and* Corydon thee, O Alexis. Each is drawn away by some peculiar Pleasure.

See, the *labouring* Steers bring home the Plough borne lightly on the Yoke, and the retreating Sun doubles the growing Shadows: But me Love *still* consumes. For what Bounds can be set to Love? Ah, Corydon, Corydon; what Frenzy hath possessed thee? Half-pruned is thy Vine *propped* on the leafy Elm. Why rather triest thou not to weave, of Osiers and pliant Rushes, some one or other at least of those Implements which thy Work requires? Thou wilt find another Alexis, if this disdains thee.

NOTES.

Things that prove destructive to them; the Southwind by its hot sultry Quality being noxious to Flowers. Hence *Papin.* Lib. III. *Sylv.*

Pubentesque rosæ primos moriuntur ad austros.

61. *Dardaniusque Paris.* Paris was exposed by his Father in a Wood, in order to elude the Oracle, which foretold that he was to be the Destruction of *Troy*.

61. *Pallas condidit.* Meaning, that she first invented and taught to build stately Structures.

66. *Suspensa.* Moving lightly, as Things that are suspended in a Balance.

ECLOGA

ECLOGA III.

MENALCAS, DAMOETAS, PALÆMON.

M. DIC mihi, Damœta, cujum pecus? an Meliboei?
D. Non; verùm Ægonis. Nuper mihi tradidit Ægon.
M. Infelix ô ſemper oves pecus! ipſe Neæram
Dum fovet, ac, ne me ſibi præferat illa, veretur;
Hic alienus oves cuſtos bis mulget in horâ,
Et ſuccus pecori, et lac ſubducitur agnis.
D. Parcius iſta viris tamen objicienda memento.
Novimus et qui te, tranſverſa tuentibus hircis,
Et quo, ſed faciles nymphæ riſere, ſacello.
M. Tum, credo, cùm me arbuſtum videre Myconis,
Atque mala vites incidere falce novellas.
D. Aut hìc ad veteres fagos, cum Daphnidis arcum

ORDO.

M. *Damœta, dic mihi cujum pecus eſt? an eſt Melibœi?* D. *Non; verùm* eſt *Ægonis. Ægon tradidit* illud *mihi nuper.* M. *O oves, ſemper infelix pecus! dum Ægon ipſe fovet Neæram, ac veretur ne illa præferat me ſibi; hic alienus cuſtos mulget oves bis in horâ: et ſuccus ſubducitur pecori, et lac* ſub-ducitur *agnis.* D *Tamen memento iſta objicienda* eſſe *viris parcius. Et novimus qui* corruperit *te, hircis tuentibus tranſverſa, et quo ſacello, ſed faciles nymphæ riſere.* M. *Credo* fuiſſe *tum, cùm* illæ *videre me incidere arbuſtum Myconis, atque* ejus *novellas vites malâ falce.* D. *Aut hìc ad veteres fagos, quum fregiſti arcum et calamos Daphnidis, quæ tu,*

TRANSLATION.

M. TELL me, Damœtas, whoſe *is* that Flock? Is it *that* of Melibœus?

D. No; but Ægon's. Ægon lately gave it to my Care.

M. Ah Sheep, ſtill a luckleſs Flock! while *the Maſter* himſelf careſſes Neæra, and fears that ſhe prefer me to him; this hireling Shepherd milks his Ewes twice in an Hour; and *by him* the Juice from the Flock, and the Milk from the Lambs, is filched away.

D. Remember, however, that theſe Scandals ſhould with more Reſerve be charged on Men. We know both who *ſeduced* you, and in what ſacred Cave, while the Goats looked aſkance; but the good-natured Nymphs *winked thereat, and* ſmiled.

M. Then, I ſuppoſe, when they ſaw me with a felonious Bill cut down Mycon's Grove and tender Vines.

D. Or here by theſe old Beeches, when *for Spite* you broke the Bow and Arrows of Daphnis: Which when you, croſs-grained Menalcas, ſaw given to the

NOTES.

Damœtas and *Menalcas*, after ſome ſmart Strokes of Country Raillery, reſolve to try who has the moſt Skill at a Song; and accordingly make their Neighbour *Palæmon* Judge of their Performance: Who, after a full Hearing of both Parties, declares himſelf unfit for the Deciſion of ſo weighty a Controverſy, and leaves the Victory undetermined.

7. *Viris.* There is a particular Emphaſis lie, on *viris*: As much as to ſay, *Such Indignities may be borne by ſuch Varlets as you, but not by Men of Honour.*

10. *Tum credo, &c.* Menalcas here ſlily accuſes *Damœtas* of what he charges himſelf with.

16. *Farci,*

perverſe Menalca, cùm vidiſti donata puero, et dolebas, et eſſes mortuus, ſi non nocuiſſes ei aliqua. M. *Quid domini* ipſi *faciant, cùm* ſervi *fures audent talia? an non ego vidi te, peſſime, excipere caprum Damonis inſidiis, Lyciſcâ latrante multum? et cùm ego clamarem: quò nunc ille* fur *proripit ſe? Tityre, coge* tuum *pecus: tu latebas poſt carecta.* D. *An non ille, victus cantando, redderet mihi caprum, quem mea fiſtula meruiſſet carminibus? ſi neſcis, ille caper fuit meus; et Damon ipſe fatebatur* id, *ſed negabat ſe poſſe reddere* eum. M. *Tu* viciſti *illum cantando? aut unquam fuit tibi fiſtula juncta cerâ? an non tu, indocte, ſolebas diſperdere miſerum carmen ſtridenti ſtipulâ in triviis?* D. *Vis ergo* ut *viciſſim experiamur inter nos, quid uterque poſſit? ego depono hanc vitulam (ne forte recuſes* eam, *bis* die *venit ad mulctram, alit binos fetus ubere) tu dic, quo pignore certes mecum.*

Fregiſti et calamos: quæ tu, perverſe Menalca,
Et, cùm vidiſti puero donata, dolebas;
Et, ſi non aliqua nocuiſſes, mortuus eſſes.
M. Quid domini faciant, audent cùm talia fures?
Non ego te vidi Damonis, peſſime, caprum
Excipere inſidiis, multum latrante Lyciſcâ?
Et, cùm clamarem: Quò nunc ſe proripit ille?
Tityre, coge pecus: tu poſt carecta latebas.
D. An mihi cantando victus non redderet ille,
Quem mea carminibus meruiſſet fiſtula, caprum?
Si neſcis, meus ille caper fuit; et mihi Damon
Ipſe fatebatur: ſed reddere poſſe negabat.
M. Cantando tu illum? aut unquam tibi fiſtula cerâ
Juncta fuit? non tu in triviis, indocte, ſolebas
Stridenti miſerum ſtipulâ diſperdere carmen?
D. Vis ergo inter nos, quid poſſit uterque, viciſſim
Experiamur? ego hanc vitulam (ne ſortè recuſes,
Bis venit ad mulctram, binos alit ubere fetus)
Depono: tu dic, mecum quo pignore certes.

TRANSLATION.

Boy, you both repined; and, hadſt thou not by ſome Means or other done him a Miſchief, thou hadſt burſt *for Envy*.

M. What may *not* Maſters do, when pilfering Slaves are ſo audacious? Miſcreant! did not I ſee thee inſidiouſly ſnap the Goat of Damon, while his Mongrel barked with Fury? And when I cried out, Whither is he now ſneaking off? Tityrus, gather your Flock together: You ſkulked away behind the Sedges.

D. Ought he not when vanquiſhed in piping to give me the Goat which my Flute by its Muſic won? If you know not, *I will let you know*, that Goat was my own; and Damon himſelf owned to me *the Debt*, but alleged he was not able to pay.

M. You *vanquiſh* him in piping? Or was there ever a Wax-jointed Pipe in your Poſſeſſion? Waſt thou not wont, thou Dunce, in the Croſs-ways to murder a pitiful Tune on a ſqueaking Straw?

D. Are you willing then that we ſhall each of us try by Turns what we can do? This young Heifer I ſtake, and, leſt you ſhould poſſibly reject it, ſhe comes twice a Day to the Milking-pail, two Calves ſhe ſuckles with her Udder: Say you what Stake you will lay againſt me.

NOTES.

16. *Fures*, i. e. *Slaves*; becauſe Slaves were much addicted to Pilfering: Hence *Plautus*, ſpeaking to a Slave, ſays: *Tu trium literarum homo, vituperas me?* i. e. *tu fur*.

18. *Lyciſca*. The Mongrel Breed of a Wolf and a Bitch, from λυκος, *lupus*, and κυων, *canis*.

20. *Coge*. i. e. *Examine that none of them be wanting*.

31. *Mecum quo pignore certes*. Literally, *With what Stake you will contend with me*.

M. De grege non ausim quicquam deponere tecum:
Est mihi namque domi pater, est injusta noverca:
Bisque die numerant ambo pecus, alter et hœdos.
Verùm, id quod multò tute ipse fatebere majus,
Insanire libet quoniam tibi, pocula ponam
Fagina, cœlatum divini opus Alcimedontis:
Lenta quibus torno facili superaddita vitis
Diffusos ederâ vestit pallente corymbos.
In medio duo signa, Conon: et, quis fuit alter,
Descripsit radio totum qui gentibus orbem;
Tempora quæ messor, quæ curvus arator haberet?
Necdum illis labra admovi, sed condita servo.
D. Et nobis idem Alcimedon duo pocula fecit:
Et molli circum est ansas amplexus acantho:
Orpheaque in medio posuit, silvasque sequentes.
Necdum illis labra admovi, sed condita servo.
Si ad vitulam spectas, nihil est quod pocula laudes.
M. Nunquam hodiè effugies: veniam quocunque vocàris.

M. *Non ausim deponere quicquam de grege tecum: namque est mihi pater domi, est injusta noverca: bisque die ambo numerant pecus, et alter* numerat *hœdos. Verùm, quoniam libet tibi insanire, ponam id, quod tute ipse fatebere esse majus* pignus, scilicet, duo *fagina pocula, cœlatum opus divini Alcimedontis: quibus* poculis *lenta vitis, superaddita facili torno, vestit corymbos diffusos pallente hederâ. In medio* sunt *duo signa, Conon: et, quis fuit alter,* ille *qui descripsit totum orbem gentibus radio, quæ tempora messor, quæ* tempora *curvus arator haberet? necdum admovi* mea *labra illis, sed servo* illa *condita.* D. *Et idem Alcimedon fecit duo pocula nobis, et est circum amplexus ansas* eorum *molli acantho: posuitque Orphea in medio, silvasque sequentes* eum. *Necdum admovi* mea *labra illis, sed servo* illa *condita. Si spectes ad vitulam, est nihil* propter *quod laudes pocula.* M. *Nunquam effugies* certamen *hodiè: veniam quocunque vocàris* me.

TRANSLATION.

M. I dare not stake any thing from the Flock: For I have a Sire at home, I have a harsh Step-dame: And twice a Day they number the Cattle both, and one the Kids. But, what thyself shalt own of far greater Value, since thou choosest to be mad, I will pawn my beechen Bowls, the carved Work of divine Alcimedon: Round with a curling Vine, superadded by the easy *skilful* Carver's Art, mantles the clustering Berries diffusely spread from a pale Ivy-*bough*. In the midst two Figures *are embossed*, Conon *the one:* And, who was the other? He who with his Wand distributed among the Nations the whole Globe; *Who taught* what Seasons the Reaper, what the bending Ploughman should observe? Nor have I yet applied my Lips to them, but keep them carefully laid up.

D. For me too the same Alcimedon made two Bowls, and with soft Foliage wreathed their Handles round: Orpheus in the midst he placed, and the Woods following. Nor have I yet applied my Lips to them, but keep them carefully laid up. If you consider the Heifer, you have no Reason to praise *so much* your Bowls.

M. By no Means shalt thou this Day escape: I will descend to any Terms you

NOTES.

38. *Lenta quibus, &c.* These two Verses are somewhat intricate, and the Commentators have made them much more by their Glosses. *Ruæus* takes *vitis* for *vimen*, but quotes no Authority: And the whole of his Interpretation appears harder than the Original. *Vitis* I take in the usual Sense: By *torno facili, the easy carving Tool,* understand the ingenious Carver, who handles the graving Tool with Ease and Address: And by *diffusos edera pallente corymbos,* the Berries diffused on the Ivy-boughs. So that the plain Meaning will be, that each of these Cups was engraved with Vine and Ivy-branches interwoven, in such sort, that the Ivy-berries were shaded by the mantling Vine.

40. *Quis fuit alter?* Supposed to mean either *Aratus* or *Archimedes*.

45. *Acantho.* Acanthus is properly the Plant called *Bear's foot*, or *Bear's-Breech*.

49. *Nunquam hodiè effugies.* Damœtas seemed

Tantùm vel ille qui venit audiat hæc, ecce, Palæmon: efficiam, ne laceſſas quemquam voce poſthac. D. Quin age, ſi habes quid; non erit ulla mora in me: nec fugio quemquam. Tantùm, vicine Palæmon, reponas hæc imis ſenſibus mentis, res non eſt parva. P. Dicite; quandoquidem conſedimus in molli herbâ: et nunc omnis ager, nunc omnis arbos parturit: nunc ſilvæ frondent, nunc annus eſt formoſiſſimus. Incipe, Damœta, tu deinde ſequêre, Menalca. Dicetis alternis carminibus: Camenæ amant alterna carmina. D. Muſæ, principium ſit ab Jove: omnia ſunt plena Jovis: ille colit terras, mea carmina ſunt illi curæ. M. Et Phœbus amat me: ſunt Phœbo ſemper apud me ſua munera, lauri, et ſuave rubens hyacinthus. D. Galatea, laſciva puella, petit me malo, et fugit ad ſalices, et cupit ſe videri à me antè quam fugiat. M. At meus ignis Amyntas offert ſeſe mihi ultro; ut non Delia ſit notior noſtris canibus.

Audiat hæc tantùm vel qui venit, ecce, Palæmon:
Efficiam poſthàc ne quemquam voce laceſſas.
D. Quin age, ſi quid habes; in me mora nón erit ulla:
Nec quemquam fugio. Tantùm, vicine Palæmon,
Senſibus hæc imis, res eſt non parva, reponas.
P. Dicite; quandoquidem in molli conſedimus herbâ:
Et nunc omnis ager, nunc omnis parturit arbos:
Nunc frondent ſilvæ, nunc formoſiſſimus annus.
Incipe Damœta: tu deinde ſequêre, Menalca.
Alternis dicetis: amant alterna Camenæ.
D. Ab Jove principium, Muſæ: Jovis omnia plena:
Ille colit terras, illi mea carmina curæ.
M. Et me Phœbus amat: Phœbo ſua ſemper apud me
Munera ſunt, lauri, et ſuave rubens hyacinthus.
D. Malo me Galatea petit, laſciva puella;
Et fugit ad ſalices, et ſe cupit ante videri.
M. At mihi ſeſe offert ultro meus ignis Amyntas:
Notior ut jam ſit canibus non delia noſtris.

TRANSLATION.

name. Let but that very Perſon who comes (lo, it is Palæmon) liſten to this *Debate*: I'll take care you ſhall not challenge *any* henceforth at ſinging.

D. Come on then, if thou haſt any *Manhood*; in me there ſhall be no Delay: Nor do I decline any *Judge*. Only, *good* Neighbour Palæmon, weigh this Debate with the deepeſt Attention, it is a Matter of no ſmall Importance.

P. Sing *then*; ſince we are ſeated on the ſoft Graſs: And now every Field, now every Tree is budding forth: Now the Woods look green, now the Year is in its higheſt Beauty. Begin Damœtas: Then you, Menalcas, follow. Ye ſhall ſing in alternate Meaſures: Alternate Meaſures pleaſe the Muſes.

D. From Jove, ye Muſes, let us begin: All Things are full of Jove: He cheriſhes the Earth, my Songs are his Regard.

M. And me Phœbus loves: For Phœbus are ſtill with me his *ſacred* Gifts, the Laurel, and ſweet-bluſhing Hyacinth.

D. Galatea, a wanton Girl, pelts me with Apples; *then* to the Sallows flies, but wiſhes firſt to be ſeen.

M. But my Darling Amyntas voluntarily offers himſelf to me; that now not Delia's ſelf is more familiar to our Dogs.

NOTES.

ed to conſtrue *Menalcas*'s Backwardneſs to ſtake a Heifer as an Attempt to evade the Combat, and ſtill inſiſted on that Condition: Upon which *Menalcas* turns ſhort upon him, retorts the Charge of Faint-heartedneſs, and takes him on his own Terms: *Nunquam hodiè, &c.* Think not that any of your evaſive Arts will ſerve your Turn; *veniam quocunque vocaris*; I will deſcend to any Terms you name; if you inſiſt on my ſtaking a Heifer, be it ſo; I agree to that, or any other Condition you name.

54. *Senſibus imis.* Literally, *Lay up theſe Matters in your deepeſt Thoughts.*

63. *Lauri—hyacinthus.* The Laurel and Hyacinth were ſacred to *Apollo*; the one on account of *Daphne*, *Apollo*'s Miſtreſs, who was transformed

D. Parta meæ Veneri ſunt munera: namque notavi
Ipſe locum, aëriæ quo congeſſere palumbes.
M. Quod potui, puero ſilveſtri ex arbore lecta
Aurea mala decem miſi; cras altera mittam.
D. O quoties, et quæ nobis Galatea locuta eſt!
Partem aliquam, venti, Divûm referatis ad aures.
M. Quid prodeſt, quod me ipſo animo non ſpernis, Amynta,
Si, dum tu ſectaris apros, ego retia ſervo?
D. Phyllida mitte mihi: meus eſt natalis, Iola.
Cum faciam vitulâ pro frugibus, ipſe venito.
D. Phyllida amo ante alias, nam me diſcedere flevit;
Et, longum formoſe vale, vale, inquit, Iola.
D. Triſte lupus ſtabulis; maturis frugibus imbres;
Arboribus venti: nobis Amaryllidis iræ.
M. Dulce ſatis humor; depulſis arbutus hœdis;
Lenta ſalix feto pecori; mihi ſolus Amyntas.

D. *Munera ſunt parta meæ Veneri: namque ego ipſe notavi locum*, in *quo aëriæ palumbes congeſſere* nidamenta. M. Ego *miſi decem aurea mala puero* Amyntæ, *lecta ex ſilveſtri arbore, quod* unum *potui facere: cras mittam altera.* D. *O quoties, et quæ* verba *Galatea eſt locuta nobis!* vos *venti referatis aliquam partem* eorum *ad aures Divûm.* M. *Quid prodeſt* mihi, *Amynta, quod* tu *ipſe non ſpernis me animo, ſi ego ſervo retia, dum tu ſectaris apros?* D. *Iola, mitte Phyllida mihi, eſt meus natalis* dies. *Cum faciam* ſacra *vitulâ pro frugibus*, tu *ipſe venito.* M. *Iola, amo Phyllida ante alias* fœminas, *nam flevit me diſcedere; et inquit, formoſe* Menalca, *vale longum* tempus, *vale.* D. *Lupus* eſt *triſte ſtabulis; imbres* ſunt *maturis frugibus; venti* ſunt *arboribus; iræ Amaryllidis* ſunt triſte *nobis.* M. *Humor* eſt *dulce ſatis; arbutus* eſt *depulſis hœdis; lenta ſalix* eſt *feto pecori; Amyntas ſolus* eſt dulce *mihi.*

TRANSLATION.

D. I have a Preſent provided for my Love: For I myſelf marked the Place where the airy Ring-doves have built *their Neſt.*

M. What I could I ſent to my Boy, ten golden Apples gathered from a Tree in the Wood: To-morrow I will ſend him other *ten.*

D. Oh how often, and what *charming* Things Galatea ſpoke to me! Some Part, ye Winds, waft to the Ears of the Gods.

M. What avails it, O Amyntas, that you deſpiſe me not in your Heart, if, while you hunt the Boars, I watch the Toils, *and ſhare not with you the Danger?*

D. Iolas, ſend *home* to me *the charming* Phyllis: It is my Birth-day. When for the Fruits I ſacrifice a Heifer, come thyſelf.

M. Iolas, I love Phyllis above others, for at my Departure ſhe wept; and ſaid, Adieu, fair Youth, a long Adieu.

D. The Wolf is * fatal to the Flocks; Showers of Rain to ripened Corn; *ſhaking* Winds to Trees; to me the Wrath of Amaryllis.

M. Moiſture is grateful to the ſpringing Corn; the Arbutus to weaned Kids; limber Willows to the teeming Cattle; to me Amyntas only.

* *A ſad Thing.*

NOTES.

transformed into the Laurel; and the other of *Hyacinthus* his favourite Boy, whom he accidentally killed with a Quoit, and from whoſe Blood ſprung the Flower of his Name. *See Banier Mythology.*

74. *Quid prodeſt, &c.* Damœtas mentions the Happineſs he had enjoyed in his Miſtreſs's Preſence and Converſe; and in her Abſence ſolaces himſelf with the delightful Remembrance thereof; *Menalcas* here ſtrives to go beyond him in Sentiments of Love and Tenderneſs, and ſhews that it is impoſſible for him to have any Enjoyment of himſelf while *Amyntas* is abſent, nay, unleſs he ſhare with him every Danger.

77. *Faciam vitulâ*, i. e. *Faciam ſacra ex vitulâ.*

80. *Stabulis.* Stalls, here put for Herds or Flocks of Cattle.

82. *Arbutus.* The Strawberry-tree, ſo called from the Reſemblance of its Fruit to a Strawberry.

D. Pollio amat nostram Musam, quamvis sit rustica: Pierides, pascite vitulam vestro lectori. M. *Et Pollio ipse facit nova carmina: pascite illi taurum,* qui *jam petat cornu, et qui spargat arenam pedibus.* D. *Qui amat te, Pollio, veniat, quò gaudet te quoque venisse: mella fluant illi, et asper rubus ferat amomum.* M. *Qui non odit Bavium* poëtam, *amet tua carmina, Mævi: atque idem jungat vulpes* jugo, *et mulgeat hircos.* D. *O pueri, qui legitis flores, et fraga nascentia humi, fugite hinc, frigidus anguis latet in herbâ.* M. *Oves, parcite procedere nimiùm; non creditur bene ripæ: etiam aries ipse nunc siccat vellera.* D. *Tityre, reîce pascentes capellas à flumine:* ego *ipse lavabo omnes in fonte, ubi erit tempus.* M. *Pueri, cogite oves* in ovile: *si æstus præceperit lac, ut nuper, frustra pressabimus ubera* earum *palmis.*

D. Pollio amat nostram, quamvis est rustica, Musam:
Pierides, vitulam lectori pascite vestro.
M. Pollio et ipse facit nova carmina: pascite taurum,
Jam cornu petat, et pedibus qui spargat arenam.
D. Qui te, Pollio, amat, veniat, quò te quoque gaudet:
Mella fluant illi, ferat et rubus asper amomum.
M. Qui Bavium non odit, amet tua carmina, Mævi:
Atque idem jungat vulpes, et mulgeat hircos.
D. Qui legitis flores, et humi nascentia fraga,
Frigidus, ô pueri, fugite hinc, latet anguis in herbâ.
M. Parcite oves nimiùm procedere; non bene ripæ
Creditur: Ipse aries etiam nunc vellera siccat.
D. Tityre, pascentes à flumine reîce capellas:
Ipse, ubi tempus erit, omnes in fonte lavabo.
M. Cogite oves, pueri: si lac præceperit æstus,
Ut nuper, frustra pressabimus ubera palmis.

TRANSLATION.

D. Pollio loves my Muse, though rustic: Ye Pierian Sisters, feed a Heifer for your Reader.

M. Pollio himself too composes noble Verses: Feed *for him* the Bull which already butts with the Horn, and spurns the Sand with his Feet.

D. Let him who loves thee, Pollio, rise *to those Honours* to which he joys that thou *hast risen*. For him let Honey flow, and the prickly Bramble bring forth Amomum.

M. Who hates not Bavius's Verse, may he love thine, O Mævius: And the same *Fool* may join Foxes *in the Yoke*, and milk He-goats.

D. Ye Swains who gather Flowers, and Strawberries that grow *lowly* on the Ground, oh fly hence, a cold *deadly* Snake lurks in the Grass.

M. Forbear, *my* Sheep, to advance too far; 'tis not safe trusting to the Bank: The Ram himself is but now drying his Fleece.

D. Tityrus, from the River remove your browzing Goats: I myself, when it is time, will wash them all in the Pool.

M. Pen up the Sheep, ye Swains: If the Heat shall dry up the Milk, as of late, in vain shall we squeeze the Teats with our Hands.

NOTES.

86. *Nova*, i. e. *Magna miranda*, such as are rare and unmatched.

88. *Veniat quò.* May he arrive at the Consulship, and all those Honours which you have attained.

89. *Amomum.* What is commonly called *amomum Plinii*, or *Berry-bearing Nightshade*: But *Salmasius* thinks the Ancients called every sweet Odour *amomum*.

98. *Præceperit.* Shall take it before us, or prevent us of it.

D. Eheu, quam pingui macer est mihi taurus in arvo!
Idem amor exitium pecori est, pecorisque magistro.
M. His certè neque amor causa est: vix ossibus hærent:
Nescio quis teneros oculus mihi fascinat agnos.
D. Dic, quibus in terris, et eris mihi magnus Apollo,
Tres pateat cœli spatium non amplius ulnas.
M. Dic, quibus in terris inscripti nomina Regum
Nascantur flores; et Phyllida solus habeto.
P. Non nostrum inter vos tantas componere lites:
Et vitulâ tu dignus, et hic; et quisquis amores
Aut metuet dulces, aut experietur amaros
Claudite jam rivos, pueri: sat prata biberunt.

D. Eheu, quàm macer taurus est mihi in pingui arvo! idem amor est exitium pecori, magistroque pecoris. M. Certè neque amor est causa his meis ovibus cur sunt macræ: *vix hærent ossibus: nescio quis oculus fascinat teneros agnos mihi. D. Dic in quibus terris, spatium cœli pateat tres ulnas, et non amplius, et eris magnus Apollo mibi. M.* Tu *dic, in quibus terris flores nascantur, inscripti* quoad *nomina regum, et* tu *solus habeto Phyllida.* P. *Non est nostrum componere tantas lites inter vos: et tu* es *dignus vitulâ, et hic; et quisquis aut metuet dulces, aut experietur amaros amores. Jam, pueri, claudite rivos: prata biberunt sat.*

TRANSLATION.

D. Alas, how lean is my Bullock in a fertile Field! the same Love is the Bane of the Herd, and of the Herdsman.

M. Surely Love is not the Cause why these *too are so lean:* They scarce stick to their Bones: I know not what *malignant* Eye bewitches my tender Lambs.

D. Tell me, and you shall be my great Apollo, where Heaven's Circuit extends not farther than three Ells.

M. Tell me where Flowers grow, inscribed with the Names of Kings; and have Phyllis to thyself alone.

P. 'Tis not in me to determine this weighty Controversy between you: Both you and he deserve the Heifer; and whoever *so well* shall sing the Fears of sweet *successful* Love, and experimentally describe the Bitterness *of Disappointment.* Now, Swains, shut up your Streams: The Meads have drunk enough.

NOTES.

105. *Tres pateat, &c.* May mean, *In the Bottom of a Well.*

106. *Inscripti nomina regum, &c.* The Flower here meant is probably the Hyacinth, of which *Pliny* says: *Hyacinthum comitatur fabula duplex, luctum præferens ejus quem Apollo dilexerat, aut ex Ajacis cruore editi, ita discurrentibus venis, ut figura literarum Græcarum* Ai, *legatur inscripta*, Lib. XXI. Cap. 2. This Account, I doubt, is like many others in *Pliny*, built but on a slight Foundation: But it is sufficient for *Virgil* if there was such a Tradition.

110. *Metuet dulces, &c.* Literally, *Shall either fear sweet Amours, or experience the bitter;* i. e. *shall sing the Fears and Jealousies that mingle with sweet successful Love, and from Experience describe the Pangs and bitterness of Disappointment.* The one was the Case of *Menalcas*, *Dulce satis humor, &c.* the other that of *Damœtas*, *Triste lupus stabulis, &c.* In the Language of Poetry, Persons are said to do what they naturally describe. So Ecl. VI. 62.

Tum Phaëthontiadas musco circumdat amaræ Corticis, &c.

111. *Claudite, &c.* An allegorical Expression, denoting that it was Time to give over their Songs, now that they had given sufficient Proof of their Talent.

ORDO.

Musæ Sicelides, canamus paulò majora carmina. Arbusta, humilesque myricæ, non juvant omnes. Si canimus silvas, silvæ sint dignæ consule. Jam ultima ætas Cumæi carminis venit: jam magnus ordo seculorum nascitur ab integro. Et jam Virgo Astræa *redit, Saturnia regna redeunt: jam nova progenies demittitur alto cælo. Tu modò, casta* Juno *Lucina, fave nascenti puero,* sub *quo ferrea* gens *primùm desinet, ac aurea gens surget* in *toto mundo: jam tuus Apollo regnat. Adeòque hoc decus ævi inibit, te, Pollio, te consule: et magni menses incipient procedere.*

SIcelides Musæ, paulò majora canamus.
Non omnes arbusta juvant, humilesque myricæ.
Si canimus silvas, silvæ sint Consule dignæ.
Ultima Cumæi venit jam carminis ætas:
Magnus ab integro seclorum nascitur ordo.
Jam redit et Virgo, redeunt Saturnia regna:
Jam nova progenies cœlo demittitur alto.
Tu modò nascenti puero, quo ferrea primùm
Desinet, ac toto surget gens aurea mundo,
Casta fave Lucina: tuus jam regnat Apollo.
Teque adeò decus hoc ævi, te consule, inibit
Pollio: et incipient magni procedere menses.

TRANSLATION.

YE Sicilian Muses, let us sing somewhat higher Strains. The Groves and lowly Tamarisks delight not all. If rural Lays we sing, let those Lays be worthy a Consul's Ear. The last Æra, *the Subject* of Cumæan Song, is now arrived: The great Series of *revolving* Ages begins anew. Now too returns the Virgin *Astræa*, returns the Reign of Saturn: Now a new Progeny from high Heaven descends. Be thou but propitious to the Infant Boy, by whom first the Iron Age shall cease, and the golden Age over all the World arise. O chaste Lucina; now thy own Apollo reigns. While thou too, Pollio, while thou art Consul, this Glory of our Age shall make his Entrance; and the

NOTES.

Among the various Conjectures about the Design of this Pastoral, the most probable is, that *Virgil* therein celebrates the Birth of the famous *Marcellus*, the Nephew of *Augustus* by *Octavia*; the same who died in the Flower of his Age, and whose Memory the same Poet has perpetuated by that celebrated Funeral Elogy in the sixth Æneid. The Time of his Birth agrees to the Year of *Pollio*'s Consulship, *A. U. C.* 714, when the Child here described is said to have come into the World. This Event fell out in a happy Conjuncture, just after *Augustus* and *Antony* had ratified a League of Peace, and *Octavia*, by marrying *Antony*, sealed that Peace; which restored Plenty to *Rome*, re-established the Tranquillity of the Empire, as in the Times of the golden Age. Yet many, not without Ground, think this Pastoral a Prophecy of *Our Blessed Saviour*, there being several remarkable Passages in it applicable to Him.

1. *Sicelides Musæ.* Sicilian or pastural Muses; because *Theocritus*, the original pastoral Poet, was a Native of *Sicily*.

3. *Silvæ.* Woods, here put for pastoral, rural Subjects.

5. *Magnus ordo.* Thought to refer to the great *Platonic* Year, which *Cicero* says, *tum efficitur, cum Solis, et Lunæ, et quinque errantium ad eandem inter se comparationem confectis omnium spatiis, est facta conversio*, 2 de Nat. Deor. And *Clavis*, C. 1. *Sphæræ quo tempore quidam volunt omnia, quæcunque in mundo sunt, eodem ordine esse reditura, quo nunc cernuntur.*

11. *Inibit.* Is a much finer Word, and more emphatic, than any of those the Commentators substitute in the Room of it: It implies, he shall enter on the Happiness of his Life, and Glories of his Reign.

Te duce, si qua manent sceleris vestigia nostri,
Irrita perpetua solvent formidine terras.
Ille Deum vitam accipiet, Divisque videbit
Permistos heroas, et ipse videbitur illis:
Pacatumque reget patriis virtutibus orbem.
At tibi prima, puer, nullo munuscula cultu,
Errantes hederas passim cum baccare tellus,
Mistaque ridenti colocasia fundet acantho.
Ipsæ lacte domum referent distenta capellæ
Ubera, nec magnos metuent armenta leones.
Ipsa tibi blandos fundent cunabula flores.
Occidet et serpens, et fallax herba veneni
Occidet: Assyrium vulgo nascetur amomum.
At simul heroum laudes, et facta parentis
Jam legere, et quæ sit poteris cognoscere virtus:
Molli paulatim flavescet campus arista,
Incultisque rubens pendebit sentibus uva:
Et duræ quercus sudabunt roscida mella.
Pauca tamen suberunt priscæ vestigia fraudis,
Quæ tentare Thetim ratibus, quæ cingere muris
Oppida, quæ jubeant telluri infindere sulcos.
Alter erit tum Tiphys, et altera quæ vehat Argo
Delectos heroas; erunt etiam altera bella;

Te duce, si qua vestigia nostri sceleris manent, illa irrita solvent terras perpetua formidine. Ille puer accipiet vitam Deorum, videbitque heroas permistos Divis, et ipse videbitur illis: regetque pacatum orbem patriis virtutibus. At tellus fundet prima munuscula tibi, puer, nullo cultu, errantes hederas passim cum baccare, fundetque colocasia mista ridenti acantho. Capellæ ipsæ referent ubera domum, distenta lacte: nec armenta metuent magnos leones. Cunabula ipsa fundent blandos flores tibi. Et serpens occidet, et fallax herba veneni occidet: Assyrium amomum nascetur vulgo. At simul poteris jam legere laudes heroum, et facta tui parentis, et cognoscere quæ virtus sit: tunc campus flavescet paulatim molli arista, rubensque uva pendebit incultis sentibus: et duræ quercus sudabunt roscida mella. Tamen pauca vestigia priscæ fraudis suberunt, quæ jubeant homines tentare Thetim ratibus, quæ jubeant cingere oppida muris, quæ jubeant infindere sulcos telluri. Tum erit alter Tiphys gubernator, et altera navis Argo, quæ vehat delectos heroas: etiam altera bella erunt;

TRANSLATION.

great Months begin to roll. Under thy Conduct, whatever Vestiges of our Guilt remain, shall *by* being done away release the Earth from Fear for ever. He shall partake the Life of Gods, shall see Heroes mingled in Society with Gods, himself be seen by them, and rule the peaceful World with his Father's Virtues. Mean while the Earth, *sweet* Boy, as her first Offerings, shall pour thee forth every where without Culture creeping Ivy with Ladies-glove, and Egyptian Beans with smiling Acanthus intermixed. The Goats of themselves shall homeward convey their Udders distended with Milk: Nor shall the Herds dread huge overgrown Lions. The very Cradle shall pour thee forth fair attractive Flowers. The Serpent shall die, and the Poison's fallacious Plant shall die: The Assyrian Spikenard shall grow in every Soil. But soon as thou shalt be able to read the Praises of Heroes, and the Achievements of thy Sire, and to understand what Virtue is; the Field shall by Degrees grow yellow with soft Ears of Corn, blushing Grapes shall hang on the rude Brambles, and hard Oaks shall distil the dewy Honey. Yet some few Footsteps of ancient Vice shall *still* remain, to prompt *Men* to tempt the Sea in Ships, to inclose Cities with Walls, and cleave Furrows in the Earth. Another Tiphys then shall be, and another Argo to waft chosen Heroes *over the Main:* There shall be likewise other Wars, and

NOTES.

19. *Hederas.* He promises him Ivy as a future Poet, Ecl. VII. 25.

Pastores hedera crescentem ornate poëtam.

19. *Baccare.* The Herb *Baccar*, or *Ladies Glove*, thought to have Virtue against Fascination.

26. *At simul.* i. e. *As soon as you shall arrive at Youth.*

26. *Facta parentis.* This is referred to *Augustus*, the adoptive Father of *Marcellus*.

atque magnus Achilles mittetur iterum ad Trojam. Hinc, ubi jam firmata ætas fecerit te virum, et vector ipſe cedet mari; nec nautica pinus mutabit merces: omnis tellus feret omnia. Non humus patietur raſtros, non vinea patietur falcem: jam quoque robuſtus arator ſolvet juga tauris. Nec lana diſcet mentiri varios colores: ſed aries ipſe, in pratis, mutabit ſua vellera, jam ſuave rubenti murice, jam croceo luto. Sandyx veſtiet paſcentes agnos ſuâ ſponte. Sorores *Parcæ, concordes ſtabili numine fatorum, dixerunt ſuis fuſis, ô talia ſecla currite. O clara ſoboles Deûm, magnum incrementum Jovis, Aggredere magnos honores, jam tempus aderit. Aſpice mundum convexo pondere nutantem, terraſque, tractuſque maris, profundumque cœlum: aſpice, ut omnia lætentur* hoc *aureo ſeclo venturo.*

Atque iterum ad Trojam magnus mittetur Achilles.
Hinc, ubi jam firmata virum te fecerit ætas,
Cedet et ipſe mari vector: nec nautica pinus
Mutabit merces: omnis feret omnia tellus.
Non raſtos patietur humus, non vinea falcem:
Robuſtus quoque jam tauris juga ſolvet arator.
Nec varios diſcet mentiri lana colores:
Ipſe ſed in pratis aries jam ſuave rubenti
Murice, jam croceo mutabit vellera luto.
Sponte ſuâ ſandyx paſcentes veſtiet agnos.
Talia ſecla, ſuis dixerunt, currite, fuſis
Concordes ſtabili fatorum numine Parcæ.
Aggredere ô magnos (aderit jam tempus) honores,
Clara Deûm ſoboles, magnum Jovis incrementum.
Aſpice, convexo nutantem pondere mundum,
Terraſque, tractuſque maris, cœlumque profundum:
Aſpice, venturo lætentur ut omnia ſeclo.

TRANSLATION.

great Achilles ſhall once more be ſent to Troy. After this, when confirmed Age ſhall now have ripened thee into Man, the Sailor ſhall of himſelf renounce the Sea: Nor ſhall the naval Pine barter Commodities: All Lands ſhall all Things produce. The Ground ſhall not endure the Harrow, nor the Vineyard the Pruning-hook: Now the ſturdy Ploughman too ſhall releaſe his Bullocks from the Yoke. Nor ſhall the Wool learn to counterfeit various Colours: But the Ram himſelf ſhall in the Meadows tinge his Fleece now with ſweet-bluſhing Purple, now with Saffron-dye. Scarlet ſhall ſpontaneous cloath the Lambs as they feed. The Deſtinies harmonious in the eſtabliſhed Order of the Fates ſung to their Spindles: "Ye ſo happy Ages run, *haſte forward to the Birth.*" Bright Offspring of the Gods, illuſtrious Progeny of Jove, ſet forward in thy Way to ſignal Honours, the Time is now at hand. See the World with its conglobed ponderous Frame nodding to thee *in ſign of gratulation*, the Earth, the Regions of the Sea, and Heaven ſublime: See how all Things rejoice at the Approach of this *happy*

NOTES.

37. *Firmata virum, &c.* Literally, *When confirmed Age ſhall now have made thee a Man,* i. e. *When thou art now arrived at the Years of full Maturity.*

44. *Luto.* Lutum is an Herb with which they dyed yellow.

46. *Talia ſecla currite.* Some make the Conſtruction to be, *currite talia ſecla,* or *per talia ſecla*; i. e. *interrupt not the Courſe of ſuch happy Ages.* The Expreſſion ſeems borrowed from *Catullus,* who has, *currite ducentes ſubtemina, currite fuſi.* I have given what I take to be the Senſe of *currite:* The Poet repreſents the Deſtinies well pleaſed in ſpinning ſuch happy Events, and haſtening to bring forth the glorious Schemes of Fate.

48. *Aggredere.* Expreſſes the Greatneſs of Mind with which he was to riſe to Honour, and ſurmount all Difficulties that oppoſed his Advancement; the aſſuming that Power to himſelf with which he was to ſubdue Vice and eſtabliſh Virtue.

49. *Clara.* Others read *chara.*

50. *Aſpice convexo nutantem pondere.* Some explain it thus: *Look with Compaſſion on a World* nutantem mole vitiorum, *labouring and oppreſſed with Guilt and Miſery.*

O mihi tam longæ maneat pars ultima vitæ,
Spiritus et quantum sat erit tua dicere facta!
Non me carminibus vincet nec Thracius Orpheus,
Nec Linus; huic mater quamvis, atque huic pater adsit,
Orphei Calliopea, Lino formosus Apollo.
Pan etiam Arcadiâ mecum si judice certet,
Pan etiam Arcadiâ dicat se judice victum.
Incipe, parve puer, risu cognoscere matrem:
Matri longa decem tulerunt fastidia menses:
Incipe, parve puer: cui non risere parentes,
Nec Deus hunc mensâ, Dea nec dignata cubili est.

O utinam *ultima pars tam longæ vitæ maneat mihi, et tantum spiritus, quantum erat sat dicere tua facta!* non quivis vincet me *carminibus, nec Thracius Orpheus, nec Linus; quamvis mater Calliopea adsit huic Orphei, atque pater formosus Apollo* adsit huic *Lino. Si etiam* Deus *Pan* ipse *certet mecum, Arcadiâ judice, etiam Pan* ipse *dicat se* esse *victum, Arcadiâ judice. Parve puer, incipe cognoscere matrem risu: decem menses tulerunt longa fastidia* tuæ *matri. Incipe, parve puer: cui* puero *parentes non risere, nec Deus* est dignatus *hunc mensâ, nec Dea est dignata* hunc *cubili.*

TRANSLATION.

Age. O that my last Stage of Life may continue so long, and so much Breath as shall suffice to sing thy Deeds! Neither Thracian Orpheus, nor Linus shall surpass me in Song, tho' his Mother aid the one, and the Sire the other, Calliopea Orpheus, *and* fair Apollo Linus. Should even Pan with me contend, Arcadia's self being Judge; even Pan should own himself o'ercome, Arcadia's self being Judge. Begin, sweet Babe, to distinguish thy Mother by her Smiles: Ten Months did bring thy Mother tedious Qualms. Begin, sweet Babe: That Child on whom his Parents never smiled, nor God *e'er* honoured with his Table, nor Goddess with her Bed.

NOTES.

60. *Risu cognoscere.* Some explain it, *Begin to distinguish thy Mother by smiling on her*; but the Sense we have given agrees better with the following, *cui non risere parentes.*

62. *Cui non risere parentes.* No less a Man than *Quintilian* explains it: *Those who have not smiled on their Parents*; and, which is exceeding harsh, alleges *hunc* in the following Verse, is for *hos*, *Inst.* Lib. IX. 3.

63 *Nec Deus, &c.* The Meaning seems to be this: *Begin, sweet Boy, to know thy Parents by their Smile; for thy Parents must smile upon thee before thou canst be advanced to that Life of the Gods mentioned,* Verse 15. *Ille Deûm vitam accipiet, &c.* For no God nor Goddess ever promoted any to their Society on whom their Parents did not smile.

Or it may be interpreted thus: *Begin, sweet Boy, to know thy Parents by their Smile; for thy Parents must smile upon thee before thou canst be honoured with the Table of a God,* viz. Augustus, *or Bed of a Goddess,* viz. Julia. Both which Honours *Marcellus* arrived to, by *Augustus* adopting him for his Son, and giving him *Julia* his Daughter in Marriage.

ECLOGA

ECLOGA V.

MENALCAS, MOPSUS.

ORDO.

Me. Mopse, quoniam nos convenimus, ambo boni, tu inflare leves calamos, ego dicere versus, cur non consedimus hic inter ulmos mistas corylis? Mo. Tu es major: est æquum me parere tibi, Menalca: sive sub incertas umbras Zephyris motantibus eas, sive potiùs succedimus antro: aspice, ut silvestris labrusca sparsit antrum raris racemis. Me. In nostris montibus Amyntas solus certet tibi. Mo. Quid si idem Amyntas certet superare Phœbum canendo? Me. Mopse, tu prior incipe, si habes aut quos ignes Phyllidis,

ME. CUR non, Mopse, boni quoniam convenimus ambo,
Tu calamos inflare leves, ego dicere versus,
Hìc corylis mistas inter consedimus ulmos?
MO. Tu major: tibi me est æquum parere, Menalca:
Sive sub incertas Zephyris motantibus umbras,
Sive antro potiùs succedimus: aspice, ut antrum
Silvestris raris sparsit labrusca racemis.
ME. Montibus in nostris solus tibi certet Ámyntas.
MO. Quid si idem certet Phœbum superare canendo?
ME. Incipe, Mopse, prior; si quos aut Phyllidis ignes,

TRANSLATION.

ME. SInce, Mopsus, we are *happily* met, both skilful Swains, you in piping on the slender Reed, I in singing Verses, why have we not sat down here among the Elms intermixed with Hazles?

MO. You, Menalcas, are my Superior: 'Tis just that I be ruled by you: Whether under the Shades that waver by the fanning Zephyrs, or rather into this Grotto we repair: See how the wild Vine with Clusters here and there hath mantled over the Grotto.

ME. Amyntas alone in our Mountains may vie with thee.

MO. What if the same *presumptuous Youth* should vie with Phœbus self in Song?

ME. Begin you, Mopsus, first; whether you are disposed to sing the Passion of

NOTES.

Two Shepherds, *Menalcas* and *Mopsus*, celebrate the Funeral Elegy of *Daphnis*. *Virgil* himself is *Menalcas*, as appears from Verse 85, &c. *Mopsus*, some other Poet of Reputation in *Rome*, but young, and who had probably been *Virgil*'s Disciple. *Daphnis*, some suppose to have been a Brother of his, who died in the Prime of his Age; others *Quintilius Varus*, of whom *Horace* says, *nulli flebilior quam tibi Virgili*: But here the Chronology does not agree; for *Quintilius Varus* died *A. U. C.* 730, and *Virgil* wrote this Eclogue fifteen Years before: Others therefore, with more Probability, refer it to the Death and Deification of *Julius Cæsar*.

10. *Phyllidis ignes.* Phyllis, Queen of *Thrace*, fell in Love with *Demophoon*, the Son of *Theseus*, and married him. Some time after *Demophoon* having gone to *Athens*, and being detained there beyond the Time when he had promised to return, *Phyllis*, tortured with the Pangs of a jealous Lover, grew impatient under his Absence, and at last hanged herself in Despair.

Aut Alconis habes laudes, aut jurgia Codri;
Incipe: pascentes servabit Tityrus hœdos.
Mo. Imò hæc, in viridi nuper quæ cortice fagi
Carmina descripsi, et modulans alterna notavi,
Experiar: tu deinde jubeto certet Amyntas.
Me. Lenta salix quantum pallenti cedit olivæ,
Puniceis humilis quantum saliunca rosetis;
Judicio nostro tantum tibi cedit Amyntas.
Mo. Sed tu desine plura, puer: successimus antro.
Exstinctum nymphæ crudeli funere Daphnin
Flebant, vos coryli testes, et flumina nymphis:
Cum, complexa sui corpus miserabile nati,
Atque Deos atque astra vocat crudelia mater.
Non ulli pastos illis egere diebus
Frigida, Daphni, boves ad flumina: nulla neque amnem
Libavit quadrupes, nec graminis attigit herbam.
Daphni, tuum Pœnos etiam ingemuisse leones
Interitum, montesque feri silvæque loquuntur.

aut laudes Alconis, aut jurgia Codri; incipe: Tityrus servabit pascentes hœdos. Mo. *Imò po*tiùs *experiar hæc* carmina, *quæ carmina descripsi nuper in viridi cortice fagi, et modulans notavi* ea *alterna: deinde tu jubeto* ut *Amyntas certet* mecum. Me. *Quantum lenta salix cedit pallenti olivæ, quantum humilis saliunca* cedit *puniceis rosetis; tantum Amyntas cedit tibi nostro judicio.* Mo. *Sed, puer, tu desine* loqui *plura* verba: *successimus antro. Nymphæ flebant Daphnin extinctum crudeli funere: vos coryli et flumina* estis *testes nymphis, cum mater complexa miserabile corpus sui nati, vocat atque Deos atque astra crudelia. Daphni, non ulli* pastores *egere pastos boves ad frigida flumina illis diebus: nulla quadrupes neque libavit amnem, nec attigit herbam graminis. Daphni, ferique montes silvæque loquuntur, etiam Pœnos leones ingemuisse tuum interitum.*

TRANSLATION.

Phyllis, or the Praises of Alcon, or the *glorious* Strife of Codrus; Begin: Tityrus will tend the browzing Kids.

Mo. Nay, I'll rather try those Strains, which lately I inscribed on the green Bark of the Beech-tree, and sung and noted them by Turns: Then bid Amyntas vie with me.

Me. As far as the limber Willow is inferior to the pale Olive, and humble Lavender to crimson Beds of Roses; so far is Amyntas, in my Judgment, inferior to you.

Mo. But, Shepherd, no more: Now we have reached the Grotto. The Nymphs deplored Daphnis cut off by cruel Death: Ye Hazles and ye Streams witnessed *the Mourning of* the Nymphs: When the Mother, embracing the lamented Corpse of her Son, reproaches both Gods and Stars of Cruelty. The *mourning* Swains, O Daphnis, then forgot to drive their fed Cattle to the cooling Streams: No Quadruped or tasted of the Brook, or touched a Blade of Grass. The savage Mountains, Daphnis, and the Woods, can tell that the *very* Lions

NOTES.

11. *Alconis.* A famous *Cretan* Archer, who aimed an Arrow so dexterously at a Serpent wreathed about the Body of his Son, as to kill the Animal without touching the Boy.

11. *Jurgia Codri.* Codrus was King of the *Athenians*, and signalized himself by dying for his People. For in a War between them and the *Lacedæmonians*, hearing that an Oracle had promised the Victory to that People whose King should die, and the Enemy being strictly enjoined not to kill the *Athenian* King; he disguised himself in the Habit of a Peasant, went in among the Enemy, picked a Quarrel with some of them, and was slain in the Scuffle. The Enemy no sooner found out who he was than they threw down their Swords.

24. *Non ulli.* To this *Ruæus* refers these Words of *Suetonius in Jul. C.* 81. *Proximis diebus equorum greges, quos in trajiciendo flumine Rubicone consecrârat, ac vagos et sine custode dimiserat, comperit pertinacissime a pabulo abstinere, ubertimque flere.*

38. *Par-*

Daphnis et inſtituit ſubjungere Armenias tigres curru, Daphnis inſtituit inducere thiaſos Baccho, et intexere lentas haſtas mollibus foliis. Ut vitis eſt decori arboribus, ut uvæ vitibus, ut tauri gregibus, ut ſegetes pinguibus arvis; tu es omne decus tuis. Poſtquam fata abs-tulerunt te, Dea Pales ipſa, atque Apollo ipſe reliquit agros. Sæpe, quibus ſulcis mandavimus grandia hordea, infelix lolium, et ſteriles avenæ dominantur his. Pro molli violâ, pro purpureo narciſſo, carduus et paliurus ſurgit acutis ſpinis. Paſtores, ſpargite humum foliis, et inducite umbras fontibus: Daphnis mandat talia fieri ſibi. Et facite tumulum illi, *et ſuperaddite hoc carmen tumulo: ego Daphnis* jaceo hic, *notus in ſilvis, hinc uſque ad ſidera, cuſtos formoſi pecoris, ipſe formoſior.* Me. *Divine poëta, tuum carmen* eſt *tale nobis, quale ſopor* eſt *feſſis in gramine, quale reſtinguere ſitim ſaliente rivo dulcis aquæ. Nec æquiparas magiſtrum calamis ſolùm, ſed* etiam *voce. Fortunate puer, nunc tu eris alter ab illo. Tamen nos dicemus hæc noſtra carmina tibi viciſſim, tollemuſque tuum Daphnin ad aſtra:*

Daphnis et Armenias curru ſubjungere tigres
Inſtituit, Daphnis thiaſos inducere Baccho,
Et foliis lentas intexere mollibus haſtas.
Vitis ut arboribus decori eſt, ut vitibus uvæ,
Ut gregibus tauri, ſegetes ut pinguibus arvis;
Tu decus omne tuis. Poſtquam te fata tulerunt,
Ipſa Pales agros, atque ipſe reliquit Apollo.
Grandia ſæpe quibus mandavimus hordea ſulcis,
Infelix lolium, et ſteriles dominantur avenæ.
Pro molli violâ, pro purpureo narciſſo,
Carduus, et ſpinis ſurgit paliurus acutis.
Spargite humum foliis, inducite fontibus umbras,
Paſtores: mandat fieri ſibi talia Daphnis.
Et tumulum facite, et tumulo ſuperaddite carmen:
Daphnis ego in ſilvis, hinc uſque ad ſidera notus,
Formoſi pecoris cuſtos, formoſior ipſe.
   Me. Tale tuum carmen nobis, divine poëta,
Quale ſopor feſſis in gramine; quale per æſtum
Dulcis aquæ ſaliente ſitim reſtinguere rivo.
Nec calamis ſolùm æquiparas, ſed voce magiſtrum.
Fortunate puer, tu nunc eris alter ab illo.
Nos tamen hæc quocunque modo tibi noſtra viciſſim
Dicemus, Daphninque tuum tollemus ad aſtra:

TRANSLATION.

in the Wilds of Afric mourned thy Death. Daphnis taught to yoke Armenian Tygers in the Chariot, Daphnis *taught* to lead up the Dances in Honour of Bacchus, and wreathe the pliant Spears with ſoft Leaves. As the Vine is the Glory of the Trees, as grapes are of the Vine, as the Bull is of the Flock, as ſtanding Corn of fertile Fields; ſo thou waſt all the Glory of thy Fellow-ſwains. E'er ſince the Fates ſnatched thee away, Pales herſelf, and Apollo too, have left the Plains. Luckleſs Darnel, and the barren Oats prevail in theſe Furrows where we were wont to ſow the plump Barley. In lieu of the ſoft Violet, in lieu of the empurpled Narciſſus, the Thiſtle ſprings up, and the Thorn with its ſharp Prickles. Strow the Ground with Leaves, ye Shepherds, cover the Fountains with ſhady Boughs: Theſe Rites Daphnis for himſelf ordains. And raiſe a Tomb, and on that Tomb inſcribe this Epitaph: *Here* I Daphnis of the Groves *repoſe*, from hence even to the Stars renowned, the Shepherd of a fair Flock, fairer myſelf *than they*.

Me. Such, matchleſs Poet, is thy Song to me, as Slumbers to the weary on the Graſs; as in ſcorching Heat to quench Thirſt from a ſalient Rivulet of freſh Water. Nor equal you your Maſter in the Pipe only, but *alſo* in the Voice. Happy Swain, you ſhall now be the next to him. Yet, as I can, I'll ſing in my

NOTES.

38. *Purpureo narciſſo.* There are a great many different Kinds of the Narciſſus or Daffodil; *Dioſcorides* particularly mentions one that is πορφυροειδής, *of a purple Hue.*

Daphnin ad astra feremus: amavit nos quoquè
Daphnis.
Mo. An quicquam nobis tali sit munere majus?
Et puer ipse fuit cantari dignus: et ista
Jampridem Stimichon laudavit carmina nobis.
Me. Candidus insuetum miratur limen Olympi,
Sub pedibusque videt nubes, et sidera Daphnis.
Ergo alacris silvas, et cætera rura voluptas,
Panaque, pastoresque tenet, Dryadasque puellas.
Nec lupus insidias pecori, nec retia cervis
Ulla dolum meditantur: amat bonus otia Daphnis.
Ipsi lætitia voces ad sidera jactant
Intonsi montes: ipsæ jam carmina rupes.
Ipsa sonant arbusta: Deus, Deus ille, Menalca.
Sis bonus ô felixque tuis! en quatuor aras;
Ecce duas tibi, Daphni, duoque altaria Phœbo.
Pocula bina novo spumantia lacte quotannis
Craterasque duos statuam tibi pinguis olivi:

Daphnis amavit nos quoque. Mo. An quicquam sit majus nobis tali munere? et puer ipse fuit dignus cantari; et jampridem Stimichon laudavit ista carmina nobis. Me. Nunc Daphnis, candidus, miratur insuetum limen Olympi, videtque nubes et sidera sub pedibus. Ergo alacris voluptas tenet silvas, et cætera rura, Panaque, pastoresque, puellasque Dryadas. Nec lupus meditatur insidias pecori, nec ulla retia meditantur dolum cervis: bonus Daphnis amat otia. Intonsi montes ipsi jactant voces ad sidera cum lætitia: jam rupes ipsæ modulantur carmina. Jam arbusta ipsa sonant hoc: Menalca, ille est Deus, ille est Deus. Daphni, ô sis bonus felixque tuis! en aspice quatuor aras; ecce duas tibi, Daphni, duoque altaria Phœbo. Statuam bina pocula spumantia novo lacte quotannis, duosque crateras pinguis olivi tibi.

TRANSLATION.

Turn these *Verses* of mine, and exalt your Daphnis to the Stars: Daphnis I'll raise to the Stars: Me too Daphnis loved.

Mo. Can aught be more acceptable to me, than such a Present? The Swain was both worthy himself to be celebrated, and Stimichon hath long since praised to me that Song of yours.

Me. Daphnis robed in white admires the Courts of Heaven, to which he is a Stranger, and underneath his Feet beholds the Clouds and Stars. Hence mirthful Pleasure fills the Woods and every Field, Pan, and the Shepherds, and Virgin Dryads. The Wolf does neither meditate mischievous Plots against the Sheep, nor are any Toils set to ensnare the Deer: Good Daphnis delights in Peace. For Joy, even the unshorn Mountains raise their Voices to the Stars: Now the very Rocks, the very Groves resound these Notes: A God, a God he is, Menalcas. Oh be propitious and indulgent to thy own! See *here* four Altars; lo, Daphnis, two for thee, and two for Phœbus. Two Bowls foaming with new Milk, and two Goblets of fat Oil will I present to thee each Year: And chiefly,

NOTES.

52. *Amavit nos quoquè Daphnis.* Virgil was obscure and little known in *Julius Cæsar's* Time; but *Ruæus* thinks it may be contained of the *Mantuans* in general, who, with the other People of *Cisalpine Gaul*, were cherished and protected by Cæsar.

54. *Et puer ipse.* Hence *Servius* infers, that the *Daphnis* here celebrated cannot be *Julius Cæsar*, since *puer* ill agrees to a Man of fifty six Years. *Ruæus* contends that he may be called *puer*, as being now a God, whose Privilege is to preserve immortal Youth. But these refined Criticisms are very superfluous; *Virgil*, in the Style of pastoral Poetry, represents *Daphnis*, whoever he was, as a Swain, and *puer* is the Word he uses all along in that Sense, Ecl. III. 62. VI. 14, &c.

56. *Candidus.* Servius makes this an Emblem of his Divinity, white being the Colour of the celestial Ones. *Tibull.* L. III. 6. *Candide Liber, ades*, Ov. *Trist.* V. 514. *Candidus huc venias.*

66. *Aras.* *Aræ* were altars consecrated indifferently either to the celestial or infernal Deities; but the *altaria* only to the former, and were of a larger Form: Hence *Servius* derives the Word from *altus*, high.

Et inprimis hilarans convivia multo Baccho, ante focum, si erit frigus, si erit messis, in umbrâ, fundam Arvisia vina, novum nectar è calathis. Damœtas et Lyctius Ægon cantabunt mihi: Alphesibœus imitabitur saltantes Satyros. Hæc sacra semper erunt tibi, et cum reddemus solennia vota Nymphis, et cum lustrabimus agros. Dum aper amabit juga montis, dum piscis amabit fluvios, dumque apes pascentur thymo, dum cicadæ pascentur rore; semper tuus honos, tuumque nomen, laudesque manebunt. Agricolæ facient vota tibi quotannis sic, ut Baccho Cererique; tu quoquè damnabis eos votis solvendis. Mo. *Quæ, quæ dona reddam tibi pro tali carmine? nam neque sibilus venientis Austri juvat me tantum, nec litora percussa fluctu tam juvant me, nec flumina, quæ decurrunt inter saxosas valles.* Me. *Nos donabimus te ante hâc fragili cicutâ. Hæc* cicuta docuit *nos* canere; *Corydon ardebat formosum Alexin:*

Et, multo inprimis hilarans convivia Baccho,
Ante focum, si frigus erit, si messis, in umbrâ,
Vina novum fundam calathis Arvisia nectar.
Cantabunt mihi Damœtas, et Lyctius Ægon:
Saltantes satyros imitabitur Alphesibœus.
Hæc tibi semper erunt, et cum solennia vota
Reddemus Nymphis, et cum lustrabimus agros.
Dum juga montis aper, fluvios dum piscis amabit,
Dumque thymo pascentur apes, dum rore cicadæ;
Semper honos, nomenque tuum, laudesque manebunt.
Ut Baccho Cererique, tibi sic vota quotannis
Agricolæ facient: damnabis tu quoquè votis.
Mo. Quæ tibi, quæ tali reddam pro carmine dona?
Nam neque me tantum venientis sibilus Austri,
Nec percussa juvant fluctu tam litora, nec quæ
Saxosas inter decurrunt flumina valles.
Me. Hàc te nos fragili donabimus ante cicutâ.
Hæc nos, Formosum Corydon ardebat Alexin:

TRANSLATION.

enlivening the Feast with Plenty of the Joys of Bacchus, before the Fire if it be Winter, if Harvest in the Shade, I will pour thee forth Chian Wines rich as Nectar. Damœtas and Lyctian Ægon shall sing to me: Alphesibœus shall mimic the frisking Satyrs. These Rites shall be ever thine, both when we pay our solemn anniversary Vows to the Nymphs, and when we make the Circuit of the Fields. While the Boar shall love the Tops of Mountains, while Fishes in the Floods delight, while Bees on Thyme shall feed, and Grashoppers on Dew; thy Honour, Name, and Praise, shall still remain. As to Bacchus and Ceres, so to thee the Swains shall yearly perform their Vows: Thou too shalt bind *them to* their Vows.

Mo. What *just*, what *grateful* Returns shall I make thee for so excellent a Song? For neither the Whispers of the rising South Wind, nor Shores lashed by the Wave, nor Rivers that glide down among the stony Vales, please me so much.

Me. First will I present you with this brittle Reed. This *taught* me, "Cory-

NOTES.

71. *Arvisia.* From *Arvisia*, a Promontory in the Island of Chios, famous for excellent Wines. *Novum nectar, i. e. quæ sunt novum nectar; Wines which are excellent as Nectar, the Drink of the Gods.* *Novus* here signifies *excellent*, as above, Ecl. III. 86.

80. *Damnabis tu quoque votis.* Literally, *Thou shalt condemn them to their Vows.* When the Object of the Vow or Prayer was granted, then the Person was *reus voti*, or *damnatus voti*. So that *damnare votis* is a Phrase equivalent to that of granting their Vows, or hearing their Prayers as a God.

Hæc

Hæc eadem docuit, cujum pecus? an Melibœi?
Mo. At tu sume pedum, quod, me cum sæpe rogaret,
Non tulit Antigenes, (et erat tum dignus amari)
Formosum paribus nodis atque ære, Menalca.

hæc eadem cicuta docuit nos, cujum est pecus? an est Melibœi? Mo. *At, Menalca, tu sume pedum, formosum paribus nodis atque ære, quod Antigenes non tulit, cum sæpe rogaret me (et tum ille erat dignus amari.)*

TRANSLATION.

" don for fair Alexis burned:" This same hath taught me, " Whose is this " Flock? Is it that of Melibœus?"

Mo. But do you, Menalcas, accept this Sheep-hook adorned with uniform Knobs, and *Rings of* Brass, which Antigenes never could obtain, tho' he often begged it of me, and at that time he was worthy to be loved.

ECLOGA VI.

SILENUS.

PRima Siracosio dignata est ludere versu,
Nostra nec erubuit silvas habitare Thalia.
Cum canerem reges et prœlia, Cynthius aurem
Vellit, et admonuit: pastorem, Tityre, pingues
Pascere oportet oves, deductum dicere carmen.

ORDO.

Nostra musa Thalia prima est dignata ludere Siracosio versu, nec erubuit habitare silvas. Cum canerem reges et prœlia, Cynthius Apollo *vellit* meam *aurem, et admonuit* me sic: *Tityre, oportet pastorem pascere pingues oves, et dicere deductum carmen.*

TRANSLATION.

MY Thalia is the first who deigned to sport in Sicilian Verse, nor blushed to be an Inhabitant of the Woods. When I offered to sing of Kings and Battles, Apollo twitched my Ear, and warned me *thus:* A Shepherd, Tityrus, should feed his fattening Sheep, *and* sing in humble Strain. Now *then* will I,

NOTES.

Silenus surprized in a Grotto by two Shepherds, *Chromis* and *Mnasylus*, and by the Nymph *Ægle*, is sollicited to perform the Promise he had long given them of a Song. Upon which he explains to them the Origin of the World according to the Doctrine of the *Epicureans*; and then, to gratify their Curiosity, entertains them with several Fables agreeable to the Simplicity of Pastoral. This Eclogue is supposed to have been designed as a Compliment to *Syro* the *Epicurean*, who instructed *Virgil* and *Varus* in the Principles of that Philosophy.

1. *Siracosio versu.* In *Syracusian* Verse, i. e. in Pastoral Poetry, such as *Theocritus* the *Syracusian* wrote.

4. *Pingues pascere oves,* i. e. *Pascere ut pinguescant.*

5. *Deductum dicere carmen.* A humble or slender Song; a Metaphor taken from Wool spun out till it becomes fine and slender. So *Hor.* Lib. II. 1. 225. *Tenui deducta poemata filo.* And *Tibul.* Lib. I. 3. 86. *Deducat plena stamina longa colo.*

Nunc ego (namque ſuper tibi erunt, qui dicere laudes,
Vare, tuas cupiant, et triſtia condere bella)
Agreſtem tenui meditabor arundine Muſam.
Non injuſſa cano: ſi quis tamen hæc quoquè, ſi quis
Captus amore leget; te noſtræ, Vare, myricæ,
Te nemus omne canet: nec Phœbo gratior ulla eſt,
Quàm ſibi quæ Vari præſcripſit pagina nomen.
Pergite, Pierides. Chromis et Mnaſylus in antro
Silenum pueri ſomno videre jacentem;
Inflatum heſterno venas, ut ſemper, Iaccho.
Serta procul tantùm capiti delapſa jacebant:
Et gravis attritâ pendebat cantharus anſâ.
Aggreſſi (nam ſæpe ſenex ſpe carminis ambo
Luſerat) injiciunt ipſis ex vincula ſertis.
Addit ſe ſociam, timidiſque ſupervenit Ægle,
Ægle Naïadum pulcherrima, jamque videnti
Sanguineis frontem moris et tempora pingit.
Ille dolum ridens, Quo vincula nectitis? inquit.

Nunc ego meditabor agreſtem muſam tenui arundine (namque ſuper erunt tibi, Vare, qui cupiant dicere tuas laudes, et condere triſtia bella carminibus). *Non cano* carmina *injuſſa* à Phœbo: *tamen ſi quis, ſi quis captus amore* tenuis *leget hæc quoquè; Vare, noſtræ myricæ* canent te, *omne nemus canet te: nec eſt ulla pagina gratior Phœbo, quàm* illa *quæ præſcripſit nomen Vari ſibi. Pierides, pergite. Chromis et Mnaſylus* duo pueri *videre Silenum jacentem ſomno in antro, inflatum* quoad *venas heſterno Iaccho, ut ſemper* eſt mos illi. *Serta, tantùm delapſa capiti, jacebant procul* ab illo: *et gravis cantharus pendebat attritâ anſâ.* Pueri, *aggreſſi* eum, *injiciunt* illi *vincula* facta *ex ſertis ipſis (nam ſæpe ſenex* Silenus *luſerat ambo ſpe carminis.) Ægle addit ſe ſociam* pueris, *ſupervenitque* iis *timidis, Ægle pulcherrima Naïadum, pingitque frontem et tempora* ſeni *jam videnti ſanguineis moris. Ille,* Silenus, *ridens, dolum inquit, Quò nectitis vincula?*

TRANSLATION.

O Varus (for there will not be wanting ſuch as are ambitious to celebrate thy Praiſes, and record thy diſaſtrous Wars) exerciſe my rural Muſe on the ſlender Reed. I ſing not unbidden Strains, *tho' humble:* Yet whoſo enamoured *with the rural Muſe*, whoſo ſhall read even theſe; *to him*, O Varus, our *lowly* Tamariſks, *to him* each Grove ſhall ſing of thee: Nor is any Page more acceptable to Phœbus, than on whoſe Front the Name of Varus is inſcribed. Proceed, O Muſes, Chromis and Mnaſylus, the youthful Swains, ſaw Silenus lying aſleep in his Cave, his Veins, as uſual, blown up with Yeſterday's Debauch. His Garlands juſt fallen from his Head lay at ſome Diſtance, and his ponderous Tankard hung by its worn Handle. Laying hold on him (for often the Sire had amuſed them both with the Promiſe of a Song) they bind him with his own Wreaths. Ægle aſſociates herſelf with them, and comes unexpectedly upon the timorous Swains, Ægle, the faireſt of the Naids, and, juſt as he is opening his Eyes, ſhe paints his Forehead and Temples with Blood-red Mulberries. He, ſmiling at the Trick, ſays, Why theſe Bonds? Looſe me, Swains. It is enough that I have ſuffered

NOTES.

7. *Vare.* Quintilius Varus, one of *Auguſtus*'s Generals, who afterwards loſt his Life and Army in *Germany*.

9. *Injuſſa.* May mean *Strains*; *I am forbid to ſing*, viz. *Varus's Battles*.

10. *Noſtræ myricæ*, i. e. *Humble Paſtorals.*

16. *Serta.* To be crowned with Garlands was the Badge of a Drunkard.

16. *Procul.* Apart, at ſome Diſtance; for it ſeems abſurd to make *procul* here, with *Servius*, ſignify *near hand*, and at other times *far off*.

Solvite me, pueri: satis est potuisse videri.
Carmina, quæ vultis, cognoscite: carmina vobis;
Huic aliud mercedis erit. Simul incipit ipse.
Tum verò in numerum Faunosque ferasque videres
Ludere, tum rigidas motare cacumina quercus.
Nec tantùm Phœbo gaudet Parnassia rupes:
Nec tantùm Rhodope miratur et Ismarus Orphea.
Namque canebat, utì magnum per inane coacta
Semina terrarumque, animæque, marisque fuissent,
Et liquidi simul ignis: ut his exordia primis
Omnia, et ipse tener mundi concreverit orbis.
Tum durare solum, et discludere Nerea Ponto
Cœperit, et rerum paulatim sumere formas.
Jamque novum ut terræ stupeant lucescere Solem,
Altiùs atque cadant submotis nubibus imbres:
Incipiant silvæ cum primùm surgere, cumque
Rara per ignotos errent animalia montes.
Hinc lapides Pyrrhæ jactos, Saturnia regna,
Caucaseasque refert volucres, furtumque Promethei.

Solvite me, pueri: est satis me potuisse videri sic vobis. Vos cognoscite carmina quæ vultis: sunt carmina vobis; erit aliud mercedis huic Æglæ; simul ipse incipit. Tum verò videres Faunosque ferasque ludere in numerum cantus; tum videres rigidas quercus motare cacumina. Nec Parnassia rupes tantùm gaudet Phœbo, nec mons Rhodope et Ismarus tantùm miratur Orphea canentem. Namque canebat, uti semina terrarumque, animæque, marisque, et simul liquidi ignis fuissent coacta per magnum inane spatium; ut ex his primis omnia exordia, ut tener orbis mundi ipse concreverit. Tum ut solum cœperit durare, et discludere Nerea ponto, et sumere formas rerum paulatim. Jamque ut terræ stupeant novum solem lucescere, atque ut imbres cadant nubibus submotis altiùs à terrâ: cum primùm silvæ incipiunt surgere, cumque rara animalia errent per ignotos montes. Hinc refert jactos lapides Pyrrhæ, Saturnia regna, Caucaseasque volucres, furtumque Promethei.

TRANSLATION.

myself tò be seen. Hear the Song which you desire: The Song for you; for her I shall find another Reward. At the same time he begins. Then you might have seen the Fauns and Savages frisking *about him* in measured Dance, then the rigid Oaks waving their Tops. Nor rejoices the Parnassian Rock so much in Phœbus: Nor do Rhodope and Ismarus so much admire their Orpheus. For he sung how, through the mighty Void, the Seeds of Earth, and Air, and Sea, and pure *ethereal* Fire, had been together ranged: How from these Principles all the Elements, and the World's recent Globe itself combined into a System. Then how the Soil began to harden, to shut up the Waters apart within the Sea, and by Degrees to assume the Forms of Things. And how anon the Earth was struck to see the new-born Sun shine forth, and how from the Clouds, suspended high, the Showers descend: When first the Woods began to rise, and when the Animals, as yet but few, began to range the unknown Mountains. He rehearses next the *Transformation of* the Stones which Pyrrha threw, the Reign of Saturn, the Fowls of Caucasus, and the Theft of Prometheus. To these he adds the Fountain where the

NOTES.

31. *Magnum per inane.* The *Epicureans*, whose Philosophy is here sung, taught that incorporeal Space, here called *magnum inane*, and corporeal Atoms were the first Principles of all Things: Their void Space they considered as the Womb, in which the Seeds of all the Elements were ripened into their distinct Forms.

35. *Et discludere Nerea ponto.* Literally, *to shut up* Nereus *apart in the Sea*, i.e. *to separate the Waters into their Channel*: Nereus the Sea-god being here put for the Waters in general; and *ponto* for the Channel or Receptacle of these Waters.

41. *Lapides Pyrrhæ.* See the Fable, Ovid. *Met.* I. 318.

42. *Caucaseasque volucres.* Prometheus is fabled to have stolen Fire from Heaven, wherewith he animated a Man of Clay of his own Formation: For which presumptuous Theft he was chained to a Rock in Mount *Caucasus*, and had a Vulture continually preying upon his Liver, that grew as fast as it was consumed.

43. *Hylan.*

Adjungit his, quo fonte nautæ clamâſſent relictum Hylan: ut omne litus ſonaret, Hyla, Hyla. Et ſolatur reginam Paſiphaen amore nivei juvenci, fortunatam, ſi armenta nunquam fuiſſent. Ah, infelix virgo, quæ dementia cepit te? Prœtides implerunt agros falſis mugitibus: attamen non ulla earum *eſt ſecuta tam turpes concubitus pecudum, quamvis timuiſſet aratrum collo, et ſæpe quaſiviſſet cornua in levi fronte. Ah, infelix virgo, nunc tu erras in montibus! ille* taurus, *fultus* quoad *niveum latus molli hyacintho, ruminat pallentes herbas ſub nigrâ ilice, aut ſequitur aliquam* vaccam *in magno grege. Nymphæ, Dictææ nymphæ, claudite, jam claudite ſaltus nemorum:* ut videamus *ſi forte qua errabunda veſtigia bovis, obvia, ferant ſeſe noſtris oculis. Forſitan aliquæ vaccæ perducant illum ad Gortynia ſtabula, aut captum viridi herbâ, aut ſecutum armenta.*

His adjungit, Hylan nautæ quo fonte relictum
Clamâſſent: ut litus, Hyla, Hyla omne ſonaret.
Et fortunatam, ſi nunquam armenta fuiſſent,
Paſiphaen nivei ſolatur amore juvenci.
Ah, virgo infelix, quæ te dementia cepit?
Prœtides implerunt falſis mugitibus agros:
At non tam turpes pecudum tamen ulla ſecuta eſt
Concubitus; quamvis collo timuiſſet aratrum,
Et ſæpe in levi quæſiſſet cornua fronte.
Ah, virgo infelix, tu nunc in montibus erras!
Ille, latus niveum molli fultus hyacintho,
Ilice ſub nigrâ pallentes ruminat herbas,
Aut aliquam in magno ſequitur grege. Claudite nymphæ,
Dictææ nymphæ, nemorum jam claudite ſaltus:
Si qua forte ferant oculis ſeſe obvia noſtris
Errabunda bovis veſtigia. Forſitan illum
Aut herbâ captum viridi, aut armenta ſecutum;
Perducant aliquæ ſtabula ad Gortynia vaccæ.

TRANSLATION.

Argonautic Sailors had invoked aloud *their* Hylas loſt: How the whole Shore reſounded Hylas, Hylas. And *next* he ſoothes Paſiphae in her Paſſion for the Snow-white Bull; happy *Princeſs* if Herds had never been! Ah, ill-fated Maid, what Madneſs ſeized thee? The Daughters of Prœtus with imaginary Lowings filled the Fields: Yet none of them purſued ſuch vile Embraces of a Beaſt; however they might dread the Plough *to be yoked* about their Necks, and often feel for Horns on their ſmooth Foreheads. Ah, ill-fated Maid, thou now art roaming on the Mountains! He, reſting his ſnowy Side on the ſoft Hyacinth, ruminates the blanched Herbs under ſome gloomy *ever-green* Oak, or courts ſome Female in the numerous Herd. Ye Nymphs, ſhut up, now ye Dictæan Nymphs, ſhut up the Lawns and Openings of the Groves, if any where by Chance my Bullock's wandering Footſteps may offer to my Sight. Perhaps ſome Heifers may lead him on to the Gortynian Stalls, or enticed by the verdant Paſture, or in purſuance of the Herd. Then he ſings the Virgin *Atalanta* charmed with

NOTES.

43. *Hylan.* The Boy *Hylas*, *Hercules*'s Favourite, and companion in the *Argonautic* Expedition, having gone to fetch Water from a Fountain near which the *Argonauts* had landed, fell into the Well, and was drowned. *Hercules* and his fellow *Argonauts*, miſſing the Boy, went in ſearch of him along the Coaſt, calling on him aloud by his Name.

48. *Falſis mugitibus.* They imagined themſelves transformed to Heifers; therefore he calls their Lowings *falſe*, *they were only fancied, not real.*

55. *Claudite.* Here *Silenus* perſonates *Paſiphae* apoſtrophizing the Woods and Groves.

56. *Dictææ Nymphæ.* The Nymphs of *Crete*, from *Dicte*, a Mountain in that Iſland, where *Paſiphae* was Queen.

56. *Saltus.* Signifies the Lawns or open Places in Foreſts and Parks, where the Cattle have Room *ſalire, to feed and friſk about.*

62. *Tum*

Tum canit Hesperidum miratam mala puellam:
Tum Phaetontiadas musco circumdat amaræ
Corticis, atque solo proceras erigit alnos.
Tum canit, errantem Permessi ad flumina Gallum
Aonas in montes ut duxerit una Sororum:
Utque viro Phœbi chorus assurrexerit omnis;
Ut Linus hæc illi divino carmine pastor,
Floribus, atque apio crines ornatus amaro,
Dixit: Hos tibi dant calamos, en accipe, Musæ,
Ascræo quos antè seni; quibus ille solebat
Cantando rigidas deducere montibus ornos.
His tibi Grynæi nemoris dicatur origo:
Ne quis sit lucus, quo se plus jactet Apollo.
Quid loquar, ut Scyllam Nisi? ut quam fama secuta est,
Candida succinctam latrantibus inguina monstris,
Dulichias vexâsse rates, et gurgite in alto,
Ah, timidos nautas canibus lacerâsse marinis?
Aut ut mutatos Terei narraverit artus?
Quas illi Philomela dapes, quæ dona parârit?
Quo cursu deserta petiverit, et quibus ante
Infelix sua tecta supervolitaverit alis?

Tum canit puellam miratam mala Hesperidum: tum circumdat Phaetontiadas musco amaræ corticis, atque erigit eas proceras alnos solo. Tum canit, ut una sororum Musarum *duxerit Gallum errantem ad flumina Permessi in Aonas montes; utque omnis chorus Phœbi assurrexerit viro; ut Linus pastor, ornatus* quoad *crines floribus atque amaro apio, dixerit hæc illi divino carmine:* Galle, *musæ dant tibi hos calamos, en accipe eos, quos* dederant *antè seni Ascræo; quibus ille solebat deducere rigidas ornos montibus cantando. Origo Grynæi nemoris dicatur tibi his calamis: ne sit quis lucus,* in *quo Apollo jactet se plus. Quid loquar,* ut narraverit, *aut Scyllam* filiam *Nisi,* aut eam *quam, succinctam* quoad *candida inguina latrantibus monstris, fama est secuta, vexâsse Dulichias rates, et, in alto gurgite, ah, lacerâsse timidos nautas marinis canibus? aut ut narraverit artus Terei* fuisse *mutatos* in upupam? *quas dapes, quæ dona Philomela paraverit illi? quo cursu* Tereus *petiverit deserta, et quibus alis* ille *infelix supervolitaverit tecta sua ante?*

TRANSLATION.

the Apples of the Hesperides: Then how the Sisters of Phaeton were wrapped about with the Moss of bitter Bark, and how from the Ground the stately Alders rose. Then sings how Gallus, wandering by the Streams of Permessus, was led to the Aonian Mountains by one of the Sister-muses; and how the whole Choir of Phœbus rose up to do him Honour. How Linus the Shepherd of Song divine, his Locks adorned with Flowers and bitter Parsley, thus addressed him: Here take these Pipes the Muses give thee, which before *they gave* to the Ascrean Sage: By whose Music he was wont to draw down the rigid wild Ashes from the Mountains. On these the Origin of Grynium's Grove by you be sung: That in no Grove Apollo may glory more. Why should I tell or *how he sung* of Scylla the Daughter of Nisus? or of her whom, round the snowy Waist begirt with barking Monsters, Fame records to have vexed the Dulichian Ships, and in the deep Abyss, alas, torn in Pieces the trembling Sailors with Sea-dogs?-Or how he described the Limbs of Tereus transformed? What Banquets and what Presents Philomela for him prepared? With what Speed he sought the Desarts, and with what Wings, ill-fated *Prince*, he fluttered over the Palace once his own?

NOTES.

62. *Tum Phaetontiadas.* Literally, *Then he infolds the Sisters of* Phaeton *in the Moss of bitter Bark, and rears the tall Alders from the Grove*; i. e. *He sings their Transformation, and describes it to the Life.* See the Note on Ecl. III. 110.

64. *Permessi.* Permessus, a River in *Beotia*, issuing from Mount *Helicon*.

65. *Aonas in montes.* Helicon and Citheron, Mountains in *Beotia*; so called from *Aon*, the Son of *Neptune*, who reigned there.

70. *Ascræo seni.* Hesiod, whose Country was *Ascræa*, a Village of *Beotia*.

72. *Grynæi nemoris.* Grynium, according to *Strabo*, was a City of *Æolis*, where *Apollo* had a Temple of white Marble, and a sacred Grove, where was a famous Oracle. See *Banier's Mythology*.

74, 78, 79. *Scyllam—Terei—Philomela.* See

ille Silenus canit omnia, quæ beatus fluvius Eurotas audiit, Phœbo quondam meditante, jussitque lauros ediscere: pulsæ valles referunt carmina ad sidera. Donec vesper jussit pastores cogere oves stabulis, referreque numerum earum, et processit Olympo invito.

Omnia quæ, Phœbo quondam meditante, beatus
Audiit Eurotas, jussitque ediscere lauros,
Ille canit: pulsæ referunt ad sidera valles.
Cogere donec oves stabulis, numerumque referre
Jussit, et invito processit vesper Olympo.

TRANSLATION.

All those *Airs* he sings, which happy Eurotas heard, and bade its Laurels learn, when Phœbus played of old. The Vallies struck *with the Sound* re-echo to the Stars; till Vesper warned *the Shepherds* to pen their Sheep in the Folds, and recount their Number; and advanced on the Sky, full loth *to lose the Song*.

NOTES.

all these Fables in *Ovid*, and the other Books of Mythology, and the History of them in *Banier*.

86. *Invito Olympo.* This beautifully represents the Sun and Sphere of Day, listening to the Sweetness of the Song, which described their own Formation; and unwillingly giving way to the Evening-star, that came unseasonably, as it were, to interrupt their Pleasure.

ECLOGA VII.

MELIBOEUS, CORYDON, THYRSIS.

ORDO.

M. Forte Daphnis consederat sub argutâ ilice, Corydonque et Thyrsis compulerant greges in unum; Thyrsis compulerat oves, Corydon compulerat capellas distentas lacte. Ambo florentes ætatibus, ambo Arcades, et pares cantare, et parati respondere. Hic caper ipse, vir gregis, deerraverat mihi: dum defendo teneras myrtos à frigore: atque ego aspicio Daphnin:

M. FOrte sub argutâ consederat ilice Daphnis,
Compulerantque greges Corydon et Thyrsis in unum;
Thyrsis oves, Corydon distentas lacte capellas:
Ambo florentes ætatibus, Arcades ambo:
Et cantare pares, et respondere parati.
Hic mihi, dum teneras defendo à frigore myrtos,
Vir gregis ipse caper deerraverat: atque ego Daphnin

TRANSLATION.

M. DAphnis by chance sat down under a whispering ever-green Oak, and Corydon and Thyrsis had drove their Flocks together; Thyrsis his Sheep, Corydon his Goats distended with Milk: Both in the Flower of their Age, Arcadians both: Equally matched at singing, and ready to answer *each other's Challenge*. Here, while I am fencing my tender Myrtles from the Cold, the He-goat himself, the Husband of the Flock, from me had strayed away: and *lo* I espied

NOTES.

Melibœus here gives us the Relation of a sharp poetical Contest between *Thyrsis* and *Corydon*; at which he himself and *Daphnis* were present, who both declared for *Corydon*.

16. Et

Aſpicio: ille ubi me contrà videt, ocyùs, inquit.
Huc ades, ô Melibœe; caper tibi ſalvus, et hœdi;
Et, ſi quid ceſſare potes, requieſce ſub umbrâ.
Huc ipſi potum venient per prata juvenci.
Hìc viridis tenerà prætexit arundine ripas
Mincius, eque ſacrâ reſonant examina quercu.
Quid facerem? neque ego Alcippen, nec Phyllida habebam,
Depulſos à lacte domi quæ clauderet agnos:
Et certamen erat, Corydon cum Thyrſide, magnum.
Poſthabui tamen illorum mea ſeria ludo.
Alternis igitur contendere verſibus ambo
Cœpêre: alternos Muſæ meminiſſe volebant.
Hos Corydon, illos referebat in ordine Thyrſis.
C. Nymphæ, noſter amor, Libethrides, aut mihi carmen,
Quale meo Codro, concedite: (proxima Phœbi
Verſibus ille facit) aut ſi non poſſumus omnes,
Hìc arguta ſacrâ pendebit fiſtula pinu.
T. Paſtores ederâ creſcentem ornate poëtam
Arcades, invidià rumpantur ut ilia Codro.

ubi ille videt me contrà, inquit, ô Melibœe, ades huc ocyùs; caper eſt ſalvus tibi, et hœdi; et, ſi potes ceſſare quid temporis, *requieſce ſub umbrâ. Juvenci ipſi venient per prata huc potum.* Hìc viridis *Mincius prætexit ripas tenerâ arundine, examinaque* apium *reſonant è ſacrâ quercu. Quid facerem? ego habeam neque Alcippen, nec Phyllida, quæ clauderet domi agnos depulſos à lacte: et erat magnum certamen, Corydon cer*tabat *cum Thyrſide. Tamen poſthabui mea ſeria* negotia *ludo illorum. Igitur ambo* cœpere *contendere alternis verſibus: Muſæ volebant* me *meminiſſe alternos* verſus. *Corydon refere*bat *hos, Thyrſis referebat illos in ordine.* C. *Nymphæ Libethrides, noſter amor, aut concedite* tale *carmen mihi, quale* conceſ-ſiſtis *meo Codro: (ille facit* carmina *proxima verſibus Phœbi:) aut, ſi* nos *omnes non poſſumus* aſſequi tale, *hìc arguta fiſtula pendebit ſacrâ pinu.* T. Vos *paſtores Arcades, ornate creſcentem poëtam hederâ, ut ilia rumpantur Codro invidiâ.*

TRANSLATION.

Daphnis: When he again ſaw me, ſtrait he cries, come hither, Melibœus; your Goat and Kids are ſafe; and, if you can ſtay a while, reſt under this Shade. Hither thy Bullocks of themſelves will come acroſs the Meads to drink. Here Mincius hath fringed the verdant Banks with tender Reed, and from the ſacred Oak Swarms *of Bees* reſound. What could I do? *On the one Hand,* I had neither Alcippe, nor Phyllis, to ſhut up at home my weaned Lambs: And *on the other Hand,* there was a mighty Match *propoſed,* Corydon againſt Thyrſis. After all, I poſtponed my ſerious Buſineſs to their Play. In alternate Verſes therefore the two began to contend: Alternate *Verſes* the Muſes would have me record. Theſe Corydon, thoſe Thyrſis, *each* in his Turn recited.

C. Ye Libethrian Nymphs, my Delight, or favour me with ſuch a Song as you did my Codrus (he makes Verſes next to thoſe of Phœbus), or, if we cannot all attain to this, here on this ſacred Pine my tuneful Pipe ſhall hang.

T. Ye Arcadian Shepherds, deck with Ivy your riſing Poet, that Codrus's Sides may burſt with Envy. Or, if he praiſe me beyond what I deſire, bind

NOTES.

16. *Et certamen erat, Corydon cum Thyrſide.* There is no Occaſion here for having Recourſe, with *Servius*, and other Commentators, to the Antiptoſis, or Subſtitution of one Caſe for another: *Corydon cum Thyrſide* is an Ellipſis for *Corydon certabat cum Thyrſide*; and full as eaſily underſtood as if the Verb had been expreſſed.

19. *Alternos, &c.* See Dr. *Trapp*'s Note on this Paſſage.

21. *Nymphæ Libethrides.* The Muſes are called *Libethrian Nymphs*, from *Libethra*, a Fountain in *Magneſia*, or, according to others, in *Bœotia*; over which they preſided.

Aut si laudârit cum ultrà placitum, cingite ejus frontem baccare, ne mala lingua noceat futuro vati. C. Delia, parvus Mycon offert hoc caput setosi apri tibi, et ramosa cornua vivacis cervi. Si hoc fuerit proprium mihi, *stabis tota de lævi marmore, evincta* quoad *suras puniceo cothurno. T. Priape, est sat te exspectare sinum lactis et hæc liba quotannis: es custos pauperis horti. Nunc fecimus te marmoream pro tempore: at tu esto aureus, si fœtura suppleverit gregem.* C. O *Galatea Nerine, dulcior mihi thymo Hyblæ, candidior cycnis, formosior albâ hederâ: cum primum pasti tauri repetent præsepia, si qua cura tui Corydonis habet te, venito.* T. *Imò ego videar tibi amarior Sardois herbis, horridior rusco, vilior projectâ algâ, si hæc lux non est jam longior mihi toto anno. Pasti juvenci, ite domum, ite, si est* vobis *quis pudor.*

Aut si ultrà placitum laudârit, baccare frontem
Cingite, ne vati noceat mala lingua futuro.
C. Setosi caput hoc apri, tibi, Delia, parvus
Et ramosa Mycon vivacis cornua cervi.
Si proprium hoc fuerit, lêvi de marmore tota
Puniceo stabis suras evincta cothurno.
T. Sinum lactis, et hæc te liba, Priape, quotannis
Exspectare sat est: custos es pauperis horti.
Nunc te marmoreum pro tempore fecimus: at tu,
Si fetura gregem suppleverit, aureus esto.
C. Nerine Galatea, thymo mihi dulcior Hyblæ,
Candidior cycnis, ederâ formosior albâ:
Cum primùm pasti repetent præsepia tauri,
Si qua tui Corydonis habet te cura, venito.
T. Imò ego Sardois videar tibi amarior herbis,
Horridior rusco, projectâ vilior algâ,
Si mihi non hæc lux toto jam longior anno est.
Ite domum pasti, si quis pudor, ite juvenci.

TRANSLATION.

my Brow with Lady's glove, lest his ill Tongue should hurt your future Poet.

C. To thee, Diana, young Mycon *for me presents* this Head of a bristly Boar, and the branching Horns of a long-lived Stag. If this Success be lasting, thou shalt stand at thy full Length in polished Marble, thy Legs with Scarlet Buskins bound.

T. A Pail of Milk, and these Cakes, Priapus, is enough for you to expect *from me:* You are the Keeper of a poor ill-furnished Garden. Now we have raised thee of Marble such as the Times admit: But, if the Breed recruit my Flock, thou shalt be all of Gold.

C. Divine Galatea, sweeter to me than Hybla's Thyme, whiter than Swans, fairer than white Ivy: Soon as the *full-fed* Steers shall return to their Stalls, come, if thou hast any Regard for Corydon.

T. Nay, may I, *sweet Maid*, appear to thee more bitter than Sardinian Herbs, more rugged than the Furze, more worthless than Sea-weed thrown out *upon the Shore*, if this Day be not longer to me than a whole Year. Go home, my *well-fed* Bullocks, if you have any Shame, go home.

NOTES.

27. *Laudârit, baccare frontem.* Immoderate Praise was thought to be of a fascinating Nature. Hence says *Pliny*, Lib. VII. 2. *Esse in Africa familias quasdam effascinantium; quarum laudatione intereant probata, arescant arbores, emoriantur infantes.* Therefore, to avert the malignant Influence, they wore a Garland of *Baccar* or *Lady's-glove*, by way of Amulet.

31. *Si proprium, &c.* The Meaning is, *If you continue to give me such Success in Hunting.*

35. *Pro tempore.* Literally, *according to the Time*; i. e. *in proportion to my present Ability.*

37. *Nerine Galatea.* He compliments his Mistress, by giving her the Name of *Galatea*, the Daughter of *Nereus*; as much as to say, *equal to her in Charms.*

41. *Sardois herbis.* An Herb like Smallage, or, as some say, Holly-bush, growing in *Sardinia*, which, being bitter, causeth convulsive Laughter, with great Grinning. Hence *Sardonicus risus, a forc'd Laughter.*

53. *Hirsuta*

C. Muſcoſi fontes, et ſomno mollior herba,
Et quæ vos rarâ viridis tegit arbutus umbrâ,
Solſtitium pecori defendite: jam venit æſtas
Torrida; jam læto turgent in palmite gemmæ.
T. Hic focus, et tædæ pingues; hic plurimus ignis
Semper, et aſſiduâ poſtes fuligine nigri.
Hic tantum Boreæ curamus frigora, quantum
Aut numerum lupus, aut torrentia flumina ripas.
C. Stant et juniperi, et caſtaneæ hirſutæ;
Strata jacent paſſim ſua quæque ſub arbore poma;
Omnia nunc rident: at ſi formoſus Alexis
Montibus his abeat, videas et flumina ſicca.
T. Aret ager; vitio moriens ſitit aëris herba;
Liber pampineas invidit collibus umbras:
Phyllidis adventu noſtræ nemus omne virebit:
Jupiter et læto deſcendet plurimus imbri.
C. Populus Alcidæ gratiſſima, vitis Iaccho,
Formoſæ myrtus Veneri, ſua laurea Phœbo;

C. Vos *muſcoſi fontes, et herba mollior ſomno, et viridis arbutus, quæ tegit vos rarâ umbrâ, defendite ſolſtitium pecori: jam torrida æſtas venit; jam gemmæ turgent in læto palmite.* T. *Hic eſt focus, et pingues tædæ; hic eſt plurimus ignis ſemper, et poſtes nigri aſſiduâ fuligine. Hic curamus frigora Boreæ tantum, quantum aut lupus* curat *numerum ovium, aut torrentia flumina* curant *ripas.* C. *Et juniperi, et hirſutæ caſtaneæ ſtant; poma jacent ſtrata paſſim, quæque ſub ſuâ arbore; nunc omnia rident: at ſi formoſus Alexis abeat his montibus, videas et flumina ſicca.* T. *Ager aret; herba ſitit moriens vitio aëris; Liber invidit pampineas umbras collibus: omne nemus virebit adventu noſtræ Phyllidis: et plurimus Jupiter deſcendet læto imbri.* C. *Populus eſt gratiſſima Alcidæ, vitis Iaccho, myrtus formoſæ Veneri, ſua laurea Phœbo.*

TRANSLATION.

C. Ye moſſy Fountains, and Graſs more ſoft than Sleep, and the green Arbute-tree that clothes you with its Shade, ward off the ſolſtitial Heat from my Flock: Now ſcorching Summer comes; now the Buds ſwell on the fruitful Tencrils *of the Vine.*

T. Here is a *glowing* Hearth, and unctuous Pines; here is always a ſwinging Fire, and Lintels ſooted with continual Smoke. Here we juſt as much regard the Cold of Boreas, as either the Wolf *does* the Number *of Sheep*, or impetuous Rivers their Banks.

C. *Now* Junipers and prickly Cheſnuts crown the Boughs; beneath each Tree its Apples here and there lie ſtrowed; now all Nature ſmiles: But, were fair Alexis to go from theſe Hills, you would ſee even the Rivers dry.

T. The Field is parched; by the Intemperature of the Air the Herbage thirſts and dies; Bacchus has envied our Hills the Shadows of his Vine: At the Approach of our Phyllis every Grove ſhall look green; and Jove full liberal deſcend in joyous Showers.

C. The Poplar *is* moſt grateful to Hercules, the Vine to Bacchus, to lovely Venus the Myrtle, to Phœbus his own Laurel; Phyllis loves the Hazles: Theſe

NOTES.

53. *Hirſutæ.* Of the Kind that were rough and prickly, in oppoſition to the ſoft and ſmooth Ones mentioned Ecl. I. *ad fin.* Or in general *they ſtand rough*; i. e. *ſtill in the Shells.*

53. *Stant.* Servius renders it *plenæ ſunt*, viz. *fructu, they are loaded with Fruit*, taking *juniperi* and *caſtaneæ* for the Trees. I underſtand them, with others, of the Fruit, and ſo conſider *ſtant* in oppoſition to *ſtrata jacent* in the next Verſe: The one ſtand or hang ripening on the Boughs; the other in rich Profuſion ſtrow the Ground.

54. *Sua, &c.* We muſt either read *quaque*, or *ſua* muſt be contracted into one Syllable *ſa*, as *Ennius* ſays, *ſis* for *ſuis.*

61. *Populus Alcidæ.* The Poplar-tree was ſacred to *Hercules*, becauſe he wore a Crown of

Phyllis amat corylos: dum Phyllis amabit illas, nec myrtus, nec laurea Phœbi vincet corylos. T. *Fraxinus eſt pulcherrima in ſilvis, pinus in hortis, populus in fluviis, abies in altis montibus: at ſi tu, formoſe Lycida, reviſas me ſæpius, fraxinus in ſilvis, et pinus in hortis cedet tibi.* M. *Memini hæc carmina, et Thyrſum victum contendere fruſtra. Ex illo tempore Corydon eſt Corydon nobis.*

Phyllis amat corylos: illas dum Phyllis amabit,
Nec myrtus vincet corylos: nec laurea Phœbi.
T. Fraxinus in ſilvis pulcherrima, pinus in hortis,
Populus in fluviis, abies in montibus altis:
Sæpius at ſi me, Lycida formoſe, reviſas;
Fraxinus in ſilvis cedet tibi, pinus in hortis.
M. Hæc memini, et victum fruſtra contendere Thyrſin.
Ex illo, Corydon, Corydon eſt tempore nobis.

TRANSLATION.

ſo long as Phyllis loves, neither the Myrtle, nor the Laurel of Phœbus ſhall ſurpaſs the Hazles.

T. The Aſh *is* faireſt in the Woods, the Pine-trees in the Gardens, the Poplar by the Rivers, the Fir on lofty Mountains: But if, my charming Lycidas, you make me more frequent Viſits, the Aſh tree in the Woods ſhall yield to thee, and the Pine-tree in the Gardens.

M. Theſe Verſes I remember, and that vanquiſhed Thyrſis did in vain contend. From that Time 'tis Corydon, Corydon for me.

NOTES.

of that Tree when he went down to Hell. The Vine to *Bacchus*, becauſe he was the Inventor of Wine. The Myrtle to *Venus*, either for its delicious Smell, or becauſe it grows often along the Shore of the Sea, out of whoſe Foam *Venus* ſprung. The Laurel to *Apollo*, on account of *Daphne*, as is ſaid above.

ECLOGA VIII.

PHARMACEUTRIA.

Damon, Alphesiboeus.

PAstorum Musam, Damonis et Alphesibœi,
Immemor herbarum quos est mirata juvenca
Certantes, quorum stupefactæ carmine lynces,
Et mutata suos requiêrunt flumina cursus:
Damonis Musam dicemus et Alphesibœi.
Tu mihi, seu magni superas jam saxa Timavi,
Sive oram Illyrici legis æquoris; en erit unquam
Ille dies, mihi cum liceat tua dicere facta!
En erit, ut liceat totum mihi ferre per orbem
Sola Sophocleo tua carmina digna cothurno!
A te principium: tibi desinet. Accipe jussis

ORDO.

Dicemus *Musam pastorum Damonis et Alphesibœi, quos certantes* quæque *juvenca, immemor herbarum, est mirata, carmine quorum lynces* sunt *stupefactæ, et flumina mutata*, quoad *suos cursus, requiêrunt: dicemus Musam Damonis et Alphesibœi. Tu*, Pollio, fave *mihi, seu jam superas saxa magni Timavi, sive legis oram Illyrici æquoris; en unquam ille dies erit, cum liceat mihi dicere tua facta! en* illud tempus *erit, ut liceat mihi ferre tua carmina, sola digna Sophocleo cothurno per totum orbem* terrarum! duxi *principium* meorum laborum *à te*: labor *desinet tibi.*

TRANSLATION.

THE Muse of the Shepherds, Damon and Alphesibœus, whom the Heifers mindless of their Pasture admired, contending, and to whose Song the Lynxes listened with Astonishment, and the Rivers, having changed their Courses, stood still: The Muse of Damon and Alphesibœus I sing.

Aid thou me, *great Pollio*, whether thou overpass the Rocks of broad Timavus, or cruize along the Coast of the Iberian Sea; say, shall that Day ever come, when I shall be indulged to sing thy *glorious* Deeds? Say, shall it come, that I may be indulged to diffuse through all the World thy Verse which sole merits *to be praised* in Sophocles's lofty Style? With thee, my Muse commenced, with thee

NOTES.

This Pastoral contains the Songs of *Damon* and *Alphesibœus*. The first of them bewails the Loss of his Mistress, and repines at the Success of his Rival *Mopsus*. The other repeats the Charms of some Enchantress, who endeavoured by her Spells and Magic to make *Daphnis* in love with her.

4. *Requiêrunt.* Here may be active, as in *Propertius*, Lib. II. 18. 25. *Jupiter Alcmenæ geminas requieverat Arctos.*

10. *Tua carmina.* Some by this understand my Verses, in which your Praises are celebrated; but this seems very harsh.

10. *Sophocleo cothurno.* In *Sophocles*'s Buskins; *i. e. in his sublime tragic Style.* The *Cothurnus* signifies the higher Kind of Shoe wore by Tragedians, hence put for Tragedy itself; as the *Soccus* the lower Kind of Shoe is for Comedy. *Hor. de Art. Poet.* 90.

Indignatur item privatis ac prope socco
Dignis carminibus narrari cœna Thyestæ.

Carmina cœpta tuis: atque hanc ſine tempora circum
Inter victrices ederam tibi ſerpere lauros.
Frigida vix cœlo noctis deceſſerat umbra,
Cum ros in tenerâ pecori gratiſſimus herbâ;
Incumbens tereti Damon ſic cœpit olivæ.
D. Naſcere, præque diem veniens age Lucifer almum:
Conjugis indigno Niſæ deceptus amore
Dum queror; et Divos, quanquam nil teſtibus illis
Profeci, extremâ moriens tamen alloquor horâ.
Incipe Mænalios mecum, mea tibia, verſus.
Mænalus argutumque nemus pinoſque loquentes
Semper habet; ſemper paſtorum ille audit amores,
Panaque, qui primus calamos non paſſus inertes.
Incipe Mænalios mecum, mea tibia, verſus.
Mopſo Niſa datur! quid non ſperemus amantes?
Jungentur jam gryphes equis: ævoque ſequenti
Cum canibus timidi venient ad pocula damæ.
Mopſe, novas incide faces: tibi ducitur uxor.
Sparge, marite, nuces: tibi deſerit Heſperus OEtam.

Accipe carmina cœpta tuis juſſis, atque ſine hanc ederam ſerpere inter victrices lauros circum tempora tibi. Vix frigida umbra noctis deceſſerat cœlo, cum ros, gratiſſimus pecori, eſt in tenerâ herbâ; Damon, incumbens tereti olivæ, cœpit ſic. D. Lucifer, naſcere, prævenienſque age almum diem: dum ego, deceptus indigno amore conjugis Niſæ, queror; et moriens, tamen extremâ horâ vitæ, alloquor Deos, quanquam profeci nil illis teſtibus. Mea tibia, incipe Mænalios verſus mecum. Mænalus ſemper habet argutumque nemus, loquenteſque pinos: ille mons ſemper audit amores paſtorum, *Panaque* ipſum Deum eorum, *qui primus non* fuit *paſſus calamos* eſſe *inertes. Mea tibia, incipe Mænalios verſus mecum. Niſa datur Mopſo! quid nos amantes non ſperemus? jam præſenti* ævo *gryphes jungentur equis: ſequentique ævo, timidi damæ venient cum canibus ad pocula. Mopſe, incide novas faces: uxor ducitur tibi. Marite, ſparge nuces: Heſperus deſerit* montem *OEtam tibi.*

TRANSLATION.

my Muſe ſhall end: Accept my Songs begun by thy Command, and permit this Ivy to creep around thy Temples among thy victorious Laurels.

Scarce had the cold Shades of Night retired from the Sky, what Time the Dew on the tender Graſs *is* moſt grateful to the Cattle, *when* Damon leaning againſt a tapering Olive thus began:

D. Ariſe, *fair* Lucifer, and previous uſher in the cheerful Day: While I, deceived by the feigned Paſſion of my Miſtreſs Niſa, *to her* complain; and to the Gods, now that I die (though it hath *hitherto* availed me nought that I took them to Witneſs) yet in my laſt Hour appeal. Begin with me, my Pipe, Mænalian Strains. *Mount* Mænalus has Groves for ever filled with Melody, and Pines *for ever* vocal; he ever hears the Loves of Shepherds, and *the Muſic of* Pan, the firſt who ſuffered not the Reeds to be neglected. Begin with me, my Pipe, Mænalian Strains. Niſa is given away to Mopſus! What may we Lovers not expect? Griffins now ſhall match with Horſes, and in the ſucceeding Age the timorous Does with Dogs ſhall come to drink. Mopſus, cut your freſh nuptial Torches: For thee a Wiſe is conducting home. Strow the Nuts, Bridegroom;

NOTES.

18. *Conjugis Niſæ*, i. e. *His deſigned Wiſe*, as *maritus* is put for a Lover or intended Huſband, Æn. IV. 536.

Quos ego ſum toties jam dedignata maritos.

30. *Sparge nuces.* This Ceremony of ſtrowing Nuts, that the Boys might ſcramble for them, was uſual at Nuptials; for which ſeveral Reaſons are aſſigned by *Pliny*.

30. *Tibi deſerit Heſperus OEtam.* OEta was a Mountain, or Range of Mountains, in *Theſſaly*, of a very great Height; which, as *Ruæus* obſerves, being weſtward of *Attica* and *Beotia*, the

Incipe Mænalios mecum, mea tibia, versus.
O digno conjuncta viro! dum despicis omnes,
Dumque tibi est odio mea fistula, dumque capellæ,
Hirsutumque supercilium, prolixaque barba;
Nec curare Deum credis mortalia quemquam
Incipe Mænalios mecum, mea tibia, versus.
Sepibus in nostris parvam te roscida mala
(Dux ego vester eram) vidi cum matre legentem.
Alter ab undecimo tum me jam ceperat annus:
Jam fragiles poteram à terrâ contingere ramos.
Ut vidi, ut perii, ut me malus abstulit error!
Incipe Mænalios mecum, mea tibia, versus.
Nunc scio quid sit Amor: duris in cotibus illum
Ismarus, aut Rhodope, aut extremi Garamantes,
Nec nostri generis puerum, nec sanguinis edunt.
Incipe Mænalios mecum, mea tibia, versus.
Sævus amor docuit natorum sanguine matrem
Commaculare manus: crudelis tu quoquè mater:
Crudelis mater magis, an puer improbus ille?
Improbus ille puer: crudelis tu quoquè mater.

Mea tibia, incipe Mænalios versus mecum. O Nisa conjuncta digno viro! dum despicis omnes alios præter illum Mopsum; *dumque mea fistula est tibi odio, dumque* meæ *capellæ, hirsutumque supercilium, prolixaque barba* sunt odio; *nec credis quemquam Deûm curare mortalia. Mea tibia, incipe Mænalios versus mecum.* Ego *vidi te parvam, legentem roscida mala cum matre in nostris sepibus (ego eram vester dux). Jam tum alter annus ab undecimo ceperat me: jam poteram contingere fragiles ramos à terrâ. Ut vidi, ut perii* amore, *ut malus error abstulit me! Mea tibia, incipe Mænalios versus mecum. Nunc scio quid Amor sit: Ismarus, aut Rhodope, aut extremi Garamantes edunt illum in duris cotibus,* illum *puerum nec nostri generis, nec* nostri *sanguinis. Mea tibia, incipe Mænalios versus mecum. Sævus amor docuit matrem* Medeam *commaculare manus sanguine natorum: tu, mater, fuisti crudelis quoquè:* an *mater* fuit *magis crudelis, an ille puer* magis *improbus? ille puer* fuit *improbus, tu crudelis quoquè, mater.*

TRANSLATION.

Hesperus for thee forsakes OEta. Begin with me, my Pipe, Mænalian Strains. O *rarely* matched to a worthy Spouse! while you disdain all the World besides, and while you detest my Pipe and Goats, my shaggy Eye-brows, and my overgrown Beard; nor believe that any God regards the Affairs of Mortals. Begin with me, my Pipe Mænalian Strains. When thou wast but a Child, I saw thee with thy Mother gathering the dewy Apples on our Hedges, I was your Guide; I had then just entered on the Year next after eleven: I was then just able to reach the slender Boughs from the Ground. How I looked, how I languished, how the fatal Delusion stole my Heart away! Begin with me, my Pipe, Mænalian Strains. Now I know what Love is: Ismarus, or Rhodope, or the remotest Garamantes, produced him on rugged Cliffs, a Boy nor of our Race, nor of our Blood. Begin with me, my Pipe, Mænalian Strains. Relentless Love taught the Mother to imbrue her Hands in her own Childrens Blood: A cruel Mother too thou wast: Whether more cruel was the Mother, or more impious the Boy? Impious was the Boy: Thou, Mother, too wast cruel.

NOTES.

the Inhabitants of those Countries used to observe the Stars set and retire out of Sight behind that Mountain. So that, with respect to them, *Hesperus leaves OEta,* is the same as to say, *the Evening-star is now setting.* And the same Way of speaking was adopted by Poets of other Countries, tho' differently situated.

39. *Alter ab undecimo.* Literally, *The Year next after eleven had then just taken hold of me.* *Servius* makes it the thirteenth Year; for *alter,* he says, is said only of two. But *alter ab illo,* Ecl. V. 49, plainly signifies *the next after,* and so it would seem to do here.

44. *Ismarus—Rhodope.* Two Mountains in *Thrace,* very wild and horrid. The *Garamantes* again were a savage People inhabiting the more inland Parts of *Libya.*

47. *Matrem.* This cruel Mother is *Medea,* who, to be revenged on *Jason* for preferring another Mistress to her, slew her Sons whom she bore to him before his Eyes.

56. *Arien.*

Mea tibia, incipe Mænalios versus mecum. Nunc et lupus fugiat oves ultro: duræ quercus ferant aurea mala: alnus floreat narcisso: myricæ sudent pinguia electra corticibus; et ululæ certent cycnis; Tityrus sit alter *Orpheus; Orpheus in silvis, Arion inter delphinas. Mea tibia, incipe Mænalios versus mecum. Omnia fiant vel medium mare: silvæ vivite et* valete. *Deferar præceps de speculâ aërii montis in undas: habeto hoc extremum munus morientis* amatoris. *Tibia, desine, jam desine Mænalios versus. Damon* dixit *hæc: vos, Pierides, dicite, quæ Alphesibœus responderit. Omnes non possumus facere omnia.* A. *Effer aquam* huc, famula, *et cinge hæc altaria molli vittâ: adoleque pingues verbenas, et mascula thura: experiar avertere sanos sensus* mei *conjugis magicis sacris. Nibil nisi carmina desunt hic.*

Incipe Mænalios mecum, mea tibia, versus.
Nunc et oves ultro fugiat lupus: aurea duræ
Mala ferant quercus: narcisso floreat alnus:
Pinguia corticibus sudent electra myricæ;
Certent et cycnis ululæ: sit Tityrus Orpheus;
Orpheus in silvis, inter delphinas Arion.
Incipe Mænalios mecum, mea tibia, versus.
Omnia vel medium fiant mare: vivite silvæ.
Præceps aërii speculâ de montis in undas
Deferar: extremum hoc munus morientis habeto.
Desine Mænalios, jam desine, tibia, versus.
Hæc Damon: vos, quæ responderit Alphesibœus,
Dicite, Pierides. Non omnia possumus omnes.
A. Effer aquam, et molli cinge hæc altaria vittâ:
Verbenasque adole pingues, et mascula thura:
Conjugis ut magicis sanos avertere sacris
Experiar sensus. Nihil hìc nisi carmina desunt.

TRANSLATION.

Begin with me, my Pipe, Mænalian Strains. Now let the Wolf of himself fly from the Sheep: The hard Oaks bear golden Apples: The Alder with Narcissus bloom: The Tamarisks distil rich Amber from their Barks: Let Owls with Swans contend; be Tityrus an Orpheus; an Orpheus in the Woods, an Arion among the Dolphins. Begin with me, my Pipe, Mænalian Strains. All *the World for me* may even become one great Abyss: Ye Woods, farewel. From the Summit of yon aerial Mountain will I fling me headlong down into the Waves: Take this last Present from thy dying *Swain*. Cease, my Pipe, now cease Mænalian Strains.

Thus Damon: Ye Pierian *Muses*, say what Alphesibœus responsive sung. All Things we cannot all.

A. Bring forth the Water, and bind these Altars with a soft Fillet: Burn thereon fat *unctuous* Vervain, and male Frankincense: That I may try by sacred Magic Spells to dispossess my Love of a sound Mind. Nothing here but Charms

NOTES.

56. *Arion.* A Lyric Poet, who, in his Return to *Corinth* his native Country, from *Italy*, where he had enriched himself, was by the covetous Mariners thrown over board, while he was playing on his Lyre: But a Dolphin, charmed with his Music, is said to have taken him on its Back, and carried him to *Tænarus.*

59. *Speculâ*, Signifies an Eminence which commands the Prospect of all the Country round.

64. *Effer aquam*, &c. Here *Alphesibœus* personates the Enchantress, whom we must now suppose to be entering on her magic Rites, in order to recover the lost Affection of *Daphnis*: And these Words she addresses to her Maid *Amaryllis*, who is mentioned Verse 78.

65. *Verbenas.* According to the best Interpreters is here to be taken for all sorts of Herbs used in such Kind of Rites: The Herb Vervain however was peculiarly appropriated to magical Operations, *Plin.* Lib. XXII. 2.

65. *Mascula thura*, i. e. *The purest and best*, as *La Cerda* explains it from *Dioscorides.*

66. *Conjugis*, &c. To turn away the sound Mind of him who was to have been my Spouse, *i. e.* to throw him into the frantic Passion of Love for me whom he has rejected.

Ducite ab urbe domum, mea carmina, ducite Daphnin.
Carmina vel cœlo possunt deducere Lunam:
Carminibus Circe socios mutavit Ulyssei:
Frigidus in pratis cantando rumpitur anguis.
Ducite ab urbe domum, mea carmina, ducite Daphnin.
Terna tibi hæc primùm triplici diversa colore
Licia circumdo; terque hæc altaria circum
Effigiem duco. Numero Deus impare gaudet.
Ducite ab urbe domum, mea carmina, ducite Daphnin.
Necte tribus nodis ternos, Amarylli, colores:
Necte, Amarylli, modò: et, Veneris, dic, vincula necto.
Ducite ab urbe domum, mea carmina, ducite Daphnin.
Limus ut hic durescit, et hæc ut cera liquescit
Uno eodemque igni; sic nostro Daphnis amore.
Sparge molam, et fragiles incende bitumine lauros.
Daphnis me malus urit; ego hanc in Daphnide laurum.

Mea carmina, ducite, ducite Daphnin ab urbe domum. Carmina vel possunt deducere Lunam cœlo: Circe mutavit socios Ulyssei carminibus: frigidus anguis, in pratis, rumpitur cantando. Mea carmina, ducite, ducite Daphnin ab urbe domum. Primum circumdo hæc tria licia tibi, diversa triplici colore, ducoque tuam *effigiem ter circum hæc altaria. Deus gaudet impare numero. Mea carmina, ducite, ducite Daphnin ab urbe domum.* Famula *Amarylli, necte teneros colores tribus nodis: Amaryllis, necte* eos *modò: et dic* hæc verba, *necto vincula Veneris. Mea carmina, ducite, ducite Daphnin ab urbe domum. Ut hic limus durescit, et ut hæc cera liquescit uno eodemque igni; sic Daphnis* durescat aliis, et liquescat *nostro amore. Sparge molam, et incende fragiles lauros bitumine. Malus Daphnis urit me; ego uro hanc laurum in Daphnide.*

TRANSLATION.

are wanting. My Charms bring *Daphnis* from the Town, bring Daphnis home *to me.* Charms can even draw down the Moon from Heaven: Circe by Charms transformed the Associates of Ulysses: The cold Snake is in the Meads by Incantation burst. My Charms bring *Daphnis* from the Town, bring Daphnis home *to me.* First these three Threads with threefold Colours varied I round thee twine: and thrice lead thy Image round these Altars. The Gods delight in the uneven Number. My Charms bring *Daphnis* from the Town, bring Daphnis home *to me.* Bind, Amaryllis, three Colours in three Knots: Bind them, Amaryllis, now: And say I bind the Chains of Venus. My Charms bring *Daphnis* from the Town, bring Daphnis home *to me.* As this Clay hardens, and as this Wax with one and the same Fire dissolves; so *may* Daphnis by my Love. Sprinkle the salt Cake, and burn the crackling Laurels in Bitumen. Me cruel Daphnis burns, I on Daphnis *burn* this Laurel. My Charms bring

NOTES.

71. *Cantando.* i. e. *Dum incantatur*, as Geor. II. 250.

Sed picis in morem ad digitos lentescit habendo. i. e. *Dum habetur tractaturque digitis.*

82. *Fragiles.* Either *crackling, quasi fragorem edentes*: In which Sense *Lucretius* uses the Word, Lib. VI. 3.

Interdum perscissa furit petulantibus Euris,
Et fragiles sonitus chartarum commeditatur.

Or, which is the same thing, *withered*, and so apt to crackle: Thus *fragilis* is opposed to *succosus* in *Celsus*: *Succosa firmiora quam fragilia*, *Cel.* II. 18. That the Crackling of the Laurel was a good Omen we learn from *Tibullus*, II. 5. 81.

Et succensa sacris crepitet bene laurea flammis,
Omine quo felix, et sacer annus erat.

Mea carmina, ducite, ducite Daphnin ab urbe domum. Talis amor teneat Daphnin, qualis est, bucula cum fessa quærendo juvencum per nemora, atque altos lucos, perdita procumbit in viridi herbâ propter rivum aquæ, nec meminit decedere seræ nocti: talis amor teneat eum; nec sit mihi cura mederi ejus amori. Mea carmina, ducite, ducite Daphnin ab urbe domum. Ille perfidus olim reliquit has exuvias mihi, cara pignora sui: quæ nunc ego mando tibi, terra, in limine ipso: hæc pignora debent Daphnin mihi. *Mea carmina, ducite, ducite Daphnin ab urbe domum. Mœris ipse dedit mihi has herbas, atque hæc venena lecta Ponto: plurima* venena *nascuntur Ponto. Ego vidi Mœrin sæpe fieri lupum his, et condere se silvis, sæpe excire animas imis sepulcris, atque traducere satas messes aliò. Mea carmina ducite, ducite Daphnin ab urbe domum. Amarylli, fer cineres foras; jaceque eos trans caput fluenti rivo: ne respexeris.*

Ducite ab urbe domum, mea carmina, ducite Daphnin.
Talis amor Daphnin, qualis, cum fessa juvencum
Per nemora, atque altos quærendo bucula lucos
Propter aquæ rivum viridi procumbit in herbâ
Perdita, nec seræ meminit decedere nocti:
Talis amor teneat; nec sit mihi cura mederi.
Ducite ab urbe domum, mea carmina, ducite Daphnin.
Has olim exuvias mihi perfidus ille reliquit,
Pignora cara sui: quæ nunc ego limine in ipso
Terra, tibi mando: debent hæc pignora Daphnin.
Ducite ab urbe domum, mea carmina, ducite Daphnin.
Has herbas, atque hæc Ponto mihi lecta venena
Ipse dedit Mœris: nascuntur plurima Ponto.
His ego sæpe lupum fieri, et se condere silvis
Mœrin, sæpe animas imis excire sepulcris,
Atque satas aliò vidi traducere messes.
Ducite ab urbe domum, mea carmina, ducite Daphnin.
Fer cineres, Amarylli, foras; rivoque fluenti,

TRANSLATION.

Daphnis from the Town, bring Daphnis home *to me*. Such Love on Daphnis, as when a Heifer, tired with ranging after the Bull through Lawns and lofty Groves, *at length* in absolute Despair lies down on the green Rushes by a Rivulet of Water, nor is mindful to withdraw from the late *Hour of* Night: Let such Love *on Daphnis* seize; nor let his Cure be my Concern. My Charms bring *Daphnis* from the Town, bring Daphnis home *to me*. These Garments the faithless *Shepherd* left with me some time ago, the dear Pledges of himself: Which to thee, O Earth, in the very Entrance I now commit: These Pledges owe *to me the Return of* Daphnis. My Charms bring *Daphnis* from the Town, bring Daphnis home *to me*. These Herbs, and these baneful Plants, in Pontus gathered, Mœris himself gave me: In Pontus they numerous grow. By these have I seen Mœris transform himself into a Wolf, and skulk into the Woods, often from their deep Graves call forth the Ghosts, and transfer the springing Harvests to another Ground. My Charms bring *Daphnis* from the Town, bring Daphnis home *to me*. Bring forth the Ashes, Amaryllis; throw them into a

NOTES.

91. *Exuvias.* The Clothes he had once wore, which were thought to further the Effect of Enchantments. For which Reason *Dido* orders the Garments of *Æneas* to be laid on the Pile which she pretended to have raised for the Performance of magical Rites:

—arma viri, thalamo quæ fixa reliquit
Impius exuviasque omnes—superimponas.

92. *In ipso limine.* In the Porch of *Vesta's* Temple, says *Servius*. But *Turnebus* explains it, *In the Entrance to* Daphnis's *House*. Others, with more Reason, understand it of the Entrance to her own House: For it appears that the Enchantress performed all these Rites near her own House, Verse 64, 107.

101. *Rivoque fluenti.* The same as *in rivum fluentem*, of which Construction many Examples occur in *Virgil*. See Æn. I. 293. II. 250. V. 451. VI. 191. VIII. 591. IX. 664. XII. 283.

When

Transque caput jace: ne respexeris. His ego Daphnin
Aggrediar: nihil ille Deos, nil carmina curat.
Ducite ab urbe domum, mea carmina, ducite Daphnin.
Aspice, corripuit tremulis altaria flammis
Sponte suâ, dum ferre moror, cinis ipse: bonum sit.
Nescio quid certè est: et Hylax in limine latrat.
Credimus? an, qui amant, ipsi sibi somnia fingunt?
Parcite, ab urbe venit, jam parcite, carmina, Daphnis.

Ego aggrediar Daphnin his: ille nihil curat Deos, nil curat carmina. Mea carmina, ducite, ducite Daphnin ab urbe domum. Aspice cinis ipse corripuit altaria tremulis flammis suâ sponte, dum moror ferre eum: sit bonum. Certè, est nescio quid: et canis Hylax latrat in limine. Credimus? an qui amant, ipsi fingunt somnia sibi? mea *carmina, parcite, jam parcite, Daphnis venit ab urbe* domum.

TRANSLATION.

flowing Brook, and over thy Head: Look not back. Daphnis with these I will assail: Nought he regards the Gods, nought he regards my Charms. My Charms bring *Daphnis* from the Town, bring Daphnis home *to me*. See, the very Ashes have spontaneous seized the Altars with quivering Flames, while I delay to remove them: May it be *a* happy *Omen*. Something here, I know not what, appears: And Hylax in the Entrance barks. Can I believe? or do those in love form to themselves fantastic Dreams? Cease, for Daphnis comes from the Town, now cease, my Charms.

ECLOGA IX.

LYCIDAS, MOERIS.

L. QUò te, Mœri, pedes? an, quò via ducit, in urbem?
M. O Lycida, vivi pervenimus, advena nostri,
Quod nunquam veriti sumus, ut possessor agelli,

ORDO.

L. *Mœri, quò pedes* ducunt *te? an in urbem* Mantuam, *quò via ducit?* M. *O Lycida,* nos *vivi pervenimus eò miseriæ, ut advena possessor nostri agelli diceret (quod nunquam sumus veriti).*

TRANSLATION.

L. WHither is Mœris bound? Are you for the Town, whither the Way leads?

M. Ah Lycidas, we have lived to see the Day when an Alien Possessor of my

NOTES.

When *Virgil*, by the Favour of *Augustus*, had recovered his Patrimony near *Mantua*, and went in hope to take Possession, he was in Danger to be slain by *Arius* the Centurion, to whom those Lands had been assigned by the Emperor, in Reward of his Service against *Brutus* and *Cassius*. This Pastoral therefore is filled with Complaints of his hard Usage, and the Persons introduced are alleged to be the Bailif of *Virgil*, or his Father, represented by *Mœris*, and his Friend *Lycidas*, a *Mantuan* Shepherd.

1. *Quò te, Mœri, pedes.* i. e. *Quò pedes ducunt te.*

2. *Vivi pervenimus.* i. e. *Vivendo pervenimus eò.*

6. *Quod*

hæc arva sunt mea; vos *veteres coloni migrate.* Nos *nunc victi, tristes, quoniam Fors versat omnia, mittimus hos hœdos illi* (quod munus, utinam, *nec vertat bene* illi.) L. *Certè equidem audieram, vestrum Menalcan servasse omnia arva carminibus, quà colles incipiunt subducere se, demitterque jugum molli clivo, usque ad aquam, et cacumina veteris fagi jam fracta.* M. *Audieras* illud, *et fama fuit* sic: *sed, Lycida, nostra carmina valent tantùm inter Martia tela, quantùm dicunt Chaonias columbas* valere, *aquila veniente. Quòd nisi sinistra cornix monuisset me antè, ab cavâ ilice, incidere novas lites quâcumque* ratione; *nec hic tuus Mœris, nec Menalcas ipse viveret.* L. *Heu, tantum scelus cadit in quemquam! Heu Menalca, tua solatia* sunt *penè rapta nobis simul tecum! quis* igitur *caneret nymphas? quis spargeret humum florentibus herbis? aut induceret fontes viridi umbrâ?*

Diceret: Hæc mea sunt; veteres migrate coloni.
Nunc victi, tristes, quoniam Fors omnia versat,
Hos illi (quod nec bene vertat) mittimus hœdos.
L. Certè equidem audieram, quà se subducere colles
Incipiunt, mollique jugum demittere clivo,
Usque ad aquam, et veteris jam fracta cacumina fagi,
Omnia carminibus vestrum servasse Menalcan.
M. Audieras, et fama fuit: sed carmina tantum
Nostra valent, Lycida, tela inter Martia; quantum
Chaonias dicunt, aquilâ veniente, columbas.
Quòd nisi me quâcumque novas incidere lites
Antè sinistra cavâ monuisset ab ilice cornix;
Nec tuus hic Mœris, nec viveret ipse Menalcas.
L. Heu, cadit in quemquam tantum scelus! heu tua nobis
Penè simul tecum solatia rapta, Menalca!
Quis caneret nymphas? quis humum florentibus herbis
Spargeret, aut viridi fontes induceret umbrâ?

TRANSLATION.

little Farm (what we never apprehended) may say: These are mine; old Tenants, begone. Now vanquished and disconsolate, since Fortune turns all Things topsy turvy, to him I convey these Kids, of which I wish him little good.

L. Sure I heard that your Menalcas had saved by his Verse all that Ground where the Hills begin invisibly to withdraw, and by an easy Declension to sink down their Ridges as far as the Stream, and now broken Tops of the old Beech.

M. Thou heardst it, Lycidas, and it was reported: But our Verse just as much avails amidst martial Arms; as they say the Chaonian Pigeons do, when the Eagle comes *upon them*. But had not the ill-boding Raven, from an hollow ever-green Oak warned me by any Means to break off new Pleas; neither your Mœris here, nor Menalcas himself had been *this Day* alive.

L. Alas, is any one capable of so great Wickedness! Alas, Menalcas, the Charms of thy Poetry were almost snatched from us with thyself! Who *then* had sung the Nymphs? Who with flowery Herbs had strewed the Ground, or co-

NOTES.

6. *Quod nec bene vertat*, Literally, *Which may it not turn out well to him.* The common Form of congratulating one upon receiving a Favour was *Bene vertat, I wish you Joy, much Good may it do you.*

13. *Chaonias columbas.* The Pigeons of *Dodona*, in *Chaonia* or *Epirus*, said to have delivered Oracles. *Epirus* was called *Chaonia* from the *Chaonians* who inhabited a Part of that Country.

17. *Heu cadit.* Literally, *Can such Wickedness fall to the Share of any one.*

20. *Fontes induceret umbrâ.* Induco is used in the same Sense by *Cæsar*, 2 *Bel. Gal.* 33. *Scutis ex cortice factis, aut viminibus intextis, quæ subito (ut temporis exiguitas postulabat) pellibus induxerunt.*

Vel quæ ſublegi tacitus tibi carmina nuper,
Cum te ad delicias ferres Amaryllida noſtras?
Tityre, dum redeo, brevis eſt via, paſce capellas:
Et potum paſtas age, Tityre: et, inter agendum,
Occurſare capro, cornu ferit ille, caveto.
M. Imò hæc, quæ Varo necdum perfecta canebat:
Vare, tuum nomen (ſuperet modò Mantua nobis,
Mantua væ miſeræ nimiùm vicina Cremonæ!)
Cantantes ſublime ferent ad ſidera cycni.
L. Sic tua Cyrneas fugiant examina taxos:
Sic cytiſo paſtæ diſtentent ubera vaccæ.
Incipe, ſi quid habes. Et me fecere poëtam
Pierides: ſunt et mihi carmina: me quoque dicunt
Vatem paſtores: ſed non ego credulus illis:
Nam neque adhuc Varo videor, nec dicere Cinnâ
Digna; ſed argutos inter ſtrepere anſer olores.
M. Id quidem ago; et tacitus, Lycida, mecum ipſe voluto,
Si valeam meminiſſe: neque eſt ignobile carmen.
Huc ades, ô Galatea: quis eſt nam ludus in undis?

vel caneret *carmina, quæ* ego *tacitus ſublegi tibi nuper, cum ferres te ad Amaryllida, noſtras delicias?* Quorum carminum hoc eſt fragmentum: *Tityre, paſce* meas *capellas, dum redeo, via eſt brevis: et Tityre, age* eas *paſtas potum: et, inter agendum, caveto occurſare capro, ille ferit cornu.* M. *Imò* potiùs *hæc* carmina, *quæ canebat Varo, necdum perfecta.* Quorum hoc eſt fragmentum: *Vare, cantantes cycni ferent tuum nomen ſublime ad ſidera,* ſi *modò Mantua ſuperet nobis, Mantua, væ, nimiùm vicina miſeræ Cremonæ!* L. *Sic tua examina* apium *fugiant Cyrneas taxos: ſic* tuæ *vaccæ, paſtæ cytiſo, diſtentent ubera* lacte. *Incipe, ſi habes quid. Et Pierides fecere me poëtam: et ſunt mihi carmina: paſtores quoque dicunt me* eſſe *vatem: ſed ego non* ſum *credulus illis: nam adhuc videor dicere* carmina *digna neque Varo, nec Cinnâ; ſed* velut *anſer, ſtrepere inter argutos olores.* M. *Quidem ago id; et, Lycida,* ego *ipſe tacitus voluto mecum, ſi valeam meminiſſe* illud: *neque eſt ignobile carmen.* Jam memini: *ades huc, ô Galatea: quiſnam ludus eſt in undis?*

TRANSLATION.

vered with verdant Shade the Springs? Or who *had ſung* thoſe Songs which lately I ſecretly ſtole from you, when you reſorted to our darling Amaryllis? "Feed, Tityrus, my Goats, till I return, ſhort is the Way: And when they are fed, drive them, Tityrus, to watering: And while you are ſo doing, beware of meeting the He-goat, he butts with the Horn."

M. Nay rather theſe, which to Varus, and yet unfiniſhed, he ſung: "Varus, the tuneful Swans ſhall raiſe thy Name aloft to the Stars, if Mantua remain but in our Poſſeſſion, Mantua, alas, too near unfortunate Cremona!"

L. If thou retaineſt any, begin: So may thy Swarms avoid Cyrnean Yews: So may thy Heifers, fed with Cytiſus, diſtend their Dugs. Me too the Muſes have dubbed a Poet: I too have my Verſes; and *our* Shepherds call me Bard; but to them I give no Credit: For as yet methinks I ſing nothing worthy of a Varus or a Cinna; but only gabble *as* a Gooſe among ſonorous Swans.

M. That, Lycidas, is what I am about; and now con it over in Silence with myſelf, if I can recollect it: Nor is it a vulgar Song. "Come hither, Galatea: For what Pleaſure have you among *the roaring* Waves? Here is

NOTES.

30. *Cyrneas taxos.* The Bees that feed on Yews yield Honey very harſh and bitter to the Taſte; and theſe Trees abounded in *Corſica,* which Iſland the *Greeks* called *Cyrne.*

35. *Varo—Cinnâ.* Quintilius Varus mentioned Ecl. VI. 7. and *Cornelius Cinna,* Pompey's Grandſon, who became a Favourite of *Auguſtus.*

Hìc ver purpureum : varios hìc flumina circum
Fundit humus flores : hìc candida populus antro
Imminet, et lentæ texunt umbracula vites.
Huc ades : insani feriant sine litora fluctus.
L. Quid, quæ te purâ solum sub nocte canentem
Audieram ? numeros memini, si verba tenerem.
M. Daphni, quid antiquos signorum suspicis ortus ?
Ecce Dionæi processit Cæsaris astrum :
Astrum, quo segetes gauderent frugibus ; et quo
Duceret apricis in collibus uva colorem.
Insere, Daphni, pyros : carpent tua poma nepotes.
Omnia fert ætas, animum quoquè. Sæpe ego longos
Cantando puerum memini me condere soles.
Nunc oblita mihi tot carmina : vox quoque Mœrim
Jam fugit ipsa : lupi Mœrim videre priores.
Sed tamen ista satis referet tibi sæpe Menalcas.
L. Causando nostros in longum ducis amores.
Et nunc omne tibi stratum silet æquor : et omnes,
Aspice, ventosi ceciderunt murmuris auræ.

hìc est purpureum ver : hìc humus fundit varios flores circum flumina : hìc candida populus imminet antro, et lentæ vites texunt umbracula. Ades huc : sine ut insani fluctus feriant litora. L. *Quid verò ?* quæ sunt illa carmina, *quæ audieram te solum canentem sub purâ nocte ? memini numeros, si tenerem verba.* M. *Daphni, quid* semper *suspicis antiquos ortus signorum ? ecce astrum Dionæi Cæsaris processit : astrum, quo segetes gauderent frugibus ; et quo uva duceret colorem in apricis collibus. Daphni, insere pyros : nepotes carpent tua poma. Ætas fert omnia,* et *animum quoquè. Ego memini me puerum sæpe condere longos soles cantando. Nunc tot carmina sunt oblita mihi : jam vox ipsa quoque fugit Mœrim : lupi priores videre Mœrim. Sed tamen Menalcas* ipse *referet ista carmina tibi sæpe satis.* L. *Tu ducis nostros amores in longum* tempus *causando. Et nunc aspice, omne æquor stratum silet tibi, et omnes auræ ventosi murmuris ceciderunt.*

TRANSLATION.

blooming Spring: Here, about the Rivers, Earth pours forth her various Flowers: Here the white Poplar overhangs the Grotto, and the limber Vines weave shady Bowers. Come hither: Leave the mad Billows to buffet the Shores."

L. *But* what *are these,* which I heard you singing in a clear Night alone? I remember the Air, if I could recollect the Words.

M. Daphnis, why gaze you with Admiration on the Risings of the Signs, which are of ancient Date? Lo Dionæan Cæsar's Star is entered on its Course: The Star, at whose Rising the Fields were to rejoice with Corn; at whose Rising the Grapes on sunny Hills were to take on their *purple* Hue. Daphnis, plant thy Pear-trees. Posterity shall pluck the Fruit of thy Plantations. Age impairs all Things, even the Mind itself. Often, I remember, when a Boy, I sung long Summer-days quite down the Sky. Now all these Songs I have forgot: Now the Voice itself has left Mœris; the Wolves have seen Mœris first. But these Menalcas himself will often enough recite to you.

L. By framing Excuses you tediously suspend my fond Desire. And now the whole Surface of the Main for thee lies smooth and still; and mark how every

NOTES.

47. *Dionæi Cæsaris.* Cæsar of the *Julian* Family, which sprung from *Æneas*, the Son of *Venus*, whom Mythology makes the Daughter of *Jupiter* and *Dione*.

50. *Carpent tua poma nepotes.* Here *Mœris* abruptly breaks off, as if his Memory had failed him, and thence takes Occasion to make the following Reflection, than which nothing can be more natural: *Omnia fert ætas,* &c.

54. *Lupi Mœrim videre priores.* Alluding to a superstitious Notion, that, if a Wolf saw a Man before it was seen by him, it made him lose his Voice.

60. *Bianorts,*

Hinc adeò media eſt nobis via: namque ſepulcrum
Incipit apparere Bianoris. Hìc, ubi denſas
Agricolæ ſtringunt frondes, hìc, Mœri, canamus;
Hìc hœdos depone: tamen veniemus in urbem.
Aut ſi, nox pluviam ne colligat ante, veremur,
Cantantes licet uſque, minus via lædet, eamus.
Cantantes ut eamus, ego hoc te faſce levabo.
M. Deſine plura, puer, et, quod nunc inſtat agamus.
Carmina tum melius, cum venerit ipſe, canemus.

Adeò hinc eſt nobis media via: namque ſepulcrum Bianoris incipit apparere. Hìc, ubi agricolæ ſtringunt denſas frondes, hìc, Mœri, canamus: hìc depone hœdos: tamen veniemus in urbem. Aut ſi veremur, ne nox colligat pluviam ante, licet ut eamus cantantes uſque (via minus lædet.) Ut eamus cantantes, ego levabo te hoc faſce. M. *Puer, deſine* loqui *plura* verba: *et agamus, quod nunc inſtat. Canemus carmina melius tum, cum* Menalcas *ipſe venerit.*

TRANSLATION.

whiſpering Breeze of Wind hath died away. Beſides Half of our Journey ſtill remains: For Bianor's Tomb begins to appear. Here, where the Swains are ſtripping off the thick Leaves, here, Mœris, let us ſing. Here lay down your Kids: Yet we ſhall reach the Town *betimes*. Or if we are afraid leſt the Night ſhould gather Rain before *we arrive, yet* we may ſtill go on ſinging, the Way will be leſs tedious. That we may go on ſinging, I will eaſe you of this Burden.

M. Shepherd, urge me no more, and let us mind the Buſineſs now in hand. We ſhall ſing thoſe Tunes to more Advantage when *Menalcas* himſelf arrives.

NOTES.

60. *Bianoris.* The Son of the River *Tyber*, and the prophetic Nymph *Manto*, who founded *Mantua*, and called it after the Name of his Mother.

ECLOGA X.

GALLUS.

ORDO.

Arethusa, concede hunc extremum laborem mihi. Pauca carmina sunt dicenda meo Gallo, sed quæ Lycoris ipsa legat. Quis neget carmina Gallo? sic amara Doris non intermisceat suam undam tibi, cum labere subter Sicanos fluctus. Dea incipe, *dicamus sollicitos amores Galli, dum simæ capellæ attendent tenera virgulta. Non canimus surdis; silvæ respondent omnia. Quæ nemora, aut qui saltus habuere vos, puellæ Naiades, cum Gallus periret indigno amore? nam neque juga Parnassi, nam neque ulla* juga *Pindi, neque Aganippæ* fons *Aoniæ fecere moram vobis.*

Extremum hunc, Arethusa, mihi concede laborem.
Pauca meo Gallo, sed quæ legat ipsa Lycoris,
Carmina sunt dicenda. Neget quis carmina Gallo?
Sic tibi, cum fluctus subter labêre Sicanos,
Doris amara suam non intermisceat undam.
Incipe: sollicitos Galli dicamus amores,
Dum tenera attondent simæ virgulta capellæ.
Non canimus surdis; respondent omnia silvæ.
Quæ nemora, aut qui vos saltus habuere, puellæ
Naiades, indigno cum Gallus amore periret?
Nam neque Parnassi vobis juga, nam neque Pindi
Ulla moram fecere, neque Aoniæ Aganippæ.

TRANSLATION.

Indulge me, Arethusa, this last Essay. A few Verses, but such as Lycoris herself may read, I must sing to my Gallus. Who can deny a Verse to Gallus? So, when thou glidest beneath the Sicilian Waves, may brackish Doris not intermingle her Stream *with thine*. Begin: Let us sing the anxious Loves of Gallus, while the flat-nosed Goats browze the tender Shrubs. We sing not to the Deaf; the Woods reply to all. What Groves, ye Virgin Naids, or what Lawns detained you, while Gallus pined away with ill-requited Love? For neither any of Parnassus's Tops, nor those of Pindus, nor Aonian Aganippe, *the*

NOTES.

Gallus, a great Patron of *Virgil*, and an excellent Poet, was very deeply in love with one *Cytheris*, whom he calls *Lycoris*; and who had forsaken him for the Company of a Soldier. The Poet therefore supposes his Friend *Gallus* retired in his Height of Melancholy into the Solitudes of *Arcadia* (the celebrated Scene of Pastorals), where he represents him in a very languishing Condition, with all the rural Deities about him, pitying his hard Usage, and condoling his Misfortunes.

This *Gallus* is he who, *Suetonius* tells us, raised himself from a mean Station to high Favour with *Augustus*, and had from him the Government of *Egypt* after the Death of *Antony* and *Cleopatra*. *Suet. in Aug.* LXVI.

1. *Arethusa.* A Fountain or Fountain-nymph in *Sicily*, where *Theocritus* flourished.

5. *Doris amara.* Doris is one of the Sea-nymphs, here put for the Sea itself. For the fabulous Story of *Alpheus* and *Arethusa*, see Æn. III. 694.

10. *Indigno amore.* Either *unworthily requited, qui dignus erat meliore amore:* Or taking *indignus* in the Sense of *fœdus, crudelis*, as *Donatus* interprets it; and as it is used in the second Æneid:

Quæ causa indigna serenos—fœdavit vultus?

11. *Nam neque*, &c. The Meaning is, that neither *Parnassus*, *Pindus*, nor any Place sacred to the Muses, could retard you from *Gallus*; for there the very Trees and Shrubs mourned in Concert with his elegiac Muse, and must have melted you into Pity, had you been in those Retreats; they were so far from retarding, that they would have invited you to aid the Love-sick, dying Swain.

11. *Parnassi—Pindi.* Parnassus is a Mountain

Illum etiam lauri, illum etiam flevere myricæ:
Pinifer illum etiam solâ sub rupe jacentem
Mænalus, et gelidi fleverunt saxa Lycæi.
Stant et oves circum, nostrî nec pœnitet illas;
Nec te pœniteat pecoris, divine poëta:
Et formosus oves ad flumina pavit Adonis.
Venit et upilio: tardi venere bubulci:
Uvidus hibernâ venit de glande Menalcas.
Omnes, unde amor iste, rogant, tibi? venit Apollo:
Galle quid insanis? inquit. Tua cura Lycoris,
Perque nives alium, perque horrida castra secuta est.
Venit et agresti capitis Silvanus honore,
Florentes ferulas et grandia lilia quassans.
Pan Deus Arcadiæ venit: quem vidimus ipsi
Sanguineis ebuli baccis minioque rubentem.
Et quis erit modus? inquit: Amor non talia curat.
Nec lacrymis crudelis amor, nec gramina rivis,
Nec cytiso saturantur apes, nec fronde capellæ.
Tristis at ille: tamen cantabitis, Arcades, inquit,

Etiam lauri, etiam myricæ flevere illum. Etiam pinifer Mænalus, et saxa gelidi Lycæi fleverunt illum jacentem sub solâ rupe. Et oves stant circum eum, nec pœnitet illas nostrî; nec pœniteat te pecoris, ô divine poëta: et formosus Adonis pavit oves ad flumina. Et upilio venit: tardi bubulci venere: Menalcas uvidus de hibernâ glande venit. Omnes rogant, unde est tibi iste amor? Apollo venit: inquit, Galle, quid insanis? Lycoris tua cura est secuta alium perque nives, perque horrida castra. Et Silvanus venit, cum agresti honore capitis, quassans florentes ferulas, et grandia lilia. Pan Deus Arcadiæ venit: quem nos ipsi vidimus, rubentem sanguineis baccis ebuli, minioque. Et ille inquit, quis erit modus? amor non curat talia. Nec crudelis amor saturatur *lacrymis, nec gramina rivis, nec apes saturantur cytiso, nec capellæ fronde. At ille* Gallus *tristis inquit, tamen, Arcades,* vos *cantabitis.*

TRANSLATION.

Fountain of the Muses, did retard you. *There* the very Laurels, the very Tamarisks condoled him: Even Pine-top'd Mænalus *bemoaned* him as he lay beneath a lonely Rock, and over him the Stones of cold Lycæus wept. His Sheep too stand *mourning* around him, nor are they ashamed to share our Griefs; nor of thy Flock, divine Poet, be thou ashamed: Even fair Adonis tended Sheep along the Streams. The Shepherd too came up: The slow-paced Neat-herds came: Menalcas came wet from *gathering* Winter-maste. All interrogate whence this thy Love? Apollo came: Gallus, he says, why ravest thou *thus?* Lycoris, for whom you pine, is following another *Lover* through Snows, and horrid Camps. Silvanus too came up with rural Honours on his Head, waving the flowery Fennels and big Lilies *that adorned his Brow*. Pan, the God of Arcadia, came: Whom we ourselves beheld stained with the Elder's purple Berries and Vermilion. What Bounds, he says, will you set *to Mourning?* Love regards not such *vain Lamentations*. Nor cruel Love with Tears, nor grassy Meads with Streams, nor Bees with Cytisus, nor Goats with Browze are satisfied. But he overwhelmed with Grief: yet you, Arcadians, he says, shall sing these *my Woes*

NOTES.

tain in *Phocis*, and *Pindus* in *Bœotia*; both of them sacred to the Muses. Out of this last the Fountain *Aganippe* springs, and is here called *Aonian*, from *Aonia*, the same as *Bœotia*.

15. *Mænalus, Lycæi.* Mænalus and Lycæus are two Mountains of *Arcadia*, the Scene of this Pastoral. The one abounded with Pines, the other is often covered with Snow.

16. *Nostrî nec pœnitet illas*, i.e. *Nec pœnitet illas ingemiscere nostrâ causâ.*

19. *Bubulci.* Others read *subulci*.

22. *Tua cura Lycoris.* Lycoris thy Care, or the Object of thy Love.

 33 Quam

Montibus hæc vestris: soli cantare periti
Arcades. O mihi tum quàm molliter ossa quiescent,
Vestra meos olim si fistula dicat amores!
Atque utinam ex vobis unus, vestrique fuissem
Aut custos gregis, aut maturæ vinitor uvæ!
Certè sive mihi Phyllis, sive esset Amyntas,
Seu quicunque furor; (quid tum, si fuscus Amyntas?
Et nigræ violæ, sunt et vaccinia nigra)
Mecum inter salices lentâ sub vite jaceret:
Serta mihi Phyllis legeret, cantaret Amyntas.
Hìc gelidi fontes, hìc mollia prata, Lycori,
Hìc nemus: hìc ipso tecum consumerer ævo.
Hunc insanus amor duri me Martis in armis,
Tela inter media, atque adversos detinet hostes.
Tu procul à patriâ (nec sit mihi credere) tantùm
Alpinas, ah dura! nives, et frigora Rheni,
Me sine sola vides. Ah te ne frigora lædant!
Ah tibi ne teneras glacies secet aspera plantas!
Ibo, et Chalcidico quæ sunt mihi condita versu

hæc mea mala vestris montibus: vos Arcades soli periti cantare. O quàm molliter tum ossa quiescent mihi, si olim vestra fistula dicat meos amores! atque utinam ego fuissem unus ex vobis, autque custos vestri gregis, aut vinitor maturæ uvæ! Certè sive esset mihi Phyllis, sive Amyntas, seu quicunque furor; (quid tum, si Amyntas sit fuscus: et violæ sunt nigræ, et vaccinia sunt *nigra) jaceret mecum inter salices sub lentâ vite: Phyllis legeret serta mihi, Amyntas cantaret* mihi. *Hìc* sunt *gelidi fontes, hìc* sunt *mollia prata, Lycori, hìc* est *nemus: hìc consumerer tecum ævo ipso. Nunc insanus amor detinet me in armis duri Martis, inter media tela, atque adversos hostes. Tu, procul à patriâ (nec sit mihi credere) vides tantùm Alpinas nives, et frigora Rheni, ah dura! sola sine me. Ah, ne frigora lædant te! ah, ne aspera glacies secet teneras plantas tibi! Ibo, et modulabor carmina avenâ Siculi pastoris* Theocriti,

TRANSLATION.

on your Mountains: Ye Arcadians only skilled in Song. O how softly then my Bones shall rest, if your Pipe in future Times shall sing my Loves! And would to Heaven I had been one of you, and either Keeper of your Flock, or Vintager of the ripe Grape! Sure whether Phyllis or Amyntas, or whoever else had been my Love, (what tho' Amyntas be swarthy? The Violet is black, and Hyacinths are black) they would have reposed with me among the Willows under the limber Vine: Phyllis had gathered Garlands for me, *and* Amyntas should have sung. Here *are* cool Fountains, here, Lycoris, soft *flowery* Meads, here a *delicious* Grove: Here with thee I could consume my whole Life away. Now Love frantic *through Despair* detains me in the Service of rigid Mars, in the midst of Darts, and adverse Foes. Thou, far from thy native Land (*yet* let me not believe it) beholdest nothing but Alpine Snows, and the Colds of the Rhine, ah, hard-hearted *Fair!* alone, *and* without me. Ah Heaven forbid that these Colds should hurt thee! that the sharp Ice should wound thy tender Feet! I will go, and warble on the Sicilian Shepherd's Reed those Songs which are

NOTES.

33. *Quàm molliter ossa, &c.* They seem to have had a superstitious Dread lest the Bodies of the Dead should be oppressed with the Weight of the Earth that was laid upon them: And therefore they took care it should first be pounded and crumbled into Dust before it was laid on the Grave; using this Form of Words: *Sit tibi terra levis, may the Earth be light upon thee.*

36. *Vinitor.* Is one who prunes or takes care of Vines. As it is here joined not with *vitis*, but *uvæ*, it would seem to import the same as *custos vineæ*, as *Mancinellus* explains it; or *vindemiator*, the *Vintager*.

45. *Adversos*, i. e. says *Servius*, *se pellusque suum pugnæ objicientes*; *rectâ fronte, intrepido et viris animo occurrentes.*

48. *Me sine sola.* Lycoris had followed *Gallus*'s Rival to the Wars, as is said in the Argument; therefore the Meaning of *me sine sola*, is, *that she was alone as to him.*

50. *Chalcidico versu.* In Elegiac Verse, such

Carmina, pastoris Siculi modulabor avenâ.
Certum est in silvis, inter spelæa ferarum
Malle pati; tenerisque meos incidere amores
Arboribus: crescent illæ: crescetis amores.
Interea mistis lustrabo Mænala Nymphis:
Aut acres venabor apros. Non me ulla vetabunt
Frigora Parthenios canibus circundare saltus.
Jam mihi per rupes videor, lucosque sonantes
Ire: libet Partho torquere Cydonia cornu
Spicula: tanquam hæc sint nostri medicina furoris;
Aut Deus ille malis hominum mitescere discat.
Jam neque Hamadryades rursus, nec carmina nobis
Ipsa placent: ipsæ rursus concedite silvæ.
Non illum nostri possunt mutare labores;
Nec si frigoribus mediis Hebrumque bibamus,
Sithoniasque nives hiemis subeamus aquosæ:

quæ sunt condita mihi Chalcidico versu. Est certum, malle pati in silvis, inter spelæa ferarum, incidereque meos amores teneris arboribus: illæ arbores crescent: vos mei amores crescetis. Interea lustrabo Mænala nymphis mistis, aut venabor acres apros. Non ulla frigora vetabunt me circundare Parthenios saltus canibus. Jam videor mihi ire per rupes, sonantesque lucos: libet mihi torquere Cydonia spicula Partho cornu: tanquam hæc sint medicina nostri furoris; aut ille Deus discat mitescere malis hominum. Jam rursus neque Hamadryades, nec carmina ipsa placent nobis: rursus vos silvæ ipsæ concedite. Nostri labores non possunt mutare illum Deum; nec si bibamusque Hebrum mediis frigoribus, subeamusque Sithonias nives aquosæ hyemis:

TRANSLATION.

by me composed in Euphorion's *elegiac* Strain. I am resolved, rather *than pursue thee thus in vain*, to submit *to Toils and Dangers* in the Words, among the Dens of wild Beasts, and to inscribe my Loves upon the tender Trees: As they grow up, so you, my Loves, will grow. Mean while with mingled *Troops of* Nymphs over Mænalus will I range, or hunt the fierce Boars. No Colds shall hinder me from traversing with my Hounds the Parthenian Lawns around. Now over Rocks and resounding Groves methinks I roam: Pleased I am to shoot Cydonian Shafts from the Parthian Bow: *Fool that I am!* as if these were a Cure for the Rage of Love; or *as if* that God were capable of being softened by human Woes. Now neither the Nymphs of the Groves, nor Songs themselves charm me any more: Even to you, ye Woods, once more I bid adieu. No Sufferings can alter him; not tho' in midst of Frosts we drink of Hebrus, and undergo the Sithonian Snows of rainy Winter; nor should we tend our Flocks

NOTES.

as *Euphorion* of *Chalcis* wrote. *Servius* informs us, that *Gallus* had translated his *Greek* Elegies into *Latin* Verse; and *Ruæus* and most Interpreters take this to be the Meaning of the Words *condita Chalcid'eo versu*: *Quæ versibus traduxi è Chalcidensi poëta*, says *Ruæus*. But, though this may be true, it is not to be made out of *Virgil's* Words, without great straining; for they imply no more than simply that *Gallus* had composed some Songs or Elegies in the same kind of Verse as the Poet of *Chalcis* wrote. *Catrou* seems to me to have hit upon the true Meaning, namely, That he would forsake *Euphorion* for *Theocritus*; *i. e.* Elogy for the pastoral kind of Poetry.

51. *Pastoris Siculi.* Theocritus.

59. *Partho cornu.* The *Parthian* Bow; because the *Parthians* were famed for handling the Bow, which they made of Horn.

59. *Cydonia spicula.* Cydonian Shafts, from *Cydon*, a Town in *Crete*, whose Arrows were much esteemed.

62. *Hamadryades.* The Nymphs of the Woods or Trees, from ἅμα, *simul*, and δρῦς, *an Oak*, because their Fate was connected with that of particular Trees, with which they lived and died.

65. *Hebrum.* Hebrus, one of the greatest Rivers in *Thrace*, rising out of Mount *Rhodope*.

66. *Sithoniasque nives.* Sithonian Snows, from *Sithonia*, a Part of *Thrace*.

nec ſi, cum moriens liber aret in altâ ulmo, verſemus oves Æthiopum ſub ſidere Cancri. Amor vincit omnia: et nos cedamus amori. Divæ Pierides, erit ſat, veſtrum poëtam cecinisse hæc carmina, dum ſedet, et texit fiſcellam gracili hibiſco: vos facietis hæc carmina maxima Gallo: Gallo, amor cujus creſcit mihi tantum in ſingulas horas, quantum viridis alnus ſubjicit ſe novo vere. Surgamus: umbra ſolet eſſe gravis cantantibus; umbra juniperi eſt gravis; umbræ nocent et frugibus. Vos capellæ, ſaturæ, ite domum, ite, Heſperus venit.

Nec ſi, cum moriens altâ liber aret in ulmo,
Æthiopum verſemus oves ſub ſidere Cancri.
Omnia vincit amor: et nos cedamus amori.
Hæc ſat erit, Divæ, veſtrum ceciniſſe poëtam,
Dum ſedet, et gracili fiſcellam texit hibiſco,
Pierides: vos hæc facietis maxima Gallo:
Gallo, cujus amor tantum mihi creſcit in horas,
Quantum vere novo viridis ſe ſubjicit alnus.
Surgamus: ſolet eſſe gravis cantantibus umbra:
Juniperi gravis umbra: nocent et frugibus umbræ.
Ite domum ſaturæ, venit Heſperus, ite capellæ.

TRANSLATION.

in Ethiopia, beneath the Sign of Cancer, when the dying Rhind is withered on the ſtately Elm. Love conquers all; and let us yield to Love. These *Verſes*, ye divine Muſes, it ſhall ſuffice your Poet to have ſung, while he ſat, and wove his little Baſket of ſlender Oſiers: Theſe you will make acceptable to Gallus: To Gallus, for whom my Love grows as much every Hour, as the green Alder ſhoots up in the Infancy of Spring. Let us ariſe: The *Evening*-ſhade uſes to prove noxious to Singers; even the Juniper's Shade, *at other Times the moſt wholſome*, now grows noxious; the *Evening* ſhades are hurtful even to the Corn. Go home, the Evening-ſtar ariſes, my full-fed Goats, go home.

NOTES.

76. *Gravis cantantibus umbra*, The Even- | ing Shade, as is plain from what follows;

BUCOLICORUM FINIS.

P. VIRGILII MARONIS

GEORGICA.

LIBER I.

QUID faciat lætas ſegetes; quo ſidere terram
Vertere, Mæcenas, ulmiſque adjungere vites
Conveniat; quæ cura boum, qui cultus habendo
Sit pecori; atque apibus quanta experientia parcis,
Hinc canere incipiam. Vos, ô clariſſima mundi
Lumina, labentem cœlo quæ ducitis annum;

ORDO.

Quid faciat lætas ſegetes; quo ſidere conveniat vertere terram, O Mæcenas, adjungereque vites ulmis; quæ cura boum ſit, qui cultus ſit pecori habendo; atque quanta experientia ſit parcis apibus, hinc incipiam canere. Vos, ô clariſſima lumina mundi, quæ ducitis annum labentem cœlo;

TRANSLATION.

WHAT makes the Fields of Corn joyous; under what Sign, Mæcenas, it is proper to turn the Earth and join the Vines to Elms; what Care *is requiſite* for Kine, the Nurture for breeding Sheep *and leſſer Cattle*; and what Experience for *managing* the frugal Bees, hence will I begin to ſing. Ye brighteſt Luminaries of the World, that lead the Year ſliding along the Sky; *thou*

NOTES.

The Poet, in the firſt four Lines, ſhews the Deſign of each of the four Books of the Georgics in their Order. And, after a ſolemn Invocation of all the Gods who are any way related to his Subject, he addreſſes himſelf in particular to *Auguſtus*, whom he compliments with Divinity; and after ſtrikes into his Buſineſs. He ſhews the different Kinds of Tillage proper to different Soils, traces out the Original of Agriculture, gives a Catalogue of the Huſbandman's Tools, ſpecifies the Employments peculiar to each Seaſon, deſcribes the Changes of the Weather, with the Signs in Heaven and Earth that forebode them; inſtances many of the Prodigies that happened near the Time of *Julius Cæſar*'s Death; and ſhuts up all with a Supplication to the Gods for the Safety of *Auguſtus*, and the Preſervation of *Rome*.

4. *Pecori.* Pecus here, as oppoſed to *boves*, ſignifies *the leſſer Cattle*, as Sheep and Goats, but eſpecially Sheep; as the Word, I think, always ſignifies in *Virgil* when it ſtands by itſelf. See Ecl. I. 75. III. 1, 20, 34. V. 87. Geor. II. 371.

5. *Hinc,* May either mean *henceforth*, or *with thoſe Subjects*, as Geor. II. 444.

5. *Vos, ô clariſſima mundi, &c.* Varro, in his ſeventh Book of Agriculture, invocates the Sun and Moon, then *Bacchus* and *Ceres*, as *Virgil* does here: Which ſufficiently confutes thoſe who take the Words, *vos, ô clariſſima lumina*, to be meant of *Bacchus* and *Ceres*.

8. *Chaoniam*,

Liber et alma Ceres si, vestro munere, tellus mutavit Chaoniam glandem pingui aristâ, miscuitque Acheloïa pocula uvis inventis: et vos Fauni, præsentia numina agrestium virorum; Faunique puellæque Dryades simul ferte pedem meis carminibus: *cano vestra munera. Tuque, ô Neptune, cui prima tellus, percussa magno tridenti, fudit frementem equum: et tu,* Aristæe, *cultor nemorum, cui ter centum nivei juvenci tondent pinguia dumeta* insulæ *Ceæ: tu ipse, Pan, custos ovium, linquens patrium nemus, saltusque* montis *Lycæi, si tua Mænala* sunt *tibi curæ, ô* Pan *Tegeæe, adsis favens* nobis: *Minervaque inventrix oleæ, puerque, ô* Triptoleme, *monstrator unci aratri; et tu, Silvane, ferens teneram cupressum ab radice: omnesque Dî Deæque, quibus studium est tueri arva,*

Liber, et alma Ceres; vestro si munere tellus
Chaoniam pingui glandem mutavit aristâ,
Poculaque inventis Acheloïa miscuit uvis:
Et vos agrestum præsentia numina Fauni;
Ferte simul Faunique pedem, Dryadesque puellæ:
Munera vestra cano. Tuque ô, cui prima frementem
Fudit equum magno tellus percussa tridenti,
Neptune: et cultor nemorum, cui pinguia Ceæ
Ter centum nivei tondent dumeta juvenci:
Ipse nemus linquens patrium, saltusque Lycæi,
Pan ovium custos, tuâ si tibi Mænala curæ,
Adsis, ô Tegeæe, favens: oleæque Minerva
Inventrix: uncique puer monstrator aratri;
Et teneram ab radice ferens, Silvane, cupressum:
Dique Deæque omnes, studium quibus arva tueri,

TRANSLATION.

Bacchus and fostering Ceres, if by your Bounty Mortals exchanged Chaonian Maste for fattening Ears of Corn, and mingled Draughts of Achelous with the invented *Juice of the* Grape: And ye Fauns propitious to the Swains, ye Fauns and Virgin Dryads both come tripping up together: Your bounteous Gifts I sing. And thou, O Neptune, to whom the Earth, struck with thy mighty Trident, first poured forth the neighing steed; and thou inhabitant of the Groves, for whom three hundred Snow-white Bullocks cropt Cæa's fertile Thickets: Thou too, O Pan, Guardian of the Sheep, O Tegeæan *God*, if thy own Mænalus be thy Care, draw nigh propitious, leaving *a while* thy native Grove, and the Lawns of Lycæus: And *thou*, Minerva, Inventress of the Olive; and thou, O Boy, who taught the Use of the crooked Plough. And thou, Silvanus, bearing a tender Cyprus plucked up by the Root: Ye Gods and Goddesses all,

NOTES.

8. ***Chaoniam.*** Because the Woods of *Dodona* in *Epirus* or *Chaonia* abounded with Oaks and Maste-bearing Trees.

9. *Pocula Acheloïa.* Draughts of *Achelous*, i. e. *of pure Water*. *Achelous* was a River in *Ætolia*, said to be the first that arose out of the Earth, and therefore was frequently put for Water by the Ancients.

12. *Tuque, &c.* Meaning *Aristæus*.

13. *Equum.* La Cerda contends it should be read *aquam*; but what then becomes of the Epithet *frementem*?

14. *Ceæ.* Cæa, one of the *Cyclades* Islands, where *Aristæus* settled, leaving *Thebes*, after his Son *Actæon* was torn in Pieces by a Pack of Hounds, for gazing upon *Diana* as she was bathing herself.

16. ***Lycæi—Mænala.*** Lycæus and *Mænalus* were two Mountains in *Arcadia*, sacred to *Pan*.

17. *Si.* Here, according to some, has the Force of *etsi, though thy own* Mænalus, *&c. be thy Care, yet draw nigh.* But others explain it: *If thou hast any Care for these Pasturages, aid my Song, whence so much Honour and Advantage will accrue to those Places.*

18. *Tegeæe.* Pan, so called from *Tegea*, a City of *Arcadia*, sacred to *Pan*.

19. *Uncique puer.* Triptolemus, who, according to Fable, first taught the *Greeks* Agriculture, wherein he himself had been instructed by *Ceres*.

20. *Ab radice.* Achilles Statius tells us, that *Silvanus* was represented on ancient Coins and Marbles, bearing a Cypress-tree plucked up by the Roots.

Quique novas alitis nullo de semine fruges;
Quique satis largum cœlo demittitis imbrem.
Tuque adeò, quem mox quæ sint habitura Deorum
Concilia, incertum est: urbisne invisere Cæsar,
Terrarumque velis curam, et te maximus orbis
Auctorem frugum, tempestatumque potentem
Accipiat, cingens maternâ tempora myrto:
An Deus immensi venias maris, ac tua nautæ
Numina sola colant: tibi serviat ultima Thule,
Teque sibi generum Tethys emat omnibus undis:
Anne novum tardis sidus te mensibus addas,
Quà locus Erigonen inter, Chelasque sequentes
Panditur: ipse tibi jam brachia contrahit ardens
Scorpius, et cœli justâ plus parte relinquit.
Quidquid eris; (nam te nec sperent Tartara regem,
Nec tibi regnandi veniat tam dira cupido:

quique alitis novas fruges de nullo semine; quique demittitis satis largum imbrem cœlo. Adeòque tu, Cæsar, quem est incertum, quæ concilia Deorum sint habitura mox, velisne invisere urbes, curamque terrarum, et maximus orbis accipiat te auctorem frugum, potentemque tempestatum, cingens tempora tui capitis *maternâ myrto: an venias Deus immensi maris, ac nautæ colant tua numina sola: ultima Thule serviat tibi, Tethysque emat te generum sibi omnibus undis: anne addas te novum sidus tardis mensibus, quà locus panditur inter Erigonen, Chelasque sequentes* eam: *jam ardens Scorpius ipse contrahit brachia tibi, et relinquit* tibi *plus justâ parte cœli. Quidquid* numen *eris; (nam nec Tartara sperent te regem, nec tam dira cupido regnandi veniat tibi:*

TRANSLATION.

whose Province it is to guard the Fields, both ye who nourish the infant Fruits *that Spring* from no Seed *sown by the Hand of Man*; and ye who on the sown *Fruits* send down the liberal Shower from Heaven.

And chiefly thou, *great* Cæsar, whom 'tis yet uncertain which Council of the Gods is soon to have: Whether thou wilt vouchsafe to visit Cities, and *undertake* the Care of Countries, and the widely extended Globe receive thee, Giver of the Fruits, and Ruler of the Seasons, binding thy Temples with thy Mother's Myrtle: Or whether thou comest God of the unmeasured Ocean, and Mariners worship thy Divinity alone: Whether remotest Thule is to be subject to thee, and Tethys to purchase thee for her Son-in-law with all her Waves: Or whether thou wilt *take thy Seat among the Stars*, join thyself to the slow Months, a new Constellation, where Space lies open *for thy Reception* between Erigone and the *Scorpion*'s pursuing Claws: The Scorpion himself, impatient *for thy Coming*, already contracts his Arms, and leaves for thee more than an equal Proportion of the Sky. Whatever *Deity* thou wilt be; (for let not Tartarus expect thee for its King, nor let such dire Lust of Sway once enter thy

NOTES.

22. *Nullo de semine.* This is the Reading which *Pierius* found in several Manuscripts, and the Sense confirms it to be the true one: For, as Mr. *Martin* rightly observes, the Poet in these two Lines invokes first those Deities who take care of Spontaneous Plants, and then those who shed their Influence on Plants that are sown. Thus, at the Beginning of the second Georgic, he tells us, that some Trees come up of their own Accord without Culture, and that others are sown:

Principio arboribus varia est natura creandis.
Namque aliæ, nullis hominum cogentibus, ipsæ
Sponte sua veniunt————
Pars autem posito surgunt de semine.

27. *Tempestatumque.* Not Storms, as some translate it; for that belongs to the Class of Sea-divinities mentioned afterwards. Besides, to be Ruler or Arbiter of the Seasons, is a much higher Compliment.

30. *Thule.* An Island in the *Scottish* Seas, between *Norway* and *Scotland*.

32. *Tardis mensibus.* Either the Summer Months, call'd slow, because the Days are then longer: Or, as Mr. *Martin* has it from Dr. *Halley*, because the four Signs of *Leo*, *Virgo*, *Libra*, and *Scorpio*, are really slower in their Ascension than the other eight.

34. *Ardens.* Impatient for thy Coming. This Sense I choose rather than to make it an Epithet of *Scorpio*.

quamvis Græcia miratur Elyſios campos, nec Proſerpina repetita curet ſequi matrem) da facilem curſum, atque annue noſtris audacibus cœptis; miſeratuſque agreſtes ignaros viæ mecum ingredere, et jam nunc aſſueſce vocari votis. In *novo vere, cum gelidus humor liquitur è canis montibus, et putris gleba reſolvit ſe Zephyro; jam tum taurus incipiat ingemere mihi depreſſo aratro, et vomer attritus ſulco* incipiat *ſplendeſcere. Illa ſeges demum reſpondet votis avari agricolæ, quæ* ſeges *ſenſit bis ſolem, bis frigora; immenſæ meſſes ruperunt horrea* illius agricolæ. *At priuſquam ſcindimus ignotum æquor ferro, cura ſit, prædiſcere ventos, et varium morem cœli, ac patrios cultuſque habituſque locorum; et quid quæque recuſet. Hîc ſegetes* veniunt felicius, *illic uvæ veniunt felicius:*

Quamvis Elyſios miretur Græcia campos,
Nec repetita ſequi curet Proſerpina matrem) 39
Da facilem curſum, atque audacibus annue cœptis;
Ignaroſque viæ mecum miſeratus agreſtes,
Ingredere, et votis jam nunc aſſueſce vocari.
Vere novo, gelidus canis cum montibus humor
Liquitur, et Zephyro putris ſe gleba reſolvit;
Depreſſo incipiat jam tum mihi taurus aratro 45
Ingemere, et ſulco attritus ſplendeſcere vomer.
Illa ſeges demum votis reſpondet avari
Agricolæ, bis quæ Solem, bis frigora ſenſit:
Illius immenſæ ruperunt horrea meſſes.
At prius ignotum ferro quàm ſcindimus æquor,
Ventos, et varium cœli prædiſcere morem 51
Cura ſit, ac patrios cultuſque habituſque locorum;
Et quid quæque ferat regio, et quid quæque recuſet.
Hìc ſegetes, illic veniunt feliciùs uvæ:

TRANSLATION.

Mind: Tho' Greece admires her Elyſian Fields, and Proſerpine redemanded cares not to follow her Mother *to the upper World)* grant me an eaſy Courſe, favour my adventrous Enterprize; and, pitying with me the Swains who are Strangers to their Way, commence *a God*, and accuſtom thyſelf even now to be invoked by Prayers.

In early Spring, when the melted Snows glide down the hoary Hills, and the crumbling Glebe unbinds itſelf by the Zephyr; then let my Steer begin to groan under the deep-preſſed Plough, and the Share worn on the Furrow *begin* to glitter. That Field at laſt anſwers the Wiſhes of the covetous Farmer, which twice hath felt the *Summer*'s Sun, *and* twice the Colds *of Winter:* Harveſts immenſe have *even* burſt his Barns.

But, before we cut an unknown Plain with the Coulter, let it be our Care previouſly to learn the Winds, and various Quality of the Climate, the Ways of Culture practiſed by our Forefathers, and the Genius and Habits of the Soil; what each Country is apt to produce, and what to refuſe. Here Corn, there

NOTES.

43. *Gelidus humor.* Literally, *the cold Moiſture.*

48. *Bis quæ ſolem, &c.* i. e. *Which is ſuffered to lie fallow two Years.*

49. *Ruperunt, &c.* Meaning, *That his Barns have not been able to contain ſo great Plenty.*

50. *Ferro.* Any Inſtrument of Iron.

51. *Ventos.* To what Winds it ſtands moſt expoſed.

51. *Cœli morem.* Whether moiſt or dry, cold or hot; and how the Soil agrees with each.

52. *Patrios cultus, &c.* This I explain in Servius's Senſe. *Sciendum eſt*, ſays he, *ager et quemadmodum à majoribus cultus ſit, et quid melius ferre conſueverit.* A Soil, by being cultivated in a certain Way, acquires a Habit or Aptitude to produce ſome Grain better than others; which is the *habitus locorum*, chiefly its acquired Habit or Genius; for the natural Genius is expreſſed in the following Words, *Quid quæque ferat*, &c.

Arborei fetus alibi, atque injuſſa vireſcunt
Gramina. Nonne vides, croceos ut Tmolus odores,
India mittit ebur, molles ſua thura Sabæi?
At Chalybes nudi ferrum, viroſaque Pontus
Caſtorea, Eliadum palmas Epiros equarum?
Continuò has leges, æternaque fœdera certis
Impoſuit natura locis, quo tempore primùm
Deucalion vacuum lapides jactavit in orbem:
Unde homines nati, durum genus. Ergo age, terræ
Pingue ſolum primis extemplò à menſibus anni
Fortes invertant tauri: glebaſque jacentes
Pulverulenta coquat maturis ſolibus æſtas.
At ſi non fuerit tellus fecunda, ſub ipſum
Arcturum tenui ſat erit ſuſpendere ſulco:
Illic, officiant lætis ne frugibus herbæ:
Hic, ſterilem exiguus ne deſerat humor arenam.

arborei fetus, atque gramina injuſſa vireſcunt alibi. Nonne vides ut mons Tmolus mittit croceos odores, ut India mittit ebur, ut molles Sabæi mittunt ſua thura? At nudi Chalybes mittunt ferrum, Pontuſque mittit viroſa caſtorea, et Epiros mittit palmas Eliadum equarum? Continuò natura impoſuit has leges æternaque fœdera certis locis, quo tempore primùm Deucalion jactavit lapides in vacuum orbem: unde homines, durum genus, ſunt nati. Ergo age, fortes tauri invertant pingue ſolum terræ extemplò à primis menſibus anni: pulverulentaque æſtas coquat jacentes glebas maturis ſolibus. At ſi tellus non fuerit fecunda, erit ſat ſuſpendere eam tenui ſulco ſub Arcturum ipſum: illic facies ut juſſi, ne herbæ officiant lætis frugibus: hic facies ne exiguus humor deſerat ſterilem arenam.

TRANSLATION.

Grapes more happily grow: Nurſeries of Trees elſewhere, and Herbs ſpontaneous bloom. Don't you ſee, how Tmolus ſends *us* Saffron Odours, India Ivory, the ſoft Sabæans their Frankincenſe? But the naked Chalybes Steel, Pontus ſtrong-ſcented Caſtor, Epirus the Prime of the Olympic Mares? Theſe Laws and eternal Regulations Nature from the Beginning impoſed on certain Places, what Time Deucalion firſt threw *thoſe* Stones into the unpeopled World, whence Men, a hardy Race, ſprung up. Come then, let your ſturdy Steers turn up a Soil that is rich forthwith from the firſt Months of the Year: And let the duſty Summer bake the lying Clods with Suns mature *and vigorous*. But, if the Land be not fertile, it will be ſufficient to raiſe it up with a light Furrow, even *ſo late as* towards the Riſing of Arcturus: In the former Caſe, leſt Weeds obſtruct the joyous Corn: In the latter, leſt the ſcanty Moiſture forſake the barren ſandy Soil.

NOTES.

55. *Arborei fetus.* Signifies *Nurſeries of Trees in general*, as Verſe 75.

56. *Tmolus.* A Mountain in *Lydia*, famous for the beſt Saffron.

57. *Sabæi.* The Inhabitants of *Arabia Felix*, in whoſe Country only the Frankincenſe-tree is ſaid to grow, Geor. II. 117.

Solis eſt Thurea virga Sabæis.

58. *Chalybes nudi.* The *Chalybes*, according to *Juſtin*, were a People in *Spain*, here called *Nudi*, becauſe the Heat of their Forges made them work naked.

58. *Viroſa caſtorea.* Caſtor, according to *Pliny*, is the Beaver's Teſticles: It is of a medicinal Nature, and the Smell of it ſo powerful, that it is ſaid to make Women miſcarry. *Lucretius* ſays, the Smell of it affects them in certain Circumſtances with a kind of Lethargy, and makes them drop the Work they are about out of their Hands, Lib. VI. 794.

Caſtoreoque gravi mulier ſopita recumbit,
Et manibus nitidum teneris opus effluit ei,
Tempore eo ſi odorata eſt, quo menſtrua ſolvit.

Hence *Virgil* gives it the Epithet *viroſa*, *poiſonous* or *deady*. The Moderns have diſcovered that the Caſtor is not contained in the Teſticles of the Beaver, but in odoriferous Glands about the Groin.

59. *Eliadum palmas equarum.* Palmas here ſignifies the Prime or Choice of the Mares, ſuch as were wont to carry the Palm at the *Olympic* Games in the Plains of *Elis*. Thus Æn. V. 339. *Nunc tertia palma Diores*; i. e. *Diores tertius victor.*

67. *Sub ipſum Arcturum.* About the middle of *September*.

Tu idem patiere tonsas novales terras cessare alternis annis, *et segnem campum durescere situ. Aut ibi seres flava farra, sidere mutato, unde priùs sustuleris lætum legumen quassante siliquâ, aut tenues fetus viciæ, fragilesque calamos tristis lupini, sonantemque silvam. Enim seges lini urit campum, seges avenæ urit* eum: *papavera perfusa Lethæo somno urunt* eum. *Sed tamen labor* est *facilis alternis* annis; *tantùm ne pudeat te saturare arida sola pingui fimo; neve jactare immundum cinerem per effetos agros. Sic quoque arva requiescunt fetibus mutatis, nec interea est nulla gratia inaratæ terræ.*

Alternis idem tonsas cessare novales,
Et segnem patiere situ durescere campum.
Aut ibi flava seres, mutato sidere, farra,
Unde prius lætum siliquâ quassante legumen,
Aut tenues fetus viciæ, tristisque lupini
Sustuleris fragiles calamos, silvamque sonantem.
Urit enim lini campum seges, urit avenæ;
Urunt Lethæo perfusa papavera somno.
Sed tamen alternis facilis labor; arida tantùm
Ne saturare fimo pingui pudeat sola; neve
Effetos cinerem immundum jactare per agros:
Sic quoque mutatis requiescunt fetibus arva.
Nec nulla interea est inaratæ gratia terræ.

TRANSLATION.

You shall likewise suffer your Lands after Reaping to rest every other Year, and the Field to harden, *and be overgrown* with Scurf. Or, changing the Season, you shall sow there yellow Wheat, whence before you have taken up *a* joyful *Crop of* Pulse, with rattling Pods, or the Vetch's slender Offspring, and the bitter Lupine's brittle Stalks, and rustling Grove. For a Crop of Flax burns the Land; as also Oats and Poppies impregnated with Lethæan Sleep. But yet your Labour will be easy, *even tho' you should sow these kinds of Grain* every other Year, provided only you be not backward to saturate the parched Soil with rich Dung; nor to scatter sordid Ashes upon the exhausted Lands: Thus too, *with this Precaution*, your Land will rest *merely* by changing the Grain. Mean while, should your Field remain untilled *for one Year*, it would not be ungrateful.

NOTES.

71. *Novales.* Novalis terra is properly Ground new broke up, *unde vetus silva excisa est*, says *Pliny*. Hence it is transferred to signify *Fallow-ground*, because by resting it is recruited, and as it were renewed.

72. *Situ.* Situs is properly the foul Weeds, the Scurf or Squalour which overspread the Ground for want of Culture.

73. *Mutato sidere.* Or *semine*, as in *Pierius*.

74. *Lætum legumen.* By this it is probable *Virgil* understood Beans, which were esteemed the principal sort of Pulse; and *Pliny*, quoting this Passage, for *lætum legumen* substitutes *faba*.

76. *Silvam.* A thick luxuriant Crop of any kind is called *silva*.

77. *Urit enim.* The Connexion is, if you are to change the Grain, it must be with Pulse, Beans, Vetches, or Lupines, but not with Flax, *&c.* for these burn and exhaust the Moisture of the Land.

83. *Nec ulla.* Literally, *Nor mean while is there no Gratitude in the Land that is untilled*, i. e. *left fallow every other Year*. This whole Paragraph, as it is explained by the Commentators, is so perplexed and confused, that one knows not what to make of it. The Sense of the whole seems to be shortly this: The Poet, Verse 71, advises to let the Ground lie fallow every other Year; or, if Circumstances will not admit of this, then he advises, Verse 73, to change the Grain, and sow, after Corn, Pulse of several kinds: But not Flax, nor Oats, nor Poppies, because, Verse 77, these burn out the Substance of the Ground. Yet these too may be used in their Turn, provided Care be taken to recruit and again enrich the Soil with fat Dung and Ashes, after it has been parched with those hot Grains, Verse 79. But he concludes, that should the Ground be left fallow, and quite untilled, instead of being sown with any of these Grains in the alternate Year, it would not be ungrateful, *i. e.* it would make it well worth the Farmer's While, by producing proportionably more in those Years when it is cultivated.

Sæpe etiam ſteriles incendere profuit agros,
Atque levem ſtipulam crepitantibus urere flammis:
Sive inde occultas vires, et pabula terræ
Pinguia concipiunt; ſive illis omne per ignem
Excoquitur vitium, atque exſudat inutilis humor;
Seu plures calor ille vias et cæca relaxat
Spiramenta, novas veniat quà ſuccus in herbas;
Seu durat magis, et venas aſtringit hiantes;
Ne tenues pluviæ, rapidive potentia ſolis
Acrior, aut Boreæ penetrabile frigus adurat.
  Multum adeò, raſtris glebas qui frangit inertes,
Vimineaſque trahit crates, juvat arva (neque illum
Flava Ceres alto nequicquam ſpectat Olympo)
Et qui, proſciſſo quæ ſuſcitat æquore terga,
Rurſus in obliquum verſo perrumpit aratro,
Exercetque frequens tellurem, atque imperat arvis.
  Humida ſolſtitia, atque hiemes orate ſerenas,
Agricolæ. Hiberno lætiſſima pulvere farra,
Lætus ager. Nullo tantum ſe Myſia cultu
Jactat, et ipſa ſuas mirantur Gargara meſſes.

Sæpe etiam profuit incendere ſteriles agros, atque urere levem ſtipulam crepitantibus flammis. Sive inde terræ concipiunt occultas vires et pabula; ſive per ignem omne vitium excoquitur illis, atque inutilis humor exſudat; ſeu ille calor relaxat plures vias, et cæca ſpiramenta, quà ſuccus veniat in novas herbas; ſeu magis durat terram, et aſtringit hiantes venas, ne tenues pluviæ, acriorve potentia rapidi ſolis, aut penetrabile frigus Boreæ adurat eam. *Adeò* ille *multum juvat arva, qui frangit inertes glebas raſtris, trahitque vimineas crates (neque flava Ceres nequicquam ſpectat illum ab alto Olympo) et,* ille etiam juvat arva *qui rurſus perrumpit tellurem quæ ſuſcitat terga, proſciſſo æquore, aratro verſo in obliquum, frequenſque exercet* eam, *atque imperant arvis. Agricolæ, orate* Deos *humida ſolſtitia, atque ſerenas hiemes. Farra* ſunt *lætiſſima, et ager* eſt *lætus hiberno pulvere. Myſia jactat ſe tantum nullo cultu, et Gargara ipſa mirantur ſuas meſſes.*

TRANSLATION.

Often too it has been of uſe to ſet fire to barren Lands, and burn light Stubble in crackling Flames: Whether the Land from thence receives ſecret Strength and rich Nouriſhment, *as is the Caſe with Land that is poor*; or whether every vicious Diſpoſition is exhaled by the Fire, and the ſuperfluous Moiſture ſweats off, *as it happens if the Soil be watery*; or whether the Heat opens more Paſſages, and ſecret Pores, through which the Sap may be derived into the new-born Herbs, *which is the Caſe of the ſtiff Clay*; or whether it hardens more, and binds the gaping Veins, *as happens to a ſpungy Soil*; that the ſmall Showers, or keen Influence of the violent Sun, or penetrating Cold of Boreas may not † hurt it.

He too greatly improves the Lands who breaks the ſluggiſh Clods with Harrows, and drags Oſier Hurdles over them (nor does yellow Ceres view him with an unpropitious Eye from high Olympus) and he alſo who, after the Plain has *once* been torn, again breaks through the Land that raiſes up its Ridges, *and gives it a ſecond Furrow*, turning the Plough acroſs, and vexes it with frequent Exerciſe, and rules his Lands imperiouſly.

Pray, ye Swains, for moiſt Summers, and ſerene Winters. In Winter's Duſt moſt joyful is the Corn, joyful is the Field. This improves *the fertile* Myſia more than all her Culture, and *hence* even Gargarus admires his own Harveſts.

† *Scorch it.*

NOTES.

100. *Solſtitia.* Generally applied by the Poets to ſignify the Summer Solſtice. See *La Cerda.*

102. *Myſia.* There were two Countries of this Name; the one in *Europe*, between *Macedonia*, *Thrace*, and *Dacia*; and the other in the Weſt of *Aſia*, bounding *Troas* on the inland Sides. This laſt is here meant.

103. *Gargara.* A Part of Mount *Ida*, and a City in *Troas.*

Quid dicam de illo, qui, semine jacto, statim insequitur arva, ruitque cumulos male pinguis arenæ? deinde inducit fluvium, sequentesque rivos satis? et cum exustus ager æstuat morientibus herbis, ecce ducit undam e supercilio clivosi tramitis: illa unda, cadens per aspera saxa, ciet raucum murmur, temperatque arva arentibus scaturiginibus. Quid dicam de eo, qui, ne culmus gravidus procumbat spicis, depascit luxuriem segetum in tenera herba, cum primum sata æquant sulcos? quique deducit humorem paludis collectum bibula arena? præsertim si amnis abundans incertis mensibus exit, et tenet omnia late obducto limo, unde cavæ lacunæ sudant tepido humore. Nec tamen (cum labores hominumque boumque sint experti hæc mala versando terram) improbus anser, Strymoniæque grues, et intyba amaris fibris, officiunt nihil, aut umbra nocet nihil. Pater Deorum ipse haud voluit viam colendi terram esse facilem, primusque movit agros per artem, acuens mortalia corda curis;

Quid dicam, jacto qui semine cominùs arva
Insequitur, cumulosque ruit malè pinguis arenæ?
Deinde satis fluvium inducit rivosque sequentes?
Et, cum exustus ager morientibus æstuat herbis,
Ecce, supercilio clivosi tramitis undam
Elicit: illa cadens raucum per lævia murmur
Saxa ciet, scatebrisque arentia temperat arva.
Quid, qui, ne gravidis procumbat culmus aristis,
Luxuriem segetum tenerâ depascit in herbâ,
Cum primùm sulcos æquant sata? quique paludis
Collectum humorem bibulâ deducit arenâ?
Præsertim incertis si mensibus amnis abundans
Exit, et obducto latè tenet omnia limo;
Unde cavæ tepido sudant humore lacunæ.
Nec tamen (hæc cum sint hominumque boumque labores
Versando terram experti) nihil improbus anser,
Strymoniæque grues, et amaris intyba fibris
Officiunt, aut umbra nocet. Pater ipse colendi
Haud facilem esse viam voluit, primusque per artem
Movit agros, curis acuens mortalia corda;

TRANSLATION.

Why should I speak *of him*, who immediately after sowing the Seed persecutes the Lands *anew*, and levels the Heaps of barren Sand? Then on the springing Corn derives the Stream and ductile Rills? And when the Field is scorched with raging Heat, the Herbs all dying, lo from the Brow of a hilly Tract he decoys the Torrent: Which falling down the smooth-*worn* Rocks awakes the hoarse Murmur, and with gurgling Streams allays the thirsty Lands.

What *of him* who, lest the Stalk with over-loaded Ears fall to the Ground, feeds down the Luxuriance of the Crop in the tender Blade, when first the springing Corn is equal with the Furrow? And who drains from soaking Sand the collected Moisture of the Marsh? Chiefly when, in the variable *rainy* Months, the overflowing River bursts *from its Banks* away, and overspreads all around with slimy Mud, whence the hollow Dykes sweat with tepid Vapour.

Nor after all (when the Labours of Men and Oxen have thus been tried in cultivating the Ground) does the destroying Goose, the Strymonian Cranes, and Succory with its bitter Roots nought hurt *the growing Corn*, or *nought* the Shade injure. Father *Jove* himself willed the Ways of Tillage not to be easy, and first commanded to cultivate the Fields by Art, whetting the Minds of Mor-

NOTES.

115. *Incertis mensibus*, i. e. *In those Months when the Weather is more variable.*

118. *Cum sint*, &c. Servius, and the whole Herd of Interpreters after him, explain these Words thus: *Tho' the Labours of Men and Oxen have provided against these Evils.* But the first Sense I have offered in reading the Passage is what is given in the Translation: Which seems to agree full better with the Context, since the Poet does not so much insist on the bad Qualities of Land, as on the Means of meliorating and correcting them.

119 *Improbus anser.* Columella, Lib. VIII. 13. complains of the Goose, *Quicquid tenerum contingere potest carpit.* And Pallad. Lib. I. 23. *Anser in satis satis contrarius innocuum est.*

123. *Movit.* Literally, *Stirred or sollicited*, i. e. *He taught or commanded Mortals to cultivate the Ground.*

127. *In*

Nec torpere gravi passus sua regna veterno.
Ante Jovem nulli subigebant arva coloni:
Nec signare quidem, aut partiri limite campum
Fas erat. In medium quærebant; ipsaque tellus
Omnia liberiùs, nullo poscente, ferebat.
Ille malum virus serpentibus addidit atris,
Prædarique lupos jussit, pontumque moveri;
Mellaque decussit foliis, ignemque removit,
Et passim rivis currentia vina repressit:
Ut varias usus meditando extunderet artes
Paulatim, et sulcis frumenti quæreret herbam,
Et silicis venis abstrusum excuderet ignem.
Tunc alnos primùm fluvii sensere cavatas:
Navita tum stellis numeros et nomina fecit,
Pleïadas, Hyadas, claramque Lycaonis Arcton.
Tum laqueis captare feras, et fallere visco,
Inventum; et magnos canibus circumdare saltus.
Atque alius latum fundâ jam verberat amnem,
Alta petens: pelagoque alius trahit humida lina.
Tum ferri rigor, atque argutæ lamina serræ:

nec est passus sua regna torpere gravi veterno. Ante Jovem nulli coloni subigebant arva; nec quidem erat fas signare, aut partiri campum limite. Quærebant victum in medium; tellusque ipsa ferebat omnia liberiùs, nullo poscente. Ille Jupiter addidit malum virus atris serpentibus, jussitque lupos prædari, pontumque moveri; decussitque mella foliis, removitque ignem, et repressit vina currentia passim rivis: ut meditando usus extunderet varias artes paulatim, et quæreret herbam frumenti sulcis, et excuderet abstrusum ignem venis silicis. Tunc primùm fluvii sensere cavatas alnos: tum navita fecit numeros et nomina stellis, appellans Pleïadas, Hyadas, claramque Arcton filiam Lycaonis. Tum est inventum captare feras laqueis, et fallere aves visco; et circumdare magnos saltus canibus. Atque alius jam verberat latum amnem fundâ, petens alta, aliusque trahit humida lina pelago. Tum rigor ferri, atque lamina argutæ serræ venere:

TRANSLATION.

tals with Care; nor suffered he his Reign to lie inactive in heavy Sloth. Before Jove no Husbandmen subdued the Fields; nor was it so much as lawful to mark out, or by Limits divide the Ground. They enjoyed all Things in common, and Earth of herself produced every Thing freely, without any Solicitation. He infused the noxious Poison into the horrid Serpent, commanded the Wolves to prowl, and the Sea to be put into Commotion; he shook the Honey from the Leaves, removed Fire *out of Mortals Sight*, and restrained the Wine that ran commonly in Rivulets: That Experience by Dint of Thought might gradually hammer out the various Arts *of Life*, in Furrows seek the Blade of Corn, and from the Veins of Flint strike out the hidden Fire. Then first the Rivers felt the hollowed Alders: Then the Seaman gave the Stars their Numbers and their Names, the Pleiades, Hyades, and the bright Bear of Lycaon. Then was invented the catching of wild Beasts in Toils, and the deceiving with Bird-lime, and the encompassing the spacious Lawns with Hounds. And now one, seeking the Depths, lashes the broad River with his Casting-net: And on the Sea another drags his humid Lines along. Then the rigid Force of Steel, and the

NOTES.

127. *In medium quærebant.* They made Acquisition for the public, or common Stock.

136. *Cavatas alnos.* The first Vessels were nothing but Hulks scarcely hallowed out of Trees.

138. *Lycaonis Arcton.* The *Ursa Major* called *Lycaon's Bear*, because his Daughter *Calisto* was transformed by *Juno* into a Bear, and by *Jove*, to whom she had been kind, translated to the Stars.

145. *Improbus.*

(nam primi homines ſcindebant fiſſile lignum cuneis) tum variæ artes venere. Improbus labor vicit omnia, et egeſtas urgens in duris rebus. Ceres prima inſtituit mortales vertere terram ferro: cum jam glandes atque arbuta ſacræ ſilvæ deficerent, et Dodona negaret victum. Et mox labor eſt additus frumentis: ut mala rubigo eſſet culmos, ſegniſque carduus horreret in arvis. Segetes intereunt; aſpera ſilva ſubit, lappæque, tribulique: interque nitentia culta arva, infelix lolium et ſteriles avenæ dominantur. Quòd niſi inſectabere terram aſſiduis raſtris, et terrebis aves ſonitu, et premes umbras opaci ruris falce, vocaveriſque imbrem votis; heu, fruſtra ſpectabis magnum acervum alterius, ſolabereque famem concuſſâ quercu in ſilvis. Et eſt dicendum, quæ arma ſint duris agreſtibus; ſine quis meſſes potuere nec ſeri, nec ſurgere. Primùm vomis, et grave robur inflexi aratri,

(Nam primi cuneis ſcindebant fiſſile lignum)
Tum variæ venere artes. Labor omnia vicit
Improbus, et duris urgens in rebus egeſtas.
Prima Ceres ferro mortales vertere terram
Inſtituit: cum jam glandes, atque arbuta ſacræ
Deficerent ſilvæ, et victum Dodona negaret.
Mox et frumentis labor additus: ut mala culmos
Eſſet rubigo, ſegniſque horreret in arvis
Carduus. Intereunt ſegetes; ſubit aſpera ſilva,
Lappæque, tribulique: interque nitentia culta
Infelix lolium et ſteriles dominantur avenæ.
Quòd niſi et aſſiduis terram inſectabere raſtris,
Et ſonitu terrebis aves, et ruris opaci
Falce premes umbras, votiſque vocaveris imbrem;
Heu, magnum alterius fruſtra ſpectabis acervum;
Concuſſàque famem in ſilvis ſolabere quercu.
    Dicendum, et quæ ſint duris agreſtibus arma;
Queis ſine nec potuere ſeri, nec ſurgere meſſes.
Vomis, et inflexi primùm grave robur aratri,

TRANSLATION.

flat Lingot of the grating Saw (for the firſt *Mortals* clove the fiſſile Wood with Wedges) then various Arts enſued. Inceſſant Labour and Want, in Hardſhips urgent, ſurmounted every Obſtacle. Firſt Ceres taught Mortals with Steel to turn the Ground: When now the Maſte and Arbutes of the ſacred Wood failed, and Dodona denied *her wonted* Suſtenance. Soon too was Diſtreſs inflicted on the Corn: That noxious Mildew ſhould eat the Stalks, and the lazy *uſeleſs* Thiſtle ſhoot up *its* horrid *Spikes* in the Field. The Crops of Corn die; Burrs and Caltrops, a rugged prickly Wood, ſucceed: And, amidſt the *gay* ſhining Fields, unhappy Darnels, and barren *wild* Oats bear ſway. But unleſs you both vex the Ground with aſſiduous Harrows, fright away the Birds with Noiſe, and with the Pruning-knife reſtrain the Shades of the darkened Field, and by Prayers call down the Showers; alas, *while thy Labour proves* in vain, thou ſhalt view another's ample Store, and in the Woods ſolace thy Hunger by ſhaking *Acorns* from the Oak.

We muſt alſo deſcribe what are the Inſtruments uſed by the hardy Swain; without which the Crops could neither be ſown nor ſpring. Firſt the Share, and heavy Timber of the Plough, and the ſlow-rolling Wains of the Eleuſinian

NOTES.

146. *Improbus.* Indefatigable, or unwearied, as Æn. XII. 687.

Fertur in abruptum magno mons improbus actu.

150. *Labor additus.* Labor here I take to ſignify *Calamity* or *Diſtreſs*; and *additus* has the Senſe of *datus* or *aſſignatus*, as *Hor.* 3 Lib. Ode IV. 78.

Incontinentis nec Tityi jecur
Relinquit ales, nequitiæ additus
Cuſtos.

So Æn. VI. 90.

—Nec Teucris addita Juno
Uſquam aberit.

158. *Spectabis.* The *Medicean* Manuſcript reads *exſpectabis.*

163. *Eleu-*

Tardaque Eleusinæ matris volventia plaustra,
Tribulaque, traheæque, et iniquo pondere rastri:
Virgea præterea Celei, vilisque supellex,
Arbuteæ crates, et mystica vannus Iacchi.
Omnia quæ multò ante memor provisa repones;
Si te digna manet divini gloria ruris.
Continuò in silvis magnâ vi flexa domatur
In burim, et curvi formam accipit ulmus aratri,
Huic à stirpe pedes temo protentus in octo,
Binæ aures, duplici aptantur dentalia dorso.
Cæditur et tilia ante jugo levis, altaque fagus;
Stivaque, quæ currus à tergo torqueat imos.
Et suspensa focis explorat robora fumus.
  Possum multa tibi veterum præcepta referre,
Ni refugis, tenuisque piget cognoscere curas.
Area cum primis ingenti æquanda cylindro,

tardaque volventia plaustra Eleusinæ matris, Cereris, *tribulaque, trabeæque, et rastri iniquo pondere: præterea virgea vilisque supellex Celei, arbuteæ crates, et mystica vannus Iacchi. Omnia quæ provisa multo antè* tu *memor repones, si digna gloria divini ruris manet te. Continuò in silvis flexa ulmus domatur magná vi in burim, et accipit formam curvi aratri. Huic* buri *temo, protentus à stirpe in octo pedes, binæ aures,* et *dentalia duplici dorso aptantur. Et ante levis tilia cæditur jugo, altaque fagus, stivaque, quæ torqueat imos currus à tergo. Et fumus explorat* illa *robora suspensa focis. Possum referre tibi multa præcepta veterum, ni refugis, pigetque* te *cognoscere* tam *tenues curas. Cum primis area* est *æquanda ingenti cylindro,*

TRANSLATION.

Mother Ceres, the Planks and Sleds *for pressing out the Corn*, and the Harrows of unwieldy Weight: Besides the mean Osier Furniture of Celeus, Arbute Hurdles, and the mystic Van of Bacchus. All which with mindful Foresight you will provide long before-hand, if the blissful Country has due Honour in Store for thee. Straight in the Woods a *stubborn* Elm bent with vast Force is subdued into the Plough-tail, and receives the Form of the crooked Plough. To this at the lower End are fitted a Beam extended eight Feet in Length, two Earth-boards, and Share-beams with their double Back. The light Lime-tree also is felled before-hand for the Yoke, and the tall Beech, and the Plough-staff, to turn the Bottom of the Carriage behind. And the Smoke seasons the Wood hung up in Chimnies.

I can recite to you many Precepts of the Ancients, unless you decline them, and think it not worth while to learn these trifling Cares. The Threshing-floor chiefly must be levelled with the huge cylindric Roller, and wrought with the

NOTES.

163. *Eleusinæ matris*, i. e. *Such as were invented by* Ceres, *who was worshipped at* Eleusis *in* Attica.

164. *Tribula.* The *Tribulum*, or *Tribula*, was an Instrument used by the Ancients to thresh their Corn. It was a kind of Plank or Waggon pointed with Stones or Pieces of Iron, with a Weight laid upon it; and so was drawn over the Corn by Oxen. Thus it is described by *Varro*: *Id fit è tabula lapidibus, aut ferro asperata, quo imposito auriga, aut pondere gravi, trahitur jumentis junctis, ut discutiat è spica grana.*

164. *Trabeæque.* The *Trabea* again was a Carriage without Wheels, used for the same Purpose as the former.

165. *Celei.* Celeus was the Father of *Triptolemus*, whom *Ceres*, as has been said, instructed in Husbandry.

168. *Si te digna manet*, &c. Literally, *If due Honour awaits thee from the divine Country*; i. e. *If thou expectest to see thy blest rural Labours crowned with due Honour.* The *Country* or *Country-life* is called *divine*, because of its Innocence and divine Pleasures.

172. *Duplici dentalia dorso.* See at the End of Mr. *Martin*'s first Georgic a Draught of a Plough such as is used at this Day in *Mantua*; pretty much the same with that which *Virgil* here describes. There the Share-beams (*dentalia*) joined to the two Handles, form that Shape which *Virgil* calls the *double Back.*

173. *Levis.* Light, that it may not oppress the Oxen with its Weight.

174. *Currus.* The Plough so called, because it ran upon Wheels, as do several modern Ones, particularly that of *Mantua* above mentioned.

187. *Nux.*

et vertenda manu, et solidanda tenaci cretâ, ne herbæ subeant, neu victa pulvere fatiscat. Tum variæ pestes illudunt: sæpe exiguus mus posuitque domos sub terris, atque fecit horrea: aut talpæ, capti oculis, fodere cubilia. Bufoque inventus cavis, et plurima alia *monstra, quæ terræ ferunt: curculioque, atque formica, metuens inopi senectæ, populat ingentem acervum farris.* Tu *item contemplator, cum* in *silvis, plurima nux induet se in florem, et curvabit olentes ramos: si fetus* harum *superant, pariter frumenta sequentur, magnaque tritura veniet cum magno calore. At si umbra exuberat luxuriâ foliorum, nequicquam area teret culmos pingues paleâ. Vidi equidem multos* homines *serentes medicare semina, et priùs perfundere* ea *nitro et nigra amurcâ, ut fetus esset grandior fallacibus siliquis. Et, quamvis properata exiguo igni maderent,*

Et vertenda manu, et cretâ solidanda tenaci;
Ne subeant herbæ, neu pulvere victa fatiscat.
Tum variæ illudunt pestes: sæpe exiguus mus
Sub terris posuitque domos, atque horrea fecit:
Aut oculis capti fodêre cubilia talpæ.
Inventusque cavis bufo, et quæ plurima terræ
Monstra ferunt: populatque ingentem farris acervum
Curculio, atque inopi metuens formica senectæ.
  Contemplator item, cum se nux plurima silvis
Induet in florem, et ramos curvabit olentes:
Si superant fetus, pariter frumenta sequentur,
Magnaque cum magno veniet tritura calore.
At si luxuriâ foliorum exuberat umbra,
Nequicquam pingues paleâ teret area culmos.
  Semina vidi equidem multos medicare serentes,
Et nitro priùs, et nigrâ perfundere amurcâ,
Grandior ut fetus siliquis fallacibus esset.
Et, quamvis igni exiguo properata maderent,

TRANSLATION.

Hand, and consolidated with binding Chalk; that Weeds may not spring up, and that overpowered with Drought it may not chap. Then various Pests mock *your Hopes:* Oftentimes the tiny Mouse has built its Cell, and made its Granaries: Or the Moles, deprived of Sight, have dug their Lodges under Ground. And in the Cavities has the Toad been found, and Vermin which the Earth produces in Abundance: The Weevil plunders vast Heaps of Corn, and the Ant, fearful of indigent old Age.

Observe also, when the Almond shall clothe itself abundantly with Blossoms in the Woods, and bend its fragrant Boughs: If the rising Fruit exceed *the Leaves* in Number, in like Quantity the Corn will follow, and a great Threshing with great Heat will ensue. But, if the shady Boughs abound with Luxuriance of Leaves, in vain the Floor shall bruise the Stalks fertile *only* in Chaff.

'Tis true I have seen many Sowers artificially prepare their Seeds, and steep them first in Nitre and black Leas of Oil, that the Produce might be larger in the fallacious Pods. And tho', to precipitate them, they were soaked over a slow

NOTES.

187. *Nux.* By this Interpreters generally understand the Almond-tree, agreeably to what is said of it in other Authors. *Isid.* Lib. XVII. 47. *Amygdala nomen Græcum est, quæ Latine nux longa vocatur—de qua Virgilius, cum se nux plurima silvis induet in florem.* So *Theophyl. in Natural. Prob.* Cap. 17 'Ορα την αμυγδαλην, &c. *Amygdalum cerne fructu ingravescentem, adeo ut præ fetu et exuberantia incurvetur, et terram pene contingat. Est hoc, O Polycrates, argumentum maximum fertilitatis.* Plut. Lib. II. *de Vita Moysis,* Γινεται μεντοι και ταν, &c. *Fertur è vernis arboribus prima florere Amygdalus proventum prænuntians fructuum arborum.* Mr. *Martin* however contends it is to be meant of the Walnut-tree.

192. *Nequicquam.* Servius renders *nequicquam pingues* by *non pingues;* but it may justly be questioned, whether *Virgil* ever uses the Word in that Sense; those other Examples which *Servius* produces are very dubious.

200. *Sub-*

Vidi lecta diu, et multo ſpectata labore
Degenerare tamen: ni vis humana quotannis
Maxima quæque manu legeret. Sic omnia fatis
In pejus ruere, ac retrò ſublapſa referri;
Non aliter, quàm qui adverſo vix flumine lembum
Remigiis ſubigit, ſi brachia forte remiſit,
Atque illum in præceps prono rapit alveus amni.
  Præterea tam ſunt Arcturi ſidera nobis,
Hœdorumque dies ſervandi, et lucidus Anguis;
Quam quibus in patriam ventoſa per æquora vectis
Pontus et oſtriferi fauces tentantur Abydi.
  Libra die ſomnique pares ubi fecerit horas,
Et medium luci atque umbris jam dividet orbem;
Exercete viri tauros, ſerite hordea campis,
Uſque ſub extremum brumæ intractabilis imbrem.
Nec non et lini ſegetem, et Cereale papaver
Tempus humo tegere, et jamdudum incumbere raſtris,
Dum ſiccâ tellure licet, dum nubila pendent.

vidi ea, diu lecta, et ſpectata multo labore, degenerare tamen; niſi humana vis quotannis legeret quæque maxima manu. Sic vidi omnia ruere fatis in pejus, ac ſublapſa retrò referri: Non aliter quam nauta, qui vix ſubigit lembum remigiis adverſo flumine, ſi forte remiſit brachia, ruit atque alveus rapit illum in præceps prono amni. Præterea tam ſidera Arcturi, dieſque hœdorum ſunt obſervandi nobis, et etiam lucidus Anguis; quam nautis, quibus, vectis per ventoſa æquora in patriam, pontus et fauces oſtriferi Abydi tentantur. Ubi libra fecerit horas diei ſomnique pares, et jam dividet medium orbem luci atque umbris; viri, exercete tauros, ſerite hordea campis, uſque ſub extremum imbrem intractabilis brumæ. Nec non eſt tempus tegere et ſegetem lini, et Cereale papaver humo, et jamdudum incumbere raſtris, dum licet ſiccâ tellure, dum nubila pendent.

TRANSLATION.

Fire, ſelected long, and proved with much Labour, yet have I ſeen them degenerate: Unleſs human Induſtry with the Hand culled out the largeſt every Year. Thus all Things, by Deſtiny, haſte into Decay, and, gliding away, inſenſibly are driven backward: Not otherwiſe than he who rows his Boat with much ado againſt the Stream, if by chance he ſlackens his Arms, *is inſtantly gone*, and the Tide hurries him headlong down the River.

Further, the Stars of Arcturus, and the Days of the Kids, and the ſhining Dragon muſt be as much obſerved by us, as by thoſe who, homeward borne acroſs the Main, attempt the *Euxine* Sea, and the Streights of Oyſter-breeding Abydus.

When *Libra* makes the Hours of Day and Night equal, and now divides the Globe in the Middle between Light and Shades; *then* work your Bullocks, ye Swains, ſow Barley in the Fields, till towards the laſt Shower of the inclement Winter Solſtice. *Then* too is the Time to hide in the Ground a Crop of Flax, and the Poppy of Ceres, and high Time to ply your Harrows, whilſt, the Ground *yet* dry, you may, whilſt the Clouds are *yet* ſuſpended.

NOTES.

200. *Sublapſa.* Signifies *gliding inſenſibly*, as Æn. XII. 686.

——————*Seu turbidus imber*
Proluit, aut annis ſolvit ſublapſa vetuſtas.

203. *Atque, &c.* Moſt Interpreters explain *atque* by *ſtatim*, upon the Authority of *A. Gellus*. But, as none of them have produced any parallel Example from a claſſical Author, I have ventured to recede from the common Explication, by ſuppoſing an Ellipſis which every one will eaſily ſupply in the Reading. Thus: *Omnia in pejus ruere, ac retrò ſublapſa referri, non aliter quàm ille* ruit ac retrò ſublapſus refertur, *&c.* As the ingenious Author of the Eſſay on the Georgics had conſidered the Paſſage in the ſame Light, I have ſupplied the Ellipſis with his Words.

212. *Cereale papaver.* Probably the white Poppy, whoſe Seed was ſerved up by the Ancients with the Deſert, *Plin.* XIX. 8. *Servius* aſſigns ſeveral Reaſons why the Poppy is called *Ceres*'s: But all of them appear fabulous. It is ſufficient for explaining the Author to know that Poppies were conſecrated to *Ceres*,

Est satio fabis vere: tum putres sulci accipiunt te quoque, Medica: et annua cura venit milio; cum candidus taurus aperit annum auratis cornibus, et canis, cedens averso astro, occidit. At si exercebis humum in triticeam messem, robustaque farra, instabisque aristis solis: Eoæ Atlantides Pleiades abscondantur tibi, Gnossiaque stella ardentis coronæ decedat ante, quàm committas debita semina sulcis, quàmque properes credere spem anni invitæ terræ. Multi cœpere ante occasum Maiæ; sed exspectata seges elusit illos vanis aristis. Verò si seres viciamque, vilemque faselum, nec aspernabere curam Pelusiacæ lentis; cadens Bootes mittet haud obscura signa tibi. Incipe, et extende sementem ad medias pruinas.

Vere fabis satio: tum te quoque, Medica, putres
Accipiunt sulci: et milio venit annua cura;
Candidus auratis aperit cum cornibus annum
Taurus, et averso cedens Canis occidit astro.
At si triticeam in messem robustaque farra
Exercebis humum, solisque instabis aristis;
Ante tibi Eoæ Atlantides abscondantur,
Gnosiaque ardentis decedat stella Coronæ,
Debita quàm sulcis committas semina; quàmque
Invitæ properes anni spem credere terræ.
Multi ante occasum Maiæ cœpere; sed illos
Exspectata seges vanis elusit avenis.
Si verò viciamque seres, vilemque faselum,
Nec Pelusiacæ curam aspernabere lentis;
Haud obscura cadens mittet tibi signa Bootes.
Incipe, et ad medias sementem extende pruinas.

TRANSLATION.

In the Spring is the Sowing of Beans: Then thee too, O Medic *Plant!* the rotten Furrows receive, and Millet comes, an annual Care; when the bright Bull with gilded Horns opens the Year, and the Dog sets, giving Way to the backward Star. But if you labour the Ground for a Wheat Harvest, and strong Grain, and are bent on bearded Ears alone; let the Pleiades in the Morning be set, and let the Gnosian Star of *Ariadne*'s blazing Crown emerge from the Sun, before you commit to the Furrows the Seed designed and before you hasten to trust the unwilling Earth with the Hopes of the Year. Many have begun before the Setting of Maia; but the expected Crop hath mocked them with empty Ears. But if you are to sow Vetches, and mean Kidney-beans, nor despise the Care of the Egyptian Lentil; setting Bootes will afford thee Signs not obscure. Begin, and extend thy Sowing to the Middle of the Frosts.

NOTES.

Ceres, and that most of her Statues are adorned with them.

215. *Medica*. Burgundy Trefoil, or *Medic-fodder*, so called, because, it was brought from *Media* into *Greece*.

216. *Annua cura*. Thy annual Care, in Opposition to the *Medic* Plant which lasts many Years; *Pliny* says it lasts thirty.

218. *Averso astro*. The backward Star or Constellation, *viz*. of the Bull, so called because he rises backwards.

221. *Eoæ Atlantides*. The *Pleiades* are called *Atlantides*, because they were fabled to be the Daughters of *Atlas*. *Eoæ*, in the Morning, *i. e.* when they set or go below our western Horizon about the Sun-rising, which is called their *Cosmical Setting*.

222. *Gnosia stella coronæ*. Ariadne's Crown, so called from *Gnosus*, a City of *Crete*, where *Minos*, the Father of *Ariadne*, reigned.

222. *Decedat*. I have followed the Stream of the Commentators in rendering this Word by *emerges*, viz. *from the Sun*, i. e. *rises heliacally*; because the heliacal Rising of this Constellation, and not the Setting, happens at the Time here mentioned by *Virgil*, tho' I believe the Word is hardly to be found any where else in this Sense.

225. *Maiæ*. Maia, one of the *Pleiades*, here put for the whole.

227. *Vilem*. Because they were very common among them, and therefore of little Estimation.

229. *Cadens Bootes*. About the Beginning of *November*.

Idcircò certis dimensum partibus orbem
Per duodena regit mundi Sol aureus astra.
Quinque tenent cœlum zonæ: quarum una corusco
Semper Sole rubens, et torrida semper ab igni:
Quam circum extremæ dextrâ lævâque trahuntur,
Cæruleâ glacie concretæ, atque imbribus atris. 236
Has inter mediamque, duæ mortalibus ægris
Munere concessæ Divûm: et via secta per ambas,
Obliquus quà se signorum verteret ordo. 239
Mundus ut ad Scythiam Riphæasque arduus arces
Consurgit; premitur Libyæ devexus in Austros.
Hic vertex nobis semper sublimis: at illum
Sub pedibus Styx atra videt Manesque profundi.
Maximus hìc flexu sinuoso elabitur anguis
Circum, perque duas in morem fluminis Arctos:
Arctos Oceani metuentes æquore tingi. 246
Illic, ut perhibent, aut intempesta silet nox
Semper, et obtentâ densantur nocte tenebræ;

Idcircò aureus sol regit orbem dimensum certis mensibus, per duodena astra mundi. Quinque zonæ tenent cœlum: quarum una est semper rubens corusco sole, et semper torrida ab igni: circum quam extremæ zonæ trahuntur dextrâ lævâque parte, concretæ cæruleâ glacie, atque atris imbribus. Inter has mediamque zonam, duæ sunt concessæ ægris mortalibus munere Divûm, et via est secta per ambas, quà obliquus ordo signorum verteret se. Ut mundus consurgit arduus ad Scythiam Riphæasque arces; ita premitur devexus in Austros Libyæ. Hic vertex nobis est semper sublimis: at atra Styx videt, profundique manes vident *illum sub pedibus. Hìc* ad superiorem polum *maximus anguis elabitur circum sinuoso flexu, inque morem fluminis per duas Arctos: Arctos, metuentes tingi æquore oceani. Illic, ut perhibent, aut intempesta nox semper silet, et tenebræ densantur nocte obtentâ;*

TRANSLATION.

For this Purpose the golden Sun, through the Twelve Constellations of the World, rules the Globe measured out into certain Portions. Five Zones embrace the Heavens: Whereof one is ever glowing with the flashy Sun, and scorched for ever by his Fire: Round which *two others* on the Extremities *of the Globe* to right and left are extended, *pinched and* frozen up with cærulean Ice, and horrid Showers *of Snow*. Between these and the middle *Zones*, two by the Bounty of the Gods are given to weak Mortals, and a Path cut thro' both, where the Series of the Signs might revolve obliquely. As the World rises up on high towards Scythia and the Riphæan Hills; *so* bending towards the South Winds of Lybia it is depressed. The one Pole to us is still elevated: But the other under our Feet is seen by gloomy Styx and the infernal Ghosts. Here, after the Manner of a River, the huge Dragon glides away with tortuous Windings, around and through between the Two Bears, the Bears that fear to be dipt in the Ocean. There, as they report, either dead Night for ever reigns in Silence, and, outspread, wraps

NOTES.

232. *Mundi.* Either *orbem mundi*, or rather *astra mundi*; as Æn. IX. 93.

Filius huic contra, torquet qui sidera mundi.

236. *Concretæ.* Frozen up as *concretum flumen*, or *thick and foggy*, as *Cicero* says, *Crassus hic et concretus aer.* Dr. *Trapp* translates it *stiff*, which, however it may agree to *cærulea glacie*, is incongruous to *atris imbribus*, and therefore he adopts another Epithet, *black with lowering Clouds. Imber*, 'tis true, sometimes signifies *Clouds fraught with Rain*, as Æn. III. 193.

Tum mihi cæruleus supra caput astitit imber.

But here I am inclined to think it means *Snows*, as being joined with Ice, and because of the Epithet *concretæ*. In this *Sense Virgil*'s Description of the two frigid Zones agrees with that of other Poets, *Ov. Met.* I. 56. *Nix tegit alta duos.*

248. *Et obtentâ*, &c. Literally, *And, Night being outstretched, Darkness is thickened.*

Aut redit à nobis Aurora, diemque reducit:
Nosque ubi primus equis Oriens afflavit anhelis,
Illic sera rubens accendit lumina Vesper.
  Hinc tempestates dubio prædiscere cœlo
Possumus, hinc messisque diem, tempusque serendi;
Et quando infidum remis impellere marmor
Conveniat: quando armatas deducere classes,
Aut tempestivam silvis evertere pinum.
Nec frustra signorum obitus speculamur et ortus,
Temporibusque parem diversis quatuor annum.
  Frigidus agricolam si quando continet imber,
Multa, forent quæ mox cœlo properanda sereno,
Maturare datur. Durum procudit arator
Vomeris obtusi dentem: cavat arbore lintres:
Aut pecori signum, aut numeros impressit acervis.
Exacuunt alii vallos, furcasque bicornes;
Atque Amerina parant lentæ retinacula viti.
Nunc facilis rubeâ texatur fiscina virgâ:
Nunc torrete igni fruges, nunc frangite saxo.

aut Aurora redit à nobis, reducitque diem: ubique primus sol oriens afflavit nos anhelis equis, illic rubens vesper accendit sera lumina. Hinc possumus prædiscere tempestates dubio cælo, hinc possumus prædiscere diemque messis, tempusque serendi; et quando conveniat impellere infidum marmor remis: quando conveniat deducere armatas classes, aut evertere tempestivam pinum silvis. Nec frustra speculamur obitus et ortus signorum, annumque parem quatuor diversis temporibus. Si quando frigidus imber continet agricolam domi; tempus datur maturare ea, quæ mox forent properanda cælo sereno. Arator procudit durum dentem obtusi vomeris, et cavat lintres arbore: impressit aut signum pecori, aut numeros acervis frugum. Alii exacuunt vallos, bicornesque furcas, atque parant Amerina retinacula lentæ viti. Nunc facilis fiscina texatur rubeâ virgâ: nunc torrete fruges igni, nunc frangite eas molari saxo.

TRANSLATION.

all things up in Darkness; or else Aurora returns *thither* from us, and brings *them* back the Day: And, when the rising *Sun* first breathes on us with panting Steeds, there ruddy Vesper lights up his late Illuminations.

Hence we are able to foreknow the Seasons when the Sky is dubious, hence the Days of Harvest, and the Time of sowing; and when it is proper to sweep the faithless Sea with Oars, when to launch the armed Fleets, or to fell the Pine Tree in the Woods in Season. Nor in vain do we study the Settings and the Risings of the Signs, and the Year equally divided into Four different Seasons.

If at any Time a bleak Shower confines the Husbandman, then is his Time to provide many Things, which as soon as the Sky is serene, must be done precipitantly. *Then* the Ploughman sharpens the hard Point of the blunted Share: Scoops little Boats from Trees: Or stamps the Mark on his Sheep, or the Number on his Sacks *of Corn*. Others point Stakes, and Two horned Forks, and prepare Amerine *Osier* Bands for the limber Vine. Now let the pliant Basket of Bramble-Twigs be wove: Now parch your Grain over the Fire, now grind it with the *Mill*.

NOTES.

255. *Deducere.* To draw them down from the Docks.

262. *Lintres* Either *little Boats*, or *Troughs*, such as they used for carrying their Grapes, *Tib.* L. I. El. 5.

Hæc mihi servabit plenis in lintribus uvas.

265. *Amerina retinacula.* Amerine Bands, so called from *Ameria*, a Town in *Umbria*, which abounded with Osiers.

266. *Rubeâ virgâ.* Bramble-twigs: Others render it *Rubean Wicker*, from *Rubi*, a Town in *Italy*, which *Horace* mentions in his Journey to *Brundusium*. But, as *Pliny* mentions the Bramble among the Twigs that are fit for such Purposes, it is more probable that these are here meant.

Quippe etiam festis quædam exercere diebus
Fas et jura sinunt. Rivos deducere nulla
Religio vetuit: segeti prætendere sepem,
Insidias avibus moliri, incendere vepres,
Balantumque gregem fluvio mersare salubri.
Sæpe oleo tardi costas agitator aselli
Vilibus aut onerat pomis: lapidemque revertens
Incusum, aut atræ massam picis urbe reportat.
  Ipsa dies alios alio dedit ordine Luna
Felices operum. Quintam fuge: pallidus Orcus,
Eumenidesque satæ. Tum partu Terra nefando
Cœumque Iapetumque creat, sævumque Typhœa,
Et conjuratos cœlum rescindere fratres.
Ter sunt conati imponere Pelio Ossam
Scilicet, atque Ossæ frondosum involvere Olympum:
Ter Pater exstructos disjecit fulmine montes.
Septima post decimam felix, et ponere vitem,
Et prensos domitare boves, et licia telæ
Addere: nona fugæ melior, contraria furtis.

Quippe etiam fas et jura sinunt exercere quædam festis diebus. Nulla religio vetuit deducere rivos, prætendere sepem segeti, moliri insidias avibus, incendere vepres, mersareque gregem balantum ovium *salubri fluvio. Sæpe agitator tardi aselli onerat costas* illius *oleo aut vilibus pomis: revertensque* domum *reportat incusum lapidem, aut massam atræ picis* ex *urbe. Luna ipsa dedit alios* dies *felices operum alio ordine. Fuge quintum* diem: illâ die *pallidus Orcus, Eumenidesque* sunt *satæ. Tum nefando partu Terra creat Cœumque, Iapetumque, sævumque Typhœa, et fratres conjuratos rescindere cœlum. Scilicet, ter sunt conati imponere Ossam Pelio, atque involvere frondosum Olympum Ossæ: ter pater* Jupiter *disjecit* hos *exstructos montes fulmine. Septima* dies *post decimam* est *felix, et ponere vitem, et domitare prensos boves, et addere licia telæ. Nona* dies est *melior fugæ, contraria furtis.*

TRANSLATION.

stone. For even on Holy-days divine and human Laws permit to perform some Works. No Religion hath forbid to drain the Fields, to raise a Fence before the Corn, to lay Snares for Birds, to fire the Thorns, and plunge in the wholesome River a Flock of bleating *Sheep*. Oftentimes the Driver of the sluggish Ass loads his Ribs with Oil, or low-rated Apples: And, in his Return from the Town, brings back an indented *Mill*-stone, or a Mass of black Pitch.

The Moon too hath allotted Days auspicious to Works, some in one Order, some in another. Shun the fifth: *On this* pale Pluto and the Furies were born. Then at a hideous Birth the Earth brought forth Cœus, Iapetus, and stern Typhœus; and all the *Giant*-Brothers who conspired to scale the Skies. For thrice they did essay to lay Ossa upon Pelion, and to roll woody Olympus upon Ossa: Thrice Father *Jove*, with his Thunder, overthrew the piled-up Mountains. The seventh, next to the Tenth, is lucky both to plant the Vine, and break the Oxen *first* caught *in the Yoke*, and to add the Woof to the Web: The ninth is

NOTES.

269. *Rivos deducere.* Not to float the Ground, as some will have it; for that, as we learn from *Servius*, was prohibited by the Priests on Holy-days: but to drain the Pools, and make the Rivulets run off the Fields; which was allowed, as we read in *Columella: Feriis autem ritus majorum etiam illa permittit— Piscinas, lacus, fossas veteres tergere, et purgare.* To float the Fields, in *Virgil*'s Stile, is *inducere rivos*, as Verse 106. in opposition to which *deducere humorem* signifies *to drain*, Verse 113.

272. *Fluvio salubri.* Columella observes, upon this Passage, that it was unlawful to wash the Sheep on Holy-days for the sake of the Wool: But that it was allowed to wash them, for the Cure of their Diseases. Hence *Virgil* mentions the *wholesome River*, to shew that he meant it by way of Medicine.

284. *Septima post decimam.* The seventh next to the tenth; Or, as others, the seventeenth.

Adeò multa dedere se meliùs gelidâ nocte; aut cum Eous irrorat terras novo sole. Nocte leves stipulæ meliùs, nocte arida prata tondentur meliùs: lentus humor non deficit noctes. Et quidam pervigilat ad seros ignes hiberni luminis, inspicatque faces acuto ferro. Interea conjux, solata longum laborem cantu, percurrit telas arguto pectine: aut decoquit humorem dulcis musti Vulcano, et despumat undam trepidi aheni foliis. At rubicunda Ceres succiditur medio æstu, et area terit tostas fruges medio æstu. Tu *nudus ara, nudus sere: hiems est ignava colono. Agricolæ plerumque fruuntur parto frigoribus hiemis, lætique curant mutua convivia inter se: genialis hiems invitat ad hæc, resolvitque curas eorum. Ceu cum jam pressæ carinæ tetigere portum, et læti nautæ imposuere coronas puppibus. Sed tamen tunc* est *tempus stringere et quernas glandes, et baccas lauri, oleamque, cruentaque myrta.*

Multa adeò gelidâ meliùs se nocte dedere;
Aut cum sole novo terras irrorat Eous.
Nocte leves meliùs stipulæ, nocte arida prata
Tondentur: noctes lentus non deficit humor.
Et quidam seros hiberni ad luminis ignes
Pervigilat, ferroque faces inspicat acuto;
Interea longum cantu solata laborem
Arguto conjux percurrit pectine telas:
Aut dulcis musti Vulcano decoquit humorem,
Et foliis undam trepidi despumat aheni.
At rubicunda Ceres medio succiditur æstu;
Et medio tostas æstu terit area fruges.
Nudus ara, sere nudus: hiems ignava colono.
Frigoribus parto agricolæ plerumque fruuntur,
Mutaque inter se læti convivia curant:
Invitat genialis hiems, curasque resolvit.
Ceu pressæ cum jam portum tetigere carinæ,
Puppibus et læti nautæ imposuere coronas.
Sed tamen et quernas glandes tunc stringere tempus,
Et lauri baccas, oleamque, cruentaque myrta.

TRANSLATION.

better for a Journey, *but* adverse to Thefts. Many Works too have succeeded better in the cool Night; or when, at the Rising of the Sun, the Morn sprinkles the Dews upon the Earth. By Night the light Stubble, by Night the parched Meadows are better shorn: The clammy Dews fail not by Night. And some by the late Fires, their Winter Light, watch all Night long, and with the sharp Steel shape Matches into a tapering Point. Meanwhile, by Song, his Spouse cheering her tedious Labour, runs over the Webs with the shrill *sounding* Shuttle: Or over the Fire boils away the Liquor of the luscious Must, and scums with Leaves the Tide of the trembling Caldron.

But reddening Ceres is cut down in Noontide Heat, and in Noontide Heat the Floor threshes out the parched Grain. Plow naked, *and* sow naked: Winter is an inactive Time for the Hind. In the Colds *of Winter* the Farmers mostly enjoy the Fruit of their Labour, and, rejoicing with one another, provide mutual Entertainments: The genial Winter invites them, and relaxes their Cares. As Weather-beaten Ships, when now they have reached the Port, and the joyous Mariners have planted Garlands on the Sterns. But yet then is the Time both to stripe the Maste of Oak, and the Bay-Berries, the Olive, and the Bloody Myrtle-

NOTES.

295. *Dulcis musti.* The use of this boiled Must is to put into some Sorts of Wine, to make them keep. *Columella* recommends the sweetest Wine for this Purpose so that *dulcis* in this Passage is no idle Epithet to *musti*.

303. *Pressæ.* Weather-beaten. Others render it *laden*. But the former Sense figures more aptly the Toils of the Farmer; and agrees better to the Words *ceu pressæ carinæ cum jam, &c.* the *cum jam* denotes that the Ships had been in Distress.

307. *Pe-*

Tunc gruibus pedicas, et retia ponere cervis,
Auritosque sequi lepores: tum figere damas,
Stuppea torquentem Balearis verbera fundæ;
Cum nix alta jacet, glaciem cum flumina trudunt.
Quid tempestates autumni, et sidera dicam?
Atque ubi jam breviorque dies, et mollior æstas,
Quæ vigilanda viris? vel cum ruit imbriferum
ver;
Spicea jam campis cum messis inhorruit, et cum
Frumenta in viridi stipulâ lactentia turgent;
Sæpe ego, cum flavis messorem induceret arvis
Agricola, et fragili jam stringeret hordea culmo,
Omnia ventorum concurrere prœlia vidi;
Quæ gravidam latè segetem ab radicibus imis
Sublime expulsam eruerent: ita turbine nigro
Ferret hiems culmumque levem stipulasque volantes.
Sæpe etiam immensum cœlo venit agmen aquarum,

Tunc est tempus cum ponere pedicas gruibus, et retia cervis, sequique auritos lepores: tum figere damas, torquentem stupea verbera Balearis fundæ, cum alta nix jacet, cum flumina trudunt glaciem. Quid dicam tempestates et sidera autumni? atque quæ sint vigilanda viris, ubi jam diesque est brevior, et æstas est mollior? vel cum imbriferum ver ruit; cum spicea messis jam inhorruit campis, et cum lactentia frumenta turgent in viridi stipulâ? Sæpe ego, cum agricola induceret messorem flavis arvis, et jam stringeret hordea fragili culmo, vidi omnia prœlia ventorum concurrere, quæ latè eruerent gravidam segetem, ab imis radicibus, expulsam sublime: ita, nigro turbine, hiems ferret levemque culmum, volantesque stipulas. Sæpe etiam immensum agmen aquarum venit cœlo,

TRANSLATION.

berries. Then to set Springs for Cranes, and Nets for Stags, and to pursue the long-eared Hares: And whirling the hempen Thongs of the Balearian Sling, to pierce the Does, when the Snow lies deep, when the Rivers shove the Ice along.

Why should I speak of the Storms and Constellations of Autumn? And what *Accidents* must be guarded against by the Swains when now the Day is shorter, and the Summer more soft *and mild?* Or when the showery Spring pours down *its Stores;* what Time the spiky Harvest bristles in the Fields, and when the milky Corn swells on the green Stalk? Often have I seen, when the Farmer had just brought the Reaper into the yellow Fields, and was now binding up the Barley with the brittle Straw, often have I seen all the Fierceness of the Winds combine, which far and wide tore up the full-loaded Corn, from the lowest Roots, and tossed it up on high: Just so with blackening Whirlwind a wintery Storm would drive light Straw and flying Stubble. Often also an immense Band of Vapours gathers on

NOTES.

307. *Pedicas.* Springes for catching Birds or Beasts by the Legs.

317. *Stringeret.* Was binding up. *Servius* renders it *secaret*, and quotes Verse 305.

Et quernas glandes tum stringere tempus.

But surely *stringere* there signifies *to gather or strip off with the Hand.*

322. *Sæpe etiam—cœlo venit.* The common Way of explaining this Line, in a great Measure, destroys the whole Beauty of the Passage, takes away the Solemnity of the Description and renders it somewhat preposterous. It turns that lofty Expression, *ruit arduus æther*, into a Tautology, and breaks into the Description before the Reader is prepared for it.

To see the Passage in its just Light, we are to consider that the Poet is here describing one of those Storms that are fraught with Thunder, Hail, Lightning, Rain, and which come gradually on by sensible Approaches. First the Clouds or Vapours come marching up together in Bands, *agmen aquarum*, till they have overcast the whole Face of the Sky.

Sæpe etiam immensum cœlo venit agmen aquarum.

Then, by gathering themselves in thicker Wreaths, they cease the Darkness, and brew the Storm more deep and threatening:

Et fœdam glomerant tempestatem imbribus atris,
Collectæ ex alto nubes.

After

Et fœdam glomerant tempestatem imbribus atris
Collectæ ex alto nubes: ruit arduus æther,
Et pluviâ ingenti sata læta boumque labores
Diluit: implentur fossæ, et cava flumina crescunt
Cum sonitu, fervetque fretis spirantibus æquor.
Ipse Pater, mediâ nimborum in nocte, coruscâ
Fulmina molitur dextrâ: quo maxima motu
Terra tremit: fugêre feræ, et mortalia corda
Per gentes humilis stravit pavor. Ille flagranti
Aut Atho, aut Rhodopen, aut alta Ceraunia telo
Dejicit: ingeminant Austri, et densissimus imber;
Nunc nemora ingenti vento, nunc litora plangunt.
Hoc metuens, cœli menses et sidera serva;
Frigida Saturni sese quò stella receptet;
Quos ignis cœli Cyllenius erret in orbes.
In primis venerare Deos; atque annua magnæ
Sacra refer Cereri, lætis operatus in herbis,
Extremæ sub casum hiemis, jam vere sereno.

et nubes, collectæ ex alto mari, glomerant fœdam tempestatem atris imbribus: arduus æther ruit, et ingenti pluviâ diluit læta sata, laboresque boum: fossæ implentur, et cava flumina crescunt cum sonitu, æquorque fervet spirantibus fretis. Pater Jupiter *ipse molitur fulmina coruscâ dextrâ, in mediâ nocte nimborum: quo motu maxima terra tremit: feræ fugere, et humilis pavor stravit mortalia corda per gentes. Ille dejicit aut* montem *Atho, aut Rhodopen, aut alta Ceraunia flagranti telo: Austri et densissimus imber ingeminant; nunc nemora, nunc litora plangunt ingenti vento. Metuens hoc,* ob*serva menses et sidera cœli quo* loco *frigida stella Saturni receptet sese; in quos orbes cœli Cyllenius ignis erret. In primis venerare Deos; atque refer annua sacra magnæ Cereri, operatus in lætis herbis, sub casum extremæ hiemis, jam sereno vere.*

TRANSLATION.

the Sky, and Clouds collected from the Deep brew thick a deformed Storm of black Showers: The lofty Sky pours down, and with Torrents of Rain sweeps away the joyful Corns, and Labours of the Oxen: The Ditches are filled, and the deep Rivers swell with roaring Noise, and in the steaming frothy Friths the Sea boils and rages. Father *Jove* himself, amidst a Night of Clouds, lances the flashy Thunders with his Right Hand: With the Violence of which Earth trembles to its utmost Extent: The Beasts are fled, and through the Nations humble Fear hath sunk the Hearts of Men. He with his flaming Bolt strikes down or Athos, or Rhodope, or the high Ceraunia: The South Winds redouble, and the Shower is more and more condensed; now the Woods, now the Shores in howling Notes resound with the tempestuous Wind.

In fear of this, observe the Months and Constellations of the Heavens; which Way the cold Star of Saturn shapes his Course, towards which of the heavenly Orbs Mercury's fiery Planet wanders. Above all, pay Veneration to the Gods; and renew to great Ceres the sacred annual Rites, offering up thy Sacrifice upon the joyous Turf, at the expiring of the last Days of Winter, when now the Spring

NOTES.

After this solemn Apparatus, the Storm bursts, the Clouds discharge such a Deluge of Rain as if the whole Sky were dissolved, and poured down at once, *ruit arduus æther*.

Venit cœlo therefore is here of the same Import with *venit in cœlum*, or *convenit in cœlo*, agreeable to *Virgil*'s Stile in many other Places. Thus *Æn.* I. 293. *Hunc tu accipies cœlo* for *accipies in cœlum*. *Æn.* V. 451. *It clamor cœlo*, for *ad cœlum*, or *per cœlum*, See also *Æn.* VI. 191. VIII. 591. IX. 664. XII. 283.

324. *Ex alto.* Servius explains it *ab Aquilone, from the North*; because the North-pole is elevated with respect to us: But this seems forced. *Alto* is often put elsewhere for *the Sea*, and seems to be so here.

332. *Atho.* Athos is a Mountain in *Macedonia* that overlooks the *Ægean* Sea. *Rhodope* is a Mountain in *Thrace*, a Part of Mount *Hemus*, which extends itself as far as *Scythia*, taking different Names according to the different Places it passes through.

332. *Ceraunia.* The *Ceraunian* Mountains again are in *Epirus*; they were formerly so called

Tunc agni pingues, et tunc molliſſima vina:
Tunc ſomni dulces, denſæque in montibus umbræ.
Cuncta tibi Cererem pubes agreſtis adoret.
Cui tu lacte favos, et miti dilue Baccho:
Terque novas circum felix eat hoſtia fruges:
Omnis quam chorus, et ſocii comitentur ovantes;
Et Cererem clamore vocent in tecta: neque antè
Falcem maturis quiſquam ſupponat ariſtis,
Quàm Cereri, tortâ redimitus tempora quercu,
Det motus incompoſitos, et carmina dicat.
  Atque hæc ut certis poſſimus diſcere ſignis,
Æſtuſque, pluviaſque, et agentes frigora ventos,
Ipſe Pater ſtatuit, quid menſtrua Luna moneret;
Quo ſigno caderent Auſtri, quid ſæpe videntes
Agricolæ, propius ſtabulis armenta tenerent.
  Continuò ventis ſurgentibus, aut freta ponti
Incipiunt agitata tumeſcere, et aridus altis
Montibus audiri fragor: aut reſonantia longè
Litora miſceri, et nemorum increbreſcere murmur.

Tunc agni ſunt pingues, et tunc vina ſunt molliſſima: tunc ſomni ſunt dulces, umbræque ſunt denſæ in montibus. Cuncta agreſtis pubes tibi adoret Cererem. Cui tu dilue favos lacte, et miti Baccho: terque felix hoſtia eat circum novas fruges: quam hoſtiam *omnis chorus, et ovantes ſocii comitentur; et vocent Cererem clamore in tecta: neque quiſquam ſupponat falcem maturis ariſtis, antè quàm, redimitus* quoad ſua *tempora torta quercu, det incompoſitos motus, et dicat carmina Cereri. Atque ut poſſumus diſcere hæc certis ſignis, æſtuſque, pluviaſque et ventos agentes frigora: pater* Jupiter *ipſe ſtatuit, quid menſtrua Luna moneret; quo ſigno Auſtri caderent; quid agricolæ videntes ſæpe tenerent armenta propius ſtabulis. Continuò, ventis ſurgentibus, aut freta ponti agitata incipiunt tumeſcere, et aridus fragor* incipit *audiri altis montibus: aut litora reſonantia longè miſceri, et murmur nemorum increbreſcere.*

TRANSLATION.

comes on ſerene. Then the Lambs are fat, and then the Wines moſt mellow: Then Slumbers on the Hills are ſweet, and thick the Shades. Let the Buſh let all the rural Youths adore Ceres. In Honour of whom mix thou the Honey-comb with Milk and gentle Wine, and thrice let the auſpicious Victim go round the recent Grain: Which let the whole Chorus *of the Village* and thy Aſſociates accompany in jovial Mood; and with Acclamation invite Ceres into their Dwellings: Nor let any one put the Sickle to the ripe Corn, till, in Honour of Ceres, having his Temples bound with wreathed Oak, he perform the ruſtic artleſs Dance, and ſing Hymns.

And that we may learn theſe Things by certain Signs, both Heats and Rains, and Cold-bringing Winds, Father *Jove* himſelf has appointed what the monthly Moon ſhould betoken; with what Signs *concomitant* the Southwinds ſhould fall; from what common Obſervations the Huſbandman ſhould learn to keep his Herds nearer their Stalls.

Straight, when the Winds are riſing, the Friths of the Sea with Toſſings begin to ſwell, and a dry craſhing Noiſe to be heard in the high Mountains: Or the far ſounding Shores *begin* to be diſturbed, and the Murmurs of the Grove to

NOTES.

called from κεραυνὸς, *Thunder*, becauſe their Height expoſed them much to Thunder. They are now called *Monti del la Chimera*.

342. *Tunc ſomni dulces.* Both *dulces ſomni* and *denſæ umbræ* I think are to be conſtrued with *in montibus*; for the Meaning is plainly, that Slumbers then are ſweet on the Hills under Trees, which then begin to be covered with thick Shade: Not as if Sleep were ſweeter then than at other Seaſons, as one would imagine Dr. *Trapp* and other Interpreters underſtand it.

354. *Caderent.* Seems here to have the Signification of *incumberent*; in which Senſe *Varro* ſays, *adverſo venti reciderunt*.

357. *Aridus fragor.* Such a Sound as is made by dry Trees when they break.

Jam tum unda malè temperat sibi à curvis carinis, cum celeres mergi revolant ex medio æquore, feruntque clamorem ad litora, cumque marinæ fulicæ ludunt in sicco; ardeaque deserit notas paludes, atque volat supra altam nubem. Sæpe etiam, vento impendente, videbis stellas labi præcipites cœlo; longosque tractus flammarum albescere à tergo per umbram noctis: sæpe levem paleam et caducas frondes volitare: aut plumas nantes in summâ aquâ colludere. At cum fulminat de parte trucis Boreæ, et cum domus Eurique Zephyrique tonat, omnia rura natant plenis fossis, atque omnis navita legit humida vela ponto. Imber nunquam obfuit imprudentibus. Aut aëriæ grues fugêre illum imbrem *surgentem imis vallibus: aut bucula, suspiciens cœlum, captavit auras patulis naribus: aut arguta hirundo circumvolitavit lacus: et ranæ cecinere veterem querelam in limo.*

Jam sibi tum à curvis malè temperat unda carinis,
Cum medio celeres revolant ex æquore mergi,
Clamoremque ferunt ad litora; cumque marinæ
In sicco ludunt fulicæ; notasque paludes
Deserit, atque altam supra volat ardea nubem.
Sæpe etiam stellas, vento impendente, videbis
Præcipites cœlo labi; noctisque per umbram
Flammarum longos à tergo albescere tractus:
Sæpe levem paleam, et frondes volitare caducas:
Aut summâ nantes in aquâ colludere plumas.
At Boreæ de parte trucis cum fulminat, et cum
Eurique Zephyrique tonat domus, omnia plenis
Rura natant fossis, atque omnis navita ponto
Humida vela legit. Nunquam imprudentibus imber
Obfuit: aut illum surgentem vallibus imis
Aëriæ fugêre grues: aut bucula cœlum
Suspiciens, patulis captavit naribus auras:
Aut arguta lacus circumvolitavit hirundo:
Et veterem in limo ranæ cecinere querelam.

TRANSLATION.

rise louder and louder. Now hardly the Billows refrain from the crooked Ships, when the Cormorants fly swiftly back *to Land* from the midst of the Sea, and send their Screams to the Shore; and when the Sea-coots sport on the Beach; and the Heron forsakes the well-known Fens, and soars above the lofty Cloud. Often too, when Wind is approaching, you shall see the Stars shoot precipitant from the Sky: and behind them long Trails of Flame whiten athwart the Shades of Night: Often the light Chaff and fallen Leaves flutter about: Or Feathers swimming on the Surface of the Water frisk together.

But when it lightens from the Quarter of surly Boreas, and when the House of Eurus and of Zephyrus thunders, all the Fields are floated with full Ditches, and every Mariner on the Sea furls his humid Sails. Showers never hurt any unforewarned: Either the airy Cranes have shunned it in the deep Vallies as it rose: Or the Heifer, looking up to Heaven, hath snuffed the Air with wide Nostrils: Or the chattering Swallow hath fluttered about the Lakes: And the Frogs croaked

NOTES.

374. *Aut illum surgentem vallibus imis*, &c. Some construe the Words thus, *grues fugere ex imis vallibus*. Others take the Meaning to be, that the Shower rises out of the Vallies. The Author of the Essay on the Georgics interprets it, that the Cranes avoid the coming Storm, by retreating to the low Vallies. This Interpretation is agreeable to *Aristotle* in his History of Animals, where, treating of the Foresight of Cranes, he says, They fly on high, that they may see far off, and, if they perceive Clouds and Storms, they descend, and rest on the Ground: εαν ιδωσι νεφη, και χειμερια, καταπτασαι ησυχαζουσιν.

378. *Veterem cecinere querelam*. Either alluding to the known Fable of the Frogs in *Æsop*; or to that fabulous Tradition of the Transformation of the *Lycians* into Frogs. For which see *Ovid. Met.* VI. 374.

Sæpius et tectis penetralibus extulit ova
Angustum formica terens iter: et bibit ingens
Arcus: et è pastu decedens agmine magno
Corvorum increpuit densis exercitus alis.
Jam varias pelagi volucres, et quæ Asia circum
Dulcibus in stagnis rimantur prata Caystri,
Certatim largos humeris infundere rores;
Nunc caput objectare fretis, nunc currere in undas,
Et studio incassùm videas gestire lavandi.
Tum cornix plenâ pluviam vocat improbâ voce,
Et sola in siccâ secum spatiatur arenâ.
Nec nocturna quidem carpentes pensa puellæ
Nescivere hiemem; testâ cum ardente viderent
Scintillare oleum, et putres concrescere fungos.
 Nec minùs ex imbri Soles, et aperta serena
Prospicere, et certis poteris cognoscere signis.
Nam neque tum stellis acies obtusa videtur;
Nec fratris radiis obnoxia surgere Luna:
Tenuia nec lanæ per cœlum vellera ferri.

Et sæpius formica, terens angustum iter, extulit ova tectis penetralibus, et ingens cœlestis arcus bibit: et exercitus corvorum, decedens è pastu magno agmine, increpuit densis alis. Jam videas varias volucres pelagi, et eas quæ rimantur circum Asia prata in dulcibus stagnis Caystri, certatim infundere largos rores; nunc objectare caput fretis, nunc currere in undas, et gestire studio lavandi incassùm. Tum improba cornix vocat pluviam plenâ voce, et sola spatiatur secum in siccâ arenâ. Nec quidem puellæ, carpentes nocturna pensa, nescivere hiemem; cum viderent oleum scintillare ardente testâ, et putres fungos concrescere. Nec minùs, ex imbri, poteris prospicere, et certis signis cognoscere soles et aperta cœla serena. Nam tum neque acies videtur esse obtusa stellis, nec Luna surgere obnoxia radiis solis *fratris: nec tenuia vellera lanæ ferri per cœlum.*

TRANSLATION.

their old Complaint in the Mud. And often the Ant, wearing a narrow Path, hath conveyed her Eggs from her secret Cell: The spacious Bow hath drunk deep: And an Army of Ravens, on their Return from feeding, have beat the Air, and made a Noise, with Wings close crowded. Now you may observe the various Sea-Fowls, and those that rummage *for their Food* about the Asius's Meads, in Cayster's pleasant Lakes keenly lave the copious Dews upon their Shoulders; now *on the Banks* offer their Heads to the working Tides, now run into the Streams, and sportive joy with Eagerness to wash *their Plumes* in vain. Then the inauspicious Crow with full Throat invites the Rain, and solitary stalks by herself on the dry Sand. Nor were even the Maids, carding their Tasks *of Wool* by Night, ignorant of the *approaching* Storm: when they saw the Oil sputter in the heated Potsheard-*Lamp*, and foul fungous Clots grow thick *around the Wick*.

Nor *with* less *Ease* may you foresee, and by sure Signs discern Sunshine succeeding Rain, and open serene Skies. For neither are the Stars then seen with blunted Edge, nor the Moon to rise *obscure, as* indebted to her Brother's Beams: Nor thin fleecy Clouds to be carried through the Sky. Nor do Thetis's beloved

NOTES.

380. *Bibit ingens arcus.* According to a vulgar Notion, that the Rainbow drunk up the Vapours, to feed the Clouds for Rain.

387. *Incassùm.* Either, as *Servius* has it, because their Feathers keep their Bodies from being wet: *Quia plumarum compositio aquam minime ad corpus admittit*; or, as others, their Bustle is idle, and to no Purpose, since without so much Pains they will soon be effectually washed by the coming Rain.

393. *Ex imbri.* Some read *soles ex imbre; clear Sun shine, without Rain.*

396. *Nec fratris radiis obnoxia.* She rises bright, as if she shone with a Light unborrowed and independent on her Brother's Beams. Those, who are curious to see a critical Explication of the Word *obnoxius*, may consult *Aulus Gellius* in his *Noct. Att.* L. VII. 17.

397. *Tenuia lanæ vellera.* Signifies *thin, fleecy Clouds*, as *Pliny* explains it, Lib. XVIII.

Alcyones, dilectæ Thetidi, non pandunt pennas ad tepidum solem in litore: immundi sues non meminere jactare solutos manipulos palearum ore. At nebulæ magis petunt ima loca, recumbuntque campo: et noctua observans occasum solis de summo culmine nequicquam exercet seros cantus. Nisus apparet sublimis in liquido aëre, et Scylla dat pœnas pro purpureo capillo. Quacumque illa fugiens secat levem æthera pennis, ecce inimicus, atrox Nisus insequitur eam per auras magno stridore: quà Nisus fert se ad auras, illa fugiens raptim secat levem æthera pennis. Tum corvi ingeminant liquidas voces ter aut quater presso gutture: et sæpe altis cubilibus, læti nescio quâ dulcedine præter solitum morem,

Non tepidum ad Solem pennas in litore pandunt
Dilectæ Thetidi Alcyones: non ore solutos
Immundi meminere sues jactare maniplos.
At nebulæ magis ima petunt, campoque recumbunt:
Solis et occasum servans de culmine summo
Nequicquam seros exercet noctua cantus.
Apparet liquido sublimis in aëre Nisus,
Et pro purpureo pœnas dat Scylla capillo.
Quacumque illa levem fugiens secat æthera pennis,
Ecce inimicus, atrox, magno stridore per auras
Insequitur Nisus: quà se fert Nisus ad auras,
Illa levem fugiens raptim secat æthera pennis.
Tum liquidas corvi presso ter gutture voces,
Aut quater ingeminant: et sæpe cubilibus altis,
Nescio quâ præter solitum dulcedine læti,

TRANSLATION.

Halcyons expand their Wings upon the Shore to the warm Sun: The impure Swine are not heedful to toss about with their Snouts loosened Bundles *of Straw*. But the Mists sink down to the lower Grounds, and rest upon the Plain: And the Owl, observant of the setting Sun from the high House Top, practises her Evening Songs in vain. Nisus, transformed *into a Hawk*, in the clear Sky appears aloft, and Scylla, *in Form of the Lark*, is punished for *having cut her Father's* purple Lock. Wherever she flying cuts the light Air with her Wings, lo hostile, implacable Nisus with loud Screams pursues her through the Sky: Where Nisus mounts into the Sky, she swiftly flying cuts the light Air with her Wings. Then the Ravens with compressed Throat thrice or Four Times repeat their Notes clear *and shrill:* And often in their towering Nests, affected with I know not what

NOTES.

35. *Si nubes ut vellera lanæ spargent ur——*
equum in trid. [illegible]

399. *Dilectæ Thetidi Alcyones.* Ceyx, the King of *Trachinia*, having perished by Shipwreck in the *Ægean* Sea, his Queen *Halcyone* seeing his dead Body floating near the Shore, flung herself upon it in the Transports of her Passion, and *Jove*, in Compassion to the unhappy Lovers, transformed them into the Bird called Halcyons or King-fishers. For then the Sea is said to be smoothed seven or eleven Days about the Winter Solstice, that they may the more conveniently hatch their Young. Hence those are called Halcyon-days.

403. *Nequicquam exercet.* Among the various Glosses which Interpreters have put on these Words, the true and most obvious Meaning seems to be this: That, whereas the Hooting of the Owl is commonly a Prognostic of bad Weather, yet, when these Signs of fair Weather here mentioned occur, she hoots and sings in vain, her dreary Prognostic is not to be minded, or, if any regard it as a Sign of bad Weather, they will find themselves disappointed. Thus Verse 450, after having said that the Clearness of the Sun's Orb at Rising and Setting betokens fair Weather, he adds, *frustra terrebere nimbis*; Mists and blackening Clouds, which at other Times are Forerunners of Rain, are then not to be regarded, it is then in vain to be alarmed by them.

To those who dislike this Interpretation *Servius* proposes another, taking *nequicquam* for *non*; but it is a Question if ever the Word has that Signification either in *Virgil* or any other good Author.

403. *Seros.* The Owl is the only Bird that never sings but by Night; for, as to the Nightingale, it is well known that she sings also by Day, only her Music is not then so much regarded amidst the Chorus of other Birds.

416. *Rerum.*

Inter se foliis strepitant: juvat, imbribus actis,
Progeniem parvam dulcesque revisere nidos.
Haud equidem credo, quia sit divinitùs illis
Ingenium, aut rerum fato prudentia major:
Verùm, ubi tempestas, et cœli mobilis humor
Mutavere vias; et Jupiter humidus Austris
Densat, erant quæ rara modò, et quæ densa relaxat;
Vertuntur species animorum, et pectora motus
Nunc alios; alios, dùm nubila ventus agebat,
Concipiunt. Hinc ille avium concentus in agris,
Et lætæ pecudes, et ovantes gutture corvi.
Si verò solem ad rapidum Lunasque sequentes
Ordine respicies; nunquam te crastina fallet
Hora, neque insidiis noctis capiere serenæ.
Luna revertentes cum primùm colligit ignes,
Si nigrum obscuro comprenderit aëra cornu;
Maximus agricolis pelagoque parabitur imber.
At, si virgineum suffuderit ore ruborem,
Ventus erit: vento semper rubet aurea Phœbe.

strepitant inter se foliis: imbribus actis, juvat eos revisere parvam progeniem, dulcesque nidos. Equidem haud credo, quia ingenium sit datum illis divinitùs, aut major prudentia rerum fato: verùm ubi tempestas, et mobilis humor cœli mutavere vias; et Jupiter, humidus Austris, densat ea, quæ modò erant rara, et relaxat ea, quæ erant densa, species animorum vertuntur, et eorum pectora concipiunt nunc alios, nunc alios motus, dum ventus agebat nubila. Hinc est ille concentus avium in agris, et hinc pecudes sunt lætæ, et corvi ovantes gutture. Si verò respicies ad rapidum Solem, Lunasque sequentes eum ordine; crastina hora nunquam te fallet, neque capiere insidiis serenæ noctis. Cum primùm Luna colligit revertentes ignes, si comprenderit nigrum aëra obscuro cornu; maximus imber parabitur agricolis pelagoque. At, si suffuderit virgineum ruborem ore, erit ventus: aurea Phœbe semper rubet vento.

TRANSLATION.

unusual Joy, they caw and make a Bustle together among the Leaves: The Rains now past, they are fond to revisit their little Offspring, and beloved Nests. Not indeed, I am persuaded, as if they had a Spirit of Discernment from the Gods, or superior Knowledge of Things by Fate: But when the Temperature of the Air and fluctuating Vapours have changed their Courses; and Jove, veiled in Showers, by his South Winds condenses those Things which just before were rare, and rarefies what Things were dense; the Images of their Minds are altered, and their Breasts receive now Motions of one Sort; now of another, while the Wind rolled the Clouds. Hence that Concert of Birds in the Fields, and *hence* the Cattle frisking for Joy, and the Ravens exulting in hoarse Notes.

But if you give Attention to the rapid Sun, and the Moons in Order following; the Hour of ensuing Morn shall never cheat you, nor shall you be deceived by the treacherous Aspect of a Night *fair and* serene. When first the Moon collects the returning Rays, if with Horns obscure she inclose dusky Air; *a* vast *Storm of* Rain is preparing for the Swains and Mariners. But, if she shall spread a Virgin Blush over her Face, Wind will ensue: Golden Phœbe still reddens with

NOTES.

416. *Rerum fato prudentia major.* A superior Knowledge of Things by Fate. Some construe the Words thus: *Prudentia rerum major fato, a Knowledge of Nature superior to Fate,* i. e. as I take it, *a greater Knowledge than may be accounted for from Destiny and the established Laws of Matter and Motion.* Others, *major prudentia in fato rerum, a superior Insight into Fate.*

418. *Jupiter.* Jupiter, no doubt, often signifies *the Air*; but the Dignity of the poetical Style lies in these and the like figurative Expressions, and therefore ought not to be lost in a Translation.

427. *Luna revertentes.* These Signs, taken from the Moon, were proverbial:

Pallida luna pluit, rubicunda flat, alba serenat.

434. *Nas-*

Sin erit pura in quarto ortu (namque is eſt certiſſimus auctor) nec ibit obtuſis cornibus per cœlum; et totus ille dies, et qui naſcentur ab illo, ad exactum menſem carebunt pluviâ ventiſque: nautæ ſervati ſolvent vota in litore Glauco, et Panopeæ, et Inoo Melicertæ. Sol quoque, et exoriens, et cum condet ſe in undas, dabit ſigna. Certiſſima ſigna ſequuntur ſolem, et quæ refert manè, et quæ refert aſtris ſurgentibus. Ubi ille variaverit naſcentem ortum maculis, conditus in nubem, refugeritque medio orbe; imbres ſint ſuſpecti tibi: namque Notus ſiniſter arboribuſque, ſatiſque, pecorique urget ab alto mari. Aut ubi ſub lucem diverſi radii rumpent ſeſe inter denſa nubila; aut ubi Aurora, linquens croceum cubile Tithoni, ſurget pallida; heu, tum pampinus malè defendet mites uvas; tum multa horrida grando ſalit crepitans in tectis. Profuerit magis meminiſſe hoc etiam, cum jam ſol decedet Olympo emenſo: nam ſæpe videmus varios colores errare in vultu ipſius.

Sin ortu in quarto (namque is certiſſimus auctor)
Pura, nec obtuſis per cœlum cornibus ibit;
Totus et ille dies, et qui naſcentur ab illo,
Exactum ad menſem, pluviâ ventiſque carebunt:
Votaque ſervati ſolvent in litore nautæ
Glauco, et Panopeæ, et Inoo Melicertæ.
Sol quoque, et exoriens, et cum ſe condet in undas,
Signa dabit. Solem certiſſima ſigna ſequuntur,
Et quæ manè refert, et quæ ſurgentibus aſtris.
Ille ubi naſcentem maculis variaverit ortum
Conditus in nubem, medioque refugerit orbe;
Suſpecti tibi ſint imbres: namque urget ab alto
Arboribuſque ſatiſque Notus, pecorique ſiniſter.
Aut ubi ſub lucem denſa inter nubila ſeſe
Diverſi rumpent radii; aut ubi pallida ſurget
Tithoni croceum linquens Aurora cubile;
Heu, malè tum mites defendet pampinus uvas;
Tam multa in tectis crepitans ſalit horrida grando.
Hoc etiam, emenſo cum jam decedet Olympo,
Profuerit meminiſſe magis: nam ſæpe videmus
Ipſius in vultu varios errare colores.

TRANSLATION.

Wind. But if at her Fourth Riſing (for that is the moſt unerring Monitor) ſhe walks along the Sky pure and bright, nor with blunted Horns; both that whole Day, and all thoſe that ſhall come after it, till the Month be finiſhed, ſhall be free from Rain and Winds: And the Mariners, preſerved *from Shipwreck*, ſhall pay their Vows upon the Shore to Glaucus, Panopea, and Melicerta, Ino's Son.

The Sun too, both riſing, and when he ſets in the Waves, will give Signs. The ſureſt Signs attend the Sun, both thoſe which he brings in the Morning, and thoſe when the Stars ariſe. When he ſhall chequer his new-born Face with Spots, hid in a Cloud, and *coyly* ſhun *the Sight* with Half his Orb, you may then ſuſpect Showers: For the South Wind, pernicious to Trees, and Corn, and Flocks, haſtens from the Sea. Or when, at the Dawn, the Rays ſhall break *and ſcatter* themſelves diverſely among thick Clouds; or when Aurora, leaving the Saffron-bed of Tithonus, riſes pale; ah, the Vine Leaf will then but ill defend the mild *ripening* Grapes; ſo thick the horrid Hail bounds rattling on the Roofs. This too it will be more advantageous to remember, when, having meaſured the Heavens, he is juſt ſetting: For often we ſee various Colours wander over

NOTES.

434. *Naſcentur.* The *Roman* and *Lombard* Manuſcript, according to *Pierius*, read *naſcetur.*

446. *Diverſi rumpent.* The *Roman* Manuſcript has *rumpunt*; *Servius* and others after him read *erumpent.*

Cæruleus pluviam denuntiat: igneus Euros.
Sin maculæ incipient rutilo immiſcerier igni;
Omnia tunc pariter vento nimbiſque videbis
Fervere. Non illâ quiſquam me nocte per altum
Ire, neque à terrâ moneat convellere funem.
At ſi, cum referetque diem, condetque relatum,
Lucidus orbis erit; fruſtra terrebere nimbis,
Et claro ſilvas cernes Aquilone moveri.
 Denique, quid Veſper ſerus vehat, unde ſerenas
Ventus agat nubes, quid cogitet humidus Auſter,
Sol tibi ſigna dabit. Solem quis dicere falſum
Audeat? ille etiam cæcos inſtare tumultus
Sæpe monet, fraudemque et operta tumeſcere bella.
Ille etiam exſtincto miſeratus Cæſare Romam,
Cum caput obſcurâ nitidum ferrugine texit,
Impiaque æternam timuerunt ſecula noctem.
Tempore quanquam illo tellus quoque et æquora ponti,
Obſcœnique canes, importunæque volucres
Signa dabant. Quoties Cyclopum effervere in agros
Vidimus undantem ruptis fornacibus Ætnam,

Cæruleus color *denuntiat pluviam, igneus* denuntiat *Euros. Sin maculæ incipient immiſceri rutilo igni; tunc videbis omnia fervere pariter ventis nimbiſque. Non quiſquam moneat me ire per altum* mare *illâ nocte, neque convellere funem à terrâ. At ſi orbis* ſolis *erit lucidus, cum referetque diem, condetque* eum *relatum; fruſtra terrebere nimbis, et cernes ſilvas moveri claro Aquilone. Denique, quid ſerus Veſper vehat, unde ventus agat ſerenas nubes, et quid humidus Auſter cogitet, ſol dabit ſigna tibi. Quis audeat dicere ſolem* eſſe *falſum? ille etiam ſæpe monet cæcos tumultus inſtare, fraudemque et operta bella tumeſcere. Ille etiam eſt miſeratus Romam Cæſare extincto, cum texit nitidum caput obſcurâ ferrugine, impiaque ſecula timuerunt æternam noctem. Quanquam illo tempore, tellus quoque, et æquora ponti, obſcœnique canes, importunæque volucres dabant ſigna. Quoties vidimus Ætnam, undantem fornacibus ruptis, effervere in agros Cyclopum,*

TRANSLATION.

his Face. The Azure threatens Rain: The Fiery, Storms of Wind. But if the Spots begin to be blended with bright Fire: then you ſhall ſee all embroiled together with Wind and Drifts of Rain. Let none adviſe me that Night to launch into the Deep, nor to tear my Cable from the Land. But if, both when he uſhers in, and *when* he ſhuts up the revolving Day, his Orb is *clear and* lucid; in vain ſhall you be alarmed by the Clouds, but you ſee ſhall Woods waved by the fair North Wind.

In fine, the Sun will give thee Signs *of* what *Weather* late Veſper brings, from what Quarter the Wind will roll the Clouds ſerene *and fair*, what humid Auſter meditates. Who dares to call the Sun a Deceiver? He even forewarns often that dark Inſurrections are at Hand, and that Treachery and ſecret Wars are ſwelling to a Head. He alſo ſympathized with Rome on Cæſar's Death, when he covered his bright Head with a dark enſanguined Hue, and the impious Age feared eternal Night. Tho' at that Time the Earth too, and Ocean's watery Plains, Dogs in hideous Howlings, and Birds, by importunate unſeaſonable Screams, gave ominous Signs. How often have we ſeen *Mount* Ætna from its burſt Furnaces boil over in Waves on the Lands of the Cyclops, and ſhoot

NOTES.

458. *Cum referetque, &c.* Literally, *When he ſhall both bring back the Day, and ſhut it up when brought back.*

467. *Ferrugine.* This Word ſignifies here *a dark Red, ſomewhat reſembling that of Blood.*

470. *Obſcœnique canes,* i. e. *Dogs of Bad Omen, howling abominably.* Every Thing vile, obſcene, or impure, was by the Ancients reckoned inauſpicious; hence the Word ſignifies *direful or unlucky.*

482. *Flu-*

volveretque globos flammarum, liquefactaque saxa? Germania audiit sonitum armorum toto cœlo: et Alpes tremuerunt insolitis motibus. Ingens vox quoque est exaudita vulgò per silentes lucos, et simulacra pallentia miris modis, sunt visa sub obscurum noctis; pecudesque sunt locutæ, infandum! amnes sistunt, terræque dehiscunt; et mœstum ebur illacrymat templis, æraque sudant. Eridanus, rex fluviorum, proluit silvas, contorquens eas insano vertice, tulitque armenta cum stabulis per omnes campos. Nec eodem tempore aut minaces fibræ cessavere apparere tristibus extis, aut cruor cessavit manare puteis; et urbes resonare altè per noctem, lupis ululantibus. Non plura fulgura aliàs ceciderunt sereno cœlo; nec diri cometæ toties arsere. Ergo Philippi videre Romanas acies concurrere iterum inter sese paribus telis:

Flammarumque globos, liquefactaque volvere saxa?
Armorum sonitum toto Germania cœlo
Audiit: insolitis tremuerunt motibus Alpes.
Vox quoque per lucos vulgò exaudita silentes
Ingens, et simulacra modis pallentia miris
Visa sub obscurum noctis; pecudesque locutæ,
Infandum! sistunt amnes, terræque dehiscunt:
Et mœstum illacrymat templis ebur, æraque sudant.
Proluit insano contorquens vortice silvas
Fluviorum rex Eridanus; camposque per omnes
Cum stabulis armenta tulit. Nec tempore eodem
Tristibus aut extis fibræ apparere minaces,
Aut puteis manare cruor cessavit; et altè
Per noctem resonare, lupis ululantibus, urbes.
Non aliàs cœlo ceciderunt plura sereno
Fulgura; nec diri toties arsere cometæ.
Ergo inter sese paribus concurrere telis
Romanas acies iterum videre Philippi:

TRANSLATION.

up *into the Air* Globes of Flame, and molten Rocks? Germany heard a Clashing of Arms over all the Sky: The Alps trembled with uncommon Earthquakes. A mighty Voice too was commonly heard through the silent Groves, and Spectres, hideously pale, were seen under Cloud of Night: And the very Cattle (O horrid!) spoke. Rivers stopped their Courses, Earth yawned wide: The mourning Ivory weeps in the Temples, and the brazen Statues sweat. Eridanus, Supreme of Rivers, overflowed, whirling in his furious Eddy whole Woods along, and bore away the Herds with their Stalls over all the Plains. Nor at the same Time did either the Fibres fail to appear threatening in the baleful Entrails, or *Streams of* Blood to flow from the Wells; and Cities to resound aloud with Wolves howling by Night. Never did Lightning fall in greater Quantities from a serene Sky: Nor did direful Comets so often blaze. For this Philippi twice hath seen the Roman Armies in intestine War engage: Nor seemed it unbecoming

NOTES.

482. *Fluviorum rex Eridanus.* The Poet here, on purpose to express the Rapidity of this River, begins the Verse with two short Syllables. The *Eridanus*, or *Po*, rises from the Foot of Mount *Vesulus*, and, passing through the *Cisalpine Gaul*, falls into the *Adriatic* Sea. *Virgil* calls it the King of Rivers, because it is the largest and most famous of all the Rivers in *Italy*.

490. *Romanas acies iterum videre Philippi.* It is generally agreed that *Virgil* here means those two Battles which are so famous in History; the one between *Cæsar* and *Pompey*, and the other between *Brutus* and *Cassius* on the one Side, and *Augustus* and *M. Antony* on the other. But it is certain, from History, that the Scenes of those two Battles were widely distant from each other; for the former was fought on the Plains of *Pharsalus* in *Thessaly*, the other at *Philippi* in *Thrace*, which two Places are above two hundred Miles Distance the one from the other. It can hardly be conceived what Confusion there is among Interpreters in their Attempts to unravel this great Difficulty. *Servius*, *Stephanus* in his *Thesaurus*, *Petavius*, Dr. *Heylin*, *Torrentius*, *Desprez*, Mr. *Dacier*, Father *Sanadon*, but especially the two celebrated Writers of the *Roman*

Nec fuit indignum Superis, bis ſanguine noſtro
Emathiam, et latos Hæmi pingueſcere campos.
Scilicet et tempus veniet, cum finibus illis
Agricola, incurvo terram molitus aratro,
Exeſa inveniet ſcabrâ rubigine pila:
Aut gravibus raſtris galeas pulſabit inanes,
Grandiaque effoſſis mirabitur oſſa ſepulcris.
Dî patrii, Indigetes, et Romule, Veſtaque mater,
Quæ Tuſcum Tiberim, et Romana palatia ſervas;
Hunc ſaltem everſo juvenem ſuccurrere ſæclo
Ne prohibete. Satis jam pridem ſanguine noſtro
Laomedonteæ luimus perjuria Trojæ.

nec fuit indignum Superis, Emathiam et latos campos Hæmi pingueſcere bis noſtro ſanguine. Scilicet et tempus veniet, cum, illis finibus, agricola, molitus terram incurvo aratro, inveniet pila exeſa ſcabrâ rubigine: aut pulſabit inanes galeas gravibus raſtris, mirabiturque grandia oſſa effoſſis ſepulcris. Patrii Dî Indigetes, et Romule, materque Veſta, quæ ſervas Tuſcum Tiberim et Romana palatia; ſaltem ne prohibete hunc juvenem ſuccurrere everſo ſæclo. Jam pridem luimus perjuria Laomedonteæ Trojæ noſtro ſanguine.

TRANSLATION.

to the Gods, that Emathia, and the extenſive Plains of Hæmus, ſhould twice be fattened with our Blood. Nay, and the Time ſhall come, when in thoſe Regions the Huſbandman, labouring the Ground with the crooked Plough, ſhall find Javelins half-conſumed with corroſive Ruſt: Or with his cumbrous Harrows ſhall claſh on empty Helmets, and having dug up Graves, admire at the huge Bones.

Ye guardian Deities of my Country, ye Indigetes, and *thou*, O Romulus, and Mother Veſta, who preſideſt over the Tuſcan Tiber, and the Palaces of Rome; forbid it not at leaſt that this young Prince repair the Ruins of the Age. Long ſince have we with our Blood atoned for the Perjuries of Laomedon's Troy.

NOTES.

Roman Hiſtory, *Catrou* and *Rouille*; all theſe, and Numbers of others, will needs have it that both theſe Battles were fought on the ſame Spot. But this Opinion is quite inconſiſtent with the plaineſt Teſtimony of the moſt authentic Hiſtorians, tends to ſubvert the Credibility of all Hiſtory whatſoever, and lays a Foundation for univerſal Scepticiſm.

If the Reader would ſee a ſatisfactory Solution of this Difficulty, he may conſult a Pamphet lately publiſhed in the way of Letters by Mr. *Holdeſworth*, intituled *Pharſalia and Philippi*. The Sum of that Gentleman's Opinion is this: " That *Virgil* means by his two Battles of *Philippi*, not two Battles fought on the ſame individual Spot, but at two diſtant Places of the ſame Name, the former at *Philippi* (*alias Thebæ Phthiæ*) near *Pharſalus* in *Theſſaly*, the latter at *Philippi*, near the Confines of *Thrace*. And tho' the Hiſtorians (all except *Lucius Florus*), for Diſtinction's ſake, call the latter Battle only by the Name of *Philippi*; yet, as there was a *Philippi* likewiſe near *Pharſalia*, in Sight of which the former was fought, the Poets, for certain Reaſons (which, ſays he, I ſhall conſider hereafter) call both by the ſame Name."

As to the Reaſons that he ſays determined *Virgil* to call both Battles by the ſame Name, the Chief of them, I think, is this: " That, in Compliment to *Auguſtus*, he might impreſs the ſuperſtitious *Romans* with a Belief, that the Vengeance of the Gods againſt the Murderers of *Cæſar* was denounced by Numbers of Prodigies and Omens, and in ſo remarkable a Manner, that there appeared in it a particular Stroke of Providence, according to the Heathen Superſtition, that the ſecond Battle, which proved fatal to the *Romans*, ſhould be fought in the ſame Province with the firſt, and near a ſecond *Philippi*.

292. *Emathiam—Hæmi*. The ſame ingenious Gentleman proves that the ancient *Macedonia* or *Emathia*, according to the Language of the Poets, extended as far as the River *Neſtus* in *Thrace* to the Eaſt, and to the South comprehended all *Theſſaly*, and conſequently took in the *Pharſalian Philippi*; ſo that both Battles, here referred to, were really fought in *Emathia*, as *Virgil* here ſays. Again he ſhews that both *Philippi*'s were near Mount *Hæmus*, which, tho' commonly reckoned only a Mountain of *Thrace*, was really a Chain of Mountains like the *Alps* and *A-*

Jam pridem, ô Cæsar, regia cœli invidet te nobis, atque queritur te curare triumphos hominum. Quippe ubi fas atque nefas est versum, tot bella sunt per orbem; tam multæ facies scelerum: non ullus dignus honos habetur aratro, arva squalent colonis abductis ad militiam, et curvæ falces conflantur in rigidum ensem. Hinc Euphrates movet bellum, illinc Germania movet bellum: vicinæ urbes ferunt arma inter se legibus fœderis ruptis: impius Mars sævit toto urbe. Ut cum quadrigæ effudere sese carceribus, addunt se in spatia: et auriga, frustra tendens retinacula, fertur equis, atque currus audit habenas.

Jam pridem nobis cœli te regia, Cæsar,
Invidet, atque hominum queritur curare triumphos.
Quippe ubi fas versum atque nefas; tot bella per orbem;
Tam multæ scelerum facies: non ullus aratro
Dignus honos: squalent abductis arva colonis,
Et curvæ rigidum falces conflantur in ensem.
Hinc movet Euphrates, illinc Germania bellum:
Vicinæ ruptis inter se legibus urbes
Arma ferunt: sævit toto Mars impius orbe.
Ut cum carceribus sese effudere quadrigæ,
Addunt se in spatia, et frustra retinacula tendens
Fertur equis auriga, neque audit currus habenas.

TRANSLATION.

Long since, O Cæsar, the Courts of Heaven envy us *the Possession of* thee, and complain that thou art concerned about the Triumphs of Mortals. Since among them the Distinctions of Right and Wrong are perverted; so many Wars, so many Species of Crimes prevail throughout the World: The Plough has none of those Honours that are its due: The Fields lie waste, their Owners forced *to bear Arms*, and the crooked Scythes are forged into rigid Swords. Here Euphrates, there Germany raises War: Neighbouring Cities, having broke their mutual Leagues, take Arms *against each other:* Pitiless Mars rages over all the World. As when the four-horsed Chariots have started from the Goal, they fly out swifter and swifter to the Race, and the Charioteer, stretching in vain the Bridle, is hurried away by the Steeds, nor is the Chariot heedful of the Reins.

NOTES.

pennines; the Head or highest Part thereof was in *Thrace*, but all the other Mountains, viz. *Rhodope*, *Pangæus*, &c. quite round to *Pindus* and *Oeta*, branch out from the same Head. *Virgil* himself seems to take the Mount in this extensive View, when he cries out, Geor. II. 488.

O qui me gelidis in vallibus Hæmi
Sistat, et ingenti ramorum protegat umbrâ!

As all the other Places, mentioned in this Passage, were in *Thessaly* or *Achaia*, 'tis reasonable to suppose, that by the Vallies of *Hæmus* he means the same Country too. But, let that be as it will, there are several Passages in *Lucan* which evidently shew that *Hæmus* reached to the *Thessalian Philippi*. Thus at the latter End of the first Book he prophesies that the Battle of *Pharsalia* (which he too calls by the Name of *Philippi*) was to be fought under the Rock of *Hæmus*, Verse 681.

Latosque Hæmi sub rupe Philippos.

See also L. VII. 174, 449, 576.

511. *Impius.* Here signifies *cruel, unnatural*, that has no *pietas*, no Tenderness, no natural Affection.

P. VIRGILII MARONIS

GEORGICA.

LIBER II.

HACTENUS arvorum cultus, et ſidera cœli;
Nunc te, Bacche, canam, necnon ſilveſtria tecum
Virgulta, et prolem tardè creſcentis olivæ.
Huc, pater ô Lenæe: tuis hìc omnia plena
Muneribus: tibi pampineo gravidus autumno
Floret ager: ſpumat plenis vindemia labris:
Huc, pater ô Lenæe, veni; nudataque muſto
Tinge novo mecum direptis crura cothurnis.

ORDO.

Hactenus cecini *cultus arvorum, et ſidera cœli: nunc canam te, Bacche necnon ſilveſtria virgulta tecum, et prolem tardè creſcentis olivæ.* Adde *huc, ô pater Lenæe: omnia hìc* ſunt *plena tuis muneribus: ager floret tibi gravidus pampineo autumno: vindemia ſpumat plenis labris: Veni huc, ô pater Lenæe; et mecum tinge nudata crura novo muſto, cothurnis direptis.*

TRANSLATION.

THUS far of the Culture of Fields, and of the Conſtellations of the Heavens; now, Bacchus, will I ſing of thee, and with thee of woodland Trees, and of the ſlow-growing Olive's Offspring. Hither, O Father Lenæus (here all is full of thy Bounties: For thee the Field, laden with the viny Harveſt, flouriſhes: *For thee* the Vintage foams in the full Vatts:) Hither, O Father Lenæus, come; and, having thy Buſkins ſtript off, ſtain thy naked Legs with me in new Wine.

NOTES.

The Subject of the following Book is Planting. In handling of which Argument, the Poet ſhews all the different Methods of raiſing Trees; deſcribes their Variety, and gives Rules for the Management of each in particular. He then points out the Soils in which the ſeveral Plants thrive beſt: And thence takes Occaſion to run out into the Praiſes of *Italy*. After which he gives ſome Directions for diſcovering the Nature of every Soil, preſcribes Rules for dreſſing of Vines, Olives, *&c.* and concludes the Georgic with a Panegyric on a Country Life.

2. *Silveſtria virgulta.* Foreſt-trees, chiefly thoſe that were uſed in propping the Vine, as the Poplar, Elm, Oſier, Aſh, *&c.*

4. *Lenæe.* A Name of *Bacchus* of *Greek* Derivation, from ληνος, *torcular*, a *Wine-preſs*.

8. *Direptis cothurnis.* The Cothurnus or Buſkin was a Part of *Bacchus*'s Dreſs. *Tac.* L. II. *In celebrando vindemiæ ſimulacra, Silius Bacchum referens hedera vinctus erat, et cothurnos gerebat.*

8. *Tinge.* Alludes to the Cuſtom of treading out the Grapes with their Feet.

Principio est varia natura creandis arboribus: namque aliæ veniunt ipsæ suâ sponte, nullis hominum cogentibus eas; tenentque campos latè et curva flumina: ut molle siler, lentæque genistæ, populus, et canentia salicta glaucâ fronde. Autem pars surgunt de posito semine: ut altæ castaneæ, æsculusque maxima nemorum, quæ frondet Jovi, atque quercus habitæ oracula à Graiis. Densissima silva pullulat aliis ab radice: ut cerasis, ulmisque: etiam parva Parnassia laurus subjicit se sub ingenti umbrâ matris. Natura primùm dedit hos modos: his modis omne genus silvarum fruticumque, sacrorumque nemorum viret. Sunt alii modi, *quos usus ipse repperit sibi* aliquâ *viâ. Hic* homo, *abscindens plantas de tenero corpore matrum, deposuit eas sulcis: hic obruit arvo stirpes, quadrifidasque sudes, et vallos acuto robore:*

Principio arboribus varia est natura creandis:
Namque aliæ, nullis hominum cogentibus, ipsæ
Sponte suâ veniunt; camposque, et flumina latè
Curva tenent: ut molle siler, lentæque genistæ,
Populus, et glaucâ canentia fronde salicta.
Pars autem posito surgunt de semine: ut altæ
Castaneæ, nemorumque Jovi quæ maxima frondet
Æsculus, atque habitæ Graiis oracula quercus.
Pullulat ab radice aliis densissima silva:
Ut cerasis, ulmisque: etiam Parnassia laurus
Parva sub ingenti matris se subjicit umbrâ.
Hos natura modos primùm dedit: his genus omne
Silvarum, fruticumque viret, nemorumque sacrorum.
Sunt alii, quos ipse viâ sibi repperit usus.
Hic plantas tenero abscindens de corpore matrum,
Deposuit sulcis: hic stirpes obruit arvo,
Quadrifidasque sudes, et acuto robore vallos:

TRANSLATION.

First, Nature is various in producing Trees: For some, without any cogent Means applied by Men, come freely of their own Accord, and widely overspread the Plains and winding Rivers: As the soft Osier, and limber Broom, the Poplar and the whitening Willows, with Sea-green Leaves. But some arise from deposited Seed: As the lofty Chesnuts, and the Æsculus, most majestic of the Groves, which, in Honour of Jove, shoots forth its Leaves, and the Oaks reputed oracular by the Greeks. To others a most luxuriant Wood *of Suckers* springs from the Roots: As the Cherries, and the Elms: Thus too the little Bay of Parnassus raises itself under its Mother's diffusive Shade. Nature at first ordained these Means *for the Production of Trees:* By these every Species blooms, of Woods, and Shrubs, and sacred Groves. Others there are, which Experience has found out for itself by Art. One, cutting off the Suckers from the tender Body of their Mother, sets them in the Furrows: Another buries the Stocks in the Ground, and Stakes, *whose Bottom is* split in four, and Poles with the Wood

NOTES.

16. *Æsculus.* A kind of Oak, which some take to be what we call the Bay-oak. This Tree was consecrated to *Jupiter.*

19. *Se subjicit.* i. e. *Sursum jacit, shoots up.* See Ecl. X. 74.

22. *Viâ.* Arte, as *Cic. de Cl. Or.* XLVI *Artea neminem solitum viâ nec arte, sed accurate nomen, et de scripto pleresque dicere.*

23. *Hic plantas, &c.* This refers to the Propagation of Trees by Suckers.

25. *Quadrifidasque sudes.* This is the Method of Propagation, by fixing the large Branches like Stakes in the Earth.

25. *Acuto robore.* Trunco exacuto et in mucronem fastigiato, as *Pliny* has it. The *quadrifidas sudes* is when the Bottom is slit across both Ways; the *acuto robore* is when it is cut into a Point, which is called the *Colt's Foot. Essay on the Georgics.*

26. *Silva-*

Silvarumque aliæ preſſos propaginis arcus
Exſpectant, et viva ſuâ plantaria terrâ.
Nil radici egent aliæ: ſummumque putator
Haud dubitat terræ referens mandare cacumen.
Quin et caudicibus ſectis, mirabile dictu,
Truditur è ſicco radix oleagina ligno.
Et ſæpe alterius ramos impunè videmus
Vertere in alterius, mutatamque inſita mala
Ferre pyrum, et prunis lapidoſa rubeſcere corna.
Quare agite, ô proprios generatim diſcite cultus,
Agricolæ, fructuſque feros mollite colendo:
Neu ſegnes jaceant terræ: juvat Iſmara Baccho
Conſerere, atque oleâ magnum veſtire Taburnum.

aliæ arbores ſilvarum exſpectant preſſos arcus propaginis, et viva plantaria defodi in ſuâ terrâ. Aliæ egent radicis nil: putatorque haud dubitat mandare ſummum cacumen, referens illud terræ. Quin et, mirabile dictu, radix oleagina, caudicibus ſectis, truditur è ſicco ligno. Et ſæpe videmus ramos alterius arboris vertere impunè in ramos alterius, pyrumque mutatam ferre mala inſita ſibi, et lapidoſa corna rubeſcere prunis. Quare agite, ô agricolæ, diſcite proprios cultus generatim, molliteque feros fructus colendo eos: neu ſegnes terræ jaceant: juvat conſerere Iſmara Baccho, atque veſtire magnum Taburnum oleâ.

TRANSLATION.

ſharpened to a Point: Some Trees *luxuriant* expect the bent-down Arches of a Layer, and living Nurſeries in their own *native* Soil. Others have no need of any Root: And the Planter makes no Scruple to commit to Earth the topmoſt Shoots, giving them back *to her Care.* Nay (what is wondrous to relate) even after her Trunk is cut in Pieces, the Olive Tree ſhoots forth Roots from the dry Wood. Often we ſee the Boughs of one Tree transformed, with no Diſadvantage, into thoſe of another, and a Pear Tree *thus* changed bear ingrafted Apples, and ſtony Cornelian Cherries grow upon Plumb Tree Stocks.

Wherefore come on, O Huſbandmen, learn the Culture proper to each Kind, and ſoften the Wild Fruits by Cultivation: Nor let *even poor and* infertile Grounds lie neglected: It is worth while to plant *even rugged Mountains ſuch as* Iſmarus with Vines, and clothe vaſt Taburnus with Olives.

NOTES.

26. *Silvarum.* Trees very luxuriant, and abounding with Shoots that look like a little Wood.

26. *Preſſos propaginis arcus exſpectant.* This deſcribes the Method of raiſing Trees by Layers, *i. e.* by bending down a Branch from the Mother-tree, and planting it in the Ground, till it take Root firm enough to nouriſh itſelf; which, according to *Columella*, is in the third Year: Then it may be ſeparated from the Mother.

27 *Exſpectant.* i. e. By their Luxuriance and bending down to the Earth they ſeem to expect Propagation, and to deſire, as it were, that their Shoots may be ſet in the Ground.

27. *Viva.* i. e. Not ſeparated from their Mother-tree.

29. *Referens mandare.* This is the Method of Propagation, which is called by *Cuttings. Referens* ſignifies *giving them back to the Earth, whence they came.*

30. *Caudix.* Is properly the Body of the Tree ſeparate from the Root, as *truncus* is the Body ſeparate from the Head.

37. *Neu ſegnes jaceant terræ.* Dr. *Trapp* renders it, *Let not your Land lie idle.* And in like Manner all the other Interpreters I have ſeen. But the Conſtructions ſeems rather to be, *neu ſegnes terræ jaceant, nor let Land however naturally infertile lie neglected*; which both preſerves the Connexion with what goes before, and ſhews the Propriety of adding *juvat Iſmara Baccho conſerere,* &c. Mountains by Nature rugged, and whoſe Soil is *ſegnis*, infertile, and backward to produce, yet by Culture will turn to good Account: Thus *Iſmarus* bears excellent Vines, and *Taburnus* is famous for the Production of Olives.

37. *Iſmara.* Iſmarus, a Mountain in the maritime Parts of *Thrace.*

38. *Taburnum.* Taburnus, a Mountain in *Campania*, between *Capua* and *Nola*, fertile in Olives. Its modern name is *Taburo.*

39. *De-*

Tuque ades, decurreque inceptum laborem unà mecum, ô decus, ô meritò maxima pars noſtræ famæ, Mæcenas, volanſque da vela patenti pelago. Ego non opto amplecti cuncta meis verſibus: non, ſi ſint mihi centum linguæ, centumque ora, et ferrea vox: ades, et lege oram primi litoris. Terræ ſunt in noſtris *manibus: non tenebo te hìc ficto carmine, atque per ambages et longa exorſa.* Arbores, *quæ tollunt ſe in oras luminis ſuâ ſponte, ſurgunt infecunda quidem, ſed læta et fortia: quippe natura ſubeſt ſolo. Tamen ſi quis inſerat hæc quoque, aut mandet* hæc *mutata ſubactis ſcrobibus, exuerint ſilveſtrem animum: frequentique cultu, haud tarda ſequentur, in quaſcunque artes voces* illa. *Nec non et* illa *quæ exit ſterilis ab imis ſtirpibus, faciet hoc, ſi ſit digeſta per vacuos agros: nunc altæ frondes, et rami matris opacant* eam, *adimuntque fetus* illi *creſcenti, uruntque* eam *ferentem* fructus.

Tuque ades, inceptumque unà decurre laborem,
O decus, ô famæ meritò pars maxima noſtræ,
Mæcenas; pelagoque volans da vela patenti.
Non ego cuncta meis amplecti verſibus opto:
Non, mihi ſi linguæ centum ſint, oraque centum,
Ferrea vox: ades, et primi lege litoris oram.
In manibus terræ: non hìc te carmine ficto,
Atque per ambages, et longa exorſa tenebo.
  Sponte ſuâ quæ ſe tollunt in luminis oras,
Infecunda quidem, ſed læta et fortia ſurgunt:
Quippe ſolo natura ſubeſt. Tamen hæc quoque ſi quis
Inſerat, aut ſcrobibus mandet mutata ſubactis,
Exuerint ſilveſtrem animum: cultuque frequenti,
In quaſcunque voces artes, haud tarda ſequentur.
Nec non et ſterilis quæ ſtirpibus exit ab imis,
Hoc faciet, vacuos ſi ſit digeſta per agros:
Nunc altæ frondes, et rami matris opacant,
Creſcentique adimunt fetus, uruntque ferentem.

TRANSLATION.

And thou, my Glory, *to whom I juſtly owe* the greateſt Portion of my Fame, be preſent, O Mæcenas, purſue with me this Taſk begun, and flying, ſet ſail on this Sea, now opening wide. I chooſe not to comprize all in my Verſe: Not tho' I had an hundred Tongues, an hundred Mouths, and an Iron Voice: Be preſent, and coaſt along the neareſt Shore. The Land is *ſtill* in view: I will not here detain thee with fictitious Song, nor with Circumlocution and tedious Preamble.

Thoſe, which ſpring up ſpontaneouſly into the Regions of Light, are unfruitful indeed; but they riſe vigorous and ſtrong: For in the Soil lies hid ſome natural Quality *peculiarly ſuited to them.* Yet, if any one ingraft even theſe, or depoſit them tranſplanted in Trenches well prepared, they will put off their ſavage Nature, and by frequent Culture will not be ſlow to follow whatever Arts *and Methods of Improvement* you call them to. And *the Suckers* alſo, which ſprout up barren from the low Roots, will do the ſame, if they be diſtributed through Fields where they have room *to ſtrike their Roots:* Now *in their natural State* the high Shoots and Branches of the Mother overſhadow them, and hinder them from bearing Fruit as they grow up, or pinch and ſtarve them when they bear.

NOTES.

39. *Decurre.* This is the ſame Alluſion with that in Verſe 41. *Pelagoque volans da vela patenti*; *decurro* being applied to proſperous Sailing, when the Ship runs with a gliding Motion along the Waves; as Æn. V. 212.

Prona petit maria, et pelago decurrit aperto.

41. *Pelagoque volans,* &c. And flying ſet Sail into the open Sea, i. e. accompany and conduct me through this immenſe Work, which now opens itſelf to my View like an expanded Ocean.

50. *Mutata.* i. e. *Mutato loco, tranſplanted.*

56. *Uruntque ferentem.* Pinch or ſtarve it in bearing, by intercepting the Sun and Air.

Jam, quæ ſeminibus jactis ſe ſuſtulit arbos,
Tarda venit, ſeris factura nepotibus umbram:
Pomaque degenerant ſuccos oblita priores:
Et turpes avibus prædam fert uva racemos.
Scilicet omnibus eſt labor impendendus, et omnes
Cogendæ in ſulcum, ac multâ mercede domandæ,
Sed truncis oleæ meliùs, propagine vites
Reſpondent; ſolido Paphiæ de robore myrtus.
Plantis eduræ coryli naſcuntur, et ingens
Fraxinus, Herculeæque arbos umbroſa coronæ,
Chaoniique patris glandes: etiam ardua palma
Naſcitur, et caſus abies viſura marinos.
  Inſeritur verò ex fetu nucis arbutus horrida:
Et ſteriles platani malos geſſere valentes.
Caſtaneæ fagus, ornuſque incanuit albo
Flore pyri: glandemque ſues fregere ſub ulmis.
Nec modus inſerere, atque oculos imponere ſimplex.
Nam quà ſe medio trudunt de cortice gemmæ,
Et tenues rumpunt tunicas; anguſtus in ipſo
Fit nodo ſinus: huic alienâ ex arbore germen
Includunt, udoque docent inoleſcere libro.

Jam arbos, quæ ſuſtulit ſe jactis ſeminibus, venit tarda, factura umbram ſeris nepotibus: pomaque degenerant, oblita priores ſuccos: et uva fert turpes racemos prædam avibus. Scilicet labor eſt impendendus omnibus, et omnes ſunt cogendæ in ſulcum, ac domandæ multâ mercede. Oleæ provenientes è truncis, vites è propagine meliùs reſpondent, et myrtus Paphiæ de ſolido robore. Eduræ coryli naſcuntur plantis, et ingens fraxinus, populuſque *umbroſa arbos Herculeæ coronæ, glandeſque Chaonii patris* Jovis: *etiam ardua palma naſcitur, et abies viſura marinos caſus. Verò horrida arbutus inſeritur ex fetu nucis, et ſteriles platani geſſere valentes malos. Fagus incanuit* flore *caſtaneæ, ornuſque albo flore pyri: ſueſque fregere glandem ſub ulmis. Nec eſt ſimplex modus inſerere atque imponere oculos. Nam quà gemmæ trudunt ſe de medio cortice, et rumpunt tenues tunicas, anguſtus ſinus fit in nodo ipſo: includunt germen* acciſum *ex alienâ arbore huc, docentque* illud *inoleſcere udo libro.*

TRANSLATION.

The Tree again, that is raiſed from Seed thrown *into the Ground*, grows up ſlowly, ſo as to form a Shade for late Poſterity: And *its* Fruits degenerate, forgetting their former Juices: *Thus* even the Vine bears ſorry Cluſters, a Prey for Birds. For Labour muſt be beſtowed on all, and all muſt be reduced into the Trench, and tamed, *and made prolific* with vaſt Pains. But Olives anſwer *our Wiſhes* better *when propagated* by Truncheons, Vines by Layers, the Myrtles of the Paphian *Goddeſs by Setts* from the ſolid Wood. From Suckers the hard Hazels grow, the huge Aſh, and the ſhady *Poplar*-Tree *that furniſhed* Hercules his Crown, and the Oaks of the Chaonian Father *Jove*: *Thus* alſo the lofty Palm is propagated, and the Fir-Tree, doomed to viſit the Dangers of the Main.

But the rugged Arbute is ingrafted on the Offſpring of the Walnut, and barren Planes have borne ſtout Apple-Trees. Cheſnut-Trees *have borne* Beeches, and the Mountain-Aſh hath whitened with the ſnowy Bloſſoms of the Pear: And Swine have crunched Acorns under Elms. Nor is the Method of ingrafting and that of inoculating one and the ſame. For *inoculating is thus*, where the Buds thruſt themſelves forth from the Middle of the Bark, and burſt the ſlender Coats, a ſmall Notch is made in the very Knot: Hither they incloſe an Eye from another

NOTES.

59. *Pomaque.* Poma here, and in many other Places, ſignifies *all Sorts of Fruits*. See Verſe 82. and *Plin.* L. XVII. 10.

63. *Truncis.* Truncheons called by *Columella* and *Cato*, *Taleæ*: They are the thick Branches ſawn in Pieces.

67. *Chaoniique patris glandes.* Glandes, Acorns, are here put for the Oaks that bear them. *Chaonii patris* is *Jupiter* worſhipped at *Dodona* in *Chaonia*, or *Epirus*, to whom the Oak was ſacred.

Aut rursum enodes trunci resecantur, et via finditur alte in solidum cuneis: deinde feraces plantae immittuntur. Nec est tempus longum, et ingens arbos exiit ad coelum felicibus ramis, miraturque novas frondes, et poma non sua. Praeterea haud est unum genus, nec fortibus ulmis, nec salici, loto, neque Idaeis cyparissis: nec pingues olivae nascuntur in unam faciem, Orchites, et radii, et pausia amara bacca; pomaque, et silvae Alcinoi: nec est idem surculus Crustumiis, Syriisque piris, gravibusque volemis. Eadem vindemia non pendet nostris arboribus, quam vindemiam Lesbos carpit de Methymnaeo palmite. Sunt Thasiae vites, sunt et albae Mareotides;

Aut rursum enodes trunci resecantur, et altè
Finditur in solidum cuneis via: deinde feraces
Plantæ immittuntur: nec longum tempus, et ingens
Exiit ad cœlum ramis felicibus arbos,
Miraturque novas frondes, et non sua poma.
Præterea genus haud unum nec fortibus ulmis,
Nec salici, lotoque, nec Idæis cyparissis:
Nec pingues unam in faciem nascuntur olivæ,
Orchites, et radii, et amara pausia baccâ;
Pomaque, et Alcinoi silvæ: nec surculus idem
Crustumiis, Syriisque piris, gravibusque volemis.
Non eadem arboribus pendet vindemia nostris,
Quam Methymnæo carpit de palmite Lesbos.
Sunt Thasiæ vites, sunt et Mareotides albæ;

TRANSLATION.

Tree, and teach it to unite with the moist Rind. Or again, *in ingrafting* the knotless Stocks are cut, and a Passage is cloven deep into the Solid *Wood* with Wedges: Then fertile Cions are inserted: And in no long Time a huge Tree shoots up to Heaven with prosperous Boughs, and admires its new Leaves, and Fruits not its own.

Moreover, the Species is not single, neither of strong Elms, nor of Willows, of the Lote-Tree, nor of the Idæan Cypresses: Nor do the fat Olives grow in one Form, the *Orchites*, and the *Radii*, and the *Pausia* with bitter Berries: Nor Apples, and the Orchards of Alcinous: Nor are the Shoots the same of the Crustumian and Syrian Pears, and of the heavy Volema. The same Vintage hangs not on our Trees, which *Lesbos* gathers from the Methymnæan Vine. There are the Thasian Vines, and there are the white Mareotides; these fit for

NOTES.

85. *Orchites.* This is the Reading of Servius, which appears to be right, because it is found in that Manner in the Prose Writers of Agriculture. Thus *Pliny*: *Genera olearum tria dixit Virgilius, Orchites, et radios, et pausias.* The *Orchis* is a round Olive, so called from ὄρχις a Testicle.

86. *Radii.* The *radius* is a long Olive, so called from its Semblance to a Weaver's Shuttle.

86. *Amara pausia baccâ.* The Poet mentions the bitter Berry of this sort of Olive, because it is to be gathered before it is quite ripe; for then it has a bitter or austere Taste.

88. *Crustumiis, Syriisque piris, gravibusque volemis.* The *Crustumia*, so called from *Crustumium* in Italy, were reckoned the best sort of Pears. The *Syrian* Pears, called also *Tarentine*, are thought by some to be the *Bergamot*. The *Volema*, so called from their Largeness, *quia volam impleant*, because they fill the *Palm of the Hand*. *Ruæus* takes them for the *Bon Cretien*; others for the *Libralis* or *Pounder*.

90. *Methymnæo palmite.* So called from *Methymna*, a City of *Lesbos*, an Island in the *Ægean* Sea, famous for good Wine.

91. *Thasiæ vites.* So called from *Thasus*, another Island in the same Sea.

91. *Mareotides albæ.* Most probably an *Egyptian* Wine, from *Mareotis*, a Lake near *Alexandria*. Which Opinion *Horace* seems to countenance; for he represents *Cleopatra* intoxicated with it:

"*Mentemque lymphatam Mareotico*
Redegit in veros timores
Cæsar."

Others understand this of a *Libyan* Wine, from *Marea*, a Part of *Africa*.

93. *Passo*

Pinguibus hae terris habiles, levioribus illae:
Et passo Psithia utilior, tenuisque Lageos,
Tentatura pedes olim, vincturaque linguam:
Purpureae, preciaeque: et quo te carmine dicam,
Rhaetica? nec cellis ideo contende Falernis.
Sunt etiam Aminneae vites, firmissima vina:
Tmolius et assurgit quibus, et rex ipse Phanaeus:
Argitisque minor: cui non certaverit ulla,
Aut tantum fluere, aut totidem durare per annos.
Non ego te, mensis et Dis accepta secundis,
Transierim, Rhodia, et tumidis, Bumaste, racemis.
Sed neque quam multae species, nec nomina quae sint,
Est numerus: neque enim numero comprendere refert:
Quem qui scire velit, Libyci velit aequoris idem
Discere, quam multae Zephyro turbentur arenae:

[illegible]

TRANSLATION.

a rich Soil, and those for a lighter one: And the Psithian more serviceable when dried, and the thin light Lageos, which will try the Feet at length, and bind the Tongue: The Purple, and the Rathripe. And in what Numbers shall I sing of thee, O Rhaetian Grape? Nor therefore vie thou with the Falernian Cellars. There are also Aminnean Vines, best-bodied Wines: Which even Tmolus and Phanae King of Mountains honour: And the smaller Argitis, which none can rival, either in yielding so much Juice, or in lasting so many Years. I must not pass thee over, Rhodian Grape, grateful to the Gods and second Courses, nor thee Bumastus, with thy swelling Clusters. But we neither can recount how numerous the Species, nor what are their Names, nor imports it to comprize their Number: Which whoever would know, the same may seek to learn how numerous are the Sands of the Lybian Sea raised by the

NOTES.

93. *Passo Psithia, &c.* Passum is a Wine made from Raisins, or dried Grapes. The Psithia vitis is probably so called from some City in Greece; for Columella calls it Graecanicam.

93. *Lageos.* So called from λαγώς, a Hare, on account of its Colour.

95. *Preciae.* Quasi praecoquae, i.e. Rathripe, because they are first ripe.

96. *Falernis.* Campanian Wine, so called from Falernus, a Mountain in Campania.

96. *Rhaetica.* So called from Rhaetia, a Country bordering upon Italy. This Wine is praised by Cato, Strabo, and other Authors.

97. *Aminneae.* 'Tis not certain what Wine is here meant.

98. *Tmolus.* A Mountain in Lydia, very famous for Wine.

98. *Rex Phanaeus.* From Phanae the Name of a Mountain in Chios, whose Wines are [illegible].

101. *Dis et mensis accepta secundis.* i.e. it was so excellent as to be fit for being offered in Libations, which were made at the second Courses.

102. *Bumaste.* From the Greek [illegible], because its Clusters swelled out big, somewhat resembling a Cow's Teats.

aut, ubi Eurus violentior incidit navigiis, nosse, quot Ionii fluctus veniant ad litora. Nec verò omnes terræ possunt ferre omnia genera arborum. Salices nascuntur fluminibus, alnique crassis paludibus, steriles orni saxosis montibus, et litora sunt lætissima myrtetis: denique Bacchus amat apertos colles. taxi amant Aquilonem, et frigora. Aspice et orbem domitum extremis cultoribus, Eoasque domos Arabum, pictosque Gelonos. Patriæ sunt divisæ arboribus. India sola fert nigrum ebenum, et thurea virga est Sabæis solis. Quid referam tibi balsamaque sudantia ex odorato ligno, et baccas semper frondentis acanthi? quid referam nemora Æthiopum canentia molli lanâ? utque Seres depectant tenuia vellera foliis? aut quos lucos India propior Oceano, sinus extremi orbis, gerit? ubi haud ullæ sagittæ potuere vincere summum aëra.

Aut, ubi navigiis violentior incidit Eurus,
Nosse, quot Ionii veniant ad litora fluctus.
Nec verò terræ ferre omnes omnia possunt.
Fluminibus salices, crassisque paludibus alni
Nascuntur: steriles saxosis montibus orni.
Litora myrtetis lætissima: denique apertos
Bacchus amat colles: Aquilonem et frigora taxi.
Aspice et extremis domitum cultoribus orbem,
Eoasque domos Arabum, pictosque Gelonos.
Divisæ arboribus patriæ. Sola India nigrum
Fert ebenum: solis est thurea virga Sabæis.
Quid tibi odorato referam sudantia ligno
Balsamaque, et baccas semper frondentis acanthi?
Quid nemora Æthiopum molli canentia lanâ?
Velleraque ut foliis depectant tenuia Seres?
Aut quos Oceano propior gerit India lucos,
Extremi sinus orbis? ubi aëra vincere summum

TRANSLATION.

Zephyr: Or to know how many Waves of the Ionian Sea come *rolling* to the Shores, when Eurus, more violent, falls upon the Ships.

But neither can all Soils bear all Sorts *of Trees.* Willows grow along the Rivers, and Elders in miry Fens: The barren wild Ashes on rocky Mountains. The Shores rejoice most in Myrtle-groves: Bacchus in fine loves open Hills: The Yews the North Wind and the Colds.

Survey also *those Parts of* the Globe *that are* subdued *and cultivated* by Hinds most remote, both the eastern Habitations of the Arabians, and the painted Geloni. Countries are distinguished by their Trees. India alone bears black Ebony: The Frankincense-Tree belongs to the Sabæans only. Why should I mention to thee Balms distilling from the fragrant Woods, and the Berries of the ever-green Acanthus? Why the Forests of the Ethiopians whitening with downy Wool? And how the Seres comb the fine *silky* Fleeces from the Leaves? Or the Groves which India, nearer the Ocean, produces, the utmost Skirts of the Globe?

NOTES.

115. *Pictos Gelonos.* The *Geloni* were a People of *Scythia*, who painted their Faces.

116. *Sola India—fert ebenum.* Theophrastus was of the same Opinion, that Ebony was peculiar to *India*; but other Authors tell us that the best Ebony is brought from *Ethiopia.*

119. *Balsamaque.* According to the best Accounts of modern Authors the true Country of the Balsam-plant is *Arabia Felix.* The Balsam flows out of the Branches by making Incisions in the Summer Months.

119. *Baccas semper frondentis acanthi.* There are two Sorts of the *Acanthus*; the one an *Egyptian* Tree, of which the Poet here speaks; and the other an Herb, to which he elsewhere refers. It is observed that the Flowers grow in little Balls, which *Virgil* might poetically call Berries.

120. *Nemora Æthiopum molli canentia lanâ.* The Forests abounding with Cotton-trees.

121. *Velleraque ut foliis depectant tenuia Seres?* The *Seres* were a People of *India* who furnished the other Parts of the World with Silk. The Ancients were generally ignorant of the Manner in which it was spun by the Silk-worms, and imagined it was a Sort of Down gathered from the Leaves of Trees.

125. *Media*

Arboris haud ullæ jactu potuere sagittæ:
Et gens illa quidem sumtis non tarda pharetris.
Media fert tristes succos, tardumque saporem
Felicis mali: quo non præsentius ullum,
Pocula siquando sævæ infecere novercæ,
Miscueruntque herbas, et non innoxia verba,
Auxilium venit: ac membris agit atra venena.
Ipsa ingens arbos, faciemque simillima lauro:
Et, si non alium latè jactaret odorem,
Laurus erat. Folia haud ullis labentia ventis:
Flos apprima tenax. Animas et olentia Medi
Ora fovent illo, et senibus medicantur anhelis.
Sed neque Medorum silvæ, ditissima terra,
Nec pulcher Ganges, atque auro turbidus Hermus,
Laudibus Italiæ certent; non Bactra, neque Indi,
Totaque thuriferis Panchaïa pinguis arenis.
Hæc loca non tauri spirantes naribus ignem
Invertêre, satis immanis dentibus hydri;
Nec galeis, densisque virûm seges horruit hastis:

arboris jactu: et tamen illa gens quidem non est tarda pharetris sumtis. Media fert tristes succos tardumque saporem felicis mali: quo non ullum præsentius auxilium venit, ac agit atra venena membris, siquando sævæ novercæ infecere pocula, miscueruntque herbas, et non innoxia verba. Ipsa est ingens arbos, simillimaque lauro quoad *faciem: et, si non jactaret alium odorem latè, erat laurus. Folia haud* sunt *labentia ullis ventis:* ejus *flos* est *apprima tenax: Medi fovent animas et olentia ora, et medicantur anhelis senibus illo* flore. *Sed neque silvæ Medorum, ditissima terra, nec pulcher Ganges, atque Hermus turbidus auro certent laudibus Italiæ: non Bactra, neque Indi, totaque Panchaïa pinguis thuriferis arenis. Non tauri, spirantes ignem naribus, invertêre hæc loca, dentibus immanis hydri satis; nec seges virûm horruit galeis densisque hastis:*

TRANSLATION.

Where no Arrows by their Flight have been able to surmount the airy Summit of the Trees: And yet that Nation is not unskilful in Archery. Media bears the bitter Juices, and the permanent Relish of the happy Apple: Than which no Remedy comes more seasonable, and *more effectually* expels the black Venom from the Limbs, what Time cruel Stepmothers have poisoned a Cup, and mingled Herbs, and not innoxious Spells. The Tree itself is stately, and in Form most like a Bay: And, if it did not widely diffuse a different Scent, would be a Bay. Its Leaves fall not off by any Winds: Its Blossoms are exceedingly tenacious. With it the Medes correct their Breaths and unsavoury Mouths, and cure their asthmatic old Men.

But neither the Forests of Media, that richest Country, nor the beautiful Ganges, and Hermus, turbid with golden Sands, can match the Praises of Italy: Not Bactra, nor the Indians, and Panchaia, all enriched with Incense-bearing Soil. Bulls breathing Fire from their Nostrils never plowed these Regions, to be sown with a hideous Dragon's Teeth; nor did *ever* a Crop of Men shoot dreadful up

NOTES.

126. *Media fert tristes succos.* The Fruit here mentioned is certainly the Citron; for *Dioscorides* says expresly, that the Fruit, which the *Greeks* call *Medicum*, is in *Latin* called *Citrium.* Its Rhind is bitter and its Seeds covered with a bitter Skin; hence *tristes succos.* By its *tardum saporem* again is probably meant a Taste which dwells long upon the Palate.

127. *Felicis mali.* The Citron is probably called *happy* on account of its great Virtues.

137. *Auro turbidus Hermus.* Hermus is a River of *Lydia*; it receives the *Pactolus* famous for its golden Sands.

140. *Hæc loca.* Alluding to the Story of *Jason*, who went to *Colchis* for the golden Fleece; where he conquered the Bulls which breathed forth Fire from their Nostrils, &c.

ſed gravidæ fruges, et Maſſicus humor Bacchi implevere ea, oleæque lætaque armenta tenent ea. Hinc bellator equus, arduus, inſert ſeſe campo; hinc albi greges, et taurus, maxima victima, ſæpe perfuſi tuo ſacro flumine, ô Clitumne, duxere Romanos triumphos ad templa Deûm. Hic eſt *aſſiduum ver, atque æſtas* cum *alienis menſibus.* Hic *pecudes* ſunt *bis* anno *gravidæ, et arbos bis utilis pomis. At rabidæ tigres, et ſæva ſemina leonum abſunt; nec aconita fallunt miſeros legentes: nec ſquameus anguis rapit immenſos orbes per humum, neque colligit ſe in ſpiram tanto tractu,* quanto in quibuſdam aliis regionibus. *Adde tot egregias urbes, laboremque operum; tot oppida congeſta manu præruptis ſaxis; fluminaque labentia ſubter antiquos muros* urbium. *An memorem mare, quod* alluit Italiam *ſupra, quodque alluit* eam *infra?*

Sed gravidæ fruges, et Bacchi Maſſicus humor
Implevere, tenent oleæque, armentaque læta.
Hinc bellator equus campo ſeſe arduus inſert;
Hinc albi, Clitumne, greges, et maxima taurus
Victima, ſæpe tuo perfuſi flumine ſacro,
Romanos ad templa Deûm duxere triumphos.
Hic ver aſſiduum, atque alienis menſibus æſtas:
Bis gravidæ pecudes, bis pomis utilis arbos.
At rabidæ tigres abſunt, et ſæva leonum
Semina; nec miſeros fallunt aconita legentes:
Nec rapit immenſos orbes per humum, neque tanto
Squameus in ſpiram tractu ſe colligit anguis.
Adde tot egregias urbes, operumque laborem;
Tot congeſta manu præruptis oppida ſaxis;
Fluminaque antiquos ſubter labentia muros.
An mare quod ſupra, memorem, quodque alluit infra?

TRANSLATION.

with Helmets and crowded Spears: But teeming Corn and Bacchus's Campanian Juice have filled *the Land*, Olives and joyous Herds poſſeſs it. Hence the Warrior Horſe with ſtately Port advances into the Field; hence, Clitumnus, thy white Flocks, and the Bull, Chief of Victims, which, after they have been often plunged in thy ſacred Stream, accompany the Roman Triumphs to the Temples of the Gods. Here is perpetual Spring, and Summer in Months not her own: Twice *a Year* the Cattle are big with Young, twice the Trees productive of Fruit. But here are no ravening Tygers, nor the Savage Breed of Lions: nor *poiſonous* Wolfsbane deceives the wretched Gatherers: Nor *here* the ſcaly Serpent ſweeps his immenſe Orbs along the Ground, nor with ſo vaſt a Train collects himſelf in Spires. Add ſo many magnificent Cities, and Works of elaborate Art; ſo many Towns upreared with the Hand on craggy Rocks; and Rivers gliding under ancient Walls. Or need I mention the Sea which waſhes it above, and that

NOTES.

143. *Maſſicus humor.* Maſſicus is a Mountain of *Campania*, celebrated for Wine.

146. *Albi, Clitumne, greges.* The Banks of the *Clitumnus*, a River of *Italy*, in *Umbria*, were famous for feeding white Flocks, which *Pliny* makes to have been the Effect of the Water. But, whatever be in that, they were ſought for Sacrifice, the white Colour being thought more acceptable to the Gods. For which Reaſon the Victims were whitened with Chalk when the natural Colour could not be found, as in *Juvenal*, Sat X. 66.

Duc in Capitolia magnum Cretatumque bovem.

147. *Sacro.* Not only becauſe all Rivers were reputed ſacred, but becauſe Temples and Places of Worſhip were frequent on its Borders.

149. *Alienis menſibus*, i. e. In ſuch Months when other Countries do not feel the Warmth. Thus *Lucretius* uſes *alienis partibus anni* in much the ſame Senſe.

150. *Bis pomis utilis arbos.* Varro mentions an Apple-tree which bears twice, *Malus bifera, ut in agro Conſentino.*

152. *Nec miſeros fallunt*, &c. Servius, who alledges that the *Aconite* grew in *Italy*, takes the Meaning to be, that it deceives nobody, becauſe it is ſo well known. But this Senſe is ſo low, that one can hardly imagine *Virgil* capable of it; beſides, why ſhould the Gatherers,

Annc lacus tantos? te, Lari maxime; teque
Fluctibus et fremitu aſſurgens, Benace, marino?
An memorem portus, Lucrinoque addita clauſtra?
Atque indignatum magnis ſtridoribus æquor,
Julia quà ponto longè ſonat unda refuſo,
Tyrrhenuſque fretis immittitur æſtus Avernis?
Hæc eadem argenti rivos, æriſque metalla
Oſtendit venis, atque auro plurima fluxit.
Hæc genus acre virûm, Marſos, pubemque Sabellam,
Aſſuetumque malo Ligurem, Volſcoſque verutos
Extulit: hæc Decios, Marios, magnoſque Camillos,
Scipiadas duros bello, et te, maxime Cæſar;
Qui nunc extremis Aſiæ jam victor in oris,

anne memorem *tantos lacus? an te, maxime Lari; teque, Benace, aſſurgens fluctibus et marino fremitu? an memorem portus, clauſtraque addita* Lacui *Lucrino,* atque *æquor* circa illas, *indignatum magnis ſtridoribus, quâ* parte *Julia unda ſonat ponto longè refuſo, Tyrrhenuſque æſtus immittitur Avernis fretis? hæc eadem* Italia *oſtendit rivos argenti, metallaque æris* in *venis, atque fluxit plurima auro. Hæc* Italia *extulit acre genus virûm, Marſos, Sabellamque pubem, Ligurem que aſſuetum malo, Volſcoſque verutos: hæc* extulit *Decios, Marios, magnoſque Camillos, Scipiadas duros bello, et te, maxime Cæſar; qui jam nunc victor in extremis oris Aſiæ,*

TRANSLATION.

below? Or its Lakes ſo vaſt? Thee, Larius, of largeſt Extent, and thee, Benacus, ſwelling with the Waves and Roaring of a Sea? Or ſhall I mention its Ports, and the Moles raiſed to dam the Lucrine *Lake*, and the *impriſoned* Sea raging indignant with loud Murmurs, where the Julian Wave afar reſounds, the Sea being driven back, and *where* the Tuſcan Tide is let into the Streights of Avernus? This ſame Land hath in its Veins diſcloſed Rivers of Silver and Mines of Copper, and copious flowed with Gold. The ſame hath produced a warlike Race of Men, the Marſi, and the Sabellian Youth, and the Ligurian inured to Hardſhip, and the Volſcians armed with ſharp Darts: This ſame *produced* the Decii, the Marii, and the great Camilli, the Scipios invincible in War, and thee, moſt mighty Cæſar; who, at this very Time victorious in Aſia's remoteſt

NOTES.

ers be called *miſeri*, *miſerable*, if they all knew it ſo well as never to miſtake it? Therefore the Meaning muſt either be, that this Herb grows not at all, or but very rarely, in *Italy*. *Fallunt* has the Force of *interimunt*, becauſe poiſonous Herbs only deſtroy thoſe who are ignorant of their noxious Qualities. So Ecl. IV. 24. *Fallax herba veneni*.

159. *Lari.* The *Larius* is a great Lake at the Foot of the *Alps*, in the *Milaneſe*, now called *Lago di Coma*.

160. *Benace.* The *Benacus* is another great Lake in the *Veroneſe*, now called *Lago di Garda*; out of which flows the *Mincius*, on the Banks whereof *Virgil* was born.

161. *Lucrinoque addita clauſtra*, &c. Lucrinus and *Avernus* are two Lakes of *Campania*; *Auguſtus* made a Haven of them, to which he gave the Name of the *Julian Haven*. As in *Suetonius*: *Portum Julium apud Baias, immiſſo in Lucrinum et Avernum lacum mari, effecit.*

164. *Tyrrhenuſque fretis immittitur æſtus Avernis.* The Lake *Avernus*, *Strabo* tells us, lay near the *Lucrine* Bay, but more within Land. Hence it appears that a Canal was made between the two Lakes, which the Poet here calls the Streights of *Avernus*.

165. *Æris metalla.* Æs is commonly tranſlated *Braſs*, but Copper is the native Metal; Braſs being made of Copper melted with *Lapis Calaminaris*.

168. *Aſſuetumque malo.* Some explain it *accuſtomed to Deceit*. But it is not likely that the Poet would mention the Vices of the People, where he is celebrating the Praiſes of *Italy*. Therefore *malum* here muſt ſignify *Hardſhip* or *Labour*; which agrees with the character given of the *Ligurians* by *Dionyſius*, who ſays they lead a laborious Life, and live by the Chace.

169. *Marios.* Julius Cæſar was related to this Family by Marriage: So that the Poet makes a Compliment to *Auguſtus*, by celebrating the *Marian* Family.

171. *Qui nunc*, &c. I take the Meaning of this Paſſage to be, that the mere Fame of thy Victories hath ſo terrified the *Indians*, that they

avertis imbellem Indum Romanis arcibus. Salve, Saturnia tellus, magna parens frugum, magna parens virûm: tibi ingredior res antiquæ laudis et artis, ausus recludere sanctos fontes ejus; canoque Ascræum carmen per Romana oppida. Nunc est locus dicendis ingeniis arvorum; quæ robora sint *cuique, quis* sit *color, et quæ natura sit rebus ferendis. Primùm, difficiles terræ, malignique colles, ubi* est *tenuis argilla, et calculus dumosis arvis, gaudent Palladiâ silvâ vivacis olivæ. Plurimus oleaster, surgens eodem tractu, est indicio, et agri strati silvestribus baccis. At humus, quæ* est *pinguis, lætaque dulci uligine, campusque qui* est *frequens herbis, et fertilis ubere, qualem sæpe solemus despicere cavâ convalle montis; amnes liquuntur summis rupibus huc, trahuntque felicem limum: quique* campus est *editus Austro, et pascit invisam filicem curvis aratris;*

Imbellem avertis Romanis arcibus Indum.
Salve, magna parens frugum, Saturnia tellus,
Magna virûm: tibi res antiquæ laudis et artis
Ingredior; sanctos ausus recludere fontes;
Ascræumque cano Romana per oppida carmen.
  Nunc locus arvorum ingeniis; quæ robora cuique,
Quis color, et quæ sit rebus natura ferendis.
Difficiles primùm terræ, collesque maligni,
Tenuis ubi argilla, et dumosis calculus arvis,
Palladiâ gaudent silvâ vivacis olivæ.
Indicio est tractu surgens oleaster eodem
Plurimus, et strati baccis silvestribus agri.
At quæ pinguis humus, dulcique uligine læta,
Quique frequens herbis, et fertilis ubere campus,
Qualem sæpe cavâ montis convalle solemus
Despicere; huc summis liquuntur rupibus amnes,
Felicemque trahunt limum: quique editus Austro,
Et filicem curvis invisam pascit aratris;

TRANSLATION.

Limits, avertest from the Roman Towers the Indian peaceful and disarmed. Hail, Saturnian Land, great Parent of Fruits; great Parent of Heroes; for thee I enter on a Subject of ancient Renown and Art, adventuring to disclose the sacred Springs; and sing the Ascræan Strain through Roman Cities.

Now it is Time to describe the Geniuses of Soils; what Strength *and Energy* to each *belongs*, what Colour, and what its Nature is aptest to produce. First untractable Lands, and unfruitful Hills, where lean Clay *abounds*, and Pebbles in the bushy Fields, rejoice in Pallas's Wood of long-lived Olives. The wild Olive rising copious in the same Soil is an Indication, and the Fields strewed with Woodland Berries. But the Ground that is fat, and gladdened with sweet Moisture, and the Plain that is luxuriant in Grass, and of a fertile Soil, such as we are often wont to look down upon in the hollow Valley of a Mountain; hither Streams glide from the high Rocks, and draw a rich fattening Slime *along:* And that which is raised to the South, and nourishes the Fern abhorred by the crooked

NOTES.

dare not take up Arms against the *Romans*, but are fain to sue for Peace. Agreeably to what is reported both by *Suetonius* and *Diodorus Siculus*. So that *victor avertis* is, "*In Consequence of these thy victories thou deterrest.*"

176. *Ascræum carmen.* By *Ascræan* Verse he means that he follows *Hesiod*, who was of *Ascra* in *Bœtia*.

179. *Collesque maligni.* That are envious, as it were, illiberal, and yield but scanty increase.

119. *Filicem.* Masvicius has *silicem*, which Reading is not without Foundation; for *Columella* says Flints are beneficial to Vines. And Mr. *Millar*, the Author of *the Gardener's Dictionary*, observes, that the Land which abounds with Fern is always very poor and unfit for Vines: But the flinty Rocks which abound in *Chianti* are always preferred, and the Vines there produced are esteemed the best in *Italy*.

192. *Pa-*

Hic tibi prævalidas olim, multoque fluentes
Sufficiet Baccho vites: hic fertilis uvæ,
Hic laticis, qualem pateris libamus et auro,
Inflavit cum pinguis ebur Tyrrhenus ad aras,
Lancibus et pandis fumantia reddimus exta.
Sin armenta magis studium, vitulosque tueri,
Aut fetus ovium, aut urentes culta capellas;
Saltus, et saturi petito longinqua Tarenti;
Et qualem infelix amisit Mantua campum,
Pascentem niveos herboso flumine cycnos.
Non liquidi gregibus fontes, non gramina desunt:
Et quantum longis carpent armenta diebus,
Exiguâ tantum gelidus ros nocte reponet.
Nigra ferè, et presso pinguis sub vomere terra,
Et cui putre solum (namque hoc imitamur arando)
Optima frumentis. Non ullo ex æquore cernes
Plura domum tardis decedere plaustra juvencis:
Aut undè iratus silvam devexit arator,
Et nemora evertit multos ignava per annos,
Antiquasque domos avium cum stirpibus imis

hic campus *olim sufficiet tibi vites prævalidas, fluentesque multo Baccho: hic erit fertilis uvæ, hic erit fertilis laticis, qualem libamus pateris et auro, cum pinguis Tyrrhenus inflavit ebur ad aras, et reddimus* Diis *fumantia exta* victimarum *pandis lancibus. Sin* est *magis studium tueri armenta vitulosque, aut fetus ovium, aut capellas urentes culta* arbusta; *petito saltus, et longinqua* arva *saturi Tarenti; et* talem *campum qualem infelix Mantua amisit, pascentem niveos cycnos herboso flumine. Non liquidi fontes, non gramina desunt gregibus: et quantum* herbarum *armenta carpent longis diebus, gelidus ros reponet tantum exiguâ nocte. Terra ferè nigra, et pinguis sub presso vomere, et cui est putre solum (namque imitamur hoc arando)* est *optima frumentis. Non cernes plura plaustra,* tracta *à tardis juvencis, decedere domum ex ullo æquore. Aut* illa terra *undè iratus arator devexit silvam, et evertit ignava nemora per multos annos, eruitque antiquas domos avium cum imis stirpibus;*

TRANSLATION.

Ploughs; this in Time will afford thee Vines exceeding strong, and flowing with Plenty of generous Wine: This *will be* prolific of Grapes, this of such Liquor as we pour forth in Libation from golden Bowls, when the fat Tuscan has blown the Ivory Trumpet at the Altars, and we offer up the smoking Entrails in the bending Chargers.

But if you are studious to preserve Herds *of Kine* and Calves, or the Offspring of the Sheep, or Kids that kill the Nurseries; seek the Lawns and distant Fields of fruitful Tarentum; and Plains like those which hapless Mantua hath lost, feeding Snow-white Swans in the grassy Stream. *There* neither limpid Springs nor Pastures will be wanting to the Flocks: And as much as the Herds will crop in the long Days, so much will the cool Dews in *one* short Night restore.

A Soil that is blackish and fat under the deep piercing Share, and whose Mould is loose and crumbling (for this we imitate by ploughing) is generally best for Corn. From no Plain will you see more Waggons move homeward with slow *heavy-loaded* Oxen: Or *that* from which the angry Ploughman has bore away a Wood, and felled the Groves that have been at a Stand for many Years, and with their lowest Roots grubbed up the ancient Habitations of the Birds;

NOTES.

192. *Pateris et auro.* This the Commentators observe to be equivalent to *pateris aureis*, which is true as to the Sense. But we are to remember that *auro* is used for any Vase of Gold; as Æn. I. 743 —*pleno se proluit auro.*

193. *Pinguis Tyrrhenus.* The ancient *Tuscans* were famous for indulging their Appetites, which made them generally fat.

201. *Quantum longis,* &c. What the Poet here says of the prodigious Growth of the Grass in a Night's Time seems incredible; *yet Varro* informs that *Cæsar Vopiscus* affirmed, that, at *Rosea*, a Vine-pole, being fixed in the Ground, would be lost in the Grass the next Day.

211. *Eruit.*

illæ aves petiere altum aëra nidis relictis: at campus priùs rudis enituit vomere impulſo. Nam quidem jejuna glarea clivoſi ruris, et ſcaber tophus, et creta exeſa nigris chelydris, vix miniſtrat humiles caſias roremque apibus: negant alios agros ferre æquè dulcem cibum, et præbere curvas latebras ſerpentibus. Illa terra, *quæ exhalat tenuem nebulam, volucreſque fumos, et bibit humorem, et ipſa remittit eum ex ſe, cum vult; quæque ſemper veſtit ſe ſuo viridi gramine, nec lædit ferrum ſcabie et ſalſâ rubigine; illa,* inquam, *intexit ulmos tibi lætis vitibus; illa eſt ferax oleæ: experiere, colendo, illam* eſſe *et facilem pecori, et patientem unci vomeris. Dives Capua, et ora vicina jugo Veſevo, et* amnis *Clanius non æquus vacuis Acerris, arat talem* terram. *Nunc dicam, quo modo poſſis cognoſcere quamque* terram. Si *requiras* an *ſit rara, an ſit denſa ſupra morem;*

Eruit; illæ altum nidis petiere relictis:
At rudis enituit impulſo vomere campus.
Nam jejuna quidem clivoſi glarea ruris,
Vix humiles apibus caſias roremque miniſtrat:
Et tophus ſcaber, et nigris exeſa chelydris
Creta, negant alios æquè ſerpentibus agros
Dulcem ferre cibum, et curvas præbere latebras.
Quæ tenuem exhalat nebulam, fumoſque volucres,
Et bibit humorem, et, cum vult, ex ſe ipſa remittit;
Quæque ſuo viridi ſemper ſe gramine veſtit,
Nec ſcabie, et ſalſâ lædit rubigine ferrum;
Illa tibi lætis intexet vitibus ulmos;
Illa ferax oleæ eſt: illam experiere colendo,
Et facilem pecori, et patientem vomeris unci.
Talem dives arat Capua, et vicina Veſevo
Ora jugo; et vacuis Clanius non æquus Acerris.
Nunc, quo quamque modo poſſis cognoſcere, dicam.
Rara ſit, an ſupra morem ſit denſa, requiras;

TRANSLATION.

they abandoning their Neſts ſoar on high: But the Field looks gay as ſoon as the Share is driven into it. For lean hungry Gravel of a hilly Field ſcarce furniſhes humble Caſſia and Roſemary for the Bees: And the rough rotten Stone, and Chalk corroded by black Water Snakes, no other Lands, they ſay, yield ſo ſweet Food to Serpents, or afford them ſuch winding Coverts. That *Land* which exhales thin Miſts and flying Smoke, and drinks in the Moiſture, and emits it at Pleaſure; and which always clothes itſelf with its own verdant Graſs, nor hurts the Coulter with Scurf and ſalt Ruſt; that will entwine thy Elms with joyous Vines; that is fertile of Olives: That Ground you will experience in manuring both to be friendly to Cattle, and ſubmiſſive to the crooked Share. Such a Soil rich Capua tills, and the Territory adjoining to Mount Veſuvius, and the Clanius not kind to depopulated Acerræ.

Now will I tell by what Means you may diſtinguiſh each. If you deſire to know whether it be rare *and looſe*, or unuſually denſe *and ſtiff*; (becauſe the

NOTES.

211. *Enituit.* Signifies it looked *ſleek*, *ſmooth*, and *ſhining*, as, when new taken-in Ground, if it be of a rich Mould, it commonly does when firſt ploughed.

213. *Caſias.* Virgil, ſays Mr. *Martin*, mentions two Sorts of *Caſſia*; the one is an aromatic Bark, not much unlike Cinnamon, and is probably what we call *Caſſia Lignea.* Of this he ſpeaks, Verſe 466th of this Georgic.

Nec Caſia liquidi corrumpitur uſus olivi.

The other ſeems to be the Plant which bears the *Granum Gnidium*, called *Spurge flax*, or *Mountain-widow Waile*, and grows in rough Mountains in the warmer Climates.

214. *Tophus ſcaber.* This the ſame Author takes to be what we call *Rotten Stone. Pliny* ſays it is of a crumbling Nature. *Nam Tophus ſcaber natura friabilis expetitur quoque ab autoribus.*

225. *Vacuis Clanius non æquus Acerris.* Acerræ is the Name of a very ancient City of *Campania*, which was almoſt depopulated by the frequent Inundations of the River *Clanius.*

Altera frumentis quoniam favet, altera Baccho;
Densa magis Cereri, rarissima quæque Lyæo:
Antè locum capies oculis, altèque jubebis
In solido puteum demitti, omnemque repones
Rursus humum, et pedibus summas æquabis arenas.
Si deerunt; rarum, pecorique et vitibus almis
Aptius uber erit: sin in sua posse negabunt
Ire loca, et scrobibus superabit terra repletis,
Spissus ager; glebas cunctantes, crassaque terga
Exspecta, et validis terram proscinde juvencis.
  Salsa autem tellus, et quæ perhibetur amara,
Frugibus infelix, (ea nec mansuescit arando,
Nec Baccho genus, aut pomis sua nomina servat)
Tale dabit specimen. Tu spisso vimine qualos,
Colaque prælorum fumosis deripe tectis.
Hùc ager ille malus, dulcesque à fontibus undæ
Ad plenum calcentur: aqua eluctabitur omnis
Scilicet, et grandes ibunt per vimina guttæ.
At sapor indicium faciet manifestus, et ora
Tristia tentantum sensu torquebit amaror.

quoniam altera favet frumentis, altera favet Baccho; densa magis favet Cereri, quæque rarissima magis favet *Lyæo: antè, capies locum oculis, jubebisque puteum demitti altè in solido loco, rursusque repones omnem humum, et æquabis summas arenas pedibus. Si deerunt* ad replendum locum; *uber erit rarum, aptiusque pecori et almis vitibus: sin negabunt* se *posse ire in sua loca, et terra superabit, scrobibus repletis, ager* est *spissus; exspecta cunctantes glebas, crassaque terga, et proscinde terram validis juvencis. Autem salsa tellus, et quæ perhibetur amara,* est *infelix frugibus, (ea nec mansuescit arando, nec servat* suum *genus Baccho, aut sua nomina pomis) dabit tale specimen* sui. *Tu deripe qualos spisso vimine, colaque prælorum fumosis tectis. Ille malus ager, dulcesque undæ* haustæ *à fontibus calcentur huc ad plenum: scilicet omnis aqua eluctabitur, et grandes guttæ ibunt per vimina. At manifestus sapor faciet indicium, et amaror torquebit tristia ora tentantium sensu.*

TRANSLATION.

one is fit for Corn, the other for Wine; the stiff for Ceres best, and the most loose for Bacchus:) First you shall mark out a Place with your Eye, and order a Pit to be sunk deep in solid Ground, and again return all the Mould into its Place, and level with your Feet the Sands at Top. If they prove deficient, the Soil is loose, and more fit for Cattle and bounteous Wines: But if they deny the Possibility of returning to their Places, and there be an Overplus of Mould after the Pit is filled up, then it is a dense Soil; expect reluctant Clods, and stiff *tenacious* Ridges, and tear up the Land with sturdy Bullocks.

But saltish Ground, and what is accounted bitter, where Corn can never thrive (it neither mellows by ploughing, nor preserves to Grapes their Kind, nor to Fruits their Qualities) will give an experimental Proof to this Effect. Snatch from the smoky Roofs' Baskets of close-woven Twigs, and the Strainers of thy Wine-Presses. Hither let some of that vicious Mould, and sweet Water from the Spring be pressed Brim full: Be sure all the Water will strain out, and big Drops pass through the Twigs. But the Taste will clearly make Discovery, and its Bitterness will distort the Countenances of the Tasters, offended with the Sensation.

NOTES.

233. *Almis.* Vines are called *almæ* in the same sense as *Ceres, the Earth*, &c. from *alo*, because they invigorate and give Nourishment.

237. *Validis terram proscinde juvencis.* He mentions the Strength of the Bullocks, to signify that this Soil must be plowed deep.

240. *Sua nomina.* Nomen, when applied to Wines and Fruits, signifies their Qualities: Thus *Cato* says, *Ne vinum* nomen *perdat.*

Item discimus denique hoc pacto, quæ tellus sit pinguis: ea jactata manibus haud unquam fatiscit, sed lentescit ad digitos habendo eam, in morem picis. Humida tellus alit majores herbas, ipsaque est lætior justo. Ah, ne illa sit nimium fertilis mihi, neu ostendat se prævalidam primis aristis! quæ terra est gravis, prodit se tacitam pondere ipso; quæque est levis prodit se. Est promtum prædiscere nigram oculis, et quis color sit cuique. At est difficile exquirere sceleratum frigus: tantùm piceæ, nocentesque taxi interdum, aut nigræ ederæ pandunt vestigia. His animadversis, memento excoquere terram multò antè, et circundare magnos montes scrobibus: ostendere supinatas glebas Aquiloni ante quàm infodias lætum genus vitis. Sunt putri solo optima arva: venti, gelidæque pruinæ, et robustus fossor, movens labefacta jugera, curant id.

Pinguis item quæ sit tellus, hoc denique pacto
Discimus: haud unquam manibus jactata fatiscit.
Sed picis in morem ad digitos lentescit habendo.
Humida majores herbas alit, ipsaque justo
Lætior. Ah, nimiùm ne sit mihi fertilis illa,
Neu se prævalidam primis ostendat aristis!
  Quæ gravis est, ipso tacitam se pondere prodit;
Quæque levis. Promtum est oculis prædiscere nigram,
Et quis cui color. At sceleratum exquirere frigus
Difficile est: piceæ tantùm, taxique nocentes
Interdum, aut ederæ pandunt vestigia nigræ.
  His animadversis, terram multò antè memento
Excoquere, et magnos scrobibus circundare montes:
Ante supinatas Aquiloni ostendere glebas,
Quàm lætum infodias vitis genus. Optima putri
Arva solo: id venti curant, gelidæque pruinæ,
Et labefacta movens robustus jugera fossor.

TRANSLATION.

Again, what Land is fat, we briefly learn thus: When squeezed by the Hand it never crumbles, but in handling, it sticks to the Fingers like Pitch. The moist Soil produces Herbs of a larger Size, and is itself luxuriant beyond due Measure. Ah, may none of mine be *thus* too fertile, nor shew itself too strong at the first Springing of the Grain!

The heavy *Land* betrays itself by its very Weight, without my telling you; and *likewise* the light. 'Tis obvious to distinguish the black at first Sight, and whatever is the Colour *of each.* But to search out the mischievous Cold is no easy Task: Only Pitch-Trees, and sometimes noxious Yews, or black Ivy, disclose its Signs.

These Rules observed, remember to dry and bake the Soil long before, to encompass the spacious Hills with Trenches, *and* expose the turned-up Clods to the North Wind, before you plant the Vine's joyous Race. Fields of a loose crumbling Soil are best: This Effect the Winds and cold Frosts produce, and the sturdy Delver, close plying his Acres, tossed and turned upside down.

NOTES.

254. *Tacitam.* Without my telling you. In the same Sense the Word occurs. *Æn.* VI. 841.

255. *Oculis prædiscere.* To distinguish it at first Sight, or to learn it by the Eye previously to all Trial.

257. *Taxique nocentes.* The Berries of the Yew are said by *Pliny* and other Authors to be poisonous. The Leaves also are found to be destructive to Horses.

260. *Circundare.* This *Pierius* assures us to be the Reading of the *Roman* Manuscript, which seems preferable to *concidere* in the common Editions.

268. *Semina.*

At si quos haud ulla viros vigilantia fugit;
Antè locum similem exquirunt, ubi prima paretur
Arboribus seges, ex quò mox digesta feratur;
Mutatam ignorent subitò ne semina matrem.
Quin etiam cœli regionem in cortice signant:
Ut, quo quæque modo steterit, quà parte calores
Austrinos tulerit, quâ terga obverterit axi,
Restituant. Adeò in teneris consuescere multum est.
Collibus, an plano melius sit ponere vitem,
Quære priùs. Si pinguis agros metabere campi,
Densa sere; in denso non segnior ubere Bacchus:
Sin tumulis acclive solum, collesque supinos;
Indulge ordinibus: nec seciùs omnis in unguem
Arboribus positis secto via limite quadret.
Ut sæpe ingenti bello cum longa cohortes
Explicuit legio, et campo stetit agmen aperto,
Directæque acies, latè fluctuat omnis

At si haud ulla vigilantia fugit quos viros; hi antè exquirunt similem locum, unum ubi prima seges paretur arboribus, et alterum quo mox ea digesta per ordines feratur: ne semina ignorent matrem subitò mutatam. Quin etiam signant regionem cœli in cortice: ut restituant unamquamque arborem eo modo quo quæque steterit, eâ parte quâ quæque tulerit Austrinos calores, qua obverterit terga axi. Est adeò multum consuescere in teneris annis. Quære priùs, an sit melius ponere vites collibus, an plano. Si metabere agros pinguis campi, sere vites densa: Bacchus non est segnior denso ubere. Sin eligis solum acclive tumulis, supinosque colles; indulge ordinibus: nec seciùs omnis via quadret secto limite arboribus positis in unguem. Ut sæpe ingenti bello, cum longa legio explicuit cohortes, et agmen stetit aperto campo, aciesque sunt directæ, ac omnis tellus fluctuat latè

TRANSLATION.

But those, whom not any Vigilance escapes, first seek out a Piece of Ground similar *to that whence the Plants are taken,* where the first Nursery may be provided for their Trees, and whither it may soon be transplanted in Rows; lest the Slips take not kindly to this *new* Mother that is suddenly changed upon them. Nay, they even mark on the Bark the Quarter of the Sky, that in whatever Manner each stood, in what Part it bore the Southern Heats, what Sides it turned to the *Northern* Pole, they may restore *to it the same Position.* Of such Avail is Custom in tender Years.

Examine first whether it is better to plant your Vines on Hills or on a Plain? If you lay out the Fields of a rich Plain, plant thick; Bacchus will not be the more backward to grow in *such* a Soil *when* planted thick: But if *you lay out* a Soil rising with a gentle Ascent, and sloping Hills; give room to your Ranks: Yet so as that, your Trees being exactly ranged, each Space may square with the Path cut *across it.* As often in dreadful War, when the extended Legion hath ranged its Cohorts, the Battalions stand marshalled on the open Plain, the Armies set in Array, and the whole Ground wide waves with gleaming Brass,

NOTES.

268. *Semina.* In this Place signifies *young Plants,* as also Verse 301.

——————Neu ferro læde retuso
Semina.

In the same Sense it is often used by *Pliny, Columella,* &c.

275. *Denso.* Denso here seems to be the same as *denso consito.* Mr. *Martin* construes *ubere* with *segnior,* taking *ubere* for Fertility, and makes *denso* the same as *in denso, ordine* being understood. Others follow *Ruæus,* who takes *ubere* for *agro,* as it seems to be, *Æn.* III.

———Quæ vos à stirpe parentum
Prima tulit tellus, eadem vos ubere læto
Accipiet reduces. And above, Verse 234.

277. *Nec seciùs omnis,* &c. The Order of the Words seems to be thus: *Nec seciùs omnis via quadret secto limite, arboribus positis in unguem:* "And no less let every Path, or Space, square with the cross Path, the Trees being planted exactly." *Martin.* Where *via* signifies *the*

renidenti ære, nec dum mifcent horrida prœlia, fed dubius Mars errat in mediis armis. Sic omnia intervalla *viarum fint dimenfa paribus numeris; non modò uti profpectus pafcat inanem animum; fed quia non aliter terra dabit æquas vires omnibus, neque rami poterunt extendere fe in vacuum* aëra. *Forfitan et quæras quæ faftigia fint fcrobibus. Aufim committere vitem vel tenui fulco. Arbos defigitur altiùs ac penitùs terræ; in primis Efculus: quæ quantum* tendit *vertice ad æthereas auras, tantum tendit radice in Tartara. Ergo non hiemes, non flabra, neque imbres convellunt illam: manet immota, perque multos annos volvens multa fecula virûm durando vincit* ætatem eorum. *Tum latè tendens fortes ramos et brachia huc illuc, ipfe media fuftinet ingentem umbram. Neve vineta vergant tibi ad cadentem folem; neve fere corylum inter vites: neve*

Ære renidenti tellus, nec dum horrida mifcent
Prœlia, fed dubius mediis Mars errat in armis:
Omnia fint paribus numeris dimenfa viarum;
Non animum modò utì pafcat profpectus inanem;
Sed quia non aliter vires dabit omnibus æquas
Terra; neque in vacuum poterunt fe extendere
rami.
Forfitan et fcrobibus quæ fint faftigia quæras.
Aufim vel tenui vitem committere fulco.
Altiùs, ac penitùs terræ defigitur arbos;
Efculus in primis: quæ quantum vertice ad auras
Æthereas, tantum radice in Tartara tendit.
Ergo non hiemes illam, non flabra, neque imbres
Convellunt: immota manet, multofque per annos
Multa virûm volvens durando fecula vincit.
Tum fortes latè ramos et brachia tendens
Huc illuc, media ipfa ingentem fuftinet umbram.
Neve tibi ad folem vergant vineta cadentem;
Neve inter vites corylum fere: neve flagella

TRANSLATION.

nor as yet are they engaged in horrid Battle, but Mars hovers dubious in the Midft of Arms: Thus let all your Vineyards be laid out in equal Proportions; not only that the Profpect may feed the Mind with vain Delight; but becaufe the Earth will not otherwife fupply equal Strength to all; nor will the Branches be able to extend themfelves at large.

Perhaps too you may demand what Depth is proper for the Trenches. I could venture to commit my Vine even to a flight Furrow. Trees again are funk deeper down, and far into the Ground; efpecially the Efculus, which fhoots downward to Hell with its Roots, as far as *it rifes* with its Top to the ethereal Regions. Therefore not wintery Storms, nor Blafts of Wind, nor Showers, can overthrow it: It remains unmoved, and, rolling many Ages of Men away, outlafts them for many Years. Then ftretching wide its fturdy Boughs and Arms this Way and that Way, itfelf in the Midft fuftains a mighty Shade.

Nor let thy Vineyards lie towards the fetting Sun; nor plant the Hazle among your Vines; Nor gather your Cuttings from the Top of the Tree, *but*

NOTES.

Spaces between the Rows; *limes* again *the Crofs-path*, which in the fquare Figure cuts the other at right Angles.

284. *Numeris.* Signifies *Harmony, Order, Proportion.*

285. *Inanem.* i. e. *Without reaping any other Advantage thence but the bare pleafing of the Eye.*

290. *Altiùs, ac penitùs terræ defigitur arbos.* I take the conftruction to be, *arbos defigitur altiùs, ac penitùs terræ*, not *ac arbos defigitur. Virgil* here makes a Diftinction between *vitis* and *arbos*; for Vines were not accounted Trees, but Shrubs, or fomething of a middle Nature between both. Thus *Columella*: *Nam ex furculo vel arbos procedit, ut olea; vel frutex, ut palma campeftris: vel* tertium quiddam, *quod nec* arborem, *nec fruticem propriè dixerim, ut eft* vitis.

300. *Flagella*

Summa pete, aut summas defringe ex arbore plantas:
(Tantus amor terræ) neu ferro læde retuso
Semina: neve oleæ silvestres insere truncos.
Nam sæpe incautis pastoribus excidit ignis,
Qui furtim pingui primùm sub cortice tectus,
Robora comprendit, frondesque elapsus in altas,
Ingentem cœlo sonitum dedit; inde secutus
Per ramos victor, perque alta cacumina regnat,
Et totum involvit flammis nemus, et ruit atram
Ad cœlum piceâ crassas caligine nubem: —
Præsertim si tempestas à vertice silvis
Incubuit, glomeratque ferens incendia ventus.
Hoc ubi; non à stirpe valent, cæsæque reverti
Possunt, atque imâ similes revirescere terrâ:
Infelix superat foliis oleaster amaris.
Nec tibi tam prudens quisquam persuadeat auctor,
Tellurem Boreâ rigidam spirante movere.

pete summa flagella, aut defringe summas plantas ex arbore (est illis tantus amor terræ) neu læde semina retuso ferro: neve insere silvestres truncos oleæ. Nam sæpe ignis excidit incautis pastoribus, qui ignis, primùm tectus sub pingui cortice, comprendit robora, elapsusque in altas frondes, dedit ingentem sonitum cœlo: inde secutus, victor regnat per ramos, perque alta cacumina, et involvit totum nemus flammis, et crassius piceâ caligine ruit atram nubem ad cœlum: præsertim si tempestas incubuit silvis à vertice, ventusque glomerat incendia ferens ea. *Ubi hoc* contigerit, vites *non valent reverti à stirpe, cæsæque, possunt reverti, atque revirescere similes imâ terrâ: infelix oleaster amaris foliis so*lus *superat. Nec quisquam, tam prudens, auctor persuadeat tibi movere terram Boreâ spirante.*

TRANSLATION.

those that are near the Roots, which will thrive best, having already contracted a Fondness for the Earth; so much Love to the Earth avails. Nor hurt your Shoots with blunted Steel: Nor plant among them the Truncheons of the wild Olive. For Fire is often let fall from the unwary Shepherds, which at first secretly lurking under the unctuous Bark catches the solid Wood, and, shooting up into the topmost Leaves, raises a loud Crackling to Heaven: thence pursuing its Way, reigns victorious among the Branches and the lofty Tops, involves the whole Grove in Flames, and, condensed in pitchy Vapour, darts the black Cloud to Heaven; chiefly if a Storm over Head rests its Fury on the Woods, and the driving Wind whirls the Flames *aloft*. When this *happens*, their Strength decays from the Root, nor can they recover, *tho'* cut, or sprout up from the deep Earth such as they were: The unblest wild Olive with its bitter Leaves, *alone* survives *the Disaster*.

Let no Counsellor be so wise in your Eyes to persuade you to stir the rigid Earth when Boreas breathes. Then Winter shuts up the Fields with Frost;

NOTES.

300. *Flagella summa pete.* Columella uses the same Word *flagella* for Shoots. The *summa flagella* Mr. *Martin* takes to be, not the topmost Shoots, as it is commonly understood, but the upper Part of the Shoot, which expert Gardeners advise to cut off, because the upper Parts of the Shoot are never so well ripened as the lower Parts.

310. *A vertice.* From on high, as the Southwind is mentioned to come *ab alto*, as Geor. I. 443.

——————*Namque urget ab alto*
Arboribusque satisque Notus, pecorique sinister.

312. *Hoc ubi; non. &c.* Others point it thus, *hoc ubi non*; when this is not the Case, these wild Olives, mentioned before, are vigorous at the Root, and are able to recover themselves, tho' cut, and will sprout up such as they were.

320. Candida

Tum hiems claudit rura gelu, nec, ſemine jacto, patitur affigere concretam radicem terræ. Satio eſt optima vinetis, cum, rubenti vere, candida avis, Ciconia, inviſa longis colubris venit: vel ſub prima frigora autumni, cum rapidus ſol nondum contingit hiemem equis, ſed jam æſtas præterit. Ver eſt adeò utile *frondi nemorum,* ver adeò *utile ſilvis: vere terræ tument, et poſcunt genitalia ſemina. Tum omnipotens pater, Æther, deſcendit in gremium terræ lætæ conjugis fecundis imbribus,* et ipſe *magnus, commiſtus magno corpore* terræ, *alit omnes fetus. Tum avia virgulta reſonant canoris avibus: et armenta repetunt Venerem certis diebus. Almus ager parturit, arvaque laxant ſinus tepentibus auris Zephyri: tener humor ſuperat omnibus* agris: *graminaque audent credere ſe tutò in novos ſoles: nec pampinus metuit ſurgentes Auſtros, aut imbrem actum è cœlo magnis Aquilonibus: ſed trudit gemmas, et explicat omnes frondes.*

Rura gelu tum claudit hiems; nec ſemine jacto
Concretam patitur radicem affigere terræ.
Optima vinetis ſatio, cum vere rubenti
Candida venit avis longis inviſa colubris:
Prima vel autumni ſub frigora, cum rapidus Sol
Nondum hiemem contingit equis, jam præterit æſtas.
Ver adeò frondi nemorum, ver utile ſilvis:
Vere tument terræ, et genitalia ſemina poſcunt.
Tum pater omnipotens fecundis imbribus Æther
Conjugis in gremium lætæ deſcendit, et omnes
Magnus alit, magno commiſtus corpore, fetus.
Avia tum reſonant avibus virgulta canoris:
Et Venerem certis repetunt armenta diebus.
Parturit almus ager, Zephyrique tepentibus auris
Laxant arva ſinus: ſuperat tener omnibus humor:
Inque novos ſoles audent ſe gramina tutò
Credere: nec metuit ſurgentes pampinus Auſtros,
Aut actum cœlo magnis Aquilonibus imbrem:
Seu trudit gemmas, et frondes explicat omnes.

TRANSLATION.

nor, when the Slip is planted, ſuffers the frozen Root to faſten to the Earth. The Plantation of the Vineyards is beſt, when in the bluſhing Spring the white Bird comes in, which the long Snakes abhor: Or towards the firſt Colds of Autumn, when the vehement Sun does not yet touch the Winter with his Steeds, the Summer is juſt gone. The Spring is chiefly beneficial to the Foliation of the Groves, the Spring is beneficial to the Woods: In Spring the Lands ſwell, and demand the genial Seeds. Then Almighty Father Æther deſcends in fructifying Showers into the Boſom of his joyous Spouſe, and great himſelf, mingling with her great Body, nouriſhes all her Offspring. Then the retired Brakes reſound with tuneful Birds: And the Herds renew their Loves on the ſtated Days. *Then* beauteous Earth is teeming to the Birth, and the Fields open their Boſoms to the warm Breezes of the Zephyr: In all a gentle Moiſture abounds: And the Herbs dare ſafely truſt themſelves to the Infant Suns: Nor are the Vine's tender Shoots afraid of the riſing South Winds, or of a Shower precipitated from the Sky by the violent North Winds: But put forth their Buds, and unfold all their

NOTES.

320. *Candida avis.* The Stork, which is a Bird of Paſſage, and in ſuch Eſteem, *Pliny* tells us, for deſtroying Serpents, that in *Theſſaly* it was a capital Crime to kill them.

325. *Tum pater omnipotens.* The Æther or Sky, which in the Heathen Mythology is the ſame with *Jupiter,* or *the Almighty Father.* Thus *Lucretius:*

Poſtremo pereunt imbres, ubi eos pater Æther
In gremium matris Terrai præcipitavit.

332. *Audent,* &c. i. e. *When they are ſtrong enough to ſuſtain the firſt Heats of the Sun.*

342. *Immiſſæ-*

Non alios primâ crescentis origine mundi
Illuxisse dies, aliumve habuisse tenorem
Crediderim; ver illud erat: ver magnus agebat
Orbis, et hibernis parcebant flatibus Euri:
Cum primùm lucem pecudes hausere, virûmque
Ferrea progenies duris caput extulit arvis,
Immissæque feræ silvis, et sidera cœlo.
Nec res hunc teneræ possent perferre laborem,
Si non tanta quies iret frigusque caloremque
Inter, et exciperet cœli indulgentia terras.
Quod superest, quæcunque premes virgulta per agros,
Sparge fimo pingui, et multâ memor occule terrâ:
Aut lapidem bibulum, aut squalentes infode conchas.
Inter enim labentur aquæ, tenuisque subibit
Halitus, atque animos tollent sata. Jamque reperti,
Qui saxo super, atque ingentis pondere testæ
Urgerent: hoc, effusos munimen ad imbres:
Hoc, ubi hiulca siti findit Canis æstifer arva.
Seminibus positis, superest deducere terram
Sæpius ad capita, et duros jactare bidentes:

Crediderim non alios dies illuxisse primâ origine crescentis mundi, habuisseve alium tenorem; illud tempus erat ver: magnus orbis agebat ver, et Euri parcebant hibernis flatibus: cum primùm pecudes hausere lucem, ferreaque progenies virûm extulit caput duris arvis, feræque fuerunt immissæ silvis, et sidera cœlo. Nec teneræ res possent ferre hunc laborem, si tanta quies non iret inter frigusque caloremque, et indulgentia cœli exciperet terras. Quod superest, quæcunque virgulta premes per agros, memor sparge ea pingui fimo, et occule ea multâ terrâ: aut infode bibulum lapidem, aut squalentes conchas circa ea. Enim inter ea aquæ labentur, tenuisque halitus subibit, atque sata tollent animos. Jamque sunt reperti, qui urgerent ea super saxo atque pondere ingentis testæ: hoc est munimen ad effusos imbres: hoc est munimen, ubi æstifer Canis findit hiulca arva siti. Seminibus positis, superest deducere terram sæpius ad capita, et jactare duros ferreos bidentes:

TRANSLATION.

Leaves. No other Days, methinks, had shone at the first Origin of the rising World; it was *reigning* Spring; the spacious Globe enjoyed Spring, and the East Winds withheld their wintery Blasts: When first the Cattle drew in the Light, and Man's laborious Race upreared their Heads from the hard Glebe, and the Woods were stocked with wild Beasts, and the Heavens with Stars. Nor could the tender Productions *of Nature* bear this Labour, if so great Rest did not intervene between the Cold and Heat, and if Heaven's indulgent Season did not visit the Earth in its Turn.

For what remains, whatever Layers you bend down over all the Fields, overspread them with fat Dung, and carefully cover them with copious Earth: Or bury about them spungy Stones, or rough Shells. For *thus* the Rains will soak through, the subtile Vapour penetrate *into their Pores*, and the Plants become stout and vigorous. We find some too who are for pressing them from above with a Stone, and the Weight of a great Potsherd: This is a Defence against the pouring Rains: This *a Defence* when the sultry Dog-Star cleaves the gaping Fields with Drought.

After your Layers are planted, it remains to convey Earth often to the Roots, and ply the hard Drags: Or to labour the Soil under the impressed Share, and

NOTES.

342. *Immissæque feræ silvis, et sidera cœlo.* Literally, *And the wild Beasts were sent into the Woods, and Stars into the Heavens.*

355. *Capita.* Caput vitis, or arboris, signifies always *the Top*; but, as the Poet is here speaking of Layers, *caput* by consequence signifies *the Root*, since the Shoots are planted with their Heads downward.

361. Ta-

aut exercere solum sub presso vomere, et flectere luctantes juvencos inter vineta ipsa: tum aptare viti lêves calamos, et hastilia rasæ virgæ, fraxineasque sudes, bicornesque furcas; viribus quarum assuescant eniti, et contemnere ventos, sequique tabulata per summas ulmos. Ac est parcendum teneris vitibus, dum prima ætas earum adolescit novis frondibus: et, dum lætus palmes agit se ad auras, immissus per purum aëra laxis habenis, acies ipsa falcis nondum est tentanda; sed frondes sunt carpendæ, interlegendæque uncis manibus. Inde ubi jam vites, amplexæ ulmos validis stirpibus, exierint, tum stringe comas, tum tonde brachia earum; antè reformidant ferrum: tum denique exerce dura imperia, et compesce fluentes ramos. Etiam sepes sunt texendæ, et omne pecus est tenendum à vitibus: præcipuè dum frons est tenera, imprudensque laborum; cui frondi, super indignas hiemes, potentemque solem,

Aut presso exercere solum sub vomere, et ipsa
Flectere luctantes inter vineta juvencos:
Tum lêves calamos, et rasæ hastilia virgæ,
Fraxineasque aptare sudes, furcasque bicornes;
Viribus eniti quarum, et contemnere ventos
Assuescant, summasque sequi tabulata per ulmos.
Ac, dum prima novis adolescit frondibus ætas,
Parcendum teneris: et, dum se lætus ad auras
Palmes agit laxis per purum immissus habenis
Ipsa acies falcis nondum tentanda; sed uncis
Carpendæ manibus frondes, interque legendæ.
Inde ubi jam validis amplexæ stirpibus ulmos
Exierint, tum stringe comas, tum brachia tonde;
Antè reformidant ferrum: tum denique dura
Exerce imperia, et ramos compesce fluentes.
Texendæ sepes etiam, et pecus omne tenendum;
Præcipuè dum frons tenera, imprudensque laborum;
Cui, super indignas hiemes, solemque potentem,

TRANSLATION.

guide your struggling Bullocks through the very Vineyards: Then to adapt *to the Vines* smooth Reeds, and Spears of peeled Rods, and ashen Stakes, and two-horned Forks: By whose Strength they may learn to shoot up, to contemn the Winds, and climb from Stage to Stage along the highest Elms.

And, while their Infant-Age sprouts with new-born Leaves, you must spare the tender Vines: And while the joyous Shout raises itself on high, wantoning through the open Air with loose Reins, the Edge of the Pruning-Knife itself must not be applied; but the Leaves should be plucked with the in-bent Hand, and culled here and there. Thereafter when now they have shot forth, embracing the Elms with firm Stems, then cut their Locks, then lop their Arms. Before this they dread the Steel: Then, and not till then, exercise severe Dominion *over them*, and check the loose straggling Boughs.

Fences too should be woven *around them*, and all Cattle must be restrained; especially while the Shoots are tender and unacquainted with Hardships; which, besides the rigorous Winters, and vehement *Heat of the* Sun, the wild Buffaloes

NOTES.

361. *Tabulata.* The *tabulata* are the Branches of Elms extended at proper Distances, to sustain the Vine. Thus *Columella: Cum deinde adolescere incipient, falce formandæ, et* tabulata *instituenda sunt: hoc enim nomine usurpant agricolæ ramos truncosque prominentes, eosque vel propius ferro compescunt, vel longius promittunt, ut vites laxius diffundantur, &c.*

364. *Laxis per purum immissus habenis.* This is a Metaphor taken from Horses, in Imitation of *Lucretius:*

Arboribus datum'st variis exinde per auras
Crescendi magnum immissis certamen habenis.

Per purum in *Virgil* signifies the same as *per auras* in *Lucretius.* *Horace* uses it also for the Air:

————————*Per* purum *tonantes*
Egit equos.

374. *Sil-*

Silvestres uri assiduè, capreæque sequaces
Illudunt; pascuntur oves, avidæque juvencæ.
Frigora nec tantum canâ concreta pruinâ,
Aut gravis incumbens scopulis arentibus æstas;
Quantum illi nocuere greges, durique venenum
Dentis, et admorso signata in stirpe cicatrix.
Non aliam ob culpam Baccho caper omnibus aris
Cæditur, et veteres ineunt proscenia ludi:
Præmiaque ingeniis pagos, et compita circum,
Theseidæ posuere; atque inter pocula læti
Mollibus in pratis unctos saliere per utres.

silvestres uri, sequacesque capreæ assiduè illudunt; oves, avidæque juvencæ pascuntur frondibus vitium. *Nec frigora concreta canâ pruinâ, aut gravis æstas incumbens arentibus scopulis nocent* vitibus *tantum, quantum illi greges, venenumque duri dentis et cicatrix signata in admorso stirpe nocuere. Ob non aliam culpam caper cæditur Baccho omnibus ari, et veteres ludi ineunt proscenia: Theseidæque posuere præmia ingeniis circum pagos et compita: atque inter pocula læti saliere per unctos utres in mollibus pratis.*

TRANSLATION.

and persecuting Goats continually insult; the Sheep and greedy Heifers browze upon them. Nor do the Colds condensed in hoary Frost, or the severe Heat beating upon the scorched Rocks, hurt them so much as the Flocks and Poison of their hard Teeth, and a Scar imprinted on the gnawed Stem.

For no other Crime is the Goat sacrificed to Bacchus on every Altar, and the ancient Plays come upon the Stage: And *for this* the Athenians proposed to the *tragic* Wits Prizes *of Goats* about the Villages and Crossways; and amidst their Cups full joyous danced in the soft Meadows on *Goat-Skin* Bottles be-

NOTES.

374 *Silvestres uri.* The *urus*, as described by *Cæsar*, is a wild Bull of prodigious Strength and Swiftness, being almost as big as an Elephant: But this cannot be the *urus* mentioned by *Virgil*, being an Animal utterly unknown in *Italy*. It is more probably what is now called the *Buffalo*.

377. *Aut gravis incumbens scopulis arentibus æstas.* The Meaning seems to be, That Vineyards planted on a rocky Soil, which therefore suffer most in dry Weather, are not so much injured by the most scorching Heat, as by the Biting of Cattle.

381. *Proscenia.* In the *Roman* Theatre there was first the *Porticus* or Gallery for the Populace, where the Seats were formed like Wedges, growing narrower as they came nearer the Centre of the Theatre, and therefore called *cunei*, or *Wedges*. 2. The *Orchestra*, in the Centre and lowest Part of the Theatre, where the Senators and Knights sat, and where the Dancers and Musicians performed. 3. The *Proscenium*, or Space before the Scenes, which was raised above the *Orchestra*, and where the Actors spoke.

382. *Ingeniis.* The usual Reading is *ingentes*, which is a very useless Epithet in this Place. But *Pierius* found *ingeniis* in all the most ancient Manuscripts. The Poets here alludes to the ancient Custom, amongst the *Greeks*, of proposing a Goat for a Prize to him who should be judged to excel in satirical Verse. Thus *Horace:*

Carmine qui tragico vilem certavit ob hircum.

There is a Line in *Horace* not much unlike this of *Virgil:*

"*Quis circum pagos, et circum compita pugnax,*
Magna coronari contemnat Olympia."———

383. *Theseidæ.* The *Athenians*, so called from *Theseus* their King, who first civilized and taught them to live in Cities. Tragedy had its Beginning among the *Athenians*. *Thespis*, an *Athenian* Poet, is said to have invented it, as we find in *Horace*,

Ignotum tragicæ genus invenisse Camænæ
Dicitur, et plaustris vexisse poëmata Thespis;
Quæ canerent agerentque peruncti fæcibus ora.

384. *Unctos saliere per utres.* The *utres* were Bags made of Goats Skins. These Skins were blown up like Bladders, and besmeared with Oil. They were set in the Fields, and it was the Custom to dance upon them with one Leg at the Feasts of *Bacchus:* The Skins being very slippery, the Dancers often fell down, which occasioned a great Laughter.

Nec non Ausonii coloni, gens missa Trojâ, ludunt incomtis versibus, solutoque risu; sumuntque horrenda ora cavatis corticibus. Et vocant te, Bacche, per læta carmina, suspenduntque mollia oscilla ex altâ pinu. Hinc omnis vinea pubescit largo fetu: cavæque valles, profundique saltus complentur, et quocumque Deus Bacchus *circumegit honestum caput. Ergo ritè dicemus suum honorem Baccho patriis carminibus, feremusque lances et liba* illi: *et hircus, sacer* illi, *ductus cornu, stabit ad aram; torrebimusque* ejus *pinguia exta in colurnis verubus. Est etiam ille alter labor curandis vitibus, cui nunquam est satis exhausti* laboris: *namque omne solum* est *scindendum terque quaterque quotannis, glebaque* est *frangenda aternùm versis bidentibus, et omne nemus* est *levandum fronde.*

Nec non Ausonii, Trojâ gens missa, coloni
Versibus incomtis ludunt, risuque soluto;
Oraque corticibus sumunt horrenda cavatis:
Et te, Bacche, vocant per carmina læta, tibique
Oscilla ex altâ suspendunt mollia pinu.
Hinc omnis largo pubescit vinea fetu:
Complentur vallesque cavæ, saltusque profundi;
Et quocumque Deus circum caput egit honestum.
Ergo ritè suum Baccho dicemus honorem
Carminibus patriis, lancesque et liba feremus:
Et ductus cornu stabit sacer hircus ad aram;
Pinguiaque in verubus torrebimus exta colurnis.
Est etiam ille labor curandis vitibus alter;
Cui nunquam exhausti satis est: namque omne quotannis
Terque quaterque solum scindendum, glebaque versis
Æternùm frangenda bidentibus: omne levandum

TRANSLATION.

smeared *with Oil. On the same Account* the Ausonian Colony also, a Race derived from Troy, sport in unpolished Strains, and unbounded Laughter; assuming horrid Masks of hollowed Barks of Trees: And thee, O Bacchus, they invoke in jovial Songs, and to thee hang up soft Images from a tall Pine. Hence every Vineyard shoots forth with large Produce: The hollow Vales and deep Lawns are filled *with Plenty*, and wherever the God hath moved around his graceful Head. Therefore will we solemnly ascribe to Bacchus his due Honours in our Country's Lays, and offer *to him* Chargers and the consecrated Cakes; and the sacred Goat led by the Horn shall stand at his Altar, and we will roast the fat Entrails on Hazle Spits.

There is also that other Toil in dressing the Vines; in *executing* which you can never bestow Pains enough: For the whole Soil must be plowed three or four Times every Year, and the Clods are continually to be broken with bended

NOTES.

389. *Oscilla.* The Commentators are much divided about the meaning of this Word. The most probable Opinion is, that they were little earthen Images of *Bacchus* suspended to the Branches of Trees, where they swung, and were blown about by the Wind, and were thought to bestow Fertility on the Vines which way soever they turned their Faces. Whence he adds:

Et quocumque Deus circum caput egit honestum.

392. *Circum caput egit.* Some think this alludes to the Custom of carrying the Statues of *Bacchus* round the Fields and Vineyards in Procession.

396. *Verubus colurnis.* On Hazle Spits, because the Hazles were destructive to the Vines. Hence he says above, Verse 299.

——*Neve inter vites corylum sere.*

400. *Omne levandum fronde nemus.* It is usual to thin the Leaves, to give the Sun a greater Power to ripen the Fruit.

Fronde nemus. Redit agricolis labor actus in orbem;
Atque in ſe ſua per veſtigia volvitur annus.
Et jam olim ſeras poſuit cum vinea frondes,
Frigidus et ſilvis Aquilo decuſſit honorem;
Jam tum acer curas venientem extendit in annum
Ruſticus; et curvo Saturni dente relictam
Perſequitur vitem attondens, fingitque putando.
Primus humum fodito, primus devecta cremato
Sarmenta, et vallos primus ſub tecta referto:
Poſtremus metito. Bis vitibus ingruit umbra:
Bis ſegetem denſis obducunt ſentibus herbæ:
Durus uterque labor. Laudato ingentia rura;
Exiguum colito. Nec non etiam aſpera ruſci
Vimina per ſilvam, et ripis fluvialis arundo
Cæditur; incultique exercet cura ſalicti.

Labor, actus in orbem, redit agricolis, atque annus volvitur in ſe per ſua veſtigia. Et jam olim cum vinea poſuit ſeras frondes, et frigidus Aquilo decuſſit honorem ſilvis; jam tum acer ruſticus extendit curas in venientem annum, et perſequitur vitem relictam, attondens eam *curvo dente Saturni, fingitque* eam am-*putando. Primus fodito humum, primus cremato ſarmenta devecta* domum, *et primus referto vallos ſub tecta: poſtremus metito. Bis umbra ingruit vitibus: bis herbæ obducunt ſegetem denſis ſentibus: uterque labor* eſt *durus. Laudato ingentia rura; colito exiguum rus. Nec non etiam aſpera vimina ruſci per ſilvam* cæduntur, *et fluvialis arundo cæditur ripis; curaque inculti ſalicti exercet* nos.

TRANSLATION.

Days; the whole Grove muſt be diſburdened of its Leaves. The Farmer's paſt Labour returns in a Circle, and the Year rolls round on itſelf in its own Steps. And now when at length the Vineyard has ſhed its late Leaves, and the cold North Wind ſhook from the Groves their Honours; even then the active Swain extends his Cares to the enſuing Year, and cloſe plies the *deſolate* forſaken Vine, cutting off *the ſuperfluous Roots* with Saturn's crooked Hook, and forms it by pruning. Be the firſt to trench the Ground, be the firſt to carry home and burn the *ſuperfluous* Shoots, and the firſt to return beneath your Roof the Stakes *that propped your Vines:* Be the laſt to reap the Vintage. Twice a *luxuriant* Shade *of Leaves* aſſails the Vines: Twice thick prickly Weeds overrun the Field: Each *a Subject of* hard Labour. Commend large Farms; cultivate a ſmall one. Beſides all this, the rough Twigs of Butcher's Broom are to be cut throughout the Woods, and the Watery Reed on the Banks; and the Care of the uncultivated Willow gives *him* new Toil. *And now his Labour ſeems at*

NOTES.

405. *Curas venientem extendit in annum.* This autumnal Pruning is really providing for the next Year.

406. *Curvo Saturni dente.* The Scithe or Pruning-hook, which was *Saturn*'s Symbol.

406. *Relictam.* Servius explains it, *a ſe paulo ante deſertam.* But I rather think it repreſents the Vine forſaken of its Fruits and Leaves in the Situation of a forlorn Mother bereft of her Children; as Æn. IX. 290.

At tu, oro, ſolare inopem, et ſuccurre relictæ.

407. *Attondens.* This is what the *Roman* Writers on Agriculture call *ablaqueatio*, i. e the opening the Ground, and cutting away the Roots that grow near the Surface called the Day-roots. So *attondens* is underſtood by *Cerda* and others.

408. *Primus devecta cremato,* i. e. Be the firſt in performing every Piece of Labour that belongs to Vines, ſuch as trenching the Ground, pruning, &c. except the gathering of the Grapes, which are the better, the longer Time they have to ripen.

412. *Laudato ingentia rura,* &c. The Meaning ſeems to be, that you may admire the Splendor of a large Vineyard, but that you had better cultivate a ſmall one: Becauſe the Labour of cultivating Vines is ſo great, that the Maſter cannot extend his Care over a large Spot of Ground.

413. *Ruſci.* The *ruſcus* in *Pliny* is the ſame with the *Oxymyrſine:* " *Caſtor Oxymyrſinen myrti foliis acutis, ex qua fiunt ruri ſcopæ ruſcum vocavit,* And *Dioſcorides* deſcribes our

Jam vites sunt vinctæ; jam arbusta reponunt falcem; jam effetus vinitor canit extremos antes: tamen tellus est solicitanda, pulvisque est movendus; et jam Jupiter est metuendus maturis uvis. Contra, non est ulla cultura oleis: neque illæ exspectant procurvam falcem, tenacesque rastros: cum semel hæserunt arvis, tuleruntque auras. Tellus ipsa, cum recluditur unco dente, sufficit humorem satis oleis, et sufficit gravidas fruges, cum recluditur vomere. Hoc nutritor olivam pinguem et placitam paci. Poma quoque, ut primùm sensere valentes truncos, et habuere suas vires, nituntur ad sidera raptim propriâ vi, haudque indiga nostræ opis.

Jam vinctæ vites; jam falcem arbusta reponunt;
Jam canit extremos effetus vinitor antes:
Solicitanda tamen tellus, pulvisque movendus;
Et jam maturis metuendus Jupiter uvis.
Contra, non ulla est oleis cultura: neque illæ
Procurvam exspectant falcem, rastrosque tenaces;
Cum semel hæserunt arvis, aurasque tulerunt.
Ipsa satis tellus, cum dente recluditur unco,
Sufficit humorem, et gravidas, cum vomere, fruges.
Hoc pinguem et placitam paci nutritor olivam.
Poma quoque, et primùm truncos sensere valentes,
Et vires habuere suas; ad sidera raptim
Vi propriâ nituntur, opisque haud indiga nostræ.

TRANSLATION.

an End, now the Vines are tied; now the Vineyard lays aside the Pruning Hook; now the exhausted Vintager salutes in Song his utmost Rows: Yet must the Earth be vexed *anew*, and the Mould *still* put in Motion; and now, *after all*, Jove and *the Weather* are to be dreaded by the ripened Grapes.

On the other hand, the Olives require no Culture: Nor do they expect the crooked Pruning-Hook, and tenacious Harrows; when once they are rooted in the Ground, and have sustained the Air. Earth of herself supplies the Plants with Moisture, when opened by the hooked Slipping-Iron, and weighty Fruits, when *opened* by the Share. Nourish with this the Fat and Peace-delighting Olive. *The other* Fruit-Trees too, as soon as they feel their Trunks vigorous, and acquire their Strength, quickly shoot up to the Stars by their own *inherent* Virtue, and need not our Assistance. At the same Time, every Grove is in like Manner *with-*

NOTES.

Butcher's Broom under the Name of *μυρσίνην ἀγρίαν*, or *wild Myrtle*. It was probably used to bind the Vines in *Virgil*'s Time, since it is mentioned in this Place.

416 *Reponunt.* The Vines are poetically said to lay aside the Pruning-hook, when they have no more occasion for it.

417. *Canit extremos antes.* Literally, *Sings his last or utmost Rows.*

423. *Dente unco.* May signify any crooked Instrument of one Tine, for opening the Ground about the Roots of the Vine. Mr. *Martin* renders it *a Drag*, but that is a *bidens*, an Instrument with two Tines; it seems rather to be that Instrument which we call a Slipping-iron.

424. *Cum vomere.* Servius takes *cum vomere* to be the same as *per vomerem*; *Ruæus*, whom Dr. *Trapp* follows, renders it *statim cum vomere*, an Hyperbole to denote the Quickness of the Produce. All of them forced But the Construction will be easy, if we only supply *recluditur* which goes before, thus: *Tellus sufficit humorem cum recluditur dente unco, et gravidas fruges cum recluditur vomere.* Plowing, as Mr. *Martin* observes, being universally thought to increase the Product of the Olives.

425. *Hoc.* Servius, and all the Commentators after him, explain this as if it were *ob hoc*. But the Author of the Essay on the Georgics, who appears to have thoroughly understood Agriculture, and therefore has penetrated more fully into the Sense of his Author, justly observes that the Sense is much better, as well as easier, by construing *hoc* with *vomere*.

426. *Poma.* Here put for Fruits or Fruit-trees in general.

426. *Truncos sensere valentes.* Others understand by this, *so soon as they have taken to the strong Trunks on which they are engrafted.*

429. *Fetu.*

Nec minus interea fetu nemus omne gravefcit;
Sanguineifque inculta rubent aviaria baccis.
Tondentur cytifi, tædas filva alta miniftrat,
Pafcunturque ignes nocturni, et lumina fundunt.
Et dubitant homines ferere, atque impendere curam?
Quid majora fequar? falices, humilefque geniftæ,
Aut illæ pecori frondem, aut paftoribus umbram
Sufficiunt, fepemque fatis, et pabula melli.
Et juvat undantem buxo fpectare Cytorum,
Naryciæque picis lucos: juvat arva videre,
Non raftris hominum, non ulli obnoxia curæ.
Ipfæ Caucafeo fteriles in vertice filvæ,
Quas animofi Euri affiduè franguntque feruntque,
Dant alios aliæ fetus: dant utile lignum
Navigiis pinos, domibus cedrofque cupreffofque.
Hinc radios trivere rotis, hinc tympana plauftris
Agricolæ, et pandas ratibus pofuere carinas.

Nec minus interea omne nemus incultum gravefcit fetu, incultaque aviaria rubent fanguineis baccis. Cytifi tondentur, alta filva miniftrat tædas, quibus *nocturni ignes pafcuntur, et fundunt lumina. Et homines dubitant ferere* has plantas, *atque impendere curam* iis? *Quid fequar majora* commoda? *falices, humilefque geniftæ, illæ* ipfæ *fufficiunt aut frondem pecori, aut umbram paftoribus, fepemque fatis, et pabula melli. Et juvat fpectare* montem *Cytorum undantem buxo, lucofque Naryciæ picis: juvat videre arva obnoxia non raftris hominum, non ulli curæ. In Caucafeo vertice fteriles filvæ ipfæ, quas animofi Euri affiduè franguntque feruntque, aliæ dant alios fetus: dant pinos, lignum utile navigiis, cedrofque cupreffofque* utiles *domibus. Hinc agricolæ trivere radios rotis, hinc* trivere *tympana plauftris, et pofuere pandas carinas ratibus.*

TRANSLATION.

out Culture loaded with Offspring, and the uncultivated Haunts of Birds glow with Blood-red Berries. The Cytifus is browzed on *by Cattle,* the tall Wood fupplies us with Torches, and *thence our* nocturnal Fires are fed, and fhed *on us* beamy Light. And *after this* do Men hefitate about planting and beftowing Care?

Why fhould I infift on greater Things? The *very* Willows and lowly Broom, *even* thefe fupply either Browze for Cattle, or Shade for Shepherds, Fences for the Corn, and Materials for Honey. It is delightful to behold Cytorus waving with the Groves of Narycian Pitch: It is delightful to fee the Fields not indebted to the Harrows, or any Care of Men. Even the barren Woods on the Top of Caucafus, which the fierce Eaft Winds continually are crufhing and tearing, yield each their different Produce: They yield Pines, an ufeful Wood for Ships, and Cedars and Cypreffes for Houfes. Hence the Hufbandmen have laboured Spokes for Wheels; hence they have framed folid Orbs for Waggons,

NOTES.

429. *Fetu.* Here is not Fruit, but *Produce* of Trees, as Geor. I. 55.

Arborei fetus alibi——virefcunt.

And Verfe 440 of this fecond Book,

Ipfæ Caucafeo fteriles in vertice filvæ,
Quas animofi Euri affiduè franguntque feruntque,
Dant alios aliæ fetus: dant utile lignum
Navigiis pinos.

We are to obferve farther, that *inculta* in the fecond Line is alfo to be fupplied to the firft, thus: *Omne nemus* incultum *gravefcit*; for that is plainly the Senfe.

437. *Et juvat.* Ut juvat would feem to be more in *Virgil*'s Style, and more coherent.

437. *Cytorum.* Cytorus is a Mountain in *Paphlagonia.*

438. *Naryciæ picis.* Naryx, or Narycia, was a City of the *Locrians* in that Part of *Italy* which is over againft *Greece.*

440. *Caucafeo.* Caucafus is a famous Range of Mountains running from the *Black* Sea to the *Cafpian.*

444. *Tympana.* Servius explains it *the Coverings of the Waggons*; but others, feemingly with more Reafon, underftand it of the Wheels of Waggons that are folid, made without Spokes, and fomewhat fhaped like Drums.

Salices ſunt *fecundæ viminibus*, et *ulmi frondibus: at myrtus* eſt bona *validis haſtilibus*, *et cornus bona bello: taxi torquentur in Ityræos arcus. Nec leves tiliæ, aut buxum raſile torno, non accipiunt formam, cavanturque acuto ferro. Nec non et levis alnus, miſſa Pado, innatat torrentem undam: Nec non et apes condunt examina cavis corticibus, alveoque vitioſæ ilicis. Quid æquè memorandum Baccheïa dona tulerunt? Bacchus et dedit cauſas ad culpam: ille domuit letho furentes Centauros, Rhœtumque Pholumque, et Hylæum minantem Lapithis magno cratere. O agricolas nimiùm fortunatos, ſi nôrint ſua bona! quibus* agricolis *procul à diſcordibus armis, juſtiſſima tellus ipſa fundit facilem victum humo.* Si apud illos *alta domus*, cum *ſuperbis foribus, non vomit ingentem undam* hominum *ſalutantium* eos *manè totis ædibus; nec inhiant varios poſtes pulchrâ teſtudine,*

Viminibus ſalices fecundæ, frondibus ulmi:
At myrtus validis haſtilibus, et bona bello
Cornus: Ityræos taxi torquentur in arcus.
Nec tiliæ leves, aut torno raſile buxum,
Non formam accipiunt, ferroque cavantur acuto.
Nec non et torrentem undam levis innatat alnus
Miſſa Pado: nec non et apes examina condunt
Corticibuſque cavis, vitioſæque ilicis alveo.
Quid memorandum æquè Baccheïa dona tulerunt?
Bacchus et ad culpam cauſas dedit: ille furentes
Centauros letho domuit, Rhœtumque Pholumque,
Et magno Hylæum Lapithis cratere minantem.
   O fortunatos nimiùm, ſua ſi bona nôrint,
Agricolas! quibus ipſa procul diſcordibus armis,
Fundit humo facilem victum juſtiſſima tellus.
Si non ingentem foribus domus alta ſuperbis
Manè ſalutantum totis vomit ædibus undam;
Nec varios inhiant pulchrâ teſtudine poſtes,

TRANSLATION.

and bending Keels for Ships. The Willows are fertile in Twigs, the Elms in Leaves *for Cattle:* The Myrtle again is uſeful for ſturdy Spears, and the Corneil for War: The Yews are bent into Ityrean Bows. In like Manner the ſmooth-grained Limes, or Box that poliſhes with the Lathe, receive *any* Shape, and are hollowed with ſharp Steel. Thus too the light Alder launched on the Po ſwims the rapid Stream: Thus too the Bees hide their Swarms in the hollow Bark, and in the Heart of a rotten Holm. What have the Gifts of Bacchus produced ſo worthy of Record? Bacchus has given Occaſion to Offence and Guilt: He quelled by Death the furious Centaurs, Rhœtus, and Pholus, and Hylæus, threatening the Lapithæ with a huge Goblet.

Thrice happy Swains, did they but know their own Bliſs! to whom, at Diſtance from diſcordant Arms, Earth, of herſelf moſt liberal, pours from her Boſom their eaſy Suſtenance. If *there* the Palace high raiſed with proud Gates vomits not forth from all its Apartments a vaſt Tide of Morning Viſitants; and *if they* doat not on Porticoes variegated with beauteous Tortoiſe-Shell, and on

NOTES.

446. *Frondibus ulmi.* The Cattle were fed with Leaves of Elms.

448. *Ityræos.* The *Ityræi* were a People of *Cœlo-Syria*, famous for ſhooting with the Bow.

458. *Nimiùm.* Here, and in ſome other Places, ſignifies not *too much*, but *exceedingly*, or, as we ſay, *beyond Meaſure or Expreſſion.*

460. *Facilem.* Simple and natural, ſuch as is eaſily procured; in oppoſition to what is far fetched, and not to be had without great Difficulty: What *Horace* calls *cibos longè petitos.*

460. *Juſtiſſima. Proprie,* ſays *Servius, nam ſi juſtus eſt qui, quod acceperit, reddit; terra utique juſtiſſima eſt quæ majore fœnere ſemina accepta reſtituit.* Or the Earth may be called *moſt juſt*, in ſatisfying all the natural Demands of her Children.

463. *Inhiant.* This Verb does not always ſignify to pant after the Enjoyment of a Thing, but to hold it in high Eſteem and Admiration. As *Hor.* 1 Sat. I. 70.

—Congeſtis undique ſaccis indormis inhians.

So that the Meaning is, *What tho' they have not*

Illusasque auro vestes, Ephyreïaque æra;
Alba nec Assyrio fucatur lana veneno;
Nec casiâ liquidi corrumpitur usus olivi:
At secura quies, et nescia fallere vita,
Dives opum variarum: at latis otia fundis,
Speluncæ, vivique lacus; at frigida Tempe,
Mugitusque boum, mollesque sub arbore somni
Non absunt. Illic saltus, ac lustra ferarum,
Et patiens operum, parvoque assueta juventus;
Sacra Deûm, sanctique patres: extrema per illos
Justitia excedens terris vestigia fecit.
  Me verò primùm dulces ante omnia Musæ,
Quarum sacra fero ingenti percussus amore,
Accipiant; cœlique vias, et sidera monstrent;
Defectus Solis varios, Lunæque labores;

vestesque illusas auro, Ephyreïaque æra; nec apud illos alba lana fucatur Assyrio veneno, nec usus liquidi olivi corrumpitur casiâ: at secura quies, et vita nescia fallere, dives variarum opum: at otia in latis fundis, speluncæ, vivique lacus; at frigida Tempe, mugitusque boum, mollesque somni sub arbore non absunt. Illic sunt saltus, ac lustra ferarum, et juventus patiens operum, assuetaque parvo; sacra Deûm, sanctique patres: Dea Justitia excedens terris fecit extrema vestigia per illos. Verò dulces Musæ accipiant me primùm ante omnia, Musæ, quarum sacra ego sacerdos fero percussus ingenti amore earum; monstrentque mihi vias cœli et sidera, varios defectus solis, laboresque lunæ;

TRANSLATION.

Vestments curiously embroidered with Gold, and on *Vases of* Corinthian Brass; and if *for them* the white Wool is not stained with the Assyrian Drug; nor the Use of the pure Oil corrupted with Cassia's aromatic Bark: Yet *theirs is* Peace secure, and a Life of solid unfallacious Bliss, rich in various Opulence: Yet *theirs are* peaceful Retreats in ample Fields, Grottoes, and living Lakes; yet *to them* cool delicious Vales, the Lowings of Kine, and soft Slumbers under a Tree are not wanting. There are Lawns, and Dens for Beasts of Chace, and Youth patient of Toil, and inured to Thrift; the Worship of the Gods, and Fathers held in Veneration: Justice, when she left the World, took her last Steps among them.

But me may the sweet Muses, whose sacred Symbols I bear, smit with the violent Love *of philosophic Song*, first, above all Things else, receive *into Favour*; and shew me the Paths of Heaven, and Constellations; the various Eclipses of the

NOTES.

not these Things in their Possession, nor place their Happiness in them.

464. *Illusasque. In quibus artifex ludens auro aliqua depinxerat,* says *Servius.*

464. *Ephyreïque æra.* Corinthian Brass, from *Ephyre*, the original Name of *Corinth.*

466. *Nec casiâ.* See the Note on Verse 213.

467. *At nescia fallere vita.* A Life that knows not to deceive; *i. e.* A Life of solid and substantial Bliss, in opposition to the Pleasures of Courts and Palaces, which are showy, false, and deceitful. This Sense agrees perfectly well to the Context, and is far more elegant than what is given by others. This Passage is finely imitated by Mr. *Thomson* in his *Autumn* 1236.

Oh knew he but his Happiness, of Men
The happiest he! who far from public Rage,
Deep in the Vale, with a choice few retir'd,
Drinks the pure Pleasures of the rural Life.
What tho' the Dome be wanting, &c.
What tho' depriv'd of these fantastic Joys,
That still amuse the Wanton, still deceive;
A Face of Pleasure, but a Heart of Pain!
Their hollow Moments undelighted all!
Sure Peace is his; a solid Life estrang'd
To Disappointment, and fallacious Hope;
Rich in Content, in Nature's Bounty rich,
In Herbs, and Fruits, &c.

471. *Illic saltus,* i. e. *There are the Pleasures of the Chace*; which at the same Time leads him to mention the Hardiness and Temperance of the Youth.

475. *Dulces Musæ.* Tho' the Poet praises so much the Pleasures of Agriculture, and a Country Life; yet he prefers the more noble Entertainments

unde tremor sit *terris; quâ vi alta maria tumescant objicibus ruptis, rursusque residant in se ipsa; quid hiberni soles tantum properent tingere se Oceano, vel quæ mora obstet tardis noctibus. Sin frigidus sanguis circum præcordia obstiterit, ne possim accedere has partes naturæ; rura et rigui amnes in vallibus placeant mihi, et inglorius amem flumina silvasque.* O si essem *ubi* sunt *campi, Sperchiusque* amnis, *et Taygeta baccata Lacænis virginibus! O* sit *qui sistat me in gelidis vallibus* montis *Æmi, et protegat* me *ingenti umbrâ ramorum!* est *felix, qui potuit cognoscere causas rerum, atque subjecit omnes metus et inexorabile fatum, strepitumque avari Acherontis* suis *pedibus! et ille* est *fortunatus, qui novit agrestes Deos, Panaque, senemque Silvanum, sororesque Nymphas! non fasces populi, non purpura regum, et discordia agitans infidos fratres,*

Unde tremor terris; quâ vi maria alta tumescant
Objicibus ruptis, rursusque in se ipsa residant;
Quid tantum Oceano properent se tingere Soles
Hiberni, vel quæ tardis mora noctibus obstet.
Sin, has ne possim naturæ accedere partes,
Frigidus obstiterit circum præcordia sanguis;
Rura mihi, et rigui placeant in vallibus amnes;
Flumina amem, silvasque inglorius. O, ubi campi,
Sperchiusque, et virginibus bacchata Lacænis
Taygeta! ô, qui me gelidis in vallibus Æmi
Sistat, et ingenti ramorum protegat umbra!
Felix, qui potuit rerum cognoscere causas;
Atque metus omnes, et inexorabile Fatum
Subjecit pedibus, strepitumque Acherontis avari!
Fortunatus et ille, Deos qui novit agrestes,
Panaque, Silvanumque senem, Nymphasque sorores!
Illum non populi fasces, non purpura regum
Flexit, et infidos agitans discordia fratres;

TRANSLATION.

Sun, and Labours of the Moon; whence the trembling of the Earth; from what powerful Cause the Seas swell high, bursting their Barriers, and again sink back into themselves: Why the Winter Suns make such Haste to dip themselves in the Ocean, or what Delay retards the slow-paced *Summer* Nights.

But if the cold Blood about my Heart hinders me from penetrating into those Parts of Nature; let Fields and Streams gliding in the Vallies be my Delight; may I court the Rivers and the Woods, inglorious and obscure. O *to be* where are the *pleasant Thessalian* Plains, and *the River* Sperchius, and Taygetus, the Scene of Bacchanalian Revels to Spartan Maids! O for one to set me down in the cool Vallies of Hæmus, and shelter me with a thick Shade of Boughs! Happy he who was able to trace out the Causes of Things, and who cast beneath his Feet all Fears, and inexorable Destiny, and the Noise of devouring Acheron! Blest too is he who has known the rural Deities, Pan, and old Silvanus, and the Sister Nymphs! Him neither the Fasces of the People has moved, nor the Purple of Kings, nor Discord persecuting faithless Brothers; nor the Dacian de-

NOTES.

tertainments of the Mind, the Charms of Poetry and Philosophy: For 'tis plain that by *Musæ* here we are to understand not only Poetry, but also philosophic Science.

485. *Rigui.* Properly that ooze or refresh the Vallies with Moisture.

486. *Campi.* As the other Places here mentioned are in *Thessaly*; so 'tis probable that by these *campi* we are to understand the pleasant Plains of *Thessaly* called *Tempe*, as in his *Culex*:

O pecudes, O Panes, et ô gratissima Tempe
Fontis Hamadryadum———

486. *O ubi—ô qui me gelidis*, &c. These are not Questions, but Exclamations, which are usually elliptic in all Languages. The Sentence, when full, would run thus: *O si*, or *O utinam essem ubi sint campi—O utinam esset qui*, &c.

492. *Strepitumque.* Strepitus here may signify the fabulous Noise and Bustle that is made about the infernal Regions. Or the Meaning is, Who, by conforming his Life to the Precepts of Truth and Philosophy, conquered the Fears of Death and future Punishment.

449. *Aut*

Aut conjurato descendens Dacus ab Istro:
Non res Romanæ, perituraque regna: neque ille
Aut doluit miserans inopem, aut invidit habenti.
Quos rami fructus, quos ipsa volentia rura
Sponte tulere suâ, carpsit: nec ferrea jura,
Insanumque forum, aut populi tabularia vidit.
  Sollicitant alii remis freta cæca, ruuntque
In ferrum: penetrant aulas, et limina regum.
Hic petit excidiis urbem, miserosque Penates,
Ut gemmâ bibat, et Sarrano dormiat ostro.
Condit opes alius, defossoque incubat auro.
Hic stupet attonitus rostris: hunc plausus hiantem
Per cuneos (geminatur enim) Plebisque Patrumque,
Corripuit: gaudent perfusi sanguine fratrum;
Exsilioque domos, et dulcia limina mutant,
Atque alio patriam quærunt sub Sole jacentem.
Agricola incurvo terram dimovit aratro;
Hinc anni labor: hinc patriam, parvosque nepotes

aut Dacus descendens ab conjurato Istro flexit illum: non Romanæ res, regnaque peritura flexerunt illum: *neque ille, aut doluit miserans inopem, aut invidit habenti* divitias. *Carpsit fructus, quos rami, quos volentia rura ipsa tulere suâ sponte: nec vidit ferrea jura, insanumque forum, aut tabularia populi. Alii solicitant cæca freta remis, ruuntque in ferrum: penetrant aulas et limina regum. Hic petit urbem miserosque Penates excidiis, ut bibat è gemmâ, et dormiat Sarrano ostro. Alius condit opes, incubatque defosso auro. Hic stupet attonitus rostris: plausus plebisque patrumque per cuneos* theatri *(enim geminatur) corripuit hunc hiantem:* alii *gaudent perfusi sanguine fratrum, mutantque domos et dulcia limina exilio, atque quærunt patriam jacentem sub alio sole. Agricola dimovit terram incurvo aratro; hinc* est *labor anni: hinc sustinet patriam, parvosque nepotes;*

TRANSLATION.

scending from the conspiring Danube: Nor the Revolutions of Rome, and perishing Kingdoms: He neither pined with Grief, lamenting the Poor, nor envied he the Rich. What Fruits the Boughs, what *Fruits* the willing Fields yielded of themselves spontaneous, he gathered: Nor saw the *rigorous* Iron Laws, the madly litigious Bar, or the public Courts.

Some vex the dangerous Seas with Oars, *some* rush into Arms: *Some* work their Way into Courts, and the Palaces of Kings. One destines a City and wretched Families to Destruction, that he may drink in Gems, and sleep on Tyrian Purple. Another hoards up Wealth, and broods over buried Gold. One, astonished with *the Eloquence of* the Rostra, grows giddy: Another, Peals of Applause, (for it is redoubled along the Rows both of the People and the Fathers) have captivated, and set agape: Some rejoice *in being* stained with their Brother's Blood; and exchange their Homes and sweet Mansions for Exile, and seek a Country lying under another Sun. The Husbandman cleaves the Earth with the crooked Plough; hence the Labours of the Year: Hence he sustains his Country,

NOTES.

499. *Aut doluit.* Some explain it of his being in that happy Situation where there are no miserable Objects to disturb him, and excite his Sorrow. To be sure it cannot mean that he is insensible to the Impressions of Humanity and Compassion, but that he is free from the lasting Influence of Grief, Anxiety, Envy, and the like Passions, that prevail elsewhere; and enjoys a more unruffled State of Tranquillity than is to be found among the Rich and Great.

502. *Tabularia* Properly the Place where the Records and public Registers were kept.

503. *Cæca.* Ruæus renders it *profunda*; but it seems rather to mean *unseen*, i. e. *full of unseen Dangers.*

503. *Ruuntque.* Alii must be supplied to all the three Verbs.

506. *Sarrano,* Tyrian, from *Sarra*, the first Name of *Tyre.*

514. *Anni labores.* Labores here is not to be understood of the Husbandman's Labours, as Dr. *Trapp* explains it; but of the laboured Productions of the Year, as elsewhere, *hominumque boumque labores.* This is plain enough from

hinc ſuſtinet *armenta boum, meritoſque juvencos. Nec eſt requies, quin annus exuberet aut pomis, aut fetu pecorum, aut mergite Cerealis culmi: oneretque ſulcos proventu, atque vincat horrea. Hiems venit; Sicyonia bacca teritur trapetis, ſues læti glande redeunt, ſilvæ dant arbuta: et autumnus ponit varios fetus; et mitis vindemia coquitur altè in apricis ſaxis. Interea dulces nati pendent circum oſcula* parentum; *caſta domus ſervat pudicitiam; vaccæ demittunt lactea ubera; pinguesque hœdi luctantur inter ſe adverſis cornibus in læto gramine. Ipſe agitat feſtos dies; fuſuſque per herbam, ubi* eſt *ignis in medio, et* ubi *ſocii coronant cratera, libans* vinum *vocat te, Lenæe: ponitque magiſtris pecoris certamina velocis jaculi in ulmo, nudatque prædura corpora agreſti palæſtrâ. Veteres Sabini olim coluere hanc vitam, et Remus et Frater* Romulus coluere *hanc: ſic fortis Etruria crevit;*

Suſtinet; hinc armenta boum, meritoſquejuvencos.
Nec requies, quin aut pomis exuberet annus,
Aut fetu pecorum, aut Cerealis mergite culmi:
Proventuque oneret ſulcos, atque horrea vincat.
Venit hiems; teritur Sicyonia bacca trapetis,
Glande ſues læti redeunt, dant arbuta ſilvæ:
Et varios ponit fetus autumnus; et altè
Mitis in apricis coquitur vindemia ſaxis.
Interea dulces pendent circum oſcula nati;
Caſta pudicitiam ſervat domus; ubera vaccæ
Lactea demittunt; pinguiſque in gramine læto
Inter ſe adverſis luctantur cornibus hœdi.
Ipſe dies agitat feſtos; fuſuſque per herbam,
Ignis ubi in medio, et ſocii cratera coronant,
Te libans, Lenæe, vocat; pecoriſque magiſtris
Velocis jaculi certamina ponit in ulmo;
Corporaque agreſti nudat prædura palæſtrâ:
  Hanc olim veteres vitam coluere Sabini;
Hanc Remus et Frater: ſic fortis Etruria crevit;

TRANSLATION.

and his little Offspring; hence his Herds of Kine, and deſerving Steers. Nor is there any Intermiſſion, but the Year either abounds with Apples, or with the Breed of the Flocks, or with Bundles of Ceres's Stalks: Loads the Furrows with Increaſe, and overſtocks the Barns. Winter comes; the Sicyonian Berry is pounded in the Oil-preſſes, the Swine come home gladdened with Acorns, the Woods yield their Arbutes, *and wild Fruits:* And the Autumn lays down its various Productions; and high on the ſunny Rocks the mild Vintage is ripened. Meanwhile the ſweet Babes twine round their Parent's Neck: His chaſte Family maintain a virtuous Oeconomy; the Cows hang down their Udders full of Milk; and the fat *friſky* Kids wreſtle together with butting Horns on the cheerful Green. The Swain himſelf celebrates Feſtival-days; and extended on the Graſs, where a Fire is in the Middle, and where his Companions crown the Bowl, invokes thee, O Lenæus, making Libation; and on an Elm ſets forth to the Maſters of the Flock Prizes to be contended for with the winged Javelin; and ſtrips their hardy Bodies in the ruſtic Ring.

This Life of old the ancient Sabines: this Remus and his Brother ſtrictly obſerved: Thus Etruria grew to its Strength; nay, and thus did Rome become

NOTES.

from what follows, *Nec requies quin*, &c. which does not ſignify there is no Intermiſſion of his Labour, but of the Productions of the Year.

519. *Sicyonia bacca.* Olives, ſo called from *Sicyon* a City of *Achaia*, fertile in Olive-trees.

524 *Caſta pudicitiam ſervat domus.* The Meaning is, That his whole Family is regulated with great Order and Oeconomy: All are bred to honeſt Induſtry, which is the beſt Preſervative of their Virtue and Chaſtity. To the ſame Purpoſe he ſays of the frugal, thrifty Houſewife, That ſhe is induſtrious in order to preſerve her Huſband's Bed chaſte, *Æn.* VIII. 411.

———*Famulaſque ad lumina longo*
Exercet penſo; caſtum ut ſervare cubile
Conjugis, et poſſit parvos educere natos.

527. *Agitat.* Agere, ſome obſerve, is applied even to a Thing done by Force and Neceſſity; but *agitare* only to Things of Choice and Pleaſure.

533. *Hanc Remus et Frater,* Romulus and

Remus

Scilicet et rerum facta est pulcherrima Roma,
Septemque una sibi muro circumdedit arces.
Ante etiam sceptrum Dictæi regis, et ante
Impia quàm cæsis gens est epulata juvencis;
Aureus hanc vitam in terris Saturnus agebat.
Necdum etiam audierant inflari classica; necdum
Impositos duris crepitare incudibus enses.
Sed nos immensum spatiis confecimus æquor;
Et jam tempus equûm fumantia solvere colla.

scilicet sic Roma est facta pulcherrima urbs rerum, unaque circumdedit septem arces sibi muro. Etiam ante sceptrum Dictæi regis Jovis, et antequam impia humana gens est epulata cæsis juvencis; aureus Saturnus agebat hanc vitam in terris. Necdum etiam homines audierant classica inflari; necdum audierant enses impositos duris incudibus crepitare. Sed nos confecimus immensum æquor spatiis, et jam est tempus solvere fumantia colla equûm jugo.

TRANSLATION.

the Glory and Beauty of the World, and single hath encompassed for herself seven Hills with a Wall. This Life too golden Saturn led on Earth, before the sceptered Sway of the Dictæan King, and before an impious Race *of Mortals* feasted on slain Bullocks. Nor as yet had Mankind heard the warlike Trumpets blown; nor yet the Swords laid on the hard Anvils clatter.

But we have finished this immensely extended Field; and now 'tis Time to loose the smoking Necks of our Steeds.

NOTES.

Remus were educated amongst the Shepherds, and were employed themselves in tending Sheep, as we learn from *Livy*.

541. *Immensum spatiis—æquor.* The *Spatia*, as has been said elsewhere, signifies the Stages or whole Bounds marked out for a Race; so that *æquor immensum spatiis* may perhaps be a poetical Phrase to signify *a Digression*: A Field or Plain not measured by Stages, or that did not lie within the Bounds of my proposed Race. Taking *immensum* for *non mensum*.

P. VIRGILII MARONIS

GEORGICA.

LIBER III.

ORDO.
Nos *canemus te quoquè, magna Pales, et te* Apollo, *paſtor memorande ab Amphryſo* fluvio; canemus *vos, ſilvæ, amneſque Lycæi. Omnia cætera carmina, quæ tenuiſſent vacuas mentes, jam ſunt vulgata. Quis neſcit aut durum Euryſthea, aut aras illaudati Buſiridis?*

TE quoquè, magna Pales, et te memorande canemus
Paſtor ab Amphryſo; vos ſilvæ, amneſque Lycæi.
Cætera, quæ vacuas tenuiſſent carmina mentes,
Omnia jam vulgata. Quis aut Euryſthea durum,
Aut illaudati neſcit Buſiridis aras?

TRANSLATION.

THEE too, great Pales, and thee, O Shepherd, famed from Amphryſus; ye Woods, and Arcadian Rivers, will I ſing. Other Songs, that might have entertained diſengaged Minds, are now all trite and common. Who is unacquainted or with ſevere Euryſtheus, or the Altars of infamous Buſiris? By

NOTES.

This Book begins with the Invocation of ſome rural Deities, and a Compliment to *Auguſtus*: After which *Virgil* directs himſelf to *Mæcenas*, and enters on his Subject. He lays down Rules for the Breeding and Management of Horſes, Oxen, Sheep, Goats, and Dogs; and interweaves ſeveral pleaſant Deſcriptions of a Chariot-race, of the Battle of the Bulls, of the Force of Love, and of the *Scythian* Winter. In the latter Part of the Book he relates the Diſeaſes incident to Cattle, and ends with the Deſcription of a fatal Murrain that formerly raged among the *Alps*.

1. *Pales*. The Goddeſs of Shepherds and Flocks.

2. *Ab Amphryſo*. Amphryſus was a River in *Theſſaly*, where *Apollo*, in his Exile from Heaven for killing the *Cyclops*, fed the Flocks of *Admetus*.

4. *Euryſthea*. Euryſtheus, King of *Mycenæ*, who, at *Juno*'s Inſtigation, impoſed on *Hercules*, ſubjected to him by Command of the Oracle, the moſt ſevere Trials of Fortitude, commonly called *the twelve Labours of* Hercules; hence he is deſigned by the Epithet *durus*, *rigid*, or *ſevere*.

5. *Illaudati Buſiridis*. Buſiris, King of *Egypt*, ſuch a Monſter of Cruelty, that he butchered as a Sacrifice to his Gods the Strangers who viſited his Dominions. *Illaudati*, an

Epithet

Cui non dictus Hylas puer, et Latonia Delos?
Hippodameque, humeroque Pelops insignis eburno,
Acer equis? tentanda via est, quâ me quoquè possim
Tollere humo, victorque virûm volitare per ora.
Primus ego in patriam mecum, modò vita supersit,
Aonio rediens deducam vertice Musas:
Primus Idumæas referam tibi, Mantua, palmas:
Et viridi in campo templum de marmore ponam
Propter aquam, tardis ingens ubi flexibus errat
Mincius, et tenerâ prætexit arundine ripas.
In medio mihi Cæsar erit, templumque tenebit.
Illi victor ego, et Tyrio conspectus in ostro,
Centum quadrijugos agitabo ad flumina currus.

Cui Hylas puer non est dictus, et Latonia Delos, Hippodameque, Pelopsque insignis eburno humero, et acer equis? via est tentanda mihi, quâ possim tollere me quoquè humo, victorque possim volitare per ora virûm. Ego primus, rediens ab Aonio vertice, deducam Musas mecum in patriam, modò vita supersit mihi: primus referam Idumæas palmas tibi, Mantua: et, in viridi campo, ponam templum de marmore propter aquam, ubi ingens fluvius Mincius errat tardis flexibus, et prætexit ripas tenerâ arundine. In medio erit mihi Cæsar, tenebitque templum. Illi, ego victor, et conspectus in Tyrio ostro, agitabo centum quadrijugos currus ad flumina.

TRANSLATION.

whom has not the Boy Hylas been recorded, and Latonian Delos? Hippodame, and Pelops signalized by his Ivory Shoulder, victorious in the Race? I too must attempt a Way, whereby to lift me from the Ground, and victorious spread my flying Fame through the Mouths of Men.

I first returning from the Aonian Mount will (provided Life remain) bring along the Muses with me into my Country: For thee, O Mantua, I first will gain the Idumæan Palms: And on thy verdant Plain erect a Temple of Marble, fast by the Stream, where the great Mincius winds in slow Meanders, and hath fringed the Banks with tender Reed. In the Middle will I have Cæsar, and he shall command the Temple. In Honour of him will I victorious, and in Tyrian Purple conspicuous, drive an hundred four-horsed Chariots

NOTES.

Epithet which some have censured as too weak for so infamous a Character, implies a great deal more than merely *not praised*; for, according to the Idiom of the Language, these Negatives imply not only the Want of some good Quality, but the Possession of the contrary; Thus *inutilis humor*, *inutilis filix*, in the Georgics, signify not only *useless*, but *noxious*; so here *illaudatus* is one who, far from meriting Praise, is quite infamous.

6. *Hylas.* See the Note on Ecl. VI. 44.

7. *Hippodame.* Or *Hippodamia*, the Daughter of *Oenomaus*, King of *Elis*, who having learned from an Oracle that he was to be slain by his Son-in-law; in order to elude his Destiny he obliged his Daughter's Suitors to try their Skill with him in the Chariot-race, presuming on the Swiftness of his Steeds. The Law of the Combat was, that whoever of them gained the Victory should win his Daughter; or if vanquished die. After thirteen of them had lost their Lives in the Trial, *Pelops* at length gained the beauteous Prize, by bribing *Myrtillus*, *Oenomaus*'s Charioteer.

7. *Humeroque Pelops insignis eburno.* Tantalus, the Father of *Pelops*, had invited the Gods to a Banquet, at which, having a mind to try their Divinity, he dressed his Son, and set his Flesh before them. All the Gods abstained from this horrid Food, except *Ceres*, who eat the Shoulder. *Jupiter* afterwards restored *Pelops* to Life, and gave him an Ivory Shoulder, instead of that which had been eaten.

11. *Aonio vertice.* Aonia was the Name of the mountainous Part of *Beotia*, whence all *Beotia* came to be called *Aonia*. In this Country was the famous Mountain *Helicon*, sacred to the Muses.

17. *Tyrio conspectus in ostro.* Those who offered Sacrifice amongst the *Romans*, on account of any Victory, were clothed in the *Tyrian* Colour.

18. *Ad flumina.* At first the *Circensian* Games

Mibi cuncta Græcia, linquens fluvium Alpheum, lucosque Molorchi, decernet cursibus et crudo cæstu. Ego ipse, ornatus quoad *caput foliis tonsæ olivæ, feram dona. Jam nunc juvat* me *ducere solennes pompas ad delubra, videreque cæsos juvencos; vel* videre, *ut scena discedat frontibus versis, utque intexti Britanni tollant purpurea aulæa. In foribus* templi *faciam, ex auro solidoque elephanto, pugnam Gangaridum, armaque victoris Quirini: utque* hic pingam *Nilum, undantem bello, magnumque fluentem, ac columnas surgentes navali ære. Addam* his *domitas urbes Asiæ, pulsumque Niphatem, Parthumque fidentem fugâ versisque sagittis; et duo tropæa, rapta manu ex diverso hoste, gentesque bis triumphatas ab utroque litore.*
Et Parii lapides stabunt spirantia signa,

Cuncta mihi, Alpheum linquens, lucosque Molorchi,
Cursibus, et crudo decernet Græcia cæstu.
Ipse caput tonsæ foliis ornatus olivæ
Dona feram. Jam nunc solennes ducere pompas
Ad delubra juvat, cæsosque videre juvencos;
Vel scena ut versis discedat frontibus; utque
Purpurea intexti tollant aulæa Britanni.
In foribus pugnam ex auro, solidoque elephanto
Gangaridum faciam, victorisque arma Quirini:
Atque hìc undantem bello, magnumque fluentem
Nilum, ac navali surgentes ære columnas.
Addam urbes Asiæ domitas, pulsumque Niphatem,
Fidentemque fugâ Parthum, versisque sagittis;
Et duo rapta manu diverso ex hoste tropæa,
Bisque triumphatas utroque ab litore gentes.
Stabunt et Parii lapides, spirantia signa,

TRANSLATION.

along the River. For me all Greece, leaving Alpheus, and the Groves of Molorchus, shall contend in Races and the rigid Gauntlet. I myself, graced with Leaves of the shorn Olive, will dispense the Prizes. Even now I am well pleased to lead on the solemn Pomps to the Temple, and to see the Bullocks slain; or how the Scene with shifting Front retires; and how the inwoven Britons lift up the purple Curtain. On the Doors will I delineate in Gold and solid Ivory, the Battle of the Gangarides, and the Arms of conquering Quirinus: And here the Nile surging with War, flowing majestic, and Columns rising with naval Brass. I will add the vanquished Cities of Asia, and subdued Niphates, and the Parthian presuming on his Flight, and Arrows shot backward, and two Trophies by personal Valour snatched from two widely distant Foes, and Nations twice triumphed over on either Shore. *Here* too shall stand in Parian Marble,

NOTES.

Games were celebrated on the Banks of a River, to which *Virgil* here alludes.

19. *Alpheum.* A River of *Elis*, in the *Peloponnesus*, where the *Olympian* Games were celebrated, which Games are therefore by this Metaphor intended. As by *lucos Molorchi*, the Groves of *Molorchus*, we are to understand the *Nemæan* Games, *Molorchus* being the Name of that Shepherd who had been *Hercules*'s Host, and in Favour of whom that Hero slew the *Nemæan* Lion.

22. *Pompas.* The Pomps or Pageants were Images of the Gods carried in Procession before the People at the *Circensian* Games.

27. *Gangaridum.* The *Gangarides* were an *Indian* Nation near the *Ganges*.

27. *Victorisque arma Quirini.* As it was debated in the Senate, whether *Augustus* or *Quirinus* should be the Name of him who before was called *Octavianus*; this is thought to refer to that Debate. If so, we must agree with *Catrou* that this Verse was inserted in the Year of *Rome* 734: For that Debate happened in the Year 727, three Years after the Publication of the Georgics; and it was not till the Year 734, that *Augustus* conquered the *Indians* or *Gangarides*.

32. *Duo tropæa——bisque triumphatas gentes.* Probably refers to *Augustus*'s two Victories over *Antony*, one at *Actium*, on the *European* Coast, and the other at *Alexandria*, on the *African* Coast.

Aſſaraci proles, demiſſæque ab Jove gentis
Nomina, Troſque parens, et Trojæ Cynthius auctor.
Invidia infelix Furias amnemque ſeverum
Cocyti metuet, tortoſque Ixionis angues,
Immanemque rotam, et non exſuperabile ſaxum.
Interea Dryadum ſilvas, ſaltuſque ſequamur
Intactos, tua, Mæcenas, haud mollia juſſa.
Te ſine nil altum mens inchoat: en age ſegnes
Rumpe moras: vocat ingenti clamore Cithæron,
Taygetique canes, domitrixque Epidaurus equorum;
Et vox aſſenſu nemorum ingeminata remugit.
Mox tamen ardentes accingar dicere pugnas
Cæſaris, et nomen famâ tot ferre per annos,
Tithoni primâ quot abeſt ab origine Cæſar.
Seu quis, Olympiacæ miratus præmia palmæ,
Paſcit equos, ſeu quis fortes ad aratra juvencos,
Corpora præcipuè matrum legat. Optima torvæ
Forma bovis, cui turpe caput, cui plurima cervix,

proles Aſſaraci, nominaque gentis demiſſæ ab Jove. Troſque parens Aſſaraci, et Cynthius Apollo auctor Trojæ. Invidia infelix metuet furias, ſeverumque amnem Cocyti, tortoſque angues Ixionis immanemque rotam, et ſaxum Siſyphi non exſuperabile. Interea ſequamur ſilvas Dryadum, ſaltuſque intactos aliis, tua haud mollia juſſa, Mæcenas. Mea mens inchoat nil altum ſine te: en age, rumpe ſegnes moras: montes Cithæron vocat nos ingenti clamore, caneſque montis Taygeti, Epidauruſque urbs domitrix equorum; et vox, ingeminata aſſenſu nemorum, remugit. Tamen mox accingar dicere ardentes pugnas Cæſaris, et ferre famâ ejus nomen per tot annos, quot Cæſar abeſt ab primâ origine Tithoni. Seu quis, miratus præmia Olympiacæ palmæ, paſcit equos, ſeu quis paſcit fortes juvencos ad aratra, legat præcipuè corpora matrum. Forma bovis eſt optima, cui eſt turpe caput, cui eſt plurima cervix,

TRANSLATION.

breathing Statues, the Offspring of Aſſaracus, and the Chiefs of the Jove-deſcended Race, both Tros, the great Anceſtor *of Rome*, and the Cynthian Apollo Founder of Troy. *Here* baneful Envy ſhall dread the Furies and grim River of Cocytus, Ixion's twiſted Snakes, the enormous racking Wheel, and the Stone's unſurmountable Labour.

Mean while let us purſue the Woods of the Dryads, and untrodden Lawns, thy Commands, Mæcenas, of no eaſy Import. Without thee my Mind enterprizes nothing ſublime: Come then, break off lazy Delays. Cithæron with loud Hallowing calls, and the Hounds of Taygeta, and Epidaurus, the Tamer of of Horſes, and the Voice doubled by the aſſenting Groves re-echoes. Yet ere long ſhall I be prepared to ſing of Cæſar's ardent Battles, and to tranſmit his Name with Honour through as many Years, as Cæſar is diſtant from the firſt Origin of Tithonus.

Whether any one, aſpiring to the Prizes of the Olympian Palm, breeds Horſes, or whether any one *breeds* ſturdy Bullocks for the Plough, let him chooſe with ſpecial Care the Bodies of the Mothers. The four-looking Heifer's Form is beſt, whoſe Head is hideouſly large, whoſe Neck is brawny, and from the

NOTES.

37. *Invidia infelix.* The Source of Unhappineſs to its Sons.

38. *Ixionis.* Ixion, for making an Attempt on *Juno*, was caſt into Hell, and bound with twiſted Snakes to a Wheel which was continually turning.

39. *Non exſuperabile ſaxum.* Siſyphus infeſted *Attica* with Robberies, for which he was ſlain by *Theſeus*; and condemned in Hell to roll a Stone to the Top of a Hill which always turned back again.

44. *Taygetique canes.* Taygetus was a Mountain in *Laconia*, near *Sparta*, famous for Hunting.

44. *Epidaurus.* A City in *Epirus*, according to *Servius*; or in the *Peloponneſus*, according to others.

52. *Turpe caput.* This is commonly meant of

Et crurum tenus à mento palearia pendent.
Tum longo nullus lateri modus: omnia magna;
Pes etiam; et camuris hirtæ sub cornibus aures.
Nec mihi displiceat maculis insignis et albo,
Aut juga detrectans, interdumque aspera cornu,
Et faciem tauro propior, quæque ardua tota,
Et gradiens imâ verrit vestigia caudâ.
Ætas Lucinam, justosque pati Hymenæos
Desinit ante decem, post quatuor incipit annos:
Cætera nec feturæ habilis, nec fortis aratris.
Interea, superat gregibus dum læta juventus,
Solve mares: mitte in Venerem pecuaria primus;
Atque aliam ex aliâ generando suffice prolem.
Optima quæque dies miseris mortalibus ævi
Prima fugit: subeunt morbi, tristisque senectus,
Et labor; et duræ rapit inclementia mortis.
Semper erunt, quarum mutari corpora malis.
Semper enim refice: ac, ne pòst amissa requiras,
Anteveni, et sobolem armento sortire quotannis.

et cui palearia pendent à mento tenus crurum. Tum est *nullus modus longo lateri: omnia* mem*bra* sunt *magna; pes etiam; et hirtæ aures sub camuris cornibus. Nec vacca, insignis maculis et albo, displiceat mihi, aut detrectans juga, interdumque aspera cornu, et* quoad *faciem propior tauro, quæque* est *tota ardua, et gradiens verrit vestigia imâ caudâ. Ætas* vacca*rum pati Lucinam justosque Hymenæos desinit ante decem* annos, *incipit post quatuor annos: cætera* ætas earum est *nec habilis feturæ, nec fortis aratris. Interea, dum læta juventus superat gregibus, solve mares:* tu *primus mitte pecuaria in Venerem, et suffice aliam prolem ex aliâ generando. Quæque optima dies ævi prima fugit miseris mortalibus: morbi, tristisque senectus, et labor subeunt; et inclementia duræ mortis rapit* eos. *Erunt semper* pecudes, *quarum corpora* tu *malis mutari. Enim semper refice* armentum: *ac, ne pòst requiras amissa, anteveni* damnum, *et sortire sobolem armento quotannis.*

TRANSLATION.

Chin down to the Legs her Dewlaps hang. Then no Measure in her Length of Side: All her Parts huge; even her Foot; and rough Ears under her crankled Horns. Nor would I dislike her if streaked with white Spots, or if she refuses the Yoke, and sometimes is surly with her Horn, and in Aspect approaches nearer to a Bull, and if she is stately throughout, and sweeps her Steps with the Extremity of her Tail as she goes along.

The Age to undergo Lucina, and just Hymeneal Rites, ends before ten, and begins after four Years: Their other Years are neither fit for Breeding, nor strong for the Plough. Mean time, while the Flocks abound with sprightly Youth, let loose the Males: Be the first to indulge thy Cattle in the Joys of Love; and by Generation raise up one Race after another. All the best Days of Life fly first away from wretched Mortals: Diseases succeed, and disconsolate old Age, and Pain; and the Inclemency of inexorable Death snatches them away. There will always be *some* whose Bodies you would choose to have changed *for better*. Therefore continually repair them: And, that you may not regret them when lost, be before-hand, and yearly provide a new Offspring for the Herd.

NOTES.

of a Head that is deformed, and of disproportioned Magnitude.

61. *Desinit ante decem, post quatuor incipit annos.* Varro says it is better for the Cow not to admit the Bull till she is four Years old: and that they are fruitful till ten, and sometimes longer.

Nec non et pecori eſt idem delectus equino.
Tu modò, quos in ſpem ſtatues ſubmittere gentis,
Præcipuum jam inde à teneris impende laborem.
Continuò pecoris generoſi pullus in arvis
Altiùs ingreditur, et mollia crura reponit;
Primus et ire viam, et fluvios tentare minaces
Audet, et ignoto ſeſe committere ponti:
Nec vanos horret ſtrepitus. Illi ardua cervix,
Argutumque caput, brevis alvus, obeſaque terga:
Luxuriatque toris animoſum pectus (honeſti
Spadices, glaucique; color deterrimus albis,
Et gilvo). Tum, ſiqua ſonum procul arma dedere,
Stare loco neſcit, micat auribus, et tremit artus;
Collectumque premens volvit ſub naribus ignem:
Denſa juba, et dextro jactata recumbit in armo.
At duplex agitur per lumbos ſpina, cavatque
Tellurem, et ſolido graviter ſonat ungula cornu.
Talis Amyclæi domitus Pollucis habenis
Cyllarus; et, quorum Graii meminere poëtæ,

Nec non et idem delectus eſt neceſſarius *equino pecori. Tu modò impende præcipuum laborem jam inde à teneris* annis iis, *quos ſtatues ſubmittere in ſpem gentis. Continuò pullus generoſi pecoris ingreditur altiùs in arvis, et reponit mollia crura; primus audet et ire viam, et tentare minaces fluvios, et committere ſeſe ignoto ponti: nec horret vanos ſtrepitus.* Eſt *illi ardua cervix, argutumque caput, brevis alvus, obeſaque terga: animoſumque pectus luxuriat toris. Spadices, glaucique* ſunt *honeſti*; eſt *deterrimus color albis, et gilvo. Tum, ſi qua arma dedere ſonum procul, neſcit ſtare loco, micat auribus, et tremit per artus, premenſque collectum ignem volvit eum ſub naribus.* Ejus *juba* eſt *denſa, et jactata recumbit in dextro armo. At duplex ſpina agitur per lumbos, ungulaque cavat tellurem, et graviter ſonat ſolido cornu. Talis fuit Cyllarus, domitus habenis Amyclæi Pollucis, et bijuges equi Martis, quorum Graii poëtæ meminere,*

TRANSLATION.

Nor is the ſame diſcriminating Care leſs needful for a Breed of Horſes. But ſtill, on thoſe which you deſign to bring up for the Hope of the Race, beſtow your principal Diligence immediately from their tender Years. The Colt of generous Breed from the very firſt walks ſtately in the Fields, and nimbly moves his pliant Legs; he is the firſt that dares to lead the Way, and tempt the threatening Floods, and truſt himſelf to an unknown Bridge: Nor ſtarts affrighted at vain Alarms: Lofty is his Neck, his Head little and ſlender, his Belly ſhort, his Back *round and* plump, and his proud Cheſt ſwells luxuriant with brawny muſcles: (The Bay-brown and bluiſh-grey are in moſt Requeſt; the worſt Colours are the White and Dun.) Then, if he hears the diſtant Sound of Arms, he knows not how to ſtand his Ground, he pricks up his Ears, trembles in every Joint, and ſnorting rolls the collected Fire under his Noſtrils: Thick is his Main, and waving reſts on his Right-ſhoulder. A double ſpinal Bone runs down between his Loins, his Hoof ſcoops up the Ground, and deep reſounds with its ſolid Horn. Such was Cyllarus, broke by the Reins of Amyclæan Pollux, and, which the Grecian Poets have deſcribed, ſuch the harneſſed

NOTES.

75. *Continuò.* Here, and in many other Places in *Virgil*, ſignifies *from the very Beginning*, i. e. *as ſoon almoſt as he is foaled.*

83. *Tum, ſi qua ſonum procul arma dedere, ſtare loco neſcit, micat auribus, et tremit artus.* &c. It may be worth while to compare with this that noble Deſcription of a Warrior-horſe in the Book of *Job*: "He paweth in the Valley, and rejoiceth in his Strength: He goeth on to meet the armed Men. He mocketh at Fear; and is not affrighted, neither turneth he back from the Sword. The Quiver rattleth againſt him, the glittering Spear and the Shield. He ſwalloweth the Ground with Fierceneſs and Rage; neither believeth he that it is the Sound of the Trumpet. He ſaith among the Trumpets, ha, ha; and he ſmelleth the Battle afar off, the Thunder of the Captains, and the Shouting."

89. *Amyclæi.* Amyclæ was a City of *La-*

et currus magni Achillis. Talis et pernix Saturnus ipse effudit jubam equinâ cervice adventu conjugis, et fugiens implevit altum Pelion acuto hinnitu. Abde hunc domo quoquè, ubi aut gravis morbo, aut jam segnior annis deficit, et ignosce senectæ nec turpi. Senior equus est *frigidus in venerem, frustraque trahit ingratum laborem; et, si quando est ventum ad prœlia, ut quondam magnus ignis sine viribus* furit *in stipulis,* sic *ille furit incassum. Ergo notabis animos ævumque* equorum *præcipuè, hinc* notabis *alias artes* eorum, *prolemque parentum, et quis dolor* sit *cuique victo, quæ gloria palmæ* sit cuique victori. *Nonne vides? cum, præcipiti certamine, currus corripuere campum, ruuntque effusi carcere;* *cum spes juvenum* sunt *arrectæ, pulsansque pavor haurit exsultantia corda: illi* juvenes *instant* equis *torto verbere, et proni dant lora: axis fervidus vi volat. Jamque humiles, jamque elati sublime videntur*

Martis equi bijuges; et magni currus Achillis.
Talis et ipse jubam cervice effudit equinâ
Conjugis adventu pernix Saturnus, et altum
Pelion hinnitu fugiens implevit acuto.
  Hunc quoquè, aut ubi morbo gravis, aut jam segnior annis 95
Deficit, abde domo, nec turpi ignosce senectæ.
Frigidus in venerem senior, frustraque laborem
Ingratum trahit; et, si quando ad prœlia ventum est,
Ut quondam in stipulis magnus sine viribus ignis,
Incassum furit. Ergo animos, ævumque notabis
Præcipuè, hinc alias artes, prolemque parentum,
Et quis cuique dolor victo, quæ gloria palmæ.
  Nonne vides? cum præcipiti certamine campum
Corripuere, ruuntque effusi carcere currus; 104
Cum spes arrectæ juvenum, exsultantiaque haurit
Corda pavor pulsans: illi instant verbere torto,
Et proni dant lora: volat vi fervidus axis.
Jamque humiles, jamque elati sublime videntur

TRANSLATION.

Brace of Mars, and the Chariot-*horses* of great Achilles. Such Saturn too himself precipitant on the Arrival of his Wife spread out a full Main on his *assumed* Horse's Neck, and flying filled lofty Pelion with shrill Neighing.

Him too, when with Sickness oppressed, or now enfeebled with Years he fails, shut up in his Lodge, spare his not inglorious Age: When in Years he is cold to Love, and in vain drags on the ungrateful Task; and, if ever he comes to an Engagement, he is furiously keen with no Effect, *just* as at Times a great Fire *rages* without Strength among Stubble. Therefore chiefly mark their Spirit and Age; then their other Qualities, their Parentage, and what Sorrow each receives when vanquished, what Pride when victorious.

See you not? When in the rapid Race the Chariots have seized the Plain, and pouring forth rush along; when the Hopes of the Youth are elevated, and palpitating Fear heaves their throbbing Hearts: They ply the twisted Lash, and bending forward give *full* Reins: The Axle flies glowing with the Impetuosity. And now low, now high, they seem to be borne aloft through the open Air, and

NOTES.

tonio, where *Castor* and *Pollux* were brought up.

96. *Nec turpi ignosce senectæ*, i. e. *Ignosce senectæ non turpi. Spare his old Age, that is not inglorious.* This Sense agrees best with what goes before, *abde domo*; and is most suitable to the Temper of *Virgil*, who shews his Humanity even in recommending Tenderness and Compassion towards the Brute Creatures.

Aëra per vacuum ferri, atque assurgere in auras.
Nec mora, nec requies: at fulvæ nimbus arenæ
Tollitur: humescunt spumis, flatuque sequentum.
Tantus amor laudum, tantæ est victoria curæ.
Primus Erichthonius currus, et quatuor ausus
Jungere equos, rapidisque rotis insistere victor.
Fræna Pelethronii Lapithæ, gyrosque dedere
Impositi dorso; atque equitem docuere sub armis
Insultare solo, et gressus glomerare superbos.
Æquus uterque labor; æquè juvenemque magistri
Exquirunt, calidumque animis, et cursibus acrem:
Quamvis sæpe fugâ versos ille egerit hostes,
Et patriam Epirum referat, fortesque Mycenas;
Neptunique ipsa deducat origine gentem.
His animadversis, instant sub tempus, et omnes
Impendunt curas denso distendere pingui,
Quem legêre ducem, et pecori dixere maritum:
Pubentesque secant herbas, fluviosque ministrant,
Farraque; ne blando nequeat superesse labori;
Invalidique patrum referant jejunia nati.

ferri per vacuum aëra, atque assurgere in auras. Nec mora, nec requies datur iis: *at nimbus fulvæ arenæ tollitur: humescunt spumis flatuque sequentum.* Est illis *tantus amor laudum, victoria est tantæ curæ* illis. *Erichthonius primus* est *ausus jungere currus et quatuor equos, victorque insistere rapidis rotis. Pelethronii Lapithæ, impositi dorso* equorum, *dedere fræna gyrosque; atque docuere equitem sub armis insultare solo, et glomerare superbos gressus. Uterque labor* sive aurigandi sive equitandi *est æquus; magistri* utriusque artis *æquè exquirunt* equum *juvenemque, calidumque animis, et acrem cursibus:* non eligunt senem, *quamvis ille sæpe egerit hostes versos fugâ, et referat Epirum patriam, fortesque Mycenas; deducatque gentem origine Neptuni ipsâ. His animadversis, instant sub tempus* admissuræ; *et impendunt* omnes *curas distendere cum denso pingui, quem legere ducem, et dixere maritum pecori: secantque pubentes herbas, ministrantque fluvios, farraque; ne nequeat superesse blando labori, invalidique nati referant jejunia patrum.*

TRANSLATION.

to mount up into the Skies. No Stop, no Stay: But a thick Cloud of yellow Sand is tossed up: The foremost are wet with the Foam and Breath of those that follow. So powerful is the Love of Praise, so anxious the Desire of Victory.

First Erichthonius dared to yoke the Chariot and four Steeds, and over the rapid Wheels victorious to preside. The Pelethronian Lapithæ first mounted on Horseback applied the Reins, and turned him in the Ring; taught the Horseman under Arms to bound insulting over the Plain, and with proud ambling Pace to prance along. Either Toil, *that of the Chariot and of the Manage*, is equal; with equal Care the Masters in either Case seek after a *Steed that is* youthful, of warm Mettle, and sprightly in the Race: Tho' often he may have drove before him the flying Foes, may boast of Epirus, or of warlike Mycene for his Country, and derive his Race even from Neptune's Breed.

These Things observed, they are very careful about the Time *of Generation*, and bestow all their Care to plump him up with firm Fat whom they have chose Leader, and assigned Stallion to the Herd: They cut *for* him downy, *tender* Herbs, supply him with Fulness of Water and Corn, lest he should not be sufficient for the soothing Toil; and the puny Sons resemble the Meagreness of their

NOTES.

117. *Gressus glomerare superbos.* This is the same with what *Varro* calls *tolutim incedere*, and *Pliny*, *tolutim carpere gressus*, and *Martial*, *ad numeros colligere ungulas*: to move with a round ambling Pace.

120. *Quamvis sæpe fugâ*, &c. That is, says *Servius*, *Quamvis sit sæpe victor, quamvis nobili genere procreatus, tamen à magistris est ætas, magnanimitasque requirenda.*

Ipsa autem macie tenuant armenta volentes : 129
Atque, ubi concubitus primos jam nota voluptas
Sollicitat, frondesque negant, et fontibus arcent :
Sæpe etiam cursu quatiunt, et Sole fatigant,
Cum graviter tunsis gemit area frugibus, et cum
Surgentem ad Zephyrum paleæ jactantur inanes.
Hoc faciunt, nimio ne luxu obtusior usus 135
Sit genitali arvo, et sulcos oblimet inertes ;
Sed rapiat sitiens venerem, interiusque recondat.
  Rursus cura patrum cadere, et succedere matrum
Incipit ; exactis gravidæ cum mensibus errant :
Non illas gravibus quisquam juga ducere plaustris,
Non saltu superare viam sit passus, et acri 141
Carpere prata fugâ, fluviosque innare rapaces.
Saltibus in vacuis pascant, et plena secundum
Flumina ; muscus ubi, et viridissima gramine ripa,
Speluncæque tegant, et saxea procubet umbra. 145
  Est, lucos Silari circa, ilicibusque virentem
Plurimus Alburnum, volitans, cui nomen asylo

Autem illi volentes tenuant armenta ipsa macie. Atque, ubi jam nota voluptas earum solicitat primos concubitus; negantque illis frondes, et arcent eas fontibus: sæpe etiam quatiunt eas cursu, et fatigant eas Sole, cum area gemit graviter tunsis frugibus, et cum inanes paleæ jactantur ad surgentem Zephyrum. Faciunt hoc, ne nimio luxu sit obtusior usus genitali arvo, et oblimet inertes sulcos; sed ut sitiens rapiat venerem, recondatque eam interius. Rursus, cura patrum incipit cadere, et illa matrum succedere, cum illæ errant gravidæ mensibus exactis. Non quisquam sit passus illas ducere juga gravibus plaustris, non superare viam saltu, et carpere prata acri fugâ, innare que rapaces fluvios. Pascant in vacuis saltibus, et secundum plena flumina; ubi muscus sit, et ripa viridissima gramine, speluncæque tegant eas, et saxea umbra procubet illis. Est circa lucos fluvii Silari, Alburnumque montem virentem ilicibus, plurimus volitans, cui asylo est Romanum nomen,

TRANSLATION.

Sires. But they purposely extenuate the Breed-mares with Leanness : And, when now the known Pleasure solicits the first Enjoyment, they both deny them Herbs, and debar them from the Springs : Often too they shake them in the Race, and tire them in the Sun, when beneath the beaten Grain the Barn-floor deeply groans, and in the rising Zephyr the empty Chaff is tossed about. This they do, that by excessive pampering the genial Soil may not be blunted in its Use, and choak up the sluggish Passages ; but may with Eagerness drink in the Joys of Love, and lay them up more deep within.

Again the Care of the Sires begins to fail, and that of the Dams to succeed ; when now, their Months elapsed, they rove about pregnant : Let no one suffer them to drag the Yokes of heavy Waggons, nor to leap across the Way, to scamper over the Meads with sprightly Career, and swim the rapid Floods. Let them feed in spacious Lawns, and beside full Rivers ; where Moss, and grassy Banks of prime Verdure, and Caves may shelter them, and over them a shady Rock project.

About the Groves of Silarus, and Alburnus, verdant with ever-green Oaks, abounds a flying Insect, which the Romans name Asylus, and the Greeks in

NOTES.

133. *Cum graviter tunsis gemit area frugibus.* This refers to the Custom of treading out the Corn by Oxen.

144. *Viridissima gramine ripa.* Literally, *a Bank most verdant with Grass.*

145. *Est lucos Silari.* Silarus, now *Selo*, a River of *Italy* in *Lucania*, which divides that Country from the *Picene* Territory, or the Marquisate of *Ancona*.

147. *Alburnum.* Alburnus, a Mountain of that Country, now *Alborno*, out of which rises the River *Tanagrus*, *the Negro*, which is very small, and therefore mostly dry in Summer.

147. *Asylo.* The *Asylus*, or *Tabanus*, is a flying Insect, in Shape somewhat resembling a wild Bee or Wasp. The Belly is terminated by three long Rings, from the last of which proceeds

Romanum est, œstron Graii vertere vocantes;
Asper, acerba sonans: quo tota exterrita silvis
Diffugiunt armenta; furit mugitibus æther
Concussus, silvæque, et sicci ripa Tanagri.
Hoc quondam monstro horribiles exercuit iras
Inachiæ Juno pestem meditata juvencæ.
Hunc quoquè (nam mediis fervoribus acrior instat)
Arcebis gravido pecori; armentaque pasces
Sole recens orto, aut noctem ducentibus astris.
Post partum cura in vitulos traducitur omnis;
Continuòque notas, et nomina gentis inurunt:
Et quos aut pecori malint submittere habendo,
Aut aris servare sacros, aut scindere terram,
Et campum horrentem fractis invertere glebis.
Cætera pascuntur virides armenta per herbas.
Tu quos ad studium atque usum formabis agrestem
Jam vitulos hortare, viamque insiste domandi,

Graii vocantes hunc asylum *vertere œstron; asper, sonans acerba: quo tota armenta exterrita diffugiunt silvis, æther concussus mugitibus furit, silvæque, et ripa sicci Tanagri furit. Juno, meditata pestem Inachiæ juvencæ, quondam exercuit horribiles iras hoc monstro. Arcebis hunc asylum quoque gravido pecori; (nam ille acrior instat mediis fervoribus) pasce que armenta, sole recens orto, aut astris ducentibus noctem. Post partum, omnis cura traducitur in vitulos; continuòque inurunt notas et nomina gentis: et notant eos, quos aut malint submittere pecori habendo, aut servare sacros aris, aut scindere terram, et invertere horrentem campum fractis glebis. Cætera armenta pascuntur per virides herbas in*discriminatim. *Jam hortare vitulos quos tu formabis ad studium atque agrestem usum, insisteque viam domandi eos;*

TRANSLATION.

their Language have rendered Oestron; armed with a *sharp* Sting, humming harsh: With which whole Herds affrighted fly diverse through the Woods: The Sky is furiously shook with Bellowings, and the Woods, and Banks of dry Tanagrus. With this Monster did Juno once exercise her fell Revenge, having meditated a Plague for the Inachian Heifer. This too (for in the Noontide Heats it rages more keen) you shall keep off from the pregnant Cattle; and feed your Herds when the Sun is newly risen, or when the Stars usher in the Night.

After the Birth, the whole Care is transferred to the Calves; and from the first they stamp with a hot Iron the Marks and Names of the Race: And which they choose to bring up for the Increase of the Flock, or *which* to keep sacred for the Altars, or *which* to cleave the Ground, and turn up the Soil all rugged with broken Clods. The rest of the Herd *promiscuous* graze amidst the green Pastures.

Those, which you would form for Exercise and rustic Service, train up while Calves, and enter on the Way to tame them, whilst their Minds in Youth are

NOTES.

proceeds a formidable Sting. This Sting is composed of a Tube, through which the Egg is emitted, and of two Augres, which make way for the Tube to penetrate into the Skin of the Cattle. Those Augres are armed with little Knives, which prick with their Points, and cut with their Edges, causing intolerable Pain to the Animal that is wounded by them.

153. *Inachiæ juvencæ.* Io, the Daughter of *Inachus*, whom *Jove*, to blind *Juno*, transformed into a Heifer. But the Goddess, discovering the Deceit, sent an *Oestros* to torment her; with which being stung she fled into *Egypt*, where, being restored to her former Shape, she was married to King *Osiris*, and after her Death was worshipped as a Goddess under the Name of *Isis*. *See Banier's Mythology.*

162. *Cætera pascuntur*, &c. The Meaning seems to be, as Mr. *Martin* has it, that *the rest of the Herd*, that is, those which are designed for Breeding, or Sacrifice, *may feed at large in the Meadows*, for they need no other Care than

to

dum animi juvenum ſunt *faciles, dum ætas* eorum eſt *mobilis. Ac primùm ſubnecte cervici* eorum *laxos circulos de tenui vimine: dehinc ubi aſſuêrint colla* priùs *libera ſervitio, junge* duos *pares juvencos aptos è torquibus ipſis, et coge* eos *conferre gradum. Atque jam ſæpe inanes rotæ ducantur* ab *illis per terram, et ſignent veſtigia* earum *ſummo pulvere. Poſt faginus axis, nitens ſub valido pondere, inſtrepat, et æreus temo trahat orbes junctos* ſibi. *Interea carpes non gramina tantùm indomitæ pubi, nec veſcas frondes ſalicum, paluſtremque ulvam, ſed* etiam *ſata frumenta manu: nec fetæ vaccæ, more* noſtrorum *patrum, implebunt nivea mulctralia; ſed conſument tota ubera in dulces natos. Sin ſtudium eſt magis ad bellum, feroceſque turmas, aut prælabi Alphea flumina Piſæ rotis, et agitare volantes currus in luco Jovis; primus labor equi eſt, videre animos atque arma bellantum, patique lituos, ferreque rotam gementem tractu.*

Dum faciles animi juvenum, dum mobilis ætas.
Ac primùm laxos tenui de vimine circlos
Cervici ſubnecte: dehinc, ubi libera colla
Servitio aſſuêrint, ipſis è torquibus aptos
Junge pares, et coge gradum conferre juvencos:
Atque illis jam ſæpe rotæ ducantur inanes
Per terram, et ſummo veſtigia pulvere ſignent.
Poſt valido nitens ſub pondere faginus axis
Inſtrepat, et junctos temo trahat æreus orbes.
Interea pubi indomitæ non gramina tantùm,
Nec veſcas ſalicum frondes, ulvamque paluſtrem,
Sed frumenta manu carpes ſata: nec tibi fetæ,
More patrum, nivea implebunt mulctralia vaccæ;
Sed tota in dulces conſument ubera natos.
  Sin ad bella magis ſtudium, turmaſque feroces,
Aut Alphea rotis prælabi flumina Piſæ,
Et Jovis in luco currus agitare volantes;
Primus equi labor eſt, animos atque arma videre
Bellantum, lituoſque pati, tractuque gementem

TRANSLATION.

tractable, while their Age is pliant. And firſt faſten about their Necks looſe Collars of ſlender Twigs: Next, when they have accuſtomed their free Necks to Servitude, match your Bullocks in Pairs joined by thoſe ſame Collars, and make them ſtep together: And now let empty Wheels be dragged by them along the Ground, and let them print their Traces in the Surface of the Duſt. Afterwards let the beachen Axle labouring under a ponderous Load creak, and the brazen Pole draw the joined Wheels. Meanwhile for the young untamed Bullocks you ſhall crop with your Hand not only Graſs, or the Willows tender Leaves, or marſhy Sedge, but *alſo* ſpringing Corn: Nor ſhall your ſuckling Heifers, as was the Cuſtom of our Fathers, fill the ſnowy Milking-pails; but ſpend all their Udders on their ſweet Offspring.

But if thy Inclination is to War and martial Troops, or with thy Wheels to ſkim along the Brink of Piſa's Alphean Streams, and drive the flying Chariot in Jupiter's Grove; the firſt Taſk of the Horſe muſt be to view the Fierceneſs and the Arms of Warriors, to be patient of the Trumpet, and to bear the Rumbling of

NOTES.

to furniſh them with ſufficient Nouriſhment, till they arrive at their due Age. But *theſe, which are deſigned for Agriculture*, require more Care, they muſt be *tamed whilſt they are but Calves, and made tractable in their tender Years.*

170. *Rotæ ducantur inanes.* By *rotæ inanes, empty Wheels*, are either meant *empty Carriages*, or *Wheels without any Carriage laid upon them.*

180. *Alphea Piſæ. Piſa* was the Name of a Country in that Part of *Elis* thruugh which the River *Alpheus* flowed, and in which ſtood the famous Temple of *Jupiter Olympius.*

188. *In-*

Ferre rotam, et ſtabulo frænos audire ſonantes:
Tum magis atque magis blandis gaudere magiſtri
Laudibus, et plauſæ ſonitum cervicis amare.
Atque hæc jam primò depulſus ab ubere matris
Audiat; inque vicem det mollibus ora capiſtris,
Invalidus, etiamque tremens, etiam inſcius ævi.
At, tribus exactis, ubi quarta acceſſerit æſtas,
Carpere mox gyrum incipiat, gradibuſque ſonare
Compoſitis, ſinuetque alterna volumina crurum:
Sitque laboranti ſimilis. Tum curſibus auras
Próvocet; ac per aperta volans, ceu liber habenis,
Æquora, vix ſummâ veſtigia ponat arenâ.
Qualis Hyperboreis Aquilo cum denſus ab oris
Incubuit, Scythiæque hiemes, atque arida differt
Nubila: tum ſegetes altæ, campique natantes
Lenibus horreſcunt flabris; ſummæque ſonorem
Dant ſilvæ, longique urgent ad litora fluctus:
Ille volat, ſimul arva fugâ, ſimul æquora verrens.
Hic, vel ad Elei metas, et maxima campi
Sudabit ſpatia, et ſpumas aget ore cruentas:

et audire ſonantes frænos ſtabulo: tum magis atque magis gaudere blandis laudibus magiſtri, et amare ſonitum plauſæ cervicis. Atque audiat hæc jam primo depulſus ab ubere matris, inque vicem det ora mollibus capiſtris invalidus, etiamque tremens, etiam inſcius propter imbecillitatem *ævi. At, ubi quarta æſtas acceſſerit, tribus exactis, mox incipiat carpere gyrum, ſonareque compoſitis gradibus, ſinuetque alterna volumina crurum: ſitque ſimilis laboranti. Tum provocet auras curſibus; ac volans per aperta æquora, ceu liber habenis, vix ponat veſtigia ſummâ arenâ. Qualis cum denſus Aquilo incubuit ab Hyperboreis oris, differtque hiemes Scythiæ atque arida nubila: tum altæ ſegetes, natanteſque campi horreſcunt lenibus flabris, ſummæque ſilvæ dant ſonorem, longique fluctus urgent ſe ad litora. Ille volat verrens ſimul arva, ſimul æquora fugâ. Hic* equus, *vel ad metas et maxima ſpatia Elei campi, ſudabit, et aget cruentas ſpumas ore:*

TRANSLATION.

the Wheels in their Career, and in his Stall to hear the rattling Bridles: Then more and more to rejoice in the ſoothing Applauſes of his Maſter, and to love the Sound of patting his Neck. And these let him hear as ſoon as weaned from the Udder of his Dam, and now and then yield his Mouth to ſoft Head-ſtalls when weak, and yet trembling, and yet unexperienced from his Years. But, three *full Years* elapſed, when his fourth Summer is arrived, let him forthwith begin to wheel the Ring, and with regular Steps to prance, and let him bend the pliant Joints of his Legs alternately, and ſeem to labour. Then let him dare the Winds in Swiftneſs, and through the open Plains flying, as looſened from the Reins, ſcarce print his Steps on the Surface of the Sand. As when aſtringent Boreas hath ruſhed forth from the Hyperborean Regions, and drives along the Scythian Storms and dry Clouds: Then the high Fields of Corn and waving Plains tremble with the *firſt* gentle Guſts, the Tops of the Woods ruſtle, and the lengthened Waves preſs towards the Shore: He flies, ſweeping in his Career at once the Fields, at once the Seas. Such a Courſer, or round the Goals and ſpacious Bounds of the Elean Plain will ſweat, and drive the *Flakes of* bloody

NOTES.

188. *Invicem.* i. e. *Sometimes be tried with them, and ſometimes without them.* Nonnunquam, ſays Celſus, *ſit ſine capiſtris.* Dr. Trapp underſtands it in this Senſe, *now and then.*

189. *Inſcius ævi.* i. e. *Propter imbecillitatem ævi*; it is a *Greek* Conſtruction.

193. *Sitque laboranti ſimilis.* Either, *Let him practiſe to prance and curvet, however painful and fatiguing it may be to him at firſt.* Or, as Dr. Trapp and others: *Let him not really labour by reaſon of his tender Age, but be exerciſed with ſeeming Labour.*

202. *Elei campi.* i. e. *The Plains about Olympia, in the Region of* Elis, by which Name the whole Country between *Achaia, Meſſenia,* and *Arcadia*, was called.

vel meliùs feret Belgica esseda molli collo. Tum demum finito magnum corpus crescere iis *jam domitis crassa farragine: namque,* si saginentur *ante domandum, tollent ingentes animos; prensique negabunt pati lenta verbera, et parere duris lupatis. Sed non ulla industria magis firmat vires, quàm avertere venerem et stimulos cæci amoris; sive usus boum, sive equorum est gratior cui. Atque ideò relegant tauros procul, atque in sola pascua, post oppositum montem, et trans lata flumina: aut servant* eos *clausos intus ad satura præsepia. Enim femina carpit* ejus *vires paulatim, uritque* eum *videndo: nec patitur* eum *meminisse nemorum nec herbæ. Illa quidem* facit hoc *dulcibus illecebris, et sæpe subigit superbos amantes decernere inter se cornibus. Formosa juvenca pascitur in magnâ silvâ:* illi tauri *alternantes multâ vi miscent prœlia crebris vulneribus: ater sanguis lavit corpora; cornuaque adversa urgentur in* adversarios *obnixos cum vasto gemitu: silvæque et magnus Olympus reboant.*

Belgica vel molli meliùs feret esseda collo.
Tum demum crassa magnum farragine corpus
Crescere jam domitis sinito: namque ante domandum
Ingentes tollent animos; prensique negabunt
Verbera lenta pati, et duris parere lupatis.
Sed non ulla magis vires industria firmat,
Quàm venerem, et cæci stimulos avertere amoris;
Sive boum, sive est cui gratior usus equorum.
Atque ideò tauros procul, atque in sola relegant
Pascua, post montem oppositum, et trans flumina lata:
Aut intus clausos satura ad præsepia servant.
Carpit enim vires paulatim, uritque videndo
Femina: nec nemorum patitur meminisse, nec herbæ.
Dulcibus illa quidem illecebris, et sæpe superbos
Cornibus inter se subigit decernere amantes.
Pascitur in magnâ silvâ formosa juvenca:
Illi alternantes multâ vi prœlia miscent
Vulneribus crebris: lavit ater corpora sanguis;
Versaque in obnixos urgentur cornua vasto
Cum gemitu: reboant silvæque et magnus Olympus.

TRANSLATION.

Foam from his Mouth: Or will better bear the Belgic Chariots on his pliant Neck. Then at last, when they are now broke, let their ample Bodies grow with fattening Mash: For, *if full fed* before they are broke, they will swell their Mettle high, and laid hold of, refuse to bear the limber Whip, and to obey the hard Bits.

But no Industry more confirms their Strength, than to avert Venus from them, and the Stings of blind Love; whether any one be fonder of a Breed of Bullocks or of Horses. And therefore they remove the Bulls to a Distance, and to lonely Pastures, behind an obstructing Mountain, and beyond broad Rivers: Or keep them shut up within at full Cribs. For the Female insensibly consumes his Vigour, and fires him while in his Eye; Nor suffers him to mind his Groves and Pasture. Nay, she often by her attractive Charms even impels her haughty Lovers to combat together with their Horns. The beauteous Heifer feeds in the spacious Wood: *While* they by turns with mighty Force engage with repeated Wounds: Black Blood laves their Bodies; and their adverse Horns are impelled on the struggling Foes with a vast Groan: The Woods and spacious

NOTES.

211. *Tauros procul—relegant.* In like Manner Columella advises with respect to Horses. *Equos autem pretiosos reliquo tempore anni removere oportet à fœminis; ne aut, cum volent, ineant, aut, si id facere probibeantur, cupidine sollicitati noxam contrahant.*

Nec mos bellantes unà stabulare; sed alter
Victus abit, longèque ignotis exsulat oris;
Multa gemens ignominiam, plagasque superbi
Victoris, tum quos amisit inultus amores:
Et stabula aspectans regnis excessit avitis.
Ergo omni curâ vires exercet, et inter
Dura jacet pernox instrato saxa cubili,
Frondibus hirsutis, et carice pastus acutâ:
Et tentat sese, atque irasci in cornua discit
Arboris obnixus trunco; ventosque lacessit
Ictibus, et sparsâ ad pugnam proludit arenâ.
Post, ubi collectum robur, viresque receptæ,
Signa movet, præcepsque oblitum fertur in hos-
tem:
Fluctus ut, in medio cœpit cum albescere ponto,
Longiùs ex altoque sinum trahit; utque volutus
Ad terras immane sonat per saxa, nec ipso
Monte minor procumbit: at ima exæstuat unda
Vorticibus, nigramque altè subjectat arenam.

Nec est mos stabulare bellantes tauros unà; sed alter victus abit, exulatque longè ignotis oris; multa gemens ignominiam, plagasque illatas à cornibus *superbi victoris, tum amores, quos inultus amisit: et* frequenter *aspectans stabula excessit avitis regnis. Ergo exercet vires omni curâ, et pernox jacet instrato cubili inter dura saxa, pastus hirsutis frondibus et acutâ carice: et tentat sese, atque discit irasci in* sua *cornua, obnixus trunco arboris; lacessitque ventos ictibus, et proludit ad pugnam sparsâ arenâ. Post, ubi robur* est *collectum, viresque* sunt *receptæ, movet signa, præcepsque fertur in oblitum hostem: ut fluctus, cum cœpit albescere in medio ponto, trahit sinum longiùs exque alto* mari; *atque volutus ad terras sonat immane per saxa, nec minor monte ipso procumbit: at ima unda exæstuat vorticibus, subjectatque nigram arenam altè.*

TRANSLATION.

Skies rebel'ow. Nor is it usual for the Warriors to dwell together; but the one vanquished retires, and becomes an Exile in unknown distant Coasts; grievously bemoaning his Disgrace, and the Wounds of the proud Victor, in fine the Loves which unavenged he has lost: And with *many* a Retrospect on the Stalls, *which contain the Object of his Desire,* departs from his hereditary Realms. Therefore with the utmost Care he exercises his Strength, and lies all Night long among the hard Rocks, on a Couch quite bare, feeding on prickly Leaves and sharp-pointed Sedge: He essays himself, and practises his Rage upon his Horns, butting against the Trunk of a Tree; buffets the Winds with Blows, and preludes to the Fight by spurning the Sand. Afterwards, when his Strength is rallied, and his Vigour recovered, he flits his Camp, and is borne headlong on his unmindful Foe: As a Wave, when it begins to whiten in the Middle of the Sea, at Distance and from the Deep draws along a curling Train, and as rolling to the Land it roars dreadful among the Rocks, nor less even than a Mountain falls; while with Whirlpools the Water from the Bottom boils and tosses up the blackening Sand on high.

NOTES.

230. *Pernox.* This I take to be the true Reading, notwithstanding *Pierius* found *pernix* in all the Manuscripts he consulted. For *pernix* can hardly be explained consistently with the Sense of this Place. *Servius* however explains *pernix* by *perseverans*; but without producing any Authority.

230. *Instrato.* Not strewed with Leaves. The word occurs elsewhere in *Virgil*, *Lucretius*, and others, in a positive Sense, but here it seems to be taken negatively; tho' it may be construed with *Ruæus*, *cubili instrato inter*, &c.

237. *Fluctus ut in medio.* This Simile is taken from the fourth Iliad:

Ως δ' οτ' εν αιγιαλω πολυηχει κυμα θαλασσης, &c.

As when the Winds, ascending by Degrees,
First move the whitening Surface of the Seas,
The Billows float in Order to the Shore,
The Wave behind rolls on the Wave before, &c.

POPE.

Adeò omne genus in terris, hominumque ferarumque, et æquoreum genus, pecudes, pictæque volucres ruunt in furias ignemque hujusmodi; *idem amor* eſt *omnibus. Non alio tempore leæna, oblita catulorum, sævior erravit in agris; nec informes urſi dedere vulgò tam multa funera ſtragemque per ſilvas: tum aper* eſt *ſævus, tum tigris* eſt *peſſima. Heu! tum malè erratur in ſolis agris Libyæ. Nonne vides, ut tremor pertentet tota corpora equorum, ſi tantùm odor attulit notas auras? ac jam neque fræna virûm, neque ſæva verbera, non ſcopuli, cavæque rupes, atque objecta flumina, torquentia montes correptos undâ, retardant eos. Sabellicus ſus ipſe ruit, exacuitque dentes, et proſubigit terram pede, fricat coſtas arbore, atque durat humeros hinc atque illinc ad vulnera. Quid juvenis* facit, *cui durus amor verſat magnum ignem in oſſibus? nempe* ille, *ſerus cæcâ nocte, natat freta turbata abruptis procellis: ſuper quem ingens porta cœli tonat, et æquora illiſa ſcopulis reclamant:*

Omne adeò genus in terris hominumque ferarumque,
Et genus æquoreum, pecudes, pictæque volucres,
In furias ignemque ruunt; amor omnibus idem.
Tempore non alio catulorum oblita leæna
Sævior erravit campis; nec funera vulgò
Tam multa informes urſi, ſtragemque dedere
Per ſilvas: tum ſævus aper, tum peſſima tigris.
Heu! malè tum Libyæ ſolis erratur in agris.
Nonne vides, ut tota tremor pertentet equorum
Corpora, ſi tantùm notas odor attulit auras?
Ac neque eos jam fræna virûm, nec verbera ſæva,
Non ſcopuli, rupeſque cavæ, atque objecta retardant
Flumina, correptoſque undâ torquentia montes.
Ipſe ruit, denteſque Sabellicus exacuit ſus,
Et pede proſubigit terram, fricat arbore coſtas,
Atque hinc atque illinc humeros ad vulnera durat.
Quid juvenis, magnum cui verſat in oſſibus ignem
Durus amor? nempe abruptis turbata procellis
Nocte natat cæcâ ſerus freta: quem ſuper ingens
Porta tonat cœli, et ſcopulis illiſa reclamant

TRANSLATION.

And indeed every Kind on Earth, both Men and Savages, the ſcaly Race, the Beaſts, and parti-coloured Birds, ruſh into *this* Fire and Fury; Love rages in all the ſame. At no other Time does the Lioneſs, forgetful of her Whelps, range the Plains more fierce; nor do the unſhapely Bears uſually ſpread ſo numerous Ravages and ſuch Havock in the Woods: Then ferocious is the Boar, then moſt fell the Tyger. 'Tis then, alas! unhappy wandering in the deſolate Fields of Libya. See you not how tremulous Ardour ſhoots through the Horſe's whole Body, if his Smell has but ſucked in the well-known Gales? And now neither Bridles of Men, nor cruel Whips, nor Cliffs, nor hollow Rocks, and oppoſed Rivers, that whirl with their Torrent *whole* Mountains ſwept away, can retard him. Even the Sabellian Boar ruſhes, and whets his Tuſks, and with his Feet tears up the Ground, rubs his Flanks againſt a Tree, and on this Side and that Side hardens his Shoulders to Wounds. What *does* the Youth, in whoſe Vitals relentleſs Love fans the mighty Fire? Why, late in the darkſome Night he ſwims the Frith boiſterous with burſting Storms: Over whom the ſpacious Gate of Heaven thunders, and the Seas daſhing againſt the Rocks remurmur: Nor can

NOTES.

247. *Informes urſi. Vel magni*, ſays *Servius*; *vel qui tempore quo naſcuntur forma carent: dicitur enim caro quædam naſci, quam mater lambendo in membra componit.*

255. *Sabellicus ſus.* He mentions the *Sabellian* Boar, becauſe the Country of the *Sabines* was covered with Foreſts, the Haunt of Boars.

259. *Nempe abruptis.* Alluding to the Story of *Hero* and *Leander*. For which ſee *Ovid*.

261. *Porta tonat cœli.* This is a poetical Way of ſpeaking common to moſt Languages. The Burſting of the Clouds are conſidered under the Notion of the Heavens, or Gates of Heaven opening, and darting forth Thunder and Lightning.

261. *Re-*

Æquora: nec miſeri poſſunt revocare parentes,
Nec moritura ſuper crudeli funere virgo.
Quid lynces Bacchi variæ, et genus acre luporum,
Atque canum? quid? quæ imbelles dant prœlia cervi?
Scilicet ante omnes furor eſt inſignis equarum:
Et mentem Venus ipſa dedit, quo tempore Glauci
Potniades malis membra abſumſere quadrigæ.
Illas ducit amor trans Gargara, tranſque ſonantem
Aſcanium: ſuperant montes, et flumina tranant:
Continuòque avidis ubi ſubdita flamma medullis,
Vere magis (quia vere calor redit oſſibus) illæ
Ore omnes verſæ in Zephyrum, ſtant rupibus altis,
Exceptantque leves auras: et ſæpe ſine ullis
Conjugiis, vento gravidæ, mirabile dictu,
Saxa per, et ſcopulos, et depreſſas convalles
Diffugiunt; non, Eure, tuos, neque Solis ad ortus;
In Boream, Caurumque; aut unde nigerrimus Auſter
Naſcitur, et pluvio contriſtat frigore cœlum.
Hinc demum, hippomanes vero quod nomine dicunt

nec miſeri parentes poſſunt revocare eum, *nec virgo* ipſa *moritura ſuper* ejus *crudeli funere. Quid variæ lynces Bacchi, et acre genus luporum, atque canum* faciunt? *quid cervi* faciunt, et *quæ prœlia* illi *imbelles dant? ſcilicet ante omnes furor equarum eſt inſignis: et Venus ipſa dedit* illis hanc *mentem. quo tempore Potniades quadrigæ abſumſere membra Glauci malis. Amor ducit illas trans Gargara, tranſque ſonantem Aſcanium: ſuperant montes, et tranant flumina: continuòque, ubi flamma* eſt *ſubdita avidis medullis, magis vere (quia calor redit oſſibus vere) omnes illæ verſæ in Zephyrum ore, ſtant altis rupibus, exceptantque leves auras: et ſæpe ſine ullis conjugiis,* factæ *gravidæ vento, mirabile dictu, diffugiunt per ſaxa et ſcopulos, et depreſſas convalles; non* ad *tuos ortus, Eure, neque ad ortus Solis, in Boream, Caurumque, aut unde nigerrimus Auſter naſcitur, et contriſtat cœlum pluvio frigore. Hinc demum lentum virus, quod paſtores dicunt hippomanes vero nomine*

TRANSLATION.

his diſtreſſed Parents recal him, nor the Maid, who will be ſure to die in Conſequence of his diſaſtrous Fate. What *do* the ſpotted Lynxes of Bacchus, and the fierce Race of Wolves and Dogs? What the timorous Stags? what dreadful Wars they wage! Yet know the Fury of the Mares is moſt of all extraordinary: And this Spirit Venus herſelf inſpired, what time his four Potnian Mares tore the Limbs of Glaucus to Pieces with their Jaws. Love drives them acroſs the *pathleſs* Gargarus, and roaring Aſcanius: They climb the Mountains, ſwim the Rivers: And forthwith, when the Flame is ſecretly conveyed into their craving Marrow, chiefly in the Spring (for in the Spring the *genial* Heat returns into their Bones) they all, with their Mouths turned towards the Zephyr, ſtand on high Rocks, and catch the gentle Gales: And often, wondrous to relate! without any Mate, impregnated by the Wind, over Rocks and Cliffs, and hollow Vales they ſcour; not towards thine, O Eurus, nor the Sun's riſing, nor towards Boreas and Caurus, or whence grimly Auſter ariſes, and ſaddens the Sky with bleak Rain. Hence at laſt, what the Shepherds call by its true Name Hippomanes, a clam-

NOTES.

261. *Reclamant.* Either ſimply *rear back*, or *remurmur*, as we have tranſlated it; or ſeem by their roaring Noiſe to forbid any one's venturing out to Sea.

268. *Potniades.* Beotian, from *Potnia*, a Village in *Beotia*, whereof *Glaucus* was a Native.

269. *Gargara.* Gargarus was a Part of Mount *Ida* in *Troas*.

270. *Aſcanium.* Aſcanius is the Name of a River of *Bithynia* in *Aſia*, here put for River in general.

280. *Hippomanes.* See the Note on *Æn.* IV. 516.

destillat ab inguine earum. Hippomanes, quod sæpe malæ novercæ legêre, miscueruntque herbas huic, *et non innoxia verba. Sed interea tempus fugit, fugit irreparabile, dum capti amore describendi vectamur circum singula. Hoc est satis armentis. Altera pars nostræ curæ superat, nempe agitare lanigeros greges, hirtasque capellas. Hic est labor: fortes coloni sperate laudem hinc. Nec ego sum dubius animi, quàm magnum opus sit vincere ea verbis, et addere hunc honorem angustis rebus. Sed amor dulcis raptat me per ardua deserta Parnassi: juvat ire jugis, quà nulla orbita priorum divertitur molli clivo ad Castaliam* undam. *Nunc, Pales veneranda, nunc est sonandum magno ore. Incipiens, edico oves carpere herbam in mollibus stabulis, dum mox frondosa æstas reducitur: et sternere duram humum multâ stipulâ, maniplisque filicum subter* ovibus; *ne frigida glacies lædat molle pecus, feratque scabiem, turpesque podagras.*

Pastores, lentum destillat ab inguine virus.
Hippomanes, quod sæpe malæ legêre novercæ,
Miscueruntque herbas, et non innoxia verba.
Sed fugit interea, fugit irreparabile tempus,
Singula dum capti circumvectamur amore.
Hoc satis armentis. Superat pars altera curæ,
Lanigeros agitare greges, hirtasque capellas.
Hic labor: hinc laudem fortes sperate coloni.
Nec sum animi dubius, verbis ea vincere magnum
Quàm sit, et angustis hunc addere rebus honorem.
Sed me Parnassi deserta per ardua dulcis
Raptat amor: juvat ire jugis, quà nulla priorum
Castaliam molli devertitur orbita clivo.
Nunc, veneranda Pales, magno nunc ore sonandum.
Incipiens, stabulis edico in mollibus herbam
Carpere oves, dum mox frondosa reducitur æstas:
Et multâ duram stipulâ, filicumque maniplis
Sternere subter humum; glacies ne frigida lædat
Molle pecus, scabiemque ferat, turpesque podagras.

TRANSLATION.

my Poison distils from their Groins. Hippomanes, which wicked Stepdames often have gathered, and mixed *therewith* Herbs, and noxious Spells. But Time flies mean while, flies irretrievable, while we, enamoured *of the pleasing Theme*, minutely trace Particulars.

Thus far of Herds. Another Part of our Care remains, to manage the fleecy Flocks, and shaggy Goats. A Labour this: Hence hope for Praise ye sturdy Swains. Nor am I ignorant, how difficult it is to raise such Subjects by *Dignity of* Style, and add these *poetical* Ornaments to Things so low. But the sweet Love *of the Muses* transports me through the thorny Desarts of Parnassus: Pleased I am to range those Mountain-tops, where no Tract of the Ancients winds down with gentle Declination to Castalia.

Now, adorable Pales, now must I sing in lofty Strain. To begin, I appoint the Sheep to be foddered in soft Cotes, till first the flowery Spring return: And that the hard Ground underneath them be strewed with Plenty of Straw, and Bundles of Ferns; lest the cold Ice hurt the tender Cattle, and bring on the Scab,

NOTES.

291. *Parnassi.* Parnassus, a Mountain of *Phocis*, sacred to *Apollo* and the Muses. At the Foot of which was the Fountain of *Castalia*, sacred also to the Muses.

296. *Æstas.* The Spring. See the Note on Verse 322.

299. *Turpesque podagras.* Columella mentions two Kinds of Distempers that affect the Feet of Sheep, to which he gives the Name of *Clavi*. One is when there is a Filth and Galling in the Parting of the Hoof; the other, when there is a Tubercle in the same Place, with a Hair in the Middle, and a Worm under it. For both which he prescribes the proper Cure.

300. *Fron-*

Poſt, hinc digreſſus, jubeo frondentia capris
Arbuta ſufficere, et fluvios præbere recentes;
Et ſtabula à ventis hiberno opponere Soli
Ad medium converſa diem; cum frigidus olim
Jam cadit, extremoque irrorat Aquarius anno.
Hæ quoquè non curâ nobis leviore tuendæ;
Nec minor uſus erit: quamvis Mileſia magno
Vellera mutentur Tyrios incocta rubores.
Denſior hinc ſoboles; hinc largi copia lactis.
Quàm magis exhauſto ſpumaverit ubere mulctra;
Læta magis preſſis manabunt flumina mammis.
Nec minus interea barbas, incanaque menta
Cinyphii tondent hirci, ſetaſque comantes,
Uſum in caſtrorum, et miſeris velamina nautis.
Paſcuntur verò ſilvas, et ſumma Lycæi,
Horrenteſque rubos, et amantes ardua dumos.
Atque ipſæ memores redeunt in tecta, ſuoſque
Ducunt, et gravido ſuperant vix ubere limen.
Ergo omni ſtudio glaciem, ventoſque nivales,

Poſt, digreſſus hinc, jubeo ſufficere frondentia arbuta capris, et præbere iis *recentes fluvios, et opponere ſtabula* tuta *à ventis hiberno Soli converſa ad medium diem; cum jam olim frigidus Aquarius cadit, irroratque extremo anno. Hæ* capræ *quoquè* ſunt *tuendæ nobis non leviore curâ, nec uſus* earum *erit minor: quamvis Mileſia vellera* ovium, *incocta* quoad *Tyrios rubores, mutentur magno* pretio. *Soboles hinc* eſt *denſior,* eſt *hinc copia largi lactis. Quàm magis mulctra ſpumaverit ubere exhauſto; læta flumina magis manabunt preſſis mammis. Nec minus interea* paſtores *tondent barbas, incanaque menta, comanteſque ſetas Cinyphii hirci, in uſum caſtrorum, et* in *velamina miſeris nautis. Verò paſcuntur ſilvas, et ſumma* cacumina *Lycæi, horrenteſque rubos, et dumos amantes ardua* loca. *Atque ipſæ memores redeunt in tecta, ducuntque ſuos* fetus, *et vix ſuperant limen gravido ubere. Ergo avertes glaciem nivaleſque ventos* ab illis *omni ſtudio,*

TRANSLATION.

and foul Gouts. Next, leaving them, I order to provide the Goats with leafy Arbutes, and to ſupply them with freſh Streams; and, *ſheltered* from the Woods, to oppoſe their Cotes to the Winter Sun, turned towards the South; when cold Aquarius now ſets at length, and in the Extremity of the Year ſheds his Dews. Nor are theſe to be tended by us with leſs Care; nor will their Uſefulneſs be leſs: Tho' Mileſian Fleeces, that have drunk the Tyrian Glow, be ſold for much. From theſe *ariſes* a more numerous Breed, from theſe a greater Quantity of Milk. The more the Pail froths with their exhauſted Udder, the more will joyous Streams flow from their preſſed Dugs. Mean while *the Shepherds* alſo ſhear the Beards and houry Chins, and long waving Hair of the Cinyphian He-goat, for the Service of the Camp, and for Coverings to the adventurous Mariners. And then they *eaſily* find Paſture from the Woods, from the Summits of Lycæus, from the rough Brambles, and from Brakes that love the craggy Rocks. And mindful *of their Time* the Goats of themſelves return Home, and bring their Young with them, and can ſcarce get over the Threſhold with their teeming Udders. Therefore the leſs they themſelves provide againſt the Wants of Mortality, the more careful muſt you be to defend them from the Ice and ſnowy

NOTES.

300. *Frondentia arbuta.* Virgil uſes *arbutus* elſewhere for the Tree. See Ecl. III. 82. VII. 46. Geor. II. 69. and *arbutum* for the Fruit, as Geor. I. 148. II. 520. But here *arbuta frondentia* muſt ſignify the Tree, which is called *frondens*, becauſe it is an Ever-green, and therefore ſupplies the Goats with Browze in Winter, of which Seaſon *Virgil* is now ſpeaking.

313. *Uſum in caſtrorum, et miſeris velamina nautis.* So *Varro* obſerves that Goats were ſhorn for the Uſe of Sailors and Engines of War, namely, to cover the moving Turrets, under which the Aſſailants made their Approaches in a Siege: *Ut fructum ovis è lana ad veſtimentum; ſic capra pilis miniſtrat ad uſum nauticum, et ad bellica tormenta, et fabrilia vaſa.*

322. *Æſtat.*

Quò minus est illis curæ mortalis egestas,
Avertes; victumque feres, et virgea lætus
Pabula: nec totâ claudes fœnilia brumâ.
At verò, Zephyris cum læta vocantibus æstas,
In saltus utrumque gregem, atque in pascua mittes:
Luciferi primo cum sidere frigida rura
Carpamus; dum mane novum, dum gramina canent,
Et ros in tenerâ pecori gratissimus herbâ.
Inde, ubi quarta sitim cœli collegerit hora,
Et cantu querulæ rumpent arbusta cicadæ;
Ad puteos, aut alta greges ad stagna jubeto
Currentem ilignis potare canalibus undam:
Æstibus at mediis umbrosam exquirere vallem,
Sicubi magna Jovis antiquo robore quercus
Ingentes tendat ramos: aut sicubi nigrum
Ilicibus crebris sacrâ nemus accubet umbrâ.
Tum tenues dare rursus aquas, et pascere rursus
Solis ad occasum: cum frigidus aëra Vesper
Temperat, et saltus reficit jam roscida Luna,
Litoraque Alcyonen resonant, et acanthida dumi.

quò minus est illis egestas mortalis curæ; lætusque feres victum, et virgea pabula illis: *nec claudes fœnilia totâ brumâ. At verò, cum læta æstas* imminebit *Zephyris vocantibus, mittes utrumque gregem* ovium et caprarum *in saltus atque in pascua: cum primo sidere Luciferi, carpamus frigida rura* illis; *dum mane* est *novum, dum gramina canent, et ros, gratissimus pecori, est in tenerâ herbâ. Inde, ubi quarta hora collegerit sitim cœli, et querulæ cicadæ rumpent arbusta cantu; jubeto greges ad puteos, aut ad alta stagna, potare undam currentem ilignis canalibus: at mediis æstibus exquirere umbrosam vallem, sicubi magna quercus Jovis, antiquo robore, tendat ingentes ramos: aut sicubi nemus, nigrum crebris ilicibus, accubet sacrâ umbrâ. Tum* jube famulos *dare* illis *tenues aquas rursus, et pascere* illos *rursus ad occasum Solis: cum frigidus Vesper temperat aëra, et jam roscida Luna reficit saltus, litoraque resonant Alcyonen, et dumi* resonant *acanthida.*

TRANSLATION.

Winds; and you shall cheerfully bring them Food, and Browze of tender Twigs: Nor shut up from them your Stores of Hay all the Winter long.

But when the gay Summer *comes* * invited by the Zephyrs, you shall send *forth* both Flocks into the Lawns and Pastures: † When Lucifer first arises, ‡ let them crop the Fields *yet* cold; while the Morning is new, while the Grass is hoary, and the Dew, most grateful to the Cattle, is on the tender Herb. Then, as soon as the fourth Hour of Day shall have brought on Thirst, and the plaintive Grashoppers shall rend the Groves with their Song; order the Flocks to drink the Water running in Oaken troughs, *or* at the Wells, or at the deep Pools: But in the Noontide Heats *let them* seek out a shady Vale, wherever Jove's stately Oak of ancient Wood extends its huge Boughs: Or wherever a Grove, embrowned with thick ever-green Oaks, projects its sacred Shade. Then give them once more the translucent Streams, and once more feed them at the Setting of the Sun: When cool Vesper tempers the Air, and now the dewy Moon refreshes the Lawns, and the Shores resound with Halcyone, and the Bushes with the Gold-finch.

* *The Zephyrs inviting.* † *With the Star of Lucifer.* ‡ *Let us crop*, i. e. let us send them to crop.

NOTES.

322. *Æstas.* Virgil, agreeably to the Manner of many of the Ancients, divides the Year both here and elsewhere into two Seasons only, the Summer and Winter. See Verse 296.

331. *Æstibus at mediis umbrosam exquirere vallem.* So *Varro*: *Circiter meridianos æstus, dum defervescant, sub umbriferas rupes, et arbores patulas subjiciunt, quoad refrigerato aëre vespertino, rursus pascant ad solis occasum.* To this Custom, which was common in all the warmer Climates, we find an Allusion in the *Canticles*: "Tell me, O thou whom my Soul loveth, where thou feedest, where thou makest thy Flock to rest at Noon."

338. *Acanthida.* Others read *acalanthida.* This Bird is thought to be either the Gold-finch,

Quid tibi paſtores Libyæ, quid paſcua verſu
Proſequar, et raris habitata mapalia tectis?
Sæpe diem, noctemque, et totum ex ordine menſem
Paſcitur, itque pecus longa in deſerta ſine ullis
Hoſpitiis: tantum campi jacet. Omnia ſecum
Armentarius Afer agit, tectumque, Laremque,
Armaque, Amyclæumque canem, Creſſamque pharetram.
Non ſecus ac patriis acer Romanus in armis
Injuſto ſub faſce viam cum carpit, et hoſti
Ante exſpectatum poſitis ſtat in agmine caſtris.
At non, quà Scythiæ gentes, Mæoticaque unda,
Turbidus et torquens flaventes Iſter arenas;
Quàque redit medium Rhodope porrecta ſub axem:
Illic clauſa tenent ſtabulis armenta; neque ullæ
Aut herbæ campo apparent, aut arbore frondes:
Sed jacet aggeribus niveis informis, et alto
Terra gelu latè, ſeptemque aſſurgit in ulnas.

Quid proſequar tibi verſu paſtores Libyæ, quid paſcua, et mapalia habitata raris tectis? Sæpe pecus paſcitur diem noctemque, et totum menſem ex ordine, itque in longa deſerta ſine ullis hoſpitiis: tantum campi jacet. Afer armentarius agit omnia ſua ſecum, tectumque, Laremque, armaque, Amyclæumque canem, Creſſamque pharetram. Non ſecus ac acer Romanus, in patriis armis, cum carpit viam ſub injuſto faſce, et caſtris poſitis ante exſpectatum hoſti ſtat in agmine. At non fit ſic, quà Scythiæ gentes ſunt, Mæoticaque unda, et Iſter turbidus, et torquens flaventes arenas; quàque Rhodope porrecta ſub medium axem redit: illic tenent armenta clauſa ſtabulis; neque aut ullæ herbæ apparent campo, aut frondes apparent arbore: ſed terra jacet latè informis niveis aggeribus, et alto gelu, aſſurgitque in ſeptem ulnas.

TRANSLATION.

Why ſhould I trace in Song the Shepherds and Paſtures of Libya, and their Cottages, where * ſcatteringly they dwell? Their Flocks often graze both Day and Night, and for a whole Month together, and repair into long Deſarts without any Shelter: So wide the Plain extends. The African Shepherd carries his All with him, his Houſe, and Houſhold-god, his Arms, his Amyclæan Dog, and Cretan Quiver. Juſt as the fierce Roman, when, † armed for his Country, he takes his Way under the unequal Load, and having pitched his Camp ſtands in Battalia againſt the Foe, before he is expected.

But not ſo, where are the Scythian Nations, and the Mæotic Waves, and the turbid ‡ Iſter whirling his yellow Sand; and where Rhodope winds about, ſtretching itſelf under the Middle of the Pole: There they keep their Herds ſhut up in Stalls; nor are either any Herbs to be ſeen in the Fields, nor Leaves on the Trees: But the Country lies deformed with Mounts of Snow, and deep Ice all around, and riſes ſeven Ells in Heighth. *It is* always Winter, always

* *In Houſes thinly diſperſed.* † *In his Country's Arms.* ‡ *The Danube.*

NOTES.

finch, Linnet, or Nightingale; but it is uncertain which.

345. *Amyclæumque canem.* Amyclæ was a City of *Laconia*, which Region was famous for the beſt Dogs.

346. *Non ſecus ac patriis.* The Poet here compares the *African* loaded with his Arms and Baggage to a *Roman* Soldier on an Expedition. We learn from *Cicero*, that the *Romans* carried not only their Shields, Swords and Helmets, but alſo Proviſions for above Half a Month, Utenſils and Stakes: *Noſtri exercitus primum unde nomen habeant vide: deinde qui labor, quantus agminis: ferre plus dimidiati menſis cibaria: ferre ſiquid ad uſum velint: ferre vallum: nam ſcutum, gladium, galeam in onere noſtri milites non plus numerant, quam humeros, lacertos, manus.*

347. *Hoſti.* Vegetius in his firſt Book of *the Art of War*, quoting this Paſſage, reads *Hoſtem ante expectatum.*

349. *Scythiæ gentes.* The Ancients called all the northern Nations *Scythian.*

359. Oceani

Eſt ſemper hiems, ſunt ſemper Cauri ſpirantes frigora. Tum Sol haud unquam diſcutit pallentes umbras: nec cum invectus equis petit altum æthera: nec cum lavit præcipitem currum rubro æquore Oceani. Subitæ cruſtæ concreſcunt in currenti flumine: jamque unda ſuſtinet ferratos orbes rotarum *tergo*, *illa* unda *hoſpita priùs patulis puppibus, nunc plauſtris. Æraque diſſiliunt vulgò, veſteſque indutæ rigeſcunt, cæduntque vina humida ſecuribus, et totæ lacunæ vertêre* ſe *in ſolidam glaciem, horridaque ſtiria induruit impexis barbis. Interea non ſeciùs ningit toto aëre; pecudes intereunt; magna corpora boum ſtant circumfuſa pruinis; cervique, conferto agmine, torpent* ſub *novâ mole, et vix exſtant ſummis cornibus.* In*colæ non agitant hos canibus immiſſis, non ullis caſſibus, pavidoſve formidine puniceæ pennæ: ſed cominus obtruncant ferro* eos, *fruſtra trudentes oppoſitum montem* nivis *pectore.*

Semper hiems, ſemper ſpirantes frigora Cauri.
Tum Sol pallentes haud unquam diſcutit umbras:
Nec cum invectus equis altum petit æthera; nec cum
Præcipitem Oceani rubro lavit æquore currum.
Concreſcunt ſubitæ currenti in flumine cruſtæ:
Undaque jam tergo ferratos ſuſtinet orbes,
Puppibus illa priùs patulis, nunc hoſpita plauſtris.
Æraque diſſiliunt vulgò, veſteſque rigeſcunt
Indutæ, cæduntque ſecuribus humida vina,
Et totæ ſolidam in glaciem vertêre lacunæ,
Stiriaque impexis induruit horrida barbis.
Interea toto non ſeciùs aëre ningit;
Intereunt pecudes; ſtant circumfuſa pruinis
Corpora magna boum; confertoque agmine cervi
Torpent mole novâ, et ſummis vix cornibus exſtant.
Hos non immiſſis canibus, non caſſibus ullis,
Puniceæve agitant pavidos formidine pennæ:
Sed fruſtra oppoſitum trudentes pectore montem,

TRANSLATION.

Northweſt-winds blowing cold. Then the Sun never diſſipates the pale Shades: Neither when borne on his Steeds he climbs the lofty Sky; nor when he bathes his Chariot in the Ocean's ruddy Plain. Cruſts *of Ice* ſuddenly are congealed in the running River: Now on its Back the Wave ſuſtains Wheels bound with Iron, the Wave hoſpitable to broad Ships before, to Waggons now. Vaſes of Braſs frequently burſt aſunder, their Garments grow ſtiff on their Backs, they cut with Axes the liquid Wine, whole Pools turn to ſolid Ice, and the horrid Icicle hardens on their uncombed Beards. Mean while it ſnows inceſſantly over all the Air; the Cattle periſh; the large Bodies of Oxen ſtand wrapt about with Hoarfroſt; and the Deer crowding all together lie benumbed under the unuſual Load, and ſcarce appear with the Tips of their Horns. Theſe they purſue not with Hounds let looſe, nor with any Toils, nor ſcared with the Terror of the Crimſon Plume: But, as in vain they are ſhoving with their Breaſts the oppoſed

NOTES.

359. *Oceani rubro æquore.* The Sea is here called *red*, on account of the Reflection of the ſetting Sun. It is however frequent among the Poets to call the Sea *Purple*. Thus in the fourth Georgic:

Eridanus, quo non alius per pinguia culta
In mare purpur*eum violentior influit amnis.*

This Colour the Waves exhibit at certain Times. Thus *Cicero* deſcribes the Waves of the Sea as growing *purple*, when cut with Oars: "*Quid? mare nonne cæruleum? at ejus unda, cum eſt pulſa remis*, purpuraſcit."

364. *Cæduntque ſecuribus humida vina.* The Epithet *humida* ſeems uſed to denote the great Intenſeneſs of the Cold; that even Wine, which above all other Liquors preſerves its Fluidity in the coldeſt Weather in other Countries, is ſo hard frozen in thoſe northern Regions, as to require to be cut with Hatchets.

376. *In*

Cominus obtruncant ferro; graviterque rudentes
Cædunt; et magno læti clamore reportant.
Ipsi in defossis specubus, secura sub altâ
Otia agunt terra, congestaque robora, totasque
Advolvere focis ulmos, ignique dedere:
Hìc noctem ludo ducunt; et pocula læti
Fermento atque acidis imitantur vitea sorbis.
Talis Hyperboreo Septem subjecta trioni
Gens effrena virûm Riphæo tunditur Euro:
Et pecudum fulvis velantur corpora setis.
Si tibi lanicium curæ; primum aspera silva.
Lappæque tribulique absint: fuge pabula læta:
Continuòque greges villis lege mollibus albos.
Illum autem, quamvis aries sit candidus ipse,
Nigra subest udo tantùm cui lingua palato,
Rejice; ne maculis infuscet vellera pullis
Nascentum; plenoque alium circumspice campo.
Munere sic niveo lanæ, si credere dignum est,
Pan Deus Arcadiæ captam te, Luna, fefellit,

cædunt que eos rudentes graviter, et læti reportant eos magno clamore. Scythæ ipsi agunt secura otia in defossis specubus sub altâ terrâ, advolvere congestaque robora, totasque ulmos focis, dedereque eas igni: hìc ducunt noctem ludo; et læti imitantur vitea pocula fermento atque acidis sorbis. Talis effræna gens virûm, subjecta Hyperboreo septemtrioni, tunditur Riphæo Euro: et corpora velantur fulvis setis. Si lanicium est tibi curæ; primùm aspera silva, lappæque, tribulique absint ovibus: fuge læta pabula: continuòque lege albos greges mollibus villis. Autem, quamvis aries ipse sit candidus, rejice illum, cui tantùm nigra lingua subest udo palato, ne infuscet vellera nascentum pullis maculis; circumspiceque alium pleno campo. Sic Pan Deus Arcadiæ fefellit te, Luna, captam niveo munere lanæ, si est dignum credere,

TRANSLATION.

Mountain *of Snow*, they stab them with the Sword close at hand, and put them to Death piteously braying, and with loud Acclamation bear them off triumphant. The Inhabitants themselves in Caves dug deep under Ground enjoy undisturbed Rest, and roll to their Hearths piled up Oaks, and whole Elms, and give them to the Flames. Here they spend the Night in Play, and joyous imitate the * Juice of the Grape with their † Beer and acid ‡ Cyder. Such is that savage Race of Men lying under the northern Sign of *Ursa Major*, buffeted by the Riphæan Eastwind, and whose Bodies are cloathed with the tawny Furrs of Beasts.

If the woollen Manufacture be thy Care; first let prickly Woods, and Burrs, and Caltroops be far away: Shun rich Pastures: And from the Beginning choose Flocks that are white with soft Wool. And that Ram, tho' he himself be of the purest White, under whose moist Palate there lurks but a black Tongue, reject; lest he should sully the Fleeces of the new-born Lambs: And look out for another over the well-stocked Field. Thus Pan, the God of Arcadia, if the Story be worthy of Credit, deceived thee, O Moon, captivated with a snowy

* *Draughts of the Vine.* † *Fermented Liquor.* ‡ *Service Berries.*

NOTES.

376. *In defossis specubus.* This agrees with History: Thus *Pomponius Mela*, speaking of the *Sarmatæ*, says, they dig Holes in the Earth for their Habitations: *Demersis in humum sedibus, specus aut suffossa habitant, totum braccati corpus, et, nisi qua vident, etiam ora vestiti.* And *Tacitus* also says, the *Germans* used to make Caves to defend them from the Severity of Winter: *Solent et subterraneos specus aperire, eosque insuper multo fimo onerant, suffugium hiemi, et receptaculum frugibus.*

381. *Septem subjecta trioni.* The *Triones*, or *Septemtriones*, are the two northern Constellations, commonly known by the Names of the *Greater* and *Lesser Bear*, in each of which are seven Stars placed nearly in the same Order, and which were fancied by the Ancients to represent a Waggon, and were therefore called ἁμάξαι and *Plaustra*. *Aulus Gellius* tells us, from *Varro*, that *Triones* is as it were *Terriones*, and was a Name by which the old Husbandmen called a Team of Oxen.

391. *Munere sic niveo.* We are told by *Probus*, that Pan, being in Love with the *Moon*

vocans te in alia nemora; nec tu es aspernata eum vocantem te. At cui est amor lactis, ipse ferat cytisum lotosque frequentes, salsasque herbas præsepibus. Hinc et amant fluvios magis, et magis tendunt ubera, et referunt occultum saporem salis in lacte. Jam multi prohibent excretos hœdos à matribus, præfiguntque prima ora ferratis capistris. Quod mulsere die surgente, horisque diurnis, premunt id nocte; quod jam mulsere tenebris et sole cadente, pastor, exportans id calathis sub lucem, adit oppida: aut contingunt id parco sale, reponuntque hiemi. Nec cura canum fuerit postrema tibi; sed unà pasce veloces catulos Spartæ, acremque Molossum pingui sero. Nunquam, illis custodibus, horrebis nocturnum furem stabulis, incursusque luporum, aut impacatos Iberos urgentes à tergo.

In nemora alta vocans; nec tu aspernata vocantem.
At cui lactis amor, cytisum, lotosque frequentes
Ipse manu, salsasque ferat præsepibus herbas
Hinc et amant fluvios magis, et magis ubera tendunt,
Et salis occultum referunt in lacte saporem.
Multi jam excretos prohibent à matribus hœdos,
Primaque ferratis præfigunt ora capistris.
Quod surgente die mulsere horisque diurnis,
Nocte premunt; quod jam tenebris et Sole cadente,
Sub lucem exportans calathis adit oppida pastor:
Aut parco sale contingunt, hiemique reponunt.
Nec tibi cura canum fuerit postrema; sed unà
Veloces Spartæ catulos, acremque Molossum
Pasce sero pingui. Nunquam custodibus illis
Nocturnum stabulis furem, incursusque luporum,
Aut impacatos à tergo horrebis Iberos.

TRANSLATION.

Offering of Wool, inviting thee into the deep Groves; nor didst thou scorn his Invitation.

But let him, who is studious of Milk, carry to their Cribs with his own Hand the Cytisus, and Plenty of Water-lilies, and salt Herbs. Hence they are both more desirous of the River, and distend their Udders the more, and in their Milk return a faint Relish of the Salt.

Many restrain the Kids as soon as grown up from their Dams, and fasten Muzzles with Iron Spikes about the Extremity of their Mouths. What they milk at the Sun-rising and the Hour of Morn, they press at Night; what they milk now in the Evening and at Sun setting, the Shepherd at Day-break carries to Town in Baskets *: Or they season it with a small Quantity of Salt, and lay it up for Winter.

Nor let your Care of Dogs be the last; but feed at once with fattening Whey the swift Hounds of Sparta, and the fierce Mastiff of Molossus. While these are your Guards, you shall never dread the nightly Robber to your Stalls, nor the Incursions of the Wolves, nor the restless Iberians coming upon you † by Stealth.

* i. e. Carries it made into Butter and Cheese. † *From behind.*

NOTES.

offered her the Choice of any Part of his Flock; that she, choosing the whitest, was deceived, because they were the worst Sheep. But, if the whitest Sheep were the worst in the Flock, it would not have answered *Virgil*'s Purpose to have alluded to the Fable. It is therefore more probable that the Fable, to which *Virgil* refers, was, as *Philargyrius* and others have related it, that *Pan* changed himself into a Ram as white as Snow, by which the *Moon* was deceived, as *Europa* was by *Jupiter*, in the Form of a white Bull.

399. *Ferratis capistris.* The Muzzles, of which the Poet speaks, are not such as confine the Mouth of the Lamb or Kid, for then it could not eat. They are Iron Spikes fastened about the Snout, which prick the Dam, if she offers to let her young One suck.

403. *Impacatos à tergo Iberos.* The *Spaniards*, or *Iberians*, were so famous for their Robberies, that the Poet makes use of their Name, in this Place, for Robbers in general.

408. *Iberos.* The *Spaniards*, so called from the River *Iberus*, now the *Ebro*.

417. *Vipera.*

Sæpe etiam cursu timidos agitabis onagros,
Et canibus leporem, canibus venabere damas.
Sæpe volutabris pulsos silvestribus apros
Latratu turbabis agens; montesque per altos
Ingentem clamore premes ad retia cervum.
Disce et odoratam stabulis accendere cedrum,
Galbaneoque agitare graves nidore chelydros.
Sæpe sub immotis præsepibus aut mala tactu
Vipera delituit, cœlumque exterrita fugit;
Aut tecto assuetus coluber succedere et umbræ,
Pestis acerba boum, pecorique aspergere virus,
Fovit humum: cape saxa manu, cape robora, pastor;
Tollentemque minas, et sibila colla tumentem
Dejice: jamque fugâ timidum caput abdidit altè,
Cum medii nexus, extremæque agmina caudæ
Solvuntur, tardosque trahit sinus ultimus orbes.
Est etiam ille malus Calabris in saltibus anguis,
Squammea convolvens sublato pectore terga,

Sæpe etiam agitabis timidos onagros cursu, et venabere leporem canibus, venabere damas canibus. Sæpe turbabis latratu apros pulsos silvestribus volutabris, agens eos; perque altos montes premes ingentem cervum ad retia clamore. Disce et accendere odoratam cedrum stabulis, agitareque graves chelydros Galbaneo nidore. Sæpe sub immotis præsepibus, aut vipera mala tactu delituit, exterritaque fugit cœlum; aut coluber, acerba pestis boum, assuetus succedere tecto et umbræ aspergereque virus pecori, fovit humum: pastor, cape saxa manu, cape robora; dejiceque eum tollentem minas, et tumentem sibila colla; jamque fugâ abdidit timidum caput altè, cum medii nexus, agminaque extremæ caudæ solvuntur, ultimusque sinus trahit tardos orbes. Est etiam ille malus in Calabris saltibus, convolvens squammea terga sublato pectore,

TRANSLATION.

Often too in the Chace you shall pursue the timorous wild Asses, and with Hounds you shall hunt the Hare, with Hounds the Hind. Often, driving on with full Cry, you shall give Chace to the Boar rouzed from his silvan Soil; and over the lofty Mountains with hallowing pursue the stately Stag into the Toil.

Learn also to burn fragrant Cedar in the Folds, and to drive away the rank Water-snakes with the Scent of Galbanum. Often under the Mangers, when not moved, either the Viper of pernicious Touch lies concealed, and affrighted flies the Light: Or that Snake, the direful Pest of Kine, which uses to shelter itself under a Roof and Shade, and shed its Venom on the Cattle, keeps close to the Ground: Snatch up Stones, Shepherds, snatch up Clubs; and while he rears his threatening Gorge, and swells his hissing Neck, knock him down: And now in Flight he has hid his dastardly Head full deep, while his Middle-knots and the Wreaths in his Tail's Extremity are unfolded, and his last tortuous Joint now drags its slow Spires along. There is also that baneful Snake in the Calabrian Lawns, winding up his scaly Back, with Breast erect, and his long

NOTES.

417. *Vipera.* Probably so called *quod vivum pariat*: This Animal differing from most other Serpents in bringing forth its Young alive.

418. *Coluber—pestis acerba boum.* Mr. *Martin* takes the Serpent here meant to be that which *Pliny* calls *Boas*; because it feeds on Cow's Milk, as we read in that Author, who affirms that they grow sometimes to a prodigious Bigness, and that a Child was found in the Belly of one of them, in the Reign of *Claudius*.

422. *Timidum.* Some Manuscripts read *tumidum*.

425. *Est etiam ille malus.* It is universally agreed that the Poet here describes the *Chersydrus*, which is so called from χέρσος, *Earth*, and ὕδωρ, *Water*, because it lives in both these Elements.

437. Cum

atque maculoſus quoad *longam alvum grandibus notis: qui, dum ulli amnes rumpuntur fontibus, et dum terræ madent udo vere ac pluvialibus Auſtris, colit ſtagna, habitanſque ripis, hic improbus explet atram ingluviem piſcibus, loquacibuſque ranis. Poſtquam palus eſt exhauſta, terræque dehiſcunt ardore, exſilit in ſiccum* campum, *et torquens flammantia lumina ſævit agris, aſperque ſiti, atque exterritus æſtu. Tum ne libeat mihi carpere molles ſomnos ſub dio, neu jacuiſſe dorſo nemoris per herbas;* cum ille *novus, exuviis poſitis, nitiduſque juventâ, relinquens aut catulos aut ovâ tectis, volvitur arduus ad ſolem, et micat triſulcis linguis ore. Docebo te quoque cauſas et ſigna morborum. Turpis ſcabies tentat oves, ubi frigidus imber perſedit altiùs ad vivum, et bruma horrida cano gelu: vel cum ſudor illotus adhæſit* iis *tonſis, et hirſuti vepres ſecuerunt corpora* earum. *Idcirco magiſtri perfundunt omne pecus dulcibus fluviis, arieſque udis villis merſatur in gurgite, miſſuſque defluit ſecundo amni:*

Atque notis longam maculoſus grandibus alvum:
Qui, dum amnes ulli rumpuntur fontibus, et dum
Vere madent udo terræ, ac pluvialibus Auſtris,
Stagna colit; ripiſque habitans, hic piſcibus atram
Improbus ingluviem, raniſque loquacibus explet.
Poſtquam exhauſta palus, terræque ardore dehiſcunt,
Exſilit in ſiccum; et flammantia lumina torquens
Sævit agris, aſperque ſiti, atque exterritus æſtu.
Ne mihi tum molles ſub dio carpere ſomnos,
Neu dorſo nemoris libeat jacuiſſe per herbas;
Cum poſitis novus exuviis, nitiduſque juventâ
Volvitur; aut catulos tectis, aut ova relinquens,
Arduus ad Solem, et linguis micat ore triſulcis.
 Morborum quoquè te cauſas, et ſigna docebo.
Turpis oves tentat ſcabies, ubi frigidus imber
Altiùs ad vivum perſedit, et horrida cano
Bruma gelu: vel cum tonſis illotus adhæſit
Sudor, et hirſuti ſecuerunt corpora vepres.
Dulcibus idcirco fluviis pecus omne magiſtri
Perfundunt, udiſque aries in gurgite villis
Merſatur, miſſuſque ſecundo defluit amni:

TRANSLATION.

Belly ſpeckled with broad Spots: Who, while any Rivers burſt from their Fountains, and while the Lands are moiſt with the dewy Spring, and rainy Southwinds, haunts the Pools, and, lodging in the Banks, intemperately gorges his horrid Maw with Fiſhes and croaking Frogs. After that the Fen is burnt up, and the Earth gapes with Drought, he darts forth on dry Ground, and rolling his inflamed Eyes rages in the Fields, exaſperated with Thirſt, and aghaſt with Heat. Let me not then chooſe to indulge ſoft Slumbers in the open Air, or to lie along the Graſs in the Slope of a Wood; when, renewed and ſleek with Youth by caſting his Slough, he rolls along: leaving either his Young or Eggs in his Den, reared to the Sun, and in his Mouth quivers a three-forked Tongue.

I will alſo teach thee the Cauſes and the Signs of their Diſeaſes. The filthy Scab infects the Sheep, when the raw Shower hath pierced deep into the Quick, and Winter rough with hoary Froſt: Or, when the Sweat unwaſhed away adheres to them after Shearing, and prickly Briers have torn their Bodies. On this Account the Shepherds drench the whole Flock in ſweet Rivers, and the Ram with humid Fleece is plunged in the Pool, and ſent to float along the

NOTES.

437. *Cum poſitis novus exuvii, &c.* Pliny tells us, Lib. VIII. 27. *Anguis hiberno ſitu membranâ corporis obductâ, fœniculi ſucco impedimentum illud exuit, rutiluſque vernat. Exuit autem à capite primum, &c.*

449. *Spumas*

Aut tonsum tristi contingunt corpus amurcâ,
Et spumas miscent argenti, vivaque sulfura,
Idæasque pices, et pingues unguine ceras,
Scillamque, elleborosque graves, nigrumque bitumen.
Non tamen ulla magis præsens fortuna laborum est,
Quàm si quis ferro potuit rescindere summum
Ulceris os: alitur vitium, vivitque tegendo;
Dum medicas adhibere manus ad vulnera pastor
Abnegat, et meliora Deos sedet omnia poscens.
Quin etiam ima dolor balantum lapsus ad ossa
Cum furit, atque artus depascitur arida febris;
Profuit incensos æstus avertere, et inter
Ima ferire pedis salientem sanguine venam:
Bisaltæ quo more solent, acerque Gelonus,
Cum fugit in Rhodopen, atque in deserta Getarum,
Et lac concretum cum sanguine potat equino.

aut contingunt tonsum corpus tristi amurcâ, et miscent spumas argenti, vivaque sulfura, Idæasque pices, et ceras pingues unguine, scillamque, gravesque elleboros, nigrumque bitumen. Tamen non est ulla magis præsens fortuna laborum, quàm si quis potuit rescindere summum os ulceris ferro: vitium alitur, vivitque tegendo; dum pastor abnegat adhibere medicas manus ad vulnera, et sedet poscens Deos omnia meliora. Quin etiam cum dolor, lapsus ad ima ossa balantum, furit, atque arida febris depascitur artus; profuit avertere incensos æstus, et ferire venam salientem sanguine inter ima loca pedis: quo more Bisaltæ solent aperire *venam, acerque Gelonus, cum fugit in Rhodopen, atque in deserta Getarum, et potat lac concretum cum equino sanguine.*

TRANSLATION.

Stream: Or they besmear their Bodies after Shearing with bitter Lees of Oil, and mix *with it* Litharge, native Sulphur, Idæan Pitch, and fat unctuous Wax, and the Sea-leek, rank Hellebore, and black Bitumen. But there is not any more effectual Remedy for their Distress, than to lance the Head of the Ulcer with Steel: The Distemper is nourished and lives by being covered; while the Shepherd refuses to apply his healing Hand to the Wound, or sits still begging the Gods to order all for the better.

Moreover when the Malady, penetrating into the inmost Bones of the bleating Sheep, rages, and the scorching Fever preys upon their Limbs, it has been of use to drive out the kindled Inflammation, and between the under Parts of the Feet to open a Vein spouting with Blood: In such Manner as the Bisaltæ use, and the fierce Gelonian, when he flies to Rhodope, and the Desarts of the Getes, and drinks Milk thickened with Horses Blood.

NOTES.

449. *Spumas argenti.* Some have supposed the Poet to mean *Quicksilver.* But *Quicksilver* was never called *spuma argenti,* by which Name the Ancients seem to understand what we call *Litharge.*

450. *Idæasque pices.* Pitch is called *Idæan,* because Pitch-trees abounded on Mount *Ida.*

451. *Scillam.* The Squill, or Sea-Onion, is a bulbous Root, like an Onion, but much larger.

451. *Elleborosque graves.* There are two Kinds of Hellebore, the Black, and the White. Mr. *Martin* takes it to be the white Hellebore that *Virgil* means. Which, says he, is serviceable in Diseases of the Skin, if it be externally applied; but it is too rough to be taken inwardly, as the black Sort is. Hence he thinks *Virgil* added the Epithet *graves* to express the white Hellebore.

461. *Bisaltæ.* The *Bisaltæ* were a People of *Macedon.*

461. *Acerque Gelonus.* The *Geloni,* again, were a *Scythian* People.

473. *Spemque*

Quam procul aut molli succedere sæpius umbræ
Videris, aut summas carpentem ignaviùs herbas,
Extremamque sequi, aut medio procumbere campo
Pascentem, et seræ solam decedere nocti;
Continuò culpam ferro compesce, prius quàm
Dira per incautum serpant contagia vulgus.
Non tam creber agens hiemem ruit æquore turbo,
Quam multæ pecudum pestes. Nec singula morbi
Corpora corripiunt; sed tota æstiva repentè,
Spemque gregemque simul, cunctamque ab origine gentem.
Tum sciat, aërias Alpes, et Norica si quis
Castella in tumulis, et Iapidis arva Timavi,
Nunc quoque post tantò videat, desertaque regna
Pastorum, et longè saltus latèque vacantes.
Hîc quondam morbo cœli miseranda coorta est
Tempestas; totoque autumni incanduit æstu;
Et genus omne neci pecudum dedit, omne ferarum;
Corripuitque lacus; infecit pabula tabo.

Quam ovem videris, aut succedere sæpius molli umbræ, aut carpentem summas herbas ignaviùs, extremamque sequi cæteras, *aut pascentem procumbere medio campo, et solam decedere seræ nocti; continuò compesce culpam ferro, priusquam dira contagia serpant per incautum vulgus. Turbo, agens hiemem, non ruit tam creber æquore, quàm multæ* sunt *pestes pecudum. Nec morbi corripiunt singula corpora; sed tota æstiva repentè, spemque, gregemque simul, cunctamque gentem ab origine. Tum sciat* hoc esse verum quod dixi, *si quis* etiam *nunc quoque, tantò* tempore *post* talem vastationem, *videat aërias Alpes, et Norica castella in tumulis, et arva Iapidis* fluminis *Timavi, desertaque regna pastorum, et saltus vacantes longè latèque. Hîc quondam tempestas miseranda est coorta morbo cœli, incanduitque toto æstu autumni, et dedit omne genus pecudum,* omne genus *ferarum neci, corruptique lacus,* et *infecit pabula tabo.*

TRANSLATION.

Whatever Sheep thou seest either creep away at a Distance *from the rest* under the mild Shade, or listlesly crop the Tops of the Grass, and follow *the Flock* in the Rear, or lie down, as she is feeding in the Middle of the Plain, and return by herself late in the Evening; forthwith * cut off the faulty *Animal,* before the dire Contagion spreads among the unwary Flock.

The Whirlwind, that brings on a wintery Storm, rushes not so frequent from the Sea, as the Plagues of Cattle are numerous. Nor do Diseases only sweep away single Bodies; but on a sudden whole † Folds, the Off-spring and the Flock at once, and the whole Stock from the first Breed. Whoever views the aerial Alps, and the Bavarian Castles on the Hills, and the Fields of Iapidian Timavus, and the Realms of the Shepherds even now after so long a Time deserted, and the Lawns lying waste far and wide, he may then be Judge *of this sad Truth.* Here in former Times a doleful sweeping Plague arose from the Distemper of the Air, and grew more and more inflamed through the whole Heat of Autumn; and delivered over to Death all the Race of Cattle, all the savage Race; poisoned the Lakes, and tainted the Pastures with Contagion. Nor was the

* *Put a Stop to the Disease with the Steel.* † *Æstiva, Summer-quarters.*

NOTES.

473. *Spemque gregemque.* *Agnos cum matribus.* Servius.

474. *Norica.* Noricum was a Region of *Germany,* bordering on the *Alps*; great Part of it is what is now called *Bavaria.*

475. *Iapidis arva Timavi.* The *Timavus,* now *Timavo,* is called *Iapidian* from *Iapidia,* which was in the *Venetian* Territory, where the *Timavus* flows. This Part of *Italy* is now called *Friuli.*

482. *Nec*

Nec via mortis erat simplex: sed ubi ignea venis
Omnibus acta sitis miseros adduxerat artus,
Rursus abundabat fluidus liquor; omniaque in se
Ossa minutatim morbo collapsa trahebat.
Sæpe in honore Deûm medio stans hostia ad aram,
Lanea dum niveâ circumdatur infula vittâ,
Inter cunctantes cecidit moribunda ministros.
Aut si quam ferro mactaverat ante sacerdos;
Inde neque impositis ardent altaria fibris,
Nec responsa potest consultus reddere vates:
Ac vix suppositi tinguntur sanguine cultri,
Summaque jejunâ saniê infuscatur arena.
Hinc lætis vituli vulgò moriuntur in herbis,
Et dulces animas plena ad præsepia reddunt.
Hinc canibus blandis rabies venit; et quatit ægros
Tussis anhela sues, ac faucibus angit obesis.
Labitur infelix studiorum, atque immemor herbæ,
Victor equus; fontesque avertitur, et pede terram
Crebra ferit; demissæ aures; incertus ibidem

Nec via mortis erat simplex; sed ubi ignea sitis, acta omnibus venis, adduxerat miseros artus, rursus fluidus liquor abundabat; trahebatque omnia ossa collapsa morbo minutatim in se. Sæpe in medio honore Deûm hostia, stans ad aram, dum lanea infula circumdatur niveâ vittâ, cecidit moribunda inter cunctantes ministros. Aut si sacerdos mactaverat quam hostiam *ante* quam ceciderat; *inde neque altaria ardent fibris impositis, nec vates consultus potest reddere responsa: ac cultri suppositi vix tinguntur sanguine, summaque arena* vix *infuscatur jejunâ saniê. Hinc vituli vulgò moriuntur in lætis herbis, et reddunt dulces animas ad plena præsepia. Hinc rabies venit blandis canibus, et anhela tussis quatit ægros sues, ac angit* eos *obesis faucibus. Equus victor labitur infelix studiorum, atque immemor herbæ, avertiturque fontes, et crebra ferit terram pede;* aures sunt *demissæ*; *incertus sudor* est *ibidem,*

TRANSLATION.

Way of their Death simple and uncomplicated: But when the burning Fever, revelling in every Vein, had shrunk up their wretched Limbs, again the waterish *pestilential* Humour overflowed, and converted into its Substance all the Bones Piece-meal consumed by the Disease. Often-times amidst the Service of the Gods, the Victim standing at the Altar, while the woollen Fillet with snowy Label binds *its Temples*, dropt down gasping to Death in the Hands of the lingering Executioners. Or, if the Priest had stabbed any one before *it fell*, neither do its Entrails when laid on the Altars burn, nor is the Augur when consulted able from thence to give Responses: And the Knives applied are scarce tinged with Blood, and the Surface of the Sand hardly stained with the *thin* meagre Gore. Hence the Calves every where expire in the luxuriant Pastures, and render up their sweet Lives at the full Cribs. Hence the gentle Dogs are seized with Madness; and wheezing Cough shakes the diseased Swine, and suffocates them with Tumours in the Throat. The *once* victorious Steed, having *now* lost all Heart to his Exercises, and forgetful of his Pasture, pines away, loathes the Springs, and often paws the Ground with his Foot; his Ears

NOTES.

482. *Nec via mortis erat simplex.* There is no Occasion for departing here from the usual Sense of the Word *simplex*, as all the Commentators have done, in Complaisance to *Servius*. 'Tis full stronger to say, the Kind of Death was complicated with a Variety of disastrous Circumstances, than barely to say, it was not a common Kind of Death.

492. *Suppositi.* See the Note on Æn. VI. 248.

493. *Jejunâ sanie.* In these morbid Bodies, the Liquids were almost wasted, and, instead of Blood, there came out only a corrupted Matter.

498. *Labitur infelix studiorum.* All the Interpreters, I have seen, construe *infelix* with *studiorum*: But the Construction will be more easy, if we make it *immemor studiorum atque herbæ*.

500. *Ibidem.* Seems to denote that their Sweat

et ille ſudor *quidem frigidus* equis *morituris* : ejus *pellis aret*, *et dura ad tactum, reſiſtit tractanti* eam. *Dant hæc ſigna primis diebus ante exitium. Sin in proceſſu* temporis *morbus cœpit crudeſcere*; *tum verò oculi* ſunt *ardentes, atque ſpiritus attractus ab alto* pectore *interdum* eſt *gravis gemitu*; *imaque ilia tendunt* ſe *longo ſingultu* : *ater ſanguis it naribus*; *et aſpera lingua premit obſeſſas fauces*. Primo *profuit infundere Lenæos latices inſerto cornu*; *ea* eſt *viſa una ſalus morientibus* : *Mox hoc ipſum erat exitio* illis; *refectique* vino *ardebant furiis, ipſique, jam ſub ægrâ morte, laniabant ſuos artus diſciſſos nudis dentibus* : *Dî* dent *meliora piis, illumque errorem hoſtibus. Autem ecce taurus fumans ſub duro vomere concidit, et vomit cruorem miſtum ſpumis ore, cietque extremos gemitus. Triſtis arator it, abjungens* alterum *juvencum mœrentem fraternâ morte, atque relinquit defixa aratra in medio opere.*

Sudor, et ille quidem morituris frigidus: aret
Pellis, et ad tactum tractanti dura reſiſtit.
Hæc ante exitium primis dant ſigna diebus.
Sin in proceſſu cœpit crudeſcere morbus;
Tum verò ardentes oculi, atque attractus ab alto
Spiritus interdum gemitu gravis; imaque longo
Ilia ſingultu tendunt: it naribus ater
Sanguis; et obſeſſas fauces premit aſpera lingua.
Profuit inſerto latices infundere cornu
Lenæos; ea viſa ſalus morientibus una:
Mox erat hoc ipſum exitio; furiiſque refecti
Ardebant, ipſique ſuos, jam morte ſub ægrâ,
(Dî meliora piis, erroremque hoſtibus illum)
Diſciſſos nudis laniabant dentibus artus.
Ecce autem duro fumans ſub vomere taurus
Concidit, et miſtum ſpumis vomit ore cruorem,
Extremoſque ciet gemitus. It triſtis arator,
Mœrentem abjungens fraternâ morte juvencum,
Atque opere in medio defixa relinquit aratra.

TRANSLATION.

hang down; there intermitting Sweat *breaks out*, and that too cold at the Approaches of Death: His Skin withered, feels hard, and in handling reſiſts the Touch. Theſe Symptoms they give before Death in the firſt Days *of their Illneſs*. But if in Proceſs of Time the Diſeaſe begins to rankle, then are their Eyes inflamed, and the Breath fetched from the Bottom of the Breaſt is ſometimes mixed with a heavy Groan; and with a long Sob they diſtend their inmoſt Bowels: Black Blood guſhes from their Noſtrils, and the rough Tongue clings to their choaked up Jaws. At firſt it was of Service to * pour Wine down their Throats; this appeared the ſole Remedy for them dying: Soon after, this very thing proved their Deſtruction; and being recruited they burned with hideous Rage; and they themſelves, now † in the Agonies of Death (the Gods award better Things to the Good, and ſuch ‡ Frenzy to our Foes!), tore their own mangled Limbs with their naked Teeth. Lo the Bull *too* ſmoking under the oppreſſive Share drops down, and vomits out of his Mouth Blood mingled with Foam, and fetches his laſt Groans. The Ploughman, unyoking the Steer that mourns his Brother's Death, goes away ſad, and in the midſt of his Work

* *To pour in Lenæan Liquors from a Horn put into their Mouths.* † *At the Approach of painful Death.* ‡ *Errorem anſwers to the* Greek *σφαλμα, which ſignifies either* error *or* clades.

NOTES.

Sweat, was particularly about their Neck and Ears, as *Lucretius* alſo has obſerved:

Sudoriſque madens per collum ſplendidus humor.

501. *Aret pellis.* The Dryneſs of the Skin ſeems inconſiſtent with the Sweating juſt mentioned. We muſt therefore underſtand the Poet, not to mean that all theſe Symptoms were found in every Horſe, but that they were variouſly affected.

514. *Diſciſſos nudis laniabant dentibus artus.* The Word *nudis*, ſays Dr. *Trapp*, ſeems to imply, that, by tearing their Fleſh, they at the ſame time tore the Gums from their Teeth. *Philargyrius* ſays, *Ut fœditatem exprimeret, adjecit nudis*. That is, to denote the filthy Sight of their Gums being ulcerated and rotted away from their Teeth.

525. *Quid*

Non umbræ altorum nemorum, non mollia poſſunt
Prata movere animum, non qui per ſaxa volutus
Purior electro campum petit amnis: at ima
Solvuntur latera, atque oculos ſtupor urget inertes;
Ad terramque fluit devexo pondere cervix.
Quid labor, aut benefacta juvant? quid vomere terras
Invertiſſe graves? atqui non Maſſica Bacchi
Munera, non illis epulæ nocuere repoſtæ.
Frondibus, et victu paſcuntur ſimplicis herbæ:
Pocula ſunt fontes liquidi, atque exercita curſu
Flumina; nec ſomnos abrumpit cura ſalubres.
Tempore non alio dicunt regionibus illis
Quæſitas ad ſacra boves Junonis; et uris
Imparibus ductos alta ad donaria currus.
Ergo ægrè raſtris terram rimantur, et ipſis
Unguibus infodiunt fruges: monteſque per altos
Contentâ cervice trahunt ſtridentia plauſtra.
Non lupus inſidias explorat ovilia circum,
Nec gregibus nocturnus obambulat: acrior illum
Cura domat. Timidi damæ, cervique fugaces,
Nunc interque canes et circum tecta vagantur.

Non umbræ altorum nemorum, non mollia prata poſſunt movere ejus *animum, non amnis, qui volutus per ſaxa purior electro petit campum: at* ejus *ima latera ſolvuntur, atque ſtupor urget inertes oculos; cervixque fluit ad terram devexo pondere. Quid labor, aut benefacta* collata homini *juvant? Quid* prodeſt *invertiſſe graves terras vomere? Atqui non Maſſica munera Bacchi, non epulæ repoſitæ nocuere illis. Paſcuntur frondibus, et victu ſimplicis herbæ: pocula ſunt liquidi fontes, atque flumina exercita curſu; nec cura abrumpit ſalubres ſomnos. Dicunt, non alio tempore, boves* fuiſſe *quæſitas illis regionibus ad ſacra Junonis, et* ejus *currus* fuiſſe *ductos ad alta donaria* ab *imparibus uris. Ergo* agricolæ *ægrè rimantur terram raſtris, et infodiunt fruges unguibus ipſis, trahuntque ſtridentia plauſtra contentâ cervice per altos montes. Lupus non explorat inſidias circum ovilia, nec nocturnus obambulat gregibus: acrior cura domat illum. Timidi damæ fugaceſque cervi nunc vagantur inter canes et circum tecta.*

TRANSLATION.

leaves the Plough fixed down *in the Earth.* Neither the Shades of the deep Groves, nor the ſoft Meadows can affect his Mind, nor the River which rolling over the Rocks glides to the Plain more pure than Amber: But his deep Sides grow lank, Deadneſs reſts upon his heavy Eyes; and his Neck with unwieldy Weight droops to the Ground. What do their Labours or good Offices now avail them? What their having turned the heavy Lands with the Share! Yet they never injured themſelves by the * rich Gifts of Bacchus, nor by ſumptuous Banquets. They feed on Leaves, and the Nouriſhment of ſimple Herbs: the cryſtal Springs and † running Rivers are their Drink, and no Care interrupts their healthful Slumbers. *Then, and* at no other Time, they tell us that Kine were wanting in thoſe Regions for Juno's ſacred Rites, and that the Chariots were drawn to her lofty Shrine by Buffaloes ill-matched. Therefore, with painful Labour they tear the Ground with Harrows, and with their very Nails ſet the Corn, and over the high Mountains drag the creaking Waggons with their ſtrained Necks. The Wolf *now* meditates no Ambuſcades around the Folds, nor *prowling* roams about the Flocks by Night: A ſharper Care ſubdues him. The timorous Does and fugitive Stags *now* ſaunter among the Dogs, and about

* Maſſici, *i. e. of* Maſſic, *or* Campanian *Wine.* † *Exercised with Running.*

NOTES.

525. *Quid labor,* &c. Theſe ſix Lines are ſo admired by *Scaliger,* that he ſays, he had rather have been the Author of them, than to have had the Favour of *Cræſus* or *Cyrus.*

Jam fluctus proluit prolem immensi maris, et omne genus natantium in extremo litore, ceu naufraga corpora: phocæ insolitæ fugiunt in flumina. Et vipera moritur frustra defensa curvis latebris, et hydri attoniti squammis astantibus. Aër non est æquus avibus ipsis, et illæ præcipites relinquunt vitam sub altâ nube. Præterea, nec jam refert pabula mutari, artesque medendi quæsitæ nocent: magistri medicinæ Phillyrides Chiron, Amythaoniusque Melampus cessere. Et pallida Tisiphone, emissa Stygiis tenebris in lucem, sævit: agitque morbos metumque ante se, surgensque in dies effert avidum caput altius. Amnes, arentesque ripæ, supinique colles, sonant balatu pecorum, et crebris mugitibus. Jamque Tisiphone *dat stragem catervatim, atque in stabulis ipsis aggerat cadavera dilapsa turpi tabo: donec discant tegere ea humo, ac abscondere ea foveis.*

Jam maris immensi prolem, et genus omne natantum,
Litore in extremo, ceu naufraga corpora, fluctus
Proluit: insolitæ fugiunt in flumina phocæ.
Interit et curvis frustra defensa latebris
Vipera, et attoniti squammis astantibus hydri.
Ipsis est aër avibus non æquus: et illæ
Præcipites altâ vitam sub nube relinquunt.
Præterea, nec jam mutari pabula refert;
Quæsitæque nocent artes: cessere magistri,
Phillyrides Chiron, Amythaoniusque Melampus.
Sævit et in lucem Stygiis emissa tenebris
Pallida Tisiphone: morbos agit ante metumque;
Inque dies avidum surgens caput altius effert.
Balatu pecorum, et crebris mugitibus amnes,
Arentesque sonant ripæ, collesque supini:
Jamque catervatim dat stragem, atque aggerat ipsis
In stabulis turpi dilapsa cadavera tabo:
Donec humo tegere, ac foveis abscondere discunt.

TRANSLATION.

the Houses. Now the Waves wash out upon the Extremity of the Shore the Breed of the immense Ocean, and all the * scaly Race, like shipwrecked Bodies: And Sea-calves fly to the Rivers *their* unusual *Haunt*. The Viper too, in vain defended by her winding Den, expires, and the astonished Water-snakes erecting their Scales *expire*. To the very Birds the Air becomes unkindly, and they falling headlong leave their Lives beneath the lofty Cloud.

Nor moreover avails it now *the Cattle* to have their Pasture changed; the *medicinal* Arts to which they had Recourse prove noxious: The *able* Masters *in the Science* failed, Chiron, the Son of Phillyra, and Melampus, the Son of Amythaon. Pale Tisiphone, sent from the Stygian Glooms to Light, rages: Drives before her Diseases and Dismay; and daily rising higher exalts her baneful Head. With *plaintive* Bleating of the Flocks, and frequent Lowings, the Rivers, the withered Banks, and sloping Hills resound: And now by Droves and Flocks she deals Destruction, and in the very Stalls heaps up Carcases rotting away with foul Contagion: Till they learn to bury them in the Ground, and

* *The Race of swimming Creatures.*

NOTES.

541. *Jam maris immensi prolem.* The Poet here contradicts *Aristotle*, who says, that a pestilental disease does not seem ever to invade Fishes.

550. *Phillyrides Chiron, Amythaoniusque Melampus.* Chiron was the Son of *Saturn* and *Phillyra*; he instructed *Æsculapius* in Physic, *Hercules* in Astronomy, and *Achilles* in Music. *Melampus* again was the Son of *Amythaon* and *Dyripe*; a famous Physician and Southsayer. They lived before the *Argonautic* Expedition. Hence Mr. *Martin* infers, that the Plague here described happened not less than five hundred Years before the famous Plague of *Athens*, viz. in the Age of *Chiron* and *Melampus*. But I incline rather to think with others that the Names of these two famed Physicians are here put for the famous Masters of Physic in general, and those who were skilled in Divination; and mean no more, than that all the

Nam neque erat coriis usus; nec viscera quisquam
Aut undis abolere potest, aut vincere flammâ:
Nec tondere quidem morbo illuvieque peresa
Vellera, nec telas possunt attingere putres.
Verùm etiam, invisos si quis tentârat amictus,
Ardentes papulæ, atque immundus olentia sudor
Membra sequebatur: nec longo deinde moranti
Tempore, contactos artus sacer ignis edebat.

Nam neque erat illis *usus coriis* eorum: *nec quisquam potest aut abolere viscera* eorum *undis, aut vincere* ea *flammâ. Nec quidem possunt tondere vellera peresa morbo illuvieque, nec attingere putres telas. Verùm etiam si quis tentârat invisos amictus, ardentes papulæ, atque immundus sudor sequebatur olentia membra: deinde sacer ignis edebat contactos artus* illi *moranti* dimittere eos amictus, *nec longo tempore.*

TRANSLATION.

hide them in Pits. For neither were their Hides for Use; nor could any cleanse their Flesh with Water, or * purge it by Fire: Nor dare they so much as shear the Fleeces corrupted with Disease and filthy Sores, nor touch the putrid Stuffs. But yet, if any one tried the odious Vestments, fiery Blains and filthy Sweat overspread his noisome Body: And then, no long Time intervening, the pestilential Fire preyed upon his infected Limbs.

* Aut vincere flamma, *Or, conquer and correct the Infection by Fire.*

NOTES.

the Methods of Cure, all Religion, and Applications to the Gods by sacred Rites, proved ineffectual.

559. *Viscera.* The Flesh in general. See the Note on Æn. V. 103.

562. *Telas.* There is no Occasion for explaining this with Dr. *Trapp*, of the Wool; for it appears from what follows, that some of that infected Wool was actually made into Garments, which consequently must first have been wrought in the Loom. So that the Meaning of the whole Passage is, That they were forced at length to abstain even from shearing the Fleeces, or touching the Wool, because those who had done so, especially those who had worn any of that Cloth, had been such miserable Sufferers thereby.

564. *Ardentes papulæ.* Seems, as Mr. *Martin* observes, to mean *Carbuncles*, which are enumerated among the Symptoms of a Pestilence, and are described to be a small Pimple, which on the Wasting of its Liquor becomes a crusty Tubercle, encompassed with a Circle as red as Fire, rising at first with an Itching, and afterwards being accompanied with a vehement Pain and intense Heat.

566. *Sacer ignis.* Seems to mean an *Erysipelas*, or St. *Antony's Fire*. Thus also *Lucretius*:

Et simul, ulceribus quasi inustis, omne rubere
Corpus, ut est per membra sacer cum diditur ignis.

P. VIRGILII MARONIS

GEORGICA.

LIBER IV.

ORDO.

Protinus exequar cœlestia dona aërii mellis. Aspice etiam hanc partem Georgicorum, *Mæcenas. Dicam spectacula levium rerum admiranda tibi, magnanimosque duces* apum, *moresque totius gentis ordine, et studia, et populos, et prœlia* earum.

PROTINUS aërii mellis cœlestia dona
Exsequar. Hanc etiam, Mæcenas, aspice partem.
Admiranda tibi levium spectacula rerum,
Magnanimosque duces, totiusque ordine gentis
Mores, et studia, et populos, et prœlia dicam.

TRANSLATION.

NEXT will I set forth the heavenly Gift of aerial Honey. Vouchsafe, Mæcenas, thy regard to this Part too *of my Work.* I'll sing a Spectacle worthy of your Admiration, tho' of Things minute; the magnanimous Leaders, the Manners and Employments, the Tribes and Battles of the whole Race in

NOTES.

Virgil has taken care to raise the Subject of the *Georgics:* In the first Part he has only dead Matter on which to work. In the second he just steps on the World of Life, and describes that Degree of it, which is to be found in Vegetables. In the third he advances to Animals, And in the last singles out the Bee, which may be reckoned the most sagacious of them, for his Subject.

In this Georgic he shews us what Station is most proper for the Bees, and when they begin to gather Honey: How to call them home when they swarm; and how to part them when they are engaged in Battle. From hence he takes Occasion to discover their different Kinds; and, after an Excursion, relates their prudent and politic Administration of Affairs, and the several Diseases that often rage in their Hives, with the proper Symptoms and Remedies of each Disease. In the last Place he lays down a Method of repairing their Kind, supposing their whole Breed lost; and gives at large the History of its Invention.

1. *Aërii mellis.* Honey is called *airy,* because, according to the Opinion of *Aristotle* and others of the Ancients, it came from the Dews that are engendered in the Air.

7. *Lava,*

In tenui labor, at tenuis non gloria; ſi quem
Numina læva ſinunt, auditque vocatus Apollo.
Principio ſedes apibus ſtatioque petenda,
Quò neque ſit ventis aditus, (nam pabula venti
Ferre domum prohibent) neque oves hœdique petulci
Floribus inſultent, aut errans bucula campo
Decutiat rorem, et ſurgentes atterat herbas.
Abſint et picti ſqualentia terga lacerti
Pinguibus à ſtabulis, meropeſque, aliæque volucres;
Et manibus Progne pectus ſignata cruentis.
Omnia nam latè vaſtant, ipſaſque volantes
Ore ferunt, dulcem nidis immitibus eſcam.
At liquidi fontes, et ſtagna virentia muſco
Adſint, et tenuis fugiens per gramina rivus;
Palmaque veſtibulum aut ingens oleaſter obumbret:
Ut, cum prima novi ducent examina reges
Vere ſuo, ludetque favis emiſſa juventus,

Labor eſt in tenui argumento, at gloria non eſt tenuis; ſi læva numina ſinunt quem ſcriptorem exequi id, Apolloque vocatus audit eum. Principio, ſedes ſtatioque eſt petenda apibus, quò neque ſit aditus ventis, (nam venti prohibent eas ferre pabula domum) neque oves petulcique hœdi inſultent floribus, aut bucula, errans campo, decutiat rorem, et atterat ſurgentes herbas. Et lacerti, picti quoad *ſqualentia terga, abſint à pinguibus ſtabulis* apum, *meropeſque, aliæque volucres; et Progne ſignata* quoad *pectus cruentis manibus* abſint ab iis. *Nam vaſtant omnia latè, feruntque volanteſque* apes *ipſas ore,* futuras *dulcem eſcam immitibus nidis. At liquidi fontes, et ſtagna virentia muſco, et tenuis rivus, fugiens per gramina, adſint; palmaque, aut ingens oleaſter obumbret veſtibulum: ut, cum novi reges ducent, prima examina ſuo vere, juventuſque, emiſſa favis, ludet,*

TRANSLATION.

Order. Laborious Eſſay on a mean Subject! But not mean the Praiſe; if the adverſe Deities permit any one *to execute the Taſk*, and Apollo invocated hear.

Firſt, a Seat and Station muſt be ſought for the Bees, where neither Winds may have Acceſs, for the Winds hinder them from carrying home their Food, nor Sheep and friſky Kids may inſult the Flowers, or Heifer, ſtraying in the Plain, ſpurn off the Dews, and bruiſe the riſing Herbs.

And let the Lizards with ſpeckled ſcaly Backs be far from the rich Hives, and Wood-peckers, and other Birds; and Progne, whoſe Breaſt is ſtained with her bloody Hands. For they lay all Things waſte around, and in their Mouths bear away the Bees themſelves while on the Wing, a ſweet Morſel for their merciless Young. But let clear Springs, and Pools edged with green Moſs be near, and a ſmall Rivulet ſwiftly running through the Meads; and let a Palm or ſtately Wild-olive overſhade the Entrance: That, when the new Kings ſhall lead forth the firſt Swarms in their own Spring, and the Youth ſport it iſſu-

NOTES.

7. *Læva.* Adverſe, or, as others render it, *auſpicious*, for the Word is uſed in either Senſe.

15. *Manibus Progne pectus ſignata cruentis.* *Progne* and *Philomela*, according to Mythology, were the Daughters of *Pandion*, King of *Athens*. *Progne* was married to *Tereus*, King of *Thrace*, by whom ſhe had a Son named *Itys*. *Tereus* afterwards violated *Philomela*, and cut out her Tongue, to prevent her telling her Siſter: She found Means however to diſcover his Wickedneſs; to revenge which the two Siſters murdered *Itys*, and gave his Fleſh to his Father to eat. When the Banquet was over, they produced the Head of the Child, to ſhew *Tereus* in what Manner they had entertained him. He, being highly enraged, purſued them with his drawn Sword, and was transformed into a Hooper (*Upupa*), *Philomela* into a Nightingale, *Progne* into a Swallow, which has the Feathers of its Breaſt ſtained with red; and *Itys* into a Pheaſant.

30. *Caſiæ.*

vicina ripa invitet eas decedere calori, obviaque arbos teneat eas frondentibus hospitiis. Conjice transversas salices, et grandia saxa in medium humorem, *seu humor stabit iners, seu profluet, ut possint consistere* his veluti *crebris pontibus, et pandere alas ad æstivum solem; si fortè præceps Eurus sparserit* eas *morantes, aut immerserit Neptuno. Circum hæc virides casiæ, et serpylla olentia latè, et copia thymbræ spirantis graviter floreat: violariaque bibant irriguum fontem. Autem alvearia ipsa, seu* fuerint *suta tibi cavatis corticibus, seu fuerint texta lento vimine, habeant angustos aditus; nam hiems cogit mella frigore, calorque remittit eadem liquefacta: utraque vis* est *pariter metuenda apibus: neque illæ* apes *nequicquam certatim linunt tenuia spiramenta cerâ in tectis, explentque oras fuco et floribus; servantque gluten, collectum ad hæc munera ipsa, lentius et visco, et pice Phrygiæ Idæ. Sæpe etiam fovere larem sub terrâ, effossis latebris, (si fama est vera)*

Vicina invitet decedere ripa calori,
Obviaque hospitiis teneat frondentibus arbos.
In medium, seu stabit iners, seu profluet humor,
Transversas salices et grandia conjice saxa;
Pontibus ut crebris possint consistere, et alas
Pandere ad æstivum solem; si fortè morantes
Sparserit, aut præceps Neptuno immerserit Eurus.
Hæc circum casiæ virides, et olentia latè
Serpylla, et graviter spirantis copia thymbræ
Floreat: irriguumque bibant violaria fontem.
 Ipsa autem seu corticibus tibi suta cavatis,
Seu lento fuerint alvearia vimine texta,
Angustos habeant aditus; nam frigore mella
Cogit hiems, eademque calor liquefacta remittit:
Utraque vis apibus pariter metuenda: neque illæ
Nequicquam in tectis certatim tenuia cerâ
Spiramenta linunt, fucoque et floribus oras
Explent; collectumque hæc ipsa ad munera gluten,
Et visco et Phrygiæ servant pice lentius Idæ.
Sæpe etiam effossis (si vera est fama) latebris,

TRANSLATION.

ing from the Hives, the neighbouring Bank may invite them to withdraw from the Heat, and the Tree just in their Way may receive them in its leafy Shelter. Into the Midst of the *neighbouring* Water, whether it stagnates idle, or purling runs, throw Willows across and huge Stones; that they may rest upon frequent Bridges, and spread their Wings to the Summer Sun, if the impetuous East-wind has by chance dispersed those that lag behind, or immersed them in the Flood. Around these Places let green Casia, and far-smelling wild Thyme, and Store of strong-scented Savory, flower: And let Beds of Violets drink an irriguous Fountain.

But as for your Hives themselves, whether they be compacted of hollow Bark, or wove with limber Osier, let them have their Inlets narrow; for Winter congeals the Honey with its Cold, and the Heat melts and dissolves the same: Either Force is equally dreaded by the Bees: Nor is it in vain they smear with Wax the minute Vents in their Houses, and fill up the Edges with *Fucus* and Flowers, and preserve for those very Uses collected Glue more clinging than Birdlime, or the Pitch of Phrygian Ida. Often too, if Fame be true, they have cherished

NOTES.

30. *Casiæ.* See the Note on Book II. 213. Some take the Casia to be the same with *Rosemary:* But *Columella*, speaking of the Plants which ought to grow about an Apiary, mentions Casia and Rosemary as two different Plants. *Nam sunt etiam remedio languentibus cytisi, tum deinde casiæ, atque pini, et rosmarinus.*

39. *Fuco.* The *fucus* is properly a sort of Sea-weed, which was anciently used in dying, and in colouring the Faces of Women. Hence all kind of daubing obtained the Name of *Fucus.*

43. *Fovere*

Sub terrâ fovere larem: penitusque repertæ
Pumicibusque cavis, exesæque arboris antro.
Tu tamen et lêvi rimosâ cubilia limo
Unge, sovens circum, et raras superinjice frondes.
Neu propius tectis taxum sine: neve rubentes
Ure foco cancros; altæ neu crede paludi:
Aut ubi odor cœni gravis, aut ubi concava pulsu
Saxa sonant, vocisque offensa resultat imago.
Quod superest, ubi pulsam hiemem sol aureus egit
Sub terras, cœlumque æstivâ luce reclusit;
Illæ continuò saltus silvasque peragrant,
Purpureosque metunt flores, et flumina libant
Summa leves. Hinc, nescio quâ dulcedine lætæ,
Progeniem nidosque fovent: Hinc arte recentes
Excudunt ceras, et mella tenacia fingunt.
Hinc ubi jam emissum caveis ad sidera cœli
Nare per æstatem liquidam suspexeris agmen,
Obscuramque trahi vento mirabere nubem;
Contemplator: aquas dulces, et frondea semper
Tecta petunt: huc tu jussos asperge sapores,

penitusque sunt repertæ cavisque pumicibus, antroque exesæ arboris. Tamen tu et unge rimosa cubilia circum lêvi limo fovens eas, et superinjice raras frondes cubilibus. Neu sine taxum esse propius tectis earum, neve juxta ure rubentes cancros foco; neu crede altæ paludi: aut ubi odor gravis cœni est, aut ubi concava saxa sonant pulsu sonitus, imagoque vocis offensa resultat. Quod superest, ubi aureus sol egit hiemem pulsam sub terras, reclusitque cœlum æstivâ luce; continuò illæ apes peragrant saltus silvasque, metuntque purpureos flores, et leves libant summa flumina. Hinc illæ, nescio quâ dulcedine lætæ, fovent suam progeniem nidosque: hinc excudunt recentes ceras arte, et fingunt tenacia mella. Hinc ubi jam suspexeris agmen apium, emissum caveis, nare ad sidera cœli per liquidam æstatem, obscuramque nubem earum trahi vento; tu contemplator: semper petunt dulces aquas et frondea tecta: tu asperge jussos sapores huc,

TRANSLATION.

their Families in Cells dug under Ground; and have been found deep down in hollow Pumice-stones, and the Cavity of a rotten Tree. But do thou, to keep them warm, daub their chinky Chambers round with smooth Mud, and strew it thinly over with Leaves. Nor suffer a Yew near their Lodges; nor burn in the Fire the reddening Crabs; nor trust them to a deep Fen: Or where a noisome Smell of Mud, or where hollow Rocks re-echo to the impulsive Sound, and the struck Image of the Voice rebounds.

For what remains, when the golden Sun has driven the Winter under Ground, and opened the Heavens with Summer Light; they forthwith traverse the Lawns and Woods, crop the empurpled Flowers, and lightly skim the Surface of the Streams. Hence, gladdened with I know not what agreeable Sensation, they grow fond of their Offspring and young Breed: Hence they labour out with Art new waxen Cells, and form the clammy Honey. In consequence of this, when now you shall behold the Swarm issued from their Hives into the open Air, swim through the serene Summer Sky, and the blackening Cloud driven about by the Wind, mark them well: They always seek the Waters and leafy Co-

NOTES.

43. *Fovere larem.* The common Reading is *fodere*, but, as Mr. *Martin* justly observes, it seems to be a Tautology to say *fodere effossis latebris*. It is *fovere* in the *Medicean* and *King's* Manuscripts: And the same Reading is admitted by *Heinsius* and *Masvicius*.

57. *Excudunt ceras.* The Word *excudunt* is a Metaphor taken from the Smith, who strikes out, *excudit*, Instruments of Iron. In like Manner he compares the Bees busied in their several Works, to the *Cyclops* labouring at the Anvil, Verse 170.

†

Trita melisphylla, et cerinthæ ignobile gramen :
Tinnitusque cie, et Matris quate cymbala circum.
Ipsæ consident medicatis sedibus ; ipsæ
Intima more suo sese in cunabula condent.
Sin autem ad pugnam exierint ; (nam sæpe duobus
Regibus incessit magno discordia motu)
Continuòque animos vulgi, et trepidantia bello
Corda licet longè præsciscere : namque morantes
Martius ille æris rauci canor increpat ; et vox
Auditur, fractos sonitus imitata tubarum.
Tum trepidæ inter se coeunt, pennisque coruscant ;
Spiculaque exacuunt rostris, aptantque lacertos :
Et circa regem atque ipsa ad prætoria densæ
Miscentur, magnisque vocant clamoribus hostem.
Ergo, ubi ver nactæ sudum, camposque patentes,
Erumpunt portis, concurritur : æthere in alto
Fit sonitus : magnum mistæ glomerantur in orbem,

trita melisphylla, et ignobile gramen cerinthæ : cieque tinnitus, et quate cymbala Cybeles matris Deorum *circum. Ipsæ consident medicatis sedibus ; ipsæ condent sese in intima cunabula suo more. Autem sin exierint ad pugnam ; (nam sæpe discordia incessit duobus regibus magno motu) continuò licet præsciscere longè animosque vulgi, et corda trepidantia bello : namque ille Martius canor rauci æris increpat eas morantes, et vox imitata fractos sonitus tubarum auditur. Tum trepidæ coeunt inter se, coruscantque pennis, exacuuntque spicula rostris, aptantque lacertos, et densæ miscentur circa regem, atque ad* ejus *prætoria ipsa, vocantque hostem magnis clamoribus. Ergo, ubi* sunt *nactæ sudum ver, patentesque campos, erumpunt portis, concurritur : sonitus fit in alto æthere : mistæ glomerantur in magnum orbem,*

TRANSLATION.

verts: Here sprinkle the *fragrant* Juices *that are* prescribed, bruised Baum, and the vulgar Herb of Honey-wort: Awake the tinkling Sounds, and beat the Cymbals of Mother *Cybele* round. They of themselves will settle on the medicated Seats; they of themselves after their Manner will retreat into the inmost Chambers.

But if they shall go forth to Battle; for often Discord with huge Commotion seizes two *rival* Kings, you may from the Beginning know long before-hand both the Animosity of the Populace, and their Hearts in Trepidation for War: For that martial Clang of hoarse Brass rouzes the Laggers, and a Voice is heard resembling the Trumpets broken Sounds. Then in a Hurry they assemble together, quiver with their Wings, sharpen their Stings with their Beaks, fit their Claws, crowd thick around their King and to his Pavilion, and with loud Hummings challenge the Foe.

As soon therefore as they find the vernal Sky serene, and the Fields of Air open, forth they rush from their Gates; they join Battle: Buzzing Sounds arise in the Sky above: Mingled they cluster in a mighty Round, and fall headlong: Hail rains not thicker from the Air, nor such Quantities of Acorns from the

NOTES.

63. *Melisphylla.* Melisphyllon seems to be a Contraction of *Melissophyllon, the Bee-herb,* and is thought to be the same with what is called by a *Latin* Name *Apiastrum.* The Description given of it by *Dioscorides* agrees very well with the *Melissa* or *Baum* so common in *English* Gardens.

63. *Cerinthæ.* The Name of this Plant is derived from κηρίον, *a Honeycomb*; because the Flower abounds with a sweet Juice like Honey; and is therefore called *Honey-wort* in *English.* This Herb grows common in *Italy,* whence the Poet calls it *ignobile gramen.*

75. *Prætoria.* Virgil here calls the Cells of the Kings poetically *Prætoria,* by a Metaphor taken from the *Roman* Camp, where his Pavilion who had the Command of the War (an Office that belonged at first to the Prætor, and afterwards was vested in the Consuls) had the Name of *Prætorium.*

91. *Squalen-*

Præcipitesque cadunt: non densior aëre grando,
Nec de concussâ tantum pluit ilice glandis.
Ipsi per medias acies, insignibus alis,
Ingentes animos angusto in pectore versant:
Usque adeò obnixi non cedere, dum gravis aut hos,
Aut hos versa fugâ victor dare terga subegit.
Hi motus animorum, atque hæc certamina tanta,
Pulveris exigui jactu compressa quiescent.
  Verùm ubi ductores acie revocaveris ambos;
Deterior qui visus, eum, ne prodigus obsit,
Dede neci: melior vacuâ sine regnet in aulâ.
Alter erit maculis auro squalentibus ardens:
(Nam duo sunt genera) hic melior, insignis et ore,
Et rutilis clarus squamis: ille horridus alter
Desidiâ, latamque trahens inglorius alvum.
  Ut binæ regum facies, ita corpora gentis.
Namque aliæ turpes horrent; ceu pulvere ab alto
Cum venit, et terram sicco spuit ore viator
Aridus: elucent aliæ, et fulgore coruscant,
Ardentes auro, et paribus lita corpora guttis.
Hæc potior soboles: hinc cœli tempore certo

caduntque præcipites: non densior grando pluit aëre, nec tantum glandis pluit de concussâ ilice. Reges *ipsi*, volantes *per medias acies, insignibus alis, versant Ingentes animos in angusto pectore: usque adeò obnixi non cedere, dum gravis victor subegit aut hos aut hos dare terga versa fugâ. Hi motus animorum, atque hæc tanta certamina, compressa jactu exigui pulveris, quiescent. Verùm ubi revocaveris ambos ductores acie; qui fuerit visus deterior* bello, *dede eum neci, ne prodigus obsit* consumendo cibos: *sine ut melior* bello *regnet in vacuâ aulâ. Alter erit ardens maculis squalentibus auro: (nam sunt duo genera) hic est melior, et insignis ore, et clarus rutilis squamis: ille alter est horridus desidiâ, ingloriusque trahens latam alvum. Ut facies regum* sunt *binæ, ita corpora gentis* sunt. *Namque aliæ* apes *turpes horrent, ceu cum aridus viator venit ab alto pulvere, et spuit terram sicco ore: aliæ elucent, et coruscant fulgore, ardentes auro, et corpora* sunt *lita paribus guttis. Hæc soboles est potior: hinc premes dulcia mella certo tempore cœli:*

TRANSLATION.

shaken Oak. *The Kings* themselves amidst the Hosts, distinguished by their Wings, exert mighty Souls in little Bodies: Obstinately determined not to yield, till the dread Victor has compelled either these or those to turn their Backs in Flight. These Commotions of their Minds, and this so mighty Fray, quashed by the Throw of a little Dust, will cease.

But, when you have recalled both Leaders from the Battle, put him to Death that appears the baser, lest by *idle* Prodigality he do hurt: And suffer the more valorous *King* to reign in the Court without a Rival. The one will glow with refulgent Spots of Gold: For there are two Sorts, this is the better, distinguishable both by his Make, and conspicuous with glistering Scales: The other is horribly deformed with Sloth, and ingloriously drags a large Belly.

As the Kings are of two *different* Figures, so are the Bodies of their People. For the one looks hideously ugly; as when a parched Traveller comes from a deep dusty Road, and spits the Dirt out of his dry Mouth: The others shine and sparkle with Brightness, burnished with Gold, and their Bodies spangled with equal Drops. This is the better Breed: From these at the stated Season

NOTES.

91. *Squalentibus.* Servius renders it *splendentibus*, and derives the Word from *squama Nam si à squalore est*, says he, *sordidum significat.* It seems to signify *speckled or streaked with golden Marks like Scales.*

nec tantum dulcia, quantum mella *et liquida, et domitura durum saporem Bacchi. At cum examina volant incerta, luduntque cœlo, contemnuntque favos, et relinquunt tecta frigida; prohibebis instabiles animos inani ludo. Nec est magnus labor prohibere* eos; *tu eripe alas regibus: non quisquam audebit ire altum iter, illis re*gibus *cunctantibus, aut vellere signa è castris. Horti, balantes croceis floribus, invitent* eas; *et tutela Hellespontiaci Priapi, custos furum atque avium, cum salignâ falce, servet* eas. *Ipse, cui talia* sunt *curæ, ferens thymum pinosque de altis montibus, ferat* eos *latè circum tecta* apium. *Ipse terat* suam *manum duro labore* plantationis, *ipse figat feraces plantas humo, et irriget amicos imbres. Atque equidem, ni jam, sub extremo fine laborum, traham vela, et festinem advertere proram terris;*

Dulcia mella premes: nec tantum dulcia, quantum
Et liquida, et durum Bacchi domitura saporem.
At cum incerta volant, cœloque examina ludunt,
Contemnuntque favos, et frigida tecta relinquunt;
Instabiles animos ludo prohibebis inani.
Nec magnus prohibere labor; tu regibus alas
Eripe: non illis quisquam cunctantibus altum
Ire iter, aut castris audebit vellere signa.
Invitent croceis halantes floribus horti;
Et custos furum atque avium, cum falce salignâ
Hellespontiaci servet tutela Priapi.
Ipse thymum pinosque ferens de montibus altis,
Tecta ferat altè circum, cui talia curæ:
Ipse labore manum duro terat: ipse feraces
Figat humo plantas, et amicos irriget imbres.
Atque equidem extremo ni jam sub fine laborum
Vela traham, et terris festinem advertere proram;

TRANSLATION.

of the Year you shall press the luscious Honey: Yet not so luscious as pure, and fit to correct the harsher Relish of the Grape.

But when the roving Swarms fly about and sport in the Air, disdain their Hives, and leave their Habitations cold; you shall restrain their unsettled Minds from their vain Play. Nor is there great Difficulty to restrain them; do you but clip the Wings of their Kings: Not one will dare, while they stay behind, to fly aloft, or pluck up the Standard from the Camp.

Let Gardens fragrant with Saffron Flowers invite them; and the Protection of Hellespontiac Priapus, the Averter of Thieves and Birds, with his Willow Scithe preserve them. Let him, who makes such Things his Care, bring Thyme himself and Pines from the high Mountains, to plant them far and wide about their Hives: Let him wear his Hands with the hard Labour: Set himself the fruitful Plants in the Ground, and water them with kindly Showers.

And *here* indeed, were I not just furling my Sails at the last Period of my Labours, and hasting to turn my Prow to Land; perhaps I might both

NOTES.

104. *Frigida tecta relinquunt.* Servius explains *frigida* by *empty* or *inactive*; *Non opere, ut prius, ferventia. Melle vacua alvearia, inspersa*: In opposition to what is said afterwards when their Activity is described, *fervet opus.*

108. *Vellere signa.* This Phrase was used by the *Romans* to express the Moving of their Camp. For, when they pitched their Camp, they stuck their Ensigns into the Ground before the General's Tent, and plucked them up when they decamped. Thus Æn. XI. 19.

———————*Ubi primum vellere signa*
Annuerint Superi, pubemque educere castris.

111. *Hellespontiaci servet tutela Priapi.* The Statue of *Priapus* was commonly set up in Gardens, to protect them from Thieves, and to scare away the Birds. So that the Meaning is, that they should be invited by such Gardens as deserve to be under the Protection of that Deity.

111. *Hellespontiaci.* Priapus was chiefly worshipped at *Lampsacum*, a City on the *Hellespont.*

Forsitan et, pingues hortos quæ cura colendi
Ornaret, canerem, biferique rosaria Pæsti;
Quoque modo potis gauderent intyba rivis;
Et virides apio ripæ; tortusque per herbam
Cresceret in ventrem cucumis: nec sera comantem
Narcissum, aut flexi tacuissem vimen acanthi.
Pallentesque ederas, et amantes litora myrtos.
Namque sub Oebaliæ memini me turribus altis,
Quà niger humectat flaventia culta Galesus,
Corycium vidisse senem, cui pauca relicti
Jugera ruris erant; nec fertilis illa juvencis,
Nec pecori opportuna seges, nec commoda Baccho.
Hic rarum tamen in dumis olus, albaque circum
Lilia, verbenasque premens, vescumque papaver,
Regum æquabat opes animis: seràque revertens
Nocte domum, dapibus mensas onerabat inemtis.
Primus vere rosam, atque autumno carpere poma;
Et cum tristis hiems etiam nunc frigore saxa
Rumperet, et glacie cursus frænaret aquarum;

forsitan et canerem, quæ cura colendi ornaret pingues hortos, rosariaque biferi oppidi Pæsti; quoque modo intyba gauderent rivis potis, et ripæ virides apio, cucumisque, tortus per herbam, cresceret in ventrem: nec tacuissem Narcissum comantem serâ, aut vimen flexi acanthi, pallentesque ederas, et myrtos amantes litora. Nam, sub altis turribus Oebaliæ, quà niger fluvius Galesus humectat flaventia culta arva, memini me vidisse Corycium senem, cui erant pauca jugera relicti ruris; illa seges nec fertilis juvencis, nec opportuna pecori, nec commoda Baccho. Tamen hic premens rarum olus in dumis, albaque lilia circum, verbenasque, vescumque papaver, æquabat opes regum animis: revertensque domum serâ nocte, onerabat mensas inemtis dapibus. Erat primus carpere rosam vere, atque poma autumno; et cum tristis hiems etiam nunc rumperet saxa frigore, et frænaret cursus aquarum glacie;

TRANSLATION.

sing what Method of Culture would adorn rich Gardens, and the Rose-beds of twice-blooming Pæstum; and how Endive and verdant Banks of Parsley delight in drinking the Rills; and how the Cucumber winding along the Grass swells into a Belly: Nor had I passed in Silence the late-flowering Daffodil, nor the Stalks of the flexile Acanthus, nor the pale Ivy, and the Myrtles that love the Shores. For I remember that, under the lofty Turrets of Oebalia, where black Galesus moistens the yellow Fields, I saw an old Corycian, who had a few Acres of neglected Land; nor was the Soil rich enough for the Plough, nor proper for Flocks, nor commodious for Vines. Yet here among the Bushes planting a few Pot-herbs, white Lilies, Vervain, and esculent Poppies all around, he equalled in a *contented* Mind the Wealth of Kings, and, returning late at Night, loaded his Board with unbought Dainties. The first to gather the Rose in Spring, and Fruits in Autumn; and even when sad Winter now split the Rocks with Cold, and bridled up the Current of the Rivers with Ice; in that very

NOTES.

119. *Biferique rosaria Pæsti.* Pæstum, says *Servius*, is a Town in *Calabria*, where the Roses blow twice a Year.

125. *Oebaliæ.* Tarentum, a City in the South of *Italy*; rebuilt by *Phalantus*, who came from *Oebalia* or *Laconia*.

127. *Corycium.* Corycius here is either the Name of the old Man here spoken of, or rather the Name of his Country. For *Coryeus* is the Name of a Mountain and City of *Cilicia*. *Pompey* had made War on the *Cilicians*, of which People some being received into Friendship, were brought by him, and planted in *Calabria*, about *Tarentum*. *Virgil*'s old Man may therefore reasonably be supposed to be one of *Pompey*'s *Cilicians*.

Ille jam tum tondebat comam mollis acanthi, increpitans seram æstatem, morantesque Zephyros. Ergo idem solebat primus abundare fetis apibus, atque multo examine, et cogere spumantia mella pressis favis: erant illi tiliæ atque uberrima pinus: quotque pomis fertilis arbos induerat se in novo flore, tenebat totidem matura autumno. Ille etiam distulit seras ulmos in versum, eduramque pyrum, et spinos jam ferentes pruna, platanumque jam ministrantem umbras potantibus. Verùm equidem ego ipse, exclusus iniquis spatiis, prætereo hæc, atque relinquo talia memoranda post me aliis poëtis. Nunc agè, expediam, quas naturas Jupiter ipse addidit apibus: pro quâ mercede consequendâ, hæ secutæ canoros sonitus Curetum, crepitantia æra, pavere Jovem regem cœli sub Dictæo antro.

Ille comam mollis jam tum tondebat acanthi,
Æstatem increpitans seram, Zephyrosque morantes.
  Ergo apibus fetis idem atque examine multo
Primus abundare; et spumantia cogere pressis
Mella favis: illi tiliæ, atque uberrima pinus:
Quotque in flore novo pomis se fertilis arbos
Induerat, totidem autumno matura tenebat.
Ille etiam seras in versum distulit ulmos,
Eduramque pyrum, et spinos jam pruna ferentes,
Jamque ministrantem platanum potantibus umbras.
Verùm hæc ipse equidem, spatiis exclusus iniquis,
Prætereo, atque aliis post me memoranda relinquo.
  Nunc agè, naturas apibus quas Jupiter ipse
Addidit, expediam: pro quâ mercede, canoros
Curetum sonitus crepitantiaque æra secutæ,
Dictæo cœli regem pavere sub antro.

TRANSLATION.

Season he was cropping the Locks of the soft Acanthus, chiding the late Summer, and the lingering Zephyrs.

He therefore was the first to abound with pregnant Bees, and numerous Swarms; and to strain the frothing Honey from the pressed Combs: He had Limes and Pines in great Abundance: And as many Fruits as the fertile Tree had been cloathed with in early Blossom, so many it retained ripe in Autumn. He too transplanted into Rows the late *far-grown* Elms, and hard Pear-trees, and Sloe-trees now bearing Damsons, and the Plane now ministering Shade to Drinkers. But these I for my Part wave, restrained by the narrow Bounds I have prescribed myself, and leave to others hereafter to record.

Come now, I will unfold the Qualities which Jupiter himself has implanted in the Bees: For which Reward accompanying the shrill Sounds and tinkling Brass of the Curetes, they fed the King of Heaven under the Dictæan Cave.

NOTES.

139. *Ergo apibus fetis.* The Poet always takes care, in his Digressions, not to forget the principal Subject. Therefore he mentions in this Place the Benefits which accrued to the old Corycian from this extraordinary Care of his Garden with respect to Bees.

144. *Seras ulmos.* Ruæus renders *seras* by *tarde crescentes*, that are late of arriving to their Growth. I rather think the Poet means far grown, *i. e.* when they had stood so long in the Ground as to be fit for transplanting: Agreeable to what is said of the other Trees here mentioned. The Sloe-trees, when they were so big as to bear Fruit, and the Planes, when so large as to yield Shade, and form a Bower.

150. *Canoros Curetum sonitus.* According to the Fable, *Saturn* intended to have devoured the Infant *Jupiter*, to avoid which he was concealed among the *Curetes* in *Crete*, the Clangor of whose brazen Armour and Cymbals, as they danced, would drown his Cries. *Melissus* is said at that Time to have been King of *Crete*, whose Daughters having nursed *Jupiter* with Goats Milk and Honey, hence arose the Fable that *Jupiter* was nursed by a Goat named *Amalthea*, and by Bees, *i. e.* by the *Melissæ*, the Daughters of King *Melissus*, which in the *Greek* Language signifies *Bees*. For which Service the Goat was placed by *Jupiter* amongst the Stars, and its Horn given to

Solæ communes natos, consortia tecta
Urbis habent, magnisque agitant sub legibus ævum:
Et patriam solæ, et certos novere penates:
Venturæque hiemis memores, æstate laborem
Experiuntur, et in medium quæsita reponunt.
Namque aliæ victu invigilant, et fœdere pacto
Exercentur agris; pars intra septa domorum,
Narcissi lacrymam, et lentum de cortice gluten,
Prima favis ponunt fundamina, deinde tenaces
Suspendunt ceras; aliæ, spem gentis, adultos
Educunt fetus; aliæ purissima mella
Stipant, et liquido distendunt nectare cellas.
Sunt, quibus ad portas cecidit custodia sorti;
Inque vicem speculantur aquas et nubila cœli:
Aut onera accipiunt venientum; aut, agmine facto,
Ignavum fucos pecus à præsepibus arcent.
Fervet opus, redolentque thymo fragrantia mella.

Hæ *solæ* animalium *habent communes natos, et consortia tecta urbis, agitantque ævum sub magnis legibus: et solæ novere patriam et certos penates: memoresque hiemis venturæ, experiuntur laborem æstate, et reponunt quæsita in medium. Namque aliæ invigilant victu, et pacto fœdere exercentur agris; pars, intra septa domorum, ponunt lacrymam Narcissi, et lentum gluten de cortice, prima fundamina favis, deinde suspendunt tenaces ceras; aliæ educunt adultos fetus, spem gentis; aliæ stipant purissima mella, et distendunt cellas liquido nectare. Sunt aliæ, quibus custodia ad portas cecidit sorti; inque vicem speculantur aquas et nubila cœli, aut accipiunt onera venientum; aut, agmine facto, arcent fucos ignavum pecus à præsepibus.*

Opus fervet, fragrantiaque mella redolent thymo.

TRANSLATION.

They alone *of all the Animal Creation* make their Young the public Care, share the Buildings of a City in common, and pass their Lives under inviolable Laws: And they alone have a Country of their own, and a fixed Abode. Mindful of the coming Winter, they experience Toil in Summer, and lay up their Acquisitions into the common Stock. For some are provident for Food, and by fixed Compact are employed in the Fields; some within the Inclosure of their Hives lay Narcissus' Tears, and clammy Gum from Bark of Trees for the first Foundation of the Combs, then build into Arches the viscid Wax; others bring up to their full Growth the Young, the Hope of the Nation; others condense the purest Honey, and distend the Cells with liquid Nectar. Some there are to whose Lot is fallen the Watching at the Gates, and these by turns observe the Waters and Clouds of Heaven: Or receive the Loads of those who return: or, forming a Band, drive from the Hives the Drones, a sluggish Generation. The Work is warmly plied, and the Honey smells fragrant of Thyme.

NOTES.

the Nymphs, with this Quality added to it, that whatever they wished for should flow to them copiously from that Horn. The Bees again, that before were no wiser than other Insects, were henceforth endued with an extraordinary Degree of Wisdom and Sagacity.

160. *Narcissi lacrymam.* The Flowers of the Narcissus or Daffodil form a Cup in the Middle. These Cups are supposed to contain the Tears of the Youth *Narcissus* who pined to Death. To this *Milton* beautifully alludes in his *Lycidas:*

Bid Amaranthus *all his Beauty shed,*
And Daffodillies *fill their Cups with Tears,*
To strew the Laureat Herse where Lycid *lies.*

162. *Adultos educunt fetus.* Educendo adultos faciunt, *they foster them till they be full grown.* So *Servius* explains it: But the Words may also signify, *they lead forth their full-grown Young.*

Ac veluti, cum Cyclopes properant fulmina lentis massis, alii accipiunt redduntque auras taurinis follibus; alii tingunt stridentia æra lacu: Ætna gemit incudibus impositis: illi, inter sese, tollunt brachia magnâ vi in numerum, versantque ferrum tenaci forcipe. Non aliter, si licet componere parva magnis, innatus amor habendi mellis urget Cecropias apes, quamque suo munere. Oppida sunt curæ grandævis, et munire favos, et fingere Dædala tecta. At minores natu fessæ referunt se multâ nocte, plenæ quoad crura thymo; pascuntur et arbuta passim, et glaucas salices, casiamque, rubentemque crocum, et pinguem tiliam, et ferrugineos hyacinthos. Quies operum est una omnibus, labor est unus omnibus. Manè ruunt portis, est nusquam mora. Rursus,

Ac veluti, lentis Cyclopes fulmina massis
Cum properant, alii taurinis follibus auras
Accipiunt redduntque; alii stridentia tingunt
Æra lacu: gemit impositis incudibus Ætna:
Illi inter sese magnâ vi brachia tollunt
In numerum, versantque tenaci forcipe ferrum.
Non aliter, si parva licet componere magnis,
Cecropias innatus apes amor urget habendi,
Munere quamque suo. Grandævis oppida curæ,
Et munire favos, et Dædala fingere tecta.
At fessæ multâ referunt se nocte minores,
Crura thymo plenæ; pascuntur et arbuta passim,
Et glaucas salices, casiamque, crocumque rubentem,
Et pinguem tiliam, et ferrugineos hyacinthos,
Omnibus una quies operum, labor omnibus unus.
Manè ruunt portis; nusquam mora. Rursus easdem

TRANSLATION.

As when the Cyclops urge on the Thunderbolts from the stubborn Masses, some receive and render back the Air in the Bull-hide Bellows; some dip the sputtering Brass in the Trough: Ætna groans under the Weight of their Anvils: They alternately with vast Force lift their Arms in Time, and turn the Iron with the griping Pincers. Just so, if we may compare small Things with great, the innate Love of Gain prompts the Cecropian Bees, each in his proper Function. The elder have the Care of their Towns, and to fortify the Combs, and frame the artificial Cells. But the younger return fatigued late at Night, their Thighs laden with Thyme; they feed at large on Arbutes, and grey Willows, on Casia, and glowing Crocus, on the gummy Lime, and purple Hyacinths; all have one Rest from Work, all one *Time of* Labour. In the Morning they rush out of the Gates without Delay. Again, when the Evening

NOTES.

175. *In numerum.* That is, in a certain Order, making a sort of Harmony with the regular Strokes of their Hammers of different Weights. We learn from *Jamblichus*, that the Sound of the Smith's Hammers taught *Pythagoras* to invent the Monochord, an Instrument for measuring the Quantities and Proportions of Sounds geometrically. See *Jamblichus de vita Pythag.* C. XXVI.

177. *Cecropias apes.* Attic, or *Athenian* Bees, from *Cecrops*, the first King of *Athens*. The *Attic* Honey was much celebrated, especially that from *Hymettus*.

183. *Ferrugineos hyacinthos.* Ferrugineus here seems to signify *a dusky Red*, as in the first Georgic, 465, speaking of the Sun,

Cum caput obscura nitidum ferrugine texit.

Mr. *Martin* takes the Hyacinth of the Poets to be the *Lilium floribus reflexis*, or *Martagon*. The Flowers, he says, of most Sorts of *Martagons* have many Spots of a deeper Colour; and sometimes I have seen these Spots run together in such a Manner, as to form the Letters A I in several Places, as the Hyacinth of the Poets is represented.

194. *Saepe*

Vesper ubi è pastu tandem decedere campis
Admonuit; tum tecta petunt, tum corpora curant:
Fit sonitus, mussantque oras et limina circum.
Post, ubi jam thalamis se composuere, siletur
In noctem, fessosque sopor suus occupat artus.
Nec verò à stabulis, pluviâ impendente, recedunt
Longiùs; aut credunt cœlo, adventantibus Euris:
Sed circum tutæ sub mœnibus urbis aquantur,
Excursusque breves tentant; et sæpe lapillos,
Ut cymbæ instabiles, fluctu jactante, saburram,
Tollunt: his sese per inania nubila librant.
Illum adeò placuisse apibus mirabere morem,
Quòd nec concubitu indulgent, nec corpora segnes
In venerem solvunt, aut fetus nixibus edunt.
Verùm ipsæ è foliis natos, et suavibus herbis
Ore legunt: ipsæ regem parvosque Quirites
Sufficiunt; aulasque et cerea regna refingunt.

ubi vesper admonuit easdem tandem decedere campis è pastu, tum petunt tecta, tum curant corpora: sonitus fit, mussantque circum oras et limina alvearis. *Post, ubi jam composuere se thalamis, siletur in noctem, suusque sopor occupat fessos artus. Nec verò, pluviâ impendente, recedunt longiùs à stabulis; aut credunt se cœlo, Euris adventantibus: sed, tutæ sub mœnibus urbis, aquantur circum* alvearia, *tentantque breves excursus: et sæpe tollunt lapillos, ut instabiles cymbæ* tollunt *saburram, fluctu jactante: librant sese his* lapillis *per inania nubila.* Tu *adeò mirabere illum morem placuisse apibus, quod nec indulgent concubitui, nec segnes solvunt corpora in venerem, aut edunt fetus nixibus. Verùm ipsæ legunt natos è foliis te suavibus herbis ore: ipsæ sufficiunt regem parvosque Quirites; refinguntque aulas et cerea regna.*

TRANSLATION.

at length has warned them to return from feeding in the Fields, then they seek their Habitations, and then refresh their Bodies. The *drowzy* Hum arises, and they buzz about the Borders and Entrance *of their Hives*. Soon after, when they have composed themselves in their Cells, all is hushed for the Night, and their proper Sleep seizes on their weary Limbs. Nor remove they to a great Distance from their Hives when Rain impends, nor trust the Sky when East-winds approach: But in Safety supply themselves with Water all around under the Walls of their City, and attempt but short Excursions; and often take up little Stones, as unsteady Vessels do Ballast in a tossing Sea: With these they poise themselves through the void airy Regions.

Chiefly you will admire this Custom peculiar to the Bees, that they neither indulge in conjugal Embrace, nor softly dissolve their Bodies in the Joys of Love, nor bring forth Young with a Mother's Throwes. But the Individuals spontaneous cull their Progeny with their Mouths from Leaves and fragrant Herbs: They themselves raise up a new King and little Subjects, and build *for them* new Palaces and waxen Realms.

NOTES.

194. *Sæpe lapillos.* So *Aristotle:* Οταν δε ανεμος η μεγας, φερουσι λιθον εφ εαυταις, ερμα προς το πνευμα.

197. *Illum adeò placuisse.* This Account of the Generation of Bees is justly exploded by modern Philosophers, who assert, with Reason, that no Animal is produced without a Concurrence of the two Sexes. However, the Doctrine of equivocal Generation was so generally admitted by the Ancients, that it is no Wonder the Poet should mention it. The same Opinion is related both by *Aristotle* and *Pliny*. But the Moderns have been more happy in discovering the Nature of these wonderful Insects. The labouring Bees don't appear to be of either Sex: The Drones are found to have the male Organs of Generation; and the Monarch is found to be of the female Sex. This Queen is wholly employed in the Increase of the Family, laying several thousand Eggs every Summer, from each of which is hatched a small white Worm, which in due Time changes either to a Drone or a Bee.

210. *Regem*

Sæpe etiam attrivere alas errando in duris cotibus, ultroque dedere animam sub fasce: est illis *tantus amor florum, et gloria generandi mellis. Ergo quamvis terminus angusti ævi excipiat ipsas (neque enim plus* quam *septima æstas ducitur* ab illis) *at genus* earum *manet immortale, fortunaque domûs stat per multos annos, et avi avorum numerantur. Præterea non Ægyptus, et ingens Lydia, nec populi Parthorum, aut Medus Hydaspes sic observant regem. Rege* earum *incolumi, est una mens omnibus;* rege *amisso, rupere fidem; ipsæque diripuere constructa mella, et solvere crates favorum. Ille* rex est *custos operum, admirantur illum, et omnes circumstant* illum *denso fremitu, frequentesque stipant, et sæpe attollunt* illum *humeris, et objectant* sua *corpora bello* pro illo, *petuntque pulchram mortem per vulnera* tuendo illum. *Quidam,* inducti *his signis, atque secuti hæc exempla* prudentiæ apium, *dixere, partem divinæ mentis, et æthereos haustus esse apibus: namque* dixerunt, *Deum ire per omnes*

Sæpe etiam, duris errando in cotibus, alas
Attrivere, ultroque animam sub fasce dedere:
Tantus amor florum, et generandi gloria mellis.
Ergo ipsas quamvis angusti terminus ævi
Excipiat; (neque enim plus septima ducitur æstas)
At genus immortale manet, multosque per annos
Stat fortuna domûs, et avi numerantur avorum.

Præterea regem non sic Ægyptus, et ingens
Lydia, nec populi Parthorum, aut Medus Hydaspes
Observant. Rege incolumi, mens omnibus una est;
Amisso, rupere fidem, constructaque mella
Diripuere ipsæ, et crates solvere favorum.
Ille operum custos, illum admirantur, et omnes
Circumstant fremitu denso, stipantque frequentes,
Et sæpe attollunt humeris, et corpora bello
Objectant, pulchramque petunt per vulnera mortem.

His quidam signis, atque hæc exempla secuti,
Esse apibus partem divinæ mentis, et haustus
Æthereos dixere: Deum namque ire per omnes

TRANSLATION.

Often too in wandering among the flinty Rocks have they tore their Wings, and voluntarily yielded up their Lives under their Burthen: So ardent is their Passion for Flowers, and such their Glory in making Honey. Therefore tho'* they themselves be limited to a narrow Term of Life; (for † it is not prolonged beyond the seventh Summer) yet the immortal Race remains, and for many Years the Fortune of the Family subsists, and they count Grandsires of Grandsires *in a long Series of Generations.*

Besides, not Egypt's Self, nor great Lydia, nor the Nation of the Parthians, nor Median Hydaspes, are so obsequious to their King. Whilst the King is safe, all live in perfect Harmony; when he is dead, they dissolve their Union, they themselves tear to Pieces the Fabric of their Honey, and demolish the Contexture of their Combs. He is the Guardian of their Works, him they admire, and all encircle him with thick Humming, and guard him in a numerous Body; often they lift him up on their Shoulders, *in his Defence* expose their Bodies in War, and through Wounds seek a glorious Death.

Some from these Appearances, and led by these Examples *of Sagacity,* have alledged that there is in Bees a Portion of the divine Mind, and heavenly Emanation: For that the Deity pervades the whole Earth, the Tracts of Sea, and

* *Tho' the Limits of a narrow Life bound the Individuals.* † *For no more than the seventh Summer is pass'd over.*

NOTES.

210. *Regem non sic Ægyptus.* The *Egyptians* were remarkable Adorers of their Monarchs; many of the Heathen Gods being the deified Kings of that People.

211. *Populi Parthorum.* The *Parthians* are reported to have been so submissive to their Kings, as to kiss his Foot, and to touch the Ground with their Mouths, when they approached him.

211. *Medus Hydaspes.* The River here designed seems to be what is commonly called the *Choaspes,* which, rising in *Media,* flows thro' *Susiana,* near the City *Susa,* one of the Capitals of the *Persian* Empire.

221. *Deum namque ire per omnes.* Plutarch, in his second Book of the Opinions of Philosophers,

Terrasque tractusque maris, cœlumque profundum.
Hinc pecudes, armenta, viros, genus omne ferarum.
Quemque sibi tenues nascentem arcessere vitas.
Scilicet huc reddi deinde, ac resoluta referri
Omnia: nec morti esse locum; sed viva volare
Sideris in numerum, atque alto succedere cœlo.
  Si quando sedem angustam, servataque mella
Thesauris relines: priùs haustus sparsus aquarum
Ore fove, fumosque manu prætende sequaces.
Bis gravidos cogunt fetus, duo tempora messis;
Taygete simul os terris ostendit honestum
Pleias, et Oceani spretos pede reppulit amnes:
Aut eadem sidus fugiens ubi Piscis aquosi
Tristior hibernas cœlo descendit in undas.

terrasque tractusque maris, profundumque cœlum. Hinc pecudes, armenta, viros, omne genus ferarum, denique quemque nascentem arcessere tenues vitas sibi. Scilicet dixerunt deinde omnia reddi, ac resoluta referri huc; nec esse locum morti; sed viva volare quæque *in numerum* sui *sideris, atque succedere alto cœlo. Si quando relines angustam sedem* earum, *mellaque servata thesauris: priùs fove ore haustus aquarum, sparsus* illis, *prætendeque manu fumos sequaces apium. Bis cogunt gravidos fetus,* sunt illis *duo tempora messis; simul ac Taygete Pleias ostendit honestum os terris, et reppulit spretos amnes Oceani pede: aut ubi eadem* Pleias, *fugiens sidus aquosi Piscis, descendit tristior cœlo in hibernas undas.*

TRANSLATION.

Depth of Heaven. That hence the Flocks, the Herds, Men, and all the Race of Savages, each at its Birth derive their slender Lives. Accordingly that all of them when dissolved return hither hereafter: Nor is there any Place for Annihilation; but that they mount up alive *each* into his proper Order of Star, and take their Seat in the high Heaven.

What Time you are to rifle their august Mansion, and their Honey preserved in their Treasures; first gargle your Mouth with a Draught of Water, and squirt it out *upon them,* and carry in your Hand before you persecuting Smoke. Twice they press the teeming Cells, there are two Seasons of that Harvest; *one,* as soon as the Pleiad Taygete has displayed her comely Face to the Earth, and spurns with her Foot the despised Waters of the Ocean: Or when the same Star, flying the Constellation of the watery Fish, descends in Sadness from the Sky into the wintery Waves. They are wrathful above Measure, and when provoked infuse

NOTES,

sophers, informs us that all of them, except *Democritus, Epicurus,* and the rest who asserted the Doctrine of a *Vacuum* and *Atoms,* held the Universe to be animated, and governed by Providence: Οἱ μεν αλλοι παντες εμψυχον τον κοσμον και προνοια διοικουμενον Δημοκριτος δε και Επικουρος και ὁσοι τα ατομα εισηγουνται και το κενον, ουτε εμψυχον ουτε προνοια διοικεισθαι, φυσει δε τινι αλογω.

229. *Relines.* Unseal or disclose, a Word applied to Vessels and other Things that use to be close stopped and sealed up: Thus *relinere epistolam* is to take off the Wax, and open a Letter.

229. *Priùs haustus, &c.* This is a very difficult Passage. In explaining it I have followed *Servius,* who takes *sparsus* for *spargens.* But perhaps it ought to be read *priùs haustu sparsis aquarum,* i. e. *illis,* having first squirted Water upon them, *sparsis ore fove,* &c. blow up with your Mouth, and hold before you in your Hand a smoking Torch.

231. *Cogunt.* Signifies, they, *viz* the Beemasters, gather or squeeze the Honey, as Verse 140. And by the *fœtus gravidos* I understand the Cells or Combs full of Honey, which are the *Fœtus* or *Productions* of the Bees.

234. *Sidus fugiens ubi Piscis aquosi.* The Setting of the *Pleiades* means the latter End of *October,* or Beginning of *November.* And the *sidus Piscis aquosi* seems to be *the Dolphin* as it rises sooner after the Setting of the *Pleiades* than any other Fish delineated on the Sphere. *Pisces* cannot be the Constellation here meant, for the Sun does not enter that Sign till the Middle of *February.*

Eſt illis apibus ira ſupra modum, læſæque inſpirant venenum morſibus; et, affixæ venis, relinquunt cæca ſpicula, ponuntque animas in vulnere. Sin metues duram hiemem, parceſque futuro, miſerabereque contuſos animos, et fractas res earum: At quis dubitet ſuffire eas thymo, et recidere inanes ceras? nam ſæpe ignotus ſtellio adedit favos, et cubilia ſunt *congeſta blattis lucifugis: fucuſque immunis laborum, ſedens ad aliena pabula, aut aſper crabro* cum *imparibus armis immiſcuit ſe* his; *aut durum genus tineæ, aut aranea inviſa Minervæ, ſuſpendit laxos caſſes in foribus* alveariorum. *Quò magis fuerint exhauſtæ, hoc acriùs omnes incumbent ſarcire ruinas lapſi generis, complebuntque foros, et texent horrea floribus.*

Illis ira modum ſupra eſt, læſæque venenum
Morſibus inſpirant, et ſpicula cæca relinquunt
Affixæ venis;-animaſque in vulnere ponunt.
. Sin duram metues hiemem, parceſque futuro,
Contuſoſque animos, et res miſerabere fractas:
At ſuffire thymo, ceraſque recidere inanes
Quis dubitet? nam ſæpe favos ignotus adedit
Stellio, et lucifugis congeſta cubilia blattis;
Immuniſque ſedens aliena ad pabula fucus.
Aut aſper crabro imparibus ſe immiſcuit armis;
Aut durum tineæ genus; aut inviſa Minervæ
In foribus laxos ſuſpendit aranea caſſes.
Quò magis exhauſtæ fuerint, hoc acriùs omnes
Incumbent generis lapſi ſarcire ruinas,
Complebuntque foros, et floribus horrea texent.

TRANSLATION.

Venom into their Stings, and leave their hidden Darts fixed in the Veins, and lay down their Lives in the Wound.

Yet, if you are afraid of a hard Winter, you ought to ſpare their future Nouriſhment, and have Pity on their drooping Spirits and afflicted State: But who would heſitate to fumigate *their Hives* with Thyme, and cut away the empty Wax? For often the Lizard preys unſeen upon the Combs, and the *vacant* Cells are ſtuffed with Grubs that ſhun the Light; the Drone alſo that ſits exempt from Duty at another's repaſt, or the fierce Hornet has engaged them with unequal Arms; or the Moth's direful Breed; or the Spider, hateful to Minerva, has ſuſpended her looſe Nets in their Gates.

The more they are exhauſted, the more vigorouſly will they all labour to repair the Ruins of their decayed Race, to fill up the Cells, and weave their Magazines of Flowers. But, ſeeing Life has on Bees too entailed our Misfortunes,

NOTES.

239. *Parceſque futuro.* This I take to be an Inſtruction by itſelf, and not a Motive to enforce the following Inſtruction, as all the Interpreters ſeem to have conſidered it, and by that Means ſtrangely embarraſs the Senſe. The Meaning is, If you are afraid of a rigid Winter, and that the Bees will not be able to ſuſtain the Cold, unleſs they be ſtrong and well fed, you ought to ſpare their Honey, their future Nouriſhment; where the Poet ſhews his Tenderneſs and Humanity, as upon all other Occaſions: For whereas others only adviſe to reſerve to them a Third, or two Thirds at moſt of the Honey, he, in Compaſſion to thoſe painful Inſects, would have his Swarm maſter to ſpare it all, leſt they ſhould not be able to ſtand through the hard Winter. But adds, *At ſuffire thymo—quis dubitet*, i. e. However you think proper to comply with this Inſtruction, yet there is one Rule ſtrictly to be obſerved, and about which no Doubt is to be made, and that is to *fumigate the Hives*, &c.

243. *Stellio et.* The common Editions want the *et*; but *Pierius* found it in all the Manuſcripts he conſulted.

246. *Inviſa Minervæ aranea.* Arachne, a *Lydian* Maid, is ſaid, according to the Fable, to have diſputed with *Minerva* the Preference in weaving Tapeſtry. *Arachne* performed her Work to Admiration. But, as ſhe had repreſented in it the Crimes of ſeveral of the Gods, *Minerva* in a Rage deſtroyed it; at which *Arachne* hanged herſelf for Grief. The Goddeſs in Compaſſion changed her into a Spider. See *Ovid. Met.* L. V.

Si verò (quoniam casus apibus quoquè nostros
Vita tulit) tristi languebunt corpora morbo;
Quod jam non dubiis poteris cognoscere signis;
Continuò est ægris alius color; horrida vultum
Deformat macies; tum corpora luce carentum
Exportant tectis, et tristia funera ducunt:
Aut illæ pedibus connexæ ad limina pendent;
Aut intus clausis cunctantur in ædibus omnes,
Ignavæque fame, et contracto frigore pigræ.
Tum sonus auditur gravior, tractimque susurrant:
Frigidus ut quondam silvis immurmurat Auster;
Ut mare sollicitum stridet refluentibus undis;
Æstuat ut clausis rapidus fornacibus ignis.
Hic jam galbaneos suadebo incendere odores;
Mellaque arundineis inferre canalibus, ultro
Hortantem, et fessas ad pabula nota vocantem.
Proderit et tunsum gallæ admiscere saporem,

Si verò (quoniam vita tulit nostros casus apibus quoquè) corpora earum *languebunt tristi morbo, quod jam poteris cognoscere non dubiis signis: continuò est ægris alius color; horrida macies deformat vultum; tum exportant corpora carentum luce vitæ è tectis, et ducunt tristia funera; aut illæ, connexæ* aliæ *pedibus* aliarum, *pendent ad limina* alvearis, *aut omnes cunctantur intus in clausis ædibus, ignavæque fame, et pigræ frigore contracto. Tum gravior sonus auditur, susurrantque tractim: ut quondam frigidus Auster immurmurat silvis; ut mare sollicitum stridet undis refluentibus; ut rapidus ignis æstuat clausis fornacibus. Hic jam suadebo te incendere galbaneos odores, inferreque illis mella arundineis canalibus, ultro hortantem, et vocantem* eas *fessas ad nota pabula. Et proderit admiscere tunsum saporem gallæ,*

TRANSLATION.

if their Bodies shall languish with a sore Disease, which you may know by undoubted Signs; immediately the Sick change Colour; horrid Leanness deforms their Countenance, then they carry the Bodies of their Dead out of their Houses, and lead the mournful Funeral Processions; or, clinging together by the Feet, hang about the Entrance, and loiter all within their Houses shut up, listless through Famine, and benumbed with contracted Cold. Then a hoarser Sound is heard, and in drawling Hums they buz: As at Times the South Wind whispers through the Woods; as the ruffled Sea murmurs with refluent Waves; as rapid Fire in the pent Furnace roars. In this Case now I would advise to burn gummy Odours, and to put in Honey through Pipes of Reed, kindly tempting and inviting the drooping *Insects* to their known Repast. It will be of Service also to mix with it the Juice of pounded Galls, and dried Roses, or Wine thickened

NOTES.

256. *Tristia funera ducunt.* Thus *Pliny* says the Bees accompany the Bodies of their Dead, after the Manner of a Funeral Procession: *Quin et morbos suapte natura sentiunt. Index eorum tristitia torpens, et cum, ante fores in teporem solis promotis, aliæ cibos ministrant, cum defunctas progerunt, funerantiumque more comitantur exequias.*

267. *Gallæ.* The Gall, says Mr. *Martin*, is an Excrescence or Nest of an Insect, formed on the Oaks in *Italy*, after the same Manner that Oak-apples are in *England*. All Parts of the Oak are astringent, especially the Galls; they are therefore very proper for the Purging to which the Bees are subject in the Spring, occasioned, according to *Columella*, by their feeding greedily on Spurge after their Winter Penury.

 269. *Desruta*

Arentesque rosas, aut igni pinguia multo
Defruta, vel Psythiâ passos de vite racemos,
Cecropiumque thymum, et grave olentia centaurea.
Est etiam flos in pratis, cui nomen amello
Fecere agricolæ; facilis quærentibus herba:
Namque uno ingentem tollit de cespite silvam,
Aureus ipse; sed in foliis, quæ plurima circum
Funduntur, violæ sublucet purpura nigræ.
Sæpe Deûm nexis ornatæ torquibus aræ;
Asper in ore sapor: tonsis in vallibus illum
Pastores, et curva legunt prope flumina Mellæ.
Hujus odorato radices incoque Baccho;
Pabulaque in foribus plenis appone canistris.
Sed si quem proles subitò defecerit omnis,
Nec, genus unde novæ stirpis revocetur, habebit;
Tempus est Arcadii memoranda inventa magistri
Pandere; quoque modo cæsis jam sæpe juvencis
Insincerus apes tulerit cruor: altiùs omnem
Expediam primâ repetens ab origine famam.

arentesque rosas, aut pinguia vina *defruta multo igni, vel passos racemos de Psythiâ vite, Cecropiumque thymum, et grave olentia centaurea. Est etiam flos in pratis, cui amello agricolæ fecere nomen, herba facilis quærentibus. Namque tollit ingentem silvam de uno cespite, ipse* aureus; *sed in foliis, quæ plurima funduntur circum, purpura nigræ violæ sublucet. Sæpe aræ Deûm* sunt *ornatæ torquibus nexis* ex eo. *Sapor* ejus est *asper in ore; pastores legunt illum* amellum *in tonsis vallibus, et prope curva flumina Mellæ. Incoque radices hujus odorato Baccho, apponeque* ea *pabula plenis canistris in foribus* alvearis. *Sed si omnis proles subitò defecerit quem, nec habebit, unde genus novæ stirpis revocetur; est tempus pandere memoranda inventa Arcadii magistri* apum, *quoque modo jam insincerus cruor tulerit apes, juvencis sæpe cæsis.* Ego *expediam omnem famam* hujus facti *altiùs, repetens* eam *ab primâ origine.*

TRANSLATION.

over a strong Fire, or Raisins from the Psythian Vine, Cecropian Thyme, and strong smelling Centaury. There is also in the Meadows a Flower, to which the Husbandmen have given the Name of Amellus; an Herb easy to be found: For from one Root it shoots a vast Luxuriance of Stalks, itself of golden Hue; but on the Leaves, which full thick are spread around, the Purple of the dark Violet sheds a Gloss. The Altars of the Gods are often decked with plaited Wreathes *of this Flower*; its Taste is bitterish in the Mouth: the Shepherds gather it in new-shorn Vallies, and near the winding Streams of Mella. Boil the Roots thereof in favorous Wine; and present it *as* their Food in full Baskets at their Door.

But if the whole Stock shall fail any one on a sudden, and he shall have no Means to recover a new Breed; it is Time to unfold the memorable Invention of the Arcadian Master, and how the tainted Gore of Bullocks slain has often produced Bees: I'll disclose the whole Tradition, tracing it high from its first Source.

NOTES.

269. *Defruta.* Defrutum was a Mixture made of new Wine, whereof the one Half, or a Third, was boiled away, into which several sweet Herbs and Spices were put.

270. *Psythiâ passos,* &c. i. e. Raisin-wine, for which the *Psythian* Grape was most proper.

271. *Est etiam flos in pratis.* We may venture to affirm, says the same Author, that the Plant here described is the *Aster Atticus,* or *Purple Italian Star wort.*

273. *Cespite.* Mr. *Martin* understands this of a Root with bushy Fibres.

278. *Mellæ.* Mella, or Mela, was the Name of a River in *Cisalpine Gaul.*

287. *Gens*

Nam quà Pellæi gens fortunata Canopi
Accolit effuſo ſtagnantem flumine Nilum,
Et circum pictis vehitur ſua rura phaſelis;
Quàque pharetratæ vicinia Perſidis urget,
Et viridem Ægyptum nigrâ fecundat arenâ,
Et diverſa ruens ſeptem diſcurrit in ora,
Uſque coloratis amnis devexus ab Indis;
Omnis in hâc certam regio jacit arte ſalutem.
Exiguus primùm, atque ipſos contractus ad uſus,
Eligitur locus; hunc anguſtique imbrice tecti,
Parietibuſque premunt arctis: et quatuor addunt
Quatuor à ventis obliquâ luce feneſtras.
Tum vitulus, bimâ curvans jam cornua fronte,
Quæritur: huic geminæ nares, et ſpiritus oris
Multa reluctanti obſtruitur; plagiſque peremto
Tunſa per integram ſolvuntur viſcera pellem.

Nam quà fortunata gens Pellæi Canopi accolit Nilum ſtagnantem agris flumine effuſo, et vehitur circum ſua rura pictis phaſelis; quàque urget vicinia pharetratæ Perſidis et fecundat viridem Ægyptum nigrâ arenâ, et quà amnis, devexus uſque ab coloratis Indis, ruens diſcurrit in ſeptem diverſa ora; omnis regio jacit certam ſalutem in hâc arte. Primùm exiguus locus eligitur, atque contractus ad hos *uſus ipſos; premunt hunc locum imbriceque anguſti tecti, arctiſque parietibus: et addunt quatuor feneſtras obliquâ luce à quatuor ventis. Tum vitulus, jam curvans cornua bimâ fronte, quæritur: geminæ nares* obſtruuntur, *et ſpiritus oris obſtruitur huic reluctanti multa: viſceraque, tunſa per integram pellem, ſolvuntur* huic *peremto plagis.*

TRANSLATION.

For where the happy Nation of Pellæan Canopus inhabit on the Banks of Nile floating *the Plains* with his overflowing River, and ſail around their Fields in painted Gondolas; and where the River, that rolls down as far as from the ſwarthy Indians, preſſes on the Borders of quivered Perſia, and fertilizes verdant Egypt with black *ſlimy* Sand, and pouring along divides itſelf into ſeven different Mouths; all the Country grounds infallible Relief on this Art. Firſt a Space of Ground of ſmall Dimenſions, and contracted for this very Purpoſe, is made choice of; this they ſtrengthen with a narrow Tile-roof and confined Walls: And add four Windows of ſlanting Light from the four Winds. Then a Bullock, juſt bending the Horns in his Forehead two Years old, is ſought out:, Whilſt he ſtruggles exceedingly, they cloſe up both his Noſtrils, and the Breath of his Mouth: And, having beaten him to Death, his battered Bowels burſt within the

NOTES.

287. *Gens fortunata.* Egypt, called a happy Nation, becauſe of its fertile Soil.

287. *Pellæi Canopi.* That is, of *Canopus*, a City of *Egypt*, in the Neighbourhood of *Alexandria*, which was founded by *Alexander*, born in *Pella* of *Macedonia*.

290. *Quàque pharetratæ vicinia Perſidis urget.* We are not to underſtand here *Perſia* ſtrictly ſo called, for that is very far diſtant from *Egypt*; but the Empire of the *Perſians* as it was extended by *Cyrus*. *Xenophon* tells us, that great Monarch left behind him an Empire bounded on the Eaſt by the *Mare Erythræum*, on the North by the *Black Sea*, on the Weſt by *Cyprus* and *Egypt*, and on the South by *Ethiopia*. Here we ſee plainly how the *Nile* may preſs the Borders of *Perſia*, ſince the *Perſians* extended their Dominions as far as *Egypt*.

290. *Pharetratæ Perſidis.* The *Perſians* are every where celebrated for their Skill in Archery.

290. *Vicinia.* The Senſe naturally leads one to take *vicinia* here in the Plural from *vicinium*. *Ruæus* ſeems not to have underſtood it ſo.

291. *Viridem Egyptum.* Viridis here is a proper Epithet to expreſs the rich Verdure and great Fertility which *Egypt* enjoys, in conſequence of its being overflowed by the *Nile*.

293. *Amnis devexus ab Indis.* The River *Nile* riſes out of the Mountains of the Moon in *Ethiopia*, all which Country was anciently called by the common Name of *India*. See *Ruæus*'s Note on Geor. II. 172.

295. *Exiguus primùm, &c.* It was the general Opinion of Antiquity that Bees were produced from the putrid Bodies of Cattle: Which ſeems to be confirmed from the Story of *Sampſon* in the fourteenth Chapter of *Judges*. The Truth is, ſuch Carcaſes are a proper Receptacle for their Young; and therefore the female Parent chooſes there to lay her Eggs, that the Warmth of the fermenting Juices may help to hatch them.

Linquunt eum positum sic in clauso loco; *et subjiciunt ramea fragmenta, thymum, recentesque casias costis ejus. Hoc geritur, Zephyris primùm impellentibus undas, antequàm prata rubeant novis coloribus, antequàm garrula hirundo suspendat nidum tignis. Interea tepefactus humor in teneris ossibus æstuat: et animalia visenda, miscentur miris modis, trunca pedum primò, et mox stridentia pennis, magis magisque carpunt tenuem aëra: donec, ut imber effusus æstivis nubibus, erupere; aut ut sagittæ e pulsante nervo, si quando leves Parthi ineunt prima prælia. Musæ, quis, quis Deus extudit hanc artem nobis? unde hæc nova experientia hominum cepit ingressus. Pastor Aristæus, fugiens Peneïa Tempe,*

Sic positum in clauso linquunt; et ramea costis
Subjiciunt fragmenta, thymum, casiasque recentes.
Hoc geritur, Zephyris primùm impellentibus undas,
Ante novis rubeant quàm prata coloribus, ante
Garrula quàm tignis nidum suspendat hirundo.
Interea teneris tepefactus in ossibus humor
Æstuat: et visenda modis animalia miris
Trunca pedum primò, mox et stridentia pennis
Miscentur; tenuemque magis magis aëra carpunt:
Donec, ut æstivis effusus nubibus imber,
Erupere; aut ut nervo pulsante sagittæ,
Prima leves ineunt si quando prælia Parthi.
Quis Deus hanc, Musæ, quis nobis extudit artem?
Unde nova ingressus hominum experientia cepit?
Pastor Aristæus fugiens Peneïa Tempe,

TRANSLATION.

Hide that remains intire. When dead, they leave him pent up; and lay under his Sides Fragments of Boughs, Thyme, and fresh Casia. This is done when first the Zephyrs stir the Waves, before the Meadows blush with new Colours, before the chattering Swallow suspends her Nest upon the Rafters. Mean while the Juices warmed in the tender Veins ferment: And Animals, wonderous to behold, first short of their Feet, and in a little while buzzing with Wings, swarm together, and more and more fan the thin Air: Till they burst away like a Shower poured down from Summer Clouds; or like an Arrow from the whizzing String, what time the swift Parthians first usher in the Fight.

What God, ye Muses, what God disclosed to us this mysterious Art? Whence took this new Experience of Men its Rise?

The Shepherd Aristæus, flying from Peneian Tempe, having lost his Bees,

NOTES.

303. *Sic positum.* When dead. Mr. *Addison* is the only one, I have seen, who has justly interpreted this Phrase; which properly signifies a dead Body laid out in order to Burial, or in a dying Posture. See *Hor.* 1 Sat. II. 106. Æn. II. 644. XI. 30.

307. *Ante quàm nidum suspendat hirundo.* The Time of the Swallow's Coming is said by *Columella* to be about the twentieth or twenty-third of *February*. But in our Climate it is a full Month later.

317. *Pastor Aristæus.* Aristæus was the Son of *Apollo*, by *Cyrene*, the Daughter of the River-god *Peneus*. He married *Autonoe*, the Daughter of *Cadmus*, by whom he had *Actæon*. After the Death of his Son, being informed by the Oracle of *Apollo*, that he should receive divine Honours in the Island *Cea*, he removed thither, where, offering Sacrifice to *Jupiter*, he obtained the ceasing of a Plague, and was therefore honoured by them as a God after his Death. He is said also to have visited *Arcadia*, *Sardinia*, *Sicily*, and *Thrace*, in all which Countries he was adored, for having taught Mankind the Uses of Oil and Honey, and the Manner of curdling Milk.

317. *Peneïa Tempe.* The River *Peneus* rises in *Pindus*, a great Mountain of *Thessaly*, and flows through the delightful Plains of *Tempe*, as it is described by *Ovid*:

Est nemus Hæmoniæ, prærupta quod undique claudit
Silva; vocant Tempe; per quæ Penëus, ab imo
Effusus Pindo, spumosis volvitur undis;
Dejectuque gravi tenues agitantia fumos
Nubila conducit, summasque aspergine silvas
Impluit; et sonitu plus quàm vicina fatigat.

323. *Thymbræus*

Amissis, ut fama, apibus morboque fameque
Tristis ad extremi sacrum caput astitit amnis,
Multa querens; atque hâc affatus voce parentem:
Mater Cyrene, mater, quæ gurgitis hujus
Ima tenes, quid me præclarâ stirpe Deorum,
Si modò, quem perhibes, pater est Thymbræus Apollo,
Invisum fatis genuisti? aut quò tibi nostrî
Pulsus amor? quid me cœlum sperare jubebas?
En, etiam hunc ipsum vitæ mortalis honorem,
Quem mihi vix frugum et pecudum custodia solers
Omnia tentanti extuderat, te matre, relinquo.
Quin age, et ipsa manu felices erue silvas;
Fer stabulis inimicum ignem, atque interfice messes;
Ure sata, et validam in vites molire bipennem:
Tanta meæ si te ceperunt tædia laudis.
  At mater sonitum thalamo sub fluminis alti
Sensit: eam circum Milesia vellera Nymphæ
Carpebant: hyali saturo fucata colore:
Drymoque, Xanthoque, Ligeaque, Phyllodoceque,

apibus amissis morboque fameque, ut est fama, astitit, tristis ad sacrum caput extremi amnis, querens multa: atque est affatus parentem hâc voce: Mater Cyrene, mater, quæ tenes ima loca hujus gurgitis, quid genuisti me, invisum fatis, de præclarâ stirpe Deorum, si modò Thymbræus Apollo, quem perhibes meum patrem, est meus pater? Aut quò est amor nostrî pulsus tibi? Quid jubebas me sperare cœlum? En, te matre, relinquo hunc honorem ipsum mortalis vitæ, quem honorem solers custodia, frugum et pecudum vix extuderat mihi tentanti omnia. Quin age, et ipsa erue meas felices silvas tua manu; fer inimicum ignem stabulis, atque interfice messes; ure sata, et molire validam bipennem in meas vites: si tanta tædia meæ laudis ceperunt te. At mater sensit sonitum vocis sub thalamo alti fluminis: circum eam nymphæ carpebant Milesia vellera, fucata saturo colore hyali: Drymoque, Xanthoque, Ligeaque, Phyllodoceque,

TRANSLATION.

as it is said, by Disease and Famine, stood mournful by the sacred Source of the rising River, dolefully complaining; and with these Accents addressed his Parent: O Mother Cyrene, O Mother, who inhabitest the Depths of this Flood, why hast thou brought me forth of the illustrious Race of Gods, if indeed, as you pretend, Thymbræan Apollo be my Sire, *thus* abhorred by Destiny? Or whither is thy Love for me banished? Why didst thou bid me hope for Heaven? Lo I, thine own Offspring, am even bereaved of this very Glory of my mortal Life, * which, amidst my watchful Care of Flocks and Agriculture, I, after infinite Essays, with much ado atchieved. Why then go on, root up with thy own Hand my happy Groves: send hostile Flames into my Stalls, and kill my Harvests; burn up my † Plantations, and wield the sturdy Bill against my Vineyards; if you are seized with such strong Aversion to my Praise.

But his Mother heard the *piteous* Sound beneath the Chambers of the deep River: Her Nymphs around her were spinning the Milesian Fleeces, dyed with rich Sea-green Tincture: Drymo and Xantho, Ligea and Phyllodoce, their

* *Which my watchful Care of Corn and Flocks struck out to me with much ado, after I had tried all Things.* † Sata, *Either Plantations, as* Geor. II. 350. *or Corn Fields.*

NOTES.

323. *Thymbræus Apollo.* Apollo had this Name from *Thymbra*, a Town of *Troas*, where he had a famous Temple.

335. *Hyali colore.* That is, a *Sea-green* or *Glass Colour*, from ὕαλος, which signifies *Glass*.

343. *Assa*

Cæsariem effusæ nitidam per candida colla;
Nesæe, Spioque, Thaliaque, Cymodoceque,
Cydippeque, et flava Lycorias; altera virgo,
Altera tum primos Lucinæ experta labores:
Clioque, et Beroe soror, Oceanitides ambæ,
Ambæ auro, pictis incinctæ pellibus ambæ;
Atque Ephyre, atque Opis, et Asia Deïopeia;
Et tandem positis velox Arethusa sagittis.
Inter quas curam Clymene narrabat inanem
Vulcani, Martisque dolos, et dulcia furta:
Atque Chao densos Divûm numerabat amores.
Carmine quo captæ, dum fusis mollia pensa
Devolvunt, iterum maternas impulit aures
Luctus Aristæi; vitreisque sedibus omnes
Obstupuere: sed ante alias Arethusa sorores
Prospiciens, summâ flavum caput extulit undâ;
Et procul: O gemitu non frustra exterrita tanto,
Cyrene soror, ipse tibi, tua maxima cura,
Tristis Aristæus, Penei genitoris ad undam
Stat lacrymans, et te crudelem nomine dicit.

effusæ quoad *nitidam cæsariem per candida colla; Nesæe, Spioque, Thaliaque, Cymodoceque, Cydippeque, et flava Lycorias; altera* adhuc *virgo, altera tum experta primus labores Lucinæ: Clioque, et Beroe* ejus *soror, ambæ Oceanitides, ambæ* incinctæ *auro, ambæ incinctæ pictis pellibus; atque Ephyre, atque Opis, et Asia Deïopeia, et velox Arethusa, sagittis tandem positis. Inter quas Clymene* sedens *narrabat inanem curam Vulcani, dolosque Martis, et* ejus *dulcia furta: numerabatque densos amores Divûm* usque *à Chao. Quo carmine dum* nymphæ *captæ devolvunt mollia pensa fusis, luctus Aristæi iterum impulit maternas aures, omnesque* sedentes *vitreis sedilibus obstupuere: sed ante alias sorores Arethusa prospiciens, extulit flavum caput è summâ undâ; et procul* dixit: *O soror Cyrene, non frustra exterrita tanto gemitu, Aristæus ipse, tua maxima cura, tristis stat lacrymans tibi, ad undam genitoris Penei, et dicit te crudelem nomine.*

TRANSLATION.

comely Hair flowing down their Snow-white Necks; Nesæe and Spio, Thalia and Cymodoce, Cydippe and golden Lycorias; the one a Virgin, the other just experienced in the first Labours of Lucina: Clio, and her Sister Beroe, both Daughters of the Ocean, both in Gold, both in parti-coloured Skins arrayed; Ephyre and Opis, and Asian Deïopeia; and swift Arethusa, having at length laid her Shafts aside. Among whom Clymene was relating Vulcan's unavailing Care, the intrigues and pleasant Thefts of Mars; and recounted the frequent Amours of the Gods down from Chaos. Whilst the Nymphs, charmed with this Song, wind off their soft Tasks from the Spindles, the Lamentations of Aristæus struck once more his Mother's Ears, and all were amazed in their Crystal Beds: But Arethusa upreared her golden Head before her Sisters, darting her eyes abroad; and afar *she cried*, O Sister Cyrene, not in vain alarmed with such piteous Moaning, thy own Aristæus overwhelmed with Sorrow, thy darling Care, stands weeping by the Water of Peneus thy Sire, and calls thee cruel by Name. To her the

NOTES.

343. *Asia Deïopeia.* This Nymph is probably called *Asian*, because she belonged to the *Asian* Fenn.

344. *Positis Arethusa sagittis.* She had been first a Huntress, and one of *Diana*'s Retinue; and was transformed by her into a River-nymph.

345. *Curam Clymene narrabat inanem Vulcani.* Venus, the Wife of *Vulcan*, was caught by her Husband in Adultery with *Mars*; in this unseemly Posture *Vulcan* threw a Net over them, and exposed them to the Laughter of all the Gods. See the eighth Book of the Odyssey. The Poet calls *Vulcan*'s Care *vain, inanem curam*, either because it had no Effect to reclaim his Wife; or because it served only to propagate his own Infamy.

Huic, percussa novâ mentem formidine mater,
Duc age, duc ad nos: fas illi limina Divûm
Tangere, ait. Simul alta jubet discedere latè
Flumina, quà juvenis gressus inferret. At illum
Curvata in montis faciem circumstetit unda,
Accepitque sinu vastu, misitque sub amnem.
Jamque domum mirans genetricis, et humida regna,
Speluncisque lacus clausos, lucosque sonantes,
Ibat, et, ingenti motu stupefactus aquarum,
Omnia sub magnâ labentia flumina terrâ
Spectabat diversa locis; Phasimque, Lycumque,
Et caput, unde altus primùm se erumpit Enipeus,
Unde pater Tiberinus, et unde Aniena fluenta
Saxosumque sonans Hypanis, Mysusque Caïcus,
Et gemina auratus taurino cornua vultu
Eridanus; quo non alius per pinguia culta
In mare purpureum violentior influit amnis.

Mater, percussa quoad *mentem novâ formidine, ait age, duc, duc* illum *ad nos:* est *fas illi tangere limina Divûm. Simul* illa *jubet alta flumina discedere latè, quà juvenis inferret gressus. At unda, curvata in faciem montis, circumstetit illum, accepitque* illum *vasto sinu, misitque* illum *sub amnem. Jamque ibat mirans domum genetricis, et ejus humida regna, lacusque clausos speluncis, sonantesque lucos, et, stupefactus ingenti motu aquarum, spectabat omnia flumina labentia sub magnâ terrâ, diversa locis; Phasimque, Lycumque, et caput, unde Enipeus primùm erumpit se, unde pater Tiberinus, et unde Aniena fluenta, Hypanisque sonans saxosum, Mysusque Caicus, et Eridanus,* cum *taurino vultu, auratus* quoad *gemina cornua, quo* Eridano *non alius amnis influit violentior per pinguia culta* arva *in purpureum mare.*

TRANSLATION.

Mother, her Soul deep seized with unusual concern, cries: Conduct, conduct him quick to us: To him it is permitted to tread the Courts of the Gods. At the same Time she commands the deep Floods to divide on all Hands, that the Youth might make his Approach. And *lo* the Water, bent into the Shape of a Mountain, stood round about him, received him into its ample Bosom, and let him pass under the River. And now admiring his Mother's Palace, and humid Realms, the Lakes pent up in Caverns, and the sounding Groves, he passed along, and, startling at the vast Motion of the Waters, surveyed all the Rivers gliding under the great Earth in different Places; Phasis and Lycus, and the Source whence deep Enipeus first bursts forth, whence Father Tiberinus, and whence Anio's Streams, and Hypanis roaring down the Rocks, and Mysian Caicus, and Eridanus, his Bull-front necked with two gilded Horns, than whom no River pours along the fertile Fields with more Violence, into the empurpled Sea.

NOTES.

364. *Speluncisque lacus clausos.* Homer makes the Ocean to be the Source of all Rivers:

—Βαθυρρειταο μεγασθενος Ωκεανοιο
Εξ ὑπερ παντες ποταμοι, &c.

Th' eternal Ocean, from whose Fountains flow
The Seas, the Rivers, and the Springs below.
Pope.

And this is also the Opinion of *Aristotle.* But *Plato*, whom *Virgil* here follows, supposes the Receptacle of all the Rivers to be in a great Cavern, which passes through the whole Earth, and is called by the Poets *Barathrum* and *Tartarus.*

373. *In mare purpureum.* See the Note on G. III. 359.

Postquam est perventum in tecta thalami pendentia pumice, et mater Cyrene cognovit inanes fletus nati: Germanæ dant liquidos fontes manibus ordine, feruntque mantilia tonsis villis. Pars earum onerant mensas epulis, et reponunt plena pocula. Aræ adolescunt Panchæis ignibus. Et mater ait, Cape carchesia Mæonii Bacchi, libemus Oceano. Simul ipsa precatur Oceanumque, patrem rerum, sororesque nymphas, quæ servant centum silvas, quæ servant centum flumina. Ter perfudit ardentem Vestam liquido nectare; ter flamma subjecta ad summum tecti reluxit. Quo omine firmans animum, ipsa sic incipit: In Carpathio gurgite Neptuni, est vates, cæruleus Proteus, qui metitur magnum æquor, invectus *piscibus, et juncto curru bipedum equorum.*

Postquam est in thalami pendentia pumice tecta
Perventum, et nati fletus cognovit inanes
Cyrene; manibus liquidos dant ordine fontes
Germanæ, tonsisque ferunt mantilia villis.
Pars epulis onerant mensas, et plena reponunt
Pocula. Panchæis adolescunt ignibus aræ.
Et mater, Cape Mæonii carchesia Bacchi,
Oceano libemus, ait. Simul ipsa precatur
Oceanumque patrem rerum, Nymphasque sorores,
Centum quæ silvas, centum quæ flumina servant.
Ter liquido ardentem perfudit nectare Vestam;
Ter flamma ad summum tecti subjecta reluxit.
Omine quo firmans animum, sic incipit ipsa:
Est, in Carpathio Neptuni gurgite, vates,
Cæruleus Proteus, magnum qui piscibus æquor,
Et juncto bipedum curru metitur equorum.

TRANSLATION.

After he was arrived under the Roof of her Bed-chamber, hung with Pumice-stones, and Cyrene informed of the idle Lamentations of her Son; the Sisters in Order serve up the Crystal Streams for the Hands, and bring smooth Towels. Some load the Boards with Viands, and plant the full Cups. The Altars blaze with Panchæan Fires. Then, the Mother: Take, says she, these Goblets of Mæonian Wine, let us offer a libation to Ocean. At the same time she herself addresses Ocean, the Parent of Things, and the Sister Nymphs, who preside over an hundred Woods, over an hundred Rivers. Thrice she sprinkled glowing Vesta with the liquid Nectar; thrice the Flame shot to the Top of the Roof, brightened.

With which Omen encouraging her Soul, she thus begins: In Neptune's Carpathian Gulf there dwells a Seer, Cærulean Proteus, who measures the great Sea with *harnessed* Fishes, and in a Chariot yoked with two legged Steeds. He

NOTES.

375. *Inanes.* These Lamentations, says *Servius*, were vain, because they were moved by a Calamity easy to be repaired.

377. *Tonsisque ferunt mantilia villis.* Mantile, or, as others spell it, *Mantele*, signifies a *Towel*, and it seems to have been made of some woolly or nappy sort of Cloth, which the nicer sort of People had shorn or clipped, for the greater Smoothness and Delicacy.

379. *Panchæis ignibus.* With *Panchæan* Incense, so called from *Panchæa*, a Region of *Arabia*, that abounded with Frankincense, Geor. III. 139.

385. *Subjecta.* Ruæus interprets it *supposita:* Which hardly makes Sense; for the Wine was poured upon the Fire, and consequently made it mount up into a Blaze. It must therefore signify *thrown up*, or *mounting up*, as *subjicio* does, Ecl. X. 74. and Æn. XII. 288.

387. *Carpathio gurgite.* Carpathus, now called *Scarpanto*, is an Island of the *Mediterranean*, over-against *Egypt*, from which the neighbouring Sea was called *Carpathian*.

388. *Proteus.* The Poets make *Proteus* to have been a Sea-god; *Homer* makes him an *Egyptian*, and *Herodotus* a King of *Egypt*. Sir *Isaac Newton* finding him cotemporary with *Amenophis*, or *Memnon*, takes him to have been only a Viceroy to that Prince, and to have governed some Part of the *Lower Egypt* in his Absence.

Hic nunc Emathiæ portus patriamque revisit
Pallenen: hunc et Nymphæ veneramur, et ipse
Grandævus Nereus; novit namque omnia vates,
Quæ sint, quæ fuerint, quæ mox ventura trahantur.
Quippe ita Neptuno visum est; immania cujus
Armenta, et turpes pascit sub gurgite phocas.
Hic tibi, nate, priùs vinclis capiendus, ut omnem
Expediat morbi causam, eventusque secundet.
Nam sine vi non ulla dabit præcepta, neque illum
Orando flectes: vim duram et vincula capto
Tende: doli circum hæc demum frangentur inanes.
Ipsa ego te, medios cum Sol accenderit æstus,
Cum sitiunt herbæ, et pecori jam gratior umbra est,
In secreta senis ducam, quò fessus ab undis
Se recipit; facilè ut somno aggrediare jacentem.

Hic nunc revisit portus Emathiæ, patriamque Pallenen: et nos nymphæ, et grandævus Nereus ipse, veneramur hunc; namque ille *vates novit omnia, quæ sint, quæ fuerint, et quæ trahantur mox ventura. Quippe ita est visum Neptuno; cujus immania armenta, et turpes phocas pascit sub gurgite. Nate, hic* Proteus est *priùs capiendus tibi vinclis, ut expediat omnem causam morbi, secundetque eventus. Nam non dabit ulla præcepta sine vi, neque flectes illum orando: tende duram vim, et vincula* illi *capto:* ejus *doli circum hæc* vincula *inanes demum frangentur. Ego ipsa, cum sol accenderit medios æstus, cum herbæ sitiunt, et jam umbra est gratior pecori, ducam te in secreta* latibula *sedis, quò fessus recipit se ab undis; ut facilè aggrediare* illum *jacentem somno.*

TRANSLATION.

now revisits the Ports of Emathia and his native Pallene: Him both we Nymphs, and old Nereus himself adore; for the Prophet knows all Things that are, that have been, and the whole Concatenation of future Events. For such is the Will of Neptune; whose unwieldy Droves, and unshapely Sea-calves, he feeds under the Deep. Him, my Son, you first must surprize with Chains, that he may explain to you the whole Cause of the Disease, and make the Issue prosperous. For no Instructions will he give without Compulsion, nor can you move him by Intreaty: Ply him, *when* taken, with rigid Force and Chains: *All* his Tricks to evade these proving vain will at length be quite baffled. I myself, as soon as the Sun has inflamed his Noon-tide Heats, when the Herbs thirst, and the Shade is now more grateful to the Cattle, I myself will conduct thee into the Senior's Recess, whither he retires from the Waves *when* fatigued; that you may easily assail him overpowered with Sleep. But when you shall hold him

NOTES.

391. *Pallenen.* Pallene is a Peninsula of *Macedon*, whereof *Virgil* makes *Proteus* a Native.

393. *Quæ mox ventura trahantur.* There is a great Propriety here in the Word *trahantur*, which denotes the Concatenation of Causes and Effects, whereby one Event is drawn on after another in a fixed Series like the Links of a Chain. *Magno judicio Poëta trahendi verbum usurpat,* says the *Variorum*; *est enim fatum præcedentium causarum, subsequentiumque perplexio quædam, et catenæ more cohærens.* Trahi *ergo dicuntur futuri rerum eventus, quia, in illa serie nexuque causarum ex æternitate pendentium, ita se consequuntur ut alius alium trahat.*

394. *Lotos.* Mr. *Martin* takes it for the Water lily, on the Credit of *Prosper Alpinus.*

399. *Flectes.* The *Medicean* and other Manuscripts read *vinces.*

 406. *Tiedent.*

Verùm ubi tenebis illum correptum manibus, vinclisque; tum variæ ſpecies, atque ora ferarum illudent tibi. Enim ſubitò fiet horridus ſus, atraque tigris, ſquamoſuſque draco, et leæna fulvâ cervice: aut dabit acrem ſonitum flammæ, atque ita excidet vinclis; aut dilapſus in tenues aquas abibit. Sed quanto magis ille vertet ſe in omnes formas, tanto magis tu, nate, contende tenacia vincla: donec erit talis, corpore mutato, qualem videris, cum tegeret lumina, ſomno incepto. Ait hæc, et diffudit liquidum odorem ambroſiæ, quo perfudit totum corpus nati. At dulcis aura ſpiravit illi crinibus compoſitis, atque habilis vigor venit membris. Eſt ingens ſpecus in latere exeſi montis, quò plurima unda cogitur vento, ſcinditque ſeſe in reductos ſinus: fuit olim tutiſſima ſtatio nautis deprenſis procellâ. Hic Proteus tegit ſe objice vaſti ſaxi.

Verùm ubi correptum manibus vincliſque tenebis;
Tum variæ illudent ſpecies, atque ora ferarum.
Fiet enim ſubitò ſus horridus, atraque tigris,
Squamoſuſque draco, et fulvâ cervice leæna:
Aut acrem flammæ ſonitum dabit, atque ita vinclis
Excidet; aut in aquas tenues dilapſus abibit.
Sed quanto ille magis formas ſe vertet in omnes,
Tanto, nate, magis contende tenacia vincla
Donec talis erit, mutato corpore, qualem
Videris, incepto tegeret cum lumina ſomno.
Hæc ait, et liquidum ambroſiæ diffudit odorem;
Quo totum nati corpus perfudit. At illi
Dulcis compoſitis ſpiravit crinibus aura,
Atque habilis membris venit vigor. Eſt ſpecus ingens
Exeſi latere in montis, quò plurima vento
Cogitur, inque ſinus ſcindit ſeſe unda reductos:
Deprenſis olim ſtatio tutiſſima nautis.
Intus ſe vaſti Proteus tegit objice ſaxi.

TRANSLATION.

faſt confined within your Arms and Chains, then various Forms and Features of wild Beaſts will mock your Graſp. For on a ſudden he will become a briſtly Boar, a fell Tyger, a ſcaly Dragon, and Lioneſs with a tawny Mane: Or he will emit the *roaring* Sound of Flame, and *ſo* eſcape the Chain; or liquified into fluid Waters glide away. But the more he ſhall transform himſelf into all Shapes, ſtill cloſer draw, my Son, the hampering Chains: Till, rechanged, he ſhall become ſuch as you ſaw him when uſhering in Sleep he cloſed his Eyes. She ſaid, and ſhed around the liquid Odour of Ambroſia, wherewith ſhe ſprinkled over the whole Body of her Son. Now from his trimmed Locks a delicious Fragrance breathed, and active Vigour was infuſed into his Limbs. In the Side of a hollowed Mountain is a ſpacious Cave, whither the Waves in great Numbers are driven by the Wind, and divide themſelves into winding Bays: At times a Station moſt ſecure for Weather-beaten Mariners. Within *this Cave* Proteus hides himſelf behind the Barrier of a huge Rock. Here the Nymph

NOTES.

406. *Illudent.* Heinſius and many old Editions read *eludent*. Pierius found *ludent* in the Roman Manuſcript, *eludent* in the *Lombard*, *Medicean*, and moſt of the ancient ones.

415. *Ambroſiæ.* Ambroſia is the Food of the Gods; and Nectar their Drink. But the two are often confounded, as here *liquidus odor* is ſaid of *Ambroſia*.

416. *Perfudit.* This is the Reading *Pierius* found in the *Roman* Manuſcript.

421. *Deprenſis.* See the Note on Æn. V. 52.

425. *Jam*

Hìc juvenem in latebris aversum à lumine Nympha
Collocat: ipsa procul nebulis obscura resistit.
Jam rapidus torrens sitientes Sirius Indos,
Ardebat cœlo, et medium Sol igneus orbem
Hauserat: arebant herbæ; cava flumina siccis
Faucibus ad limum radii tepefacta coquebant;
Cum Proteus consueta petens è fluctibus antra
Ibat: eum vasti circum gens humida Ponti
Exsultans rorem latè dispergit amarum.
Sternunt se somno diversæ in litore phocæ.
Ipse, velut stabuli custos in montibus olim,
Vesper ubi è pastu vitulos ad tecta reducit,
Auditisque lupos acuunt balatibus agni;
Considit scopulo medius, numerumque recenset.
Cujus Aristæo quoniam est oblata facultas;
Vix defessa senem passus componere membra,
Cum clamore ruit magno; manicisque jacentem
Occupat. Ille, suæ contrà non immemor artis,
Omnia transformat sese in miracula rerum,
Ignemque, horribilemque feram, fluviumque liquentem.
Verùm, ubi nulla fugam reperit fallacia, victus
In sese redit, atque hominis tandem ore locutus:

Hìc nympha collocat juvenem aversum à lumine in latebris, et ipsa resistit procul obscura nebulis. Jam rapidus Sirius, torrens sitientes Indos, ardebat cœlo, et ingens sol hauserat medium orbem: herbæ arebant, et radii coquebant cava flumina tepefacta faucibus siccis ad limum; cum Proteus ibat è fluctibus, petens consueta antra: humida gens vasti ponti, exsultans circum eum, dispergit amarum rorem. Phocæ sternunt se diversæ in litore. Ipse velut olim custos stabuli in montibus, ubi vesper reducit vitulos è pastu ad tecta, agnique acuunt lupos balatibus auditis, considit medius scopulo, recensetque numerum pecudum. *Cujus capiendi quoniam facultas est oblata Aristæo; vix passus senem Protea componere defessa membra, ruit cum magno clamore, occupatque illum jacentem manicis. Contrà ille, non immemor suæ artis, transformat sese in omnia miracula rerum, ignemque, horribilemque feram, liquentemque fluvium. Verùm ubi nulla fallacia reperit fugam, victus redit in sese, atque tandem* est *locutus ore hominis:*

TRANSLATION.

places the Youth in Ambush remote from View, she stays herself at a Distance shrouded in a misty Veil. Now the sultry Dog-star scorching the thirsty Indians blazed in the Sky, and the fiery Sun had finished Half his Course: The Herbs withered; and the Rays made the shallow overheated Rivers boil, their Channels being drained to the slimy Bottom; when Proteus, repairing to his accustomed Den, advanced from the Waves: The watery Race of the vast Ocean, gamboling around him, scatters the briny Spray far and near. The Sea-calves apart lay them down to sleep along the Shore. He himself (as at Times the Keeper of a Fold upon the Mountains, when Evening brings Home the Bullocks from the Pasture, and the Lambs with noisy Bleatings whet *the Hunger* of the Wolves) sits in the Center on a Rock, and reviews their Numbers. On *seizing* whom since so favourable an opportunity offered itself to Aristæus; scarce suffering the aged God to compose his weary Limbs, he rushes upon him with a great Shout, and surprizes him with Chains as he lay. He on the other hand, not forgetful of his Art, transforms himself into all the wonderous Shapes in Nature, Fire, and a grimly Savage, and flowing River. But when no Shifts could find him an Escape, overpowered he returns to himself, and at length *thus* spoke in human Accent:

NOTES.

425. *Jam rapidus Sirius.* Sirius, a Star of the first Magnitude in the Mouth of the *Dog*, rises about the Time of the Sun's entering into *Leo*, toward the latter End of *July*, making what we call *the Dog-days.*

435. *Auditisque.* Others read *auditique*; but the Sense would naturally lead one to *auditisque*, which is the Reading of the *Roman*, *Medicean*, and *Cambridge* Manuscripts.

447. Neque

quisnam jussit te, confidentissime juvenum, adire nostras domos? quidve petis hinc? sic inquit, At ille Aristæus ait: Proteu, scis, ipse scis, neque est cuiquam fallere te: sed tu desine velle fallere me. Nos, secuti præcepta Deûm venimus huc, quæsitum oracula lapsis rebus. [illegible] [illegible] [illegible] tum. Ad hæc denique [illegible] [illegible] ardentes oculos glauco lumine; et [illegible] graviter sic resolvit ora fatis: Iræ non nullius numinis exercent te; luis magna scelera commissa; Orpheus miserabilis suscitat tibi has pœnas, haudquaquam scelere magnas ob meritum, ni fata resistant, et sævit graviter pro conjuge rapta sibi. Illa puella quidem moritura, dum præceps fugeret te per flumina non vidit, ante pedes in altâ herbâ, immanem hydrum servantem ripas. At chorus Dryadum, æqualis ætate, implêrunt supremos montes clamore: Rhodopeiæ arces flêrunt, altaque Pangæa, et Mavortia tellus Rhesi, atque Getæ, atque Hebrus, atque Orithyia Actias.

Nam quis te, juvenum confidentissime, nostras 445
Jussit adire domos? quidve hinc petis? inquit.
At ille:
Scis, Proteu, scis ipse; neque est te fallere cuiquam:
Sed tu desine velle. Deûm præcepta secuti
Venimus huc, lapsis quæsitum oracula rebus.
Tantum effatus. Ad hæc Vates vi denique multâ
Ardentes oculos intorsit lumine glauco, 451
Et graviter frendens, sic fatis ora resolvit.
Non te nullius exercent numinis iræ:
Magna luis commissa: tibi has miserabilis Orpheus
Haudquaquam ob meritum pœnas, ni fata resistant,
Suscitat; et raptâ graviter pro conjuge sævit.
Illa quidem, dum te fugeret per flumina præceps,
Immanem ante pedes hydrum moritura puella
Servantem ripas altâ non vidit in herbâ.
At chorus æqualis Dryadum clamore supremos 460
Implêrunt montes: flêrunt Rhodopeiæ arces,
Altaque Pangæa, et Rhesi Mavortia tellus,
Atque Getæ, atque Hebrus, atque Actias Orithyia.

TRANSLATION.

Who, most presumptuous Youth, enjoined thee, he says, to approach my Habitation? Or what demandest thou here? But he: Thou knowest, O Proteus, thou knowest thyself; nor is it in any one's Power to deceive thee: But do thou cease to try *thy Wiles on me. For* in Pursuance of divine Command I came hither to consult thy Oracle about my ruined Affairs. He said. Then the Prophet at length with mighty Force rolled his Eyes flashing with azure Light, and, gnashing his Teeth fiercely, thus opened his Mouth to disclose the Fates: 'Tis the Vengeance of no mean Deity that pursues thee: Thou art making Attonement for thy heinous Crimes: These Sufferings, by no Means proportioned to thy Guilt, unhappy Orpheus entails upon thee, unless the Fates oppose; and he sorely rages for his ravished Queen. And indeed it was, whilst she fled precipitantly from you along the River, that the Maid doomed to Death was so unhappy not to see the hideous Water-snake before her Feet, as it guarded the Banks in the tall Grass. But her coeval Choir of Dryads filled the highest Mountains with their Shrieks: The Rocks of Rhodope wept, so did lofty Pangæa, and the martial Land of Rhesus, the Getes, and Hebrus, and Attic Orithyia.

NOTES.

447. *Neque est te fallere cuiquam.* This is a Grecism for *neque licet cuiquam*: Thus in the second Eclogue, *Nec sit mihi credere.* So also Horace, *Quod versu dicere non est.*

453. *Miserabilis Orpheus*, &c. Others understand the Words thus: *Orpheus unhappy for no Guilt or Demerit of his.*

454. *Orpheus.* He was the Son of *Oeagrus*, King of *Thrace*, by the Muse *Calliope*; highly celebrated for his extraordinary Skill in Music and Poetry, and was one of the *Argonauts.* The Hymns that go under his Name are with good Reason believed to be spurious.

Ipſe cavâ ſolans ægrum teſtudine amorem,
Te, dulcis conjux, te ſolo in litore ſecum,
Te veniente die, te decedente canebat.
Tænarias etiam fauces, alta oſtia Ditis,
Et caligantem nigra formidine lucum
Ingreſſus, Maneſque adiit, Regemque tremendum,
Neſciaque humanis precibus manſueſcere corda.
At cantu commotæ Erebi de ſedibus imis
Umbræ ibant tenues, ſimulacraque luce carentum:
Quàm multa in ſilvis avium ſe millia condunt,
Veſper ubi, aut hibernus agit de montibus imber:
Matres, atque viri, defunctaque corpora vitâ
Magnanimûm heroum, pueri, innuptæque puellæ,
Impoſitique rogis juvenes ante ora parentum;
Quos circum limus niger, et deformis arundo
Cocyti, tardâque palus inamabilis undâ
Alligat, et novies Styx interfuſa coërcet.
Quin ipſæ ſtupuere domus, atque intima Lethi
Tartara, cæruleoſque implexæ crinibus angues
Eumenides: tenuitque inhians tria Cerberus ora;

Orpheus *ipſe, ſolans ægrum amorem cavâ teſtudine,* canebat *te, dulcis conjux,* canebat *te ſecum in ſolo litore,* canebat *te die veniente, canebat te die decedente.* Ille, *ingreſſus Tænarias fauces, alta oſtia Ditis, et lucum caligantem nigrâ formidine, adiit Maneſque, tremendumque regem, cordaque neſcia manſueſcere, humanis precibus. At tenues umbræ, commotæ cantu* Orphei, *ſimulacraque carentum luce, ibant de imis ſedibus Erebi: quàm multa millia avium condunt ſe in ſilvis, ubi veſper, aut hibernus imber agit* eas *de montibus: matres atque viri, corporaque magnanimûm heroum defuncta vitâ, pueri, innuptæque puellæ, juveneſque impoſiti rogis ante ora parentum* ibant. *Quos niger limus, et deformis arundo Cocyti inamabiliſque palus* cum *tardâ undâ circum alligat, et Styx novies interfuſa coërcet. Quin domus ipſæ, atque intima Tartara Lethi, Eumenideſque implexæ* quoad *cæruleos angues crinibus, obſtupuere; Cerberuſque inhians tenuit tria ora;*

TRANSLATION.

Orpheus himſelf, ſoothing the Anguiſh of his Love with his concave Shell, ſung thee, *his* ſweet Eurydice, thee by himſelf on the lonely Shore, thee when the Day aroſe, thee when the Day declined *he* ſung. He entering even the Jaws of Tænarus, Pluto's Gates profound, and the Grove overcaſt with gloomy Horror, viſited the Manes, and their tremenduous King, and Hearts incapable of relenting at human Prayers. But the airy Shades, and Phantoms of the Dead, affected with his Song, advanced from the deep Manſions of Erebus, in ſuch Throngs as Birds that ſhelter themſelves by Thouſands in the Woods, when Evening, or a wintery Shower drives them from the Mountains: Matrons, and Men, and Ghoſts of gallant Heroes deceaſed, Boys, and unmarried Virgins, and Youths laid on the Funeral Piles before the Faces of their Parents; whom the black Mud, and unſightly Reeds of Cocytus, and the unlovely Lake with ſluggiſh Wave incloſes round, and Styx nine Times interfuſed confines. Nay, the very Habitations and deepeſt Dungeons of Death were aſtoniſhed, and the Furies, with whoſe Hair blue Snakes were interwoven; and yawning Cerberus repreſſed his three Mouths;

NOTES.

464. *Cavâ teſtudine.* The Lyre is called *Teſtudo,* becauſe the ancient Lyres were made of the Shells of Tortoiſes. It was a received Story, that *Mercury,* finding accidentally a dead Tortoiſe on the Banks of the *Nile,* made a Lyre of it: Whence *Horace* calls him *curvæ lyræ parentem.*

467. *Tænarias fauces.* Tænarus is a Promontory of the *Peloponneſus,* fabled to be the Entrance to the infernal Regions.

471. *Erebi.* Erebus here, and in other Places, ſignifies *the profoundeſt Manſion of Hell.*

475. *Defunctaque corpora vitâ magnanimûm heroum.* Lifeleſs Bodies of gallant Heroes. *Corpora* is likewiſe put for the airy Vehicle of departed Spirits, as Æn. VI. 303, 306.

atque rota Ixionei orbis constitit cantu. Jamque Orpheus, *referens pedem, evaserat omnes casus; Eurydiceque reddita veniebat ad superas auras, sequens* eum *ponè; namque Proserpina dederat banc legem: cum subita dementia cepit incautum amantem,* dementia *ignoscenda quidem, si Manes scirent ignoscere. Restitit, immemorque, heu! victusque animi, respexit suam Eurydicen jam sub luce ipsâ: ibi omnis labor* est *effusus, atque fœdera immitis tyranni rupta, fragorque* est *ter auditus Avernis stagnis. Illa inquit, quis perdidit et me miseram, et te, Orpheu? quis tantus furor* est *hic? En iterum crudelia fata vocant me retro, somnusque condit natantia lumina. Jamque vale: feror circumdata ingenti nocte, tendensque invalidas palmas tibi, heu! non* ampliùs *tua. Dixit; et subitò fugit diversa ex oculis* Orphei, *ceu fumus commistus in tenues auras: neque præterea vidit illum,*

Atque Ixionei cantu rota constitit orbis.
Jamque pedem referens, casus evaserat omnes;
Redditaque Eurydice superas veniebat ad auras,
Ponè sequens; namque hanc dederat Proserpina legem:
Cum subita incautum dementia cepit amantem,
Ignoscenda quidem, scirent si ignoscere Manes.
Restitit, Eurydicenque suam, jam luce sub ipsa,
Immemor, heu! victusque animi, respexit: ibi omnis
Effusus labor, atque immitis rupta tyranni
Fœdera; terque fragor stagnis auditus Avernis.
Illa, Quis et me, inquit, miseram, et te perdidit, Orpheu?
Quis tantus furor? en iterum crudelia retro
Fata vocant, conditque natantia lumina somnus.
Jamque vale: feror ingenti circumdata nocte,
Invalidasque tibi tendens, heu! non tua palmas.
Dixit; et ex oculis subitò, ceu fumus in auras
Commistus tenues, fugit diversa: neque illum,

TRANSLATION.

and the Circumrotation of Ixion's Orb was suspended by the Song. And now, tracing back his Way, he had overpassed all Dangers; and restored Eurydice was just approaching the superior Regions, following behind; for Proserpina had given him that Law: When a sudden Frenzy seized the unwary Lover, pardonable indeed, if the Manes knew to pardon. He stopt, and just on the Verge of Light, ah! unmindful, and not Master of his Mind, looked back on his Eurydice: There was all his Labour lost, and the Law of the relentless Tyrant broke, and thrice a dismal Groan heard through the Avernian Lake. *Ah!* Orpheus, she says, who hath both unhappy me, and thee undone: What deep Infatuation this? See once more the cruel Fates call me back, and Sleep closes my Swimming Eyes. And now farewell: I am snatched away, encompassed

NOTES.

484. *Cantu.* The usual Reading is *vento*, of which it is not easy to make Sense: Whereas *cantu*, which *Pierius* found in several Manuscripts, makes all easy.

493. *Fragor.* Servius understands *fragor* to mean an Exultation of the Shades at the Return of *Eurydice*, and quotes a Passage of *Lucan* in Confirmation of his Opinion:

——————*Gaudent à luce relictam*
Eurydicen, iterum sperantes Orphea Manes.

But it is observed that *fragor* is never used by *Virgil* for a Sound of Joy, but for some great Crash, or horrid Noise. Therefore it seems rather to mean here some dismal Sound.

508. *Strymonis,*

Prensantem nequicquam umbras, et multa volentem
Dicere, præterea vidit; nec portitor Orci
Ampliùs objectam passus transire paludem.
Quid faceret? quò se raptâ bis conjuge ferret?
Quo fletu Manes, quò numina voce moveret?
Illa quidem Stygiâ nabat jam frigida cymbâ.
Septem illum totos perhibent ex ordine menses,
Rupe sub aëriâ, deserti ad Strymonis undam
Flevisse, et gelidis hæc evolvisse sub antris,
Mulcentem tigres, et agentem carmine quercus.
Qualis populeâ mœrens Philomela sub umbrâ
Amissos queritur fetus, quos durus arator
Observans nido implumes detraxit: at illa
Flet noctem, ramoque sedens miserabile carmen
Integrat, et mœstis latè loca questibus implet.
Nulla Venus, nullique animum flexere Hymenæi.
Solus Hyperboreas glacies, Tanaimque nivalem,
Arvaque Riphæis nunquam viduata pruinis
Lustrabat; raptam Eurydicen, atque irrita Ditis

prensantem umbras nequicquam, et volentem dicere multa; nec portitor orci est passus eum ampliùs transire objectam paludem. Quid faceret? quò ferret se, conjuge bis raptâ? quo fletu moveret Manes, quâ voce moveret numina? Illa quidem jam frigida nabat Stygiâ cymbâ. Perhibent, illum flevisse septem totos menses ex ordine sub aëriâ rupe, ad undam deserti Strymonis, et evolvisse hæc sub gelidis antris, mulcentem tigres, et agentem quercus carmine. Qualis Philomela, mœrens sub populeâ umbrâ, queritur amissos fetus, quos durus arator, observans implumes nido, detraxit; at illa flet noctem, sedensque ramo, integrat miserabile carmen, et implet loca latè mœstis questibus. Nulla Venus, nullique Hymenæi flexere ejus animum. Solus lustrabat Hyperboreas glacies, nivalemque Tanaim, arvaque nunquam viduata Riphæis pruinis; querens Eurydicen raptam, atque dona Ditis irrita.

TRANSLATION.

with thick *Shades of* Night, and stretching forth to thee my feeble Hands, ah! thine no more. She said; and on a sudden fled from his sight a different Way, like Smoke blending with thin Air: * Nor more was seen by him grasping the Shades in vain; and in act to say a thousand Things; nor did the Ferryman of Hell suffer him again to cross the intervening Lake. What should he do? Whither should he turn him, his Love twice snatched away? With what Tears asswage the Manes, with what Accents the *infernal* Powers? She, already *a* cold *Shade*, was sailing in the Stygian Boat. For seven whole Months, 'tis said, he mourned beneath a *bleak* aërial Rock, by the Streams of desart Strymon, and revolved these Woes under the cold Caves, softening the *very* Tygers, and leading the Oaks with his Song. As mourning *Philomel* under a Poplar Shade bemoans her lost Young, which the hard-hearted Clown observing in the Nest, has stole unfledged: But she weeps through the Night, and, perched upon a Bough, renews her doleful Song, and fills the places all around with piteous Wailings. No Loves, no Hymeneal Joys could bend his Soul. Alone he traversed the Hyperborean Tracts of Ice, the snowy Tanais, and Fields never free from the Riphæan Frosts, deploring his ravished Eurydice, and Pluto's bootless Presents. For which neglected *nuptial* Rite the Ciconian Matrons,

* *Nor saw him more.*

NOTES.

508. *Strymonis.* Strymon is a River of *Macedon*, on the Borders of *Thrace*.

511. *Populeâ.* It is observed that the Poplar is judiciously chosen by the Poet on this Occasion, because the Leaves of this Tree, trembling with the least Breath of Air, make a sort of melancholy Rustling.

Quo nuptiali munere spreto, matres Ciconum, inter sacra Deûm, orgiaque nocturni Bacchi, sparsere juvenem discerptum per latos agros. Tum quoque cum Oeagrius Hebrus, portans ejus caput revulsum à marmoreâ cervice, in medio gurgite, volveret illud, ejus vox ipsa, et frigida lingua vocabat Eurydicen, ah! miseram Eurydicen, animâ fugiente: ripæ referebant Eurydicen toto flumine. Proteus ait hæc: et dedit se jactu in altum æquor; quàque dedit se, torsit spumantem undam sub vertice. At Cyrene non dedit se; namque est affata filium timentem ultro: nate, licet deponere tristes curas tuo animo. Hæc est omnis causa morbi; hinc nymphæ, cum quibus illa agitabat choros in altis lucis,

Dona querens. Spreto Ciconum quo munere matres,
Inter sacra Deûm, nocturnique Orgia Bacchi,
Discerptum latos juvenem sparsere per agros.
Tum quoquè marmoreâ caput à cervice revulsum,
Gurgite cum medio portans Oeagrius Hebrus
Volveret, Eurydicen vox ipsa, et frigida lingua,
Ah, miseram Eurydicen, animâ fugiente, vocabat:
Eurydicen toto referebant flumine ripæ.
Hæc Proteus: et se jactu dedit æquor in altum;
Quàque dedit, spumantem undam sub vortice torsit.
At non Cyrene: namque ultro affata timentem:
Nate, licet tristes animo deponere curas.
Hæc omnis morbi causa; hinc miserabile Nymphæ,
Cum quibus illa choros lucis agitabat in altis,

TRANSLATION.

amidst the sacred Service of the Gods, and nocturnal Orgies of Bacchus, having tore the Youth in Pieces, scattered his Limbs over the wide Fields. And even then, whilst Oeagrian Hebrus rolled down the Middle of its Tide, his Head torn from the Alabaster Neck, the Voice of itself, and his faultering Tongue, invoked Eurydice, Ah, unfortunate Eurydice! with his expiring Breath: The Banks re-echoed Eurydice all along the River. Thus Proteus *said:* And plunged with a Bound into the deep Sea; and, where he plunged, he tossed up the foaming Billows under the whirling Tide.

But not so Cyrene: For kindly she bespoke her trembling Son: My Son, you may ease your Mind of *all* vexatious Cares. This is the whole Cause of your Disaster; hence the Nymphs, with whom she celebrated the mingled Dances in the deep Groves, have sent this mournful Devastation on your Bees: Do

NOTES.

520. *Spreto Ciconum quo munere matres* Many Manuscripts and printed Editions of good Authority read *spretæ*. But the Sense seems to determine for *spreto*: For the Meaning is, *quo munere*, i. e. *quo* nuptiali *munere spreto*, *for the contempt of which nuptial Rite*, mentioned Verse 510.

520. *Ciconum matres.* The *Cicones* were a People of *Thrace*, living near Mount *Ismarus*, and the Mouth of the River *Hebrus*: where the Bacchanals used to perform their Revels. *Ovid* has assigned a Cause of this Matron Fury not so honourable for *Orpheus*:

——— ———Omnem refugerat Orpheus
Femineam Venerem; seu quod male cesserat illi;
Sive fidem dederat. Multas tamen ardor habebat
Jungere se vati: multæ doluere repulsæ.
Ille etiam Thracum populis fuit auctor amorem
In teneros transferre mares: citraque juventam,
Ætatis breve ver, et primos carpere flores.

But such a Guilt seems quite inconsistent with his extraordinary Passion for *Eurydice*.

524. *Oeagrius Hebrus.* The *Hebrus* is called *Oeagrian*, from *Oeagrus*, the *Thracian* King, mentioned before to have been the Father of *Orpheus*.

535. *Napæas*

Exitium misere apibus: tu munera supplex
Tende, petens pacem, et faciles venerare Napæas:
Namque dabunt veniam votis, irasque remittent.
Sed modus orandi qui sit, priùs ordine dicam.
Quatuor eximios præstanti corpore tauros,
Qui tibi nunc viridis depascunt summa Lycæi,
Delige, et intactâ totidem cervice juvencas.
Quatuor his aras alta ad delubra Dearum
Constitue, et sacrum jugulis demitte cruorem;
Corporaque ipsa boum frondoso desere luco.
Post, ubi nona suos Aurora ostenderit ortus,
Inferias Orphei Lethæa papavera mittes,
Placatam Eurydicen vitulâ venerabere cæsâ,
Et nigram mactabis ovem, lucumque revises.
Haud mora: continuò matris præcepta facessit;
Ad delubra venit; monstratas excitat aras;
Quatuor eximios præstanti corpore tauros
Ducit, et intactâ totidem cervice juvencas.
Post, ubi nona suos Aurora induxerat ortus,

misere miserabile exitium apibus. Tu supplex tende munera, petens pacem, et venerare faciles Napæas: namque dabunt veniam votis, remittentque iras. Sed dicam priùs ordine, qui sit modus orandi eas. Delige quatuor eximios tauros præstanti corpore, qui nunc depascunt summa cacumina viridis Lycæi, et cum illis totidem juvencas cervice intactâ jugo. *Constitue quatuor aras his victimis, ad alta delubra Dearum, et demitte sacrum cruorem jugulis, deserèque corpora ipsa boum frondoso luco. Post, ubi nona Aurora ostenderit suos ortus, mittes lethæa papavera inferias Orphei, venerabare placatam Eurydicen vitulâ cæsâ, et mactabis nigram ovem, revisesque lucum. Haud est mora: continuò facessit præcepta matris; venit ad delubra; excitat monstratas aras. Ducit quatuor eximios tauros præstanti corpore, et totidem juvencas cervice intactâ* jugo. *Post, ubi nona Aurora induxerat suos ortus,*

TRANSLATION.

thou humbly tender Offerings, supplicating Peace, and venerate the gentle Wood-nymphs: For at thy Supplications they will grant Forgiveness, and mitigate their Wrath. But first will I shew you in Order what must be your Manner of Worship. Single out four choice Bulls of beauteous Form, which the Tops of green Lycæus now graze for thee, and as many Heifers, whose Necks are untouched by the Yoke. For these erect four altars at the lofty Temples of the Goddesses, from their Throats emit the sacred Blood, and leave the Bodies of the Cattle in the leafy Grove. Afterwards, when the ninth Morn has displayed her rising Beams, you shall offer Lethæan Poppies by way of Funeral Rites to Orpheus, venerate appeased Eurydice with a slain Calf, sacrifice a black Ewe, and revisit the Grove.

Without Delay, he instantly executes the Orders of his Mother; repairs to the Temple; raises the Altars as directed; leads up four chosen Bulls of surpassing Form, and as many Heifers, whose Necks were untouched *by the Yoke*. Thereafter, when the ninth Morning had ushered in her rising Beams,

NOTES.

535. *Napæas.* The *Napææ* were the Nymphs of the Groves, from νάπη, *a Grove*.

545. *Inferias.* The *inferiæ* were Sacrifices offered to the *Manes*. For which see the Note, Æn. III. 66.

545. *Lethæa papavera.* The Poppy is called *Lethæan*, because it causes Sleep or Forgetfulness, from λήθη, *Oblivion*. Poppies were therefore offered to the Dead, especially to those whose Manes they designed to appease; either because Sleep, which they procure, is a lively Emblem of Death, *consanguineus leti sopor*; or because they produce Oblivion of past Injuries.

560. *Cæsar*

mittit inferias Orphei, reviſitque lucum. Hìc verò aſpiciunt monſtrum ſubitum, ac mirabile dictu; apes ſtridere toto utero per liquefacta viſcera boum, et effervere coſtis ruptis; immenſaſque nubes earum *trahi; jamque confluere ſummâ arbore, et demittere* quaſi *uvam lentis ramis. Canebam hæc ſuper cultu arvorum, pecorumque, et ſuper arboribus: dum magnus Cæſar fulminat ad altum Euphratem bello, victorque dat jura per volentes populos, affectatque viam Olympo. Illo tempore dulcis Parthenope alebat me Virgilium, florentem ſtudiis ignobilis otî: qui luſi carmina paſtorum: audaxque juventâ cecini te, Tityre, ſub tegmine patulæ fagi.*

Inferias Orphei mittit, lucumque reviſit.
Hìc verò ſubitum ac dictu mirabile monſtrum
Aſpiciunt; liquefacta boum per viſcera toto
Stridere apes utero, et ruptis effervere coſtis;
Immenſaſque trahi nubes: jamque arbore ſummâ
Confluere, et lentis uvam demittere ramis.
Hæc ſuper arvorum cultu, pecorumque canebam,
Et ſuper arboribus; Cæſar dum magnus ad altum
Fulminat Euphratem bello, victorque volentes
Per populos dat jura, viamque affectat Olympo.
Illo Virgilium me tempore dulcis alebat
Parthenope, ſtudiis florentem ignobilis otî:
Carmina qui luſi paſtorum; audaxque juventâ,
Tityre, te patulæ cecini ſub tegmine fagi.

TRANSLATION.

he offers the Funeral Rites to Orpheus, and reviſits the Grove. But here they behold a ſudden Prodigy, and wondrous to relate; Bees through all the Belly hum amidſt the putrid Bowels of the Cattle; pour forth with the fermenting Juices from the burſt Sides, and in immenſe Clouds roll along: Then ſwarm together on the Top of a Tree, and hang down in a Cluſter from the bending Boughs.

Thus of the Culture of Fields and Flocks, and of Trees, I ſung; whilſt great Cæſar at the deep Euphrates thunders in War; victorious diſpenſes Laws among the willing Nations, and purſues the Way to Heaven. At that Time did I Virgil, nouriſhed by ſweet Parthenope, flouriſh in the Studies of inglorious Eaſe: who warbled paſtoral Songs; and, adventurous through Youth, ſung thee, O Tityrus, under the Covert of a ſpreading Beech.

NOTES.

560. *Cæſar dum magnus*, &c. From this an Argument is drawn, that *Virgil* continued the Care of his Georgics as long as he lived, for the Time here mentioned is the Year before his Death. It was then that *Auguſtus* was at the Head of the *Roman* Legions in Perſon, on the Banks of the *Euphrates*, and compelled *Phraates* to reſtore the Eagles which the *Parthians* had taken from *Craſſus*, and drew the neighbouring Nations, and even the *Indians*, to make a voluntary Submiſſion to him.

564. *Parthenope.* The original Name of the City *Naples*.

565. *Audaxque juventâ.* According to *Servius*, *Virgil* was twenty-eight Years old, when he wrote the Eclogues.

GEORGICORUM FINIS.

P. VIRG.

P. VIRGILII MARONIS
ÆNEIDOS
LIBER PRIMUS.

ARMA, virumque cano, Trojæ qui primus ab oris
Italiam, fato profugus, Lavinaque venit
Littora: multùm ille et terris jactatus et alto,

ORDO.

Cano arma, virumque qui, profugus fato, primus venit ab oris Trojæ in Italiam littoraque Lavina: ille multùm fuit jactatus & terris & alto,

TRANSLATION.

ARMS I sing, and the Hero, the first who, in obedience to the Decree of Heaven, having fled from the Coasts of Troy, came to Italy, and the Lavinian Shore: Much was he tossed both on Sea and Land, * by the Powers above,

* *By the Power of the Gods.*

NOTES.

The first Book of the Æneid is reckoned by Commentators among the most finished, and particularly admired for the Harmony and Structure of its Verse, the Disposition of its Subject, the beautiful and sublime Prospect with which the Scene opens, and, above all, the Poet's Art in throwing so much Matter together in so few Words. The Proposition, the Invocation, the Reasons that kindled *Juno*'s Resentment against the *Trojans*, the Discontent of that Goddess at seeing the Fleet of *Æneas* making towards *Italy*, her Address to *Æolus*, the Description of the Storm, the Anger of *Neptune*, his chiding the Winds, their Flight, and the Calm that immediately succeeded, being all contained in no more than 150 Lines. As instances of particular Beauties, they mention that admirable Description of the Storm, which, they say, is capable of transporting the dullest, and warming the coldest Imagination; the Image of *Discord* bound up in Chains by *Peace*, and that fine Episode of the Pictures which *Æneas* surveys in the Temple of *Carthage*, where the Poet himself appears pleased, as well as in the Song of *Iopas*. But it is to be observed, though these Passages have a particular Sublimity, this is not to be understood as if the rest were not of a Piece. *Virgil* is not like some Poets, who soar very high for a while, and afterwards sink as low: He flies always far above the Earth; sometimes his Flight is more rapid and daring, and sometimes, having mounted to Heaven, he reposes himself in the Sublimity of his Flight; but his Genius never flags, nor is unequal to his Subject.

1. *Arma virumque cano*, &c. Fulvius Ursinus is of Opinion, that *Virgil*, in these first Lines of his Poem, had an Eye to the Beginning of the Odyssey: Of which the Reader may judge by comparing the two together.

> Ανδρα μοι εννεπε Μουσα πολυτροπον, ος μαλα πολλα
> Πλαγχθη, επει Τροιης ιερον πτολιεθρον επερσε.
> *The Man, for Wisdom's various Arts renown'd,*
> *Long exercis'd in Woes, Oh Muse! resound.*
> Pope's Odyssey.

The third Line in particular,

— *multum ille & terris jactatus & alto,*

comes very near to *Homer*'s,

Πολλα

vi ſuperûm, ob memorem iram ſævæ Junonis. Paſſus eſt quoque multa et in bello, dum conderet urbem, inferretque Deos Latio: unde eſt genus Latinum, patreſque Albani, atque mœnia altæ Romæ.

Vi ſuperûm, ſævæ memorem Junonis ob iram:
Multa quoquè et bello paſſus, dum conderet urbem,
Inferretque Deos Latio: genus unde Latinum,
Albanique patres, atque altæ mœnia Romæ.

TRANSLATION.

to gratify cruel Juno's unrelenting Rage; much too he ſuffered in War, till he raiſed the City Lavinium, and introduced his Gods into Latium: From whom ſprung the Latin Progeny, the Alban Fathers, and the Walls of lofty Rome.

NOTES.

Πολλὰ δ᾽ ὅγ᾽ ἐν πόντῳ πάθεν ἄλγεα.

On ſtormy Seas unnumber'd Toils he bore.

But *Virgil* always ſhews his Judgment in knowing what to take, and what to leave.

1. *Primus venit, &c.* The firſt who came, *&c.* *Antenor* arrived in *Italy* before *Æneas*, v. 246. But *Æneas* was the firſt who came from *Troy* to *Lavinium*.

2. *Fato profugus.* *Fato* may very well have a Reference to the whole Sentence: For as *Æneas* left his Country in obedience to the Will of the Gods, ſo it was by the particular Appointment of Heaven that he came to Italy, and ſettled in *Lavinium*. A Circumſtance which redounds to the Honour both of *Æneas*, and of the *Romans*, whom the Poet makes to be deſcended from him; and therefore he is careful to mention it in the Beginning of his Poem, as well as in ſeveral other Places. See v. 210 of this Book,

Tendimus in Latium; ſedes ubi fata quietas
Oſtendunt,——

And 386.

Phrygium conſcendi——æquor, data fata ſecutus.

And B. IV. v. 340.

Me ſi fata meis, &c.

3. *Laviniaque littora.* Lavinium ſtood about eight Miles from the Shore, according to *Servius*; but the neighbouring Coaſt might be diſtinguiſhed by the Name of that City.

4. *Vi ſuperûm.* By the Power of the Gods; or we may take the Expreſſion to ſignify no more than ſimply *Superis, by the Powers above*; for ſo it is uſed, Æn. VII. 432.

Cœleſtûm vis magna jubet.

The awful Majeſty of Heaven commands.

It is the ſame Idiom with the *Greeks*; thus *Homer* ſays, Βίη Ἡρακληείη, *vi Herculea*, for *Hercules*, Il. II. 658. And in the third Book of the Iliad, v. 105, Ἄξετε δὲ Πριάμοιο βίην, *adducite vim Priami*, i. e. *bring Priam*; or, as we would ſay in *Engliſh*, *bring the King's Majeſty*.

In like Manner *Virgil*, *Æn.* XI. 376, uſes *violentia Turni*, for *Turnus himſelf*.

6. *Genus unde Latinum.* *Æneas* found the *Latins* in *Italy*, how then could they be derived from him? Some ſolve the Difficulty by referring *unde* to *Latio*; *from which Country ſprung the* Latin *Race*; but, becauſe *unde* ſeems better referred to the action of *Æneas*, *Servius* offers another Solution, that *Æneas*, who, inſtead of uſing a Conqueror's Right to change or aboliſh the *Latin* Name, incorporated them and his *Trojans* into one Body, under the common Name of *Latins*, may juſtly be called the Founder of a Race he thus ſaved from Ruin and Extinction.

7. *Albanique patres.* Aſcanius, the Son of *Æneas*, after the Death of his Father, quitted *Lavinium*, and, having built *Alba*, made that the Seat of his Kingdom. It was here that *Romulus*, the Founder of the *Roman* Empire, was born. Thus the *Albans* were the Fathers or Anceſtors of the *Romans*.

8. *Muſa, mihi cauſas memora.* Virgil differs a little from *Homer* in putting the Invocation after the Propoſition of his Subject, which ſhews it to be indifferent which of them is firſt, *Homer* again invokes the Muſe for the Subject of his Poem in general. *Virgil* only mention a particular Part—*Cauſas memora.* As the Cauſes of his pious Hero's Sufferings were the Secrets of Heaven, to be known only by Inſpiration, he therefore prays the Muſe to inform him as to theſe; but that this is not to be underſtood excluſive of her general Aſſiſtance through the whole Poem, appears from his uſing the Word *cano* at the Beginning, which was properly applied to Prophets, Oracles, and thoſe that ſpoke by Inſpiration.

Gallos in limine adeſſe canebat.

Æn. VIII. 656.

Atque hæc deinde canit divino ex ore ſacerdos.

Æn. III. 373.

Extemplo tentanda fuga canit æquora Calchas.

Æn. II. 176.

8. Quo

Muſa, mihi cauſas memora, quo numine læſo,
Quidve dolens Regina Deûm, tot volvere caſus
Inſignem pietate virum, tot adire labores
Impulerit. Tantæne animis cæleſtibus iræ?
Urbs antiqua fuit, Tyrii tenuere coloni,
Carthago, Italiam contra, Tiberinaque longè
Oſtia, dives opum, ſtudiiſque aſperrima belli:
Quam Juno fertur terris magis omnibus unam

O Muſa, memora mihi cauſas, quo numine læſo, quidve Regina Deûm dolens, impulerit virum inſignem pietate volvere tot caſus, adire tot labores. Tantæne iræ ſunt animis cæleſtibus?

Urbs fuit antiqua, Tyrii coloni eam tenuere, Carthago nomine, contra Italiam, oſtiaque Tiberina longè, dives opum, aſperrimaque ſtudiis belli: quam urbem *unam Juno fertur coluiſſe magis terris omnibus,*

TRANSLATION.

Declare, O Muſe! the Cauſes *why he ſuffered*, what Deity had he offended, and why was the Queen of Heaven provoked to doom a Man of ſuch diſtinguiſhed Piety to ſtruggle with a Series of Calamities, to encounter ſo many Hardſhips: Dwells ſuch Reſentment in heavenly Minds?

An ancient City there was, *named* Carthage, inhabited by a Colony of Tyrians, fronting Italy, and the Mouth of the Tyber, *but* far remote; a City of vaſt Riches, and *yet* extremely hardy by warlike Exerciſes; which *City* Juno is ſaid to have

NOTES.

8. *Quo numine.* Some read *quo nomine læſa*, in what Particular *Juno* had been offended.

9. *Tot volvere caſus.* The Commentators would have *volvere caſus* to be for *volvi caſibus* and *volvi* again for *involvi*, which they own to be exceedingly harſh, and think to juſtify *Virgil* by the authority of *Statius*, who uſes a parallel Expreſſion. But is it not more natural, as well as more poetical, to take it in the active Senſe? *Volvere caſus* veluti *molem quandam*, ſays *H. Stephens*: *To ſtruggle with a Load of Misfortunes.* For *volvere* is a Word that imports Labour and Difficulty, like that of a Perſon ſtraining to roll forward a ponderous Stone, as,

Saxa quoque infeſto volvebant pondere.
Æn. IX. 512.

Or, *a River bearing down oppoſing Bodies* Geor. IV. 525. And at the ſame Time it implies Duration and Continuance in ſtruggling: Hence it is applied to a Beech, that ſtands through a Revolution of Ages, in ſpite of Storms and Injuries of Weather;

——— *immota manet, multoſque per annos*
Multa virum volvens durando ſecula vincit.
Geor. II. 295.

Volvere caſus then differs from *volvi caſibus*, as *to puſh*, and to be *puſhed* or *driven along*; the laſt would ſhew *Æneas* quite vanquiſhed and ſubdued by his Misfortunes, the other ſhews him in great Labour, but ſtill ſuperior to his Sufferings, and in Proſpect of Victory.

10. *Tot adire labores.* *Labores* is a much ſtronger Word than *Caſus*, and therefore this other Expreſſion ſhews the Riſe and Gradation of *Æneas*'s Sufferings. Beſides, *volvere caſus* may poſſibly refer to the long Series of Dangers which *Æneas* underwent in his ſeven Years Voyage. *Adire labores* again may denote the Toils and Hardſhips of War which he came to in *Italy*. But whatever be in that, the Word *adire* has a great Propriety, and implies the Fortitude and Reſolution with which *Æneas* bore his Trials; for it ſignifies properly to brave Danger, to look an Enemy in the Face, or advance boldly to the Encounter. Thus *Virgil*, ſpeaking of *Dares*, the redoubted Champion in the Boxing Match, ſays,

——— *nec quiſquam ex agmine tanto*
Audet adire *virum.* Æn. V. 379.

And to the ſame Purpoſe in the eleventh Book, v. 936.

Oppoſitus Remuli, quando ipſum horrebat adire,
Haſtam intorſit equo.—

14. *Dives opum.* Anſwers to ἀφνειὸς Βιότοιο in *Homer*, Il. V. 544.

14. *Studiiſque aſperrima belli.* Though *Carthage* was a wealthy City, yet her Riches had not debauched the Minds of her Citizens, and rendered them effeminate; they were rough and warlike as well as rich; unleſs we chuſe to underſtand by *opum* not Riches, but Power, as the Word may ſignify.

16. *Poſ-*

Samo etiam *poſthabitâ. Hìc* fuerunt *illius arma, hìc fuit* illius *currus: Dea* Juno *jam tum tenditque, fovetque* ſpem *hoc* futurum *eſſe regnum gentibus, ſi quà fata id ſinant. Sed enim audierat progeniem duci a Trojano ſanguine, quæ olim verteret arces Tyrias: audierat populum latè regem ſuperbumque bello venturum eſſe hinc excidio Libyæ: Parcas ſic volvere. Saturnia metuens id, memorque veteris belli,*

Poſthabitâ coluiſſe Samo. Hìc illius arma,
Hìc currus fuit: hoc regnum Dea gentibus eſſe,
Si quà fata ſinant, jam tum tenditque, fovetque.
Progeniem ſed enim Trojano à ſanguine duci
Audierat, Tyrias olim quæ verteret arces:
Hinc populum latè regem belloque ſuperbum
Venturum excidio Libyæ: ſic volvere Parcas.
Id metuens, veteriſque memor Saturnia belli,

TRANSLATION.

honoured more than any other Place of her Reſidence, preferably *even* to Samos. Here lay her Arms, here ſtood her Chariot: Here the Goddeſs even then deſigns, and fondly hopes to eſtabliſh the Seat of univerſal Empire, would the Fates permit. But ſhe had heard of a Race to be deſcended from Trojan Blood, that was one Day to overturn the Tyrian Towers: That hence a People of extenſive regal Sway, and renowned in War, was to come to the Deſtruction of Libya: So the Deſtinies ordained. This the Daughter of Saturn dreading, and bearing ſtill

NOTES.

16. *Poſthabitâ coluiſſe Samo.* *Samos*, an Iſland in the *Icarian* Sea, where Juno had her Education, or, according to ſome, her Birth, and where ſhe was married to *Jupiter*; and for that Reaſon ſhe had a magnificent Temple at *Samos*, with a Statue repreſenting her in the Habit of a Bride; and there nuptial Ceremonies were ſolemnized in her Honour. Yet ſo great was her Regard to *Carthage*, that ſhe preferred it to *Samos*.

17. *Hìc currus fuit.* Juno had two Kinds of Chariots; one wherein ſhe was wafted through the Air by Peacocks, another for Battle, drawn by Horſes of Celeſtial Breed, which *Homer* deſcribes, Iliad V. It is the Chariot of the laſt Kind that is here meant.

21. *Latè regem.* So *Horace*, *latè tyrannus*; both of them from *Homer*'s εὐρυκρείων, Il. I. 102.

22. *Sic volvere Parcas.* *Fortunas*, or *Vices*, is underſtood, as Æn. III. 375.

> ——— *ſic fata Deûm rex*
> *Sortitur, volvitque vices:* ———

In this Place there is an Alluſion to the Office of the Deſtinies, who were the Miniſters of *Jove*, to ſpin or meaſure out the Fates of Men, which they *rolled* or *wound up* in Clews, to image the Dependence that all Events have upon the firſt Cauſe, and with what cloſe Connection Things were linked together. The *Parcæ*, the Poets tell us, were three in Number, *Clotho*, *Lacheſis*, and *Atropos*; the firſt held the Diſtaff, the ſecond ſpun, the third cut the Thread of Life.

23. *Id metuens.* Dr. *Trapp* explains this as if it were *id metuens erat*, which, beſides that he brings no Authority to ſupport ſuch an odd Way of ſpeaking, would make this a detached, disjointed Sentence; whereas it ſtands in cloſe Connection both with what goes before and after; it being aſſigned as one of the Cauſes, and indeed the principal one, of *Juno*'s perſecuting *Æneas*, and therefore ſeems neceſſarily to refer to *arcebat longè Latio*; as if the Poet had ſaid, *Juno*'s Concern for *Carthage*, and the Fear of another long War with the *Trojans*, like that which ſhe had waged with them before for *Argos*, were the principal Cauſes of her barring the *Trojans* out of *Italy*. And the four Lines, from *Nec dum etiam cauſæ irarum*, to *His accenſa ſuper*, containing the Cauſes of her perſonal Reſentment, are thrown in by way of Parentheſis, and but curſorily mentioned, to ſhew how much the Poet haſtens to the Action of his Poem, according to *Horace*'s Rule,

> *Semper ad eventum feſtinat; & in medias res*
> ——— *auditorem rapit.*

23. *Veteriſque belli.* May either ſignify the late or former War, as *Dido* calls her former Love,

> —— *veteris veſtigia flammæ.* Æn. IV. 23.

or rather the War which had laſted ſo long, and which coſt *Juno* ſo much Trouble to finiſh.

23. *Veteriſque memor belli.* This, it is plain, cannot be underſtood as one of the Cauſes of *Juno*'s Anger againſt the *Trojans*, but it is a very juſt Ground of her Fear and Jealouſy for *Carthage*, and a good Reaſon for barring the

Prima quod ad Trojam pro caris gesserat Argis;
Nec dum etiam causæ irarum sævique dolores
Exciderant animo; manet altâ mente repostum
Judicium Paridis, spretæque injuria formæ;
Et genus invisum, & rapti Ganymedis honores:
His accensa super, jactatos æquore toto
Troas, relliquias Danaûm atque immitis Achillei,
Arcebat longè Latio; multosque per annos
Errabant acti fatis maria omnia circum:
Tantæ molis erat Romanam condere gentem.

quod prima gesserat ad Trojam pro Argis sibi caris; nec dum etiam causæ irarum, sævique sui dolores exciderant animo; judicium Paridis manet repostum in altâ sua mente, injuriaque formæ suæ spretæ, & genus Trojanorum sibi invisum, & honores Ganymedis rapti: accensa super his, arcebat longè à Latio Troes jactatos toto æquore, relliquias Danaûm atque Achillei immitis: errabantque per multos annos acti fatis circum omnia maria: condere gentem Romanam erat res tantæ molis.

TRANSLATION.

in Mind the long-continued War which she had the principal Hand in carrying on before Troy, in behalf of her beloved Argos; nor as yet were the Causes of her Rage and keen Resentment worn out of her Mind; the Judgment of Paris dwells deeply rooted in her Soul, the Affront *offered* to her neglected Beauty, the detested *Trojan* Race, and the Honours conferred on ravished Ganymede: she, by these Invectives fired, having tossed on the whole Ocean the Trojans, whom the Greeks and merciless Achilles had left, drove them far from Latium; and thus for many years, they were forced by Fate to roam round every Sea: So vast a Work it was to found the Roman State.

NOTES.

Access of the *Trojans* from *Italy*: For she remembered that long War which had cost her so many Anxieties, so many Quarrels with *Jupiter* and the Gods of the opposite Faction, such hard Struggles, and therefore was afraid lest she should be involved in such another War with the *Trojans*, or their Race, in Defence of *Carthage*. This seems to be the plain Sense of the Passage; for *Virgil* mentions first *Juno*'s Fears for *Carthage*, *Id metuens*, *veterisque*, &c. and then he mentions, as distinct from these, the Causes of her Anger and personal Resentment against the *Trojans*, *Nec dum etiam causæ irarum*; and then both her Fears and personal Resentments, as the concurring Causes of her afflicting *Æneas*, and endeavouring to exclude him from *Italy*; *His accensa super—Troas arcebat longè Latio*.

24. *Prima—gesserat.* Either taking *prima* adverbially, which she had *before* carried on, or rather, *prima* for *princeps*, whereof she was the principal Manager. For *Homer* represents *Jupiter* neuter in the War, or rather favourably inclined to the *Trojans*, and acting against them only by *Juno*'s Instigation. See his Speech to *Juno*, Iliad IV. 30. So that the War was chiefly conducted by *Juno* and *Pallas*, *Juno* still having the Leading and Direction.

24. *Caris—Argis.* Argus was one of the Cities where *Juno* had her particular Residence; whence she has the Name of Ἥρη Ἀργείη, Il. IV. 8. and *Juno Argiva*, Æn. III. 547. And in the same Book of the Iliad, v. 52. she names *Argos* among her favourite Cities.

27. *Judicium Paridis.* This refers to the known Story of the Dispute for the Prize of Beauty, between the three Goddesses, *Juno*, *Minerva*, and *Venus*, the Decision whereof was left to *Paris*, who gave it in favour of *Venus*.

28. *Et genus invisum.* Juno hated the whole *Trojan* Race from the Beginning, upon account of their Original; for *Dardanus*, the Founder of the Race, was the Son of *Jupiter* by *Electra*. And it is well known what irreconcileable Enmity *Juno* bore to all the Offspring of her Husband's stolen Embraces.

28. *Rapti Ganymedis.* The Office of Cupbearer to the Gods was transferred from *Hebe*, *Juno*'s Daughter, to *Ganymede*, the Son of *Tros*, a beautiful Boy, who was carried up to Heaven by an Eagle.

'Vix è conſpectu Siculæ telluris in altum
Vela dabant læti, & ſpumas ſalis ære ruebant,
Cum Juno æternum ſervans ſub pectore vulnus,
Hæc ſecum: Mene incepto deſiſtere victam?
Nec poſſe Italiâ Teucrorum avertere regem?
Quippe vetor fatis! Pallaſne exurere claſſem
Argivûm, atque ipſos potuit ſubmergere ponto,
Unius ob noxam, & furias Ajacis Oilei?
Ipſa, Jovis rapidum jaculata è nubibus ignem,
Disjecitque rates, evertitque æquora ventis:
Illum expirantem transfixo pectore flammas
Turbine corripuit, ſcopuloque infixit acuto.
Aſt ego, quæ Divûm incedo Regina, Joviſque

Vix dabant vela læti è conſpectu telluris Siculæ in altum mare, & ruebant ſpumas ſalis ære; cum Juno, ſervans vulnus æternum ſub pectore, hæc ſecum volvebat: Mene victam deſiſtere incepto, nec poſſe avertere regem Teucrorum ab Italia? quippe vetor fatis! Pallaſne potuit exurere claſſem Argivûm, atque ſubmergere ipſos ponto, ob noxam unius, & furias Ajacis Oilei? Ipſa jaculata è nubibus rapidum ignem Jovis, disjecitque rates, evertitque æquora ventis: Turbine corripuit illum (Ajacem) exſpirantem flammas è transfixo pectore, infixitque illum *ſcopulo acuto. Aſt ego, quæ incedo Regina Divûm, ſororque & conjux Jovis,*

TRANSLATION.

Scarce had the Trojans, loſing Sight of Sicily, with Joy launched out into the Deep, and began to plough the foaming Billows with their brazen Prows; when Juno, harbouring everlaſting Rancour in her Breaſt, thus *argues* with herſelf: Shall I then, baffled *thus*, deſiſt from my Purpoſe, nor have it in my Power to avert the Trojan King from Italy? And why, becauſe I am reſtrained by Fate! Was Pallas able to burn the Grecian Ships, and bury themſelves in the Ocean, and for the Offence of one, even the Frenzy of Ajax, Oileus' Son? She herſelf darting from the Clouds Jove's rapid Fire, both ſcattered their Ships, and upturned the Sea with the Winds: Him too ſhe ſnatched away in a Whirlwind, expiring Flames from his transfixed Breaſt, and daſhed *him* againſt the pointed Rock. But I, who move majeſtic, the Queen of Heaven, both Siſter and

NOTES.

34. *Vix è conſpectu, &c.* I ſhall here tranſcribe a Note that relates to this Place, from Mr. *Addiſon*'s Criticiſm on *Milton*, Spect. Vol. IV. No. 267. After he has ſhewn how *Homer*, to preſerve the Unity of his Action, haſtens into the Midſt of Things, and opens his Poem with the Diſſenſion of his Princes, artfully interweaving, in the ſeveral ſucceeding Parts of it, an Account of every Thing material which relates to them, and had paſſed before that fatal Diſſenſion, he adds: "After "the ſame Manner *Æneas* makes his firſt "Appearance in the *Tyrrhene* Seas, and within "Sight of *Italy*, becauſe the Action propoſed "to be celebrated was that of his ſettling him- "ſelf in *Latium*. But becauſe it was neceſ- "ſary for the Reader to know what had hap- "pened to him in the taking of *Troy*, and in "the preceding Parts of his Voyage, *Virgil* "makes his Hero relate it by way of Epiſode "in the ſecond and third Books of the Æneid. "The Contents of both which Books come "before thoſe of the firſt Book in the Thread "of the Story, though, for preſerving of this "Unity of Action, they follow them in the "Diſpoſition of the Poem."

35. *Ære, i. e. æratis proris*, with their brazen Prows, as Æn. IX. 122.

Quot prius æratæ ſteterant ad littora proræ.

40. *Argivûm*. Not the *Greeks* in general, but the *Locrians*, who, in their Return Home, after the Deſtruction of *Troy*, were ſhipwrecked. *Ajax* himſelf was thunderſtruck by *Pallas* for raviſhing *Caſſandra* in her Temple. *Homer* however makes him to have been drowned by *Neptune*, for impiouſly boaſting he would make his Eſcape even in ſpight of the Gods, Odyſſ. l. IV.

46. *Incedo*, Move majeſtic. *Servius* obſerves that the Word *incedo* is properly applied to Perſons

Et ſoror, et conjux, unâ cum gente tot annos
Bella gero. Et quiſquam numen Junonis adoret
Præterea, aut ſupplex aris imponat honorem ?
Talia flammato ſecum Dea corde volutans,
Nimborum in patriam, loca fœta furentibus Auſtris,
Æoliam venit. Hìc vaſto rex Æolus antro
Luctantes ventos, tempeſtateſque ſonoras
Imperio premit, ac vinclis & carcere frænat.
Illi indignantes magno cum murmure montis
Circum clauſtra fremunt. Celsâ ſedet Æolus arce,
Sceptra tenens, mollitque animos, & temperat iras.
Ni faciat, maria, ac terras, cœlumque profundum
Quippe ferant rapidi ſecum, verrantque per auras.
Sed pater omnipotens ſpeluncis abdidit atris,

gero bella tot annos cum unâ gente: & quiſquam præterea adoret numen Junonis, aut ſupplex imponat honorem ſuis altaribus? Dea volutans talia ſecum corde flammato, venit in Æoliam patriam nimborum, loca fœta auſtris furentibus. Hic rex Æolus in vaſto antro premit imperio, ac frænat vinclis & carcere ventos luctantes, tempeſtateſque ſonoras. Illi indignantes fremunt circum ſua clauſtra cum magno murmure montis. Æolus ſedet arce celsâ, tenens ſceptra: mollitque eorum *animos, & temperat iras. Quippe ni faciat* id, illi *rapidi ferant ſecum maria ac terras, cœlumque profundum, verrantque* ea *per auras. Sed pater omnipotens metuens hoc abdidit eos ſpeluncis atris:*

TRANSLATION.

Wife of Jove, muſt maintain a Series of Wars with one *poor* Race for ſo many Years. And who will henceforth adore Juno's Deity, or humbly offer Victims on her Altars ?

The Goddeſs, by herſelf revolving ſuch Thoughts in her inflamed Breaſt, repairs to Æolia, the native Land of Storms, Regions pregnant with boiſterous Winds. Here, in a capacious Cave, King Æolus controuls with imperial Sway the reluctant Winds and bluſtering Tempeſts, and confines them with Chains to *their* Priſon. They roar indignant round their Barriers, filling the *hollow* Mountain with loud Murmurs. Æolus is ſeated on a lofty Throne, wielding a Scepter, and *therewith* aſſwages their Fury, and moderates their Rage. For, unleſs he did ſo, they, in their rapid Career, would hurl away Sea and Earth, and Heaven ſublime, and ſweep them through the Air. But almighty Father *Jove*, guard-

NOTES.

Perſons of Rank and diſtinguiſhed Characters, and that it ſignifies to walk with Dignity and in State, *cum dignitate aliqua ambulare.* Hence it is again made uſe of in deſcribing Queen *Dido* advancing to the Temple in graceful Majeſty; *Regina ad templum forma pulcberrima Dido inceſſit. Juno* was believed to have a very remarkable majeſtic Gait; hence we read in *Athenæus*, Ηραιον Βαδιζει, i. e. *She walks with* Juno's *Gait.* And in like Manner *Propertius*, Lib. II. El. 2.

Et incedit vel Jove digna ſoror.
She walks with all the Dignity of the Siſter of Jove.

49. *Honorem.* This Word is uſed by *Virgil* to denote the Sacrifice and other Ceremonies of Religion that were performed in Honour of the Gods. See. v. 636.

——Divûm templis indicit honorem.

And 740.

———in menſâ laticum libavit honorem.

52. *Æoliam.* The *Æolian* Iſlands, ſituated between *Italy* and *Sicily*, which were ſeven in Number. Here *Æolus*, the Son of *Hippotas*, reigned, reputed King of the Winds, becauſe, from a Courſe of Obſervations, he had acquired ſome Knowledge of the Weather, and was capable of foretelling at Times what Wind would blow for ſome Days together, as we learn from *Diodorus* and *Pliny*.

52. *———hic vaſto rex Æolus antro*
Luctantes ventos tempeſtateſque ſonoras.

insuperque imposuit molem & montes; deditque iis regem, qui jussus sciret & premere illos certo fœdere, & dare illis laxas habenas. At quem Juno supplex tum usa est his vocibus: Æole (namque pater Divûm atque rex hominum dedit tibi & mulcere fluctus, & tollere eos vento) gens inimica mihi navigat Tyrrhenum æquor, portans Ilium in Italiam, victosque Penates. Incute vim ventis, obrueque puppes submersas: aut age eas diversas, & disjice corpora ponto. Bis septem Nymphæ sunt mibi corpore præstanti: quarum jungam tibi connubio stabili, propriamque dicabo Deïopeiam quæ est pulcherrima formâ: ut exigat omnes annos tecum pro talibus meritis, & faciat te parentem ex pulchrâ prole. Æolus contra hæc respondit: ô regina, tuus est labor explorare quid optes: fas est mihi capessere tua jussa.

Hoc metuens; molemque et montes insuper altos
Imposuit; regemque dedit, qui fœdere certo
Et premere, & laxas sciret dare jussus habenas.
Ad quem tum Juno supplex his vocibus usa est:
Æole (namque tibi Divûm pater atque hominum rex
Et mulcēre dedit fluctus, et tollere vento)
Gens inimica mihi Tyrrhenum navigat æquor,
Ilium in Italiam portans, victosque Penates.
Incute vim ventis, submersasque obrue puppes;
Aut age diversas: et disjice corpora ponto.
Sunt mihi bis septem præstanti corpore Nymphæ;
Quarum, quæ formâ pulcherrima, Deïopeiam
Connubio jungam stabili, propriamque dicabo:
Omnes ut tecum meritis pro talibus annos
Exigat, et pulchrâ faciat te prole parentem.
Æolus hæc contra: Tuus, ô Regina, quid optes
Explorare labor: mihi jussa capessere fas est.

TRANSLATION.

ing against this, hath pent them in gloomy Caves, and thrown over them the ponderous Weight of Mountains, appointing them a King, who, by fixed Laws, and at Command, knows both *when* to curb *them*, and when to relax their Reins; whom Juno then in suppliant Words thus addressed: *Great Æ*olus (for the Sire of Gods, and King of Men, hath given thee Power both to smooth the Waves, and raise them with the Wind) a Race by me detested sails the Tuscan Sea, transporting Ilium, and its conquered Gods, into Italy: Add Impulse to thy Winds, overset and sink their Ships; or drive them different Ways, and strow the Ocean with *floating* Carcases. I have twice seven lovely Nymphs, the fairest of whom, Deïopeia, I will join to thee in firm Wedlock, and assign to be thy own for ever; that with thee she may spend all her Years for this Service, and make thee Father of a beautiful Offspring.

To whom Æolus replies: To you, *illustrious* Queen, it belongs to consider what you would have done: On me it is incumbent to execute *your* Commands.

NOTES.

The Sound of these Verses is remarkably adapted to the Sense. They *labour, move slowly*, and are incumbered with Spondees, to shew the Restraint, which *Æolus* lays on his imprisoned Winds, and their Impatience under it. On the other hand, when their Prison is opened to give them Vent, their Eruption and impetuous Career, is represented in the Structure of the Verse, that runs away in a Flood of Dactyls.

Una Eurusque Notusque ruunt, creberque procellis, v. 89.

Virgil abounds with Instances of this Kind, for which the curious Reader may consult Dr. Clarke's Note on the Iliad, L. III. v. 363.

61. *Molemque & montes.* Instead of *molem montium*, a Figure which *Virgil* often uses.

71. *Sunt mihi bis septem.* This Passage is in Imitation of *Homer*, who makes the same Goddess

dess

Tu mihi quodcunque hoc regni, tu ſceptra, Jovemque
Concilias, tu das epulis accumbere Divûm,
Nimborumque facis tempeſtatumque potentem.
Hæc ubi dicta, cavum converſâ cuſpide montem
Impulit in latus: ac venti, velut agmine facto,
Quà data porta, ruunt, & terras turbine perflant.
Incubuere mari, totumque à ſedibus imis
Unà Euruſque Notuſque ruunt, creberque procellis
Africus, et vaſtos volvunt ad littora fluctus.
Inſequitur clamorque virûm ſtridorque rudentum.
Eripiunt ſubito nubes cœlumque diemque
Teucrorum ex oculis: ponto nox incubat atra.
Intonuere poli, & crebris micat ignibus æther:
Præſentemque viris intentant omnia mortem.

Tu concilias mihi hoc regni quodcunque est, tu concilias *ſceptra Jovemque: tu das* mihi *accumbere epulis Divûm, faciſque* me *potentem nimborum tempeſtatumque. Ubi hæc dicta* ſunt, *impulit cavum montem in latus cuſpide converſâ: ac venti, velut agmine facto, ruunt quà porta eſt data, & perflant terras turbine. Incubuere mari, Euruſque Notuſque, Africuſque creber procellis unà ruunt totum mare à ſedibus imis: & volvunt vaſtos fluctus ad littora. Clamorque virûm ſtridorque rudentum inſequitur. Subito nubes eripiunt cœlumque diemque ex oculis Teucrorum: atra nox incubat ponto. Poli intonuere, et æther micat crebris ignibus: omniaque intentant viris præſentem mortem.*

TRANSLATION.

To thee I owe whatever of Power I have, to thee my Scepter, and *the Smiles of* Jove. You give me to ſit at the Tables of the Gods, and make me Lord of Storms and Tempeſts.

Thus having ſaid, whirling the Point of his Spear, he ſtruck the hollow Mountain's Side: The Winds, as in a formed Battalion, ruſh forth at every Vent, and ſcour over the Lands in giddy Whirls. They ply the Ocean furiouſly, and at once, Eaſt and South, and ſtormy South-weſt, plough up the whole *Deep* from its loweſt Bottom, and roll vaſt Billows to the Shores. The Cries of the Seamen ſucceed, and the Cracking of the Cordage. In a Trice, Clouds ſnatch the Heavens and Day from the Eyes of the Trojans. Sable Nights ſits brooding on the Sea. Thunder roars from Pole to Pole, the Sky glares with repeated Flaſhes, and all Nature threatens them with immediate Death. Forthwith Æneas' Limbs are re-

NOTES.

deſs intice the God of Sleep to grant her a Favour, by promiſing him the Marriage of one of the Graces;

Ἀλλ' ἴθ', ἐγὼ δέ κέ τοι Χαρίτων μίαν ὁπλοτεράων
Δώσω ὀπυιέμεναι, καὶ σὴν κεκλῆσθαι ἄκοιτιν,
Πασιθέην, ἧς αἰὲν ἐέλδεαι ἤματα πάντα.

Hear, and obey the Miſtreſs of the Skies,
Nor for the Deed expect a vulgar Prize:
For know, thy lov'd one ſhall be ever thine,
The youngeſt Grace, Paſithae *the divine.*

Il. XIV. 301.

78. *Tu mihi.* This *Servius* underſtands in an allegorical Senſe, and thinks no more is meant by *Æolus*'s receiving his Kingdom and Scepter from *Juno*, but that the Winds are formed by the Motion of the Air or *Juno*. But ſuch Allegorizing would quite deſtroy the poetical Beauty.

79. *Epulis accumbere Divûm.* The Word *accumbere*, to lie, or recline, refers to the ancient Manner of lying or reclining on Couches at Table. And to be admitted to the Table of the Gods, imports Deification. Hence an Expreſſion of the ſame Import is uſed by *Horace* to denote *Hercules*'s Divinity, Lib. IV. Ode VIII. 29.

——— ——— ſic Jovis intereſt
Optatis epulis impiger Hercules.

81. *Hæc ubi dicta.* Thoſe who are curious may conſult *Scaliger*'s Poetics, Lib. V. where this Deſcription of the Storm is particularly examined, and compared with that of *Homer* in the fifth of the Odyſſey.

92. *Ex-*

Extemplo membra Æneæ solvuntur frigore. Ingemit, &, tendens duplices palmas ad sidera, refert talia voce: O illi terque quaterque beati, queis contigit oppetere ante ora patrum, sub altis mœnibus Trojæ! ô Tydide fortissime gentis Danaûm, mene non potuisse occumbere Iliacis campis? effundereque hanc animam tua dextra? ubi sævus Hector jacet telo Æacidæ, ubi ingens Sarpedon jacet: *ubi Simois volvit sub undis tot scuta virûm correpta, galeasque & fortia corpora.*

Procella stridens ab Aquilone adversa illi jactanti talia ferit velum, tollitque fluctus ad sidera. Remi franguntur; tum prora avertit, & dat latus undis;

Extemplo Æneæ solvuntur frigore membra.
Ingemit, et, duplices tendens ad sidera palmas,
Talia voce refert: O terque quaterque beati,
Queis ante ora patrum Trojæ sub mœnibus altis
Contigit oppetere: ô Danaum fortissime gentis
Tydide, mene Iliacis occumbere campis
Non potuisse, tuâque animam hanc effundere dextrâ?
Sævus ubi Æacidæ telo jacet Hector, ubi ingens
Sarpedon: ubi tot Simois correpta sub undis
Scuta virûm galeasque et fortia corpora volvit.
Talia jactanti, stridens Aquilone procella
Velum adversa ferit, fluctusque ad sidera tollit.
Franguntur remi: tum prora avertit, et undis

TRANSLATION.

laxed with cold shuddering Fear: He groans, and, spreading out both his Hands to Heaven, thus expostulates: O thrice happy they, who had the good Fortune to die before their Parents Eyes, under the high Ramparts of Troy! O thou, the bravest of the Grecian Race, great Tydeus' Son, why was I not destined to fall on the Trojan Plains, and pour out this Soul by thy Right-hand? *Even there*, where stern Hector lies *slain* by the Sword of Achilles; where mighty Sarpedon *lies*; where, in impetuous Whirls, Simois, *my native River*, rolls along with its Stream, the Shields, and Helmets, and Bodies of so many gallant Heroes.

Thus, while he mourns in vain, a Tempest, roaring from the North, strikes across his Sails, and heaves the Billows to the Stars. The Oars are shattered; then

NOTES.

92. *Extemplo Æneæ solvuntur.* To those who here arraign *Æneas* of Cowardice and Pusillanimity, it is sufficient to observe, that his Fear arises not from a View of Death, but only from the Apprehension of dying in an inglorious Manner. He laments that he had not died like a brave Man in the Bed of Honour,

(—pulchrumque mors succurrit in armis)

fighting for his Friends and Country, rather than to be reserved for so ignoble, not to say an accursed Death; for so Drowning was reckoned by the Ancients, not only as it deprived their Bodies of the Rites of Sepulture, but also because, as it is in *Servius*, this Kind of Death was thought as contrary to the Principle of the human Soul, as Water is to Fire; as Æn. VI. 730.

Igneus est ollis vigor, &c.

94. *O terque quaterque beati.* It may be rendered *thrice happy ye*, by way of Apostrophe, which is surely more animated and poetical.

94. *O terque quaterque beati.* Macrobius, in his Dissertation upon the Number seven, alledges that *Virgil* makes *Æneas* call them *terque quaterque beati*, or seven times happy, to express the most full and consummate Felicity, *plene & per omnia beatos exprimere volens*; seven, according to the Doctrine of the *Pythagoreans*, being a perfect Number, *numerus rerum omnium fere nodus*, as *Cicero* calls it. Which Mystery those who would see more fully explained, may consult *Macrob. in Somn. Scip.* Lib. I. Cap. 6.

99. *Æacidæ.* Achilles, the Grandson of *Æacus*.

102. *Jactanti.* Signifies while he is throwing away his Words; that is, mourning or complaining in vain. See *Virgil*, second Eclogue, v. 5.

——ibi hæc incondita solus
Montibus, & sylvis studio jactabat inani.

Hence

Dat latus; insequitur cumulo præruptus aquæ mons.
Hi summo in fluctu pendent: his unda dehiscens
Terram inter fluctus aperit: furit æstus arenis.
Tres Notus abreptas in saxa latentia torquet:
Saxa, vocant Itali mediis quæ in fluctibus Aras,
Dorsum immane mari summo. Tres Eurus ab alto
In brevia et Syrtes urget (miserabile visu)
Illiditque vadis, atque aggere cingit arenæ.
Unam, quæ Lycios fidumque vehebat Orontem,
Ipsius ante oculos ingens à vertice pontus
In puppim ferit: excutitur pronusque magister

mons aquæ præruptus cumulo insequitur. Hi pendent in summo fluctu, unda dehiscens aperit terram his inter fluctus: æstus furit arenis. Notus torquet tres abreptas in saxa latentia; quæ saxa in mediis fluctibus Itali vocant aras, immane dorsum in summo mari. Eurus urget tres ab alto in brevia & Syrtes, miserabile visu; illiditque eas vadis, atque cingit aggere arenæ. Ingens pontus ante ipsius oculos ferit à vertice in puppim unam quæ vehebat Lycios fidumque Orontem: magister excutitur pronusque

TRANSLATION.

the Prow inclines, and exposes the Side *of the Ship* to the Waves, which now swell up, one after another, into broken, *hanging* Mountains. These hang *trembling* on the towering Surge; to those the wide yawning Deep discloses the Earth between two Waves: The whirling Tide rages with *mingled* Sand. Three other *Ships*, the South-wind hurrying away, throws on latent Rocks: Rocks in the Midst of the Ocean, which the Italians call *the Altars*, *whose* huge Back just rises to the Surface of the Sea. Three from the Deep the East-wind drives on Shoals and Flats, a piteous Spectacle! and, dashing on the Shelves, inclose *them* with Mounds of Sand. A mighty Billow, falling from the Heighth *of the Ship* before the Hero's Eyes, dashes against the Stern of one which bore the Lycian Crew, and their faithful Leader Orontes: The Pilot is tossed from his Seat, and precipitantly tumbled

NOTES.

Hence it comes that *jacto* signifies to boast or bluster, which is but throwing away Words.

105. *Insequitur cumulo*, &c. The same Image is represented, Geor. III. 237.

Fluctus ut, in medio cœpit cum albescere ponto,
Longius ex altoque sinum trahit; utque volutus
Ad terras, immane sonat per saxa, nec ipso
Monte minor procumbit.

Insequitur may signify, *The next Scene is, cumulo præruptus aquæ mons*; i. e. Wave on Wave, *cumulo*, tumbling along, and still gathering Bulk, till it grows to *præruptus aquæ mons*; i. e. a broken, overhanging Mountain of Water. The Structure and Sound of the Verse shews the Image, *cumulo* expresses the Tumbling of the Waves, *præruptus* their Ruggedness and threatening Aspect, and *mons* the Weight and Noise with which they break.

107. *Terram inter*, &c. It will appear that there is nothing exaggerated in this Circumstance of the Description, if we consider that the Fleet was near Shoals and Sandbanks, v. 115. where there was no great Depth of Water.

109. *Aras*. These Rocks are thought to be the Islands *Ægates*, between *Africa*, *Italy*, and *Sicily*, where the *Romans* and *Carthaginians* struck up a Treaty of Peace, which put an End to the first *Punic* War. Hence they got the Name of the *Altars*, because of the mutual Oaths which the two Nations had there taken after the Defeat of the *Carthaginian* Army by *Lutatius Catulus*, A. U. C. 512.

114. *Pontus*. As if a whole Sea had been breaking upon the Ship at once.

114. *A vertice*. According to *Servius* is from the North, taking *vertex* for the North-pole. *Ruæus* and others explain it the Prow, Head, or Fore-part of the Ship. But the most natural Sense seems to be that of *La Cerda*, who understands by it *from above*, or *from the Top* of the Ship. And in like Manner he interprets the same expression in the second Georgic, 310.

Præsertim si tempestas à vertice sylvis
Incubuit,

119. *Gaza.*

volvitur in caput: aſt fluctus ter circum agens illam ibidem torquet, & rapidus vortex vorat æquore. Apparent rari nantes in vaſto gurgite: arma virûm apparent, tabulæque & Troïa gaza per undas. Jam hiems vicit validam navem Ilionei, jam navem fortis Achatæ; & navem quâ Abas eſt vectus, & quâ grandævus Alethes omnes naves accipiunt imbrem inimicum, compagibus laterum laxis, fatiſcuntque rimis.

Interea Neptunus ſenſit pontum miſceri magno murmure, hyememque eſſe emiſſam, & ſtagna eſſe refuſa ab imis vadis: graviter commotus, & proſpiciens alto, extulit placidum caput ſummâ undâ. Videt claſſem Æneæ disjectam toto æquore, Troas oppreſſos fluctibus, ruinâque cœli. Nec doli & iræ Junonis latuere fratrem: vocat ad ſe Eurum Zephyrumque: dehinc fatur talia;

Volvitur in caput: aſt illam ter fluctus ibidem
Torquet agens circum, et rapidus vorat æquore vortex.
Apparent rari nantes in gurgite vaſto;
Arma virûm tabulæque, et Troïa gaza per undas.
Jam validam Ilionei navem, jam fortis Achatæ,
Et quâ vectus Abas, et qua grandævus Alethes,
Vicit hiems: laxis laterum compagibus omnes
Accipiunt inimicum imbrem, rimiſque fatiſcunt.
Interea magno miſceri murmure pontum,
Emiſſamque hiemem ſenſit Neptunus, et imis
Stagna refuſa vadis: graviter commotus, et altò
Proſpiciens, ſummâ placidum caput extulit undâ.
Disjectam Æneæ toto videt æquore claſſem;
Fluctibus oppreſſos Troas, cœlique ruinâ.
Nec latuere doli fratrem Junonis, et iræ:
Eurum ad ſe Zephyrumque vocat: dehinc talia fatur:

TRANSLATION.

headlong *into the Flood*; there fixed, the Galley thrice, by the working Waves, is whirled around; and by the rapid Eddy, ſwallowed up in the Deep. Then, floating here and there on *the Face of* the vaſt Abyſs, are ſeen Men, their Arms and Planks, and the Trojan Wealth, among the Waves. Now the Storm overpowered the ſtout Veſſel of Ilioneus, now that of brave Achates, and that which Abas, and that which old Alethes bore. All, at their looſened and disjointed Sides, receive the hoſtile Stream, and gape into Chinks.

Mean while Neptune felt the Sea in vaſt Uproar and Confuſion, a Storm ſent forth *into his Domain*, and the Depths overturned from their loweſt Channels. He, in violent Commotion, and concerned for his watery Empire, reared his ſerene Aſpect above the Waves; ſees Æneas's Fleet ſcattered over the Ocean, the Trojans oppreſſed with the *conflicting* Waves *below*, and the *convulſive* Ruins of Heaven *above*. Nor were Juno's Wiles and Hate unknown to her Brother. He calls to him the Eaſt and Weſt-winds, then thus *in Wrath* beſpeaks them: And do you

NOTES.

119. *Gaza.* Originally a *Perſian* Word, which ſignifies any Kind of rich Furniture, as well as Treaſures of Silver and Gold.

123. *Imbrem.* ſignifies ſometimes Water in general, as in *Lucretius*, Lib. I. 715.

Ex igni, atque anima procreſcere, & imbri.

127. *Placidum caput.* How is this conſiſtent with his being *graviter commotus*, put in violent Commotion? In anſwer to this, *placidus* is an Epithet that denotes *Neptune*'s natural Character, the other only an occaſional Commotion and Diſturbance: Or, he was peaceful and mild with reſpect to the *Trojans*, however offended he was at the Winds: Or, laſtly, *placidum* may denote the Effect which his Aſpect had to ſtill the Sea, and produce a Calm.

132. *Veneti*

Tantane vos generis tenuit fiducia vestri?
Jam cœlum terramque, meo sine nomine, venti,
Miscere, et tantas audetis tollere moles?
Quos ego: sed motos præstat componere fluctus.
Post mihi non simili pœnâ commissa luetis.
Maturate fugam, Regique hæc dicite vestro:
Non illi imperium pelagi, sævumque tridentem,
Sed mihi sorte datum, tenet ille immania saxa,
Vestras, Eure, domos: illâ se jactet in aulâ
Æolus, et clauso ventorum carcere regnet.
Sic ait, et dicto citius tumida æquora placat:
Collectasque fugat nubes, Solemque reducit.
Cymothoe simul et Triton adnixus, acuto
Detrudunt naves scopulo: levat ipse tridenti,
Et vastas aperit Syrtes, et temperat æquor:
Atque rotis summas levibus pellabitur undas.

tantane fiducia vestri generis tenuit vos? jam audetis, ô venti, miscere cœlum terramque, sine meo numine, & tollere tantas moles? Quos ego puniam: Sed præstat componere motos fluctus. Post luetis mihi commissa pœna non simili. Maturate fugam, diciteque hæc vestro regi: imperium pelagi, sævumque tridentem, non datum illi sorte sed mihi: ille tenet saxa immania, vestras domos, ô Eure: Æolus jactet se in illa aula, & regnet in clauso carcere ventorum. Sic ait, & placat tumida æquora citius dicto, fugatque nubes collectas, reducitque solem. Simul Cymothoe & Triton adnixus detrudunt nubes acuto scopulo: ipse levat eas tridenti; & aperit vastas Syrtes, & temperat æquor, atque pellabitur summas undas levibus rotis.

TRANSLATION.

thus presume upon your Birth? Dare you, *audacious* Winds! without my sovereign Leave, to embroil Heaven and Earth, and raise such Mountains *on the Sea?* Whom I —— But first it is fit to asswage the tumultuous Waves. A Chastisement of another Nature from me awaits your next Offence. Fly apace, and bear this *Message* to your King: That not to him the Empire of the Sea, and the awful Trident, but to me by Lot are given: His Dominions are *wild*, enormous Rocks, your proper Mansions, Eurus: In that Palace let King Æolus proudly boast, and reign in the close Prison of the Winds.

So speaks *the God*, and swifter than Speech smooths the swelling Seas, disperses the collected Clouds, and brings back the Day. With him Cymothoe and Triton, with exerted Might, heave the Ships from the pointed Rock. He himself raises them with his Trident; lays open the vast Sand-banks, and calms the Sea; and in his light Chariot glides along the Surface of the Waves. And as when a

NOTES.

132. *Generis fiducia.* The Winds, according to *Hesiod*, were the Offspring of *Aurora* and *Astræus*, one of the *Titans*. *Neptune* therefore by this Reproof insinuates, that, if they imitated the Rebellion of the Giants their Ancestors, they might expect also to share their Doom.

138. *Non illi imperium.* Dr. *Trapp* alledges here, that *Virgil* makes *Neptune* say what is not good Sense, since *Æolus* pretended not to govern the Sea, but to embroil it. But in this very Thing *Æolus* was to blame; he ought to have had Permission from *Neptune* before he sent forth the Winds to embroil his Realms. For it is to be considered that *Neptune* was a God of the first Class, as absolute as *Jove* himself in his own Dominions; for the World had been shared by equal Lot between the three Brothers; and as *Jupiter* had the Earth to his Lot, so *Neptune* had the Sea, *Imperium pelagi mihi sorte datum.* Whereas *Æolus* was only a subordinate Deity, who was to act under the Command and Direction of his Superior; he was to loose and restrain the Winds, only *certo fœdere*, according to a fixed Order and Contract, *& jussus*, as he was commanded.

144. *Cymothoe.* One of the Sea-nymphs; the

Ac veluti ſæpe cum ſeditio coorta eſt in magno populo, vulguſque ignobile ſævit animis: jamque faces et ſaxa volant, furor miniſtrat arma: tum, ſi quem virum forte conſpexere gravem pietate ac meritis, ſilent, adſtantque arrectis auribus: ille regit animos, & mulcet horum pectora dictis. Sic cunctus fragor pelagi cecidit: poſtquam Genitor proſpiciens æquora, invectuſque cœlo aperto, flectit equos, volanſque ſecundo curru dat lora.

Æneadæ defeſſi contendunt petere curſu littora quæ ſunt proxima, & vertuntur ad oras Libyæ. Eſt locus in longo ſeceſſu; inſula efficit eum portum, objectu laterum; quibus omnis unda ab alto frangitur, ſcinditque ſeſe in ſinus reductos.

Ac, veluti magno in populo cum ſæpe coorta eſt
Seditio, ſævitque animis ignobile vulgus;
Jamque faces et ſaxa volant; furor arma miniſtrat:
Tum pietate gravem ac meritis ſi fortè virum quem
Conſpexere, ſilent; arrectiſque auribus adſtant:
Ille regit dictis animos, et pectora mulcet.
Sic cunctus pelagi cecidit fragor; æquora poſtquam
Proſpiciens Genitor, cœloque invectus aperto,
Flectit equos, curruque volans dat lora ſecundo.
Defeſſi Æneadæ, quæ proxima, littora curſu
Contendunt petere, et Libyæ vertuntur ad oras.
Eſt in ſeceſſu longo locus; inſula portum
Efficit, objectu laterum, quibus omnis ab alto
Frangitur, inque ſinus ſcindit ſeſe unda reductos.

TRANSLATION.

Sedition has ariſen amongſt a mighty Multitude, as often *happens*, and the Minds of the ignoble Vulgar are *all* on Fire; now Stones, now Firebrands fly; their Fury ſupplies them with Arms: If then, by Chance, they ſpy a Man revered in Piety and Worth, *all* are huſhed, and ſtand with liſtening Ears: He, by *perſuaſive* Eloquence, rules their Paſſions, and calms their Breaſts. Thus all the raging Tumult of the Ocean ſubſided, ſo ſoon as the Parent *of the Floods*, ſurveying the Seas, and wafted through the open Sky, manages his Steeds, and throws up the Reins, flying in his eaſy Chariot.

In the mean-time, the weary Trojans direct their Courſe towards the neareſt Shores, and make the Coaſts of Libya. *Here*, in a long Receſs, a Station lies; an Iſland forms it into a Harbour by her jutting Sides, againſt which every Wave from the Ocean is broke, and divided runs into a remote, winding Bay. On

NOTES.

the Name is very proper to an Inhabitant of the Sea, who glides nimbly along the Waves, being compounded of κυμα, *a Wave*, and θεειν, *to run*.

148. *Ac veluti.* This Simile is exceeding natural, juſt, and particularly exact. What more proper to repreſent the Diſorder and Havock produced by a violent Hurricane, than the Fury and Deſolation of an incenſed Mob? As, on the other Hand, the Suddenneſs with which the noiſy Waves ſubſide, and ſink into a perfect Calm, ſo ſoon as *Neptune* appears, is finely marked by the Awe and Silence with which the ſeditious Multitude are immediately ſtruck, at the Sight of a Perſon of ſuperior Merit and Authority.

159. *Eſt in ſeceſſu*, &c. This Deſcription is very beautiful in itſelf, and ſeaſonably introduced to relieve the Reader, and compoſe his Mind into an agreeable Tranquillity, after having dwelt on the former Images of Horror and Diſtreſs. *Livy* gives Account of a Port in *Spain* belonging to *New Carthage*, very like to this which *Virgil* here deſcribes: *Sinus eſt maris media fere Hiſpaniæ ora, maxime Africo vento oppoſitus, & quingentos paſſus introrſus retractus, paululo plus paſſuum in latitudinem patens. Hujus in oſtio ſinus, parva inſula objecta ab alto,* *portum*

Hinc atque hinc vaſtæ rupes, geminique minantur
In cœlum ſcopuli; quorum ſub vertice latè
Æquora tuta ſilent: tum ſylvis ſcena coruſcis
Deſuper, horrentique atrum nemus imminet umbrâ.
Fronte ſub adverſâ ſcopulis pendentibus antrum:
Intus aquæ dulces, vivoque ſedilia ſaxo,
Nympharum domus: hic feſſas non vincula naves
Ulla tenent: unco non alligat ancora morſu.
Huc ſeptem Æneas collectis navibus omni
Ex numero ſubit: ac magno telluris amore
Egreſſi, optatâ potiuntur Troes arenâ,
Et ſale tabentes artus in littore ponunt.
Ac primùm ſilici ſcintillam excudit Achates,
Suſcepitque ignem foliis, atque arida circum
Nutrimenta dedit, rapuitque in fomite flammam.
Tum Cererem corruptam undis, Cerealiaque arma
Expediunt, feſſi rerum; frugeſque receptas
Et torrere parant flammis, et frangere ſaxo.
Æneas ſcopulum interea conſcendit, et omnem

Hinc atque hinc vaſtæ rupes, geminique ſcopuli minantur in cœlum; ſub quorum vertice æquora ſilent latè tuta: tum ſcena ſylvis coruſcis, nemuſque atrum horrenti umbra deſuper imminet. Sub adverſa fronte eſt antrum in ſcopulis pendentibus, intus ſunt aquæ dulces, ſediliaque è vivo ſaxo, domus Nympharum: hic non ulla vincula tenent feſſas naves, non ulla ancora alligat eas unco morſu. Æneas ſubit huc ſeptem navibus collectis ex omni numero: ac Troes egreſſi cum magno amore telluris, potiuntur arena optata, & ponunt in littore artus tabentes ſale. Ac primùm Achates excudit ſcintillam ſilici, ſuſcepitque ignem foliis, atque dedit arida nutrimenta circum, rapuitque flammam in fomite. Tum feſſi rerum expediunt Cererem corruptam undis, armaque Cerealia: parantque et torrere flammis, et frangere ſaxo fruges receptas. Interea Æneas conſcendit ſcopulum, et petit omnem

TRANSLATION.

either Side vaſt Cliffs *ariſe*, and two Twin-like Rocks, *towering above the reſt*, threaten Heaven: Under whoſe Summit the Waters all around are calm and ſtill. Above, a ſylvan Scene, with waving Woods, and a dark Grove, with awful Shade, hangs over *the Flood*. Under the oppoſite Front a Cave *is formed* of pendant Rocks, within *which are* freſh Springs, and Seats of living Stone, the *cool* Receſs of Nymphs. Here Tempeſt-beaten Ships *ride ſafe*, though neither Cables hold, nor biting Anchors moor them. To this Retreat Æneas brings ſeven Ships, collected from all his Fleet: And the Trojans, longing much for Land, *now* diſembark, enjoy the wiſhed-for Shore, and ſtretch their *brine* drenched Limbs upon the Beach. Then firſt Achates ſtruck *the latent* Spark from a Flint, received the Fire in Leaves, round it applied dry combuſtible Matter, and inſtant blew up the Fuel into Flame. Then, ſpent with Toil and Hunger, they produce their Grain damnified with the Brine, and the Inſtruments of Ceres; and prepare *firſt* to dry over the Fire, and *then* to grind with Stones their Corn ſaved *from the Wreck*. Meanwhile, Æneas climbs a Rock, and takes a Proſpect of the wide

NOTES.

portum ab omnibus ventis, præter Africum, tutum facit.

178. *Feſſi rerum.* Virgil uſes the Word *rerum* to ſignify Diſtreſſes, as in the four-hundred and ſixty-ſecond Verſe,

Sunt lacrymæ rerum, et mentem mortalia tangunt.

prospectum latè in pelago, si quà videat Anthea jactatum vento, Phrygiasque biremes, aut Capyn, aut arma Caïci in celsis puppibus. Prospicit nullam navem in conspectu, tres vero cervos errantes in littore: tota armenta sequuntur hos à tergo; et longum agmen pascitur per valles. Constitit hic, corripuitque manu arcum celeresque sagittas, quæ tela fidus Achatas gerebat: primumque sternit ipsos ductores ferentes capita alta arboreis cornibus, tum vulgus, et agens telis inter frondea nemora miscet omnem turbam. Nec absistit priusquam victor fundat humi septem ingentia corpora, et æquet numerum cum navibus. Hinc petit portum, et partitur eos in omnes socios. Deinde dividit vina quæ bonus Acestes onerârat cadis in Trinacrio littore, be-

Prospectum latè pelago petit; Anthea si quà
Jactatum vento videat Phrygiasque biremes;
Aut Capyn, aut celsis in puppibus arma Caïci.
Navem in conspectu nullam; tres littore cervos
Prospicit errantes: hos tota armenta sequuntur
A tergo; et longum per valles pascitur agmen.
Constitit hic, arcumque manu, celeresque sagittas
Corripuit; fidus quæ tela gerebat Achates:
Ductoresque ipsos primùm, capita alta ferentes
Cornibus arboreis, sternit, tum vulgus; et omnem
Miscet agens telis nemora inter frondea turbam.
Nec prius absistit, quàm septem ingentia victor
Corpora fundat humi, et numerum cum navibus æquet.
Hinc portum petit, et socios partitur in omnes.
Vina, bonus quæ deinde cadis onerârat Acestes

TRANSLATION.

Ocean all around, if, by any Means, he can descry Antheus tossed by the Wind, and the Phrygian Gallies, or Capys, or the Arms of Caicus on the lofty Deck. He sees no Ship in View, but three Stags straying on the Shore: These the whole Herd follows, and is feeding through the Valley in a long extended Train. Here he stopped short, and snatching his Bow and winged Arrows, Weapons which the faithful Achates bore; first overthrows the Leaders, bearing their Heads high with branching Horns; next, the vulgar Throng; and disperses the whole Herd, persecuting them with Darts through the leafy Woods. Nor desists he *from the Chace*, till his conquering Arm stretches seven huge Deer on the Ground, and equals their Number with his Ships. Hence he returns to the Port, and shares *the Spoil* amongst all his Crew. Then the Hero divides the Wine which the good Acestes

NOTES.

185. *Sequuntur à tergo.* Though *à tergo* here may seem superfluous, and mere Tautology, it is agreeable to the Genius of the purest *Latin*, and is used the same Way by *Cicero*, 1 Tuscul. *Adolescentes in cursu à tergo insequens, nec opinantes assecuta est senectus.* Besides, *à tergo* signifies their following close behind, as it is the Manner of those timorous Animals to adhere close to their Leaders.

186. *Agmen.* This Word signifies a moving Body, as an Army marching; a Circumstance that makes the Prospect more delightful and picturesque, to see a Herd of Deer extended through a long Valley, and in Motion.

190. *Cornibus arboreis.* This finely marks the *Ductores* or *Leaders* from the rest, on whose lofty Heads tall branching Horns shoot up like Trees.

190. *Et omnem miscet.* *Miscere* here signifies to make them fly before him in the utmost Fear and Disorder, as Æn. X. 721.

Hunc ubi miscentem longè media agmina vidit. It answers to *Homer's* αλαπαζοντα ϛιχας ανδρων.

196. *Lit-*

Littore Trinacrio, dederatque abeuntibus, heros
Dividit, et dictis mœrentia pectora mulcet:
O socii (neque enim ignari sumus ante malorum)
O passi graviora! dabit Deus his quoque finem.
Vos, et Scyllæam rabiem, penitusque sonantes
Accêstis scopulos; vos et Cyclopea saxa
Experti: revocate animos, mœstumque timorem
Mittite; forsan et hæc olim meminisse juvabit.
Per varios casus, per tot discrimina rerum
Tendimus in Latium; sedes ubi fata quietas
Ostendunt: illic fas regna resurgere Trojæ.
Durate, et vosmet rebus servate secundis.
Talia voce refert, curisque ingentibus æger,
Spem vultu simulat: premit altum corde dolorem.

rosque dederat abeuntibus, & mulcet his dictis eorum mœrentia pectora: O socii (neque enim ignari sumus ante malorum) O vos passi graviora! Deus dabit finem his quoque. Vos accêstis & ad Scyllæam rabiem scopulosque penitus sonantes; vos experti estis & Cyclopea saxa: revocate animos, mittiteque mœstum timorem; forsan olim juvabit meminisse & hæc. Tendimus in Latium per casus varios, per tot discrimina rerum; ubi fata ostendunt nobis quietas sedes: illic fas est regna Trojæ resurgere. Durate & servate vosmet secundis rebus. Refert talia voce, ægerque ingentibus curis, simulat spem vultu, premit altum dolorem corde.

TRANSLATION.

had stowed in Casks on the Sicilian Shore, and given them at Parting, and with these Words cheers their disconsolate Hearts: O Friends and Fellow-sufferers, who have sustained severer Ills than these (for we are not Strangers to former Days of Adversity), to these too God will grant a *happy* Period; you have seen both Scylla's furious Coast, and those hideous roaring Rocks; you are acquainted even with the Dens of the Cyclops: Resume then your Courage, and dismiss your desponding Fears; perhaps the Day may come, when even these *Misfortunes* shall be remembered with Joy. Through various *Scenes of* Woe, through many perilous Adventures we steer *our Course* to Latium, where the Fates give us the Prospect of peaceful Settlements. There Troy's Kingdom is allowed once more to rise. *With Patience* persevere, and reserve yourselves for prosperous Days. So spoke *the Chief*; and *though* oppressed with *a thousand* heavy Cares, *yet* wears the Looks of well-dissembled Hope, *while he* buries deep Anguish in his Breast.

NOTES.

196. *Littore Trinacrio.* Sicily was denominated *Trinacria* from its triangular Form; the three Promontories in which its Angles terminated were called *Pachynus*, *Pelorus*, and *Lilybæum*.

198. *Ante malorum*, i. e. *Malorum* quæ *ante* fuerunt, former or past Ills.

199. *O socii,—O passi graviora:*

O fortes pejoraque passi. *Hor.* Ode I. 7. And both of them are from *Homer*, Odyss. XII.

200. *Scyllæam rabiem.* *Scylla* was a Rock in the western Part of *Italy*, adjoining to the Promontory of *Cænys*, now *Capo di Passolo.* The Violence of the Waves, and the whirling Eddies in that narrow Sea, having often proved fatal to Ships, gave the Poets a Handle to transform it into a hideous Monster, the upper Parts of whose Body resembled a beautiful Virgin; the middle that of a Wolf, and which terminated in a Fish's Tail: As in that Description *Virgil* gives of it in the third Book, v. 424.

At Scyllam cæcis cohibet spelunca latebris,
Ora exsertantem, & naves in saxa trahentem.
Prima hominis facies, & pulchro pectore virgo,
Pube tenus: postrema immani corpore Pristis,
Delphinum caudas utero commissa luporum.

201. *Cyclopea saxa.* The *Cyclops* were the primitive Inhabitants of *Sicily*, and had their chief Residence near Mount *Ætna.* They were reputed to be savage and inhospitable. Hence the Poets fabled that they were a Race of monstrous Giants, who had but one Eye, which

was

Illi accingunt ſe prædæ dapibuſque futuris; diripiunt tergora coſtis, & nudant viſcera. Pars ſecant in fruſta, figuntque ea trementia verubus: Alii locant ahena in littore, miniſtrantque flammas. Tum revocant vires ſuas victu, fuſique per herbam implentur veteris Bacchi, ferinæque pinguis. Poſtquam fames eorum eſt exempta epulis, menſæque ſunt remotæ, requirunt longo ſermone ſocios amiſſos, dubii inter ſpemque metumque; ſeu credant eos vivere, ſive pati extrema, nec vocatos jam exaudire.

Illi ſe prædæ accingunt, dapibuſque futuris;
Tergora diripiunt coſtis, et viſcera nudant.
Pars in fruſta ſecant, verubuſque trementia figunt:
Littore ahena locant alii, flammaſque miniſtrant.
Tum victu revocant vires, fuſique per herbam,
Implentur veteris Bacchi, pinguiſque ferinæ.
Poſtquam exemta fames epulis, menſæque remotæ,
Amiſſos longo ſocios ſermone requirunt;
Spemque metumque inter dubii: ſeu vivere credant,
Sive extrema pati, nec jam exaudire vocatos.

TRANSLATION.

Now they addreſs themſelves to the Spoil and future Feaſt; tear the Skin from off the Ribs, and lay the Entrails bare. Some divide *the Fleſh* into Parts, and fix on Spits the quivering Limbs: Others place the brazen Caldrons on the Shore, and prepare the Fires. Then they repair their Strength with Food, and, ſtretched along the Graſs, regale themſelves with *generous* old Wine and choice Veniſon. After the Rage of Hunger was appeaſed, and the Tables removed, in long Diſcourſe they explore the Fate of their Companions loſt, hovering in Suſpenſe between Hope and Fear, whether to believe them yet alive, or that they had finiſhed their Deſtiny, and were now deaf to the *laſt ſolemn* Invocation *of departed Ghoſts.* Above the reſt, the pious Hero, with himſelf, bemoans now the Loſs

NOTES.

was in their Forehead, and that they fed upon human Fleſh; and, from their Vicinity to Mount *Ætna*, they were given out to the *Vulcan*'s Servants, who employed them in forging *Jupiter*'s Thunderbolts.

219 *Sive extrema pati.* The *Romans* had a Shyneſs and Averſion to hear, or pronounce in direct Words that a Perſon was dead; and therefore choſe to make uſe of ſome Word that implied as much, as *fuit, vixit*; or to expreſs it by a Circumlocution, as in the Inſtance before us. *Pati* here hath the Signification of the Preterite, as in this ſame Book *Dido* ſays, *Teucrum memini venire* for *veniſſe*, v. 619.

219. *Nec jam exaudire vocatos.* This is in Alluſion to the ancient Cuſtom of calling upon the Dead, which was the laſt Ceremony performed in Funeral Obſequies, as appears from ſeveral Paſſages in the *Æneid*, particularly in the Deſcription of *Polydorus*'s Sepulture, B. III. 67.

——————— animamque ſepulchro
Condimus, & magna ſupremum voce ciemus.

After the Body was interred, the Friends three times called aloud upon the deceaſed by his Name, and after thrice repeating the Word *vale*, as the laſt Farewell, they departed. The ſame Ceremony of invocating the Dead was alſo performed towards thoſe who periſhed in Shipwreck, and whoſe Bodies could not be recovered in order to their Interment. To them a Cenotaphy, or *tumulus inanis*, was raiſed, and their departed Ghoſts were three times ſolemnly called:

Tunc egomet tumulum Rhœteo in littore inanem
Conſtitui, & magna Manes ter voce vocavi.
Æn. VI. 505.

Pliny derives the Origin of this Cuſtom from a juſt Precaution againſt burying Perſons alive. For it having been obſerved that ſome were reputed dead who were only in a Swoon or Deliquium, it was thought proper to preſerve the Body for ſeven Days, during which Time, the Friends uſed to call upon the deceaſed at certain Intervals, and after the laſt Invocation the Body was carried out to be buried, or laid on the Funeral Pile. Hence the Phraſe *conclamatum eſt* came to ſignify, *It is given up for loſt, it is paſt all Hope*; as in *Terence*, Eun. Ac. II. Sc. III. 56.

Præcipuè pius Æneas, nunc acris Orontei,
Nunc Amyci casum gemit, et crudelia secum
Fata Lyci, fortemque Gyan, fortemque Cloanthum.
Et jam finis erat, cum Jupiter æthere summo
Despiciens mare velivolum, terrasque jacentes,
Littoraque, et latos populos; sic vertice cœli
Constitit, et Libyæ defixit lumina regnis.
Atque illum tales jactantem pectore curas,
Tristior, et lacrymis oculos suffusa nitentes,

Pius Æneas præcipuè, gemit secum casum nunc acris Orontei, nunc Amyci, & crudelia fata Lyci, fortemque Gyan, fortemque Cloanthum.

Et jam erat finis, cum Jupiter è summo æthere despiciens mare velivolum terraque jacentis, littoraque, & latos populos, sic constitit in vertice cœli, & defixit lumina regnis Libyæ. Venus autem tristior, & suffusa nitentes oculos lacrymis, alloquitur illum jactantem tales curas in pectore;

TRANSLATION.

of active Orontes, now of Amycus, and then the cruel Fate of Lycus, with valiant Gyas, and *no less* valiant Cloanthus.

And now *the Day and Discourse* were ended; when Jove, from the lofty Sky, looking down upon the navigable Sea, and the Lands lying at rest, with the Shores and the Nations dispersed abroad; thus, *surveying all,* stood on the Battlements of Heaven, and fixed his Eyes on Libya's Realms. To whom, revolving such Cares in his Mind, Venus, in mournful Mood, her starry Eyes bedimmed with Tears, *thus* addresses herself: O *thou* who, with eternal Sway, rulest the Af-

NOTES.

220. *Præcipuè pius Æneas.* The most exalted and heroic Minds are most susceptible of Humanity and Compassion. Therefore *Virgil* says, *Præcipuè pius Æneas*; he was moved with generous Concern; especially for the Fate of those of distinguished Valour;

——fortemque Gyan, fortemque Cloanthum.

But at the same Time he conducts his Grief with Prudence, carefully avoids what might dispirit the rest, and therefore *gemit secum*, he keeps his Anxiety to himself; shewing his Men an Example only of Fortitude and Resolution, which rises superior to Dangers and Misfortunes. This is evident from the whole Strain of his Speech aforementioned, and particularly from what is said, Verse 209.

Spem vultu simulat: premit altum corde dolorem.

224. *Mare velivolum.* In this beautiful Epithet *Velivolum* the Poet considers the Sails of a Ship under the Notion of Wings, wherewith it flies upon the Sea. Sailing and Flying have indeed so great a Resemblance to one another, that *Virgil*, the justest Copier of Nature, uses them interchangeably. Thus Æn. III. 520. *Velorum pandimus alas*; We expand the Wings of our Sails. And, speaking of *Dedalus*'s Flight, he says, *Gelidas enavit ad arctos*; He sailed through the Air to the frozen North. And the balanced Motion of his Wings, whereby he had sped his Flight, is called *remigium alarum*, the Steerage of his Wings.

224. *Terrasque jacentes.* The Earth or Lands are said to be *jacentes*, lying still, dead, and at Rest, in opposition to the Sea, which is restless, *velivolum*, always in Motion, agitated by sailing Ships, Winds and Tides. Or *jacentes* may signify *low lying*; for the Ancients were not ignorant that the Sea rises above the Level of the Land; thus the Word is used, Æn. III. 689.

————Tapsumque jacentem.

228. *Tristior*, &c. This is the first Time *Venus* is introduced, and a very charming Appearance she makes. That Air of Melancholy with which her Looks are clowded, the Tears that dim the Lustre of her Eyes, together with her tender Anxiety for her Son, shew her in a fine Situation, and cannot but heighten her Charms in the Reader's Eye. So *Helen* is drawn in Tears the first Time she appears in the Iliad, III. 142. where her Charms extort even from the venerable Fathers of *Troy* one of the highest Encomiums that ever was pronounced on Beauty. We have also another admirable Picture of Beauty in Distress drawn by *Milton*, towards the

O tu, qui regis res hominumque Deûmque æternis imperiis, et terres fulmine; Quid tantum potuit meus Æneas, quid Troes potuere committere in te? quibus passis tot funera cunctus orbis terrarum clauditur ob Italiam? Certè pollicitus es Romanos olim, annis volventibus, ductores fore hinc, à revocato sanguine Teucri, qui tenerent mare, qui tenerent terras omni ditione: O Genitor quæ sententia vertit te? Equidem hoc solabar occasum tristesque ruinas Trojæ, rependens his fatis contraria fata.

Alloquitur Venus: O, qui res hominumque Deûmque
Æternis regis imperiis, et fulmine terres,
Quid meus Æneas in te committere tantum,
Quid Troes potuere? quibus tot funera passis,
Cunctus ob Italiam terrarum clauditur orbis?
Certè hinc Romanos olim, volventibus annis,
Hinc fore ductores, revocato à sanguine Teucri,
Qui mare, qui terras omni ditione tenerent,
Pollicitus: quæ te, Genitor, sententia vertit?
Hoc equidem occasum Trojæ, tristesque ruinas
Solabar, fatis contraria fata rependens.

TRANSLATION.

fairs of both Gods and Men, and with *thy* Thunder overawest *the World*, what so high Offence against thee could my Æneas or the Trojans be guilty of, that, after having suffered so many Deaths, they must be shut out from all the wide World upon account of Italy? *Yet* sure you promised, that in some future Age, after *a Series of* circling Years, the Romans should *descend* from them, powerful Leaders spring *even* from the Blood of Teucer restored, who should be Masters of the Sea, who should rule the Nations with absolute Sway. *Almighty* Father! whence is thy Purpose changed? *I*, indeed, was solacing *myself* with this *Promise* under Troy's Fall and sad Catastrophe, with adverse Fates balancing Fates *more prosperous*. But

NOTES.

Beginning of the fifth Book of his *Paradise Lost*, where he describes *Eve* sorrowful and dejected, for having dreamed of eating the forbidden Fruit. There are several parallel Circumstances in that Description which makes it probable *Milton* had this Passage in his Eye. I shall only transcribe those Lines where *Eve* is seen in Tears;

So chear'd he his fair Spouse, and she was chear'd,
But silently a gentle Tear let fall
From either Eye, and wip'd them with her Hair;
Two other precious Drops, that ready stood,
Each in their chrystal Juice, *he, ere they fell, Kiss'd, &c.*

That fine Circumstance, in the fourth and fifth Lines, is almost a literal Translation of *Virgil*'s *Lacrymis oculos suffusa nitentes.*

235. *Revocato à sanguine Teucri.* The Commentators are puzzled in explaining this Passage, because *Teucer* was not originally from *Italy*. *La Cerda*'s Solution, taken from *Corradus*, appears the easiest and most natural. By the *sanguine Teucri revocato*, he understands the *Trojans*, *Teucer*'s Offspring, restored to their pristine Liberty, Power, and Grandeur, in the same Sense with what *Venus* says in the End of her Speech, *Sic nos in sceptra reponis?*

239. *Fatis contraria, &c.* If *Venus* knew that *Æneas*'s future Settlement in *Italy* was promised by *Jupiter*, and destined by Fate, why was she afraid of its not being accomplished? The Answer is, That the Opposition which that Event met with from *Juno*, made her waver and doubtful of her having been mistaken. For *Jupiter* alone had a perfect Insight into Futurity, and the other Deities knew no more of it than he was pleased to reveal to them;

Quæ Phœbo pater omnipotens, mihi Phœbus Apollo
Prædixit. Æn. III. 251.

I shall here take Occasion to remark, that they do *Virgil* Injustice, who alledge he makes *Jupiter* dependent on Fate or Destiny. Whereas it appears plain, from a Variety of Passages, that his Notion of Fate is strictly just and philosophical: For he makes Fate to be nothing else but the Counsels or Decrees pronounced by the Mouth of *Jove*, as the very Etymology of the Word implies, *Fatum à fari.* Thus he is represented as the great Dispenser of Fate in the third Book of the Æneid,

—— *sic*

Nunc eadem fortuna viros tot caſibus actos
Inſequitur: quem das finem, Rex magne, laborum?
Antenor potuit, mediis elapſus Achivis,
Illyricos penetrare ſinus, atque intima tutus
Regna Liburnorum, et fontem ſuperare Timavi;
Unde per ora novem vaſto cum murmure montis
It mare proruptum, et pelago premit arva ſonanti.

Nunc eadem fortuna inſequitur viros actos tot caſibus: O magne Rex, quem finem laborum das? Antenor, elapſus mediis Achivis, potuit tutus penetrare Illyricos ſinus, atque intima regna Liburnorum, et ſuperare fontem Timavi; unde per novem ora it mare proruptum cum vaſto murmure montis, & premit arva ſonanti pelago.

TRANSLATION.

now the ſame *hard* Fortune *ſtill* purſues them, after they have been toſſed *and afflicted* with ſuch Variety of Woes. Great Sovereign *of the World*, what End to their Labours wilt thou *vouchſafe* to give? Antenor, eſcaped from amidſt the Greeks, could pierce the Illyrian Gulph, and in Safety *reach* the inmoſt Realms of Liburnia, and overpaſs the Springs of Timavus: Whence, through nine Mouths, with loud Echoing from the Mountain, it burſts away *like* a Sea impetuous, and ſweeps the Fields with a roaring Deluge. Yet *even* there he built the City Padua,

NOTES.

———— *ſic fata Deûm rex*
Sortitur, volvitque vices: is vertitur ordo.

Hence we ſee in this very Paſſage *Jupiter's* Promiſe, and Fate, are mentioned in ſynonymous Phraſes: *Certe hinc—pollicitus.*——And therefore, ſays *Venus*,

Me ſolabar fatis contraria fata rependens.

And *Jupiter* in his Anſwer opens to her more plainly the Fate of her Race, and aſſures her it was unalterably fixed and certain,

—— *manent immota tuorum fata tibi.*

For his Purpoſe was not changed, *Neque me ſententia vertit.* And he concludes, *Sic placitum*, ſuch is my Will, theſe are my Decrees. To make this ſtill more evident, *Virgil* often calls Deſtiny *fata Divûm*, which can ſignify nothing but the divine Counſels or Decrees; and if he gives Fate the Epithets of *inexpugnabile*, *inexorabile*, he muſt mean, that the Laws and Order of Nature, in a Word, all Events whatever, are fixed and immutable, as being the Reſult of conſummate Wiſdom and Foreſight, and having their Foundation in the divine Mind, which is ſubject to none of thoſe Changes that affect impotent and injudicious Mortals. As to that Paſſage in the tenth Book of the Æneid, where *Jove* to comfort *Hercules* for the Death of *Pallas*, tells him,

———— *Trojæ ſub mœnibus altis*
Tot nati cecidere Deûm; quin occidit una
Sarpedon mea progenies: etiam ſua Turnum
Fata vocant, metaſque dati pervenit ad ævi.

Whence Mr. *Dryden* infers, that the King of the Gods himſelf acknowledges he could not alter Fate, nor ſave his own Son, and prevent the Death which he foreſaw. Mr. *Pope* has given a ſatisfactory Anſwer, that this Paſſage amounts to no more than that *Jupiter* gave Way to Deſtiny.

246. *It mare proruptum.* Monſieur *Catrou* contends that this ſhould be underſtood literally, but in that Opinion he is, and, I think, always will be, ſingular. Though the *Timavus* is now but a pitiful Rivulet, yet *Servius* aſſures us, from *Varro*, it was formerly ſo large a River, as actually to get the Name of a Sea from the neighbouring Inhabitants. The *French* Tranſlator's Criticiſm would deſtroy all the Beauty of two of the fineſt Lines in *Virgil*. They bring to my Mind the Deſcription of a River ſwelled over all its Banks by Torrents of Rain in Mr. *Thomſon's* Winter:

At laſt the rouſ'd up River pours along,
Reſiſtleſs, roaring; dreadful down it comes
From the chapt Mountain, and the moſſy Wild,
Tumbling thro' Rocks abrupt, and ſounding far;
Then o'er the ſanded Valley floating ſpreads,
Calm, ſluggiſh, ſilent; till again conſtrain'd,
Betwixt two meeting Hills it burſts away,
Where Rocks and Woods o'erhang the turbid Stream;
There gathering triple Force, rapid, and deep,
It boils, and wheels, and foams, and thunders thro'.

248. *Genti*

Ille tamen locavit hic urbem Patavi ſedeſque Teucrorum, et dedit nomen genti, fixitque Troïa arma: nunc quietus compoſitus in placida pace. Nos, tua progenies, quibus annuis arcem cœli, navibus amiſſis, infandum! prodimur ob iram unius, atque disjungimur longè ab oris Italis. Hicne eſt honos pietatis? Sicne reponis nos in ſceptra?

Sator hominum atque Deorum ſubridens olli vultu quo ſerenat cœlum tempeſtateſque, libavit oſcula natæ: dehinc fatur talia: O Cytherea, parce metu; fata tuorum manent tibi immota; cernes urbem et promiſſa mœnia Lavini, fereſque magnanimum Æneam ſublimem ad ſidera cœli: neque ſententia vertit me. Hic geret ingens bellum in Italia (ego enim fabor tibi quando hæc cura remordet te, et movebo arcana fatorum, volvens ea longius)

Hic tamen ille urbem Patavi, ſedeſque locavit
Teucrorum, et genti nomen dedit, armaque fixit
Troïa: nunc placidâ compoſtus pace quieſcit.
Nos, tua progenies, cœli quibus annuis arcem,
Navibus (infandùm) amiſſis, unius ob iram
Prodimur, atque Italis longè disjungimur oris.
Hic pietatis honos? ſic nos in ſceptra reponis?
   Olli ſubridens hominum ſator atque Deorum,
Vultu quo cœlum tempeſtateſque ſerenat,
Oſcula libavit natæ: dehinc talia fatur:
Parce metu Cytherea; manent immota tuorum
Fata tibi; cernes urbem et promiſſa Lavini
Mœnia, ſublimemque feres ad ſidera cœli
Magnanimum Æneam: neque me ſententia vertit.
Hic (tibi fabor enim, quando hæc te cura remordet,
Longiùs et volvens fatorum arcana movebo)

TRANSLATION.

and eſtabliſhed a Trojan Settlement, gave the Nation a *new* Name, and ſet up the Arms of Troy. Now in calm Peace compoſed he reſts: *But* we, thy *own* Progeny, whom thou, by thy unalterable *Nod*, ordaineſt *to ſit* inthroned in Heaven, *even we (Oh the* unutterable!) having loſt our Ships, are given up *to endleſs Dangers*, driven hither and thither far from the Italian Coaſt, *and* all to gratify the Spight of one. Are theſe the Honours wherewith thou crowneſt our Piety? Is it thus thou replaceſt us on the Throne?

The Sire of Gods and Men ſmiling upon her, with that *ſerene* Aſpect wherewith he clears the tempeſtuous Sky, gently kiſſed his Daughter's Lips, then thus replies: *My* Cytherea, ceaſe from Fear: Immoveable to thee remain thy People's Fates. Thou ſhalt ſee the City and promiſed Walls of Lavinium, and ſhalt raiſe magnanimous Æneas aloft to the Stars of Heaven; nor is my Purpoſe changed. In Italy he (for I will ſpeak to thee *without Reſerve*, ſince this Care lies gnawing at thy Heart, and, tracing farther back, I will reveal the Secrets of Fate) ſhall

NOTES.

243. *Genti nomen dedit.* Livy tells us he called the Place *Troy* where they firſt landed.

250. *Nos.* *Venus* ſpeaks in the Name of *Æneas*, to ſhew how nearly ſhe had his Intereſt at Heart.

250. *Annuis.* Has a particular Propriety in this Place, as expreſſed in the Tranſlation.

251. *Infandum.* This Word is thrown in like an interjecting Sigh, when ſhe comes to the moſt moving Part of her Complaint; and the artful Pauſes in this and the two following Lines, together with the abrupt Manner in which the Speech breaks off, ſhew her quite overpowered by the Tide of her Grief.

255. *Cœlum tempeſtateſque.* For *tempeſtates cœli*, as above *molemque & montes* for *molem montium*.

262. *Movebo.* Reveal, or remove them from their Obſcurity. *Moveo* implies the Greatneſs of the Undertaking.

Bellum ingens geret Italiâ, populosque feroces
Contundet; moresque viris et mœnia ponet,
Tertia dum Latio regnantem viderit æstas,
Ternaque transierint Rutulis hiberna subactis.
At puer Ascanius, cui nunc cognomen Iülo
Additur (Ilus erat, dum res stetit Ilia regno)
Triginta magnos, volvendis mensibus, orbes
Imperio explebit, regnumque à sede Lavini
Transferet, et longam multâ vi muniet Albam.
Hìc jam tercentum totos regnabitur annos
Gente sub Hectorea; donec regina sacerdos
Marte gravis geminam partu dabit Ilia prolem.
Inde lupæ fulvo nutricis tegmine lætus
Romulus excipiet gentem, et Mavortia condet
Mœnia, Romanosque suo de nomine dicet.
His ego nec metas rerum, nec tempora pono;
Imperium sine fine dedi: quin aspera Juno,
Quæ mare nunc terrasque metu cœlumque fatigat,

contunditque feroces populos, ponetque mores et mœnia viris, dum tertia æstas viderit eum regnantem in Latio, ternaque hiberna tempora transierint, Rutulis subactis. At puer Ascanius, cui cognomen additur Iülo (Ilus erat, dum Ilia res stetit regno) explebit imperio triginta magnos orbes, mensibus volvendis, transferetque regnum ab sede Lavini, et muniet Albam Longam multâ vi. Hìc jam regnabitur tercentum totos annos sub Hectorea gente, donec Ilia, Regina sacerdos, gravis ex Marte, dabit geminam prolem partu. Inde Romulus, lætus fulvo tegmine lupæ suæ nutricis, excipiet gentem, et condet Mavortia mœnia, dicetque Romanos de suo nomine. Ego pono his nec metas rerum nec tempora: dedi illis imperium sine fine. Quin aspera Juno, quæ nunc metu fatigat mare terrasque cœlumque,

TRANSLATION.

wage a mighty War, crush a stubborn Nation, and establish Laws and Cities to his People, till the third Summer shall see him reigning in Latium, and three Winters pass after he has subdued the Rutulians. But the Boy Ascanius, who has now the additional Sirname of Iulus (Ilus he was, while the Empire of Ilium flourished) shall measure with his Reign full thirty great *solar* Circles of *twelve* revolving Months, transfer the Seat of his Empire from Lavinium, and strongly fortify Alba Longa. Here again, for full three hundred Years, the Scepter shall be swayed by Hector's Line, until Ilia, a royal Priestess, impregnated by Mars, shall bear two Infants at a Birth. Then Romulus, exulting in the tawny Hide of the Wolf his Nurse, shall take upon him the Rule of the Nation, build a City sacred to Mars, and from his own Name call *the People* Romans. To them I fix neither Limits nor Duration of Empire: Dominion have I given *them* without End. Nay more, *even* sullen Juno, who now, through jealous Fear, creates endless Disturbance to Sea, and Earth, and Heaven, *even she* shall change her

NOTES.

263. *Bellum ingens geret.* The Poet, by putting these Predictions in the Mouth of *Jove* himself, gives his Readers a very exalted Idea of his Hero, and of the Dignity of the *Romans*; while at the same Time it furnishes him with a fine Opportunity of celebrating the more remarkable Periods of their History, particularly the Victories of *Cæsar*, and the Glories of *Augustus*'s peaceful Reign, which he considers as a second golden Age, in those noted Lines,

Aspera tum positis mitescent sæcula bellis, &c.

266. *Hiberna.* *Tempora* is understood.

267. *Cui nunc cognomen Iülo.* This Circumstance is thrown in to shew the Origin of the *Julian* Family, and the important Occasion of changing its Founder's Name from *Ilus* to *Julus* or *Iülus*.

278. *Metas rerum.* *Virgil* uses the Word

referet consilia in melius, fovebitque mecum Romanos dominos rerum, gentemque togatam. Sic placitum est. Ætas veniet, lustris labentibus, cum domus Assaraci servitio premet Phthiam [et] Mycenas claras, ac dominabitur victis Argis. Cæsar nascetur Trojanus pulchrâ origine, qui terminet suum imperium Oceano, qui terminet famam astris, Julius, nomen demissum à magno Iülo. Tu secura olim accipies hunc cœlo onustum spoliis Orientis: Hic quoque vocabitur votis. Tum aspera secula mitescent, bellis positis. Cana fides, et Vesta, Quirinus cum fratre Remo, dabunt jura: diræ portæ belli claudentur ferro et arctis compagibus: impius furor sedens intus super sæva arma, et vinctus post tergum centum ahenis nodis, fremet horridus ore cruento.

Consilia in melius referet, mecumque fovebit
Romanos rerum dominos, gentemque togatam.
Sic placitum. Veniet lustris labentibus ætas,
Cui domus Assaraci Phthiam clarasque Mycenas
Servitio premet, ac victis dominabitur Argis.
Nascetur pulchrâ Trojanus origine Cæsar,
Imperium Oceano, famam qui terminet astris,
Julius, à magno demissum nomen Iülo.
Hunc tu olim cœlo, spoliis Orientis onustum,
Accipies secura: vocabitur hic quoque votis.
Aspera tum positis mitescent secula bellis:
Cana fides, et Vesta, Remo cum fratre Quirinus
Jura dabunt: diræ ferro et compagibus arctis
Claudentur belli portæ: Furor impius intus
Sæva sedens super arma, et centum vinctus ahenis
Post tergum nodis, fremet horridus ore cruento.

TRANSLATION.

Counsels for the better, and join with me in befriending the Romans, *those* Lords of the World, and the Nation of the Gown. Such is my Pleasure. An Age shall come, after a Course of Years, when the Race of Assaracus shall bring under Subjection Phthia and renowned Mycenæ, and reign over vanquished Argos. A Trojan shall be born of illustrious Race, Cæsar, whose Empire the Ocean, whose Fame the Stars shall bound, Julius his Name, from great Iülus derived. Him, loaded with the Spoils of the East, you shall receive to Heaven at length, having seen an End of all your Cares: He too shall be invoked by Vows and Prayers. Then, Wars having ceased, fiercer Nations shall soften into Peace. Faith, *with her hoary reverend Locks*, Vesta, and Quirinus, with his Brother Remus, shall *then* administer Justice. The dreadful Gates of War shall be shut with close Bolts and *Bars of* Iron. Within *the Temple* impious Fury, sitting on horrid Arms, and his Hands bound behind his Back with a hundred brazen Chains, in hideous Rage shall gnash his bloody Jaws.

NOTES.

res for Dominion or Empire, both here, and in many other Places. See above, Verse 268, and *Æneid* III. 1.

Postquam res Asiæ, &c.

282. *Gentemque togatam.* The *Toga*, or Gown, was the distinguishing Dress of the *Romans*, as the *Pallium* of the *Greeks*.

284. *Domus Assaraci.* The *Romans* descended from *Assaracus* by *Æneas*, who was his Great-grandson. *Phthia* and *Mycenæ* were the royal Seats of *Achilles* and *Agamemnon*. The Poet, say *Servius* refers to *Mummius*, who conquered *Achaia*: Others to *Paulus Æmilius*, who subdued *Macedonia*, by which Means *Thessaly*, the Country of *Achilles*, became subject to the *Romans*.

291. *Cana fides.* Alluding to the Figure of Faith, which was represented with hoary Locks, to signify that this was the peculiar Virtue of ancient Times. Hence that Exclamation, *Heu pietas, heu prisca fides!*

294. *Claudentur.* The Gates of the Temple of *Janus* were opened in Time of War, and shut in Time of Peace.

294. *Furor impius.* *Pliny* tells us that the Image of warlike Rage was drawn in this Manner

Hæc ait, et Maiâ genitum demittit ab alto,
Ut terræ, utque novæ pateant Carthaginis arces
Hoſpitio Teucris; ne, fati neſcia, Dido
Finibus arceret: volat ille per aëra magnum
Remigio alarum, ac Libyæ citus adſtitit oris.
Et jam juſſa facit: ponuntque ferocia Pœni
Corda, volente Deo: in primis Regina quietum
Accipit in Teucros animum mentemque benignam.
At pius Æneas per noctem plurima volvens,
Ut primùm lux alma data eſt, exire, locoſque
Explorare novos, quas vento acceſſerit oras;
Qui teneant (nam inculta videt) hominesne, feræne,
Quærere conſtituit, ſociiſque exacta referre.
Claſſem in convexo nemorum, ſub rupe cavata,
Arboribus clauſam circum atque horrentibus umbris

Ait hæc, et ab alto cœli demittit genitum Maia, ut terræ, utque arces novæ Carthaginis pateant hoſpitio Teucris; ne Dido neſcia fati arceret eos à ſuis finibus. Ille remigio alarum volat per magnum aëra, ac citus adſtitit oris Libyæ. Et jam facit juſſa: Pœnique ponunt ſua ferocia corda, Deo volente: imprimis Regina Dido accipit in Teucros animum quietum mentemque benignam.

At pius Æneas volvens plurima per noctem, ut primùm alma lux eſt data, conſtituit exire, explorareque locos novos, quærere in quas oras acceſſerit vento, qui teneant eas, homineſne feræne, nam videt loca *inculta, referreque ſociis exacta. Occulit claſſem in convexo nemorum, ſub cavata rupe, clauſam circum arboribus atque umbris horrentibus.*

TRANSLATION.

He ſaid, and from on high ſent down Maia's Son, that the Coaſts of Libya and the new-built Towers of Carthage might be open hoſpitably to receive the Trojans; leſt Dido, ignorant of Heaven's Decree, ſhould ſhut them out from her Ports. He, on the Steerage of his Wings, ſhoots away through the expanded Sky, and ſpeedily lighted on the Coaſts of Libya. And now he puts his Orders in Execution; and, at the Will of the God, the Carthaginians lay aſide the Fierceneſs of their Hearts. The Queen, eſpecially, entertains Thoughts of Peace, and a benevolent Diſpoſition towards the Trojans.

But the pious Æneas, by Night revolving a thouſand *Cares*, reſolved, as ſoon as cheerful Day aroſe, to ſet out, in order to view the unknown Country, *to examine* on what Coaſts he was driven by the Wind, who are the Inhabitants, whether Men or wild Beaſts (for he ſees nothing but *waſte*, uncultivated Grounds), and inform his Friends of what Diſcoveries he makes. Within *the Shelter of* a winding Grove, under a hollow Rock, he ſecretly diſpoſed his Fleet, fenced round

NOTES.

ner by *Apelles*, and dedicated by *Auguſtus* in his *Forum*: But, becauſe that *Forum* was not then dedicated, others refer it to the Statue of *Mars*, which the *Spartans* had in their City bound with Chains of Braſs, as *Virgil* here deſcribes, and as *Mars* is repreſented in *Homer*, Il. V. 386.

305. *At pius Æneas.* This is the Idea of a good Prince, Il. I. v. 25.

Ου χρη παννυχιον ευδειν βουληφορον ανδρα,
Ω λαοι τ' επιτετραφαται, και τοσσα μεμηλε.
Ill fits a Chief who mighty Nations guides,
Directs in Council, and in War preſides,
To whom its Safety a whole People owes,
To waſte long Nights in indolent Repoſe.

Pope's Il. II. 27.

In like Manner *Homer* repreſents *Agamemnon* awake, and ſolicitous for the common Intereſt, while

Ipse graditur comitatus Achate uno, crispans manu bina hastilia lato ferro.

Cui mater obvia tulit sese in media sylva, gerens os habitumque virginis, et arma virginis Spartanæ; vel talis qualis Threissa Harpalyce fatigat equos, fugâque prævertitur volucrem Hebrum. Namque venatrix humeris suspenderat habilem arcum de more, dederatque suam comam ventis diffundere, nuda genu, collectaque fluentes sinus nodo. Ac prior inquit: heus juvenes, monstrate si quam mearum sororum forte vidistis hic errantem, succinctam pharetrâ et tegmine maculosæ lyncis, aut clamore prementem cursum apri spumantis. Sic Venus locuta est: at filius Veneris contra orsus est loqui sic: nulla tuarum sororum audita est neque visa mihi. O virgo, quam memorem te! namque haud est tibi mortalis visus,

Occulit: ipse uno graditur comitatus Achate,
Bina manu lato crispans hastilia ferro.
Cui Mater mediâ sese tulit obvia silvâ,
Virginis os habitumque gerens, et virginis arma
Spartanæ; vel qualis equos Threïssa fatigat
Harpalyce, volucremque fugâ prævertitur Hebrum.
Namque humeris, de more, habilem suspenderat arcum
Venatrix, dederatque comas diffundere ventis;
Nuda genu, nodoque sinus collecta fluentes.
Ac prior, Heus, inquit, juvenes, monstrate mearum
Vidistis si quam hìc errantem forte sororum,
Succinctam pharetrâ et maculosæ tegmine lyncis,
Aut spumantis apri cursum clamore prementem.
Sic Venus; at Veneris contra sic filius orsus:
Nulla tuarum audita mihi neque visa sororum.
O, quam te memorem, virgo! namque haud tibi vultus

TRANSLATION.

with Trees and gloomy Shades: Himself marches forth, attended with Achates alone, brandishing in his Hand two Javelins of broad-pointed Steel.

To whom, in the Midst of a Wood, his Mother presents herself, wearing the Mien and Attire of a Virgin, and the Arms of a Spartan Maid: Or resembling Thracian Harpalyce, when she tires her Steeds, and in her Course outflies the swift Hebrus. For, Huntress-like, she had hung from her Shoulders a commodious Bow, and gave her Hair to wanton in the Wind; bare to the Knee, with her flowing Robes gathered in a Knot. Then first *addressing them*, pray, *gentle* Youths, she says, inform me, if by Chance ye have seen any of my Sisters wandering this Way, equipped with a Quiver, and the Skin of a spotted Lynx, or with full Cry urging the Chace of a foaming Boar? Thus Venus *spoke*, and thus her Son replied: None of your Sisters has been heard or seen by me. O Virgin *fair*, by what Name shall I address thee! for thou wearest not the Looks of a Mortal, nor

NOTES.

while the rest of the *Græcian* Princes are enjoying soft Repose, Il. X.

Αλλοι μεν παρα νηυσιν αριστηες Παναχαιων
Ευδον παννυχιοι, μαλακω δεδμημενοι υπνω·
Αλλ' ουκ Ατρειδην Αγαμεμνονα ποιμενα λαων
Υπνος εχε γλυκερος, πολλα φρεσιν ορμαινοντα.

316. *Spartanæ.* The *Lacedæmonian* Virgins, according to *Lycurgus*'s Institution, were trained up to all Sorts of manly Exercises, such as Running, Wrestling, Throwing the Coit, or Javelin, but especially to Riding and Hunting. See *Plutarch* in the Life of *Lycurgus*.

317. *Hebrum.* It is easy for a Rider to outstrip the Course of the most rapid River; therefore some Commentators ingeniously conjecture that it ought to be read *Eurum*, the East wind; which is also in *Virgil*'s Stile, who says of *Camilla*, she was able to outrun the Winds;

——*cursuque pedum prævertere ventos.*

Besides, *volucrem* is not a very proper Epithet for a River, but is very applicable to the Wind, which is usually drawn by the Poets with Wings.

323. *Maculosæ tegmine Lyncis.* It was the Custom in ancient Times for Hunters to wear the Skins of the Animals they had killed in the Chace.

Mortalis, nec vox hominem sonat. O Dea, certè!
An Phœbi soror, an Nympharum sanguinis una?
Sis felix; nostrumque leves quæcunque laborem,
Et quo sub cœlo tandem, quibus orbis in oris
Jactemur, doceas: ignari hominumque locorumque
Erramus, vento huc vastis et fluctibus acti.
Multa tibi ante aras nostrâ cadet hostia dextrâ.
Tunc Venus: Haud equidem tali me dignor honore.
Virginibus Tyriis mos est gestare pharetram,
Purpureoque altè suras vincire cothurno.
Punica regna vides, Tyrios, et Agenoris urbem;
Sed fines Libyci, genus intractabile bello.
Imperium Dido Tyriâ regit urbe profecta,
Germanum fugiens: longa est injuria, longæ
Ambages: sed summa sequar fastigia rerum.
Huic conjux Sichæus erat, ditissimus agri
Phœnicum, et magno miseræ dilectus amore;
Cui pater intactam dederat, primisque jugarat
Ominibus: sed regna Tyri germanus habebat

nec vox tua sonat hominem. O Dea certè! an soror es Phœbi an una es sanguinis Nympharum? quæcunque es sis felix nobis, levesque nostrum laborem, et doceas sub quo cœlo, in quibus oris orbis tandem jactemur: erramus ignari hominumque locorumque, acti huc vento et vastis fluctibus. Multa hostia cadet tibi ante aras nostrâ dextrâ. Tunc Venus respondit: haud equidem dignor me tali honore. Mos est Tyriis virginibus gestare pharetram, vincireque suras altè purpureo cothurno. Vides Punica regna, Tyrios, et urbem Agenoris; sed fines sunt Libyci, genus intractabile bello. Dido regit imperium, quæ profecta est Tyriâ urbe, fugiens fratrem germanum: injuria est longa, longæ sunt ambages; sed sequar summa fastigia rerum. Conjux erat huic Sichæus, ditissimus Phœnicum agri, et dilectus magno amore miseræ Didonis; cui pater dederat eam intactam, jugaratque primis omnibus: sed Pygmalion frater germanus habebat regna Tyri,

TRANSLATION.

sounds thy Voice mere human Accents. A Goddess sure! Are you the Sister of Phœbus, or one of the Race of the Nymphs? Oh! be propitious, and, whoever you are, ease our anxious Minds, and inform us under what Climate, on what Region of the Globe we at length are thrown. *For here* we wander Strangers both to the Country and the Inhabitants, driven upon this Coast by *furious* Winds and swelling Seas. *So* shall many a Victim fall a Sacrifice at thine Altars by our Right-hand. Then Venus *replies:* I, indeed, deem not myself worthy of such Honour: It is the Custom for *us*, Tyrian Virgins, to wear a Quiver, and bind the Leg *thus* high with a Purple Buskin. Before you lies the Kingdom of Carthage, a Tyrian People, and Agenor's City. But the Country is that of Libya, *and the Natives* a Race invincibly fierce in War. The Kingdom is ruled by Dido, who fled *hither* from Tyre, to shun her Brother's Hate. Tedious is *the Relation* of her Wrongs, and intricate the Circumstances *of her Story*. But I shall trace the principal Heads. Her Husband was Sichæus, the richest of the Phœnicians in Land, and passionately beloved by his unhappy Spouse. Her Father gave her to him in her Virgin Bloom, and joined her in Wedlock with the first connubial Rites. But her Brother Pygmalion then possessed the Throne of Tyre, monstrous-

TRANSLATION.

329. *An Phœbi soror.* Diana.

338. *Agenoris urbem.* *Agenor* was one of *Dido*'s Ancestors, her Great-grandfather, say some.

345. *Primisque jugarat ominibus.* As in most other Actions of Life, so particularly in Marriages, the *Romans* consulted Omens and Presages, to know whether they would prove happy or unfortunate.

348. *Quos*

immanior scelere ante alios omnes. Inter quos furor venit medius: ille impius, atque cæcus amore auri, clam superat ferro Sichæum incautum ante aras, securus amorum sororis suæ germanæ: diuque celavit factum; et malus simulans multa lusit ægram amantem vanâ spe. Sed ipsa imago conjugis inhumati venit ad eam in somnis, attollens ora pallida miris modis; nudavit aras crudeles, pectoraque trajecta ferro, retexitque omne cæcum scelus domûs. Tum suadet ei celerare fugam, excedereque patriâ; recluditque in tellure veteres thesauros auxilium viæ, ignotum pondus argenti et auri. Dido commota his parabat fugam sociosque. Conveniunt omnes quibus erat aut crudele odium aut acer metus tyranni: corripiunt naves quæ forte erant paratæ, onerantque eas auro: opes avari

Pygmalion, scelere ante alios immanior omnes.
Quos inter medius venit furor: ille Sichæum
Impius ante aras, atque auri cæcus amore,
Clam ferro incautum superat, securus amorum
Germanæ: factumque diu celavit; et ægram,
Multa malus simulans, vanâ spe lusit amantem.
Ipsa sed in somnis inhumati venit imago
Conjugis, ora modis attollens pallida miris:
Crudeles aras, trajectaque pectora ferro
Nudavit, cæcumque domûs scelus omne retexit.
Tum celerare fugam, patriâque excedere suadet;
Auxiliumque viæ veteres tellure recludit
Thesauros, ignotum argenti pondus et auri.
His commota, fugam Dido sociosque parabat.
Conveniunt, quibus aut odium crudele tyranni,
Aut metus acer erat: naves, quæ forte paratæ,
Corripiunt, onerantque auro: portantur avari

TRANSLATION.

ly wicked beyond all Mortals. Between them two an implacable Hatred arose. He, impiously inhuman, and blinded with the Love of Gold, having taken Sichæus at a Surprize, secretly assassinates him before the Altar, regardless of his Sister's Love. Long he kept the *horrid* Deed concealed, and, forging many wicked Lies, amused the love-sick *Queen* with vain Hope. But the Ghost of her unburied Husband appeared *to her* in a Dream, lifting up his Visage amazingly pale and ghastly: He opened to her View the bloody Altars, and his Breast transfixed with the Sword, and detected all the hidden Villany of the Family: Then exhorts her to fly with Speed, and quit her native Country; and, to aid her Flight, reveals a Treasure that had been long *hid* in the Earth, an unknown Mass of Gold and Silver. Dido, rouzed by this awful Message, provided Friends, and prepared to fly. *A select Band* assembles, *consisting of those* who either mortally hated, or violently dreaded the Tyrant: What Ships by Chance lay ready they seize in haste, and load with Gold. The Wealth of the covetous Pygmalion is

NOTES.

348. *Quos inter medius venit furor.* Virgil seems to ascribe *Pygmalion*'s bloody Deed not to the Instigation of a furious Passion, but to the Covetousness of his wicked Heart,

Impius—atque auri cæcus amore.

Servius therefore, and others, join the *quos inter medius venit furor* with the former Verse; which makes the Sense turn out, *that* Pygmalion had *deliberately* committed a more horrid and atrocious Crime, than any had ever been prompted to by the sudden Impulse of furious Enmity or outrageous Passion.

350. *Securus amorum.* Regardless of his Sister's Love; so *Horace*, 2 Ep. II. 17.

Ille ferat pretium pœnæ securus.

354. *Ora modis attollens pallida miris.* Not *attollens miris modis*, as *Ruæus* explains it, but *miris modis pallida*; as in *Lucretius*, from whom *Virgil* has borrowed the Expression,

Sed quædam simulacra modis pallentia miris.
Lib. I. 124.

355. *Crudeles aras.* The Altar where the cruel Deed had been acted. *Sichæus*, whom *Justin* calls *Acerbas*, was Priest of *Hercules*, and was murdered when serving the Altar.

359. *Ignotum*, &c. This is illustrated by what we read in the same Author: *Huic (Acerbæ sive Sichæo) magnæ, sed dissimulatæ opes erant:*

Pygmalionis opes pelago: dux femina facti.
Devenere locos, ubi nunc ingentia cernes
Mœnia, surgentemque novæ Carthaginis arcem;
Mercatique solum, facti de nomine Byrsam,
Taurino quantum possent circumdare tergo.
Sed vos qui tandem? quibus aut venistis ab oris?
Quòve tenetis iter? Quærenti talibus, ille
Suspirans, imoque trahens à pectore vocem:
O Dea, si primâ repetens ab origine pergam,
Et vacet annales nostrorum audire laborum;
Ante diem clauso componet vesper Olympo.
Nos Trojâ antiquâ (si vestras forte per aures
Trojâ nomen iit) diversa per æquora vectos,
Forte suâ Libycis tempestas appulit oris.
Sum pius Æneas, raptos qui ex hoste Penates
Classe veho mecum; famâ super æthera notus.
Italiam quæro patriam, et genus ab Jove summo.

Pygmalionis portantur pelago: femina erat *dux facti. Devenere* ad *locos, ubi nunc cernes ingentia mœnia, arcemque surgentem novæ Carthaginis; mercatique* sunt *solum Byrsam* dictam *de nomine facti*, tantum *quantum possent circumdare taurino tergo. Sed qui tandem* estis *vos? aut ab quibus oris venistis? quòve tenetis iter? Ille suspirans, trahensque vocem ab imo pectore*, respondit huic *quærenti talibus* verbis: *O Dea, si* ego *repetens ab prima origine pergam, et* si *vacet* tibi *audire annales nostrorum laborum, vesper ante componet diem, Olympo clauso. Tempestas forte suâ appulit Libycis oris nos vectos per diversa æquora* ab *antiqua Troja (si forte nomen Trojæ iit per vestras aures)*. Ego *sum pius Æneas, qui veho mecum* in *classe Penates raptos ex hoste, notus famâ super æthera. Quæro Italam patriam, et genus* est mihi *à summo Jove.*

TRANSLATION.

conveyed over Sea. A Woman guides the whole Exploit. Thither they came, where now you will see the stately Walls and rising Towers of new-built Carthage, and bought as much Ground as they could inclose with a Bull's Hide, *thence called* Byrsa, in Commemoration of the Action. But *say* now, who are you? Or from what Coasts ye came, or whither are you bound? To these her Demands the Hero, with heavy sighs, and slow raising his Words from the Bottom of his Breast, *thus replies:* If I, O Goddess! tracing from their early Source, shall pursue, and you have Leisure to hear the Annals of our Woes, the Evening Star will shut Heaven's Gates upon the expiring Day before *my Tale be finished.* Driven over a Length of Seas from ancient Troy (if the Name of Troy hath casually reached your Ears), a Tempest, by its *usual* Chance, threw us on *this* Libyan Coast. I am Æneas the Pious, renowned by Fame above the Skies, who carry with me in my Fleet the Gods I snatched away from the Enemy. For Italy my Course is bent, and my Descendants sprung from Jove supreme. With twice

NOTES.

erant: aurumque metu regis non tectis, sed terræ crediderat; quam rem etsi homines ignorabant, fama tamen loquebatur. Lib. XVIII. Cap. 4. The other Particulars of the History are also related in the Place here referred to, and in the following Chapter.

374.—*diem clauso componet vesper Olympo.* The Night was supposed by the Ancients to have the Charge of shutting up the Gates of Heaven, and the Day of opening them; of which many Examples occur in the Poets. This then is the Meaning of *clauso Olympo: Componet diem* again, shall bury, or seal up the Day, alludes to the poetical Way of conceiving the Morning as the Birth of a new Day, and the Evening as its Death: *Dies quidem jam ad umbilicum dimidiatus est mortuus*, says *Plautus* in *Menæch. Componere diem* therefore is to *seal*, or *close up* the expired Day, *ut reliquias in urna*, as the Bones and Ashes of the Dead use to be shut up in an Urn.

378. *Sum pius Æneas, famâ super æthera*

Conſcendi Phrygium æquor bis denis navibus, matre Deâ monſtrante mihi *viam, ſecutus fata* mihi *data: ſeptem convulſæ undis Euroque vix ſuperſunt.* Ego *ipſe ignotus, egens, peragro deſerta Libyæ, pulſus ex Europâ atque Aſia. Nec Venus paſſa* eum *querentem plura* dicere, *ſic interfata eſt* in *medio dolore: quiſquis es, carpis vitales auras, haud, credo, inviſus cœleſtibus* Diis, *qui adveneris urbem Tyriam. Perge modò, atque perfer te hinc ad limina Reginæ: namque nuntio* tibi *ſocios* eſſe *reduces claſſemque relatam, et actam in tutum* locum *Aquilonibus verſis; ni vani parentes docuere* me *augurium fruſtra.*

Bis denis Phrygium conſcendi navibus æquor;
Matre Deâ monſtrante viam, data fata ſecutus:
Vix ſeptem convulſæ undis Euroque ſuperſunt.
Ipſe ignotus, egens, Libyæ deſerta peragro;
Europâ atque Aſiâ pulſus. Nec plura querentem
Paſſa Venus, medio ſic interfata dolore eſt: 386
Quiſquis es, haud (credo) inviſus cœleſtibus auras
Vitales carpis, Tyriam qui adveneris urbem.
Perge modò, atque hinc te Reginæ ad limina perfer: 389
Namque tibi reduces ſocios, claſſemque relatam
Nuntio, et in tutum verſis Aquilonibus actam;
Ni fruſtra augurium vani docuere parentes.

TRANSLATION.

ten Ships I embarked on the Phrygian Sea in queſt of a Settlement reſerved for me by Heaven's Decree, my Goddeſs-Mother pointing out the Way. Seven, with much ado, are ſaved, *and thoſe too* torn and ſhattered by Waves and Wind. Myſelf, a Stranger, poor and deſtitute, wander through the Deſarts of Africa, baniſhed from Europe and from Aſia. Venus, unable to bear his further Complaints, thus interrupted *him* in the midſt of his Grief: Whoever you be, I truſt you live not unbefriended by the Powers of Heaven, who have arrived at a Tyrian City. *Fear nothing*, but forthwith bend your Courſe directly to the Palace of the Queen: For, that your Friends have eſcaped the Dangers of the Main, your Fleet ſaved, and, by a *favourable* Turn of the North-wind, wafted into a ſafe Harbour, I pronounce to thee with Aſſurance; unleſs my Parents, fond of a lying Art, have taught me Divination to no Purpoſe. See *theſe*

NOTES.

ectus. *Pius* may be conſidered as a Title or Name commonly given to *Æneas*, as expreſſive of his Character, and that Name by which he was beſt known. Juſt as *Ariſtides* was ſtiled *Juſtus*, and *Antoninus, Pius*. In this Senſe there is no Vanity in his taking that Appellation to himſelf. Beſides, he was then in a ſtrange Country, and addreſſing himſelf to one whom he took for a *Tyrian* Lady of the firſt Diſtinction, which made it neceſſary for him to make her acquainted with his perſonal Merit and exalted Character, that ſhe might treat him and his Followers with the greater Regard. After all, it muſt be acknowledged, that the Manners of the Age wherein *Æneas* lived, were not near ſo delicate in this Reſpect as thoſe of modern Times. *Homer*'s Heroes are every where forward to commend themſelves, and ſet their Virtues to Show. See particularly the ninth Book of the Odyſſey, Verſe 20, where *Ulyſſes* ſpeaks in the ſame Strain of Self-commendation.

382. *Matre Deâ monſtrante viam.* This perhaps is only a poetical Embelliſhment of an hiſtorical Circumſtance related by *Varro*, Lib. II. Rer. Div. *Ex quo de Troja eſt egreſſus Æneas, Veneris eum per diem quotidie ſtellam vidiſſe, donec ad agrum Laurentum veniret, in quo eam non vidit ulterius: qua re cognovit terras eſſe fatales.*

392. *Vani.* i. e. *Qui res inanes docent*, as we have rendered it; or it may ſignify *ignorant*, as Æn. X. 630.

——————*aut ego veri*
Vana feror.

Or *deluding*, as Æn. II. 80.

—*vanum etiam mendacemque improba finget.*

402. *Roſea*

Aspice bis senos lætantes agmine cycnos,
Ætheriâ quos lapsa plagâ Jovis ales aperto
Turbabat cœlo; nunc terras ordine longo
Aut capere, aut captas jam despectare videntur:
Ut reduces illi ludunt stridentibus alis,
Et cœtu cinxere polum, cantusque dedere;
Haud aliter puppesque tuæ pubesque tuorum,
Aut portum tenet, aut pleno subit ostia velo.
Perge modò, et quà te ducit via, dirige gressum.
  Dixit, et avertens roseâ cervice refulsit,
Ambrosiæque comæ divinum vertice odorem
Spiravere: pedes vestis defluxit ad imos,
Et vera incessu patuit Dea. Ille, ubi matrem

Aspice bis senos cycnos lætantes agmine, quos ales Jovis lapsa ab ætheria plaga turbabat in aperto cœlo; nunc videntur aut capere terras, longo ordine, aut despectare eas jam captas: Ut illi reduces ludunt stridentibus alis, et cinxere polum cœtu, dederequc cantus; haud aliter puppesque tuæ, pubesque tuorum aut tenet portum, aut subit ostia pleno velo. Perge modò, et dirige gressum quà via ducit te.

Dixit, et avertens refulsit roseâ cervice, comæque illius ambrosiæ spiravere divinum odorem è vertice: vestis ejus defluxit ad imos pedes, et ex incessu patuit vera Dea. Ille, ubi agnovit matrem,

TRANSLATION.

twelve Swans *now* triumphing in a Body; whom the Bird of Jove, shooting from the etherial Region, had chaced through the open Air: Now, in a long Train, they seem either to choose their Ground, or to hover over the Place where they have already chose to rest. As they, now out of Danger, sportive clap their rustling Wings, wheel about the Heavens in a *joyful* Troop, and raise their melodious Notes; just so your Ships and youthful Crew, either are *already* possessed of the Harbour, or enter the Port with full Sail. Proceed then, without further Concern, and pursue your Way where this Path directs.

She said, and, turning about, gave a bright Display of her rosy Neck, and from her Head the ambrosial Locks breathed divine Fragrance: Her Robe hung waving down to the Ground, and by her Gait the Goddess stood confessed. The Hero, soon as he knew his Mother, with these Accents pursued her as she fled:

NOTES.

402. *Roseâ cervice.* Answers to *Homer's*
—Θεας περικαλλεα δειρην.
The Goddess's beauteous Neck, Il. III. 396.
The Poets giving the Epithet of *rosy* to almost every beautiful Object or Feature. *Apuleius* describes *Venus*, *totum revincta corpus rosis micantibus.* And *Anacreon*, in his Ode to the Rose, has these Lines,

Ροδοδακτυλος μεν ηως,
The rosy-fingered Morn;
Ροδοπηχεες δε νυμφαι,
The Nymphs with rosy Arms;
Ροδοχρως δ' Αφροδιτη,
The rosy-coloured Venus.

But I see no Reason why it may not be taken here literally, as expressive of that particular Ruddiness and Blushing, which approaches near to the Colour of the Rose.

403. *Ambrosiæque comæ.* Thus *Homer* gives *Jove* ambrosial Locks:

Αμβροσιαι δ' αρα χαιται επερρωσαντο Ανακτος

He spoke, and awful bends his sable Brows,
Shakes his ambrosial Curls, and gives the Nod.
Pope's Iliad, I. 684.

And, describing *Juno's* Dress, he represents her pouring Ambrosia and other Perfumes all over her Body;

———Αλειψατο δε λιπ' ελαιῳ,
Αμβροσιῳ.

———*and round her Body pours*
Soft Oils of Fragrance, and ambrosial Show'rs.
Il. XII. 197.

Ambrosial Locks therefore may either signify *immortal and divine*, or *perfumed with Ambrosia.*

404. *Pedes vestis*, &c. This, they tell us, is one of the poetical Characteristics of Divinity, *a long sweeping Train*; and therefore *Venus*, while she chose to appear in Disguise, had concealed it, by tucking up the Skirts of her Robe,

Nuda genu, nodoque sinus collecta fluentes.

405. *Incessu patuit.* It was a current Opinion among the Heathens, that their Divinities did

ſecutus eſt eam fugientem tali voce: quid tu quoquè crudelis toties ludis cum falſis imaginibus? cur non datur mihi *jungere dextram dextræ, ac audire et reddere veras voces? incuſat* eam *talibus verbis, tenditque greſſum ad mœnia. At Venus obſcuro aëre ſepſit* eos *gradientes, et Dea circumfudit* eos *multo amictu nebulæ; ne quis poſſet cernere eos, neu quis* poſſet *contingere, vel moliri moram, aut poſcere* eos *cauſas veniendi. Ipſa ſublimis abit Paphum, lætaque reviſit ſuas ſedes; ubi templum* eſt *illi, centumque aræ calent Sabæo thure, halantque recentibus ſertis.*

Interea illi *corripuere viam, quà ſemita monſtrat: jamque aſcendebant collem, qui plurimus imminet urbi, deſuperque aſpectat arces adverſas. Æneas miratur molem, quondam magalia: miratur portas, ſtrepitumque, et ſtrata viarum.*

Agnovit, tali fugientem eſt voce ſecutus:
Quid natum toties crudelis tu quoquè falſis
Ludis imaginibus? cur dextræ jungere dextram
Non datur, ac veras audire et reddere voces?
Talibus incuſat, greſſumque ad mœnia tendit.
At Venus obſcuro gradientes aëre ſepſit,
Et multo nebulæ circum Dea fudit amictu;
Cernere ne quis eos, neu quis contingere poſſet,
Molirive moram, aut veniendi poſcere cauſas.
Ipſa Paphum ſublimis abit, ſedeſque reviſit
Læta ſuas; ubi templum illi, centumque Sabæo
Thure calent aræ, ſertiſque recentibus halant.
  Corripuere viam interea, quà ſemita monſtrat:
Jamque aſcendebant collem, qui plurimus urbi
Imminet, adverſaſque aſpectat deſuper arces.
Miratur molem Æneas, magalia quondam:
Miratur portas, ſtrepitumque, et ſtrata viarum.

TRANSLATION.

Ah, why ſo oft doſt thou too cruelly mock thy Son with borrowed Shapes? Why am I not indulged to join my Hand to thine, and to hear and anſwer thee by turns in Words ſincere and undiſſembled? Thus he expoſtulates with her, and directs his Courſe to the Town. But Venus ſkreened them in their Way with dark Clouds, and the Goddeſs ſpread around them a thick Veil of Miſt, that none might ſee, or touch, or give them Interruption, or enquire into the Reaſons of their coming. She herſelf wings her Way ſublime to Paphos, and with Joy reviſits her *happy* Seats; where, ſacred to her Honour, a Temple riſes, and a hundred Altars ſmoke with Sabean Incenſe, and with freſh Garlands perfume the Air.

Mean-while they urged their Way where the Path directs. And now they aſcended the Hill, which hangs over a great Part of the Town, and from above ſurveys its oppoſite Towers. *Here* Æneas admires the ſtately Buildings, *where* Cottages once *ſtood:* He admires the *lofty* Gates, the Hurry and Buſtle *of the Town*, and *the Magnificence of* the Streets. The Tyrians warmly ply the Work: Some

NOTES.

did not walk upon the Ground like Mortals, but ſkimmed along the Surface with a gentle gliding Motion like that in *Milton:*

So ſaying, by the Hand he took me rais'd,
And over Fields and Waters, as in Air
Smooth ſliding without Step—

Paradiſe Loſt, VIII. 300.

411. *At Venus obſcuro.* This is borrowed from *Homer*, Odyſſ. VII. near the Beginning, where *Pallas* ſpreads a Veil of Air round *Ulyſſes*, and renders him inviſible, as *Venus Æneas.* If the Reader would ſee the two compared, he may conſult *Scaliger* in the fifth Book of his Poetics.

417. *Thure calent aræ.* Incenſe, Flowers, and Perfumes were the only Offerings preſented to *Venus*, as we learn from *Tacitus*, 2 Hiſt. 2. *Hoſtiæ, ut quiſque voviſſet, mares deliguntur. Certiſſima fides hædorum fibris. Sanguinem aræ affundere vetitum; precibus & igne puro altaria adolentur.* From which Paſſage it appears, that though Victims were ſlain by her Votaries, particularly in order to conſult the Entrails, yet they were neither allowed to burn any Part of the

Inſtant ardentes Tyrii: pars ducere muros,
Molirique arcem, et manibus ſubvolvere ſaxa:
Pars aptare locum tecto, et concludere ſulco.
Jura, magiſtratuſque legunt, ſanctumque ſenatum.
Hìc portus alii effodiunt: hìc alta theatris
Fundamenta locant alii: immaneſque columnas
Rupibus excidunt, ſcenis decora alta futuris.
Qualis apes æſtate novâ per florea ruro
Exercet ſub Sole labor, cum gentis adultos
Educunt fœtus; aut cum liquentia mella
Stipant, et dulci diſtendunt nectare cellas;
Aut onera accipiunt venientum; aut, agmine facto,
Ignavum fucos pecus à præſepibus arcent:
Fervet opus, redolentque thymo fragrantia mella.

Tyrii ardentes inſtant; pars inſtat docere muros, molirique arcem, et ſubvolvere ſaxa manibus; pars aptare locum tecto, et concludere eum ſulco. Legunt jura magiſtratuſque, ſenatumque ſanctum. Hìc alii effodiunt portus: hìc alii locant alta fundamenta theatris, exciduntque rupibus immanes columnas, alta decora futuris ſcenis. Talis eſt eorum *labor qualis exercet apes in nova æſtate per florea rura; cum educunt adultos fœtus gentis, aut cum ſtipant liquentia mella, et diſtendunt cellas dulci nectare, aut accipiunt onera venientum, aut, agmine facto, arcent à præſepibus fucos pecus ignavum: Opus fervet, mellaque fragrantia thymo redolent.*

TRANSLATION.

are extending the Walls, and raiſing a Tower, or puſhing along unwieldy Stones: Some mark out the Ground for a private Building, and incloſe it with a Trench: Some chooſe *a Place* for the Courts of Juſtice, for the Magiſtrates Halls, and the venerable Senate. Here ſome are digging Ports: There others are laying the Foundations of lofty Theatres, and hewing huge Columns from the Rocks, the lofty Decorations of future Scenes. Such their Toil as in Summer's Prime employs the Bees amidſt the flowery Fields under the *warm* Sun, when they lead forth their full grown Swarms; or when they lay up the liquid Honey, and diſtend the Cells with ſweet Nectar; or when they diſburthen thoſe that come Home loaded, or, in formed Battalions, drive the inactive Drones from the Hives. The Work is hotly plied, and the fragrant Honey ſmells ſtrong of Thyme. O happy ye, Æneas ſays,

NOTES.

the Sacrifice upon her Altars, nor ſprinkle them with the Blood. Hence *Catullus* calls *Venus* the Goddeſs whoſe Altars were never ſtained with Blood:

——— Divam
Sanguinis expertem. De com. Ber

430. *Qualis apes.* The firſt Simile in *Homer*'s Iliad is taken from Bees; to which *Macrobius* compares this in *Virgil*, and allows it to have the Preference.

Ἠΰτε ἔθνεα, &c. Il. II. 87.

————The following Hoſt
Pour'd forth by Thouſands, darkens all the Coaſt.
As from ſome rocky Clef t the Shepherd ſees
Cluſt'ring in Heaps on Heaps the driving Bees,
Rolling, and black'ning, Swarms ſucceeding Swarms,
With deeper Murmurs and more hoarſe Alarms;
Duſky they ſpread, a cloſe embody'd Crowd,
And o'er the Vale deſcends the living Cloud.
So, &c. Pope.

But it is evident theſe two Compariſons are applied to quite different Purpoſes, and agree in nothing, but that they are both taken from Bees. *Homer* deſigned to image the Numbers, the Tumult, and the perpetual Egreſſion of the *Grecian* Troops iſſuing from their Tents and Ships, by a Swarm of Bees pouring out of a Rock. *Virgil* again intended to repreſent the Labour, Skill, and Aſſiduity of the *Carthaginian* Builders, by the Induſtry and Art with which thoſe curious Animals carry on their Works. Thus both the Similes are equally juſt, but cannot properly be compared together, ſince their Deſigns are ſo different.

445. Fa-

O vos fortunati, Æneas ait, quorum mœnia jam surgunt! et suspicit fastigia urbis. Infert se per medios, septus nebulâ, quod est *mirabile dictu, miscetque se cum viris, neque cernitur ulli. Lucus fuit in media urbe, letissimus umbrâ; quo in loco Pœni, jactati undis et turbine, primùm effodêre signum quod regia Juno monstrârat, caput* nempe *acris equi: nam sic* monstrârat *gentem fore egregiam bello, et facilem victu per sæcula. Hic Sidonia Dido condebat Junoni ingens templum, opulentum donis et numine Divæ: cui ærea limina surgebant gradibus, trabesque* erant *nexæ ære, cardo stridebat ahenis foribus. In hoc luco nova res oblata primùm leniit timorem: hìc Æneas primùm ausus est sperare salutem, et meliùs confidere rebus suis afflictis. Namque, dum lustrat singula sub ingenti templo, opperiens Reginam; dum miratur quæ fortuna sit urbi, manusque artificum laboremque operum inter se;*

O fortunati, quorum jam mœnia surgunt!
Æneas ait; et fastigia suspicit urbis.
Infert se septus nebulâ, mirabile dictu,
Per medios, miscetque viris, neque cernitur ulli.
Lucus in urbe fuit mediâ, lætissimus umbrâ;
Quo primùm jactati undis et turbine Pœni
Effodêre loco signum, quod regia Juno
Monstrârat, caput acris equi: sic nam fore bello
Egregiam, et facilem victu per secula gentem.
Hìc templum Junoni ingens Sidonia Dido
Condebat, donis opulentum et numine Divæ:
Ærea cui gradibus surgebant limina, nexæque
Ære trabes, foribus cardo stridebat ahenis.
Hoc primùm in luco nova res oblata timorem
Leniit: hìc primùm Æneas sperare salutem
Ausus, et afflictis meliùs confidere rebus.
Namque, sub ingenti lustrat dum singula templo,
Reginam opperiens; dum quæ fortuna sit urbi,
Artificumque manus inter se operumque laborem

TRANSLATION.

whose Walls now rise! and lifts his Eyes to the Turrets of the City. *Then,* shrowded in a Cloud, an amazing Story, he passes through the Crouds, and mingles with the Throng, nor is seen by any. In the Center of the City was a Grove, which yielded a most delightful Shade, where first the Carthaginians, driven by Wind and Wave, dug up the Head of a sprightly Coarser, an omen which royal Juno shewed. For by this *she signified*, that the Nation was to be renowned for War, brave and victorious through Ages. Here Sidonian Dido built to Juno a stately Temple, enriched with Gifts, and the Presence of the Goddess; whose brazen Threshold rose on Steps, the Beams were bound with Brass, and brazen Gates turn on the creeking Hinge. Within this Grove the View of an unexpected Scene first abated their Fear: Here Æneas first dared to promise himself Redress, and to conceive better Hopes of his afflicted State: For, while he surveys every Object in the spacious Temple, waiting the Queen's Arrival; while he is musing with Wonder on the *happy* Fortune of the City; while he compares the Hands of the Artists,

NOTES.

445. *Facilem victu.* It would be tedious to repeat here what the Commentators have offered for explaining this Passage. The Translation takes *facilem victu* to signify the same as *facilem victum*: for there are not wanting Examples where the Supines in *u*, as they are called, have an active as well as a passive Sense. And this is what agrees best to the Design of the Text, and the Nature of the Presage.

447. *Numine Divæ.* Probably refers to some rich Statue of the Goddess *Juno* that was set up in the Temple; for so *numen* is used, Æn. II. 178. where the Word is applied to the Palladium:

Omina ni repetant Argis, numenque reducant.

Miratur; videt Iliacas ex ordine pugnas,
Bellaque jam famâ totum vulgata per orbem;
Atridas, Priamumque, et sævum ambobus Achillem.
Constitit, et lacrymans, Quis jam locus, inquit, Achate,
Quæ regio in terris nostri non plena laboris?
En Priamus! sunt hìc etiam sua præmia laudi:
Sunt lacrymæ rerum, et mentem mortalia tangunt.
Solve metus: feret hæc aliquam tibi fama salutem.
Sic ait: atque animum picturâ pascit inani,
Multa gemens, largoque humectat flumine vultum.
Namque vedebat, utì bellantes Pergama circum
Hac fugerent Graii; premeret Trojana juventus:
Hac Phryges; instaret curru cristatus Achilles.

videt Iliacas pugnas ex ordine, bellaque jam vulgata fama per totum orbem; videt Atridas, Priamumque, et Achillem sævum ambobus. Constitit, et lacrymans inquit: O Achate, quis jam locus, quæve regio in terris non plena est nostri laboris? en Priamus est! etiam hic sua præmia sunt laudi: lacrymæ rerum sunt hìc, *et mortalia tangunt mentem. Solve metus; hæc fama feret tibi aliquam salutem. Sic ait: atque pascit animum* suum *inani picturâ, gemens multa, humectatque vultum largo flumine. Namque videbat, utì Graii bellantes circum Pergama fugerent hac* parte, dum *Trojana juventus premeret eos: hac* parte *Phryges fugerent,* dum *Achilles cristatus instaret iis è curru.*

TRANSLATION.

and their elaborate Works, he sees the Trojan Battles *delineated* in Order, and the War *of Troy* now blazed by Fame over all the World; *he sees* the Sons of Atreus, Priam, and Achilles implacable to both. *Amazed* he stood! and, with Tears in his Eyes, says, What Place, Achates, what Country on the Globe is not full of our Disaster? See *where* Priam *stands!* Even here praise-worthy Deeds are crowned with due Reward: Here Tears of Compassion flow, and *their* Breasts are touched with human Misery. Dismiss your Fears: This Fame of *our Misfortunes* will bring thee some Relief. This said, he feeds his Mind with the shadowy Representation, heaving many a Sigh, and bathes his *manly* Visage in Floods of Tears. For he beheld how, on the one Hand, the warrior Greeks were flying round the Walls of Troy, while the Trojan Youth closely pursued: On the other Hand, the Trojans *were flying*, while plumed Achilles, in his Chariot,

NOTES.

449. *Trabes.* Seems to mean the Door-posts and Threshold, since the Poet is only describing the Entry and Gates of the Temple.

455. *Artificumque manus.* *La Cerda* understands by these Words, not literally the Hands of the Workmen all busily employed together in cutting, polishing, or laying the Stones of the Temple; but what we call the Stile and Art of the several Masters in Painting, with whose Works the Temple was adorned. Which Sense raises, and gives a Dignity to the Expression, that would otherwise appear but mean. Mr. *Straban* is the only *English* Translator, as I know, who has taken it in this Sense:

——— *And now compares the Hands*
Of famous Artists, now admires their Works.

458. *Ambobus.* There is Mention here of three, *Agamemnon*, *Menelaus*, and *Priam*; but they may be considered only as two, the Cause, the Interests of the two Brothers, being one and the same; or *ambobus* may refer to both Armies. *La Creda* however reads *Atridem.*

462. *Sunt lacrymæ rerum.* Here *res* is to be taken in the same Sense as above, Verse 178. *Fessi rerum*, and 204. *Discrimina rerum.*

470. *Primo*

Nec procul hinc lacrymans agnoscit ex niveis velis tentoria Rhesi: quæ prodita in primo somno cruentus Tydides vastabat multâ cæde, avertitque ardentes equos in castra, priusquam gustâssent pabula Trojæ, bibissentque Xanthum. Aliâ parte Troilus fugiens, armis amissis, infelix puer, atque congressus Achilli impar! fertur equis, resupinusque hæret in inani curru, tenens lora tamen: cervixque comæque huic trahuntur per terram, et pulvis inscribitur versâ hastâ. Interea Iliades, passis crinibus, ibant ad templum Palladis non æquæ iis, ferebantque peplum suppliciter tristes, et tunsæ pectora palmis.

Nec procul hinc Rhesi niveis tentoria velis
Agnoscit lacrymans; primo quæ prodita somno
Tydides multâ vastabat cæde cruentus,
Ardentesque avertit equos in castra, prius quàm
Pabula gustâssent Trojæ, Xanthumque bibissent.
Parte aliâ, fugiens amissis Troilus armis,
Infelix puer, atque impar congressus Achilli!
Fertur equis, curruque hæret resupinus inani,
Lora tenens tamen: huic cervixque comæque trahuntur
Per terram, et versâ pulvis inscribitur hastâ.
Interea ad templum non æquæ Palladis ibant
Crinibus Iliades passis, peplumque ferebant
Suppliciter tristes, et tunsæ pectora palmis.

TRANSLATION.

thundered on their Rear. Not far from thence, weeping, he spies the Tents of Rhesus, distinguished by their Snow-white Veils; which, betrayed in that first fatal Night, cruel *Diomed* plundered, and drenched in Blood, and led away his fiery Steeds to the *Grecian* Camp, before they had tasted the Pasture of Troy, or drunk of *the River* Xanthus. In another Part *of the Temple* Troilus, flying after the Loss of his Arms, ill-fated Youth, and unequally matched with Achilles! is dragged by his Horses, and from the Chariot hangs supine, yet grasping the Reins *in Death*. His Neck and Hair trail along the Ground, and the dusty Plain is inscribed by the inverted Spear. Mean While the Trojan Matrons were marching *in solemn Procession* to the Temple of adverse Pallas, with their Hair dishevelled, and were bearing the *consecrated* Robe, like Suppliant sad, and beating their Bo-

NOTES.

470. *Primo somno.* Dr. *Trapp* translates this, —*In the first Repose by Night betray'd*; and Mr. *Strahan*,—*Betray'd in their first Sleep.* But this gives one an Idea of the Beginning of the Night; whereas *Homer* says it was towards the Approach of the Morning,—ἐγγύθι δ' ἠώς, Il. X. 251. And that *Virgil* was not forgetful of this Circumstance, appears from the Episode of *Nisus* and *Euryalus*, which is plainly an Imitation of that of *Diomed* and *Ulysses* in *Homer*, where he particularly marks the Time of their Adventure to have been about the Dawn of the Morning,—*lux inimica propinquat.* Æn. IX. 355. Therefore I take *primo somno*, with *Ruæus*, to mean *the first Night*, namely, *the first Night that* Rhesus *slept in the* Trojan *Camp*; *somnus* being put for Night, Geor. I. 208.

Libra die somnique pares ubi fecerit horas.

473. *Pabula gustâssent*, &c. Among other Fatalities of *Troy* this was one. It was foretold that *Troy* should never be taken, if once *Rhesus*'s Horses drank of the River *Xanthus*, or tasted the Grass of *Troy*.

478. *Versâ—hastâ.* The inverted Spear, not of *Troilus*, for he had dropped his Arms, Verse 474, but of *Achilles*, which was sticking in the Body of *Troilus*, and consequently, as he lay *resupinus* upon his Back, it was inverted, or had its Point downwards.

479. *Interea*, &c. This Story is related in the sixth Book of the Iliad, Verse 286, where *Hecuba*, with the other *Trojan* Matrons, carry the *Peplum* in solemn Procession to the Temple of *Minerva*, to intreat the Goddess to remove *Diomed* from the Fight. All that *Homer* says of this *Peplum* is, that it was the richest Vestment in *Hecuba*'s Wardrobe, embroidered by the *Sidonian* Women, and brought by *Paris* from *Sidon*.

Diva ſolo fixos oculos averſa tenebat.
Ter circum Iliacos raptaverat Hectora muros,
Exanimumque auro corpus vendebat Achilles.
Tum verò ingentem gemitum dat pectore ab imo,
Ut ſpolia, ut currus, utque ipſum corpus amici,
Tendentemque manus Priamum conſpexit inermes.
Se quoque principibus permiſtum agnovit Achivis,
Eoaſque acies, et nigri Memnonis arma.
Ducit Amazonidum lunatis agmina peltis
Pentheſilea furens, mediiſque in millibus ardet;
Aurea ſubnectens exſertæ cingula mammæ
Bellatrix, audetque viris concurrere virgo.
Hæc dum Dardanio Æneæ miranda videntur,
Dum ſtupet, obtutuque hæret defixus in uno;
Regina ad templum formâ pulcherrima Dido
Inceſſit, magnâ juvenum ſtipante catervâ.
Qualis in Eurotæ ripis, aut per juga Cynthi

Diva averſa tenebat oculos fixos ſolo. Achilles ter raptaverat Hectora circum Iliacos muros, vendebatque ejus exanimum corpus auro. Tum verò dat ingentem gemitum ab imo pectore, ut primum *conſpexit ſpolia, ut* conſpexit *currus ipſumque corpus amici, Priamumque tendentem inermes manus. Agnovit ſe quoque permixtum principibus Achivis, acieſque Eoas, et arma nigri Memnonis. Pentheſilea furens ducit agmina Amazonidum lunatis peltis, ardetque in mediis millibus, ſubnectens aurea cingula exſertæ mammæ, bellatrix, virgoque audet concurrere viris.*

Dum hæc miranda videntur Dardanio Æneæ, dum ſtupet, hæretque defixus in uno obtutu, Regina Dido pulcherrima formâ inceſſit ad templum, magnâ catervâ juvenum ſtipante eam. *Qualis Diana exercet choros in ripis Eurotæ, aut per juga Cynthi,*

TRANSLATION.

ſoms with their Hands. The Goddeſs of Wrath kept her Eyes fixed on the Ground. Thrice had Achilles dragged Hector round the Walls of Troy, and was ſelling his breathleſs Corpſe for Gold. Then indeed *Æneas* fetches a deep Groan from the Bottom of his Breaſt, when he ſaw the Spoils, the Chariot, and the very Body of his Friend, and Priam ſtretching forth his feeble Hands. Himſelf too he knew mingled with the Grecian Leaders, and the Eaſtern Bands, and the Arms of ſwarthy Memnon. Furious Pentheſilea leads on her Troops of Amazons, *armed* with Shields of creſcent Form, and burns *with martial Rage* amidſt the thickeſt Ranks. Below her naked Breaſt the Heroine girt a golden Belt, and the Virgin Warrior dares even Heroes to the Encounter.

Theſe wonderous Scenes while the Trojan Prince ſurveys, while he is loſt in Thought, and in one gazing Poſture dwells unmoved; Queen Dido, of ſurpaſſing Beauty, advanced to the Temple, attended by a numerous Retinue of Youth. As on Eurota's Banks, on Mount Cynthus's Top, Diana leads the circular Dances,

NOTES.

486. *Ut ſpolia, ut currus, utque ipſum corpus amici.* The languiſhing Turn of this Verſe, the artificial Pauſes, and, above all, the *ut* repeated at every Pauſe, ſhews us *Æneas* tracing theſe ſeveral affecting Objects, and every now and then fetching a Sigh; it is of the ſame Kind with that tender Line in the eighth Eclogue, 41.

Ut vidi, ut perii, ut me malus abſtulit error!

496. *Pulcherrima Dido.* This is agreeable to the Truth of Hiſtory, as we read in *Juſtin: Interim rex Tyro decedit, filio Pygmalione, et Eliſa filia, inſignis formæ virgine, hæredibus inſtitutis.* Juſt XVIII. Cap. 4.

498. *Qualis in Eurotæ.* This Simile is borrowed from the ſixth Book of the Odyſſey, Verſe 102, where *Homer* applies it to *Nauſicaa* with her Maids ſporting on the Green. *Gellius* writes, that *Valerius Probus* was of Opinion, that no Paſſage had been more unhappily copied by *Virgil* than this Compariſon. The Rea-

der

quam mille Oreades secutæ glomerantur hinc atque hinc; illa fert pharetram humero, gradiensque supereminet omnes Deas; gaudia pertentant tacitum pectus Latonæ: Dido erat talis; læta ferebat se talem per medios, instans operi regnisque futuris. Tum resedit in foribus Divæ, sub mediâ testudine templi, septa armis alteque subnixa solio. Dabat viris jura legesque, æquabatque laborem operum justis partibus, aut trahebat cum sorte, cum Æneas subito videt Anthea, Sergestumque, fortemque Cloanthum, aliosque Teucrorum accedere cum magno concursu, quos ater turbo dispulerat æquore,

Exercet Diana choros, quam mille secutæ
Hinc atque hinc glomerantur Oreades; illa pharetram
Fert humero, gradiensque Deas supereminet omnes;
Latonæ tacitum pertentant gaudia pectus:
Talis erat Dido; talem se læta ferebat
Per medios, instans operi, regnisque futuris.
Tum foribus Divæ, mediâ testudine templi,
Septa armis, solioque alte subnixa, resedit.
Jura dabat legesque viris, operumque laborem
Partibus æquabat justis, aut sorte trahebat:
Cum subito Æneas concursu accedere magno
Anthea, Sergestumque videt, fortemque Cloanthum,
Teucrorumque alios, ater quos æquore turbo

TRANSLATION.

round whom a numerous Train of Mountain Nymphs play in Rings, her Quiver hangs graceful from her Shoulder, and moving majestic she towers above the other Goddesses, *while* with silent Raptures Latona's Bosom thrills. Such Dido was, and such, with chearful Grace, she passed amidst her Train, urging forward the Labour, and her future Kingdom. Then, at the Gate of the Sanctuary, in the Middle of the Temple's Dome, she took her Seat, surrounded with her Guards, and raised on a Throne above the rest. *Here* she administered Justice, and dispensed Laws to her Subjects, and, in equal Portions, distributed their Tasks, or dispensed them by Lot; when strait Æneas sees, advancing with a vast Concourse, Antheus, Sergestus, brave Cloanthus, and other Trojans; whom a black Storm

NOTES.

der may see his Objections, and *Scaliger*'s Answer, in Mr. *Pope*'s Note upon that Place in *Homer*, where both are very fairly stated. I shall only copy these Words of *Scaliger* that point to the Particulars wherein the Comparison holds between *Diana* and *Dido*: *Quemadmodum igitur Diana in montibus; ita Dido in urbe. Illa inter Nymphas, hæc inter Matronas. Illa instans venatibus, hæc urbi.* And this is all the Use to which *Virgil* intended the Comparison, as appears from his Application of it, *Talis erat Dido, &c.*

498. *Cynthi.* *Cynthus* was a Mountain in *Delos*, *Diana*'s native Island; but it is not so easy to assign the Reason why the Banks of *Eurota* are mentioned as one of the Haunts of *Diana* and her Nymphs, unless it is that *Sparta*, near which the *Eurota* runs, was a famous Country for Hunting.

502. *Pertentant.* Signifies the brisk vibrating Motion of the Strings of a musical Instrument, hence applied by easy Analogy to the brisk Motion excited in the animal Spirits by an Object of Joy, and the pleasant Sensation with which it is accompanied:

Nonne vides ut tota tremor pertentet equorum
Corpora— Geor. III. 250.

505. *Foribus Divæ.* To the inner Part of the Heathen Temples was an Apartment, separated from the rest by a Wall or Veil, which answered to the *Sanctum Sanctorum* in the Temple of *Jerusalem*, and was called *Adytum* or *Penetrale*. Here *Virgil* supposes *Juno* to have had a Statue, or some sacred Symbol of her Presence, and therefore calls the Gate that led to her Sanctuary *Fores Divæ*, the Gate of the Goddess.

527. *Pla-*

Dispulerat, penitusque alias advexerat oras.
Obstupuit simul ipse, simul perculsus Achates,
Lætitiâque metuque, avidi conjungere dextras
Ardebant; sed res animos incognita turbat.
Dissimulant, et nube cavâ speculantur amicti,
Quæ fortuna viris; classem quo littore linquant;
Quid veniant: cunctis cum lecti navibus ibant
Orantes veniam, et templum clamore petebant.
Postquam introgressi, et coram data copia fandi,
Maximus Ilioneus placido sic pectore cœpit:
O Regina, novam cui condere Jupitur urbem,
Justitiâque dedit gentes frænare superbas,
Troes te miseri, ventis maria omnia vecti,
Oramus, prohibe infandos à navibus ignes,
Parce pio generi, et propiùs res aspice nostras.
Non nos aut ferro Libycos populare Penates

advexeratque ad oras penitus alias. Ipse simul obstupuit, simul Achates perculsus, lætitiâque metuque, avidi ardebant conjungere dextras; sed res incognita turbat eorum *animos. Dissimulant, et amicti cavâ nube speculantur quæ fortuna* sit *viris, quo* in *littore linquant classem,* ob *quid veniant: nam lecti ex cunctis navibus ibant orantes veniam, et petebant templum clamore.*

Postquam sunt *introgressi, et copia* est *data fandi coram, Ilioneus maximus sic cœpit* loqui è *placido pectore: O Regina, cui Jupiter dedit condere novam urbem, frænareque gentes superbas justitiâ,* nos *miseri Troes, vecti ventis per omnia maria, oramus te, prohibe infandos ignes à navibus, parce pio generi, et propiùs aspice nostras res. Non nos venimus aut populare Libycos Penates ferro,*

TRANSLATION.

had tossed up and down the Sea, and driven to other far distant Shores. At once Amazement seized the Hero; at once Achates was struck, and, between Joy and Fear, both ardently longed to join Hands; but the Strangeness of the Event perplexes their Minds. *Thus* they carry on their Disguise, and, shrowded under the bending Cloud, watch to learn the Fortune of their Friends; on what Coast they left the Fleet, and on what Errand they came: For a select Number was deputed from all the Ships to sue for Grace, and, with mingled Voices, made towards the Temple.

Having gained Admission and Liberty to speak before *the Queen*, Ilioneus, their Chief, with Mind composed, thus began: O Queen, to whom it is given by Jove to build this rising City, and to curb proud Nations with just Laws, we, Trojans forlorn, tossed by Winds over every Sea, implore *thy Grace*; *oh!* save our Ships from the merciless Flames; spare a pious Race, and propitiously regard our Distresses. We are not come either to ravage with the Sword your Libyan Gods

NOTES.

521. *Placido pectore.* This Expression is both more elegant and more comprehensive, than if they had said, *placido ore* or *vultu*; for the calm composed Mind regulates the Voice, the Speech, and forms the whole Deportment.

523. *Gentes frænare superbas.* The *Numidians*, and other fierce Nations in her Neighbourhood, who are thus described, *Æn.* IV. 40.

Hinc Getulæ urbes, genus insuperabile bello,
Et Numidæ infræni *cingunt, et inhospita Syrtis;*
Hinc deserta siti regio, lateque furentes
Barcæi.

527. *Libycos populare Penates.* The *Penates* were either the Tutelar Gods of a whole Province or Kingdom, of whom this Passage is to be understood; or they were the Protectors of particular Cities, as *Æn.* II. 293.

Sacra, suosque tibi commendat Troja Penates.

Or, lastly, they were the domestic Gods, the guardian Deities of private Families.

Cura penum struere, et flammis adolere Penates.
Æn. I. 704.

aut vertere raptas prædas ad littora. Ea vis non eſt animo, nec tanta ſuperbia eſt victis. Eſt locus, Graii dicunt eum Heſperiam cognomine; antiqua terra, potens armis atque ubere glebæ; Oenotrii viri eam coluere; nunc fama eſt minores dixiſſe gentem Italiam, de nomine ducis. Huc curſus fuit nobis. *Cum ſubito nimboſus Orion aſſurgens, è fluctu tulit nos in cæca vada, Auſtriſque penitus procacibus diſpulit nos per undas perque invia ſaxa, ſalo ſuperante: pauci adnavimus huc veſtris oris. Quod genus eſt hoc hominum? quæve patria permittit hunc tam barbarum morem? prohibemur hoſpitio arenæ: cient bella, vetantque nos conſiſtere* in *prima terra. Si temnitis humanum genus et mortalia arma;*

Venimus, aut raptas ad littora vertere prædas.
Non ea vis animo, nec tanta ſuperbia victis.
Eſt locus, Heſperiam Graii cognomine dicunt;
Terra antiqua, potens armis, atque ubere glebæ;
Œnotrii coluere viri: nunc fama, minores
Italiam dixiſſe, ducis de nomine gentem.
Huc curſus fuit.
Cum ſubito aſſurgens fluctu nimboſus Orion
In vada cæca tulit, penituſque procacibus Auſtris,
Perque undas, ſuperante ſalo, perque invia ſaxa
Diſpulit: huc pauci veſtris adnavimus oris.
Quod genus hoc hominum? quæve hunc tam barbara morem
Permittit patria? hoſpitio prohibemur arenæ:
Bella cient, primâque vetant conſiſtere terrâ.
Si genus humanum et mortalia temnitis arma;

TRANSLATION.

(*Settlements*), nor with rapacious Hands to bear away the Plunder to our Ships. We have no ſuch hoſtile Intention, nor does ſuch Pride of Heart become the vanquiſhed. There is a Place, called by the Greeks Heſperia, an ancient Land, renowned for martial Deeds and fruitful Soil; the Œnotrians poſſeſſed it once: Now Fame reports that their Deſcendants call the Nation Italy from their Leader's Name; hither our Courſe was bent, when ſuddenly tempeſtuous Orion riſing from the Main drove us on hidden Shelves, and by violent, outrageous South-winds, toſſed us hither and thither over Waves, and over inacceſſible Rocks, overwhelmed by the briny Deep: Hither we few have eſcaped from Shipwreck to your Coaſts. What *a ſavage* Race of Men is this, what Country ſo barbarous to allow of ſuch Manners? We are denied the Hoſpitality *even* of the *barren* Shore. In Arms they riſe, and forbid our ſetting Foot on the firſt Verge of Land. If you ſet at nought the human Kind, and the Arms of Mortals, yet know the Gods will *always* have

NOTES.

——*Et ſparſos paternâ cæde Penates.*
Æn. IV. 21.

Theſe laſt were called *parvi Penates*,

——*Exiguamque Larem, parvoſque Penates Lætus adit.* Æn. VIII. 543.

And the others were ſtiled *Magni*.

—— *Per magnos, Niſe, Penates.*
Æn. IX. 258.

As the Gods and religious Ceremonies of a Country have always been reckoned the moſt ſacred Branches of its Property, to offer Violation to them comprehends every Act of Hoſtility.

535. *Aſſurgens—Orion* Segrais infers from this Paſſage, that *Æneas* arrived at *Carthage* in the Month of *July*, when this Conſtellation riſes *heliacally*, i. e. about the ſame Time that the Sun riſes; that he ſtaid at *Carthage* till the End of Winter, when he ſet ſail for *Italy*,

Quin etiam Hiberno moliris ſidere claſſem.

where he arrived ſome Time in the Spring, as appears from thoſe Lines in the ſeventh Book, which beautifully paint that Seaſon:

Aurora in roſeis fulgebat lutea bigis:
Cum venti poſuere, omniſque repentè reſedit
Flatus, et in lento luctantur marmore tonſæ.
————————*variæ circumque ſupraque*
Aſſuetæ ripis volucres, et fluminis alveo,
Æthera mulcebant cantu, lucoque volabant.
Æn. VII. 26.

536. *Procacibus Auſtris.* To the ſame Purpoſe *Lucretius*, Lib. VI. 110.

Interdum

At ſperate Deos memores fandi atque nefandi.
Rex erat Æneas nobis, quo juſtior alter

at ſperate Deos fore memores fandi atque nefandi. Æneas erat rex nobis, quo nec fuit alter juſtior

TRANSLATION.

an unalterable Regard to Right and Wrong. We had for our King Æneas, than whom none was more juſt in performing all the Duties of Piety, none more ſig-

NOTES.

Interdum perſciſſa furit petulantibus Euris.

And *Horace*, Ode I. 26.

Tradam protervis—portare ventis.

543. *Sperate.* *Spero* ſignifies to look for, or expect, either Good or Evil, as

Hæc adeo ex illo mihi jam ſperanda fuerunt.
Æn. XI. 275.

Hunc ego ſi potui tantum ſperare dolorem.
Æn. IV. 419.

544. *Quo juſtior alter, nec pietate fuit, bello major et armis.* This is the Sum of *Æneas*'s Character, Piety and Valour,

———*pietate inſignis et armis.*
Æn. VI. 403.

And anſwers to *Homer*'s

Αμφοτερον βασιλευς τ' αγαθος, κρατερος τ' αιχμητης.
Il. III. 179.

And it is obvious to remark, that the firſt of theſe, *inſignis pietate*, agreeably to the Genius of the *Latin* Tongue, comprehends not only Devotion to the Gods, but all the Branches of Benevolence and Humanity. As *Æneas* was perfectly reſigned to the Will of Heaven, —*Ille Jovis monitis immota tenebat lumina*; ſo he was a zealous Patriot, and firmly attached to the Intereſts of his Country, which was always firſt in his Thoughts, and neareſt his Heart:

Me ſi fata meis paterentur ducere vitam
Auſpiciis, et ſponte mea componere curas;
Urbem Trojanam primum dulceſque meorum
Relliquias colerem, Priami tecta alta manerent,
Et recidiva manu poſuiſſem Pergama victis.
Æn. IV. 340.

This Piety exerts itſelf towards all his Relations, and ſhews him a tender Son, Father, Huſband. He bears his aged Sire upon his Shoulders through the Flames of *Troy*, and leads his little Son, his Wife following. What a beautiful Image has *Virgil* given of his Hero's tender Affection, in thoſe Words he puts in his Mouth,

Et me, quem dudum non ulla injecta movebant
Tela, neque adverſo glomerati ex agmine Graii;
Nunc omnes terrent auræ, ſonus excitat omnis
Suſpenſum, et pariter comitique onerique timentem. Æn. II. 726.

He ſhews the ſame Tenderneſs towards his Wife, when, having loſt her in the general Hurry and Confuſion, he ventures back into the Midſt of the Enemies to find her, and leaves not his Purſuit till her Ghoſt appears to forbid his farther Search. And as for his Son, he is the Darling of his Soul, and ingroſſes all his Affections:

Omnis in Aſcanio cari ſtat cura parentis.

Many Inſtances of the ſame Kind will occur to the Obſervation of every Reader in the Courſe of the Poem, and to inſiſt on all of them would be tedious. Thoſe, who would ſee this beautiful Character more fully illuſtrated and vindicated from Objections, may conſult Mr. *Segrais*'s Preface to his Tranſlation of the Æneid, Mr. *Dryden*'s Preface to his, and Mr. *Pope*'s Note on Iliad V. Verſe 212. From the laſt I ſhall tranſcribe two or three Sentences: "If we take a View of the whole Epiſode of this Hero (*Æneas*) in *Homer*, where he makes but an Under-part, it will appear that *Virgil* has kept him perfectly in the ſame Character in his Poem, where he ſhines as the firſt Hero. His Piety and his Valour, though not drawn at ſo full a Length, are marked no leſs in the Original than in the Copy.—As to his Valour, he is ſecond only to *Hector*, and in perſonal Bravery as great in the *Greek* Author as in the *Roman*.—He is the firſt that dares reſiſt *Achilles* himſelf at his Return to the Fight in all his Rage for the Loſs of *Patroclus*. He indeed avoids encountering two at once,—and ſhews upon the whole a ſedate and deliberate Courage, which, if not ſo glaring as that of ſome others, is yet more juſt. It is worth conſidering how thoroughly *Virgil* penetrated into all this, and ſaw into the very Idea of *Homer*; ſo to extend and call forth the whole Figure in its full Dimenſions and Colours from the ſlight eſt Hints and Sketches, which were but caſually touched by *Homer*, and even in ſome Points too, where they were rather left to be underſtood than expreſſed. And this, by the way, ought to be conſidered by thoſe Critics who object to *Virgil*'s Hero the Want of that Sort of Courage which ſtrikes us ſo much in *Homer*'s *Achilles*. *Æneas* was not the Creature of *Virgil*'s Imagination, but one whom the World was already acquainted with, &c." I ſhall only make theſe two Remaks, One is, that as *Virgil*, with the

pietate, nec major bello et armis: quem virum si fata servant, si vescitur ætheriâ aurâ, neque adhuc occubat crudelibus umbris, non sit metus nobis, nec pœniteat te priorem certâsse officio. Sunt et urbes nobis in Siculis regionibus, armaque, clarusque Acestes est à Trojano sanguine. Liceat nobis subducere classem quassatam ventis, et aptare trabes è sylvis, et stringere remos, si datur nobis *tendere* in *Italiam, sociis et rege recepto, ut læti petamus Italiam Latiumque: sin salus sit absumpta, et pontus Libyæ habet te, O optime pater Teucrûm! nec jam restat spes Iüli;*

Nec pietate fuit, nec bello major et armis:
Quem si fata virum servant, si vescitur aurâ
Ætheriâ, nec adhuc crudelibus occubat umbris;
Non metus, officio nec te certâsse priorem
Pœniteat. Sunt et Siculis regionibus urbes,
Armaque, Trojanoque à sanguine clarus Acestes.
Quassatam ventis liceat subducere classem,
Et silvis aptare trabes, et stringere remos,
Si datur Italiam, sociis et Rege recepto,
Tendere, ut Italiam læti Latiumque petamus:
Sin absumta salus, et te, pater optime Teucrûm!
Pontus habet Libyæ, nec spes jam restat Iüli;

TRANSLATION.

nalized in the Art of War, and in martial Atchievements; whom, if the Fates preserve, if *still* he breathe the vital Air, and is not yet numbered with the ruthless Shades, neither we shall despair, nor you repent your having been the first in challenging *him* to Acts of Kindness and Humanity. We have likewise Cities and Arms in Sicily, and the illustrious King Acestes is of Trojan Extraction. Permit us *then* to bring to Shore our Wind beaten Fleet, and from your Woods to chuse *Trees for* Planks, and to refit our Oars; that, if it be given us to bend our Course *once more* to Italy, upon the Recovery of our Prince and Friends, we may joyfully set out thither, and make the Latian Shore. But if our Safety is perished, and thou, O Father of the Trojans, the best of Men! now liest buried in the Libyan Sea, and no further Hope of Iülus remains, we may at least repair to the Streights

NOTES.

the greatest Justness of Thought, unites Piety towards the Gods, with all the proper Acts of Humanity, in the Person of *Æneas*; so in the Character of *Mezentius*, which is the Reverse of the other, he shews that Impiety and Inhumanity are inseparable. As that Prince is *contemptor Divûm*, so he is an implacable Tyrant, and a Monster of Cruelty:

Mortua quin etiam jungebat corpora vivis,
Componens manibusque manus, atque oribus ora,
Tormenti genus; et sanie taboque fluentes
Complexu in misero, longa sic morte necabat.
Æn. VIII. 485.

Another Remark is, that *Virgil* seems to have failed in the Propriety of his Hero's Character, by studying in some Things too closely to imitate *Homer*. Particular Instances of this occur in the ninth Book, where he makes *Æneas* sacrifice eight *Rutilians* to the Manes of *Pallas*, as *Achilles* had done twelve *Trojans* to the Ghost of *Patroclus*. This Practice, however it may suit with the furious Temper of *Achilles*, is quite incongruous to the mild, humane Disposition of *Æneas*. The same may be said of his insulting his Enemies even in their Death, and accompanying the Wounds he gives them with bitter Reproaches and Taunts. See *Æneid* X. Verses 556, 592, 600. But these, and the like, may be considered among the Blemishes which *Virgil*'s accurate Judgment would probably have corrected, had he lived to finish this Poem to that Perfection he designed.

545. *Bello—et armis*, &c. This is not a Tautology, as it may seem; the first refers to the whole Art or Conduct of War, the other to the Prowess and Bravery in the Field of Battle. *Servius.*

546. *Quem si fata*, &c. *Virgil* makes *Ilioneus* dwell on this Circumstance, in order to make the stronger Impression. Besides, such Repetitions of the same Idea in different Expressions, are common to all Poets:

Ει που ετι ζωει, και ορα φαος ηελιοιο.
If he still lives, and sees the Light of the Sun. Homer.

Vivit,

At freta Sicaniæ ſaltem, ſedeſque paratas,
Unde huc advecti, regemque petamus Aceſten.
Talibus Ilioneus: cuncti ſimul ore fremebant
Dardanidæ.
Tum breviter Dido, vultum demiſſa, profatur:
Solvite corde metum, Teucri, ſecludite curas.
Res dura, et regni novitas me talia cogunt
Moliri, et latè fines cuſtode tueri.
Quis genus Æneadum, quis Trojæ neſciat urbem?
Virtuteſque, viroſque, et tanti incendia belli?
Non obtuſa adeò geſtamus pectora Pœni;
Nec tam averſus equos Tyriâ Sol jungit ab urbe.
Seu vos Heſperiam magnam, Saturniaque arva,

at ſaltem ut petamus freta Sicaniæ, ſedeſque paratas, unde advecti ſumus huc, et regem Aceſten. Ilioneus orabat talibus verbis; cuncti Dardanidæ ſimul fremebant ore.

Tum Dido, demiſſa vultum, breviter profatur: O Teucri, ſolvite metum à corde, ſecludite curas. Mea dura res, et novitas regni, cogunt me moliri talia, et latè tueri fines meos *cuſtode: Quis neſciat genus Æneadum, quis* neſciat *urbem Trojæ? virtuteſque viroſque, et incendia tanti belli? nos Pœni non geſtamus pectora adeò obtuſa; nec Sol jungit equos tam averſus à Tyriâ urbe. Seu vos optatis Magnam Heſperiam, arvaque Saturnia,*

TRANSLATION.

of Sicily, and the Settlement there prepared for us, whence we were driven hither, and *once more* viſit King Aceſtes. So ſpoke Ilioneus. At the ſame Time the other Trojans murmured their Conſent.

Then Dido, with modeſt, downcaſt Looks, thus in brief replies: Trojans, baniſh Fear from your Breaſts, lay your Cares aſide. My hard Fate, and the Infancy of my Kingdom, force me to take ſuch Meaſures, and to ſecure my Frontiers, by *planting* Guards around. Who is a Stranger to the Æneian Race, the City Troy, her Heroes, and their valorous Deeds, and to the Devaſtations of ſo renowned a War? Carthaginian Hearts are not ſo obdurate and inſenſible; nor yokes the Sun his Steeds at ſuch a Diſtance from our Tyrian City. Whether *therefore you be deſigned for* Heſperia the Greater, and the Country where Saturn

NOTES.

Vivit, et ætherias vitales ſuſcipit auras.
He lives, and draws the vital Air.
Lucretius.

565. *Quis genus.* There are three principal Reaſons may be aſſigned why People are unacquainted with what happens in the World; either, in the firſt Place, becauſe the Events are not of Importance enough to be blazed abroad; or the People are ſtupidly unconcerned about the Affairs of others, and have no Curioſity to enquire after them; or, laſtly, they live in ſo remote a Corner of the Globe, that News cannot reach them. In this Light we may conſider *Dido* in this and the three following Lines, obviating any unfavourable Opinion *Ilioneus* might have conceived of the *Carthaginians* as ignorant and inſenſible. Think us not ſuch a Set of *Barbarians*, ſays *Dido*, as to be ignorant of the *Trojan* War, and the Exploits of its famous Heroes; theſe are Events too important not to be univerſally celebrated. *Quis genus Æneadum*, &c. Nor are we *Carthaginians* ſo ſtupid as not to concern ourſelves about other States and Kingdoms. *Non obtuſa adeò*, &c. Nor are we in ſo remote a Climate as to be cut off from Commerce and Correſpondence with the reſt of Mankind. *Nec tam averſus*, &c. Others however conſider the two laſt Lines in another Light, as if *Dido* were proving that her People could not be imagined barbarous, ſince they were not far removed from the Sun. You ought not to think us, *ſays ſhe*, obdurate, inhuman, or inſenſible; this is the Diſpoſition of thoſe Nations on whom the Sun ſeldom ſhines, or but with faint and diſtant Rays; but our Breaſts are ſoftened by his warmer Influences. Alluding to the Notion of ſome Philoſophers, that the Inhabitants of the colder Climates are leſs ſuſceptible of Humanity and Compaſſion than thoſe in warmer Countries.

570. *Ery-*

ſive fines Erycis, regemque Aceſten; dimittam vos tutos auxilio, juvaboque vos opibus. Vultiſne et pariter conſidere mecum in his regnis? Urbs, *quam urbem ſtatuo, eſt veſtra; ſubducite naves: Tros Tyriuſque agetur mihi nullo diſcrimine. Atque utinam ipſe rex veſter Æneas compulſus huc eodem Noto afforet! equidem dimittam certos* homines *per littora, et jubebo* vos *luſtrare extrema Libyæ; ſi quibus ſylvis aut urbibus ejectus errat.*

Et fortis Achates, et pater Æneas, arrecti animum his dictis, jamdudum ardebant erumpere nubem: Achates prior compellat Ænean: O nate Deâ, quæ ſententia nunc ſurgit animo? Vides omnia tuta, vides claſſem, ſocioſque receptos. Unus abeſt, quem ipſi vidimus ſubmerſum in medio fluctu: cætera reſpondent dictis tuæ matris. Vix fatus erat ea, cum nubes circumfuſa repente ſcindit ſe, et purgat ſe in apertum æthera.

Sive Erycis fines, regemque optatis Aceſten;
Auxilio tutos dimittam, opibuſque juvabo.
Vultis et his mecum pariter conſidere regnis?
Urbem quam ſtatuo, veſtra eſt; ſubducite naves:
Tros Tyriuſque mihi nullo diſcrimine eodem,
Atque utinam rex ipſe, Noto compulſus eodem,
Afforet Æneas! equidem per littora certos
Dimittam, et Libyæ luſtrare extrema jubebo;
Si quibus ejectus ſilvis, aut urbibus errat.
His animum arrecti dictis, et fortis Achates,
Et pater Æneas, jamdudum erumpere nubem
Ardebant: prior Ænean compellat Achates:
Nate Deâ, quæ nunc animo ſententia ſurgit?
Omnia tuta vides; claſſem, ſocioſque receptos,
Unus abeſt, medio in fluctu quem vidimus ipſi
Submerſum: dictis reſpondent cætera matris.
Vix ea fatus erat, cum circumfuſa repente
Scindit ſe nubes, et in æthera purgat apertum,

TRANSLATION.

reigned, or if you chuſe *to viſit* Eryx's Coaſt and King Aceſtes; I will diſmiſs you ſafe with *proper* Aſſiſtance, and ſupport you with my Wealth. Or will you ſettle with me in this Realm *of mine?* The City I *now* build ſhall be yours: Draw your Ships aſhore; Trojan and Tyrian ſhall be treated by me as if they were both the ſame. And would to Heaven the ſame Wind had driven your Prince Æneas too *upon our Coaſt*, and that he were here preſent! However, I will ſend truſty *Meſſengers* along the Coaſts, with Orders to ſearch Libya's utmoſt Bounds, if he is thrown out to wander in ſome Wood or City.

Animated by theſe *friendly* Words, brave Achates and Father Æneas had long impatiently deſired to break from the Cloud. Achates firſt addreſſes Æneas: Goddeſs-born, what Purpoſe now ariſes in your Mind? You ſee all is ſafe; your Fleet and Friends reſtored. One alone is miſſing, who ſunk before our Eyes in the Midſt of the Waves: Every Thing elſe agrees with your Mother's Prediction. Scarce had he ſaid, when ſtrait the circumambient Cloud ſplits aſunder, and diſſolves into open Air. Æneas ſtood forth, and in bright Day ſhone conſpicuous,

NOTES.

570. *Erycis.* *Eryx* was King of *Sicily*, Æn. V. 24.

573. *Urbem quam*, &c. The Conſtruction is, Urbs, *quam urbem ſtatuo, veſtra eſt.*

576. *Equidem.* *Servius* obſerves that *equidem* in *Virgil* always ſignifies *ego quidem.*

586. *Vix ea fatus erat, cum circumfuſa repente ſcindit ſe nubes*, &c. This Paſſage *Milton* ſeems to have had in his Eye, Book X. 447. where *Satan* paſſed inviſible through the Midſt of the helliſh Council, ſeated himſelf on his Throne, viewed all around him unſeen, then ſurprized them with his unexpected Appearance:

————————Down a while
He ſat, and round about him ſaw unſeen;
At laſt, as from a Cloud, his fulgent Head
And Shape Star-bright appear'd, or brighter clad,
With what permiſſive Glory ſince his Fall
Was left him, or falſe Glitter.

587. *Scindit ſe nubes.* Here again *Virgil* imitates *Homer*, who, in the ſame Manner, diſ-

Restitit Æneas, claràque in luce refulsit,
Os humerosque Deo similis: namque ipsa decoram
Cæsariem nato genitrix, lumenque juventæ
Purpureum, et lætos oculis afflarat honores.
Quale manus addunt ebori decus, aut ubi flavo
Argentum, Pariusve lapis circumdatur auro,
Tum sic Reginam alloquitur, cunctisque repente
Improvisus, ait: Coram, quem quæritis, adsum,
Troïus Æneas, Libycis ereptus ab undis.
O sola infandos Trojæ miserata labores!
Quæ nos, relliquias Danaûm, terræque marisque
Omnibus exhaustos jam casibus, omnium egenos,
Urbe, domo socias! grates persolvere dignas
Non opis est nostræ, Dido, nec quicquid ubique est
Gentis Dardaniæ, magnum quæ sparsa per orbem.
Dî tibi, si qua pios respectant numina, si quid

Æneas restitit, refulsitque in clarâ luce, similis Deo os humerosque: namque genitrix ipsa afflarat nato decoram cæsariem, purpureumque lumen juventæ, et oculis lætos honores. Tale decus quale manus addunt ebori, aut ubi argentum Pariusve lapis circumdatur flavo auro.

Tum sic alloquitur Reginam, repenteque improvisus cunctis ait; ego adsum coram, Troïus Æneas, quem quæritis, ereptus ab Libycis undis. O tu sola miserata infandos labores Trojæ! quæ urbe domo socias nos relliquias Danaûm, jam exhaustos omnibus casibus terræque marisque, et egenos omnium! O Dido, non est nostræ opis persolvere tibi dignas grates; nec est opis Dardaniæ gentis, quicquid hujus gentis ubique est, quæ sparsa est per magnum orbem: Dii (siqua numina respectant pios, siquid

TRANSLATION.

in Countenance and Make resembling a God: For *Venus* herself had adorned her Son with graceful Locks, *flushed him* with the radiant Bloom of Youth, and breathed a sprightly Lustre on his Eyes. Such Beauty as the *Artist*'s Hand superadds to Ivory, or where Silver and Parian Marble is inchased in yellow Gold.

Then suddenly addressing the Queen, he, to the Surprize of all, thus begins: Behold the Man you seek now present, Trojan Æneas, snatched from the Libyan Waves. O thou, who alone hast commiserated Troy's unutterable Calamities! who *deignest to* associate in thy Town and Palace us a Remnant saved from the Greeks, who have now been tried to the utmost by Woes in every Shape, both by Sea and Land, and are in Want of all Things! to repay thee due Thanks, great Queen, exceeds the Power of both us, and of all the Dardan Race, wherever dispersed over the wide World. The Gods, if any Powers divine regard the pi-

NOTES.

covers *Ulysses* to *Alcinous*, in the seventh Book of the Odyssey; but it is acknowledged that *Virgil* has improved upon his Original, particularly in that fine Addition at the End of the Verse, *et in æthera purgat apertum*, than which nothing can more strongly paint the Image of a Cloud just vanishing and bending with the Air.

583. *Claràque in luce refulsit.* Shone, or appeared conspicuous, as *Lucr.* V. 12. speaking of *Epicurus*,

——— *quique per artem*
Fluctibus è tantis vitam, tantisque tenebris,
In tam tranquillo, et tam clarâ luce locavit.

603. *Si qua*, &c. This Expression implies nothing of Doubt, but only puts a certain Truth into the Form of a Supposition, the more to secure and strengthen the Conclusion. It amounts to this Assertion, You shall be amply rewarded as sure as there are Gods above, as sure as there is Justice, as there is any Sense of Virtue in the World. Much like what Mr. *Addison* says:

juſtitiæ eſt uſquam) et mens conſcia ſibi recti, ferant tibi digna præmia. Quæ tam læta ſecula tulerunt te? qui tanti parentes genuere te talem? Dum fluvii current in freta, dum umbræ luſtrabunt convexa montibus, dum polus paſcet ſidera; honos, nomenque tuum, laudeſque tuæ ſemper manebunt, quæcunque terræ vocant me. Sic fatus, petit amicum Ilionea dextrâ, Sereſtumque lævâ; poſt, petit alios, fortemque Gyan, fortemque Cloanthum.

Uſquam juſtitiæ eſt, et mens ſibi conſci recti,
Præmia digna ferant: quæ te tam læta tulerunt
Secula? qui tanti talem genuere parentes?
In freta dum fluvii current, dum montibus umbræ
Luſtrabunt convexa, polus dum ſidera paſcet;
Semper honos, nomenque tuum, laudeſque manebunt,
Quæ me cunque vocant terræ. Sic fatus amicum
Ilionea petit dextrâ, lævâque Sereſtum;
Poſt, alios, fortemque Gyan, fortemque Cloanthum.

TRANSLATION.

ous, if Juſtice any where ſubſiſts, and a Mind, conſcious of its own Virtue, ſhall yield thee a juſt Recompence. What Age was ſo happy to produce thee? Who the Parents of ſo illuſtrious an Offspring? While Rivers run into the Sea, while Shadows move round the convex Mountains, while Heaven feeds the Stars; your Honour, Name and Praiſe, *with me* ſhall ever live, to whatever Climes I am called. This ſaid, he embraces his Friend Ilioneus with his Right-hand, and Sereſtus with his Left: Then the reſt *in their Turns*, the heroic Gyas, and heroic Cloanthus.

NOTES.

—— *If there's a Pow'r above us,* ——
———*he muſt delight in Virtue.*

See alſo Æneid II. 159.

———*atque omnia ferre ſub auras,*
Si qua tegunt.

Where it appears plain that ſi *qua* cannot imply any Doubt, but muſt ſignify *whatever*, or ſome Word of the like Import. Admitting therefore this to be the Signification of *ſi qua numina*, and *ſi quid juſtitiæ* in this Place, why may we not conſider it as a Prayer, which I am ſurprized to find none of the Commentators have done? *Di—ferant*, may the Gods confer upon you; the Verb, which is the optative Mood, naturally leads to this Senſe, and it is in the ſame Form with that Imprecation, B. II. 536.

Di (ſi qua eſt cœlo pietas, quæ talia curet)
Perſolvant grates dignas, et præmia reddant
Debita.

603. *Pios.* This Word ſignifies virtuous Men in general; eſpecially the kind, the beneficent, the generous. Hence *Niſus*'s generous, diſintereſted Love to *Euryalus* is called *pius amor*, Æn. V. 296. See the Note on Verſe 547.

604. *Mens ſibi conſcia recti.* Some would underſtand this not of *Dido*'s own conſcious Approbation of her Virtue, but of the divine Mind, who is conſcious to every good Action; as where *Virgil* ſays, *Mens agitat molem*, Æn. VI. 727. But, beſides that this Senſe appears forced, and a mere Repetition of the former Thought, I doubt if the Genius of the Language will admit of it. The Deity is *conſcius recti*, as he is the infallible Witneſs of Truth and Integrity; but he is *conſcius ſibi recti*, as he is conſcious of his own Uprightneſs and Sincerity. But this Expreſſion admits of another Senſe; for, inſtead of joining *et mens ſibi conſcia recti* with *Dii*, as one of the Nominatives to *ferant*, we may include it in the *Parentheſis* with *ſi qua*, &c. Thus, *if there be any Gods who regard the pious, if Juſtice any where ſubſiſts, and a Mind conſcious of Virtue.*

605. *Quæ te tam læta tulerunt ſecula.* It is the ſame Thought with that in the ſixth Æneid, 648.

Hic genus antiquum Teucri, pulcherrima proles,
Magnanimi heroës, nati melioribus annis.

It repreſents *Dido* as one of the Heroines of the happy golden Age, whoſe uncommon Worth could only be the Production of thoſe better Days.

608. *Montibus—convexa.* Either *in montibus*, or *montibus* poetically for *montium*. *Convexa* is ſeldom or never uſed by good Authors to ſignify *convex* in *Engliſh*, but rather imports the ſame as *curvus*, *bending*, *ſhelving*, or *arched*, as Æn. IV. 451. and X. 251.

Obstupuit primo aspectu Sidonia Dido,
Casu deinde viri tanto; et sic ore locuta est:
Quis te, nate Deâ, per tanta pericula casus
Insequitur? quæ vis immanibus applicat oris?
Tune ille Æneas, quem Dardanio Anchisæ
Alma Venus Phrygii genuit Simoentis ad undam?
Atque equidem Teucrum memini Sidona venire,
Finibus expulsum patriis, nova regna petentem,
Auxilio Beli: genitor tum Belus opimam
Vastabat Cyprum, et victor ditione tenebat.
Tempore jam ex illo casus mihi cognitus urbis
Trojanæ, nomenque tuum, regesque Pelasgi.
Ipse hostis Teucros insigni laude ferebat,
Seque ortum antiquâ Teucrorum à stirpe volebat.
Quare agite, O tectis, juvenes, succedite nostris:
Me quoquè per multos similis fortuna labores
Jactatam, hac demum voluit consistere terrâ.
Non ignara mali, miseris succurrere disco.

Sidonia Dido obstupuit primo aspectu, deinde tanto casu viri, et sic locuta est ore: O nate Dea, quis casus insequitur te per tanta pericula? quæ vis applicat te immanibus oris? Tune es ille Æneas, quem alma Venus genuit Dardanio Anchisæ ad undam Phrygii Simoentis? Atque equidem memini Teucrum venire Sidona, expulsum patriis finibus, petentem nova regna auxilio Beli. Genitor meus *Belus tum vastabat opimam Cyprum, et victor tenebat* eam *ditione. Casus Trojanæ urbis cognitus* est *mihi jam ex illo tempore, nomenque tuum, regesque Pelasgi. Ipse hostis ferebat Teucros insigni laude, volebatque se esse ortum ab antiqua stirpe Teucrorum. Quare, O juvenes, agite, succedite nostris tectis: similis fortuna voluit me quoque jactatam per multos labores, demum consistere in hac terrâ. Ego non ignara mali, disco succurrere miseris.*

TRANSLATION.

Sidonian Dido stood astonished first at the Presence of the Hero, then at his signal Sufferings, and thus her Speech addressed: What *hard* Fate, O Goddess-born, pursues thee through such mighty Dangers? What Power drives *thee* on *this* barbarous Coast? Are you the *great* Æneas, whom, by Phrygian Simois's Stream, fair Venus bore to Trojan Anchises? And *now* indeed I call to Mind that Teucer, expelled his native Country, came to Sidon in quest of a new Kingdom, *depending* on the Aid of Belus. My Father Belus then reaped the Spoil of wealthy Cyprus, and held it in Subjection to his victorious Arms. Ever since that Time I have been acquainted with the Fate of Troy, with your Name, and the Grecian Kings. The Enemy himself extolled the Trojans with distinguished Praise, and with Pleasure traced his Descent from the ancient Trojan Race. Come then, *heroic* Youths, enter our Walls. Me too, through a Series of Labours tossed, like Fate *with yours*, at length have doomed to settle in this Land. Myself no Stranger to Misfortune, have learned to succour the distressed.

NOTES.

619. *Teucrum—expulsum.* This is *Teucer*, the Son of *Telamon*, and Brother of *Ajax*, who upon his Return from *Troy*, was banished by his Father, for not preventing his Brother's Death, as he thought he might have done.

625. *Ipse hostis.* *Teucer*, though a *Greek* by the Father's Side, *volebat se ortum*, gave himself out, or would have himself reputed of *Trojan* Extraction, thus disclaiming Relation to his Father, and reckoning his Lineage from his Mother, who was the Daughter of *Laomedon*, King of *Troy*, descended in a direct Line from the ancient *Teucer*, the Founder of the *Teucri* or *Trojan* Race. The true Reason why *Teucer* valued himself rather on Account of his Relation to the *Trojans* by his Mother, than to the *Grecians* by his Father, was in Resentment of the ill Usage he had met with from his Father; but the Poet,

Sic memorat, ſimul ducit Æneam in regia tecta, ſimul indicit honorem templis Divûm. Interea nec minus mittit munera ſociis ad littora viginti tauros, centum horrentia terga magnorum ſuum, centum pingues agnos cum matribus, lætitiamque Dei Bacchi. At interior domus ſplendida inſtruitur regali luxu, parantque convivia in mediis tectis. Adſunt veſtes laboratæ arte, oſtroque ſuperbo: ingens argentum adeſt in menſis, fortiaque facta patrum cœlata in auro, longiſſima ſeries rerum

Sic memorat: ſimul Ænean in regia ducit
Tecta; ſimul Divûm templis indicit honorem.
Nec minus interea ſociis ad littora mittit
Viginti tauros, magnorum horrentia centum
Terga ſuum, pingues centum cum matribus agnos
Munera, lætitiamque Dei.
At domus interior regali ſplendide luxu
Inſtruitur, mediiſque parant convivia tectis.
Arte laboratæ veſtes, oſtroque ſuperbo:
Ingens argentum menſis, cœlataque in auro
Fortia facta patrum, ſeries longiſſima rerum.

TRANSLATION.

This ſaid, ſhe forthwith leads Æneas into her royal Apartments, and at the ſame Time ordains due Honours for the Temples of the Gods. Mean While, with no leſs Care, ſhe ſends Preſents to his Crew in the Ships, twenty Bulls, an hundred huge Boars with briſtly Backs, as many fat Lambs, with the Ewes, and the Joys of the God *Bacchus*. But the inner Rooms *of State* are ſplendidly furniſhed with regal Pomp, and Banquets are prepared in the Middle of the Hall. *Here are* Carpets wrought with Art, and of the richeſt Purple; the Tables *ſhine with* maſſy Silver-plate, and emboſſed in Gold *appear* the brave Exploits of her Forefathers, a lengthened Series of Hiſtory traced down through ſo many Heroes,

NOTES.

by concealing that Circumſtance, ſets this Action in ſuch a Light as to reflect no ſmall Honour on the *Trojans*.

632. *Templis indicit honorem.* It was the ancient Cuſtom to offer up Libations and other Acts of Thankſgiving to the Gods, upon the Arrival of Strangers, eſpecially to *Jupiter Zenius*, the God of Hoſpitality, or who preſides over Strangers. Thus in *Homer*, *Alcinous*, when he receives *Ulyſſes* at his Court, orders Libations to *Jove, who guides the Wanderer on his Way.* Pope's Odyſſey, VII. 240. *Servius* takes *indicit honorem* to ſignify originally to raiſe, or order Contributions to be raiſed in Honour of the Gods; becauſe the Ancients, on Account of their Poverty, were obliged to collect for their Sacrifices, or elſe they applied to that Uſe the Goods and Effects of condemned Malefactors: Hence *ſupplicia*, Puniſhments, came to ſignify Prayers: *ſupplicatio*, Thankſgivings; and *ſacer*, both holy and accurſed.

636. *Munera, lætitiamque Dei.* The Commentators are greatly divided about the Meaning of theſe Words. *Corradus* explains them *an Offering and Joy*, i. e. a grateful Offering to the God (*Neptune*) who had ſaved them from Shipwreck, taking *munera* in the ſame Senſe as Geor. IV. 534.

——————*tu munera ſupplex*
Tende, petens pacem, et faciles venerare Napæas.

Aulus Gellius reads *munera lætitiamque die*, Preſents with which they might joyfully paſs the Day; taking *die* for *diei*, as Geor. I. 208. *Servius*, and the Generality of Interpreters, conſider it as a poetical Circumlocution for *Wine*, which is the *Gift and Joy*, or *the joyful Gift of the God* (Bacchus). The Tranſlation is according to the Pointing in *Heinſius*'s Edition, where there is no Stop after *agnos*, but a Comma after *munera*; ſo that the Conſtruction runs thus, *Mittit viginti tauros munera*; ſhe ſends them Preſents of twenty Bulls, &c. *lætitiamque Dei*, and the Joy of the God (Bacchus) *i. e. Wine*. See Verſe 651, where *munera* is conſtrued the ſame Way.

640. *Argentum—auro.* Gold and Silver-plate, which was ſimply called Gold and Silver. So *Seneca de Vita Beat.* Cap. XVII. *Nec temere, et ut libet, collocatur argentum, ſed perite ſervi-*

Per tot ducta viros antiquæ ab origine gentis.
Æneas (neque enim patrius consistere mentem
Passus amor) rapidum ad naves præmittit Achatem, 644
Ascanio ferat hæc, ipsumque ad mœnia ducat.
Omnis in Ascanio cari stat cura parentis.
Munera præterea, Iliacis erepta ruinis,
Ferre jubet, pallam signis auroque rigentem,
Et circumtextum croceo velamen acantho;
Ornatus Argivæ Helenæ: quos illa Mycenis,
Pergama cum peteret, inconcessosque Hymenæos, 651
Extulerat; matris Ledæ mirabile donum.
Præterea sceptrum, Ilione quod gesserat olim,
Maxima natarum Priami, colloque monile
Baccatum, et duplicem gemmis auroque coronam. 655
Hæc celerans, iter ad naves tendebat Achates.

ducta per tot viros ab origine antiquæ gentis. Æneas (neque enim amor patrius passus est illius mentem consistere) præmittit Achaten rapidum ad naves; ut ferat hæc Ascanio, atque ipsum ad mœnia ducat: omnis cura cari parentis stat in Ascanio. Præterea jubet Ascanium ferre secum munera erepta Iliacis ruinis, pallam nempe rigentem signis auroque, et velamen circumtextum croceo acantho: ornatus Argivæ Helenæ, quos illa extulerat Mycenis, cum peteret Pergama, Hymenæosque inconcessos; qui ornatus erant mirabile donum matris Ledæ. Præterea jubet eum ferre sceptrum, quod Ilione maxima natarum Priami olim gesserat, baccatumque monile collo, et coronam duplicem gemmis auroque. Achates celerans hæc tendebat iter ad naves.

TRANSLATION.

from the first Founder of the ancient Race. Æneas (for paternal Affection suffered not his Mind to rest) with Speed sends Achates before to the Ships, to bear these Tidings to Ascanius, and bring *the Boy* himself to the City. All the fond Parent's Care centers in Ascanius. Besides, he bids him bring Presents *for the Queen* saved from the Ruins of Troy, a Mantle stiff with Gold and Figures, and a Veil woven round with Saffron-coloured Flowers of Brank-ursine, the Ornaments of Grecian Helen, which she had brought with her from Mycenæ, when bound for Troy and her lawless Marriage; her Mother Leda's curious Gift. A Scepter too, which once Ilione, Priam's eldest Daughter, bore, a Necklace strung with Pearl, and a Crown set with double Rows of Gems and Gold. This Message to dispatch, Achates directs his Course to the Ships.

NOTES.

tur. Tully IV. in Verr. *Canabat apud Eupolemum, argentum ille apposuerat.* And *Virgil* himself, in the third Æneid, 355:

——*Impositis auro dapibus.*

642. *Per tot—viros.* The whole History of the Family from *Belus*, or rather *Abibalus*, the first *Tyrian* Monarch.

644. *Rapidum—præmittit.* *Servius* thinks this is equivalent to *mittit præcipitem*, which appears forced. Rather, sends him before the Entertainment, or before the Messengers sent by *Dido*, Verse 633.

647. *Iliacis erepta ruinis.* This shews them to have been Things of the greatest Value.

648. *Pallam.* This was a Kind of Stole or long Garment, that reached down to the Feet:

Fu[illegible] sed ad teneros lutea palla pedes.

Tibull. I. [illegible]

Hence *Horace* gives it the Epithet of [illegible],

Post hunc personæ, pallæque repertor [illegible]
Æschylus. De Arte Poet. 278.

648. *Signis auroque*, i. e. *Signis aureis*, as above *molemque et montes*; and Geor. II. 192. *Pateris libamus et auro*, i. e. *pateris aureis*.

656. *Hæc celerans.* After the Manner of the *Greeks*, who used [illegible] and [illegible] the same Way.

665. *Tela*

At Cytherea versat novas artes, et nova consilia in pectore; ut nempe Cupido mutatus faciem et ora veniat pro dulci Ascanio, donisque incendat furentem Reginam, atque implicet ignem illius ossibus. Quippe timet domum ambiguam Tyriosque bilingues: atrox Juno urit eam, et cura ejus recursat sub noctem. Ergo affatur aligerum Amorem his dictis: O nate, meæ vires, mea magna potentia; nate, qui solus temnis Typhœa tela summi Patris Jovis: *confugio ad te, et supplex posco tua numina.* Hæc *nota* sunt tibi, *ut* nempe *frater tuus Æneas pelago jactetur circum omnia littora, odiis iniquæ Junonis: et tu sæpe doluisti nostro dolore. Phœnissa Dido tenet hunc, moraturque* eum *blandis vocibus; et vereor quo Junonia hospitia vertant se:* illa *haud cessabit in tanto cardine rerum. Quocirca meditor ante capere Reginam dolis, et cingere* eam *flammâ; ne quo numine mutet se; sed* potiùs ut *teneatur mecum magno amore Æneæ.*

At Cytherea novas artes, nova pectore versat
Consilia; ut faciem mutatus et ora Cupido
Pro dulci Ascanio veniat, donisque furentem
Incendat Reginam, atque ossibus implicet ignem.
Quippe domum timet ambiguam Tyriosque bilingues:
Urit atrox Juno, et sub noctem cura recursat.
Ergo his aligerum dictis affatur Amorem:
Nate, meæ vires, mea magna potentia; solus,
Nate, Patris summi qui tela Typhoëa temnis;
Ad te confugio, et supplex tua numina posco.
Frater ut Æneas pelago tuus omnia circum
Littora jactetur, odiis Junonis iniquæ,
Nota tibi: et nostro doluisti sæpe dolore.
Hunc Phœnissa tenet Dido, blandisque moratur
Vocibus; et vereor, quò se Junonia vertant
Hospitia: haud tanto cessabit cardine rerum.
Quocirca capere ante dolis, et cingere flammâ
Reginam meditor: ne quo se numine mutet;
Sed magno Æneæ mecum teneatur amore.

TRANSLATION.

But Venus revolves in her Breast new Plots *and* new Designs, that Cupid should come in place of sweet Ascanius, assuming his Mien and Features, and by the Gifts kindle in the Queen all the Rage of Love, and convey the subtle Flame into her *very* Bones. For she dreads the *false* equivocating Race, and the double-tongued, *perfidious* Tyrians: Fell Juno's Rage torments her, and with the Night her Care returns. To winged Love therefore she addresses these Words: O Son, my Strength, my mighty Power; *my* Son, who alone defiest the Typhœan Bolts of Jove supreme, to thee I fly, and suppliant implore thy Deity. Thou knowest how round all Shores thy Brother Æneas is tossed from Sea to Sea by the complicated Malice of partial Juno, and in my Grief hast often grieved. Him Phœnician Dido entertains, and amuses with smooth Speeches; and I fear what may be the Issue of Juno's Acts of Hospitality: She will not be idle in so critical a Conjuncture. Wherefore, I purpose to prevent the Queen by subtle Means, and to beset her with the Flames *of Love*, that no Power may influence her to change, but that with me she may cherish a great Fondness for Æneas. How this thou

NOTES.

665. *Tela Typhœa.* The Bolts whereby *Typhœus* and the other Giants were overthrown; a very lively poetical Expression to denote the Power of Love.

673. *Et cingere flammâ.* A Metaphor borrowed from the Manner of blocking up a Town by planting Fires round the Walls, that there was no Way left to escape:

Interea vigilum excubiis obsidere portas
Cura datur Messapo, et mœnia cingere flammis. Æn. IX. 159.

Interea Rutuli portis circum omnibus instant
Sternere cæde viros, et mœnia cingere flammis. Æn. X. 181.

681. *Idalium*

Quà facere id possis, nostram nunc accipe mentem.
Regius, accitu cari genitoris, ad urbem
Sidoniam puer ire parat, mea maxima cura;
Dona ferens, pelago, et flammis restantia Trojæ.
Hunc ego sopitum somno, super alta Cythera,
Aut super Idalium, sacratâ sede recondam;
Ne quà scire dolos, mediusve occurrere possit.
Tu faciem illius, noctem non ampliùs unam,
Falle dolo; et notos pueri puer indue vultus:
Ut, cum te gremio accipiet lætissima Dido,
Regales inter mensas, laticemque Lyæum,
Cum dabit amplexus, atque oscula dulcia figet;
Occultum inspires ignem, fallasque veneno.
Paret Amor dictis caræ genitricis, et alas
Exuit, et gressu gaudens incedit Iüli.
At Venus Ascanio placidam per membra quietem
Irrigat, et fotum gremio Dea tollit in altos
Idaliæ lucos: ubì mollis amaracus illum
Floribus, et dulci aspirans complectitur umbrâ.

Nunc accipe nostram mentem quà possis facere id. Regius puer, mea maxima cura, parat ire ad Sidoniam urbem, accitu cari genitoris, ferens dona restantia pelago et flammis Trojæ. Ego recondam hunc sopitum somno, super alta Cythera, aut super Idalium nemus in sacratâ sede; ne quà possit scire dolos, mediusve occurrere. Tu dolo falle faciem illius unam noctem non ampliùs; et ipse puer indue notos vultus pueri: ut, cum Dido lætissima accipiet te gremio, inter regales mensas Lyæumque laticem, cum dabit tibi *amplexus atque figet* tibi *dulcia oscula; inspires* ei *occultum ignem, fallasque* eam *veneno. Amor paret dictis caræ genitricis, et exuit alas, et gaudens incedit gressu Iüli. At Venus irrigat placidam quietem per membra Ascanio, et Dea tollit* eum *fotum gremio in altos lucos Idaliæ: ubi mollis amaracus aspirans, complectitur illum floribus et dulci umbrâ.*

TRANSLATION.

mayst effect, now hear what I advise. The royal Boy, my chiefest Care, at his Father's Call, prepares to visit the Sidonian City Carthage, bearing Presents *for Dido* saved from the Sea and Flames of Troy. Him having lulled to Rest, I will lay down on Cythera's Tops, or in some sacred Retreat above Idalium, lest he should discover the Plot, or, intervening, marr *its Success.* Do you artfully counterfeit his Face but for one Night, and, yourself a Boy, assume a Boy's familiar Looks; that when Dido shall take thee to her Bosom in the Heighth of her Joy amidst the royal Feasts, and Bacchus's chearing Liquor; when she shall give thee repeated Embraces, and press thee with sweet Kisses, thou mayst breathe into her the secret Flame, and by Stealth convey the Poison. The God of Love obeys the Dictates of his dear Mother, lays aside his Wings, and joyful trips along in Iulus's Gait. Mean while Venus pours the Dews of balmy Sleep on Ascanius's Limbs, and in her Bosom fondling, conveyed him to Idalia's lofty Groves, where soft Amaracus, perfuming the Air with Flowers and fragrant Shade, clasps him round.

NOTES:

681 *Idalium.* A Town and Grove of that Name in the Island of *Cyprus.*

686. *Laticemque Lyæum.* *Lyæus* is a Name given to *Bacchus,* ἀπὸ τοῦ λύειν, because Wine dissipates Care,

Cura fugit multo diluiturque mero,
———————*dissipat Evius*
Curas mordaces.
Hor. II. Ode XI. 17.

693. *Mollis amaracus.* The Herb *Marjoram,* otherwise called *Sampsucbum,* whereof *Pliny* tells us a most excellent Kind grew in *Cyprus,* and that it was baneful to Serpents: *Sampsucbum, sive amaracus, in Cypro laudatissimum et odoratissimum scorpionibus adversatur.* So that it was a very proper Bed for *Ascanius* to sleep on with Safety.

698. *Aureâ*

Jamque Cupido ibat parens dicto matris, et portabat Tyriis regia dona, lætus Achate duce. Cum venit, Regina jam composuit se super aulæis superbis, locavitque se mediam in aureâ spondâ. Jam pater Æneas, et jam Trojana juventus conveniunt, discumbiturque super strato ostro. Famuli dant lymphas manibus, expediuntque Cererem canistris, feruntque mantilia tonsis villis. Intus erant quinquaginta famulæ, quibus cura fuit struere penum longo ordine, et adolere Penates flammis. Centum erant aliæ, totidemque ministri pares ætate, qui onerent mensas dapibus, et ponant pocula. Nec non et Tyrii frequentes convenere per læta limina, jussi discumbere super pictis toris. Mirantur dona Æneæ, mirantur Iülum,

Jamque ibat dicto parens, et dona Cupido
Regia portabat Tyriis, duce lætus Achate.
Cum venit, aulæis jam se Regina superbis
Aureâ composuit spondâ, mediamque locavit.
Jam pater Æneas, et jam Trojana juventus
Conveniunt, stratoque super discumbitur ostro.
Dant famuli manibus lymphas, Cereremque canistris
Expediunt, tonsisque ferunt mantilia villis.
Quinquaginta intus famulæ, quibus ordine longo
Cura penum struere, et flammis adolere Penates.
Centum aliæ, totidemque pares ætate ministri,
Qui dapibus mensas onerent, et pocula ponant.
Nec non et Tyrii per limina læta frequentes
Convenere, toris jussi discumbere pictis.
Mirantur dona Æneæ; mirantur Iülum,

TRANSLATION.

Now, in obedience to his Instructions, Cupid went along, and bore the royal Presents to the Tyrians, pleased with Achates for his Guide. By the Time he arrived, the Queen had placed herself on a golden Couch, under a rich Canopy, and took her Seat in the Middle. Now Father Æneas, and now the Trojan Youth grace the Assembly, and plant themselves on the Purple Beds. The Attendants supply *the Guests* with Water for their Hands, dispense the Gifts of Ceres from Baskets, and furnish them with the smooth Towels. Within are fifty Handmaids, whose Task it was to prepare and marshal the Entertainments in due Order, and burn Incense to the Houshold-gods. A hundred more, and as many Servants of equal Age, are employed to crown the Boards with Dishes, and place the Cups. In like Manner the Tyrians, a numerous Train, assemble in the joyful Courts, invited to fill the embroidered Beds. They view with Wonder the Presents of Æneas, nor with less Wonder view Iülus, the glowing Aspect of the God, his

NOTES.

698. *Aureâ composuit spondâ.* Some take *aurea* in the Nominative, to agree with *regina*, but it does better in the Ablative, as Æn. VII. 190. *Aurea percussum virga*; where the two last Syllables must be pronounced like a Diphthong. See more Examples of this, Ecl. III. 96. VIII. 81. Æn. X. 487.

698. *Mediamque locavit.* The Couches whereon they lay at Table were three in Number, each of which was made for three to lie upon; hence *Triclinium* signifies a Dining-room. The Middle, according to *Servius*, was reckoned the most honourable Place, in Proof of which he brings a Quotation from *Sallust*, where *Perpenna*, entertaining *Sertorius*, sets him in the Middle: *Igitur discubuere Sertorius—in medio, &c.*

701. *Dant famuli manibus lymphas Cereremque expediunt.* It was the ancient Custom to wash before Meals. We may observe that *Virgil*, to maintain the Dignity of his Style in this simple Narration, uses the poetical Words, *Lymphas et Cererem*, for Water and Bread.

704. *Flammis adolere Penates.* *Adolere* signifies properly to burn fragrant Incense, as

Verbenasque adole pingues, et mascula thura.
Ecl. VIII. 65.

Or to perfume by Incense, as

Præterea castis adolet dum altaria tædis.
Æn. VIII. 72.

Hence

Flagrantesque Dei vultus, simulataque verba,
Pallamque, et pictum croceo velamen acantho.
Præcipuè infelix, pesti devota futuræ,
Expleri mentem nequit, ardescitque tuendo
Phœnissa; et puero pariter donisque movetur.
Ille, ubi complexu Æneæ, colloque pependit,
Et magnum falsi implevit genitoris amorem,
Reginam petit: hæc oculis, hæc pectore toto
Hæret; et interdum gremio fovet, inscia Dido
Insideat quantus miseræ Deus. At memor ille
Matris Acidaliæ, paulatim abolere Sichæum
Incipit; et vivo tentat prævertere amore
Jampridem resides animos, desuetaque corda.
Postquam prima quies epulis, mensæque remotæ;

flagrantesque vultus Dei, verbaque simulata, pallamque, et velamen pictum croceo acantho. Præcipuè infelix Phœnissa, devota futuræ pesti, nequit expleri mentem, ardescitque tuendo, et pariter movetur puero donisque. Ille, ubi pependit complexu colloque Æneæ, et implevit magnum amorem falsi genitoris, petit Reginam: hæc hæret in eo *oculis, hæc* hæret in eo *toto pectore, et Dido interdum fovet* eum *gremio, inscia quantus Deus insideat* ei *miseræ. At ille, memor matris Acidaliæ, paulatim incipit abolere Sichæum, et tentat vivo amore prævertere animos jampridem resides cordaque desueta.*

Postquam prima quies est *epulis, mensæque* sunt *remotæ;*

TRANSLATION.

swell dissembled Words, the Mantle, and Veil figured with Leaves of the Acanthus in Saffron Colours. Chiefly the unhappy Queen, henceforth devoted to Love's pestilential Fever, gazes with unwearied Delight, and is inflamed with every Glance, and is equally captivated with the Boy and with his Gifts. He on Æneas's Neck having hung with *fond* Embraces, and having fully gratified his fictitious Father's ardent Affection, advances to the Queen. She fixes her Eyes, her whole Soul *on the Boy*, and sometimes fondles him in her Lap, not thinking what a powerful God *there* sits plotting her Ruin. Meanwhile he, heedful of his Mother's *Instructions*, begins insensibly to deface *the Memory of* Sichæus, and with a living Flame tries to prepossess her languid Affections, and her Heart by long Disuse grown cold *to Love*.

Soon as the first Banquet ended, and the Tables were withdrawn, they place

NOTES.

Hence it signifies to perform Acts of Worship in general,

Junoni Argivæ jussos adolemus honores.
Æn. III. 547.

For the *Penates* see above, Verse 527.

713. *Expleri mentem nequit, ardescitque tuendo.*

Ut vidi! ut perii! ut me malus abstulit error!
Ecl. VIII. 41.

Nec prius ex illo flagrantia declinavit
Lumina, quam toto concepit pectore flammam,
Funditus, atque imis exarsit tota medullis.
Catull. in Nupt. Pelei.

719. *Insideat.* This Word is very expressive, denoting not only *Cupid*'s Situation, but his insidious Design upon *Dido*. *Heinsius* reads *insidat*, a Word of much the same Import, and is applied to Bees greedily clinging to the Summer Flowers, and rioting on the Blossoms:

——— *ubi apes æstate serenâ*
Floribus insidunt variis ———
Æn. VI. 707.

721. *Vivo amore.* May either mean with an ardent Passion, or rather a Passion for a living Object.

723. *Postquam prima quies epulis, mensæque remotæ.* The *Romans*, as *Servius* observes, brought in the several Courses in Tables, and not by single Dishes; hence we read frequently in Authors of the *prima Mensa* and *secunda Mensa*, the first and second Service. Particularly in *Cicero*'s Epistles to *Atticus*, Lib. XIV. 6. *Hæc ad te scripsi apposita secunda mensa.* This I wrote to you between the first and second Service. Whence it appears that there was a considerable Interval between the one and the other. See also his twenty-first Letter of the same Book,

ministri statuunt magnos crateras, et coronant vina. Strepitus fit in tectis, volutantque vocem per ampla atria: incensi lychni dependent ab aureis laquearibus; et funalia vincunt noctem flammis. Hic Regina poposcit pateram gravem gemmis auroque, implevitque eam mero; quam Belus et omnes à Belo soliti sunt implere. Tum silentia sunt facta in tectis: O Jupiter (nam loquuntur te dare jura hospitibus) velis hunc diem esse lætum Tyriisque, profectisque Trojâ, velisque nostros minores meminisse hujus diei. Adsit Bacchus dator lætitiæ, et bona Juno: et O vos Tyrii faventes celebrate hunc cœtum. Dixit, et libavit honorem laticum in mensa,

Crateras magnos statuunt, et vina coronant.
Fit strepitus tectis, vocemque per ampla volutant
Atria: dependent lychni laquearibus aureis
Incensi, et noctem flammis funalia vincunt.
Hic Regina gravem gemmis auroque poposcit,
Implevitque mero, pateram; quam Belus, et omnes
A Bello soliti. Tum facta silentia tectis:
Jupiter (hospitibus nam te dare jura loquuntur)
Hunc lætum Tyriisque diem, Trojâque profectis,
Esse velis, nostrosque hujus meminisse minores.
Adsit lætitiæ Bacchus dator, et bona Juno:
Et vos O cœtum Tyrii celebrate faventes.
Dixit, et in mensâ laticum libavit honorem;

TRANSLATION.

large Goblets, and crown the *sparkling* Wine. The Roofs resound with bustling Din, and *the Guests* roll through the ample Courts the bounding Voice. Down from the golden Cielings hang the flaming Lamps, and *blazing* Torches overpower the *Darkness of the* Night. Here the Queen called for a Bowl, ponderous with Gems and Gold, and with pure Wine filled it to the Brim, *a Bowl* which Belus, and all *her Ancestors* from Belus, used; then, having enjoined Silence through the Palace, *she thus began:* O Jove (for by thee, it is said, the Laws of Hospitality were given) grant this may be an auspicious Day both to the Tyrians and my Trojan Guests, and may this Day be commemorated by our Posterity. Bacchus, the Giver of Joy, and propitious Juno, be present here; and you, my Tyrians, with benevolent Hearts, solemnize this Meeting. She said, and on the Table poured an Offering *to the Gods*; and, after the Libation, first gently touch-

NOTES.

and the thirteenth Letter of the fifteenth Book.

724. *Vina coronant.* In Imitation of *Homer*, Il. I. 470.

Κυροι μεν κρητηρας επεστεψαντο ποτοιο.

The Youths crowned the Goblets with Wine: which *Athenæus* explains to mean no more than to fill them Brim full with Wine. But some understand it of adorning the Cups with Garlands. The Ancients upon certain Occasions used Goblets of a monstrous Size. The same Author describes one of Silver, so large as to contain six hundred *Amphoræ*, which amount at least to twenty Tuns of our Measure. And *Arrian* describes another so capacious as to contain the Libations *Alexander* and nine thousand Guests performed to the Gods.

726. *Dependent lychni laquearibus aureis.* This Passage *Milton* has finely improved upon in his Description of *Pandemonium*, or the Devil's Palace, in the first Book of his *Paradise Lost*, Verse 726.

——————From the arched Roof,
Pendent by subtle Magic, many a Row
Of starry Lamps, and blazing Cressets, fed
With Naphtha and Asphaltus, yielded Light
As from a Sky.

729. *Belus et omnes à Belo.* It is plain that the *Belus* here mentioned cannot refer to *Dido*'s Father (otherwise there would be no Propriety in saying *omnes à Belo*, all the Descendants or Successors of *Belus*), but to one of her Ancestors, perhaps the Founder of the Family.

736. *Libavit honorem.* This Ceremony of *Libation* consisted in pouring out some Drops of the Wine, either upon the Altar, or sometimes

upon

Primaque libato ſummo tenus attigit ore:
Tum Bitiæ dedit increpitans: ille impiger hauſit
Spumantem pateram, et pleno ſe proluit auro.
Poſt, alii proceres. Citharâ crinitus Iopas 740
Perſonat auratâ, docuit quæ maximus Atlas.
Hic canit errantem Lunam, Soliſque labores;
Unde hominum genus, et pecudes; unde imber, et ignes:
Arcturum, pluviaſque Hyadas, geminoſque Triones;
Quid tantum Oceano properent ſe tingere ſoles
Hiberni, vel quæ tardis mora noctibus obſtet. 746
Ingeminant plauſum Tyrii, Troeſque ſequuntur.
Nec non et vario noctem ſermone trahebat
Infelix Dido, longumque bibebat amorem;
Multa ſuper Priamo rogitans, ſuper Hectore multa;
Nunc, quibus Auroræ veniſſet filius armis; 751
Nunc, quales Diomedis equi; nunc, quantus Achilles.

eoque libato prima attigit reliquum tenus ſummo ore. Tum dedit Bitiæ increpitans eum: ille impiger hauſit ſpumantem pateram, et proluit ſe pleno auro: poſt eum alii proceres hauſerunt eam. *Iopas crinitus perſonat auratâ citharâ, ea quæ maximus Atlas docuit. Hic canit Lunam errantem, laboreſque Solis; unde ſit genus hominum, et pecudes; unde ſit imber, et ignes;* canit *Arcturum, Hyadaſque pluvias, geminoſque Triones;* canit *quid hyberni ſoles tantum properent tingere ſe Oceano, vel quæ mora obſtet tardis noctibus. Tyrii ingeminant plauſum, Troeſque* eos *ſequuntur.*

Nec non et infelix Dido trahebat noctem vario ſermone, bibebatque longum amorem; rogitans *multa ſuper Priamo, multa ſuper Hectore;* nunc rogitans *quibus armis filius Auroræ veniſſet; nunc quales eſſent equi Diomedis; nunc quantus* eſſet *Achilles.*

TRANSLATION.

ed *the Cup* with her Lips, then gave it to Bitias with kindly Challenge: He quickly drained the foaming Bowl, and laved himſelf with the brimming Gold; after *him* the other Lords. Long-haired Iopas *next* tunes his gilded Lyre to what the mighty Atlas taught. He ſings the wandering Moon, and the Eclipſes of the *labouring* Sun. Whence the Race of Men and Beaſts, whence Showers and fiery Meteors ariſe. *He ſings* Arcturus, the rainy Hyades, and the two *northern* Cars, why Winter Suns make ſo much Haſte to ſet in the Ocean, or what retarding Cauſe detains the ſlow *Summer* Nights. The Tyrians redouble their Applauſes *in Praiſe of the Song*, and the Trojans concur.

Mean while, unhappy Dido, with various Talk, ſpun out the Night, and drunk large Draughts of Love, queſtioning much about Priam, much about Hector. Now in what Arms Aurora's Son had come; now what were the Excellencies of Diomed's Steeds; now what Figure Achilles made. Nay, come my

NOTES.

upon the Table, as an Offering to the Gods, in Acknowledgment of their Bounty. For the Phraſe *honorem Latium* ſee above, Verſe 632.

740. *Citharâ perſonat.* In like Manner *Homer* makes *Demodocus* ſing and play at the Feaſt with which *Alcinous* entertains *Ulyſſes*, in the eighth Book of the Odyſſey. But the Subject of the Song in *Homer, the Actions of* Ulyſſes, how proper ſoever to the Occaſion, ſinks far below the Dignity of this. The Song of *Iopas* is of the ſublimeſt Kind, and there is ſuch a Sweetneſs and Majeſty in the Numbers, as lift the Soul with the Poet to Heaven, like the rapturous Muſic which he deſcribes.

749. *Infelix Dido, longumque bibebat amorem.* *Virgil* is always very happy in ſetting Objects in Contraſt to one another, as here the anxious Situation of *Dido*'s Love-ſick Mind is ſeen in a fine Light, in Oppoſition to the general Mirth and Gaiety of the banqueting Gueſts. While *Tyrians* and *Trojans* give a Looſe to Joy, and are making the Roofs reſound with their repeated Acclama-

tions,

Immò, O hospes, inquit, dic nobis à primâ origine insidias Danaûm, casusque tuorum, tuosque errores: nam septima æstas jam portat te errantem omnibus terris et fluctibus.

Immò age, et à prima, dic, hospes, origine nobis
Insidias, inquit, Danaûm, casusque tuorum,
Erroresque tuos: nam te jam septima portat
Omnibus errantem terris et fluctibus æstas.

TRANSLATION.

Guest, she says, and, from the first Original, relate to us the Stratagems of the Greeks, the Adventures of your Friends, and your own Wanderings; for now the seventh Summer brings thee *to our Coasts*, through wandering Mazes tossed on every Land and *every* Sea.

NOTES.

tions, *Æneas* alone engages *Dido*'s Thoughts and Attention; she relishes neither the Pleasures of the Feast, nor of the Song, and can listen to no Music but the Charms of his Voice.

P. VIRGILII MARONIS

ÆNEIDOS

LIBER SECUNDUS.

ORDO.

Omnes conticuere, intentique tenebant ora. Inde pater Æneas sic orsus est ab alto toro: O Regina, jubes me renovare dolorem infandum,

Conticuere omnes, intentique ora tenebant:
Inde toro pater Æneas sic orsus ab alto:
Infandum, Regina, jubes renovare dolorem:

TRANSLATION.

ALL with one Accord were silent, and fixed their Eyes upon him, eagerly attentive: Then Father Æneas thus from his lofty Couch began:
Unutterable Woes, O Queen, you urge me to renew; how the Greeks

NOTES.

This second Book is one of those which *Virgil* singled out to rehearse before *Augustus*, as a Specimen of his Work; a sure Indication of the Esteem he himself had of it.

3. *Infandum, Regina, jubes renovare dolorem.* In this Introduction *Virgil* remarkably follows the Rule laid down by *Horace, De Art. Poët.* Verse 105.

——Tristia mæstum
Vultum verba decent.

The Lines languish, and are so artfully composed, as to force the Reader to pronounce them with a slow, broken, and interrupted Voice, and shew *Æneas*, as it were, heaving out every Word with a Sigh.

Trojanas ut opes, et lamentabile regnum
Eruerint Danai; quæque ipse miserrima vidi,
Et quorum pars magna fui. Quis talia fando,
Myrmidonum, Dolopumve, aut duri miles Ulyssei
Temperet à lacrymis? et jam nox humida cœlo
Præcipitat, suadentque cadentia sidera somnos.
Sed, si tantus amor casus cognoscere nostros,
Et breviter Trojæ supremum audire laborem,
Quanquam animus meminisse horret, luctuque refugit,
Incipiam. Fracti bello, fatisque repulsi
Ductores Danaûm, tot jam labentibus annis,

narrando ut Danai eruerint Trojanas opes et lamentabile regnum; quæque miserrima ego ipse vidi, et ea quorum fui magna pars. Quis Myrmidonum, Dolopumve, aut quis miles duri Ulyssei temperet à lacrymis fando talia? et jam humida nox præcipitat se cœlo, sideraque cadentia suadent somnos. Sed si tantus amor est tibi cognoscere nostros casus, et breviter audire supremum laborem Trojæ, quanquam animus horret meminisse, refugitque luctu, incipiam. Ductores Danaûm, fracti bello, repulsique fatis, tot annis jam labentibus,

TRANSLATION.

overturned the Power *and Magnificence* of Troy, and its deplorable Realms; both what Scenes of Misery I myself beheld, and those wherein I was a principal Party. What *cruel* Myrmidon, or Dolopian, or who of hardened Ulysses's Band can, in the very Relation of such Woes, refrain from Tears! Besides, humid Night is hastening down the Sky, and the setting Stars invite to Sleep. But since you are so fond to know our Misfortunes, and briefly to hear the Catastrophe of Troy, though my Soul shudders at the Remembrance, and hath shrunk back with Grief, *yet* will I begin. The Grecian Leaders, now extremely weakened by the War, and baffled by the Fates, after a Revolution of so many Years, *being assisted* by

NOTES.

4. *Trojanas opes.* The Kingdom of *Phrygia*, whereof *Troy* was the Capital, was famous for its Riches and Magnificence even to a Proverb;

Nam tu, quæ tenuit dives Achæmenes,
Aut pinguis Phrygiæ Mygdonias opes
Permutare velis crine Licymniæ.

Hor. II. Carm. XII. 21.

5. *Eruerint Danai.* We may observe, once for all, that the *Greeks* were denominated *Danai* from *Danaus* the Brother of *Ægyptus*, who usurped the Throne of *Argos*.

7. *Myrmidonum.* The *Myrmidons* were the Troops of *Achilles*.

7. *Dolopumve.* The *Dolopians* again were the Troops which *Phenix* led to *Troy* from *Scyros*, an Island in the *Ægean* Sea.

9. *Cadentia sidera.* As the Stars rise at Night when they begin to shine out, so they set in the Morning when they disappear. This marks the Time to have been near the Morning.

12. *Luctuque refugit.* *Catrou* and others read *luctumque refugit*, declines the mournful Task, which amounts to the same Sense. The Reader here will observe, that there is a Change in the Tense, *refugit* being of the Preter-tense, whereas *horret* is in the Present; a Freedom which Dr. *Trapp* thinks very harsh. But Dr. *Clarke*, in his Remarks on *Homer*, Iliad I. Verse 37. shews that this Preterite Tense, as the Grammarians call it, refers to the Time present, as well as what is called the present Tense; only the former denotes that the Action is finished at this present Time, and the other, that it is a-doing. As *cœnat* in the Present signifies *he is at Supper*, *cœnavit* in the Preterite, *he has supped*; so here *animus refugit*, which is the very Example Dr. *Clarke* adduces to support his Opinion, signifies, *my Mind has shrunk back*, which refers to the present Time no less than *refugit*, *it shrinks, or is shrinking back.* Whence it appears, that *Virgil's* using this Tense is so far from being licentious and unwarrantable, that it is equally proper with the other, and the more emphatic of the two; for it denotes the Violence and Quickness of the Impression, that his Soul shrunk back, and recoiled at once, in a Moment, at his first calling up the mournful Subject into his Memory.

ædificant equum instar montis, divinâ arte Palladis; intexuntque costas sectâ abiete. Simulant equum esse votum pro reditu: ea fama vagatur. Hi sortiti delecta corpora virûm, furtim includunt ea huc cæco lateri; penitusque complent ingentes cavernas, uterumque armato milite. Tenedos est in conspectu, insula notissima famâ, et dives opum, dum regna Priami manebant; nunc tantum sinus, et statio male fida carinis. Ductores Danaûm *provecti huc, condunt se in deserto littore. Nos rati sumus eos abiisse, et petiisse Mycenas vento: ergo omnis Troja solvit se longo luctu; portæ panduntur; juvat* nos *ire, et videre Dorica castra,*

Instar montis equum, divinâ Palladis arte
Ædificant; sectaque intexunt abiete costas.
Votum pro reditu simulant: ea fama vagatur,
Huc delecta virûm sortiti corpora furtim
Includunt cæco lateri; penitusque cavernas
Ingentes, uterumque armato milite complent.
Est in conspectu Tenedos, notissima famâ
Insula, divus opum, Priami dum regna manebant:
Nunc tantùm sinus, et statio malefida carinis.
Huc se provecti deserto in littore condunt.
Nos abiisse rati, et vento petiisse Mycenas.
Ergo omnis longo solvit se Teucria luctu;
Panduntur portæ; juvat ire, et Dorica castra,

TRANSLATION.

the divine Skill of Pallas, build a *wooden* Horse to the Size of a Mountain, and line its Ribs with Planks of Fir. *This* they pretend an Offering, in order to procure a safe Return. Which Report is *industriously* spread. Hither having secretly conveyed a select Band, chosen out by Lot, they shut them up into the dark Sides, and cram its capacious Caverns and Womb with armed Soldiers. In sight *of Troy* lies Tenedos, an Island well known by Fame, and flourishing while Priam's Kingdom stood: now *it serves* only *for* a Bay, and a Station where Ships are hardly safe to ride: Having made this Island, they conceal themselves in that desolate Shore. We imagined they were gone, and that they had set Sail for Mycenæ. In consequence of which, all Troy is released from its long continued Distress; the Gates are thrown open; with Joy we issue forth, *with Joy* we view

NOTES.

15. *Instar montis equum.* It has been objected, that this Story of the Horse has not Probability enough to support it; since, besides, the Hardiness of the Enterprize, it is not to be imagined that the *Trojans* would be gross enough to receive within their Walls so enormous and suspicious an Engine with so implicit a Credulity. But all these Objections *Segrais* has answered in his Remarks. As to the Hardiness of the Enterprize, he observes, that modern History furnishes Examples of equally hardy and daring Enterprizes being undertaken and executed with Success; and instances, particularly, that of the *Hollanders*, forty of whom ventured to stow themselves in a Boat seemingly loaden with Turfs, and underwent these Scrutinies which are generally made for the Detection of Contraband-goods, and, having found Means of landing, retook the Town of *Breda* from the *Spaniards*. As to the other Objection, which is indeed the principal one, that the *Trojans* should be so gross as to receive the Engine within their Walls, he observes how finely the Poet has contrived Matters to make this not only plausible, but in a Manner necessary and unavoidable. He has loosed the Knot, by the seasonable Interposition of a Divinity. The *Trojans* having heard *Sinon*'s artful Story, and seeing such a strong Confirmation of the Truth of it in the terrible Disaster that befel *Laocoon* and his Sons, had all the Reason in the World to believe the Machine was an Offering sacred to *Minerva*, and that all, who offered any Violation to it, should feel the severe Vengeance of Heaven, as *Laocoon* and his Sons had done; and therefore they could not act otherwise than the Poet supposes them to have done, consistently with their Religion and System of Belief.

16. *Costas.* The *Costæ* or *Ribs* of this wooden Engine are the inner Beams, or Props to which the outer Boards are fastened.

27. *Juvat ire.* The Verb *ire* is frequently used

Deſertoſque videre locos, littuſque relictum.
Hìc Dolopum manus, hìc ſævus tendebat Achilles;
Claſſibus hìc locus; hìc acies certare ſolebant.
Pars ſtupet innuptæ donum exitiale Minervæ,
Et molem mirantur equi: primuſque Thymœtes
Duci intra muros hortatur, et arce locari;
Sive dolo, ſeu jam Trojæ ſic fata ferebant.
At Capys, et quorum melior ſententia menti,
Aut pelago Danaûm inſidias, ſuſpectaque dona
Præcipitare jubent, ſubjectiſque urere flammis;
Aut terebrare cavas uteri et tentare latebras.

locoſque deſertos, littuſque relictum. Hìc manus Dolopum tendebat, hìc tendebat ſævus Achilles; hìc erat locus claſſibus; hìc acies ſolebant certare. Pars ſtupet exitiale donum innuptæ Minervæ, et mirantur molem equi; Thymœteſque primus hortatur eum duci intra muros, et locari in arce; ſive hortatur id *dolo, ſeu fata Trojæ jam ſic ferebant. At Capys, et hi quorum menti melior erat ſententia, jubent aut præcipitare pelago inſidias ſuſpectaque dona Danaûm, urereque ea flammis ſubjectis; aut terebrare et tentare cavas latebras uteri.*

TRANSLATION.

the Grecian Camp, the *now* deſerted Plains, and the abandoned Shore. Here *lay encamped* the Dolopian Bands, there ſtern Achilles had pitched his Tent: Here were the Ships drawn up, there the Armies were wont to fight. Some view with Amazement that baleful Offering of the Virgin Goddeſs Minerva, and wonder at the ſtupendous Bulk of the Horſe; and the *venerable* Thymœtes firſt adviſes it may be dragged within the Walls, and lodged in the Tower, whether it *was* with treacherous Deſign, or that the Deſtiny of Troy now would have it ſo. But Capys, and *all* whoſe Sentiments are the Reſult of ſounder Judgment, ſtrenuouſly urge either to throw into the Sea this inſidious Engine of the Greeks, and their ſuſpected Oblation; or, by applying Flames, conſume it to Aſhes; or, *at leaſt*, to lay open, and ranſack the Receſſes of the hollow Womb. *Mean while*, the

NOTES.

uſed by *Virgil* to expreſs a precipitant, impetuous, eager Motion, as *it naribus ſanguis*, Geor. III. 507. *it mare proruptum*, Æn. I. 246. *juventus it portis*, Æn. IV. 130. And the Senſe ſhews that it ought to be ſo tranſlated here; for to be ſure the *Trojans*, after their long Reſtraint, would be extremely keen and eager to pour forth at their Gates, and view the Grounds which the Enemy had covered. Dr. *Trapp* renders it,—*and pleaſant it was to walk abroad*, as if the *Trojans* had been only going forth in a calm and ſedate Manner, to enjoy the Pleaſures of the Fields and freſh Air.

29. *Hìc Dolopum manus.* Here the Poet makes *Æneas* ſpeak in the Perſon of one of the *Trojans*, viewing the Ground where the Enemy had been encamped.

32. *Primuſque Thymœtes.* This *Thymœtes*, we are told, had to Wife *Cilla*, the Siſter of *Hecuba*, *Priam*'s Conſort, by whom he had a Son born to him on the ſame Day with *Paris*. *Priam*, being warned by the Oracle that a Child was born that Day to the Ruin of his Country, choſe rather, as was natural, to interpret the Oracle of *Thymœtes*'s Son than his own, and put him to Death. On this Account, *Thymœtes* ſtill entertained a Grudge againſt *Priam*, and for that Reaſon was ſuſpected of betraying his Country, which makes *Virgil* here ſay,—*ſive dolo hortatur*.

33. *Arce locari.* *Arx* does not always ſignify a Fort or Citadel, but the Place of greateſt Eminence in a City; as *Virgil*, ſpeaking of the ſeven Hills on which *Rome* was built, calls them *ſeptem arces*, Æn. VI. 783. The *arx* therefore here probably is to be underſtood of that Place which ſerved for a Veſtible to *Minerva*'s Temple.

34. *Sic fata ferebant.* *Virgil* all along gives us to underſtand that the Overthrow of *Troy* was ordained by Deſtiny, which adds the greater Air of Probability to this Epiſode of the wooden Horſe.

37. *Subjectiſque.* *Que* is here uſed, as it is elſewhere, for *ve*. Vid. Æn. X. 709. And indeed ſome Copies read *ſubjectiſve*.

41. *Lae-*

Vulgus incertum scinditur in contraria studia. Ibi Laocoon primus ante omnes, magnâ catervâ eum comitante, ardens decurrit ab summâ arce: et procul exclamat: O miseri cives, quæ tanta est vobis *insania? creditis hostes* esse *avectos? aut putatis ulla dona Danaûm carere dolis? an Ulysses* est *sic notus* vobis? *aut Achivi occultantur inclusi hoc ligno; aut hæc machina fabricata est in nostros muros, inspectura* nostras *domos, venturaque urbi desuper; aut aliquis error latet: O Teucri, ne credite equo. Quicquid id est, timeo Danaos, et ferentes dona. Sic fatus, validis viribus contorsit ingentem hastam in latus, inque alvum feri curvam compagibus: illa stetit tremens, uteroque recusso*

Scinditur incertum studia in contraria vulgus.
Primus ibi ante omnes, magnâ comitante catervâ,
Laocoon ardens summâ decurrit ab arce:
Et procul: O miseri, quæ tanta insania, cives?
Creditis avectos hostes? aut ulla putatis
Dona carere dolis Danaûm? sic notus Ulysses?
Aut hoc inclusi ligno occultantur Achivi;
Aut hæc in nostros fabricata est machina muros,
Inspectura domos, venturaque desuper urbi;
Aut aliquis latet error: equo ne credite, Teucri.
Quicquid id est, timeo Danaos, & dona ferentes.
Sic fatus, validis ingentem viribus hastam
In latus, inque feri curvam compagibus alvum
Contorsit: stetit illa tremens, uteroque recusso

TRANSLATION.

fickle Populace is split into opposite Inclinations. Upon this Laocoon, accompanied with a numerous Gang, Ringleader to the rest, with Ardour hastens down from the Top of the Citadel; and while yet a great Way off *cries out*, O wretched Countrymen, what desperate Infatuation *this?* Do you believe the Enemy gone? Or think you any Gifts of the Greeks can be free from Deceit? Is it thus you are acquainted with Ulysses? Either the Greeks lie concealed within this Wood, or it is an Engine framed against our Walls; to overlook our Houses, and to come down upon our City; or some mischievous Design lurks under it. Trojans, put no Faith in this Horse. However it be, I dread the Greeks, even with all the Gifts they bring. Thus said, with vigorous Efforts he hurled his massy Spear against the Sides and Belly of the Monster, where it swelled out by the compacted Boards into an Arch, the Weapon stood quivering, and, by the Shock, gi-

NOTES.

41. *Laocoon.* According to some he was Brother to *Anchises*; according to others, *Priam's* own Son, and Priest of *Apollo*, or rather of *Neptune*, as in *Petronius*,

——— ——— Namque Neptuno sacer
Crinem solutus, omne Laocoon replet
Clamore vulgus.

48. *Aliquis error. Error* signifies whatever is opposite to Truth, and is taken in a very large Sense by the *Roman* Authors: Here it signifies *Trick, Deceit, Artifice.*

49. *Timeo Danaos, et dona ferentes.* There lies a particular Emphasis in the *et*, *I am jealous of the* Greeks, *even when they bring us Presents.* Or perhaps *et dona ferentes* is to be understood in general, *I dread the* Greeks, *and all who are thus forward to offer Gifts.* It is a very just Observation, that all rash and sudden Liberality is to be suspected, but more especially when it comes from a Foe:

Namque ista subita me jubet benignitas
Vigilare, faciat ne meâ culpâ lucrum.

As *Phædrus* elegantly expresses it in the Fable; agreeable to which is that Reflection *Sophocles* puts in the Mouth of *Ajax*,

Ἐχθρῶν ἄδωρα δῶρα, κ' οὐκ ὀνήσιμα.

The Gifts of an Enemy will never benefit a Man, or make him the richer.

51. *Feri. Ferus* does not always signify a Savage or Beast of Prey; as it is here applied to a Horse, so *Virgil* uses the same Word in speaking of a tame Stag, in the seventh Æneid, Verse 789.

——— ———Petebatque ferrum.

And in like Manner *Horace* applies it to an Ass, 1 Ep. XIII. 8.

Clitellas

Insonuere cavæ gemitumque dedere cavernæ.
Et, si fata Deûm, si mens non læva fuisset,
Impulerat ferro Argolicas fœdare latebras;
Trojaque nunc stares, Priamique arx alta maneres!
Ecce, manus juvenem interea post terga revinctum
Pastores magno ad Regem clamore trahebant
Dardanidæ, qui se ignotum venientibus ultro,
Hoc ipsum ut strueret, Trojamque aperiret Achivis,
Obtulerat: fidens animi, atque in utrumque paratus;
Seu versare dolos, seu certæ occumbere morti.
Undique visendi studio Trojana juventus

cavæ cavernæ insonuere dederuntque gemitum. Et, si fata Deûm fuissent, si mens nostra non fuisset læva, impulerat nos fœdare Argolicas latebras ferro; tuque O Troja nunc stares, altaque arx Priami maneres! Ecce interea pastores Dardanidæ magno cum clamore ad regem trahebant juvenem revinctum manus post terga, qui juvenis ultro obtulerat se ignotum venientibus, ut strueret hoc ipsum, aperiretque Trojam Achivis, fidens animi, atque paratus in utrumque, seu versare dolos, seu occumbere certæ morti. Trojana juventus circumfusa ruit undique studio visendi eum,

TRANSLATION.

ven to its Sides, the hollow Caverns rung, and sent forth a Groan. And, had the Decrees of Heaven permitted, or our Minds not been infatuated, he had prevailed on us to lay open with the Sword this dark Recess of the Greeks: And thou Troy should still have stood, and thou lofty Tower of Priam now remained! In the mean Time, behold Trojan Shepherds, with loud Acclamations, came dragging to the King a Youth, whose Hands were bound behind his Back; who, to them, a mere Stranger, had voluntarily thrown himself in their Way, to promote this same treacherous Design, and open Troy to the Greeks; a resolute Soul, and prepared for either Event, whether to execute his perfidious Purpose, or submit to inevitable Death. The Trojan Youth in circling Crowds pour in from every Quarter, from

NOTES.

Clitellas ferus impingas, Afræque paternum
Cognomen vertas in risum——

53. *Gemitumque dedere.* This Groan arose from some one of the *Greeks* within, who was perhaps wounded with *Laocoon*'s Spear, or at least affrighted thereby, as *Petronius* seems to insinuate in these Words,

——————————*Fremit*
Captiva pubes intus, et dum murmurat,
Roborea moles spirat alieno metu.

57. *Ecce, manus juvenem* *Shakespeare* has given us a fine Picture of *Sinon*, answering to the Character in which he is here drawn; it is in his Poem intituled *Tarquin* and *Lucrece*. The disconsolate Lady, after the Injury of her Rape, is supposed to fix her Eyes on a Painting, in which the Destruction of *Troy* is represented; and, amongst other Figures, she sees that of the dissembling *Sinon*:

She throws her Eyes about the painted Round,
And whom she finds forlorn, she doth lament;
At last she sees a wretched Image bound,
That piteous Looks to Phrygian Shepherds lent;
His Face, though full of Cares, yet shewed Content.
Onward to Troy with these blunt Swains he goes,
So mild, that Patience seemed to scorn his Woes.
In him the Painter labour'd with his Skill,
To hide Deceit, and give the harmless Show;
An humble Gait, calm Looks, Eyes wailing still,
A Brow unbent, that seem'd to welcome Woe;
Cheeks, neither red, nor pale; but mingled so,
That blushing red no guilty Instance gave,
Nor ashy pale the Fear that false Hearts have.

62. *Seu certæ occumbere morti.* To fall a Sacrifice

certantque illudere capto. Nunc accipi insidias Danaûm, et disce omnes ab uno crimine. Namque, ut ille *constitit in medio conspectu turbatus, inermis, atque oculis circumspexit Phrygia agmina, inquit: heu, quæ tellus, quæ æquora nunc possunt accipere me; aut quid jam denique restat mihi misero! cui neque usquam locus* est *apud Danaos: et super ipsi Dardanidæ infensi poscunt pœnas cum meo sanguine. Quo gemitu* nostri *animi* sunt *conversi, et omnis impetus compressus: hortamur* eum *fari, quo sanguine* sit *cretus; memoret quid ferat; quæve fiducia sit capto. Ille, formidine tandem deposita, fatur hæc:* O *Rex,* ego *equidem, inquit, fatebor tibi cuncta vera quæcunque id fuerint;*

Circumfusa ruit, certantque illudere capto.
Accipe nunc Danaûm insidias, et crimine ab uno
Disce omnes.
Namque, ut conspectu in medio turbatus, inermis,
Constitit, atque oculis Phrygia agmina circumspexit:
Heu, quæ nunc tellus, inquit, quæ me æquora possunt
Accipere? aut quid jam misero mihi denique restat?
Cui neque apud Danaos usquam locus; et super ipsi
Dardanidæ infensi pœnas cum sanguine poscunt.
Quo gemitu conversi animi, compressus et omnis
Impetus: hortamur fari, quo sanguine cretus,
Quidve ferat; memoret quæ sit fiducia capto.
Ille hæc, depositâ tandem formidine, fatur:
Cuncta equidem tibi, Rex, fuerint quæcunque, fatebor

TRANSLATION.

Eagerness to see him, and they vie with one another in insulting the Captive. Now mark the Treachery of the Greeks, and from one Crime take a Specimen of the whole Nation.

For as he stood among the gazing Crowds perplexed, defenceless, and threw his Eyes round the Trojan Bands, Ah! says he, what Land, what Seas can now receive me? Or to what further Extremity can I, a forlorn Wretch, be reduced? For whom there is neither Shelter any where among the Greeks, and, to complete my Misery, the Trojans too, incensed against me, sue for Satisfaction with my Blood. By which mournful Accents, our Affections at once were moved towards him, and all the Keenness of our Resentment suppressed: We exhort him to say from what Race he is sprung, to declare what Message he brings, what Confidence we may repose in him now that he is our Prisoner. Then he, having at length laid aside Fear, thus proceeds: I, indeed, O King, will confess to you the whole

NOTES.

crifice to Death, the sure Reward of Miscarriage in the Attempt.

65. *Crimine ab uno.* *Catrou* observes that some Copies in *Servius*'s Time had read this Passage thus:

Accipe nunc Danaûm insidias, et crimen; ab uno
Disce omnes.

63. *Phrygia agmina circumspexit.* This is another Instance of *Virgil*'s Art in Versifying, and shews how much he studied to make *the Sound an Echo to the Sense.* *Sinon*'s affected Confusion and Terror, which he discovers in the slow, languid Cast of his Eyes around the *Trojan* Bands, is represented to the Life in the tardy Progress of the Line, occasioned partly by the Clashing of the two Vowels in *Phrygia agmina*; but especially by uniting the two Spondees in *circumspexit* at the End.

71. *Et super.* Others read *insuper.*

Vera, inquit; neque me Argolicâ de gente negabo:
Hoc primum; nec, si miserum fortuna Sinonem
Finxit, vanum etiam mendacemque improba finget.
Fando aliquid, si forte tuas pervenit ad aures
Belidæ nomen Palamedis, et inclyta famâ
Gloria; quem falsâ sub proditione Pelasgi
Insontem, infando indicio, quia bella vetebat,
Demisere neci; nunc cassum lumine lugent:
Illi me comitem, et consanguinitate propinquum,
Pauper in arma pater primis huc misit ab annis.

neque negabo me esse de Argolicâ gente: hoc est primum; nec, si improba fortuna finxit Sinonem miserum, finget eum vanum mendacemque. Si forte, fando aliquid, nomen Belidæ Palamedis, et gloria ejus inclyta famâ, pervenit ad tuas aures; quem Palamedem insontem Pelasgi, sub falsa proditione, demisere neci infando indicio, quia vetabat bella; nunc lugent eum *cassum lumine: pater* meus *pauper misit me comitem illi* Palamedi, *et propinquum ei consanguinitate, huc in arma ab primis annis.*

TRANSLATION.

Truth, says he, be the Event what will; nor will I disown that I am of Grecian Extraction, this I premise; nor shall it be in the Power of cruel Fortune, though she has made Sinon miserable, to make him also false and disengenuous. If accidentally, in the Course of common Report, the Name of Palamedes, the Descendant of Belus, and his illustrious Renown ever reached your Ears; who, though innocent, was delivered over to Death by the Greeks, under a false Accusation of Treason, upon a villanous Evidence, because he gave his Negative against the War; now they mourn him bereaved of Life: With him my Father, who was but poor, sent me in Company to the War, so soon as I was able to bear Arms, as I was his near Relation. While he remained safe in the Kingdom, and the

NOTES.

81. *Fando aliquid*, &c. The Artifice of this Speech, as *Sagrais* justly remarks, consists in mingling Truth and Lies, whereby *Sinon* effectually imposes upon his Audience. What he here premises in Relation to *Palamedes* is mostly true; what he subjoins of himself is downright Falshood.

82. *Belidæ Palamedis.* *Palamedes* was the Son of *Nauplius*, King of *Eubœa*, descended from *Belus*, King of *Africa*, by his Grand-mother *Amymone*, the Daughter of *Danaus*. The Story here referred to is briefly thus: When *Ulysses*, to be exempt from going to the *Trojan* War, under Pretence of Madness, was ploughing up the Shore, and sowing it with Salt, *Palamedes* laid down his Son *Telemachus* in his Way, and observing him to turn the Plough aside, that he might not hurt the Boy, by this Stratagem discovered his Madness to be counterfeit. For this *Ulysses* never could forgive him, and at last wrought his Ruin, by accusing him of holding Intelligence with the Enemy; to support which Charge he forged Letters from *Priam* to *Palamedes*, which he pretended to have intercepted, and conveyed Gold into his Tent, alledging it was the Bribe given him for his Treason. Upon this Presumption *Palamedes* was condemned by a Council of War, and stoned to Death. Vid. *Ovid. Met.* XIII. 56. That *Palamedes* was thus taken off through a Stratagem of *Ulysses*, was a Fact probably well known to the *Trojans*, though they might be ignorant of the Colour for his being taken off. *Sinon*, therefore, to secure the Attention and Belief of his Hearers, very artfully pretends that *Palamedes* was murdered, because he had dissuaded the *Greeks* from continuing the War against *Troy*.

85. *Nunc cassum lumine lugent.* This is agreeable to *Horace*'s Observation:

Virtutem incolumen odimus,
Sublatam ex oculis quærimus invidi.

86. *Consanguinitate propinquum.* In this he lies; for we read in the *Greek* Scholiasts, that *Sinon* was not related to *Palamedes*, but to *Ulysses*. *Anticlea*, the Mother of *Ulysses*, was Sister to *Æsimus*, *Sinon*'s Father.

87. *Primis ab annis.* *Virgil* frequently alludes to *Roman* Customs, even when he is speaking of what passed in other Nations. By *primis annis* therefore, it is probable he understands the

 military

Dum ille ſtabat incolumis in regno, regnumque vigebat ejus conſiliis, et nos geſſimus aliquod nomenque decuſque: ſed poſtquam conceſſit ab ſuperis oris invidiâ pellacis Ulyſſei (haud loquor ignota) ego *afflictus trahebam vitam in tenebris luctuque, et mecum indignabar caſum inſontis* mei *amici. Nec tacui demens; et promiſi me fore ultorem, ſiqua fors tuliſſet* occaſionem, *ſi unquam remeaſſem victor ad patrios Argos; et movi* illius *aſpera odia* meis *verbis. Hinc erat mihi prima mali labes; hinc Ulyſſes* cœpit *ſemper terrere* me *novis criminibus: hinc cœpit ſpargere voces ambiguas in vulgum, et conſcius quærere arma. Nec enim requievit, donec, Calchante miniſtro—Sed autem quid ego nequicquam revolvo hæc ingrata? quidve moror; ſi habetis omnes Achivos uno ordine,*

Dum ſtabat regno incolumis, regnumque vigebat
Conſiliis; et nos aliquod nomenque decuſque
Geſſimus: invidiâ poſtquam pellacis Ulyſſei
(Haud ignota loquor) ſuperis conceſſit ab oris;
Afflictus vitam in tenebris, luctuque trahebam,
Et caſum inſontis mecum indignabar amici.
Nec tacui demens; et me, fors ſiqua tuliſſet,
Si patrios unquam remeaſſem victor ad Argos,
Promiſi ultorem; et verbis odia aſpera movi.
Hinc mihi prima mali labes; hinc ſemper Ulyſſes
Criminibus terrere novis; hinc ſpargere voces
In vulgum ambiguas, et quærere conſcius arma.
Nec requievit enim, donec Calchante miniſtro—
Sed quid ego hæc autem nequicquam ingrata revolvo?
Quidve moror? ſi omnes uno ordine habetis Achivos,

TRANSLATION.

Community of the Grecian Princes was ſtrengthened by his Counſel. I too bore ſome Reputation and Honour: *But*, from the Time that he, by the Malice of the crafty Ulyſſes (they are well known Truths I ſpeak) quitted the Stage of this World, I, ſorely diſtreſſed, lengthened out my Life in Grief and Obſcurity, ſecretly repining at the *hard* Fate of my innocent Friend. Nor could I hold my Peace, Fool that I was, but vowed Revenge, if Fortune ſhould give me the Opportunity, if ever I returned victorious to my native Argos, and, by my *unguarded* Words provoked *his* bitter Enmity. Hence aroſe the firſt Symptom of my Miſery; henceforth Ulyſſes was always terrifying me with new Accuſations; henceforth he began to ſpread ambiguous, *dark* Surmiſes among the Vulgar, and, conſcious *of his own Guilt*, ſought the Means of my Ruin. Nor did he give over, till, by making Calchas his Tool—But why do I thus in vain unfold theſe diſagreeable *Truths!* Or why do I loſe Time? If you place all the Greeks on the ſame Foot, and your having heard *that one Circumſtance* be enough *to undo me*,

NOTES.

military Age, which among the *Romans* was about ſeventeen Years.

88. *Regno incolumis.* Either the Kingdom of *Eubœa*, of which *Nauplius*, *Palamedes*'s Father, was poſſeſſed; or rather the confederate Council, made up of all the petty Kings of *Greece*.

90. *Invidiâ---Ulyſſei.* By *invidia* we may underſtand either a general Grudge and Ill-will, which often goes under the Name of *invidia*; or that particular Envy which *Ulyſſes* bore him for having outwitted him, and acquired ſo much Reputation for Prudence and Cunning.

97. *Prima mali labes. The firſt Source of my Miſery.* As *labes* properly ſignifies a *Stain* or *Blemiſh*, I conſider it here in Alluſion to the firſt Appearance of a Plague or contagious Diſtemper breaking out on the Body in foul Spots and Blotches.

100. *Donec Calchante miniſtro. Calchas* was the Prophet or Soothſayer of the *Grecian* Army, and no Affairs were tranſacted in the Management of the War without his Counſel and Divination. This Pauſe, which *Sinon* makes juſt when he comes to a Point where he knew the

Idque audire ſat eſt; jamdudum ſumite pœnas:
Hoc Ithacus velit, et magno mercentur Atridæ.
Tum verò ardemus ſcitari, et quærere cauſas,
Ignari ſcelerum tantorum, artiſque Pelaſgæ.
Proſequitur pavitans, et ficto pectore fatur:
Sæpe fugam Danai Trojâ cupiere relictâ
Moliri, et longo feſſi diſcedere bello.
Feciſſentque utinam! ſæpe illos aſpera ponti
Intercluſit hyems, et terruit Auſter euntes.
Præcipuè, cum jam hic trabibus contextus acernis
Staret equus, toto ſonuerunt æthere nimbi.
Suſpenſi Eurypylum ſcitatum oracula Phœbi
Mittimus; iſque adytis hæc triſtia dicta reportat:

eſtque vobis *ſat audire id, jamdudum, ſumite pœnas: Ithacus* Rex *velit hoc, et Atridæ mercentur* hoc *magno* pretio.

Tum verò ardemus ſcitari, et quærere cauſas, ignari tantorum ſcelerum, artiſque Pelaſgæ. Ille *proſequitur pavitans, et fatur* ex *ficto pectore: Danai ſæpe cupiere moliri fugam, Trojâ relictâ, et diſcedere feſſi longo bello. Utinamque feciſſent! ſæpe aſpera hyems ponti interclusit, et auſter terruit illos euntes. Præcipuè, cum jam hic equus ſtaret contextus acernis trabibus, nimbi ſonuerunt* in *toto æthere.* Nos *ſuſpenſi mittimus Eurypylum ſcitatum oracula Phœbi; iſque reportat adytis hæc triſtia dicta:*

TRANSLATION.

delay not a Moment, ſtrike the fatal Blow: This the Prince of Ithaca wants, and the two Sons of Atreus would give large Sums to purchaſe. Then, indeed, we grow impatiently inquiſitive, and long to find out the *ſecret* Cauſes, unacquainted with ſuch conſummate Villany and Grecian Artifice. He proceeds with Palpitation, and ſpeaks in the Falſhood of his Heart. After quitting *the Siege of* Troy, the Greeks ſought often to ſurmount the Difficulties of their Return, and, tired out with the Length of the War, *longed* to be gone. And would Heaven they had! *But* as often did the rough Tempeſt on the Ocean bar their Flight, and the *adverſe* South Wind deterred them in their Setting out. Eſpecially when now this Horſe, framed of Maple Planks, was reared, Storms roared through all the Regions of the Air. In deep Perplexity we ſend Eurypylus to conſult the Oracle of Apollo; and from the ſacred Shrine he brings back this diſmal Reſponſe: Ye ap-

NOTES.

Curioſity of the *Trojans* would be the more inflamed, is very artful, and ſhews the great Judgment of the Poet in the Conduct of this Stratagem.

103. *Jamdudum ſumite pœnas.* I have followed the common Pointing, becauſe it ſeems more elegant than to join *jamdudum* with the former Part of the Sentence, as *Ruæus* has done: But, to make the Senſe complete, Dr. *Trapp* has well obſerved, that ſomething muſt be underſtood,—*ſumite pœnas jamdudum debitas*, or the like. Thoſe who like the other Reading better, I refer to the Note on the fourth Book, Verſe 1. *Jamdudum ſaucia.*

104. *Ithacus.* *Ulyſſes*, ſo called from *Ithaca*, where he was born, and where his Father *Laertes* reigned; it was a pitiful, little, craggy Iſland in the *Ionian* Sea; *Cicero* calls it, *Ithacam illam, in aſperrimis ſaxulis, tanquam nidulum, affixam.* *Sinon* therefore, in this Speech, gives *Ulyſſes* all along the Apellation of *Ithacus* by Way of Contempt.

104. *Magno mercentur Atridæ.* Their Religion required that a devoted Victim, who had eſcaped from the Altar, ſhould be put to Death wherever found; and *Sinon* being deſtined a Sacrifice for the Return of his Countrymen, who could not therefore expect a ſafe Voyage, unleſs he was put to Death, nothing could be more grateful to the *Greeks* than to hear that the *Trojans* had taken his Life.

112. *Trabibus contextus acernis.* This is not inconſiſtent with what he ſays above, *intexunt abiete coſtas*, and below, *pinea—laxat clauſtra*; for ſome Parts of the Engine might be of Maple, others of Pine and Fir.

114. *Eurypylum.* *Eurypylus*, a noble Augur, was the Son of *Evæmon* and *Aſtyoche*, *Priam's* Siſter;

O *Danai*, vos *placaſtis ventos ſanguine, et virgine cæſâ, cum primùm veniſtis ad Iliacas oras; reditus quærendi* ſunt vobis *ſanguine, litandumque* eſt *Argolicâ animâ. Quæ vox ut venit ad aures vulgi, animi* eorum *obſtupuere, geliduſque tremor cucurrit per ima oſſa; cui fata parent* mortem, *quem Apollo poſcat. Hìc Ithacus* rex *in medios protrahit vatem Calchanta* cum *magno tumultu; flagitat quæ ea numina Divûm ſint: et multi jam canebant mihi crudele ſcelus artificis, et taciti videbant ventura. Ille ſilet bis quinos dies, tectuſque recuſat prodere quenquam ſuâ voce, aut opponere* quenquam *morti. Tandem, vix actus magnis clamoribus Ithaci,*

Sanguine placaſtis ventos, et virgine cæſâ,
Cum primùm Iliacas Danai veniſtis ad oras;
Sanguine quærendi reditus, animâque litandum
Argolicâ: vulgi quæ vox ut venit ad aures,
Obſtupuere animi, geliduſque per ima cucurrit
Oſſa tremor; cui fata parent, quem poſcat Apollo.
Hìc Ithacus vatem magno Calchanta tumultu
Protrahit in medios; quæ ſint ea numina Divûm
Flagitat: et mihi jam multi crudele canebant
Artificis ſcelus, et taciti ventura videbant.
Bis quinos ſilet ille dies, tectuſque recuſat
Prodere voce ſuâ quenquam, aut opponere morti.
Vix tandem magnis Ithaci clamoribus actus,

TRANSLATION.

peaſed the Winds, ye Greeks, with the Blood of a Virgin ſlain, when firſt you arrived on the Trojan Coaſt; by Blood muſt your Return be purchaſed, and Atonement made by the Life of a Greek; which Intimation no ſooner reached the Ears of the Multitude, than their Minds were ſtunned, and freezing Horror thrilled through their very Bones; *anxious to know* whom Heaven deſtined *for the Sacrifice* which Apollo demanded. Upon this, Ulyſſes drags forth Calchas, the Seer, with great Buſtle and Stir, into the Midſt *of the Crowd*; importunes him to ſay what thoſe Orders of the Gods are: And, by this Time, many preſaged to me the cruel Purpoſe of the Diſſembler, and quietly foreſaw the Event. He, for twice five Days, is mute, and, cloſe ſhut up, *obſtinately* refuſes to give forth his Declaration againſt any Perſon, or doom him to Death. At length, with much ado, teazed by the importunate Clamours of Ulyſſes, he breaks Silence by Con-

NOTES.

Siſter; *Homer* ſays, he brought with him forty Ships to aſſiſt in the *Trojan* War.

116. *Sanguine placaſtis ventos.* When the *Grecian* Army was arrived at *Aulis*, ready to ſail over the *Helleſpont* to the Siege of *Troy*, *Diana*, incenſed againſt *Agamemnon* for killing one of her favourite Deers, withheld the Wind. *Calchas*, having conſulted the Oracles, reported that *Iphigenia*, *Agamemnon*'s Daughter, muſt fall a Victim to appeaſe *Diana*'s Wrath. *Ulyſſes* went and fetched the innocent Fair from the tender Embraces of her Mother, under Colour of her being to be married to *Achilles*. She was brought to the Altar, and on the Point of being ſacrificed, when *Calchas* informed that *Diana* was ſatisfied with this Act of Submiſſion, and conſented to have a Deer ſubſtituted in Room of *Iphigenia*; but that ſhe muſt be tranſported to *Tauris*, there to ſerve the Goddeſs for Life in Quality of Prieſteſs.

116. *Virgine cæſâ.* She was intentionally ſlain, and only ſaved by the unforeſeen Favour of the Goddeſs in mitigating the Sentence.

118. *Litandum.* Signifies more than *ſacrificandum*, as *Ruæus* renders it, conſiſtently with his own Note, for *litare* is to atone or make Expiation by Sacrifice, *Macrob. Sat.* Lib. III. 5.

121. *Cui fata parent.* Cui fata parent *mortem*, or *exitium*, rather than to make *fata*, with *Ruæus*, in the Accuſative.

123. *Numina Divûm.* Here *numina* is taken for the *Decrees*, *Orders*, or *Dictates* of the Gods, which Signification agrees better to the Etymology of the Word (from *nuo* to ſignify one's Will by a *Nod*) than that which it commonly bears.

125. *Taciti ventura videbant.* *Taciti* here ſignifies not *ſilent*, elſe it would contradict the former Part of the Sentence, but in *Quietneſs* and *Secrecy*, not daring openly to publiſh what they foreſaw.

133. *Salſæ*

Compositò rumpit vocem, et me destinat aræ.
Assensere omnes; et, quæ sibi quisque timebat,
Unius in miseri exitium conversa tulere.
Jamque dies infanda aderat; mihi sacra parari,
Et salsæ fruges, et circum tempora vittæ.
Eripui, fateor, leto me, et vincula rupi;
Limosoque lacu per noctem obscurus in ulvâ
Delitui, dum vela darent, si forte dedissent.
Nec mihi jam patriam antiquam spes ulla videndi,
Nec dulces natos, exoptatumque parentem;
Quos illi fors ad pœnas ob nostra reposcent
Effugia, et culpam hanc miserorum morte piabunt.

rumpit vocem compositò, et destinat me aræ. Omnes assensere, et tulere ea, quæ quisque timebat sibi, conversa esse in exitium unius miseri. Jamque infanda dies aderat; sacra cœperunt parari mibi, et salsæ fruges, et vittæ circum tempora. Eripui me leto, fateor, et rupi vincula; obscurusque delitui per noctem limoso lacu in ulvâ, dum vela darent, si forte dedissent. Nec jam ulla spes fuit mibi videndi antiquam patriam, nec dulces natos parentemque exoptatum; quos illi, fors, reposcent ad pœnas ob nostra effugia, et piabunt hanc culpam morte miserorum.

TRANSLATION.

cert, and destines me to the Altar. All assented, and were content to have the *Blow*, which they dreaded each for himself, turned off *from them*, to the Ruin of one poor Wretch. And now the rueful Day approached; for me the sacred Rites were prepared, and the salted Cake and Fillets *to bind* about my Temples. From Death, I own, I made my Escape, and broke my Bonds; and, in a slimy Fen all Night I lurked obscure among the Weeds, till they should set Sail, if I should be so happy to see that Hour. Nor have I now any Hope of being blessed with the Sight of my Country, *the* ancient *Seat of my Ancestors*, nor of my pleasant Children, and my much beloved Sire; whom they, perhaps, will sue to Vengeance for my Escape, and expiate this Offence of mine by the Death of those un-

NOTES.

133. *Salsæ fruges.* A Sort of Cake made of Bran or Meal mixed with Salt, with which they sprinkled the Head of the Victim, the Fire of the Altar, and the sacrificing Knife; it was called *Mola*, the Ceremony itself *Immolatio*, and the Verb signifying to perform that Ceremony was *Immolare*, which thence signifies to sacrifice in general.

133. *Circum tempora vittæ.* The *Vittæ* were Fillets of white Wool, with which not only the Temples of the Victim, but the Priests, and Statues of the Gods, were bound. Hence *Virgil* says below, Verse 168,

Virgineas ausi Divæ contingere vittas.

And, speaking of *Helenus*, in the third Book,

——— ———*vittasque resolvit*
Sacrati capitis.

134. *Et vincula rupi.* The Victims, as *Servius* tells us, were free, and always unbound when they were brought forward to the Altar: nor indeed is it probable that *Sinon* could have been able to make his Escape, though loose, from the Guards and Crowds of Spectators who would accompany him to the Altar. *Servius* therefore explains *vincula*, the Bonds of Religion. But he, at the same Time, observes, that the Victims were bound and confined until they were brought up to the Altar; and therefore we may very well understand by *vincula rupi*, that he secretly broke those Bonds, or that Prison wherein he had been confined against the Day of Sacrifice.

137. *Patriam antiquam. Antiquam* may either signify *ancient* in the Sense we have translated it, or it may have the same Signification with *pristinam*, former, as *Tyre* is called *Dido*'s ancient City, *i. e.* the City of her former Residence:

Nunquam suam patria antiqua cinis ater habebat.

139. *Quos illi, &c.* Here the Poet seems to have an Eye to the ancient Law among the [illegible]*mans*, which provided that the Children [illegible] expiate and suffer for some particul[illegible] Crimes [illegible]mitted by the Parents against the State, *L*[illegible] Lib. XXIV. 37. *Præsidio decedere apud R*[illegible]*nos, capitale esse; et nece liberorum etiam* [illegible] *cam legem parentes sanxisse.*

Quòd oro te per Superos et numina conscia veri, per fidem, si qua est intemerata fides quæ adhuc restat usquam mortalibus; miserere tantorum laborum, miserere animi ferentis non digna.

Damus vitam his lacrymis, et ultro miserescimus ejus. Priamus ipse primus jubet manicas atque arcta illius *vincla levari, saturque ita amicis dictis: quisquis es, hinc jam obliviscere Graios amissos; eris noster; edissereque hæc vera mihi roganti: quò statuere hanc molem immanis equi? quis* fuit *auctor? quidve petunt? quæ relligio* est? *aut quæ machina belli? dixerat* Priamus. *Ille, instructus dolis et Pelasgâ arte, sustulit ad sidera palmas exutas vinclis. Ait, testor, vos, O ignes æterni, et vestrum numen non violabile!* testor *vos, O aræ, ensesque nefandi,*

Quòd te, per Superos, et conscia numina veri,
Per, si qua est quæ restat adhuc mortalibus usquam
Intemerata fides, oro, miserere laborum
Tantorum; miserere animi non digna ferentis.
His lacrymis vitam damus, et miserescimus ultro.
Ipse viro primus manicas atque arcta levari
Vincla jubet Priamus, dictisque ita fatur amicis:
Quisquis es, amissos hinc jam obliviscere Graios;
Noster eris; mihique hæc edissere vera roganti:
Quò molem hanc immanis equi statuere? quis auctor?
Quidve petunt? quæ relligio? aut quæ machina belli?
Dixerat. Ille, dolis instructus et arte Pelasgâ,
Sustulit exutas vinclis ad sidera palmas:
Vos, æterni ignes, et non violabile vestrum
Testor numen, ait! vos aræ, ensesque nefandi,

TRANSLATION.

happy *Innocents.* But, by the Powers above, by the Gods who are conscious to Truth, by whatever Remains of inviolable Faith are any where *to be found* among Mortals, I obtest you compassionate such grievous Afflictions, compassionate a Soul suffering such unworthy Treatment.

At these Tears we gave him his Life, and pity him from our Hearts. Priam himself first gives Orders that his Manicles and strait Bonds be loosed, then thus addresses him in the Language of a Friend: Whoever you are, now henceforth forget the Greeks you have lost, ours you shall be: And *now* give me an ingenuous Reply to these Questions: To what Purpose raised they this stupendous Bulk of a Horse? Who was the Contriver? Or what do they intend *by it?* What was the religious Motive? Or what warlike Engine is it? He said. The other, practised in Fraud and Grecian Artifice, lifted up to Heaven his Hands *now* loosed from the Bonds: To you, ye everlasting Orbs of Fire, he says, and your inviolable Divinity; to you, ye Altars, and horrid Instruments of Death, which I es-

NOTES.

145. *Miserescimus ultro.* *Ultro* here I take to signify from mere Sympathy and Compassion, without Regard to any Motive but the pure Influence the Sight of his Sufferings had upon their Humanity: Though *Sinon* had supplicated their Pity, yet he needed not to have pleaded so hard for it; we pity him *ultro, frankly, voluntarily, from pure Inclination.*

151. *Quæ relligio? aut quæ machina belli?* These are elliptic Sentences, as is usual in short Questions. To supply the whole Sentence, it would run thus: What do they intend by it? Is it to fulfil some Duty of Religion? If so, *quæ relligio?* What Duty or Motive of Religion induced them to it? Or is it an Engine of War? If so, *quæ machina belli?* What warlike Engine is it?

154. *Vos, æterni ignes, &c.* *Ye everlasting Orbs of Fire.* Some by *æterni ignes* understand the Fires of the Altar; but the Epithet *æterni* agrees much better to the Stars and heavenly Luminaries, which were believed by the Ancients to be Globes of Fire, which shone for ever, and were inhabited by Divinities: And it is no new Thing

Quos fugi, vittæque Deûm, quas hostia gessi!
Fas mihi Graiorum sacrata resolvere jura;
Fas odisse viros, atque omnia ferre sub auras,
Si qua tegunt: teneor patriæ nec legibus ullis.
Tu modò promissis maneas, servataque serves
Troja fidem; si vera feram, si magna rependam.
Omnis spes Danaûm, et cœpti fiducia belli,
Palladis auxiliis semper stetit: impius ex quo
Tydides sed enim, scelerumque inventor Ulysses,
Fatale aggressi sacrato avellere templo
Palladium, cæsis summæ custodibus arcis,

quos fugi, vittæque Deûm, quas ego hostia gessi! fas est mihi resolvere sacrata jura Graiorum; fas est odisse viros, atque ferre sub auras omnia, si qua tegunt: nec teneor ullis legibus patriæ. Tu, O Troja, maneas modò in promissis, tuque servata serves tuam fidem; si ego feram vera, si rependam magna. Omnis spes Danaûm et fiducia cœpti belli semper stetit auxiliis Palladis: sed enim ex quo tempore impius Tydides, Ulyssesque inventor scelerum, aggressi avellere sacrato templo fatale Palladium, custodibus summæ arcis cæsis,

TRANSLATION.

caped; and ye Fillets of the Gods, which I a Victim wore; to you I appeal, that I am free to violate all the sacred Obligations I was under to the Greeks; I am free to hold themselves in Abhorrence, and to bring forth to Light all their dark Designs: Nor am I bound by any of the Laws of my Country: only do thou, O Troy, abide by thy Promises, and, *by my Means* preserved, preserve thy Faith *now given*; provided I disclose the Truth, provided I make thee large Amends.

The whole Hope of the Greeks, and their Confidence *in the Prosecution* of the begun War, always depended on the Aid of Pallas: But from what time the sacrilegious Diomed, and Ulysses the Projector of wicked Designs, in their Attempt to carry off by Force from her holy Temple the fatal Palladium, having slain the

NOTES.

Thing to hear them swearing by the Stars, as

——*Cœlum hoc et conscia sidera testor.*
Æn. IX. 429.

Testatur moritura Deos et conscia fati
Sidera. Æn. IV. 519.

Nor do I see how the Fire of the Altar could be called *eternal*, unless it referred to the Fire of *Vesta*.

156. *Quas hostia gessi.* In order to excite their Compassion the more, and to shew the horrid Apprehensions he had of the Thing, he speaks as if he had actually been brought a Sacrifice to the Altar, and as if that had been put in Execution which was only intended against him.

157. *Fas mihi.* That is, *fas est mihi, I am free, or it is lawful for me. Ruæus*, which *Servius*, and others, understand this to be a Prayer, *fas sit mihi*, or *liceat mihi.* But who can imagine he would pray the Gods to give him a Licence to commit the most horrid Wickedness, to violate the most sacred Ties in the World? I rather take it to be an Appeal to the Gods, that the barbarous Treatment he had met with from the *Greeks* had cancelled as his former Ties of Love and Good-will to them; the *aræ*, the Altars whereon he was to have been slain; the *enses nefandi*, the cruel Sword by which he should have bled; the *vittæ*, the Fillets with which he was to have been bound, were so many Witnesses for him, that he was now under no Obligation to mind the Interests of *Greece*, that had withdrawn all Protection from him. That this is the Meaning appears from what follows,

————*teneor patriæ nec legibus ullis.*

He does not say, *nec tenear*, *nor let me be bound*, as he ought to have done, had it been a Prayer; but *nec teneor*, *nor am I longer bound.*

165. *Fatale—Palladium.* The *Palladium* was a Statue of *Pallas*, fabled by some to have been dropped from Heaven by *Jupiter* near *Ilus*'s Tent, when he was building the Citadel of *Ilium*; or by others to have been made of *Pelops*'s Bones. All are agreed that this *Palladium* was a Pledge, on the Keeping whereof the Preservation of *Troy* depended; for which Reason *Virgil* calls it *Fa-*

corripuere ſacram effigiem; auſique ſunt contingere virgineas vittas Divæ cruentis manibus; ex illo tempore *ſpes Danaûm ſublapſa* cœpit *fluere ac referri retro; vires* eorum ſunt *fractæ,* et *mens Deæ averſa: Nec Tritonia dedit ea ſigna monſtris dubiis: vix* fuit *ſimulacrum poſitum* in *caſtris,* cum *coruſcæ flammæ arſere* ab *arrectis luminibus, ſalſuſque ſudor iit per artus* ejus, *ipſaque ter emicuit ſolo (mirabile dictu!) ferenſque parmam* ſuam *haſtamque trementem. Extemplo Calchas canit æquora* eſſe *tentanda fugâ, nec Pergama poſſe exſcindi Argolicis telis; ni repetant omina Argis, reducantque numen,*

Corripuere ſacram effigiem, manibuſque cruentis
Virgineas auſi Divæ contingere vittas;
Ex illo fluere, ac retro ſublapſa referri
Spes Danaûm; fractæ vires, averſa Deæ mens:
Ned dubiis ea ſigna dedit Tritonia monſtris: 171
Vix poſitum caſtris ſimulacrum, arſere coruſcæ
Luminibus flammæ arrectis, ſalſuſque per artus
Sudor iit; terque ipſa ſolo, mirabile dictu,
Emicuit, parmamque ferens, haſtamque trementem. 175
Extemplo tentanda fugâ canit æquora Calchas,
Nec poſſe Argolicis exſcindi Pergama telis,
Omina ni repetant Argis, numenque reducant,

TRANSLATION.

Guards of her high Tower, ſeized upon her ſacred Image, and with bloody Hands durſt *prophanely* touch the Virgin Fillets of the Goddeſs: From that day the Hope of the Greeks began to ebb, * and gradually decline; their Powers were weakened, the Mind of the Goddeſs alienated *from them:* Nor did Tritonia ſhew theſe Indications of her Wrath by dubious Prodigies: For ſcarce was the Statue ſet up in the Camp, *when* bright Flames flaſhed from her ſtaring Eye-balls, and a briny Sweat flowed over her Limbs; and, what you will be amazed to hear, ſhe herſelf ſprung thrice from the Ground, armed as ſhe was, with her Shield and quivering Spear. Forthwith Calchas declares it to be the Will of Heaven, that we attempt the Seas in our Way homeward, and that Troy can never be razed by the Grecian Sword, unleſs they repeat the Omens at Argos, and carry back the

* *And decaying to be carried backward.*

NOTES.

tale Palladium. Diomedes and *Ulyſſes*, entering the Citadel by Night, carried it off into the *Grecian* Camp.

168. *Virgineas—vittas.* The Fillets or Ribbands wore by Virgins were different from thoſe uſed by Matrons, as appears from *Propertius*, Eleg. XII. Lib. 4.

Poſt ubi jam facibus ceſſit prætexta maritis,
Vinxit et acceptas altera vitta comas.

So *Val. Flaccus*, Lib. VIII.

Ultima virgineis tum flens dedit oſcula vittis,

171. *Tritonia.* This is a Name given to *Minerva* from a Lake in *Afric* called *Tritonis*, where *Minerva* is ſaid to have been born, or at leaſt to have appeared firſt amongſt Mortals.

175. *Parmamque—haſtamque.* Theſe were the Arms by which the *Palladium* was diſtinguiſhed.

176. *Canit.* This is a Word commonly applied to Oracles and Predictions; it ſignifies that *Calchas* ſpoke by Inſpiration, and declared this to be the Mind of his God.

178. *Omina ni repetant.* This, ſays *Servius*, alludes to the Cuſtom of the *Romans*, who, if they had bad Succeſs in a Siege or Expedition, were wont to return Home, and once more take the Omens. Or, if they were far from *Rome*, appropriated for the Purpoſe Part of the Lands they had taken in the Province which was the Seat of the War, and called it the *Roman* Territory.

178. *Numenque reducant.* It ſeems moſt natural and obvious to underſtand *Numen* here to be the *Palladium*, *the Divinity*, or *Symbol of Minerva's Divinity*, which *Sinon* inſinuates to have been carried to *Argos* by the *Greeks*, and that they were obliged to fetch it back again from thence; and in the mean time, as ſome At-

tonement

Quod pelago et curvis ſecum advexere carinis.
Et nunc, quòd patrias vento petiere Mycenas,
Arma Deoſque parant comites; pelagoque remenſo,
Improviſi aderunt: ita digerit omina Calchas.
Hanc pro Palladio moniti, pro numine læſo,
Effigiem ſtatuere, nefas quæ triſte piaret:
Hanc tamen immenſam Calchas attollere molem
Roboribus textis, cœloque educere, juſſit;
Ne recipi portis, aut duci in mœnia poſſit:
Neu populum antiquâ ſub relligione tueri.
Nam ſi veſtra manus violaſſet dona Minervæ;
Tum magnum exitium (quod Dî prius omen in ipſum
Convertant) Priami imperio, Phrygibuſque futurum:
Sin manibus veſtris veſtram aſcendiſſet in urbem,
Ultro Aſiam magno Pelopeia ad mœnia bello
Venturam, et noſtros ea fata manere nepotes.

quod advexere ſecum pelago et curvis carinis. Et nunc, quòd petiere vento patrias Mycenas, parant arma Deoſque comites; aderuntque improviſi, pelago remenſo: ita Calchas digerit omina. Illi *moniti ſtatuere hanc effigiem pro Palladio, pro numine læſo, quæ* effigies *piaret triſte* illorum *nefas: Calchas tamen juſſit eos attollere hanc molem immenſam textis roboribus, educereque eam cœlo; ne poſſit recipi in portis, aut duci in mœnia; neu tueri populum ſub antiquâ relligione. Nam,* dicebat, *ſi veſtra manus violaſſet dona Minervæ, tum magnum exitium futurum* eſſe *imperio Priami Phrygibuſque, quod omen utinam Dî prius convertant in ipſum: ſin aſcendiſſet veſtris manibus in veſtram urbem, Aſiam ultro venturam magno bello ad Pelopeia mœnia, et ea fata manere noſtros nepotes.*

TRANSLATION.

Goddeſs, whom they had conveyed over Sea in their winding Ships. And now, that they have failed for their native Mycenæ with the Wind, they are providing themſelves in Arms, and the Gods to accompany *their Enterprize*; and, having meaſured back the Sea, they will be upon you in an unexpected Hour: So Calchas interprets the Omen. This Figure, warned by *Heaven*, they reared in lieu of the Palladium, in lieu *of the Symbol* of the offended Goddeſs, in order to attone for their direful Crime. But Calchas ordered to build the wooden Engine of this enormous Bulk, and raiſe it to the Skies, that it might not be admitted into the Gates, or dragged into the City, nor protect the People under *the Patronage of* their ancient Religion. For *he declared that*, if your Hands ſhould offer Violence to this Offering ſacred to Minerva, then ſignal Ruin (which Omen may the Gods rather turn on himſelf!) awaited Priam's Empire and the Trojans. But, if by your Means it mounted into the City, that Aſia, without farther Provocation given, would advance with a formidable War to the very Gates of Pelops's City *Argos*, and our Poſterity be doomed to the ſame Fate. By ſuch Treachery and

NOTES.

onement to the offended Goddeſs, had conſecrated to her the wooden Horſe.

182. *Ita digerit omina.* Others read *omnia.*

186. *Roboribus textis,* i. e. Of joined Boards; for *robora* not only ſignifies oaken Planks or Boards, but any hard Wood, as in the Georgics,

——*Cape ſaxa manu, cape robora, paſtor.*
Geor. III. 420.

188. *Antiquâ ſub relligione,* i. e. Under the religious Patronage of their ancient Guardian Goddeſs *Minerva.*

190. *In ipſum,* i. e. On *Calchas*; but it will be more emphatic if we read *in ipſos*, on the *Greeks* themſelves, as it is in ſome Copies.

193. *Ultro.* Here again *Servius* explains *ultro* to ſignify *mox, ſtatim,* without aſſigning any Authority but his own *ipſe dixit.* But to take it in the common Senſe of the Word is both eaſier and more elegant.

193. *Pelopeia mœnia.* The City *Argos*, where *Pelops* reigned, here put for *Greece* in general.

Res credita est talibus insidiis, arteque perjuri Sinonis; nosque, quos neque Tydides, nec Larissæus Achilles, quos decem anni, mille carinæ, non domuere, capti sumus dolis, coactisque lacrymis.

Hic aliud majus monstrum *multoque magis tremendum objicitur* nobis *miseris, atque turbat* nostra *improvida pectora. Laocoon, sacerdos sorte ductus Neptuno, mactabat ingentem taurum ad aras solennes. Ecce autem gemini angues à Tenedo* venientes *per alta tranquilla* maria *(horresco referens) incumbunt pelago immensis orbibus, pariterque tendunt ad littora: quorum pectora arrecta inter fluctus, jubæque sanguineæ exsuperant undas; cætera pars legit pontum ponè, sinuatque volumine immensa terga.*

Talibus insidiis, perjurique arte Sinonis,
Credita res: captique dolis, lacrymisque coactis;
Quos neque Tydides, nec Larissæus Achilles,
Non anni domuere decem, non mille carinæ.
Hic aliud majus miseris multoque tremendum
Objicitur magis, atque improvida pectora turbat.
Laocoon, ductus Neptuno sorte sacerdos,
Solennes taurum ingentem mactabat ad aras.
Ecce autem gemini à Tenedo tranquilla per alta,
(Horresco referens) immensis orbibus angues
Incumbunt pelago, pariterque ad littora tendunt:
Pectora quorum inter fluctus arrecta, jubæque
Sanguineæ exsuperant undas; pars cætera pontum
Ponè legit, sinuatque immensa volumine terga.

TRANSLATION.

Artifice of perjured Sinon, the Story is believed, and we, whom neither Diomed, nor Larissæan Achilles, nor *a* ten Years *Siege*, nor a thousand Ships subdued, are insnared by Guile and constrained Tears. Here another more affecting Scene, and far more terrible, is presented to our wretched Sight, and fills our Breasts with Surprize and Confusion. Laocoon, ordained Neptune's Priest by Lot, was sacrificing a stately Bullock at the Altars set apart for that Solemnity; when lo! from Tenedos (I shudder *even* at the Relation) two Serpents, with Orbs immense, stretch their Length along the smooth Surface of the Sea, and with equal Motion shoot forward to the Shore; whose Breasts erect amidst the Waves, and Chests bedropped with Blood, tower above the Flood; their other Parts sweep the Sea behind, and wind their spacious Backs in rolling Spires. *Lashed by their Strokes,*

NOTES.

196. *Lacrymisque coactis. By his constrained Tears.* All the ancient Manuscripts read *coacti*; but *Servius* earnestly contends for *coactis*, which Reading *Heinsius* has embraced.

197. *Larissæus Achilles.* *Achilles* is stiled *Larissæus* from *Larissa*, a Town in *Thessaly*, not far from *Phthia*, where he was born.

198. *Non mille carinæ.* *Homer*, in the Catalogue of his Ships, enumerates eleven hundred and eighty-six Sail in all.

201. *Laocoon, ductus Neptuno sorte sacerdos.* *Euphorion* writes that the Priest of *Neptune* had been stoned to Death by the *Trojans* for not hindering, by his Prayers and Sacrifices, the Arrival of the *Grecian* Army before *Troy*; and that now, being to sacrifice to that God for delivering them from their Enemies, they had chosen *Laocoon*, the Priest of *Apollo*, to officiate [illegible] *Hyginus*, who relates this Story, says the Crime, for which *Laocoon* was thus severely punished, was, that he had married a Wife, and got Children, contrary to the express Orders of *Apollo*, whose Priest he was; and that the *Trojans* had construed this Calamity which befel him as an Act of divine Vengeance for his having violated *Minerva*'s sacred Offering. *Virgil* therefore judiciously introduces this Event, not only as it is a fine Embellishment of his Poem, but also as it gives the greatest Probability to the Episode of the wooden Horse, and accounts for the Credulity of the *Trojans*.

203. *Ecce autem.* When the Poet is going to introduce some surprizing Incident, he frequently ushers it in with an *ecce*, or *ecce autem*, See Verses, 57, 270, 318.

203. *A Tenedo.* To signify, says *Servius*, that the Ships were to come from thence to demolish *Troy*.

203. *Tranquilla per alta. Along the smooth Surface of the Main.* This Circumstance gives the

Fit ſonitus, ſpumante ſalo: jamque arva tenebant,
Ardenteſque oculos ſuffecti ſanguine, et igni,
Sibila lambebant linguis vibrantibus ora.
Diffugimus viſu exſangues: illi agmine certo
Laocoonta petunt; et primùm parva duorum
Corpora natorum ſerpens amplexus uterque
Implicat, et miſeros morſu depaſcitur artus.
Pòſt ipſum auxilio ſubeuntem ac tela ferentem
Corripiunt, ſpiriſque ligant ingentibus: et jam
Bis medium amplexi, bis collo ſquamea circum
Terga dati, ſuperant capite et cervicibus altis.
Ille ſimul manibus tendit divellere nodos,
Perfuſus ſanie vittas atroque veneno:
Clamores ſimul horrendos ad ſidera tollit:
Quales mugitus, fugit cum ſaucius aram
Taurus, et incertam excuſſit cervice ſecurim.

Sonitus fit, ſalo ſpumante: jamque tenebant arva, ſuffecitque ardentes oculos ſanguine et igni, lambebant ſibila ora vibrantibus linguis. Nos diffugimus exſangues viſu: illi petunt Laocoonta certo agmine; et primùm uterque ſerpens amplexus implicat parva corpora duorum natorum, et *depaſcitur* eorum *miſeros artus morſu. Pòſt corripiunt ipſum* Laocoonta *ſubeuntem auxilio natorum ac ferentem tela, ligantque* eum *ingentibus ſpiris: et jam bis amplexi* eum *medium, bis circumdati ſquamea terga* illius *collo, ſuperant* eum *capite et altis cervicibus. Ille ſimul tendit divellere* eorum *nodos manibus, perfuſus vittas ſanie atroque veneno: ſimul tollit horrendos clamores ad ſidera;* tales, *quales mugitus* tollit *taurus, cum fugit aram ſaucius, et excuſſit cervice incertam ſecurim.*

TRANSLATION.

the Floods reſound, the briny Ocean foaming; and now they were got to Land, and, darting Fire from their glaring Blood-red Eyes, with forky Tongues licked their hiſſing Mouths. Half dead with the *horrid* Sight we fly different Ways. They, with reſolute Motion, advance towards Laocoon, and firſt either Serpent, with cloſe Embraces, twines around the little Bodies of his two Sons, and with *cruel* Fangs mangles their wretched Limbs. Next they ſeize upon himſelf, as he is coming up with Weapons to their Relief, and bind him faſt in their prodigious Folds; and now, graſping him twice about the Waiſt, twice winding their ſcaly Backs around his Neck, they overtop him by the Head and lofty Neck. He ſtrains at once with *both* Hands to tear aſunder their knotted Spires, while his *holy* Fillets are diſtained with Gore and black Poiſon: At the ſame Time he raiſes hideous Shrieks to Heaven; ſuch Bellowings, as when a Bull has fled wounded from the Altar, and has eluded with his Neck the erring Axe. Mean while, the two Serpents glide off to the high Temple, repair

NOTES.

the *Trojans* an Opportunity the better to view the whole Progreſs of the Serpents, to hear their dreadful Hiſſings, and every Laſh they give to the Waves; and conſequently adds conſiderably to the Terror of the hideous Spectacle.

210. *Ardenteſque oculos ſuffecti ſanguine, et igni.* Word for Word, *Having their glaring Eyes diſtained with Blood and Fire,* i. e. *with fiery, ſparkling red.*

211. *Vibrantibus linguis.* i. e. *Voluble, vibrating*; becauſe, as Naturaliſts obſerve, no Animal moves its Tongue with ſo much Velocity.

212. *Agmine certo. Agmen* ſignifies a moving Body, or the regular, orderly Motion of a collected Body, as of an Army of Men advancing up one after another; therefore it admirably denotes the ſpiral Motion of a Serpent ſhooting forward Fold after Fold.

215. *Morſu depaſcitur artus.* There is no Neceſſity of tranſlating this *devour*, as it is by Dr. *Trapp*, as if the Serpents had ate the Carcaſes up. This is by no Means probable, nor is the Verb *depaſcitur* always taken in that ſtrict Senſe, but ſometimes ſignifies only *mangles, preys upon, waſtes and conſumes away,* as *Virgil* himſelf, ſpeaking of a conſuming Fever, ſays,

Cum furit, atque artus depaſcitur arida febris. Geor. III. 458.

At gemini dracones lapsu effugiunt ad summa delubra, petuntque arcem sævæ Tritonidis; teguntur que sub pedibus Deæ, subque orbe clypei. Tum verò novus pavor insinuat se cunctis per pectora tremefacta; et ferunt Laocoonta merentem expendisse scelus; qui læserit sacrum robur cuspide, et intorserit sceleratam hastam tergo. Conclamant simulacrum esse ducendum ad sedes, numinaque Divæ esse oranda. Dividimus muros, et pandimus mœnia urbis. Omnes accingunt se operi; subjiciuntque pedibus equi lapsus rotarum, et intendunt stupea vincula ejus collo. Fatalis machina, fœta armis, scandit muros;

At gemini lapsu delubra ad summa dracones
Effugiunt, sævæque petunt Tritonidis arcem;
Sed pedibusque Deæ, clypeique sub orbe teguntur.
Tum verò tremefacta novus per pectora cunctis
Insinuat pavor; et scelus expendisse merentem
Laocoonta ferunt; sacrum qui cuspide robur
Læserit, et tergo sceleratam intorserit hastam.
Ducendum ad sedes simulacrum, orandaque Divæ
Numina conclamant.
Dividimus muros, et mœnia pandimus urbis.
Accingunt omnes operi; pedibusque rotarum
Subjiciunt lapsus, et stupea vincula collo
Intendunt: scandit fatalis machina muros,

TRANSLATION.

to the Fane of stern Tritonis, and are sheltered under the Feet of the Goddess, and the Orb of her Buckler. Then, indeed, uncommon Terror diffuses itself through the quaking Hearts of all; and they pronounce Laocoon to have deservedly suffered for his Crime, in having violated the sacred Wood with his pointed Weapon, and lanced his cursed Spear against its Sides. They urge with general Voice to convey the Statue to its *proper* Seat, and implore the Favour of the Goddess. We make a Breach in the Walls, and lay open the Bulwarks of the City. All keenly ply the Work; *some* under the Feet apply smooth-rolling Wheels; *others* fasten hempen Ropes to the Neck. The fatal Machine mounts our Walls, preg-

NOTES.

Agreeably to this Sense of the Word, that fine Statue, representing this Story, which *Pliny* saw in *Vespasian's* Palace, and which is still to be seen in the *Vatican Gardens*, shews *Laocoon* intwined by the Folds of the Serpents, and his two Sons lying dead on the Ground; it is not improbable that *Virgil* took this Description from that Statue.

225. *Delubra.* *Delubrum* properly was a Place before the Chapel, or near the Altar, where they washed before they entered the Church, or performed Sacrifice. Therefore the most probable Etymology of the Word is from *deluo*, to wash away. *Varro*, however, assigns another Derivation, and alledges that the *Delubrum* was the Shrine or Place where the Statue or Image of the God was dedicated; and that as the Place where the Candle was fixed was called *Candelabrum*, so the Place where the God was set up got the Name of *Delubrum*. See *Macrob* Saturn. Lib. III. C. 4.

229. *Insinuat pavor*, i. e. *Insinuat se.* *Virgil* delights in using this and such like reciprocal Verbs absolutely, as *præcipitat jam nox cœlo*, Æn. II. 9. *tum prora avertit*, I. 108. *accingunt omnes operi*, II. 235. *lateri agglomerant nostro*, II. 341. to all which *se* is understood.

230. *Sacrum—robur.* It is worth while to observe how *Virgil* diversifies his Style. To this same Horse he has found out no less than eleven different Names, all of them equally proper; *Lignum, machinam, monstrum, dolum, pinea claustra, donum, molem, effigiem equi, equum, sacrum robur, simulacrum.*

234. *Muros et mœnia.* Though these two Words are often used promiscuously, yet they are properly of two distinct Significations; *muri* signifying the bare Walls that inclose a Town, and *mœnia* (from *munio*) the Bulwarks or Fortifications; as in *Cæsar* 2. *Bel. Civ. Cum pene ædificata in muris ab exercitu nostro mœnia viderentur.*

235. *Rotarum—lapsus.* i. e. *Rotas quibus delaberetur vel deveheretur equus.* Wheels on which the Machine might roll along.

237. *Scandit—muros.* i. e. Mounts over the Ruins of the Wall.

241. *Divûm*

Fœta armis: circum pueri, innuptæque puellæ
Sacra canunt, funemque manu contingere gaudent.
Illa subit, mediæque minans illabitur urbi.
O patria, O Divûm domus Ilium, et inclyta bello
Mœnia Dardanidum! quater ipso in limine portæ
Substitit, atque utero sonitum quater arma dedere.
Instamus tamen immemores, cæcique furore,
Et monstrum infelix sacratâ sistimus arce.
Tunc etiam fatis aperit Cassandra futuris
Ora, Dei jussu non-unquam credita Teucris.

pueri innuptæque puellæ circum canunt sacra, gaudentque contingere funem manu. Illa machina subit, minansque illabitur mediæ urbi. O patria, O Ilium domus Divûm, et mœnia Dardanidum inclyta bello! quater substitit in ipso limine portæ, atque arma quater dedere sonitum ex utero. Nos tamen instamus immemores, cæcique furore, et sistimus infelix monstrum in sacratâ arce. Tunc etiam Cassandra, non unquam credita Teucris, aperit ora futuris fatis, jussu Dei.

TRANSLATION.

nant with Arms: Boys and unmarried Virgins accompany it with sacred Hymns, and are fain to touch the Rope with their Hand. It advances, and with menacing Aspect slides into the Heart of the City. O my Country, ah Ilium, the Habitation of Gods, and ye Walls of Troy by War renowned! Four Times it stopped in the very Threshold of the Gate, and four Times the Arms resounded in its Womb: Yet we, heedless *of our own Ruin*, and blind with frantic Zeal, urge on, and plant the baneful Monster in the sacred Tower. Then too, Cassandra, by the Inspiration of her God, opens her Lips to *foretel* our approaching Doom, *ill-fated Virgin*, never believed by the Trojans. Unhappy we, to whom that Day

NOTES.

241. *Divûm domus Ilium.* Ilium, *the Habitation of Gods*, either because its Walls had been built by *Neptune* and *Apollo*; or rather on Account of the numerous Temples and consecrated Places with which it abounded.

242. *Quater ipso in limine—substitit.* In reference to this *Seneca* says in his *Agamemnon:*

Fatale munus Danaûm traximus nostra
Crudele dextra: tremuitque sæpe
Limine in primo sonipes, cavernis
Conditos Reges, bellumque gestans, &c.

Some are of Opinion, that this stumbling or Halting of the Horse in the Threshold, alludes to a Notion that prevailed of its being a bad Omen for one to stumble in the Threshold, especially if he was going out to War, as is said to have happened to *Protesilaus*, the first of the *Greeks* who fell in the Plains of *Troy*. The Malignancy of this Omen was thought to proceed from the Furies, who had their Seats in the Threshold. At which *Virgil* hints in the fourth and sixth Books,

—Ultricesque sedent in limine Diræ.
————Cernis custodia qualis
Vestibulo sedeat? facies quæ limina servet?

244. *Immemores, cæcique furore.* *Servius* will have it, that *Virgil* here speaks in Allusion to the Rites of Devoting practised by the *Romans* towards their Enemies, and the Cities to which they laid Siege: In that Form of Words whereby they devoted the Cities of their Enemies, and called away from them their tutelar Gods, they poured out these Imprecations: *Eique populo, civitatique metum, formidinem*, oblivionem *injiciatis*. So that, according to him, *immemores* signifies that they were now abandoned by their Gods, and devoted to Stupidity and Infatuation.

245. *Et monstrum infelix sacratâ sistimus arce.* Here Calamity and Distress are marked in the tardy, languishing Progress of the Verse.

246. *Cassandra—non unquam credita Teucris.* *Cassandra* was *Priam*'s Daughter, and endued with the Gift of Prediction, but with no Effect, for it was her Fate never to be believed; of which

Nos miſeri, quibus ille dies eſſet ultimus, velamus delubra Deûm feſta fronde per urbem.

Interea cœlum vertitur, et nox ruit ab Oceano, involvens magna umbra terramque polumque doloſque Myrmidonum: Teucri fuſi per mœnia conticuere; ſopor complectitur feſſos eorum artus. Et jam Argiva phalanx ibat à Tenedo inſtructis navibus, per amica ſilentia tacitæ Lunæ, petens nota littora; cum regia puppis extulerat flammas, Sinonque defenſus iniquis fatis Deûm

Nos delubra Deûm miſeri, quibus ultimus eſſet
Ille dies, feſtâ velamus fronde per urbem.
Vertitur interea cœlum, et ruit Oceano nox,
Involvens umbrâ magnâ terramque polumque,
Myrmidonumque dolos: fuſi per mœnia Teucri
Conticuere; ſopor feſſos complectitur artus.
Et jam Argiva phalanx inſtructis navibus ibat
A Tenedo, tacitæ per amica ſilentia Lunæ,
Littora nota petens: flammas cum regia puppis
Extulerat; fatiſque Deûm defenſus iniquis,

TRANSLATION.

was to be our laſt, adorn the Temples of the Gods all over the City with feſtival Boughs *and Garlands*. Mean while the Heavens are rolled about, and Night advances apace from the Ocean, wrapping up in her extended Shade both Earth and Heaven, and the Wiles of the Greeks: The Trojans, diſperſed around their Walls, were huſhed and ſtill: Deep Sleep faſt binds their weary Limbs in his Embraces. And now the Grecian Troops, in their equipped Veſſels, ſet out from Tenedos, making towards the well-known Shore, *aided* by the friendly Silence of the quiet Moon-ſhine *Night*, ſo ſoon as the royal *Galley from her* Stern had ſet up the *ſignal* Fire. And Sinon, preſerved by the Will of the Gods adverſe *to Troy*,

NOTES.

which this fabulous Account is given, *Apollo*, falling in Love with *Caſſandra*, got a Promiſe of her Favour, on Condition he would endue her with the Gift of Prophecy; which, ſo ſoon as ſhe obtained, ſhe deceived the God; he, either not able, or deeming it below his Dignity, to withdraw a Boon he had once beſtowed, rendered it however uſeleſs to her, by deſtroying her Credit, and making all her Predictions to be reputed falſe.

249. *Feſtâ velamus fronde.* It was their Cuſtom, not only on Holy days and ſolemn Feſtivals, but alſo on Times of public Rejoicing, to adorn the Temples of the Gods with Branches of Laurel, Olive, Ivy, and the like.

250. *Vertitur interea cœlum. Meantime the Heavens are whirled about*, i. e. The diurnal Hemiſphere is ſunk out of Sight with the Sun, and the other Hemiſphere elevated above the Horizon, which is to be underſtood according to Appearance, the Succeſſion of Day and Night ſeemingly being made by the Revolution of the Heavens about the Earth. Thus the Ancients often ſpeak, *Cum ergo ſemper circa terram ab ortu in occaſum cœli ſphæra volvatur.* Macrob. Som. Scip. Lib. I. C. 16.

250. *Ruit Oceano nox.* As the Poets, imagining the Ocean to be at the Edge of our viſible Horizon, repreſent the Sun ſetting into the weſtern Ocean; ſo they deſcribe the Night and Darkneſs as riſing from thence in the oppoſite Quarter of the Heavens. As here *ruit Oceano nox*, and *Ovid*,

> *Lux præcipitatur aquis, et aquis nox exit ab iiſdem.* Met. Lib. IV. 92.

Milton has the ſame Thought, *P. L.* B. IV. 353.

> ——— ——— ———*For the Sun*
> *Declin'd, was haſt'ning now with prone Career*
> *To th' Ocean Iſles, and in th' aſcending Scale*
> *Of Heav'n the Stars, which uſher Ev'ning, roſe.*

251 —*Terramque polumque, Myrmidonumque dolos.* There is a great Beauty in thus ſingling out the Stratagems of the *Greeks*, as the Object of chief Attention among all the Things in Heaven and Earth which that Night concealed. It brings to my Remembrance *Sempronius*'s dying Exclamation in *Cato*,

> *O for a Peal of Thunder, that would make*
> *Earth, Sea, and Air, and Heaven, and* Cato *tremble!*

255. *Tacitæ Lunæ.* This may ſignify *of the Moon that did not ſhine*, as *Luna ſilet*, in *Pliny*, ſignifies the Moon when ſhe is new, and ſoon withdraws her Light.

256. *Flammas cum regia puppis extulerat.*

We

Incluſos utero Danaos, et pinea furtim
Laxat clauſtra Sinon: illos patefactus ad auras
Reddit equus; lætique cavo ſe robore promunt
Theſſandrus Sthenelusque duces, et dirus Ulyſſes,
Demiſſum lapſi per funem; Athamaſque, Thoaſque,
Pelideſque Neoptolemus; primuſque Machaon,
Et Menelaus, et ipſe doli fabricator Epeus.
Invadunt urbem ſomno vinoque ſepultam;
Cæduntur vigiles: portiſque patentibus omnes
Accipiunt ſocios, atque agmina conſcia jungunt.
Tempus erat, quo prima quies mortalibus ægris
Incipit, et dono Divûm gratiſſima ſerpit:
In ſomnis, ecce, ante oculos mœſtiſſimus Hector
Viſus adeſſe mihi, largoſque effundere fletus;
Raptatus bigis, ut quondam, aterque cruento

furtim laxat Danaos incluſos utero, et pinea clauſtra: equus patefactus reddit illos ad auras; Theſſandruſque Sthenelusque duces, et dirus Ulyſſes, læti promunt ſe è cavo robore, lapſi per funem demiſſum; Athamaſque, Thoaſque, Neoptolemuſque Pelides, Machaonque primus, et Menelaus, et ipſe Epeus fabricator doli. Invadunt urbem ſepultam ſomno vinoque; vigiles cæduntur; accipiuntque omnes ſocios patentibus portis, atque jungunt conſcia agmina.

Tempus erat, quo prima quies incipit ægris mortalibus, et ſerpit gratiſſima dono Divûm: ecce Hector mœſtiſſimus viſus eſt adeſſe mihi ante oculos in ſomnis, effundereque largos fletus; raptatus bigis, ut quondam, aterque cruento

TRANSLATION.

in a ſtolen Hour unlocked the wooden Priſon to the Greeks ſhut up in that *dark* Womb: The Horſe, from his expanded Caverns, pours them forth to open Air; and with Joy iſſue from the hollow Wood Theſſandrus and Sthenelus the Chiefs, and curſed Ulyſſes, ſliding down by a ſuſpended Rope, with Athamas, and Thoas, Neoptolemus the Grandſon of Peleus, and Machaon who led the Way, with Menelaus, and Epeus, he who built the fraudful Engine. They aſſault the City buried in Sleep and Wine. The Watches are knocked down; and they throw open the Gates to receive all their Friends, and join the conſcious Bands. It was the Time when the firſt Sleep invades languid Mortals, and ſteals upon them by the Indulgence of Heaven in ſweeteſt Slumbers. In that drowſy Hour, lo! Hector, extremely ſad, ſeemed to ſtand before my Eyes, and to ſhed Floods of Tears; dragged, as formerly *he had been*, by *Achilles*'s Chariot, and all deformed

NOTES.

We are to underſtand that *Helen* or *Sinon* firſt gave the Signal to *Agamemnon*, by ſhewing a lighted Torch from the Citadel, and *Agamemnon* returned the Signal to them, by letting up a Light on his Stern, as the Manner was:

Dat clarum è puppi ſignum. Æn. III 519.

258. *Incluſos utero*, &c. Word for Word. *Unlooſes, by Stealth, the Doors, or looſes the Bars of Pine, and ſets the Greeks at Liberty, who were ſhut up in this Womb.* Where we may obſerve that *Virgil* uſes the ſame Verb to *clauſtra* and *Danaos*; *he looſes the Bars, he releaſes the* Greeks; this is a Beauty which our Language will not always admit of, but often occurs in the *Latin* and *Greek* Authors: The Examples of this Kind, in *Virgil* particularly, are very numerous.

261. *Theſſandrus.* *Servius* ſays he was the Son of that *Polynices* who was ſlain in the Conteſt with his Brother *Eteocles* for the Crown of *Thebes*: If ſo, his Name ought to be written *Therſandrus* or *Therſandrus*, as in *Heinſius*'s Edition, not *Theſſandrus* or *Teſſandrus*.

265. *Somno vinoque ſepultam.* This is a ſtrong and very expreſſive Metaphor, repreſenting the whole Inhabitants of the City immerſed ſo deep in Sleep, and ſo ſilent and ſtill, as if their Beds had been their Graves; a Circumſtance which greatly moves our Pity towards the *Trojans*, and our Indignation againſt *Sinon* and the treacherous *Greeks*.

266. *Portiſque patentibus*, &c. And by the Gates wide opened they admit all their Companions.

pulvere, trajectusque lora per tumentes pedes. Hei mihi, qualis erat! quantum mutatus ab illo Hectore qui redit indutus exuvias Achillis, vel qui jaculatus est Phrygios ignes puppibus Danaûm! gerens squalentem barbam, et crines concretos sanguine, illaque vulnera quæ accepit plurima circum patrios muros: ipse flens videbar ultro compellare virum, et expromere has mœstas voces: O lux Dardaniæ! O fidissima spes Teucrûm! quæ tantæ moræ tenuere te? Hector exspectate ab quibus oris venis? ut nos defessi aspicimus te post multa funera tuorum, post varios labores hominumque urbisque? quæ indigna causa fœdavit tuos serenos vultus? aut cur cerno hæc vulnera? Ille ad hæc respondit *nihil: nec moratur me quærentem vana: sed, graviter ducens gemitus de imo pectore, ait: nate Deâ, heu! fuge, eripeque te his flammis. Hostis habet muros; Troja ruit ab alto culmine;*

Pulvere, perque pedes trajectus lora tumentes.
Hei mihi, qualis erat! quantum mutatus ab illo
Hectore, qui redit exuvias indutus Achillei,
Vel Danaûm Phrygios jaculatus puppibus ignes!
Squalentem barbam, et concretos sanguine crines,
Vulneraque illa gerens, quæ circum plurima muros
Accepit patrios: ultro flens ipse videbar
Compellare virum, et mœstas expromere voces:
O lux Dardaniæ! spes ô fidissima Teucrûm!
Quæ tantæ tenuere moræ? quibus Hector ab oris
Exspectate venis? ut te post multa tuorum
Funera, post varios hominumque urbisque labores
Defessi aspicimus? quæ causa indigna serenos
Fœdavit vultus? aut cur hæc vulnera cerno?
Ille nihil: nec me quærentem vana moratur:
Sed, graviter gemitus imo de pectore ducens,
Heu fuge, nate Dea, teque his, ait, eripe flammis.
Hostis habet muros; ruit alto à culmine Troja:

TRANSLATION.

with gory Dust, and his swollen Feet bored through with Thongs. Ah me, in what piteous Plight he was! how changed from that Hector who returned clad in the Armour of Achilles, or darting Phrygian Flames against the Ships of Greece! wearing a foul, grisly Beard, Hair clotted with Blood, and those many Wounds which he had received under his native Walls. I, methought, in Tears addressed the Hero first, and poured forth these mournful Accents: Thou, Light of Troy, the Trojans firmest Hope! ah *say* what tedious Causes have detained you so long? Whence comes my longed, my looked for Hector? How it eases my Perplexity to see thee after the many Deaths of thy *Friends*, after the various Disasters of our Men and City! What unworthy Cause has deformed *and marred* the Serenity of thy Looks? Or why do I behold those Wounds? He—not a Word, nor regards me questioning of what nought availed; but heavily, from the Bottom of his Heart, fetching a Groan, ah, fly, Goddess-born, he says, and snatch thee from these Flames: The Enemy is in Possession of the Walls: Troy tumbles down from

NOTES.

275. *Exuvias indutus Achillei.* i. e. The Arms of *Achilles*, of whom he had stripped *Patroclus* slain.

283. *Hector exspectate venis.* *Servius* will have this *exspectate* to be an Antiptosis for *exspectatus*, but I cannot understand his Reason for thinking so.

285. *Ut—defessi aspicimus.* How, *i. e* With what Joy we see thee, spent as we are with Toil!

293. *Penates,*

Sat patriæ, Priamoque datum: ſi Pergama dextra
Defendi poſſent, etiam hac defenſa fuiſſent.
Sacra ſuoſque tibi commendat Troja Penates:
Hos cape fatorum comites: his mœnia quære,
Magna pererrato ſtatues quæ denique ponto.
Sic ait, et manibus vittas, Veſtamque potentem,
Æternumque adytis effert penetralibus ignem.
Diverſo interea miſcentur mœnia luctu;
Et magis atque magis (quanquam ſecreta parentis
Anchiſæ domus, arboribuſque obtecta receſſit)
Clareſcunt ſonitus, armorumque ingruit horror.

ſat datum eſt patriæ Priamoque: ſi Pergama poſſent defendi ullâ dextrâ, fuiſſent defenſa etiam hac dextra. Troja commendat tibi ſacra, ſuoſque Penates: cape hos comites tuorum fatorum; quære mœnia his, quæ magna denique ſtatues, ponto pererrato. Sic ait, et effert manibus vittas, Veſtamque potentem, æternumque ignem ex penetralibus adytis.

Interea mœnia miſcentur diverſo luctu; et ſonitus clareſcunt magis atque magis (quanquam domus parentis Anchiſæ fuit ſecreta, receſſitque obtecta arboribus) horrorque armorum ingruit.

TRANSLATION.

its towering Tops: To Priam, to my Country all Duty has been done. Could those Walls have been ſaved by the Hand *of Man*, by this ſame *Right-hand* they had been ſaved. Troy recommends to thee her ſacred Things, her Gods; theſe take, the Companions of *thy* Fate: For theſe go in queſt of a City, which in Proceſs of Time you ſhall raiſe to a great Extent after a tedious wandering Voyage. He ſaid, and with his own Hands brings forth from the inner Temple the *holy* Fillets, *the Image of* the powerful *Goddeſs* Veſta, and the Fire which always burned.

Meanwhile the City is filled with mingled Scenes of Woe, and though my Father's Houſe ſtood in a retired Corner, remote *from Noiſe*, and incloſed around with Trees; *yet* louder and louder the Sounds riſe on the Ear, and the horrid Din of Arms aſſails us. I ſtart from Sleep, and by haſty Steps mount to the higheſt Bat-

NOTES.

293 *Penates.* *Macrobius*, in his *Saturnalia*, Lib. III. Cap. 4, explains the *Penates* to be thoſe Gods, *Per quos penitus ſpiramus, per quos habemus corpus, per quos rationem animi poſſidemus: By whom we breathe, to whom we owe our Faculties of Body and Mind*, i. e. *Jupiter*, *Juno*, and *Minerva*; to whom he joins *Veſta*, either as one of the Number, or at leaſt as their Attendant; on which Account the Conſuls, and other Magiſtrates, when they entered on their Offices, uſed to pay divine Honours to the *Penates* and *Veſta*. This ſeems to be confirmed from the Paſſage before us, where *Veſta* is delivered to *Æneas*'s Care, together with the *Penates*. Thoſe Gods he farther obſerves, were ſtyled θεοὶ μεγάλοι, *the great Gods*; whence *Virgil* gives *Juno* the ſame Appellation.

Junonis magnæ primùm prece numen adora.
Æn. III. 437.

θεοὶ χρηστοί, *beneficent Gods*, to which he refers that Line in the firſt Book,

Adſit lætitiæ Bacchus dator, et bona Juno.

Laſtly, θεοὶ δυνατοὶ *powerful Deities*; on which Account *Virgil* here gives *Veſta* the Epithet of *potentem*, *Veſtamque potentem*. *Dionyſius Halicarnaſſeus* writes, that the Symbols of theſe *Penates* at *Rome* were two wooden Statues of young Men in a ſitting Poſture, with Javelins in their Hands.

297. *Æternumque—ignem.* The ſacred Fire, which was kept perpetually burning all the Year round. It was brought by *Æneas* into *Italy*, where *Numa Pompilius* re-eſtabliſhed the Order of Veſtal Virgins, whoſe Office was to preſerve this Fire in the Temple of *Veſta*. It was ſuffered to die away on the laſt Day of the Year, and re-kindled on the firſt of *March*, not from any common Fire, but at the Sun-beams. The Original of this religious Cuſtom ſeems to have been derived to the *Egyptians* from the *Perſians*, who were famous for worſhipping the Sun, and the Fire, as an Emblem of that Luminary. This everlaſting Fire was not only preſerved in *Veſta*'s Temple, but even in private Houſes, eſpecially in

Excutior somno, et ascensu supero fastigia summi tecti, atque adsto arrectis auribus. Veluti cum flamma incidit in segetem furentibus Austris; aut torrens rapidus montano flumine sternit agros, sternit læta sata, laboresque boum, trahitque silvas præcipites; pastor inscius stupet accipiens sonitum de alto vertice saxi. Tum vero fides fuit manifesta, insidiæque Danaûm patescunt: jam ampla domus Deiphobi dedit ruinam, Vulcano superante; jam Ucalegon proximus ardet: freta Sigæa lata relucent igni. Clamorque virûm, clangorque tubarum exoritur. Ego amens capio arma, nec sat rationis erit in armis: sed animi mei ardent glomerare manum bello, et concurrere in arcem cum sociis: furor iraque præcipitant mentem,

Excutior somno, et summi fastigia tecti
Ascensu supero, atque arrectis auribus adsto.
In segetem veluti cum flamma furentibus Austris
Incidit; aut rapidus montano flumine torrens
Sternit agros, sternit sata læta, boumque labores,
Præcipitesque trahit silvas: stupet inscius alto
Accipiens sonitum saxi de vertice pastor.
Tum vero manifesta fides, Danaûmque patescunt
Insidiæ: jam Deïphobi dedit ampla ruinam,
Vulcano superante, domus: jam proximus ardet
Ucalegon: Sigea igni freta lata relucent.
Exoritur clamorque virûm, clangorque tubarum.
Arma amens capio; nec sat rationis in armis:
Sed glomerare manum bello, et concurrere in arcem
Cum sociis ardent animi: furor iraque mentem

TRANSLATION.

tlement of the Palace, and stand with listening Ears. As when a Flame is driven by the furious South-winds on standing Corn, or *as* a Torrent impetuously bursting from a Mountain-river desolates the Fields, desolates the rich Crops of Corn, and *all* the Labours of the Ox, and bears *whole* Woods headlong down; the Shepherd, struck with the Sound from the Top of a high Rock, stands amazed, not knowing *whence it arises.* Then indeed the Truth *of Hector's Words* is confirmed, and the Treachery of the Greeks disclosed. Now Deiphobus's spacious Roofs tumble down, overpowered by the Conflagration: Now, next to him, Ucalegon blazes; the Straits of Sigæum shine far and wide with the Flames. The *mingled* Shouts of Men, and Clangor of Trumpets, arise. *My* Arms I snatch with mad Haste; nor *when* in Arms have Reason enough *to use them:* But all my Soul *impatient* burns to collect a Body for the War, and rush into the Citadel with a chosen Band: Fury and Rage hurry on my Mind, and I reflect how glorious it is

NOTES.

in the Palaces of the Great, where was an Altar in the open Court to *Jupiter Hercæus,* on which Fire was kept perpetually burning. Of which some eminent Critics understand that Fire which *Virgil* says *Priam* had consecrated on the Altar at which he was slain,

Sanguine fœdantem, quos ipse sacraverat, ignes. 502.

See *Turneb. Advers.* and *Abbé Banier's Mythology.*

303. *Arrectis auribus.* With pricked up, or listening Ears, a Metaphor from the Brutes, that prick up their Ears at every Sound that gives them any Alarm.

304. *In segetem veluti.* This Simile is borrowed from *Homer,* Iliad II. Verse 455.]

310. *Deïphobi. Deiphobus* was one of *Priam's* Sons, and, after *Paris* was slain by *Pyrrhus,* married *Helen,* by whose Treachery he fell a Sacrifice to the Resentment of the *Greeks* among the first, as is described at large, *Æn.* VI. 490.

312. *Ucalegon.* One of *Priam's* Counsellors; the House is here called by the Name of the Owner. From this Verse *Juvenal* uses *Ucalegon* proverbially for any Neighbour,

—jam poscit aquam, jam frivola transfert
Ucalegon, tabulata tibi jam tertia fumant.
Juv. III. 199.

313. *Exoritur clamorque virûm, clangorque tubarum.* This is one of the finest Lines that ever was made to image the Sense in the Sound.

The

Præcipitant; pulchrumque mori succurrit in armis.
Ecce autem, telis Pantheus elapsus Achivûm,
Pantheus Otriades, arcis Phœbique sacerdos,
Sacra manu, victosque Deos, parvumque nepotem
Ipse trahit; cursuque amens ad littora tendit.
Quo res summa loco, Pantheu? quam prendimus arcem?
Vix ea fatus eram, gemitu cum talia reddit:
Venit summa dies, et ineluctabile tempus
Dardaniæ; fuimus Troes, fuit Ilium, et ingens

succurritque mihi pulchrum esse mori in armis.

Ecce autem Pantheus, elapsus telis Achivûm, Pantheus Otriades, sacerdos arcis Phœbique, ipse trahit sacra manu, Deosque victos, parvumque nepotem; amensque tendit cursu ad littora: Pantheu, in quo loco est summa res? quam arcem prendimus? Vix fatus eram ea, cum reddit talia gemitu: summa dies venit, et ineluctabile tempus Dardaniæ: nos fuimus Troes, Ilium fuit, et ingens

TRANSLATION.

to die in the Bed of Honour. Lo! then Pantheus, escaped from the Sword of the Greeks, Pantheus the Son of Otreus, the Priest of Apollo and of *Minerva*'s Tower, is hurrying away with him the holy Utensils, his conquered Gods, and little Grandchild, and with hasty Strides makes for the Shore * *like one* distracted. How is it, Pantheus, with our All? What Fortess do we seize? I scarce had said, when, with a Groan, he thus replies: Our last Day is come, and the inevitable Doom of Troy: Trojans we are no more: Adieu to Ilium, and the high Re-

* Some read *limina, the Gates of* Anchises's *Palace.*

NOTES.

the Words and Syllables are rough, hoarse, and sonorous, and so artfully put together, as to strike the Ear like the thrilling Notes of the Trumpet which they describe.

319 *Pantheus Otriades.* *Servius* informs us, that upon the Overthrow of *Troy* by *Hercules*, and the Death of *Laomedon*, *Priam* sent *Antenor*'s Son to consult the Oracle of *Delphos*, whether he should raise *Ilium* again upon the same Foundations. At that Time *Pantheus* was the Priest of *Delphic Apollo*, a Youth of exquisite Beauty, and *Antenor* was so charmed with his Shape and Mien, that he carried him off by Force to *Troy*. *Priam*, to make him some Amends for this Injury, constituted him Priest of *Apollo*. Whatever be in that, it appears from *Homer* and other Authors, that he was a Person of great Note and Authority among the *Trojans*.

319. *Arcis Phœbique sacerdos.* i. e. The Priest of *Apollo*, who was worshipped in the Citadel or Tower, together with *Pallas*, to whom it was sacred.

320. *Parvumque nepotem trahebat.* This is another Instance of *Virgil*'s applying one Verb to two Accusatives, where, in Strictness of Speech, it can only be applied to one of them. *Trahebat* is applicable enough to a young Boy, who can hardly walk, but must be half dragged along, but cannot be so well said of Things carried in one's Hand.

322. *Quo res summa loco.* By the *res summa* here I understand, with *Servius*, the Commonwealth, the common Interest of his Country, which was *Æneas*'s *summa res*, his chief, his highest Concern, and will always be nearest the Heart of every Patriot in such a Conjuncture. *Virgil*, to shew the Haste and Impatience of *Æneas*, makes him throw out these short Questions abruptly, without any previous Introduction.

324 *Venit summa dies, &c.* *Macrobius* quotes this Passage as an Instance of *Virgil*'s concise Stile, and comprehensive Eloquence; and, indeed, it is hardly possible to express more in fewer or stronger Words. And therefore he breaks forth upon it into this Exclamation. *Quis fons, quis torrens, quod mare tot fluctibus, quot hic verbis inundavit?*

325 —*Fuimus Troes, fuit Ilium.* This seems to be in Imitation of *Euripides* in the *Troades*, where *Andromache* and *Hecuba* thus alternately complain, πριν ποτ ημεν. Εκαβ. Βεβακεν ολβος Βεβηκε Τροια. *Once we were happy.* Hecuba, *Now our Happiness is gone, Troy is no more.* It

is

gloria Teucrorum; ferus Jupiter tranſtulit omnia Argos; Danai dominantur in incenſâ urbe. Arduus equus adſtans in mediis mœnibus fundit armatos viros; victorque Sinon inſultans miſcet incendia: alii adſunt portis bipatentibus, tot millia quot nunquam venere magnis Mycenis. Alii oppoſiti obſedere anguſta viarum telis: acies ferri ſtat ſtricta coruſco mucrone, parata neci; vigiles portarum primi vix tentant prœlia, et reſiſtunt cæco Marte.

Talibus dictis Otriadæ, et numine Divûm feror in flammas et in arma; quò triſtis Erinnys, quò fremitus et clamor ſublatus ad æthera vocat me. *Ripheus, et Iphitus maximus annis, Hypaniſque Dymaſque, oblati per Lunam, addunt ſe ſocios* mihi. *et adglomerant ſe noſtro lateri; juveniſque Corœbus*

Gloria Teucrorum; ferus omnia Jupiter Argos
Tranſtulit; incenſâ Danai dominantur in urbe.
Arduus armatos mediis in mœnibus adſtans
Fundit equus; victorque Sinon incendia miſcet
Inſultans: portis alii bipatentibus adſunt,
Millia quot magnis nunquam venere Mycenis.
Obſedere alii telis anguſta viarum
Oppoſiti; ſtat ferri acies mucrone coruſco
Stricta, parata neci; vix primi prœlia tentant
Portarum vigiles, et cæco Marte reſiſtunt.
Talibus Otriadæ dictis, et numine Divûm
In flammas et in arma feror; quò triſtis Erinnys,
Quò fremitus vocat, et ſublatus ad æthera clamor.
Addunt ſe ſocios Ripheus, et maximus annis
Iphitus, oblati per Lunam, Hypaniſque Dymaſque,
Et lateri adglomerant noſtro; juveniſque Corœbus

TRANSLATION.

nown of Teucer's Race: Jupiter in the Fierceneſs of his Wrath hath made over all to Argos: The Greeks bear all before them in the City *now* on Fire: The towering Horſe, planted in the Midſt of our Streets, pours fourth armed *Troops*; and Sinon, *the* victorious *Traitor*, with inſolent Triumph ſcatters the Flames. Others are ruſhing in at our wide-opened Gates, ſo many Thouſands as never came from populous Mycenæ. Others with Arms have blocked up the Lanes to oppoſe our Paſſage; the edged Sword with glittering Point ſtands unſheathed, ready to drink our Blood: Hardly the foremoſt Wardens of the Gates make an Effort to fight, and *feebly* reſiſt in the blind Encounter. By theſe Words of Pantheus, and by the Impulſe of the Gods I hurry away into *the Midſt of* Flames and Arms; whither the grim Fury, whither the tumultuous Din, and Shrieks that rend the Skies, call me on. Ripheus and Iphitus, advanced in Years, join me; Hypanis and Dymas come up with us by the *Help of* the Moon, and cloſely adhere to my Side, and young Corœbus Mygdon's Son; who at that Time had chanced to

NOTES.

is well known, that, when the *Romans* would intimate that a Perſon was dead, they frequently uſed the Words *fuit* or *vixit*, to ſhun Sounds that were ſhocking, and therefore reckoned of bad Omen. Beſides, there is a much greater Elegance in expreſſing the Death of a Perſon, or the Overthrow of a City, thus indirectly, *fuit*, *ſtetit*, &c. than in plain, direct Terms; the one is the Language of Poetry, the other flat Proſe. Who would then have imagined that Dr. *Trapp*, a Gentleman ſo well ſkilled in the *Latin* Idiom, ſhould ſo far overlook the Senſe and Spirit of theſe Words, as to give them a more literal Tranſlation, which not only ſounds wretchedly, but is hardly intelligible in *Engliſh*:

We Trojans *have been*, Ilium *once has been*.

331. *Nunquam venere.* Others read *unquam*; but the former is the ſtronger and more ſignificant.

339. *Maximus annis.* Others read *maximus armis*; but the former ſeems the true Reading from Verſe 435.

341. *Juveniſque Corœbus.* *Virgil* has applied

Mygdonides, illis qui ad Trojam forte diebus
Venerat, Insano Cassandræ incensus amore,
Et gener auxilium Priamo Phrygibusque ferebat:
Infelix, qui non sponsæ præcepta furentis
Audierat!
Quos ubi confertos audere in prœlia vidi,
Incipio super his: Juvenes, fortissima frustra
Pectora, si vobis audentem extrema cupido
Certa sequi; quæ sit rebus fortuna, videtis.
Excessere omnes adytis arisque relictis
Dî, quibus imperium hoc steterat: succurritis urbi
Incensæ: moriamur, et in media arma ruamus.
Una salus victis nullam sperare salutem.

Mygdonides, qui forte venerat ad Trojam, illis diebus, incensus insano amore Cassandræ, et gener futurus ferebat auxilium Priamo Phrygibusque: infelix, qui non audierat præcepta furentis sponsæ! Quos confertos ubi vidi audere in prœlia, his verbis super incipio: Juvenes, pectora fortissima frustra, si certa cupido est vobis sequi me audentem extrema, videtis quæ fortuna sit rebus nostris: omnes Dii, quibus hoc imperium steterat, excessere suis adytis arisque relictis: succurritis urbi incensæ: moriamur, et ruamus in media arma. Una salus est victis sperare nullam salutem.

TRANSLATION.

come to Troy, inflamed with a Passion for Cassandra to Madness; and, *in Prospect of being one Day Priam*'s Son-in-law, brought Assistance to him and the Trojans. Ill-fated *Youth*, who heeded not the Admonitions of his inspired Spouse! Whom, close united, soon as I saw resolute to engage, to animate them the more I thus begin: "*Gallant* Youths, Souls heroic and magnanimous, *but ah* in vain! if it is your resolute Purpose to follow me in this last *desperate* Attempt, what is the Situation of our Affairs you see? All the Gods, by whom this Empire stood, have deserted their Shrines and Altars abandoned *to the Enemy*: You come to the Relief of the City in Flames: Let us meet Death, and rush into the thickest of our armed Foes. The only Safety for the vanquished is to throw away all Hopes of

NOTES.

ed to *Corœbus* what *Homer* says of *Othryoneus*, in the thirteenth Book of the Iliad.

345. *Incipio super his.* I translate *super*, *over and above*, or *the more*, *viz.* to animate them. This is the Sense in which *Servius* takes it, and of which it is very capable; and it is certainly much more elegant than to understand it as *Ruæus* has done, *incipio super*, i. e. *de his*, which is so flat, that one would not choose it, if any other was possible.

348. *Juvenes, fortissima frustra.* There is a great Confusion and Neglect of Method in this Speech, to mark the Hurry and Disorder of *Æneas*'s Mind.

351. *Excessere omnes—Dî.* Before the taking of any City, it was usual for the Besiegers to invite the tutelary Deities to leave the Place, that no Sacrilege might be committed; or imagining the City could not be taken till they had deserted it. For which Reason the *Romans* took care to conceal the *Latin* Name of that God, under whose Patronage *Rome* was; and the Priests were not allowed to call the *Roman* Gods by their Names, lest, if their Names had been known, an Enemy might solicit them away. See *Macrob.* on this Verse, Saturn. Lib. III. Cap. 9. *Turnebus* however rather thinks the Poet alludes to a Tradition preserved in *Æschylus*, and other ancient Poets, that, when *Troy* was near its Doom, the Gods were seen bearing away their Statues out of the Temples.

354. *Una salus victis*, &c. This is the Argument which the brave *Leonidas* made Use of to animate his Men to sell their Lives as dear as possible: *Ita suos firmaverat, ut ire se parato ad moriendum animo ferrent: meminerint, qualitercunque præliantibus, cadendum esse.* Justin, Lib. II. Cap. 11.

Sic furor est additus animis juvenum. Inde, ceu lupi raptores in atra nebula, quos improba rabies ventris exegit cæcos, quosque catuli relicti exspectant siccis faucibus, vadimus per tela, per hostes, in mortem haud dubiam, tenemusque iter mediæ urbis: atra nox circumvolat nos cava umbra. Quis explicet cladem illius noctis, quis fando explicet funera, aut possit æquare labores lacrymis? antiqua urbs, dominata per multos annos, ruit:

Sic animis juvenum furor additus. Inde, lupi ceu
Raptores, atra in nebula, quos improba ventris
Exegit cæcos rabies, catulique relicti
Faucibus exspectant siccis, per tela, per hostes,
Vadimus haud dubiam in mortem, mediæque tenemus
Urbis iter: nox atra cava circumvolat umbra.
Quis cladem illius noctis, quis funera, fando
Explicet? aut possit lacrymis æquare labores?
Urbs antiqua ruit, multos dominata per annos:

TRANSLATION.

Safety." Thus the Courage of the Youths is kindled into Fury: Then, like ravenous Wolves in a gloomy Fog, whom the fell Rage of Hunger hath driven from their Dens, blind to Danger, and their Whelps left behind long for their Return with Jaws parched *and thirsting for Blood*; through Arms, through Enemies we march up to imminent Death, and advance through the Middle of the City: sable Night hovers around us with her deepening Shade. Who can describe the Havock, who the Deaths of that Night? Or *who* can furnish Tears equal to the Disasters? Our ancient City, the Seat of Dominion for many Years,

NOTES.

355. *Inde lupi ceu.* Dr. *Trapp* objects to this Simile, that it is quite foreign to the Purpose; nor can he imagine why Men of Courage and Virtue, endeavouring to defend their Country, though by Night, should be compared to Wolves ravening for their Prey: In a Word, he will have it, that there is nothing but the Darkness of the Night common to both. But, if I am not much mistaken, there is another very material Circumstance wherein they agree, namely, the Rage and Fury with which both of them are impelled in the Pursuit of their respective Ends. The Comparison lies not at all in the Action itself, but in the Manner of acting. This is particularly implied in the Expression *exegit cæcos*, as hungry, ravenous Wolves are driven from their safe Retreats blindfold, precipitantly, and without any Fear of Danger, so we rush desperately on our Foes, looking Death and every Danger in the Face with undaunted Boldness and Intrepidity. There is a vast Difference between the *Manners* in which even Men of Courage and Virtue may exert themselves in the Cause of their Country; some are prudent, rational, cool and sedate, while others are furious, impatient of Revenge, outrageous and desperate. Now in this last Manner the Poet shews us *Æneas* and his Party rushing headlong on their Foes, and thirsting after their Blood, like gaunt Wolves, ravening for their Prey. This is further evident from the additional Circumstance in the Comparison (which another Commentator thinks superfluous), I mean that of their Whelps gaping for their Return; by which the Poet, doubtless, designed to represent those Animals in their fiercest and most ravenous State, and therefore the more proper to image the Fierceness of the Mind driven to Despair.

356. *Atra in nebula.* Because in the Night-time, or in dark, foggy Weather, they are most bold and adventurous. A Circumstance wherein the Simile agrees.

358. *Faucibus—siccis.* Some are of Opinion, that *Virgil* here writes according to philosophical Experience and Observation: For those, who have undergone long Fasting, are observed to be more distressed with Thirst than Hunger; for which this Reason is assigned by *Plutarch*, that though the human Body is made up of the Qualities of all the four Elements, yet the strongest and most prevalent is Heat, which requires a constant Supply of Nourishment; but perhaps this is too refined.

359. *Mediæque tenemus urbis iter.* This Circumstance is mentioned to shew their Boldness and Intrepidity. On the other Hand we see *Æneas* afterwards, when he is afraid of the Enemy

Plurima perque vias sternuntur inertia passim
Corpora, perque domos, et relligiosa Deorum
Limina. Nec soli pœnas dant sanguine Teucri:
Quondam etiam victis redit in præcordia virtus,
Victoresque cadunt Danai: crudelis ubique
Luctus, ubique pavor, et plurima mortis imago.
Primus se Danaûm, magna comitante caterva,
Androgeos offert nobis, socia agmina credens,
Inscius: atque ultro verbis compellat amicis:
Festinate viri, nam quæ tam sera moratur
Segnities? alii rapiunt incensa feruntque
Pergama: vos celsis nunc primùm a navibus itis?
Dixit: et extemplo (neque enim responsa dabantur
Fida satis) sensit medios delapsus in hostes.

inertiaque corpora plurima sternuntur passim per vias, perque domos, et relligiosa limina Deorum. Nec Teucri soli dant pœnas suo sanguine; quondam virtus redit in præcordia etiam victis, Danaique victores cadunt: ubique est crudelis luctus, ubique pavor, et plurima imago mortis. Androgeos, magna caterva eum comitante, primus Danaûm offert se nobis, credens nostra agmina esse socia, inscius; atque ultro compellat nos amicis verbis: viri festinate, nam quæ tam sera segnities moratur vos? alii rapiunt feruntque Pergama incensa: vos-ne nunc primum itis a celsis navibus? Dixit, et extemplo sensit esse delapsus in medios hostes (neque enim satis fida responsa dabantur).

TRANSLATION.

tumbles to the Ground: Great Numbers of sluggish Carcases are strowed up and down, both in the Streets, in private Houses, and the sacred Temples of the Gods. Nor is it the Blood of the Trojans alone that is spilt: The vanquished too at Times resume their Courage; and the victorious Grecians bleed: Every where *appears* cruel Sorrow, every where Terror, and Death in a thousand Shapes. The first of the Greeks who comes up with us is Androgeos, accompanied by a numerous Band, unadvisedly imagining that we were confederate Troops; and he introduces himself to us with this friendly Address: Haste, *brave* Associates, what so tardy Sloth detains you? Others tear and plunder the blazing Palaces of Troy: Are you but just come from your lofty Ships? He said, and instantly perceived (for we returned him no very friendly Answer) that he had stumbled into the Midst

NOTES.

Enemy on account of his aged Father, his Wife and Son, tracing out all the By-paths and unfrequented Lanes:

——*Namque avia cursu*
Dum sequor, et nota excedo regione viarum.

364. *Plurima—sternuntur inertia—corpora.* I have here followed the Current of Interpreters, and translated *inertia corpora*, with Dr. *Trapp*, *sluggish Carcases*; but perhaps it may do better to translate *sternuntur*, *are knocked down*, as Æn. X. 429.

Sternitur Arcadiæ proles, sternuntur Etrusci.

And then there will be a great Propriety in giving *corpora* the Epithet *inertia*, to denote the more feeble and helpless of the Inhabitants even the infirm old Men and weak Women, who made no Resistance in the Streets, who could not stir from their Houses, or who fled for Refuge to the Temples of the Gods:

Plurima perque vias sternuntur inertia passim
Corpora, perque domos, et relligiosa Deorum
Limina.

366. *Nec soli pœnas dant sanguine Teucri.* Word for Word, *Nor do the* Trojans *only suffer by the Effusion of their Blood.*

367. *Quondam etiam victis*, &c. i. e. *Sometimes even Valour returns into the Breasts of the vanquished* Trojans.

372. *Ultro verbis compellat amicis.* Literally, *First addresses us with friendly Words.*

374. *Alii rapiunt*, &c. The Meaning is, that others have already gained the Victory, and are now reaping the Spoil; whereas you have not so much as begun to fight.

Obstupuit, retroque repressit pedem cum voce. Veluti qui nitens humi pressit anguem improvisum ex aspris sentibus, trepidusque repente refugit eum attollentem iras, et tumentem cærula colla: haud secus abibat Androgeos tremefactus visu. Irruimus, et circumfundimur densis armis; passimque sternimus eos ignaros loci et captos formidine: fortuna aspirat primo nostro labori. Atque hic Corœbus, exsultans successu animisque, inquit: O socii, qua fortuna prima monstrat nobis iter salutis, quaque dextra ostendit se, sequamur. Mutemus clypeos, aptemusque nobis insignia Danaûm: quis requirat in hoste dolus sit an virtus?

Obstupuit, retroque pedem cum voce repressit:
Improvisum aspris veluti qui sentibus anguem
Pressit humi nitens, trepidusque repente refugit
Attollentem iras, et cærula colla tumentem;
Haud secus Androgeos visu tremefactus abibat.
Irruimus, densis et circumfundimur armis:
Ignarosque loci passim et formidine captos
Sternimus: aspirat primo fortuna labori:
Atque hic exsultans successu animisque Corœbus,
O socii, quà prima, inquit, fortuna salutis
Monstrat iter, quaque ostendit se dextra, sequamur.
Mutemus clypeos, Danaûmque insignia nobis
Aptemus: dolus, an virtus, quis in hoste requirat?

TRANSLATION.

of Foes: He was nonplussed, and with his Words recalled his *hasty* Step. As one who, in his *heedless* Walk, hath trod upon a Snake, *shooting* unawares from rough Thorns, and in fearful Haste hath started back from him, while he is collecting all his Rage, and swelling his azure Crest; just so Androgeos, terrified at the Sight *of us*, began to withdraw. We rush in, and, with Arms to Arms close joined, inclose them round; and knocked them down here and there, Strangers as they were to the Place, and arrested with Fear: *Thus* Fortune smiles upon our first Enterprize. Upon this Corœbus exulting with Success and Courage: My Associates, says he, where Fortune thus early points out our Way to *Conquest and* Safety, and where she shews herself propitious, let us follow *her*. Let us exchange Shields, and accommodate to ourselves the Badges of the Greeks: Whether Stratagem or Valour, who questions in an Enemy? They themselves will

NOTES.

370. *Improvisum aspris veluti.* This Simile is borrowed from *Homer*; but *Virgil* is most happy in the Application, and has improved upon his Original, by the Addition of several Circumstances, that heighten the Comparison, and give it more Force and Likeness, as the learned Reader will easily see, by comparing the one with the other. *Vide* Iliad III. Vers. 33.

384. *Formidine captos.* Surely this Expression implies more than barely *territos* or *metu perculsos*, as *Ruæus* has it. *Captus formidine* signifies to be under the Power of Fear, that they were not able to exert themselves, *enchained*, *arrested*, or *nonplussed by Fear*; to be so enslaved to this Passion, that they could obey nothing but its Impulses.

386. *Corœbus.* This *Corœbus* is said to have been remarkable for nothing so much as his Stupidity; as an Instance of which *Zenobius* relates, that he used to amuse himself in counting the Waves of the Sea. Agreeably to this Character, *Virgil* tells us, he came to *Troy* when the War was almost finished, and that a mad Passion of *Cassandra* was the Motive that drew him thither; and, for the same Reason, he appears to be a very proper Person to contrive this Stratagem, so rash in itself, and so fatal in the Execution.

389. *Danaûmque insignia.* This seems to refer to the Figures or Images engraved on their Bucklers; those of the *Greeks* bearing the Image of *Neptune*, and those of the *Trojans* that of *Minerva*, as we learn from *Servius*.

391. *Comantem*

Arma dabunt ipsi. Sic fatus, deinde comantem
Androgei galeam, clypeique insigne decorum,
Induitur; laterique Argivum accommodat ensem:
Hoc Ripheus, hoc ipse Dymas, omnisque juventus
Læta, facit: spoliis se quisque recentibus armat.
Vadimus immixti Danais, haud numine nostro:
Multaque per cæcam congressi prœlia noctem
Conserimus; multos Danaûm demittimus Orco.
Diffugiunt alii ad naves, et littora cursu
Fida petunt: pars ingentem formidine turpi
Scandunt rursus equum, et nota conduntur in alvo.
Heu, nihil invitis fas quenquam fidere Divis!

Ipsi dabunt nobis arma. Sic fatus, deinde induitur comantem galeam Androgei, decorumque insigne clypei, accommodatque suo lateri Argivum ensem. Ripheus, ipse Dymas, omnisque juventus læta facit hoc: quisque armat se recentibus spoliis. Vadimus immixti Danais, haud nostro numine: congressique conserimus multa prœlia per cæcam noctem; demittimus Orco multos Danaûm. Alii diffugiunt ad naves, et cursu petunt fida littora: pars præ turpi formidine rursus scandunt ingentem equum, et conduntur in nota ejus alvo. Heu, nihil fas est quenquam fidere, Divis invitis!

TRANSLATION.

supply us with Arms: This said, he puts on the crested Helmet of Androgeos, and the rich Ornament of his Shield, and buckles to his Side a Grecian Sword. The same does Ripheus, the same does Dymas too, and all the Youth well pleased: Each arms himself with the recent Spoils. We march on, mingling with the Greeks, *but* not with Heaven on our Side; and in many a Skirmish we engage during the dark Night; many of the Greeks we send down to Pluto's Kingdom. Some fly to the Ships, and make what Haste they can to the trusty Shore: Some, through dishonest Fear, scale once more the bulky Horse, and lurk within his well-known Womb. *But* alas! on nothing ought Man to presume, while the Gods are against him. Lo! Cassandra, Priam's Virgin *Daughter*,

NOTES.

391. *Comantem Androgei galeam.* The Helmet is called *comans*, *waving with a hairy Crest*, because the Crests were made of the Hair of Beasts, as *Æn.* X. 869.

Ære caput fulgens, cristâque hirsutus equinâ.

392. *Clypeique insigne decorum.* *The rich or beauteous Ornament of his Shield*, i. e. His Shield richly ornamented, as the Manner of the Ancients was. *Insigne* therefore is not here an Epithet, but a Substantive.

394. *Hoc ipse Dymas.* Some make a Comma at *ipse*, and refer it to *Æneas*: The same did *Ripheus*, and the same did I, and *Dymas*, &c.

396. *Vadimus immixti*, This is often assigned as a Character of the valorous, that they mingle with the Enemies Ranks. Therefore *Homer* says of *Diomed*, he was so mixed with the *Trojan* Troops, that a Spectator would have been sometimes at a Loss to know whether he belonged to them or the Greeks:

Τυδειδην δ'ϰκ αν γνοιης ποτεροισι μετειη
Ηε μετα μεν Τρωεσσιν ομιλεοι, η μετ Αχαιοις.
In every Quarter fierce Tydides *rag'd,*
Amid the Greek, *amid the* Trojan *Train,*
Rapt thro' the Ranks he thunders o'er the Plain,
Now here, now there, he darts from Place to Place,
Pours on the Rear, or lightens in their Face.
Pope's Iliad, V. 110.

396. *Haud numine nostro.* By *haud nostro* here *Servius* understands either *adverse*, *not friendly to us*; or he considers it in Allusion to the Images of the Gods on the Shields, mentioned in a preceding Note: The God represented on our Shields was not ours; we had thrown away our own Bucklers, with the Image of our Patroness *Minerva*, the Symbol of Protection.

Ecce Caſſandra Priameïa virgo trahebatur paſſis crinibus a templo adytiſque Minervæ, fruſtra tendens ad cœlum ardentia lumina: lumina inquam, nam vincula arcebant ejus teneras palmas. Corœbus, furiata mente, non tulit hanc ſpeciem, et moriturus injecit ſeſe in medium agmen. Cuncti conſequimur eum, *et incurrimus denſis armis. Hic primum obruimur telis noſtrorum ex alto culmine delubri, cædeſque miſerrima oritur ex facie* noſtrorum *armorum, et errore Graiarum jubarum: tum Danai undique collecti invadunt* nos commoti *gemitu atque ira ereptæ virginis: acerrimus* erat *Ajax, et gemini Atridæ, omniſque exercitus Dolopum. Ceu venti adverſi Zephyruſque, Notuſque, et Eurus lætus Eois equis, quondam confligunt, turbine rupto; ſylvæ ſtridunt, Nereuſque ſpumeus ſævit tridenti, atque ciet æquora* ab *imo fundo.*

Ecce trahebatur paſſis Priameia virgo
Crinibus a templo Caſſandra adytiſque Minervæ,
Ad cœlum tendens ardentia lumina fruſtra:
Lumina, nam teneras arcebant vincula palmas.
Non tulit hanc ſpeciem furiata mente Corœbus,
Et ſeſe medium injecit moriturus in agmen.
Conſequimur cuncti, et denſis incurrimus armis.
Hìc primùm ex alto delubri culmine telis
Noſtrorum obruimur, oriturque miſerrima cædes,
Armorum facie, et Graiarum errore jubarum.
Tum Danai gemitu, atque ereptæ virginis ira,
Undique collecti invadunt, acerrimus Ajax,
Et gemini Atridæ, Dolopumque exercitus omnis.
Adverſi rupto ceu quondam turbine venti
Confligunt, Zephyruſque, Notuſque, et lætus Eois
Eurus equis; ſtridunt ſylvæ, ſævitque tridenti
Spumeus, atque imo Nereus ciet æquora fundo.

TRANSLATION.

with her Hair all diſhevelled, was dragged along from the Temple and Shrine of Minerva, raiſing to Heaven her glaring Eyes in vain; *I ſay* her Eyes, for Cords bound her tender Hands. Corœbus, in the Tranſports of his Soul, could not bear this Spectacle, and, reſolute on Death, flung himſelf into the Midſt of the Band. We all follow, and ruſh upon them in a Breaſt. Upon this we are firſt overpowered with the Darts of our Friends from the high Battlements of the Temple, and a moſt piteous Slaughter enſues, *occaſioned* by the Appearance of our Arms, and the *fatal* Diſguiſe of our Grecian Creſts. Next the Greeks, through Anguiſh and Rage for the Reſcue of the Virgin, fall upon us in Troops from every Quarter; Ajax moſt fierce, both the Sons of Atreus, and the whole Bands of the Dolopes. As, at Times, in a burſting Hurricane, oppoſite Winds encounter the Weſt and South, and Eurus, proud of his eaſtern Steeds; the Woods roar, foamy Nereus rages with his Trident, and toſſes up the Seas from the loweſt Bottom. / They too, whom, through the Shades, in the duſky Night,

NOTES.

405. *Fruſtra.* i. e. In vain ſhe liſted them to Heaven, imploring Pity from the Gods, now inexorable; or in vain ſeeking to move the Compaſſion of the *Greeks.*

414 *Ajax.* This is *Ajax*, the Son of *Oïleus*, by whom *Caſſandra* was raviſhed in the Temple of *Minerva.* As for the other *Ajax*, the Son of *Telamon*, he had been ſlain ſome Time before in the Diſpute for *Achilles*'s Arms, and killed himſelf for Grief at his Diſappointment.

416. *Adverſi rupto ceu quondam turbine venti.* This Simile is an Imitation of Homer, Il. IX. *ad init.* *Scaliger*, in comparing the two, finds the Preference ſo much due to *Virgil*, that he reckons him the Maſter, and *Homer* only the Scholar.

424. *Ilicet*

Illi etiam, ſi quos obſcura nocte per umbram
Fudimus inſidiis, totaque agitavimus urbe,
Apparent; primi clypeos, mentitaque tela
Agnoſcunt, atque ora ſono diſcordia ſignant.
Ilicet obruimur numero, primuſque Coroebus
Penelei dextra Divæ armipotentis ad aram
Procumbit: cadit et Ripheus, juſtiſſimus unus
Qui fuit in Teucris, et ſervantiſſimus æqui:
Dis aliter viſum. Pereunt Hypaniſque Dymaſque,
Confixi a ſociis: nec te tua plurima, Pantheu,
Labentem pietas, nec Apollinis infula, texit.
Iliaci cineres, et flamma extrema meorum!
Teſtor, in occaſu veſtro, nec tela, nec ullas
Vitaviſſe vices Danaûm; et, ſi fata fuiſſent

Illi etiam apparent, ſi quos fudimus inſidiis per umbram in obſcura nocte, agitavimuſque in tota urbe; hi primi agnoſcunt clypeos teláque mentita, atque ſignant ora noſtra ſono diſcordia. Ilicet obruimur numero, Coroebuſque primus procumbit dextra Penelei, ad aram armipotentis Divæ; et Ripheus cadit, qui fuit unus juſtiſſimus et ſervantiſſimus æqui in Teucris: viſum eſt aliter Dis. Hypaniſque Dymaſque confixi a ſociis pereunt: nec tua plurima pietas, O Pantheu, nec infula Apollinis texit te labentem. O cineres Iliaci, et extrema flamma meorum! teſtor vos, me vitaviſſe nec tela, nec ullas vices Danaûm, in veſtro occaſu; et, ſi fata fuiſſent.

TRANSLATION.

we, by Stratagem, had routed, and proſecuted all over the City, *now* make their Appearance; they are the firſt who diſcover our Shields and counterfeit Arms, and mark the Sound of our Voices to diſagree *with our Armour.* In a Moment we are overpowered by Numbers, and firſt Coroebus ſinks in Death by the Hand of Peneleus, at the Altar of the Warrior Goddeſs: Ripheus too falls, the moſt eminently virtuous among the Trojans, and *a Man* of the ſtricteſt Integrity. *But, though we may think he deſerved a better Fate,* to the Gods it ſeemed otherwiſe. Hypanis and Dymas die by the *cruel* Darts of their own Friends: Nor did thy ſignal Piety, nor the *holy* Fillets *of thy God* Apollo, ſave thee, *unhappy* Pantheus, in thy dying Hour! Ye *ſacred* Remains of Troy, ye expiring Flames of my Country! witneſs, that in your Fall I ſhunned nor Darts nor any deadly Weapon of the Greeks; and, had it been fated that I ſhould fall, I deſerved it by *this* Hand.

NOTES.

424. *Ilicet.* i. e. *Forthwith, in a Trice.* This Word anciently ſignified the ſame with *actum eſt, all is over.* It was an Expreſſion uſed by the Judge, who, when he thought fit to put an End to Buſineſs, ordered the *Crier* to pronounce the Word *ilicet*, i. e. *ire licet, all Parties may be gone, the Buſineſs of the Court is over.* Hence the Term is uſed by *Terence* in the ſame Senſe with *actum eſt*, in Adelph. *En tibi reſcivit omnem rem, id nunc clamat ilicet.* Again in Eunuch. *Actum eſt, ilicet, periiſti.* Servius.

428. *Dis aliter viſum.* I ſhall not trouble the Reader with all the Explications which Commentators have given of this Paſſage; it is obvious that the Poet could never mean to ſay, *He was the juſteſt and moſt upright Man of all the* Trojans, *but the Gods thought him not ſo;* for this would be a Contradiction, ſince, if the Gods thought him not ſo, he certainly was not the juſteſt. Yet this is Mr. *Dryden*'s Senſe of the Words:

Juſt of his Word, obſervant of the Right:
Heav'n thought not ſo.

There muſt therefore be ſomewhat underſtood to which the *Dis aliter viſum* immediately refers; and that is, the Reflection which every attentive Reader naturally makes in contemplating the unhappy Fate of ſo virtuous a Man, *Ah, what Pity ſo juſt a Man ſhould have periſhed with the reſt! ſurely he deſerved a better Fate.* This Thought would naturally ariſe in *Æneas*'s own Mind, but he checks it with the pious Reflection, *Dis aliter viſum.* See Dr. *Clarke*'s Note on *Homer*, Iliad V. 22. where he ſhews an Inſtance of the Ellipſis parallel to this.

433. *Vitaviſſe vices.* By *vices* here *Servius*

ut caderem, me *meruiſſe* hac *manu* ut caderem. *Iphitus et Pelias mecum divellimur inde*, *quorum Iphitus jam* erat *gravior ævo*, *et Pelias tardus vulnere Ulyſſei*, *protinus vocati clamore ad ſedes Priami*. *Hic vero cernimus ingentem pugnam*, *ceu cætera bella forent nuſquam*, *ceu nulli morerentur in totâ urbe*; *cernimus Martem ſic indomitum*, *Danaoſque ruentes ad tecta*, *limenque obſeſſum actâ teſtudine*. *Scalæ hærent parietibus*; Danaique *nituntur* aſcendere gradibus earum *ſub ipſos poſtes* portarum, *protectique ſiniſtris objiciunt clypeos ad tela*, *prenſant faſtigia dextris*.

Ut caderem, meruiſſe manu. Divellimur inde,
Iphitus et Pelias mecum; quorum Iphitus ævo
Jam gravior, Pelias et vulnere tardus Ulyſſei;
Protinus ad ſedes Priami clamore vocati.
Hìc verò ingentem pugnam, ceu cætera nuſquam
Bella forent, nulli totâ morerentur in urbe,
Sic Martem indomitum, Danaoſque ad tecta ruentes
Cernimus, obſeſſumque actâ teſtudine limen.
Hærent parietibus ſcalæ, poſteſque ſub ipſos
Nituntur gradibus; clypeoſque ad tela ſiniſtris
Protecti objiciunt, prenſant faſtigia dextris.

TRANSLATION.

Thence we are forced away, Iphitus, Pelias, and I; of whom Iphitus was now unwieldy through Age, and Pelias, diſabled by a Wound from Ulyſſes, forthwith to Priam's Palace called by *diſmal* Outcries. Here, indeed, a dreadful Fight riſes to our View, as though this had been the only Seat of the War, *as though* none had been dying in all the City *beſides*; with ſuch ungoverned Fury we ſee Mars raging, the Greeks ruſhing forward to the Palace, and the Gates beſieged by the Troops, advancing under the Shelter of their tortoiſed Bucklers. Scaling Ladders are fixed on the Walls, and by their Steps they mount at the very Door-poſts, and protecting themſelves by their Left-arms, oppoſe their Bucklers to the Darts, *while* with their Right-hands they graſp the Battlements. On the other

NOTES.

underſtands *Fights*, *quia per viciſſitudinem pugnabatur*, *becauſe they fought by Courſes*. *Scaliger* diſlikes this Senſe, and will have it to mean *Wounds* and *deadly Blows*, *vulnera et cædes*, becauſe Wounds in Fighting are mutually given and received. But the juſteſt Idea of the Word *vices* is that given by *Donatus*, who conſiders it as an Alluſion to Gladiators, *vito*, the Verb joining with it, being a Term uſed in Fencing, *to parry of a Thruſt*, in Oppoſition to *peto*, *to aim a Thruſt*.

434. *Meruiſſe manu*. *I deſerved it by this Hand*, *or by Fighting*. There is ſomething very noble in this Sentiment, which conſiders Death as a Prize or Reward which the valiant won by their Merit. This agrees with his former Reflection, *pulchrumque mori ſuccurrit in armis*; the ſame with *Horace's*

Dulce et decorum eſt pro patria mori.

434 *Divellimur inde*. *We are torn away*. He ſpeaks of it as a great Affliction; and, as it were, accuſes his Fate, that denied him the Honour of ſo glorious a Death.

441. *Actâ teſtudine*. By applying the *Teſtudo* or *Tortoiſe*. It was properly a Figure which the Soldiers caſt themſelves into, and is thus deſcribed by *Livy*, Lib. XLIV. 9. *Scutis ſuper capita denſatis*, *ſtantibus primis*, *ſecundis ſubmiſſioribus tertiis magis*, *et quartis*, *poſtremis etiam genu nixis*, *faſtigiatam*, *ſicut tecta ædificiorum ſunt*, *teſtudinem faciebant*: i. e. Their Targets cloſed together above their Heads, to defend them from the miſſive Weapons of the Enemy; the firſt Rank ſtood upright, the reſt ſtooped lower and lower by Degrees, till the laſt Rank kneeled down upon their Knees; ſo that every Rank covering with their Targets the Heads of all in the Rank before them, they repreſented a Tortoiſe-ſhell, or a Sort of a Penthouſe. The carrying on of an Attack againſt a Place, by this Sort of Engine, was called *agere teſtudinem*.

442. *Poſteſque ſub ipſos nituntur gradibus*. By *gradibus* here we may either underſtand the Steps that led up to the Palace, as was common in the Houſes of the Great, or rather the Steps

of

Dardanidæ contra turres ac tecta domorum
Culmina convellunt: his se, quando ultima cernunt,
Extremâ jam in morte parant defendere telis:
Auratasque trabes, veterum decora alta parentum,
Devolvunt: alii strictis mucronibus imas
Obsedere fores, has servant agmine denso.
Instaurati animi, regis succurrere tectis,
Auxilioque levare viros, vimque addere victis.
Limen erat, cæcæque fores, et pervius usus
Tectorum inter se Priami, postesque relicti
A tergo, infelix quà se, dum regna manebant,
Sæpius Andromache ferre incomitata solebat
Ad soceros, et avo puerum Astyanacta trahebat.

Contra Dardanidæ convellunt turres ac tecta culmina domorum: quando cernunt ultima, parant defendere se his telis jam in extremâ morte; devolvuntque auratas trabes, alta decora veterum parentum: alii obsedere imas fores strictis mucronibus, servant has denso agmine. Animi nostri sunt *instaurati succurrere tectis regis, levareque viros auxilio, addereque vim victis. Erat limen foresque cæcæ, et pervius usus tectorum Priami inter se, postesque relicti à tergo, quà infelix Andromache incomitata sæpius solebat ferre se ad soceros, dum regna Priami manebant, et trahebat puerum Astyanacta avo suo;*

TRANSLATION.

Hand the Trojans tear down the Turrets and Roofs of their Houses; with these Weapons, since they see the Extremity, they seek to defend themselves now in their final Catastrophe, and tumble on *their Foes* the gilded Rafters, those stately Ornaments of their Ancestors: Others with drawn Swords beset the Gates below: These they guard in a firm, compact Body. We resume all our Ardour to relieve the royal Palace, support our *labouring* Friends, and inspire their drooping Hearts with *new Life and* Vigour. There was a Passage and secret Entry that served for free Communication between the two Palaces of Priam, a neglected Postern-Gate, by which unfortunate Andromache, while the Kingdom stood, was often wont to resort to the royal Pair without Guard and Retinue, and to lead the Boy Astyanax to his Grand-sire. *By this* I mount up to the Roof of the highest

NOTES.

of the Scaling-ladders. I have translated it according to this last Sense: They mount up, or press to get up, *viz.* to the Roof by the Ladders, which were placed under the very Door-posts.

445. *Tecta domorum culmina. The covered Tops of Houses.* Though *tecta* is mostly put by itself, yet it is an Adjective, and must have *culmina*, or some such Substantive, understood.

446. *Culmina convellunt—auratasque trabes devolvunt.* This single Circumstance gives us a very lively Image of Men in Despair.

448 *Decora alta.* Some ancient Copies read *decora illa parentum*, which has a peculiar *Emphasis.*

449. *Alii—imas obsedere fores.* These I take to be *Trojan* Guards mentioned below, Verse 485. Others however understand it of the *Greeks.*

452. *Victis.* i. e. Despairing, fighting with no Hope of Victory; as in that Passage above, Verse 354.

Una salus victis nullam sperare salutem.

454. *Tectorum Priami.* Priam had two Palaces adjoining to each other, in the one resided *Hector* and *Andromache.*

455. *Infelix—Andromache.* The Mention of *Andromache's* using the secret Passage to the Palace gives a Dignity to this Circumstance, which is but low in itself.

457. *Ad soceros.* Her Fathers, or rather Parents in Law; *i. e. Priam* and *Hecuba.* Perhaps in Imitation of *Euripides*, who in his *Andromache* comprehends them both under the single Word γαμβροὺς.

457. *Astyanacta. Astyanax* was *Hector's* Son by *Andromache.* Some say he was carried off by *Ulysses*, others by *Menelaus*, in the Absence of *Pyrrhus*, and thrown over a Precipice, to void the Prophecy, which imported, that, if [illegible], he would be the Avenger of his Parents and Country.

457. *Trahebat.* This Word is used before in the

Hac evado ad faſtigia ſummi culminis, unde miſeri Teucri jactabant manu irrita tela. Nos circum *aggreſſi ferro turrim ſtantem in præcipiti, eductamque ſummis tectis ſub aſtra, unde omnis Troja* ſolita eſt *videri, et naves Danaûm ſolitæ, et Achaïca caſtra* ſolita erant videri, aggreſſi inquam turrim, *quà ſumma tabulata dabant juncturas labantes, convellimus* eam ex *altis ſedibus impulimuſque: Ea repente lapſa trahit ruinam cum ſonitu, et latè incidit ſupra agmina Danaûm: aſt alii ſubeunt; nec ſaxa* ceſſant, *nec ullum genus telorum ceſſat interea. Ante veſtibulum ipſum, inque primo limine exſultat Pyrrhus coruſcus telis et ahenâ luce.*

Evado ad ſummi faſtigia culminis, unde
Tela manu miſeri jactabant irrita Teucri.
Turrim in præcipiti ſtantem, ſummiſque ſub aſtra
Eductam tectis (unde omnis Troja videri,
Et Danaûm ſolitæ naves, et Achaïa caſtra)
Aggreſſi ferro circum, quà ſumma labantes
Juncturas tabulata dabant, convellimus altis,
Sedibus, impulimuſque: ea lapſa repente ruinam
Cum ſonitu trahit, et Danaûm ſuper agmina latè
Incidit: aſt alii ſubeunt; nec ſaxa, nec ullum
Telorum interea ceſſat genus.
Veſtibulum ante ipſum primoque in limine Pyrrhus
Exſultat, telis et luce coruſcus ahenâ:

TRANSLATION.

Battlement, whence the diſtreſſed Trojans were hurling unavailing Darts. With our Swords aſſailing all around a Turret, ſituated on a Precipice, and ſhooting up its towering Top to the Stars (whence we were wont to ſurvey all Troy, the Fleet of Greece, and the Grecian Camp), where the topmoſt Story made the Joints more apt to give Way, we tear from its ſteep Foundation, and puſh on *our Foes. The huge* Pile, on a ſudden tumbling down, brings thundering Deſolation with it, and falls with wide Havock on the Grecian Troops. But others *ſoon* ſucceed. Mean while, neither Stones, nor any Sort of miſſive Weapons, ceaſe to fly. Juſt before the Veſtible, and at the outer Gate, Pyrrhus exults, glittering in Arms and gleamy Braſs: As when a Snake *comes forth* to Light, having fed on

NOTES.

the ſame Senſe, when *Pantheus* is carrying away his Gods, and a little Boy his Grandchild, *parvumque nepotem ipſe trahit.*

458. *Evado.* I eſcape to the Top; this points to the Danger there was of his being intercepted, as Verſe 531.

460. *In præcipiti ſtantem.* If *Virgil* means no more by this, as Dr. *Trapp* and others contend, but to let us know the Tower was high, it is odd he ſhould uſe ſo many Words for that End: Firſt, *in præcipiti ſtantem,* and then, *eductam ſummis tectis ſub aſtra.* The former is certainly capable of ſignifying its threatening or projecting ſituation, that it ſtood on the outmoſt Verge of the high Wall, as on the Brink of a Precipice.

463. *Summa tabulata.* It is difficult to find out the Meaning of *Summa* in this Place, becauſe *Virgil* ſpeaks as if the whole Turret had been puſhed down, and not one Story only. I am therefore inclined to underſtand the *ſumma tabulata* of the higheſt Story of the Palace, on which the Turret ſtood. Or perhaps it means only, that the upper Part of the Tower was overthrown.

464.———*Convellimus altis*
Sedibus, impulimuſque: ea lapſa repente ruinam
Cum ſonitu trahit, et Danaûm ſuper agmina latè
Incidit

The Rumbling of theſe Verſes, and the Rapidity with which they move (being all Dactyls but the laſt Foot, in which heroic Verſe requires a Spondee), is another Inſtance of *Virgil*'s admirable Talent in making the Sound expreſs the Senſe.

470. *Luce ahenâ.* Literally *brazen Light,* i. e. The Gleam or Refulgence of his brazen Armour. So *Homer,* Il. VII.

Αὐγὴ

Qualis ubi in lucem coluber, mala gramina paſtus,
Frigida ſub terrâ tumidum quem bruma tegebat,
Nunc poſitis novus exuviis, nitiduſque juventâ,
Lubrica convolvit ſublato pectore terga
Arduus ad ſolem, et linguis micat ore triſulcis.
Unà ingens Periphas, et equorum agitator Achillis
Armiger Automedon, unà omnis Scyria pubes
Succedunt tecto, et flammas ad culmina jactant.
Ipſe inter primos, correptâ durâ bipenni,

Talis *qualis ubi coluber, paſtus mala gramina, prodit in lucem, quem tumidum frigida bruma tegebat ſub terrâ; nunc novus, exuviis poſitis, nitiduſque juventâ, convolvit lubrica terga, pectore ſublato, arduus ad ſolem, et micat linguis triſulcis in ore. Unà cum Pyrrho ingens Periphas et armiger ejus Automedon,* quondam *agitator equorum Achillis; unà* etiam *omnis Scyria pubes ſuccedunt tecto, et jactant flammas ad culmina.* Pyrrhus *ipſe inter primos, durâ bipenni correptâ*

TRANSLATION.

noxious Herbs, whom, bloated *with Poiſon*, the frozen Winter hid under the Earth, now renewed, and ſleek with Youth, after caſting his Skin, with Breaſt erect he rolls up his ſlippery Back, reared to the Sun, and brandiſhes a three-forked Tongue in his Mouth. At the ſame Time bulky Periphas, and Automedon, *formerly* Charioteer to Achilles, *now Pyrrhus*'s Armour-bearer; at the ſame Time all the Youth whom *Pyrrhus brought* from Scyros-Iſland advance to the Wall, and toſs *flaming* Brands to the Roof. *Pyrrhus* himſelf in the Front, ſnatching up a Battle-

NOTES.

αυγη χαλκειη κορυθων απο λαμπομενααν.
The blazing Splendor of the ſhining Helms.

471. *Qualis ubi in lucem. Prodit*, or ſome ſuch Word, is obviouſly underſtood. This Situation is an Improvement on that in *Homer* Il. XXII. 93. where *Hector*'s fierce Manner of expecting the Approach of *Achilles* is compared to a Snake eyeing one whom he is going to attack:

Ως δε δρακων, &c.
So roll'd up in his Den, the ſwelling Snake
Beholds the Traveller approach the Brake;
When fed with noxious Herbs his turgid Veins
Have gather'd half the Poiſons of the Plains.
Pope's Homer.

471. *Mala gramina paſtus.* This is a literal Tranſlation of *Homer*'s βεβρωκως κακα φαρμακα and agreeable to the Truth of Hiſtory: Ο. δρακοντες—μελλοντες τινα ελλοχαν. &c. *When thoſe Serpents lie in wait for either Man or Beaſt, they eat mortal Roots*, &c. Ælian. Lib. VI. Cap. 4.

473. *Poſitis novus exuviis.* We learn from *Ariſtotle*, that thoſe Animals caſt their Sloughs in the Autumn, but eſpecially in the Spring, when they come abroad after their Winter Confinement. He tells us they begin to caſt off from the Eyes, ſo as to appear at that Time quite blind to thoſe who are unacquainted with their Nature; then the Head is ſtripped, for that Part appears ſmooth before the reſt of the Body; and thus, in the Space of about a Day and a Night, they are diveſted of the Skin of their old Age, and renewed in the Beauty of Youth. *Ariſt. de Animal.* Lib. VIII. Cap. 17.

475. *Arduus ad ſolem.* It rears itſelf up to receive the Heat of the Sun, eſpecially in the Spring, when the warm Sun is moſt cheriſhing.

475. *Linguis triſulcis.* The ſame Author ſays Serpents have Tongues of a great Length, and cloven. The Poets repreſent them three forked, probably on Account of the Volubility of their Tongues, wherein they are ſaid to exceed all Animals whatſoever.

476. *Ingens Periphas. Homer* gives him the Epithet of πελωριος; for which Reaſon *Virgil* calls him *ingens, vaſt, gigantic.*

477. *Scyria pubes. Scyros* was one of the *Cyclades Iſlands*, where *Achilles*, ſent thither by his Mother *Thetis*, to the Care of *Lycomedes*, the King of the Iſland, debauched *Deidamia*, *Lycomedes*'s Daughter, and had *Pyrrhus* by her. Others ſay *Lycomedes* gave him *Deidamia* in Marriage.

478. *Succedunt tecto.* i. e. *Sub tectum cedunt*, they advance up to the Wall, ſo as to be juſt under the Roof.

perrumpit limina, vellitque æratos postes à cardine: jamque cavavit firma robora, trabe excisâ, et dedit ingentem fenestram lato ore. Domus intus apparet, et longa atria patescunt: penetralia Priami et veterum regum apparent; videntque armatos stantes in primo limine.

At interior domus miscetur gemitu miseroque tumultu; ædesque cavæ penitus ululant femineis plangoribus: clamor ferit aurea sidera. Tum pavidæ matres errant in ingentibus tectis, amplexæque postes tenent eos, atque figunt oscula illis. Pyrrhus instat patriâ vi; nec claustra, neque ipsi custodes valent sufferre eum: janua labat crebro ariete,

Limina perrumpit, postesque à cardine vellit
Æratos: jamque excisâ trabe firma cavavit
Robora, et ingentem lato dedit ore fenestram.
Apparet domus intus, et atria longa patescunt:
Apparent Priami et veterum penetralia regum;
Armatosque vident stantes in limine primo.

At domus interior gemitu miseroque tumultu
Miscetur: penitusque cavæ plangoribus ædes
Femineis ululant: ferit aurea sidera clamor.
Tum pavidæ tectis matres ingentibus errant;
Amplexæque tenent postes, atque oscula figunt.
Instat vi patriâ Pyrrhus; nec claustra, neque ipsi
Custodes, sufferre valent: labat ariete crebro

TRANSLATION.

ax, beats through the stubborn Gates, labours to tear the brazen Posts from the Hinges: And now, having hewn away the Bars, he dug through the firm Boards, and made a large, wide-mouthed Breach; *through which* the Palace within is exposed to View, and the long Galleries are discovered: The sacred Recesses of Priam and the ancient Kings are *prophanely* exposed to View, and they see the armed *Guards* standing at the Gate.

As for the inner Palace, it is filled with mingled Groans and doleful Uproar, and the hollow Rooms all throughout howl with female Yellings: Their Shrieks strike the golden Stars. Then the trembling Matrons roam through the spacious Halls, and in *fast* Embraces hug the Door-posts, and cling to them with their Lips. Pyrrhus presses on with *all* his Father's Violence: Nor Bars nor *Bolts*, nor *armed* Guards themselves are able to sustain *his Fury*. The Gate, by repeated,

NOTES.

480. *Postesque à cardine vellit.* I translate this, *he tries to tear*, or *shove the Door-posts from the Hinges*; for it cost him a great deal of hard Labour and Struggle before he accomplished his Purpose. See Verse 493.

481. *Excisâ trabe.* By the *Trabes* or *Beam*, which is a general Word, we are to understand here what answers to the Rails, or those Pieces of Timber that stretch cross the Pannels of a Door.

481. *Cavavit.* There is a particular Beauty here in the Change of the Tense: The *perrumpit limina, et vellit postes*, shews *Pyrrhus* beating down, and tearing the Gates: Then *cavavit robora, dedit fenestram*, shews the Breach, the wide Aperture he hath now made in the Door; in consequence of which *apparet domus intus*. All this is picturesque, and paints the Objects to the Life. I remember a similar Instance of the Change of Tense in *Milton*, where the Effect is the same; it is in the fifth Book of *Paradise Lost*, Verse 291, where *Raphael*'s Arrival in Paradise is described:

Their glittering Guards he pass'd; and now is come
Into the blissful Field, through Groves of Myrrh,
And flow'ring Odours, Cassia, Nard, and Balm;
A Wilderness of Sweets.

487. *Cavæ—ædes.* The Rooms with cieled or concave Roofs. Others understand by these Words the same with what was called in one Word *Cavædium, a Gallery* or *Piazza*.

490. *Amplexæque tenent postes.* This is agreeable to the *Roman* Superstition, which ascribed a Kind of Divinity to the Gates, Lintels, and Door-posts. The *Trojan* Matrons therefore embrace and kiss them, imagining these religious Rites would recommend them to the Favour and Protection of the Deities who presided over the Gates.

492. *Ariete crebro.* The *Aries* or *battering Ram*,

Janua, et emoti procumbunt cardine poſtes.
Fit via vi: rumpunt aditus, primoſque trucidant
Immiſſi Danai, et latè loca milite complent:
Non ſic, aggeribus ruptis cum ſpumeus amnis
Exiit, oppoſitaſque evicit gurgite moles,
Fertur in arva furens cumulo, campoſque per omnes
Cum ſtabulis armenta trahit. Vidi ipſe furentem
Cæde Neoptolemum, geminoſque in limine Atridas:
Vide Hecubam, centumque nurus, Priamumque per aras
Sanguine fœdantem, quos ipſe ſacraverat, ignes.
Quinquaginta illi thalami, ſpes tanta nepotum,

et poſtes emoti cardine procumbunt. Via fit vi; rumpunt aditus; Danaique immiſſi trucidant primos, et latè complent loca milite. Amnis cum exiit ſpumeus, aggeribus ruptis, evicitque oppoſitas moles gurgite, non ſic fertur in arva furens cumulo aquarum, *trahitque armenta cum ſtabulis per omnes campos.* Ego *ipſe vidi Neoptolemum furentem cæde, geminoſque Atridas in limine: vidi Hecubam, centumque* ejus *nurus, Priamumque per aras fœdantem ſanguine ignes quos ipſe ſacraverat. Quinquaginta illi thalami, tanta ſpes nepotum,*

TRANSLATION.

battering Blows, gives way, and the Door-poſts, torn from their Hinges, tumble to the Ground. *Thus* the Greeks make their Way by Force, burſt a Paſſage, and, being admitted, butcher the firſt *they meet*, and fill the Places all about with their Troops. Not with ſuch a Fury a River pours on the Fields its heavy Torrent, and ſweeps away *whole* Herds with their Stalls over all the Plains, when foaming it has burſt away from its broken Banks, and borne down oppoſing Mounds with its whirling Current. Theſe Eyes beheld Neoptolemus tranſported with bloody Rage, and the two Sons of Atreus in the Gate: I ſaw Hecuba, and her hundred Daughters-in-Law, and Priam at the Altar, defiling with his Blood the Fires which himſelf had conſecrated. Thoſe fifty Bed-chambers, whereon his great Hopes of a *numerous* Race *were raiſed*, *thoſe* Doors, that proudly ſhone with

NOTES.

Ram, as *Joſephus* deſcribes it, was a vaſt long Beam, like the Maſt of a Ship, ſtrengthened at one End with a Head of Iron, ſomething reſembling that of a Ram, whence it took its Name. This is hung by the Midſt with Ropes to another Beam, which lies croſs a Couple of Poſts; and, hanging thus equally balanced, was by a great Number of Men violently thruſt forward, and drawn backward, and ſo ſhook the Wall with its Iron Head.

501. *Centumque nurus.* It does not appear that *Hecuba*'s Daughters-in-Law were a hundred in Number. On the contrary, if *Homer*'s Account be exact, they could be no more than fifty; for, in the ſixth Iliad, he gives *Priam* only fifty Sons. And therefore we may either take *centum* for an indefinite Number, or *nurus* may ſignify her female Attendants in general, as the Word is uſed, *Ovid Met.* II. 366.

Excipit, et nuribus mittit geſtanda Latinis.
Or laſtly, thoſe fifty Sons of *Priam* might have had at leaſt a hundred Wives, taking their Concubines into the Number, after the Example of *Priam* their Father, who muſt have had ſeveral Concubines, ſince it does not appear that he had more than ſeventeen Children by his Queen.

502. *Sacraverat ignes.* In the open Court of his Palace, *Priam* had an Altar conſecrated to *Jupiter Herceus*, or *the Protector*, Verſe 512. and on this Altar we are told that hallowed Fire was kept perpetually burning. See *Turneb.* Lib. XIV. Cap. 15.

503. *Quinquaginta illi thalami.* *Homer* mentions the ſame Number of Bed-chambers in *Priam*'s Palace for his fifty Sons, Iliad VI. Verſe 244.

et poſtes ſuperbi Barbarico auro ſpoliiſque, procubuere: Danai tenent locum *quà ignis deficit.*]

Forſitan et requiras quæ fuerint fata Priami. Ubi vidit caſum captæ urbis, liminaque tectorum convulſa, et hoſtem medium in penetralibus, ſenior nequicquam circumdat arma diu deſueta humeris ſuis trementibus ævo; et inutile ferrum cingitur, ac moriturus fertur in denſos hoſtes. In mediis ædibus, ſubque nudo axe ætheris, fuit ingens ara, juxtaque veterrima laurus,

Barbarico poſtes auro ſpoliiſque ſuperbi,
Procubuere: tenent Danai, quà deficit ignis.
Forſitan et Priami fuerint quæ fata requiras.
Urbis ubi captæ caſum convulſaque vidit
Limina tectorum, et medium in penetralibus hoſtem,
Arma diu ſenior deſueta trementibus ævo
Circumdat nequicquam humeris, et inutile ferrum
Cingitur, ac denſos fertur moriturus in hoſtes.
Ædibus in mediis, nudoque ſub ætheris axe,
Ingens ara fuit, juxtaque veterrima laurus,

TRANSLATION.

Barbaric Gold, and Spoils *of conquered Nations*, were levelled with the Ground: Where the Flames relent, the Greeks take place. Perhaps, too, you are curious to hear what was Priam's *particular* Fate. So ſoon as he beheld the Cataſtrophe of the taken City, and his Palace-gates broke down, and the Enemy planted in the Middle of his private Apartments; the aged *Monarch*, with unavailing Aim, buckles on his Shoulders, trembling with Years, Arms long diſuſed, girds himſelf with his uſeleſs Sword, and ruſhes into the thickeſt of the Foes, reſolute on Death. In the Center of the Court, and under the naked Canopy of Heaven, ſtood a large Altar, and an aged Laurel by, overhanging the Altar, and encircling the

NOTES.

504. *Barbarico auro.* *Troy* by the *Romans* was ſtyled *Barbary*, as in *Horace*,

Græcia Barbariæ lento colliſa duello.

And *Phrygian* and *Barbarian* by them were underſtood to mean the ſame Thing:

Sonate miſtum tibiis carmen lyra,
Hac Dorium, illis Barbarum?
Epod. IX.

Aurum Barbaricum then is *Phrygian* Gold, for the *Phrygians* were eſteemed a very rich and wealthy People like the *Perſians*, as has been already obſerved in the Note on Verſe fourth of this Book. That the Epithet *Barbarico* is to be ſo underſtood, appears farther from *Cic. Tuſcul. Queſt.* Lib. I. 35, where he is examining whether *Priam* would not have been much happier, had he died in the flouriſhing State of the Kingdom,

Aſtante ope Barbarica
Tectis cœlatis, laqueatis.

than to have prolonged his Life through that Train of Miſeries which afterwards befel him. But, becauſe it is not ſo proper to make *Æneas* call his own Country barbarous, perhaps it may do better to underſtand, by *aurum Barbaricum*, the Gold and rich Trophies won from the foreign Nations with whom they had been at War, eſpecially ſince *ſpoliis* immediately follows, which ſeems to refer to theſe Trophies with which they uſed to adorn their Door-poſts.

505. *Tenent Danai, quà deficit ignis.* The *Greeks* are here beautifully repreſented more cruel than the mercileſs Flames. The Fire abated, and fell from its Rage, but the more mercileſs *Greeks* obſtinately periſt till all was deſtroyed.

509. *Arma deſueta.* *Juvenal* thus ſets forth *Priam* as a lively Example of Men's Folly in wiſhing for long Life, ſince, beſides the perſonal Infirmities of old Age, the foreign and external Ills which Length of Years brings about are ſo heavy and numerous:

Longa dies igitur quid contulit? omnia vidit
Everſa, et flammis Aſiam ferroque cadentem;
Tunc miles tremulus poſita tulit arma tiara.
Juv. Sat. X. 265.

But mark what Age produc'd; he liv'd to ſee
His Town in Flames, his falling Monarchy:
In fine, the feeble Sire, reduc'd by Fate,
To change his Sceptre for a Sword too late.
Mr. Dryden.

513. *Ingens ara fuit.* This is that Altar which, as we ſaid before, was conſecrated to *Jupiter*

Incumbens, aræ, atque umbrâ complexa Penates.
Hic Hecuba, et natæ nequicquam altaria circum,
Præcipites atrâ ceu tempestate columbæ,
Condensæ, et Divûm amplexæ simulacra tenebant:
Ipsum autem sumtis Priamum juvenilibus armis
Ut vidit, quæ mens tam dira, miserrime conjux,
Impulit his cingi telis? aut quo ruis? inquit.
Non tali auxilio, nec defensoribus istis,
Tempus eget: non, si ipse meus nunc afforet Hector.
Huc tandem concede: hæc ara tuebitur omnes,
Aut moriere simul. Sic ore effata, recepit
Ad sese, et sacrâ longævum in sede locavit.
Ecce autem elapsus Pyrrhi de cæde Polites,
Unus natorum Priami, per tela, per hostes,
Porticibus longis fugit, et vacua atria lustrat
Saucius: illum ardens infesto vulnere Pyrrhus

incumbens aræ, atque complexa Penates umbrâ. Illic Hecuba, et natæ ejus *nequicquam condensæ sunt circum altaria, ceu columbæ præcipites ab atrâ tempestate, et amplexæ tenebant simulacra Divûm.* Hecuba, *autem ut vidit ipsum Priamum, armis juvenilibus sumtis,* inquit: *O miserrime conjux, quæ tam dira mens impulit te cingi his telis? aut quò ruis? Tempus non eget tali auxilio, nec istis defensoribus: non, si meus Hector ipse nunc afforet. Tandem concede huc; hæc ara tuebitur omnes, aut moriere simul* nobiscum. *Illa effata sic, recepit ad sese, et locavit longævum in sacrâ sede. Ecce autem Polites, unus natorum Priami elapsus de cæde Pyrrhi, fugit in longis porticibus per tela, per hostes, et saucius lustrat vacua atria: Pyrrhus ardens insequitur illum infesto vulnere,*

TRANSLATION.

Houshold-gods with its Shade. Here Hecuba, and her Daughters (like Pigeons flying precipitantly from a blackening Tempest), crowded together, and embracing the Shrines of the Gods, sat round the Altars, hoping *for Protection* in vain. But, soon as she saw Priam clad in youthful Arms, *My* most unhappy Lord, she cries, what dire Purpose hath prompted thee to brace on these Arms? Or whither are you driving? The present Conjuncture hath no need of such *feeble* Aid, nor *Hands like* these in our Defence: Though even my Hector himself were here, it would not avail. Hither repair, now that all Hope is lost; this Altar will protect us all, or here you *and we* shall die together. Having thus said, she took her aged *Lord* to her Embraces, and placed him on the sacred Seat. But lo! Polites, one of Priam's Sons, escaped from the Sword of Pyrrhus, through Darts, through Foes, shoots across the long Galleries, and, bleeding in his Wounds, traverses the waste Halls. Pyrrhus, all on Fire, pursues him with the hostile Weapon, is just grasp-

NOTES.

Jupiter Herceus in the open Court of the Palace, to which *Ovid* refers.

Nec tibi subsidio præsens sit numen, ut illi
Cui nihil Hercæi profuit ara Jovis.
In Ibim, 283.

And *Seneca* in *Agam.*

Sparsum cruore Regis Hercæum Jovem.

Jupiter, to whom such Altars were consecrated, was called *Herceus*, from the *Greek* Word ἕρκος *septum*, a Wall or Inclosure; either because he protected the Place, or because the Altar was erected within an Inclosure.

514. *Penates*. By *Penates* here *La Cerda* would have us understand the Palace, or House, as it sometimes signifies, because this was not the Place of the *Penates* or *Houshold-gods*. But others think the Statues of the *Penates* were placed on the same Altar with *Jupiter Herceus*.

515. *Hic Hecuba*. It is well known that the Altars, and other sacred Places, were the Sanctuaries and Places of Refuge, to which it was usual for Persons to fly, to screen themselves from Danger.

529. *Infesto vulnere*. *Vulnus* is used here poetically for the wounding Weapon.

jam jamque tenet manu, et premit cum hasta. Tandem, ut evasit ante oculos et ora parentum, concidit, ac fudit vitam cum multo sanguine. Hic Priamus, quanquam jam tenetur in mediâ morte, tamen non abstinuit, nec pepercit voci iræque: at exclamat, Dî persolvant dignas grates, et reddant tibi debita præmia pro tuo scelere, pro talibus ausis, si qua pietas est cœlo quæ curet talia; tibi inquam qui fecisti me coram cernere lethum mei nati, et fœdasti patrios vultus sanguine. At ille Achilles, quo mentiris te esse satum, non fuit talis in Priamo hoste; sed erubuit jura fidemque supplicis, redditque sepulcro corpus Hectoreum exsangue,

Insequitur, jam jamque manu tenet, et premit
  hastâ.
Et tandem ante oculos evasit et ora parentum,
Concidit, ac multo vitam cum sanguine fudit.
Hìc Priamus, quanquam in mediâ jam morte
  tenetur,
Non tamen abstinuit, nec voci, iræque, peper-
  cit:
At tibi pro scelere, exclamat, pro talibus ausis,
Dî (si qua est cœlo pietas, quæ talia curet)
Persolvant grates dignas, et præmia reddant
Debita, qui nati coram me cernere lethum
Fecisti, et patrios fœdasti funere vultus:
At non ille, satum quo te mentiris, Achilles
Talis in hoste fuit Priamo; sed jura fidemque
Supplicis erubuit; corpusque exsangue seplucro

TRANSLATION.

ing him with his Hand, and presses on him with the Spear. Soon as he at length got into the Sight and Presence of his Parents he dropped down, and poured out his Life with a Stream of Blood. Upon this, Priam, though environed with Death on every Side, yet did not forbear, nor had Command of his Tongue and Passion: But may the Gods, he cries, if there be any Justice in Heaven to regard such Events, give thee ample Retribution and due Reward for this thy Wickedness, for these thy audacious Crimes, who hast made me Witness to the Death of my own Son, and defiled a Father's Eyes with *beholding filial* Blood: Yet he, from whom you falsely claim your Birth, *even* Achilles, was not thus barbarous to Priam, *for all he* was his Enemy, but paid some Regard to the Laws of Nations and a Suppliant's Right, restored my Hector's lifeless Corpse to be buried, and

NOTES.

538. *Nati coram me cernere lethum fecisti.* He does not complain of him for putting his Son to Death, but for his Barbarity in making him to be the Witness of so shocking a Spectacle.

539. *Fœdasti funere vultus. Funere*, says *Servius*, is a Carcase, a dead Body, warm, and new slain. When carried out to receive Funeral Obsequies, it is called *Exsequiæ*. The Ashes of it, when burned, are *Reliquiæ*, and the Interment of it is *Sepulchrum*.

540. *Satum quo te mentiris.* Whom you but feign to be your Father, since your Actions disprove your Birth from him. A severe Sarcasm; as much as to say, No Man, who had any Humanity in his Nature, could ever beget such a Son. The Sentiment is the same with that which *Dido* throws out in her Outrage against *Æneas*:

Nec tibi Diva parens, generis nec Dardanus auctor,
Perfide, sed duris genuit te cautibus horrens
Caucasus, Hyrcanæque admorunt ubera tigres.
Æn. IV. 365.

541. *In hoste Priamo.* When I was an active Enemy, capable of annoying him, and it would have been worth his while to put me to Death; whereas now I hardly exist, my Life is of no Avail either as a Friend or Foe.

541. *Jura fidemque supplicis erubuit.* In the twenty-fourth Book of the Iliad, *Homer* makes *Priam* repair to *Achilles*'s Tent, and ransom from him the Body of *Hector*. *Virgil* judiciously makes *Priam* forbear mentioning the Gifts by which *Achilles* was induced to restore the Body of his Enemy, and attributes his Action only to Generosity, Justice, and a Sense of Honour.

Reddidit Hectoreum, meque in mea regna remisit.
Sic fatus senior, telumque imbelle sine ictu
Conjecit; rauco quod protinus ære repulsum,
Et summo clypei nequicquam umbone pependit.
Cui Pyrrhus, referes ergo hæc, et nuncius ibis
Pelidæ genitori: illi mea tristia facta,
Degeneremque Neoptolemum, narrare memento:
Nunc morere. Hæc dicens, altaria ad ipsa trementem
Traxit, et in multo lapsantem sanguine nati:
Implicuitque comam levâ; dextrâque coruscum
Extulit, ac lateri capulo tenus abdidit ensem.
Hæc finis Priami fatorum: hic exitus illum

remisitque me in mea regna. Senior fatus est sic, conjecitque imbelle telum sine ictu; quod protinus repulsum est rauco ære, et pependit nequicquam in summo umbone clypei. Cui Pyrrhus respondit: ergo referes hæc, et ibis nuncius Pelidæ meo *genitori: memento narrare illi mea tristia facta, Neoptolemumque esse degenerem: Nunc morere. Dicens hæc, traxit* eum *trementem ad ipsa altaria, et lapsantem in multo sanguine nati: lævâque manu implicuit ejus comam; dextrâque extulit coruscum ensem, ac abdidit* eum *lateri* Priami *tenus capulo. Hæc fuit finis fatorum Priami: hic exitus tulit illum*

TRANSLATION.

sent me back into my Kingdom. Thus spoke the aged *Monarch*, and without any Force threw a feeble Dart: which was instantly repelled by the hoarse *resounding* Brass, and hung on the highest Boss of the Buckler without any Execution. To whom Pyrrhus replies: These Tidings then *yourself* shall bear, and go with the Message to my Father: Forget not to inform him of my cruel Deeds, and of his degenerate Son Neoptolemus: Now die. With these Words he dragged him up to the very Altar, *all* trembling, and sliding in a Plash of his Son's Blood, and with his Left-hand grasped his twisted Hair, and with his Right unsheathed his glittering Sword, and plunged it into his Side up to the Hilt. Such is the End of Priam's Fate: This is the final Doom allotted to him, having be-

NOTES.

543. *In mea regna remisit.* He had it in his Power to have detained *Priam*, or put him to Death; but *he blushed at the Thought of violating the Laws of Nations*, which forbid to hurt the Person of a King, require the Dead to be allowed the Rights of Burial, and the Laws of Humanity to be observed even to an Enemy when disarmed; those Laws he observed, *and that Faith which is due to a Suppliant*, whose Persons have always been held sacred by the Laws of Hospitality.

545. *Repulsum—pependit.* i. e. It was so repelled, as to fall short of wounding or killing him, yet pierced the Boss of his Buckler, and hung there quite harmless: As for the Reading, which is in some Copies, *sepultum* instead of *repulsum*, it is not worth confuting.

550. *Altaria ad ipsa trementem, &c.* Every Word here aggravates the Cruelty of this Action; *traxit*, he dragged him, *trementem*, trembling, not through Fear, but Age, and Decay of Nature; he dragged him *ad ipsa altaria*, to that very Altar where he had fled for Refuge; *et lapsantem in multo sanguine nati*; this is a very moving Circumstance, that the reverend aged Monarch should be thus trailed through a slippery Deluge of his Son's Blood, the very Sight of which was worse to him than Death. What follows, is the strong Picture of a Heart quite lost to all Sense of Humanity, and capable of perpetrating the most shocking Cruelties with the greatest Unconcern and Indifference.

550. *Altaria ad ipsa.* Others, however, write, that *Priam* was not slain at the Altar, but that *Pyrrhus*, finding him there, dragged him away to *Achilles*'s Tomb, which was near the Promontory of *Sigæum*, and thus sacrificed him to his Father's Manes. But, where there are different Traditions concerning the same Fact, the Poet is at Liberty to choose which ever of them suits his Purpose best.

554. *Hic exitus illum sorte tulit.* This is a pretty singular Idiom. *His Death carried him off by Heaven's Appointment.*

557. Jacet

ſorte, videntem Trojam incenſam et Pergama prolapſa; illum *quondam regnatorem Aſiæ ſuperbum tot populis terriſque*: ille *jacet ingens truncus* in *littore, caputque avulſum humeris, et corpus ſine nomine. At ſævus horror tum primum circumſtetit me obſtupui; imago chari genitoris ſubiit* in mentem, *ut vidi regem æquævum exhalantem vitam crudeli vulnere: Creüſa deſerta ſubiit* in mentem, *et domus direpta, et caſus parvi Iüli. Reſpicio, et luſtro quæ copia ſit circum me. Omnes defeſſi deſeruere me, et ſaltu miſere ægra corpora ad terram, aut dedere ea ignibus. Adèoque jam* ego *unus ſuper eram, cum aſpicio Tyndarida ſervantem limina Veſtæ,*

Sorte tulit, Trojam incenſam et prolapſa videntem
Pergama, tot quondam populis terriſque ſuperbum
Regnatorem Aſiæ; jacet ingens littore truncus,
Avulſumque humeris caput, et ſine nomine corpus.
At me tum primum ſævus circumſtetit horror:
Obſtupui; ſubiit cari genitoris imago,
Ut regem æquævum crudeli vulnere vidi
Vitam exhalantem: ſubiit deſerta Creüſa,
Et direpta domus, et parvi caſus Iüli.
Reſpicio, et, quæ ſit me circum copia, luſtro.
Deſeruere omnes defeſſi, et corpora ſaltu
Ad terram miſere, aut ignibus ægra dedere.
Jamque adeò ſuper unus eram, cum limina Veſtæ

TRANSLATION.

fore his Eyes Troy conſumed, and its Towers laid in Ruins; once the proud Monarch of Aſia, *who reigned* over ſo many Nations and Countries: Now he lies a Trunk at large extended *on the Shore, a* Head torn from the Shoulders, and a nameleſs Corpſe. Then, and not till then, fierce Horror aſſailed me round: I ſtood aghaſt; the Image of my dear Father aroſe to my Mind, when I ſaw the King, of equal Age, breathing out his Soul by a cruel Wound: To my Mind aroſe forlorn Creuſa, my rifled Houſe, and the Fate of tender Iülus. I look about, and ſurvey what Troops were to ſtand by me. All had left me through Deſpair, and *either* flung their fainting Bodies to the Ground, or gave them to the Flames. And thus now I remained all alone, when I ſpy Helen keeping

NOTES.

557. *Jacet ingens littore truncus.* In this and the following Circumſtances, *Virgil* is thought to have an Eye to the unhappy Fate of *Pompey*, of whom *Plutarch* gives the following Account: "The Aſſaſſins cut off his Head, then flung "his naked Body on the Shore, and left it a "Spectacle to every curious Eye."

558. *Sine nomine corpus.* The Head is, as it were, the Index, to diſtinguiſh the Perſon, and lead to the Knowledge of his Name. Or, without a Name, may ſignify *deſpicable, diſhonoured*, as *Florus* calls a Man who has no Honour, *homo ſine tribu, ſine nomine.*

567. *Jamque adeo ſuper unus eram.* There is ſome Doubt raiſed about the Genuineneſs of this Paſſage concerning *Helen*, from this to Verſe 598. *Cum mihi ſe, &c.* Thoſe who reject them connect the Verſes that go before with thoſe that follow, thus:

Deſeruere omnes defeſſi, et corpora ſaltu
Ad terram miſere, aut ignibus ægra dedere.
Tum mihi ſe, non ante oculis tam clara, videndam
Obtulit, &c.

Making *Venus*'s Appearance to be in order to reſtrain *Æneas*, who was going to kill himſelf. But, whatever may be alledged againſt theſe Verſes, thoſe, who are acquainted with *Virgil*'s Style, will eaſily diſtinguiſh them to be his; nor are the Objections againſt them ſo ſtrong, but that they admit of very ſatisfactory Anſwers. They are chiefly theſe three: 1. It is alledged, that what *Virgil* here ſays of *Helen*'s dreading the Reſentment of her Huſband *Menelaus*,—*deſerti conjugis*

Servantem, et tacitam secretâ in sede latentem,
Tyndarida aspicio: dant clara incendia lucem
Erranti, passimque oculos per cuncta ferenti.
Illa sibi infestos eversa ob Pergama Teucros,
Et pœnas Danaûm, et deserti conjugis iras,
Permetuens, Trojæ et patriæ communis Erinnys,
Abdiderat sese, atque aris invisa sedebat.

et tacitam latentem in secretâ sede: clara incendia dant lucem mihi erranti, ferentique oculos passim per cuncta. Illa, communis Erinnys Trojæ et patriæ, permetuens Teucros infestos sibi ob Pergama eversa, et pœnas Danaûm, et iras deserti conjugis, abdiderat sese, atque invisa sedebat in aris.

TRANSLATION.

Watch in the Temple of Vesta, and silently lurking in a secret Corner: The bright Flames give me Light as I am roving on, and throwing my Eyes around on every Object. She, the common Fury of Troy and her Country, dreading the Trojans, her deadly Foes upon account of their ruined Country, and the Vengeance *due to her* from the Greeks, together with the fierce Resentment of her deserted Lord, had hid herself, and was sitting by the Altars, an odious Sight.

NOTES.

jugis iras permetuens, contradicts what he tells us in the sixth Book, Verse 525, of having sought to make her Peace with *Menelaus* by betraying *Deiphobus*. But, though she endeavoured to ingratiate herself with *Menelaus* by that Piece of Treachery, it does not follow that he was actually reconciled to her, at least so fully as not to leave her guilty Mind under some Apprehensions of his Resentment. Accordingly we learn from *Euripides in Troad.* Verses, 35, 876, 1056, that *Helen* was carried away a Captive by *Menelaus* with the *Trojan* Women, with a View to have her put to Death by the *Greeks*, whose Sons had fallen in that War. Another Objection is, that *Virgil* outrages the Character of his Hero, in making him entertain a Thought of killing a Woman, and that in the Temple. Perhaps there would have been some Force in this Objection, had *Æneas* actually put *Helen* to Death; though even then I know not but he might have been justified on the Foot of those very Motives which he himself urges in Behalf of the Action:

——————Etsi nullum memorabile nomen
Fœminea in pœna est, nec habet victoria laudem;
Extinxisse nefas tamen, et sumsisse merentis
Laudabor pœnas; animumque explesse juvabit
Ultricis flammæ, et cineres satiasse meorum.

Who could have blamed him, if, in the Hurry and Confusion of mingled Passions, with which his Mind must then have been racked, he had revenged his own and his Country's Sufferings on that fair Traitness, who was chargeable with the Guilt of so many thousand Deaths, and of the utter Desolation of a whole innocent People, and once flourishing Kingdom: But when, instead of giving Way to those first Emotions of a just Resentment, he checks his Desire of Revenge, deliberates on the Merits of the Action, and is at length withheld from perpetrating it by the Interposition of his Goddess mother, or, in other Words, by the Force of superior Reason, what Shadow of Reason have even the severest Critics for censuring such a Conduct? It is objected, in the last place, that these Verses cannot be allowed to be *Virgil's*, because he cannot be supposed so unacquainted with the History of *Helen*, as not to know that she had left *Troy* long before it was taken. The History, of which it is alleged *Virgil* could not be ignorant, is that of *Herodotus*, who tells us, he had learned from some *Egyptian* Priests, who had it from *Menelaus's* own Mouth, that the *Trojans* had sent away *Helen* to *Egypt* before the *Greeks* re-demanded her: In Opinion of whose Truth *Herodotus* himself appears to have been so fully convinced, that he is at great Pains to prove it. But, whether *Virgil* was acquainted with *Herodotus's* Account or not, it is sufficient that he has poetical Tradition on his Side, and is supported by the Authority of *Homer* and *Euripides*.

567. *Limina Vestæ servantem.* *Servare domum* signifies to look after it with Anxiety, and a jealous Eye, full of Fears, and watchful of every Danger: So the Word is used by *Plautus Aulul.* 1, 2, 3. *Redi nunc jam intro, atque intus serva.* Where the Commentator says, *Servare est sollicite et suspiciose observare.*

Ignes exarsere meo animo; ira subiit ulcisci patriam cadentem, et sumere pœnas sceleratas. Hæc scilicet incolumis aspiciet Spartam patriasque Mycenas? ibitque regina, triumpho parto? videbitque conjugiumque, domumque, patres, natosque, comitata turbâ Iliadum et Phrygiis ministris? Priamus occiderit ferro? Troja arserit igni? Dardanidum littus toties sudarit sanguine? Non ita erit: Namque etsi est nullum memorabile nomen in fœmineâ pœnâ, nec ista *victoria habet laudem; tamen laudabor extinxisse nefas, et sumsisse pœnas merentis; juvabitque me explesse animum ultricis flammæ, et satiasse cineres meorum. Jactabam talia, et ferebar mente furiatâ; cum alma Parens, non visa tam clara meis oculis ante, obtulit se videndam mibi,*

Exarsere ignes animo; subit ira, cadentem
Ulcisci patriam, et sceleratas sumere pœnas.
Scilicet hæc Spartam incolumis patriasque Mycenas
Aspiciet? partoque ibit regina triumpho?
Conjugiumque, domumque, patres, natosque, videbit,
Iliadum turba et Phrygiis comitata ministris?
Occiderit ferro Priamus? Troja arserit igni?
Dardanidum toties sudarit sanguine littus?
Non ita; namque etsi nullum memorabile nomen
Fermineâ in pœnâ est, nec habet victoria laudem,
Extinxisse nefas tamen, et sumsisse merentis
Laudabor pœnas; animumque explesse juvabit
Ultricis flammæ, et cineres satiasse meorum.
Talia jactabam, et furiatâ mente ferebar;
Cum mihi se, non ante oculis tam clare, videndam

TRANSLATION.

Flames were kindled in my Soul: I burned with Rage to avenge my falling Country, and take Satisfaction on her guilty Head. Shall she then with Impunity *again* behold Sparta and her Country Mycenæ, and go off *in the Pride of* a Queen, after she has gained her Triumph? Shall she *again* see her Marriage-*bed*, her Home, her Fathers, her Sons, accompanied with a Retinue of Trojan Dames and Phrygian Women her Slaves? Shall Priam bleed? Shall Troy be consumed? Shall the Trojan Shore so often be drenched in Blood, *and yet she go unpunished?* It must not be: For though there be no Merit in punishing a Woman, nor any Honour in such a Victory; yet shall I be applauded for having extinguished a wicked Incendiary, and for inflicting on her the Punishment she deserves; besides, it will be a Pleasure to gratify my Desire of burning Revenge, and to give Satisfaction to the Manes of my Friends. Thus was I expostulating, and furiously agitated in my Soul, when my kind Parent presented herself to my View with such Brightness as I had never seen before, and amidst the *Darkness of the*

NOTES.

576. *Sceleratas sumere pœnas.* i. e. *Sumere pœnas de scelerata,* as in Verse 584. *Fœminea pœna* for *pœna de fœmina.*

577. *Patriasque Mycenas. Mycenæ* was not the Place of her own Nativity, for she was born at *Sparta*, but of her Husband *Menelaus.*

585. *Extinxisse nefas. Helen* is justly styled *nefas*, a Monster of Wickedness, who, by her Lewdness, had been the Occasion of kindling so dreadful a War. She was first ravished by *Theseus*, then married *Menelaus*; whom she forsook for the adulterous *Paris*. To him too she was unfaithful, having committed Incest in *Troy* with her Son-in-Law *Orythus*, the Son of *Paris* and *Oenone*. *Philostratus* too, in his Heroics, has celebrated the Story of her Amour with *Achilles*.

Obtulit, et purâ per noctem in luce refulsit,
Alma parens, confessa Deam, qualisque videri
Cœlicolis et quanta solet; dextrâque prehensum
Continuit; roseoque hæc insuper addidit ore:
Nate, quis indomitas tantus dolor excitat iras?
Quid furis? aut quonam nostri tibi cura recessit?
Non prius aspicies ubi fessum ætate parentem
Liqueris Anchisen? superet conjuxne Creüsa,
Ascaniusque puer? quos omnes undique Graiæ
Circum errant acies; et, ni mea cura resistat,
Jam flammæ tulerint, inimicus et hauserit ensis.
Non tibi Tyndaridis facies invisa Lacænæ,
Culpatusve Paris; Divûm inclementia, Divûm,
Has evertit opes, sternitque à culmine Trojam.
Aspice, namque omnem, quæ nunc obducta tuenti

et refulsit per noctem in purâ luce, confessa Deam, qualisque et quanta solet videri Cœlicolis; continuitque me prehensum dextrâ insuperque addidit hæc roseo ore: Nate, quis tantus dolor excitat tuas indomitas iras? ob quid furis? aut quonam cura nostri recessit tibi? non prius aspicies ubi liqueris parentem tuum *Anchisen fessum ætate? superetne conjux* tua *Creüsa, puerque Ascanius? quos omnes Graiæ acies undique circum errant; et quos flammæ jam tulerint, et inimicus ensis hauserit, ni mea cura resistat. Non invisa facies Lacænæ Tyndaridis, Parisve culpatus, sed inclementia Divûm, Divûm* inquam, *evertit has opes, sternitque Trojam à culmine. Aspice, namque eripiam omnem nubem, quæ nunc obducta tibi tuenti*

TRANSLATION.

Night shone forth in pure radiant Light, displaying all the Goddess, with such Dignity, such Grandeur *and Majesty*, as she shews to the Immortals; she restrained *me* fast held by the Right-hand, and besides let fall these Words from her rosy Lips: My Son, what high Provocation kindles *your* ungoverned Rage? Why *so* transported? Or whither are *all* thy Regards to me *now* fled? Will you not first see in what Situation you have left your Father Anchises, encumbered with Age? Whether your Spouse Creüsa be *still* in Life, and the Boy Ascanius, around whom the Grecian Troops from every Quarter reel? And, had not my Guardian-power opposed, the Flames had already carried off, or the cruel Sword drunk their Blood. Not Lacedemonian Helen, thus odious in your Eyes, nor Paris *so often* blamed; *but* the Gods, the unrelenting Gods, overthrow this powerful Realm, and level the towering Tops of Troy with the Ground. Turn your Eyes, for I will dissipate every Cloud which now intercepting the View bedims your mortal

NOTES.

590. *Obtulit alma parens. Venus* was the most proper Deity to interpose in Behalf of *Helen*, whom she had long protected, and first conferred on *Paris*, as a Reward for the Judgment he had given in her Favour against *Juno* and *Minerva*.

601. *Tyndaridis. Helen* was the Daughter of *Jupiter* and *Leda*, and is called *Tyndaris*, because *Tyndareus*, the King of *Sparta*, was married to *Leda*.

604. *Divûm inclementia, Divûm.* This Reading is much more emphatic than *verum*, or *sed enim inclementia Divûm*, and is supported by the Authority of several ancient and more correct Copies. *Homer*, in the third Iliad, makes *Priam* thus exculpate *Helen* in a warm Sally of Passion, and lay the Blame of *Troy*'s Disaster on the Gods, *Il.* III. 164.

604. *Aspice, namque, &c. Macrobius*, in *Som. Scip.* Lib. I. Cap. 3, applies this Passage to the State of the Soul, which, being immersed in Matter during its Union with the Body, is incapable of beholding Objects directly, but through a Veil, a thick Cloud, *i. e.* a gross, corporeal Medium. *Milton* seems to have had this Passage in his Eye in the eleventh Book of his *Paradise Lost*, where the Angel prepares *Adam* for beholding the future Vision of his Posterity

hebetat tuos mortales viſus, et humida circum caligat: ne tu time qua juſſa tuæ parentis, neu recuſa parere illius præceptis. Hic, ubi vides moles disjectas, ſaxaque avulſa ſaxis, fumumque undantem mixto pulvere, Neptunus quatit muros, fundamentaque emota magno tridenti, eruitque totam urbem à ſedibus. Hic ſæviſſima Juno prima tenet Scæas portas, furenſque vocat ſocium agmen à navibus, accincta ferro.

Reſpice, jam Tritonia Pallas inſedit ſummas arces, effulgens nimbo et ſævâ Gorgone.

Mortales hebetat viſus tibi, et humida circum
Caligat, nubem eripiam: tu ne qua parentis
Juſſa time, neu præceptis parere recuſa.
Hìc, ubi disjectas moles, avulſaque ſaxis
Saxa vides, mixtoque undantem pulvere fumum,
Neptunus muros magnoque emota tridenti
Fundamenta quatit, totamque à ſedibus urbem
Eruit. Hìc Juno Scæas ſæviſſima portas
Prima tenet, ſociumque furens à navibus agmen
Ferro accincta vocat.*
Jam ſummas arces Tritonia, reſpice, Pallas
Inſedit, nimbo effulgens et Gorgone ſæva.

TRANSLATION.

Sight, and ſpreads a humid Veil of Miſt around you: Fear not you the Commands of a Parent, nor refuſe to obey her Orders. Here, where you ſee *thoſe* Heaps of Ruins, and Piles from Piles of Building torn, and Smoke in Waves aſcending with mingled Duſt, Neptune ſhakes the Walls, and Foundations looſened by his mighty Trident, and overturns the whole City from its *firm* Baſis. Here *again* Juno, extremely fierce, is poſted in the Front to guard the Scæan Gate, and, *clad* in martial Array, with furious Summons calls from the Ships her ſocial Band. See *where* Tritonian Pallas hath now planted herſelf on *that* lofty Turret, refulgent with her *radiant* Cloud, and with her Gorgon terrible. Father *Jove*

NOTES.

nity and their Hiſtory, which he is going to ſet before him:

——————But to nobler Sights
Michael *from* Adam's *Eyes the Film remov'd,*
Which that falſe Fruit that promis'd clearer Sight
Had bred; then purg'd with Euphroſy and Rue
The viſual Nerve, for he had much to ſee, &c.
Book XI. 411

610. *Neptunus muros,* &c. *Virgil* makes *Neptune* an Enemy to *Troy*, on account of the Perjury of *Laomedon*, who cheated that God of his promiſed Hire, for building the Walls of *Troy*. Which Fable, according to *Servius*, ſets forth to us this hiſtorical Fact, that *Laomedon* had applied the Money, which he had deſtined for the Worſhip and Service of *Neptune*, to the Building of the Walls of *Troy*.

612. *Juno Scæas portas tenet.* The Gates of *Troy*, we are told, were ſix in Number; the Gate of *Antenor*, the Gate of *Dardanus*, the *Ilian*, the *Catumbrian*, *Trojan*, and *Scæan*. By the *Scæan* Gate, the *Trojan* Horſe is ſaid to have entered, which probably is the Reaſon why *Juno* is poſted at that Gate, rather than any other, ſhe being all along repreſented as the moſt implacable Foe to *Troy*.

616. *Nimbo effulgens.* By the *Nimbus*, *Servius* underſtands a lucid Circle, or divine Brightneſs, which the Gods wore round their Heads, and were thereby diſtinguiſhed from Mortals.

616. *Gorgone.* The three Daughters of *Phorcus*, *Meduſa*, *Euryale*, and *Stenyo*, were called *Gorgones*, *Gorgons*, or *the terrible Siſters*. *Meduſa* having been violated by *Neptune* in *Minerva*'s Temple, that Goddeſs transformed the Hair of her Head into Serpents, the very Sight of which turned Men into Stones. This Head *Perſeus* cut off, by the Aſſiſtance of *Minerva*, who lent him her Buckler, which was of Braſs, ſo finely poliſhed, that it reflected the Image of the *Gorgon*'s Head as in a Mirror, and thus ſecured him from the fatal Influence of her Eyes, and enabled him to deſtroy her. This Head *Minerva* wore upon her Buckler, to render her the more awful and tremendous.

Ipſe Pater Danais animos vireſque ſecundas
Sufficit: ipſe Deos in Dardana ſuſcitat arma.
Eripe, nate, fugam, finemque impone labori.
Nuſquam abero, et tutum patrio te limine ſiſtam.
Dixerat, et ſpiſſis noctis ſe condidit umbris.
Apparent diræ facies, inimicaque Trojæ
Numina magna Deûm.
Tum verò omne mihi viſum conſidere in ignes
Ilium, et ex imo verti Neptunia Troja
Ac veluti ſummis antiquam in montibus ornum,
Cum ferro acciſam, crebriſque bipennibus inſtant
Eruere agricolæ certatim; illa uſque minatur,
Et tremefacta comam concuſſo vertice nutat,
Vulneribus donec paulatim evicta, ſupremùm
Congemuit, traxitque jugis avulſa ruinam:

Ipſe pater Jupiter ſufficit animos vireſque ſecundas Danais: ipſe ſuſcitat Deos in Dardana arma. O nate, eripe fugam, impone que finem tuo labori. Ego nuſquam abero, et ſiſtam te tutum in patrio limine. Dixerat, et condidit ſe in ſpiſſis umbris noctis. Diræ facies apparent, magnaque numina Divûm inimica Trojæ. Tum verò omne Ilium viſum eſt mihi conſidere in ignes, et Neptunia Troja viſa eſt verti ex imo. Ac veluti cum agricolæ certatim inſtant eruere antiquam ornum in ſummis montibus, acciſam ferro crebrique bipennibus; illa omnis uſque minatur ruinam, et tremefacta comam nutat, vertice concuſſo: donec paulatim evicta vulneribus, congemuit ſupremùm, avulſaque jugis traxit ruinam.

TRANSLATION.

himſelf ſupplies them with Courage and Strength for Victory: Himſelf ſtirs up the Gods againſt the Arms of Troy. Speed thy Flight, my Son, and put a Period to thy Toils. In every Danger I will ſtand by you, and ſafe ſet you down in your Father's Palace. She ſaid, and ſunk out of Sight into the thick Shades of Night. *Now* direful Forms appear, and the great Gods, adverſe to Troy, in their awful Majeſty. Then indeed, all Ilium ſeemed at once to ſink into the Flames, and Troy, built by Neptune, to be overturned from its loweſt Foundation. And as when with emulous Keenneſs the Swains labour to fell an Aſh that long hath ſtood on a high Mountain, hewing it about with Iron Tools and many an Ax, ever and anon it threatens *a Fall*, and, waving its Locks, nods with its convulſed Top, till gradually, by Wounds ſubdued, it hath groaned its laſt, and, torn from the Ridge of the Mountain, draws along with it Ruin *and Deſolation*.

NOTES.

617. *Ipſe pater.* *Juno* and *Minerva* oppoſed the *Trojans* from partial Motives, becauſe they had been ſlighted by *Paris*; but *Jove* was an Enemy to them, becauſe their Cauſe was unrighteous, in detaining *Helen* contrary to the Law of Nations.

622. *Apparent diræ facies.* All the horrid Images of War and Deſolation.

623. *Numina magna.* The Gods were divided chiefly into two Claſſes, the *Dii majorum*, and the *Dii minorum gentium*; the Gods here referred to are of the firſt Order, *viz.* *Jupiter*, *Juno*, *Neptune*, *Minerva*, and therefore are fitly denominated *magna numina Deûm*.

626. *Ac veluti*, &c. This Simile is imitated from *Homer*, Il. XVI. 481, who applies it to the Death of *Sarpedon*; but *Macrobius* himſelf acknowledges that the Copy far exceeds the Original.

629. *Comam—nutat.* *Virgil*, conſidering a Tree in Analogy to the human Body, calls the extended Boughs its *Arms*, *brachia*, Geor. II. 296, 368, and here its Leaves, *comam*, *Hair*, or *Locks*. So alſo *Milton*, *Paradiſe Loſt*, X. 1065.

——— *while the Winds*
Blow moiſt and keen, ſhattering the graceful Locks
Of thoſe fair ſpreading Trees ——

632. *Dacinie*

Descendo, ac expedior inter flammam et hostes, Deo me ducente: tela dant locum mihi, flammæque recedunt. Ast ubi jam perventum est ad limina patriæ sedis, domosque antiquas; Genitor, quem primum optabam tollere in altos montes, petebamque primum, abnegat producere vitam, Trojâ excisâ, patique exsilium. Ait, O vos, quibus est sanguis integer ævi, quibusque vires stant solidæ suo robore, vos agitate fugam.

Descendo, ac, ducente Deo, flammam inter et hostes
Expedior: dant tela locum, flammæque recedunt.
Ast ubi jam patriæ perventum ad limina sedis,
Antiquasque domos; Genitor, quem tollere in altos
Optabam primum montes, primumque petebam,
Abnegat excisâ vitam producere Trojâ,
Exsiliumque pati. Vos O, quibus integer ævi
Sanguis, ait, solidæque suo stant robore vires,
Vos agitate fugam.

TRANSLATION.

Down I come, and, under the Conduct of the God, clear my Way amidst Flames and Foes: The Darts give Place, and the Flames retire. But now, when arrived at the Gates of my paternal Seat, and ancient Mansion-house, my Father, whom I was desirous first to remove to the high Mountains, and whom I first besought, obstinately refuses to survive the Ruins of Troy, and to suffer Exile. You, says he, who are full of youthful Blood, and whose Powers remain firm in all their Strength, do you attempt your Flight. As for me, had the Powers of Heaven

NOTES.

632 *Ducente Deo, flammam inter et hostes.* Were we to allegorize this Passage, we might say, that *Venus* conducting *Æneas* through Fire and Sword, signifies that the pious Love which burned in his Breast, first to his Country, and next to his dear Relations, rendered him insensible of every Danger that opposed the Bent of his Affection. This is the Light wherein *Spenser* has considered it in his Hymn in Honour of Love:

Thou art his God, thou art his mighty Guide,
Thou, being blind, let'st him not see his Fears,
But carriest him to that which he hath ey'd,
Thro' Seas, thro' Flames, thro' thousand Swords and Spears;
Ne ought so strong that may his Force withstand,
With which thou armest his resistless Hand.
Witness Leander *in the* Euxine *Waves,*
And stout Æneas in the Trojan *Fire.*

632. *Ducente Deo. Servius* will have it, that *Venus* here is called *God*, because the Deities partook of both Sexes. And we are particularly told, that *Venus* had a Statue in *Cyprus*, under the Name of *Venus barbata, the male Venus*, and was worshipped by the Men in the Garb of Females, and by the Women dressed like Men. But there is no Necessity of having Recourse to that Conceit; *Deus, a God,* signifies Deity in general, and may be said either of Gods or Goddesses, as *homo, Man,* is the general Word for the human Species.

633. *Expedior.* Literally, *I am disentangled or extricated, viz.* from every Danger.

636. *Primum optabam.* We learn from *Varro*, that the *Greeks* having given *Æneas* Permission to carry off what was dearest to him, he was seen trudging through the Town with his Father upon his Shoulders; while others, to whom the same Permission was given, went off loaded with Gold and Silver. The *Greeks*, struck with this eminent Example of filial Love in *Æneas*, gave him a second Option, which he made Use of in carrying off his Gods. Upon this they were induced to grant him full Liberty to take along with him his whole Family, and all his Effects. To this *Ovid* seems to allude, when he says of *Æneas*,

——— Sacra, et sacra altera, Patrem
Fert humeris, venerabile onus, Cythereius Heros
De tantisque opibus prædam pius eligit illam
Ascaniumque suum.

638. *Integer ævi sanguis,* i. e. Whose Blood is full, and not yet impaired, as in old Men; *integer ævi* is a *Greek* Construction, *causa*, or some such Word, being understood.

642. *Una*

Me si cœlicolæ voluissent ducere vitam,
Has mihi servassent sedes: satis una superque
Vidimus excidia, et captæ superavimus urbi.
Sic ô, sic positum affati discedite corpus.
Ipse manu mortem inveniam: miserebitur hostis,
Exuviasque petet: facilis jactura sepulchri.
Jampridem invisus Divis, et inutilis, annos
Demoror, ex quo me Divûm pater atque hominum rex
Fulminis afflavit ventis, et contigit igni.

Si cælicolæ voluissent me ducere vitam, servassent mihi has sedes: satis superque vidimus una excidia, et superavimus captæ urbi. O vos, affati meum corpus sic sic positum, discedite. Ego ipse inveniam mortem hac manu: hostis miserebitur mei, *petetque* meas *exuvias: jactura sepulchri* est mihi *facilis.* Ego *jampridem invisus Divis, et inutilis, demoror annos, ex quo tem*pore *pater Divûm atque rex hominum afflavit me ventis fulminis, et contigit* me *igni.*

TRANSLATION.

designed I should prolong my Life, they had preserved to me this Mansion: Enough it is, and more than enough, that I have seen one Catastrophe *of Troy*, and outlived the taking of this City. Thus, oh leave me thus with the last Farewel to my Body laid in its dying Posture. With this Hand shall I find Death myself: *Or* the Enemy will pity me, *and give it*, and lust for my Spoils. The Rites of Sepulture I can easily forego. Long have I lingered out *a Length of* Years, hated by the Gods, and useless *to the World*; from what Time the Father of Gods, and Sovereign of Men, blasted me with the Winds of his Thunder, and struck me

NOTES.

642. *Una vidimus excidia.* Because he had seen the City taken before by *Hercules*, under the Reign of *Laomedon*; a Fact not only mentioned by the Poets, but by Historians of good Authority. See *Dionys. Halic. Antiq.* Lib. I. and *Aristides in Rhodiaca.* The latter, speaking of *Troy*, says in so many Words, *Troy was once taken, once by* Hercules, *and a second Time by the* Greeks. And *Virgil* expresly says elsewhere, that *Anchises* had been twice saved from the Ruins of *Troy*, Æn. III. 476.

——— *Bis Pergameis erepte ruinis.*

644. Sic ô, *sic positum. Anchises* considers himself as already dead, and therefore desires them to take the last Farewel of him, as of a *corpus positum*, a dead Corpse laid out for Burial, or of the Funeral Pile, of which the Friends used to take a solemn Farewel, by repeating *vale, vale, vale.* We may observe farther, that there is a vast Force and Emphasis in these Particles *sic ô, sic*, insomuch that, if we take them away, we destroy the chief Beauty and Energy of the whole Line. The Repetition of the *sic* shews *Anchises*'s obstinate Purpose of dying, and his earnest Desire of being left to pursue that Resolution. It is used the same Way in the fourth Book, when *Dido*, bent on Death, is just going to plunge the Dagger into her Bosom, she breaks forth into that abrupt Eclamation,

Sic sic juvat ire sub umbras.

645. *Ipse manu mortem inveniam. Servius* understands *manu* of the Enemy, but that seems forced. The Sentence is explained by a parallel one in *Tacitus: Primum ubi vulnus Varo adactum, ubi infelici dextra et suo ictu mortem invenerit.*

645. *Miserebitur hostis.* This strongly marks the Anguish of his Soul; he was so weary of Life, that he would reckon it an Act of Pity in the Enemy to put an End to it. It is the same Sentiment with that of *Euryalus*'s Mother, who, in the Bitterness of her Grief for the Loss of her Son, thus addresses *Jupiter*:

Aut tu, magne pater Divûm, miserere, tuoque
Invisum hoc detrude caput sub Tartara telo:
Quando aliter nequeo crudelem abrumpere vitam.
Æn. IX. 495.

649. *Fulminis afflavit ventis.* The Winds by some of the Ancients were reckoned the efficient Causes of Thunder;

Jupiter, an venti, discussa nube tonarent.
Ovid. Met. XV. 70.

Anchises, according to Tradition, was blasted with Lightning, for having divulged his Intrigue with *Venus*; and some say he was thereby struck

blind:

Perſtabat memorans talia, manebatque fixus. Contra, nos effuſi lacrymis, conjuxque Creüſa, Aſcaniuſque, omniſque domus ob-ſtamur, ne pater vellet vertere cuncta ſecum, incumbereque fato urgenti. Ille abnegat, et hæret in incepto, et in iiſdem ſedibus. Rurſus feror in arma, miſerrimuſque opto mortem. Nam quod conſilium, aut quæ fortuna jam dabatur? O genitor, ſperaſtine me poſſe efferre pedem, te relicto? tantumque nefas excidit patrio ore? ſi placet Superis nihil relinqui ex tantâ urbe; et ſi hoc ſedet tuo animo, juvatque te addere teque tuoſque Trojæ perituræ; janua patet iſti letho.

Talia perſtabat memorans, fixuſque manebat.
Nos contra effuſi lacrymis, Conjuxque Creüſa,
Aſcaniuſque, omniſque domus, ne vertere ſecum
Cuncta pater, fatoque urgenti incumbere, vellet.
Abnegat, inceptoque, et ſedibus hæret in iiſdem.
Rurſus in arma feror, mortemque miſerrimus opto:
Nam quod conſilium, aut quæ jam fortuna, dabatur?
Mene efferre pedem, Genitor, te poſſe relicto
Speraſti? tantumque nefas patrio excidit ore?
Si nihil ex tantâ Superis placet urbe relinqui,
Et ſedet hoc animo, perituræque addere Trojæ
Teque tuoſque juvat, patet iſti janua letho:

TRANSLATION.

with Lightning. Such Purpoſe declaring he perſiſted, and remained unalterable. On the other hand I, my Wife Creüſa, Aſcanius, and the whole Family, burſting forth into Tears, *obteſted* my Father not to involve all with himſelf *in Ruin*, nor haſten our impending Fate. He ſtill is obſtinate, and perſeveres in his Purpoſe, and in the ſame ſettled Reſolution. *Thus* once more I fly to my Arms, and in Extremity of Diſtreſs long for Death: For what *other* Expedient had I left, or what Proſpect now of retrieving my Condition! Could you hope, *my deareſt* Sire, that I could ſtir one Foot while you was left behind? Could ſuch Impiety drop from a Parent's Lips? If it is the Will of the Gods that nothing of this great City be preſerved; if this be your ſettled Purpoſe, and you are pleaſed to involve you and yours in the Wreck of Troy; the Way lies open to that Death of which

NOTES.

blind. But, whatever others allege, *Virgil*, at leaſt, ſuppoſes him to have the Uſe of his Eyes, as Verſe 687:

Et pater Anchiſes oculos ad ſidera lætus
Extulit———

And again, Verſe 732.

——————*Genitorque per umbram*
Proſpiciens: Nate, exclamat, fuge——
Ardentes clypeos atque æra micantia cerno.

And therefore it is more probable, what others advance, that he was blaſted and diſabled in his Limbs.

653. *Fatoque urgenti incumbere vellet.* It is not very eaſy to fix the preciſe Meaning of the Word *incumbere* in this Place. Dr. *Trapp* would gladly read *occumbere*, or rather *ſuccumbere*, would the Verſe and Authority permit. As it ſtands, he thinks it is a Metaphor taken from *Falling on a Sword.* I rather take it to be a Metaphor taken from one's leaning or lying with all his Weight upon a Load which preſſes another down, ſo as to add to the Preſſure, and render it more inſupportable. *Æneas* and his Followers were already grevionſly oppreſſed and weighed down by the public Calamity, *fato urgenti*, the Fate that lay ſo heavy upon them; and therefore pray *Anchiſes* not to increaſe the Burden by the additional Weight of his perſonal Sufferings and Death.

661. *Iſti janua letho.* *Servius* ſees no Noun preceding to which *iſti* can refer, and therefore will not allow it to be a Pronoun, but, an Apocope for *iſtic*. But, if we examine *Anchiſes*'s Speech, we will ſoon find what *iſti letho* refers to: *Anchiſes* had ſaid he would find Death with his own Hand, or the Enemy would have the Pity to give him Death: In anſwer to which, *Æneas* ſays, *patet iſti janua letho*, the Door is open, you may eaſily come at that Death of yours, or that Death of which you appear ſo fond

Jamque aderit multo Priami de ſanguine Pyrrhus,
Natum ante ora patris, patrem qui obtruncat ad aras.
Hoc erat, alma parens, quod me per tela, per ignes,
Eripis, ut mediis hoſtem in penetralibus, utque
Aſcaniumque, patremque meum, juxtaque Creüſam,
Alterum in alterius mactatos ſanguine cernam?
Arma, viri, ferte arma: vocat lux ultima victos.
Reddite me Danais, ſinite inſtaurata reviſam
Prœlia: nunquam omnes hodie moriemur inulti.
Hic ferro accingor rurſus; clypeoque ſiniſtram
Inſertabam aptans, meque extra tecta ferebam.
Ecce autem complexa pedes in limine conjux
Hærebat, parvumque patri tendebat Iülum:
Si periturus abis, et nos rape in omnia tecum:
Sin aliquam expertus ſumtis ſpem ponis in armis,

Jamque Pyrrhus aderit de multo ſanguine Priami, qui Pyrrhus obtruncat natam ante ora patris, et patrem ad aras. Alma parens, ad hoc erat, quod eripis me per tela, per ignes, ut cernam hoſtem in mediis penetralibus, utque cernam Aſcaniumque, meumque patrem, juxtaque Creüſam, mactatos, alterum mactatum in ſanguine alterius? viri, ferte mihi *arma, arma; lux ultima vocat victos. Reddite me Danais, ſinite* ut *reviſam prœlia inſtaurata:* nos *omnes nunquam moriemur hodie inulti.*

Hic rurſus accingor ferro; inſertabamque ſiniſtram clypeo aptans eum, *ferebamque me extra tecta. Ecce autem conjux amplexa* meos *pedes hærebat in limine, tendebatque parvum Iülum patri. Si,* inquit, *abis periturus, rape et nos tecum in omnia: ſin expertis ponis aliquam ſpem in armis ſumtis,*

T R A N S L A T I O N.

you are ſo fond. Forthwith Pyrrhus, *reeking* from the Effuſion of Priam's Blood, will be here, who butchers the Son before the Father's Eyes, and then the Father *himſelf* at his own Altar. Was it for this, my indulgent Mother, you ſaved me through Darts, through Flames, to ſee the Enemy in the midſt of theſe Receſſes, and to ſee Aſcanius, my Father, and Creüſa by his Side, butchered in one another's Blood? Arms, my Men, bring Arms; this Day, which is our laſt, calls us *to exert ourſelves*, vanquiſhed as we are. Give me back to the Greeks: let me viſit once more the Fight renewed: Never ſhall we all die unrevenged this Day. Thus I again gird on my Sword, and thruſt my Left-hand into my Buckler, bracing it fitly on, and flung out of the Palace. But lo! my Wife clung to me in the Threſhold, graſping my Feet, and reached to his Father the tender *Boy* Iülus: If, *ſays ſhe*, you go with a Reſolution to periſh, ſnatch us too with you to *ſhare* all *your Fortune;* But if, from Experience, you repoſe *any* Confidence in thoſe

N O T E S.

fond (for *iſte* is *that Thing of yours*, as *hic* is *this of mine)*, and then he goes on to tell him how he might obtain his Wiſh:

Jamque aderit—Pyrrhus, &c.

674. *Parvumque patri tendebat Iülum.* Here *Virgil* appears to have had in his Eye that tender affecting Scene between *Hector* and *Andromache*, in the ſixth Book of the Iliad, where the Circumſtances are pretty much the ſame. *Andromache* expoſtulates with *Hector*, as *Creüſa* does with *Æneas*, and in like Manner pleads her future forlorn Condition, and that of her Child, in caſe he ſhould abandon them; and ſeems to move him from returning to Battle by the ſame innocent and natural Artifice which *Creüſa* here uſes, putting *Aſtyanax* into his Arms, as ſhe does *Iülus* into the Arm of *Æneas*.

tutare banc domum primùm: cui parvus Iülus, cui pater tuus relinquitur, et cui ego, quondam dicta tua conjux, relinquor? Illa *vociferans talia, replebat omne tectum gemitu: cum monstrum subitum, mirabileque dictu, oritur; namque, inter manus oraque mœstorum parentum, ecce levis apex visus est fundere lumen de summo vertice Iüli, flammaque innoxia visa est lambere comas ejus molli tactu, et pasci circum ejus tempora. Nos pavidi* cœpimus *trepidare metu, excutereque crinem flagrantem, et restinguere sanctos ignes fontibus. At pater* meus *Anchises latus extulit oculos ad sidera, et tetendit palmas cœlo cum voce: O Omnipotens Jupiter, aspice nos, si flecteris ullis precibus;* petimus *hoc tantum: et, o pater, si meremur pietate, da* nobis *auxilium deinde, atque firma hæc omina.*

Hanc primùm tutare domum: cui parvus Iülus,
Cui pater, et conjux quondam tua dicta relinquor?
Talia vociferans, gemitu tectum omne replebat:
Cum subitum dictuque oritur mirabile monstrum;
Namque manus inter mœstorumque ora parentum,
Ecce levis summo de vertice visus Iüli
Fundere lumen apex, tactuque innoxia molli
Lambere flamma comas, et circum tempora pasci.
Nos pavidi trepidare metu, crinemque flagrantem
Excutere, et sanctos restinguere fontibus ignes.
At pater Anchises oculos ad sidera lætus
Extulit, et cœlo palmas cum voce tetendit:
Jupiter omnipotens, precibus si flecteris ullis,
Aspice nos; hoc tantum: et, si pietate meremur,
Da deinde auxilium, pater, atque hæc omina firma.

TRANSLATION.

Arms you have assumed, let this House have your first Protection: To whom are you abandoning the tender Iülus, your *aged* Sire, and me once called your Wife? Thus expostulating loud she filled the whole Palace with her Groans, when a sudden and wondrous Prodigy rises *to my Sight:* For, *while the Boy is* in the Arms and Embraces of his mourning Parents, lo the fluttering Tuft from the Top of Iülus's Head was seen to emit a *Stream of* Light, and with gentle Touch * the lambent Flame glides harmless along his Hair, and feeds around his Temples. We, all quaking for Fear, run bustling *to his Relief,* brush the blazing Locks, and quench the holy Fire with Fountain-water. But *my* Father Anchises joyful raised his Eyes to the Stars, and stretched his Hands to Heaven with his Voice: Almighty Jove, if thou art moved by any Supplications, vouchsafe but to regard us; we ask no more: And, O *heavenly* Father, if by our Piety we deserve *it,* grant us then thy Aid, and ratify these Omens. Scarce had *my aged* Sire thus said,

* *Tactu,* others read *tractu,* a soft or gentle Train.

NOTES.

680. *Mirabile monstrum.* This Miracle is exceedingly well-timed; and, if there ever was a *dignus vindice nodus,* it is here. Had *Anchises* finally persisted in his Resolution, it must have put an End to the Poem, by involving *Æneas* and all his Followers in one common Ruin. He had been plied with all human Arguments in the strongest Manner, but with no Success; What then remained for the Poet, but to have Recourse to the seasonable Interposition of the Gods, to save his Hero in this Extremity?

691. *Hæc omina firma.* According to the Manner of the *Romans,* who deemed one Omen not sufficient, unless it was confirmed by a *second,*

Vix ea fatus erat ſenior, ſubitoque fragore
Intonuit lævum, et de cœlo lapſa per umbras
Stella facem ducens multâ cum luce cucurrit.
Illam, ſumma ſuper labentem culmina tecti
Cernimus Idæâ claram ſe condere ſylvâ,
Signantemque vias; tum longo limite ſulcus
Dat lucem, et latè circum loca ſulfure fumant.
Hìc verò victus genitor ſe tollit ad auras,
Affaturque Deos, et ſanctum ſidus adorat:
Jam jam nulla mora eſt; ſequor, et, quà ducitis, adſum.
Dì patrii, ſervate domum, ſervate nepotem:
Veſtrum hoc augurium, veſtroque in numine Troja eſt.

Senior vix fatus erat ea, lævumque cœlum intonuit ſubito fragore, et ſtella lapſa de cælo cucurrit per umbras, ducens facem cum multâ luce. Cernimus illam labentem ſuper ſumma culmina tecti, condere ſe claram in Idæâ ſylvâ, ſignantemque vias: tum ſulcus dat lucem in longo limite, et loca circum latè fumant ſulfure. Hìc verò genitor victus tollit ſe ad auras, affaturque Deos, et adorat ſanctum ſidus: ait jam jam eſt nulla mora; ſequor, et adſum, quà ducitis. O Dî patrii, ſervate domum, ſervate meum nepotem: Hoc augurium eſt veſtrum, Trojaque eſt in veſtro numine.

TRANSLATION.

when with a ſudden Peal it thundered on the Left, and a Star, that fell from the Skies, drawing a fiery Train, ſhot through the Shades with a Profuſion of Light. We ſee it, gliding over the high Tops of the Palace, loſe itſelf in the Woods of Mount Ida, full in our View, and marking out *our* Way: Then all along its Tract an indented Path ſhines, and all the Space, a great Way round, ſmokes with ſulphureous Steams. And now my Father, forced to give Way, raiſes himſelf to Heaven, addreſſes the Gods, and pays Adoration to the Holy Star: Now, now, in me is no Delay: I am all Submiſſion, and where you lead the Way I am with you. Ye Gods of my Fathers, ſave our Family, ſave my Grandſon. From you this Omen came, and Troy is in your divine Diſpoſal. *Now*, Son, I

NOTES.

cond, whence *ſecundus* and *ſecundo* came to ſignify *proſperous*, and *to proſper*. See *Cicero de Divinatione*.

693. *Intonuit lævum.* Both the *Greeks* and *Romans* agreed in their Opinion, that thoſe Omens that preſented themſelves in the Eaſtern Quarter of the Heavens were proſperous; but the *Greeks*, in taking the Auſpices, turned their Faces towards the North, and conſequently had the Eaſt on their right, as is plain from *Homer*, Il. XII. 239, where *Hector*, expreſſing his Diſregard of all Omens, ſays,

—— τῶν οὔ τι μετατρέπομ', οὐδ' ἀλεγίζω,
Εἴτ' ἐπὶ δεξί' ἴωσι πρὸς ἠῶ τ' ἠέλιόν τε,
Εἴτ' ἐπ' ἀριστερὰ τοί γε, ποτὶ ζόφον ἠερόεντα.

I heed no Omens nor Prognoſtics of Birds, whether they fly on the Right towards the Sun-riſing, or on the Left towards his Setting, i. e. whether the lucky Omens on the Right, or the unlucky ones on the Left. The *Romans*, on the other Hand, in obſerving the Auſpices, directed their Faces ſouthward, as appears from *Varro, Epiſ. Quæſ.* Lib, V. Hence they, contrary to the Manner of the *Greeks*, reckoned the Omens on the Left-hand lucky, and thoſe on the Right unlucky; becauſe the Eaſt, the Source of Light and Day, was on the Left to the *Romans*, but on the Right to the *Greeks*.

694. *Stella*, &c. *Servius* applies the ſeveral Circumſtances of this Prodigy as figurative of the particular Events that were to happen to *Æneas* and his Followers. The Star is ſaid *condere ſe Idæa ſilva*, to ſignify that the *Trojans* were to reſort to Mount *Ida multa cum luce*, to figure their future Glory and Luſtre; *ſignantem vias*, the Sparkles of Fire it left behind, are figurative of the Diſperſion of his Followers, and that they were to fix their Reſidence in different Parts: *longo limite ſulcus* marks his many Wanderings, and the Length of his Voyage: *Laſtly*, by the Smoke and ſulphureous Steams in which the Meteor expires, he underſtands the Death of *Anchiſes*.

702. *Dî patrii.* By theſe I underſtand the Guardian-gods of *Anchiſes*'s Family, thoſe whom his Anceſtors worſhipped, who preſided over parental

O nate, ego equidem cedo nec recuso ire comes tibi.

Ille dixerat: et ignis jam auditur clarior per mœnia, incendiaque volvunt æstus propius. Age ergo, o care pater, imponere nostræ cervici: ego ipse subibo te humeris meis; nec iste labor gravabit me. Quæcunque res cadent, periculum erit unum et commune, salus una erit ambobus: parvus Iülus sit comes mihi et conjux servet mea *vestigia longè. Vos famuli advertite vestris animis* ad ea *quæ dicam. Tumulus est egressis urbe, vetustumque templum desertæ Cereris;* juxtaque est *antiqua cupressus servata relligione patrum per multos annos.*

Cedo equidem, nec, nate, tibi comes ire recuso.
Dixerat ille: et jam per mœnia clarior ignis
Auditur, propiusque æstus incendia volvunt.
Ergo age, care pater, cervici imponere nostræ:
Ipse subibo humeris; nec me labor iste gravabit.
Quo res cunque cadent, unum et commune periclum,
Una salus ambobus erit: mihi parvus Iülus
Sit comes, et longè servet vestigia conjux.
Vos, famuli, quæ dicam, animis advertite vestris.
Est urbe egressis tumulus, templumque vetustum
Desertæ Cereris; juxtaque antiqua cupressus,
Relligione patrum multos servata per annos.

TRANSLATION.

resign myself indeed, nor refuse to accompany you in your Expedition. He said: And now throughout the City the *crackling* Flames are more distinctly heard, and the Conflagration rolls the Torrents of Fire nearer *to us*. Come then, dearest Father, place yourself on my Neck: With these Shoulders will I support you, nor shall that Burden oppress me. However things fall out, we both shall share either one common Danger, or one Salvation: The Boy Iülus be my Companion, and, my Spouse, trace my Steps at *some* Distance. Ye Servants heedfully attend to what I say. In your Way from the City is a rising Ground, and an ancient Temple of Ceres, *now* neglected; and hard by an aged Cypress-tree, preserved for many Years by the religious Veneration of our Forefathers. To this one

NOTES.

rental and filial Affection. These are they of whom *Cicero* makes mention in his third *Action* against *Verres*: *Rapiunt eum ad supplicium Dii patrii, quod iste inventus est, qui è complexu parentum abreptos filios ad necem duceret.*

710. *Mihi parvus Iülus.* *Donatus* reads, *mihi solus Iülus sit comes, let* Iülus *only accompany me*; which both avoids the too frequent Repetition of *parvus Iülus*, and at the same Time shews *Æneas*'s prudent Precaution to secure their Flight, since, the fewer went together, they would be the less liable to be discovered.

711. *Longè servet*, i. e. To stay behind, yet so as still to have him in View, that she might neither lose her Way, nor be far from him to help her, in case of an Attack. The Reason why he directed her not to come up close with him, has been already assigned in the former Note; it was a proper Precaution for their common Safety, that they might be the less exposed to the View of the Enemy; and pass along more quietly, by being divided into Parties. This Reason justifies *Æneas*, and there is another which made it proper for the Poet to mention that Circumstance, namely, to give Probability to his Relation of her being lost. On these Accounts, I chose rather to keep to the common Signification of *longè*, than to follow *Servius*, who explains it *valdè*, i. e. *Let my Wife carefully mark my Steps.*

712. *Quæ dicam, animis advertite.* Equivalent to *advertite animos his quæ dicam*, which is the more common Way of Speaking, as in *Ovid*,

——— *monitis animos advertite nostris.*
Met. XV. 140.

714. *Desertæ Cereris.* This Epithet, *deserted*, is applied to *Ceres*, either on Account of her being bereaved of *Proserpine*, or in regard to the particular State of her Worship, which was now neglected in the public Calamity: Or because she was now without a Priest, who is mention-

Hanc ex diverſo ſedem veniemus in unam.
Tu, genitor, cape ſacra manu, patrioſque Penates.
Me, bello è tanto digreſſum et cæde recenti,
Attrectare nefas; donec me flumine vivo
Abluero.
Hæc fatus, latos humeros, ſubjectaque colla
Veſte ſuper, fulvique inſternor pelle leonis;
Succedoque oneri: dextræ ſe parvus Iülus
Implicuit, ſequiturque patrem non paſſibus æquis.
Pone ſubit conjux. Ferimur per opaca locorum:
Et me, quem dudum non ulla injecta movebant
Tela, neque adverſo glomerati ex agmine Graii,
Nunc omnes terrent auræ, ſonus excitat omnis
Suſpenſum, et pariter comitique onerique timentem.

Nos omnes veniemus in hanc unam ſedem ex diverſo tramite. *O genitor, tu cape ſacra, patrioſque Penates* in tuâ *manu. Nefas* eſſet *me digreſſum è tanto bello, et recenti cæde, attrectare* ea ſacra; *donec abluero me vivo flumine.*

Ego *fatus hæc, ſuper inſternor latos humeros, colloque ſubjecta veſte pelleque fulvi leonis; ſuccedoque oneri: parvus Iülus implicuit ſe* meæ *dextræ, ſequiturque patrem paſſibus non æquis. Conjux ſubit pone. Ferimur per opaca* ſpatia *locorum: et nunc omnes auræ terrent, omnis ſonus excitat me, quem dudum non ulla injecta tela, neque Graii glomerati ex agmine adverſo, movebant,* me inquam *ſuſpenſum et pariter timentem comitique onerique.*

TRANSLATION.

Seat by ſeveral Ways we will repair. Do you, Father, take in thy Hand the ſacred Symbols, and the Gods of our Country. For me, juſt come from War, ſo fierce and recent Bloodſhed, to touch *them* would be Profanation, till I have purified myſelf in the living Stream. This ſaid, I ſpread a Garment and a tawny Lion's Hide over my broad Shoulders and ſubmiſſive Neck; and ſtoop to the Burden: The tender Boy is linked in my Right-hand, and trips after his Father with unequal Steps: My Spouſe comes up behind: We haſte away through the gloomy Paths. And I, whom lately not Showers of Darts could move, nor Greeks incloſing me round in a hoſtile Band, am now terrified with every Breath of Wind; every Sound alarms me anxious, and equally in Dread for my Companion and

NOTES.

ed among thoſe *Trojans* who died in the War, Æn. VI. 481.

Hic multum fleti ad Superos, belloque caduci
Dardanidæ———Glaucumque———
——————Cereríque ſacrum Polybœten.

719. *Attrectare nefas, donec me flumine vivo.* In like manner *Homer* makes *Hector* ſay, he was afraid of performing religious Worſhip to *Jupiter*, while his Hands were polluted with Blood:

Χερσὶ δ' ἀνίπτοισιν, &c.
By me that holy Office were profan'd;
Ill fits it me, with human Gore diſtain'd,
To the pure Skies theſe horrid Hands to raiſe,
Or offer Heav'n's great Sire polluted Praiſe.
Pope's Iliad, VI. 334.

It was the Cuſtom of the *Greeks* and *Romans*, and moſt other Nations, to waſh their Hands, and ſometimes their whole Bodies in Water, before they performed Acts of Religion, eſpecially if they were polluted with Bloodſhed. On ſuch Occaſions they were not allowed to uſe foul, muddy, or ſtagnant Water, but ſuch as was pure and limpid, as is that of living Fountains and running Rivers; which is the Reaſon why *Æneas* here ſays, *me flumine vivo abluero.*

726. *Et me—nunc omnes terrent auræ.* This is a very beautiful Image of *Æneas*'s pious and tender Affection, which we have taken Notice of elſewhere. With unſhaken Fortitude he faced the greateſt Dangers, when only his own Perſon was expoſed; now every Appearance of Danger ſtrikes him with Terror on account of his dear Charge. And here we may obſerve *Virgil*'s exact Judgment in making *Æneas* ſpeak in Commendation of his own Valour ſo ſeaſonably, that

Jamque propinquabam portis, videbarque evasisse omnem viam, cum creber sonitus pedum subito visus est adesse mihi *ad aures; genitorque prospiciens per umbram exclamat: nate, nate fuge;* hostes *propinquant; cerno ardentes clypeos atque micantia æra. Hic numen, nescio quod, male amicum eripuit confusam mentem mihi trepido: Namque, dum cursu sequor avia* loca, *et excedo notâ regione viarum, heu!* mea *conjux Creüsa substitit, incertum* est, *ereptane* sit *fato* mihi *misero, erravitne è via, seu resedit lassa: nec reddita est nostris oculis post. Nec respexi, reflexique animum* eam *esse amissam, priusquam venimus* ad *tumulum, sacratamque sedem antiquæ Cereris: hic, omnibus demum collectis,* Creüsa *una defuit, et fefellit comites, natumque, virumque.*

Jamque propinquabam portis, omnemque videbar
Evasisse viam, subito cum creber ad aures
Visus adesse pedum sonitus; genitorque, per umbram
Prospiciens, nate, exclamat, fuge, nate: propinquant;
Ardentes clypeos atque æra micantia cerno.
Hìc mihi nescio quod trepido male numen amicum
Confusam eripuit mentem: namque avia cursu
Dum sequor, et nota excedo regione viarum,
Heu! misero conjux fatone erepta Creüsa
Substitit, erravitne viâ, seu lassa resedit,
Incertum: nec post oculis est reddita nostris.
Nec prius amissam respexi, animumque reflexi,
Quàm tumulum antiquæ Cereris, sedemque sacratam,
Venimus: hic demum, collectis omnibus, una
Defuit, et comites, natumque, virumque fefellit.

TRANSLATION.

my *dear* Load. By this Time I was got near the Gates, and thought I had overpassed all *the Danger of* the Way, when suddenly a thick Sound of *trampling* Feet seemed to invade my Ears just at Hand: And my Father, stretching his Eyes through the Gloom, calls aloud, Fly, fly, my Son, they are upon you. I see *their* burnished Shields and glittering *Helms of* Brass. Here, in my Hurry and Consternation, some unfriendly Deity or other, confounded and bereaved me of my Reason: For while in my Journey I trace the By-paths, and forsake the known beaten Tracks, *I was so unfortunate*, alas! to drop my Wife Creüsa; whether she was snatched from me by cruel Fate, or lost her Way, or through Fatigue stopped short, is uncertain; nor did these Eyes ever see her more: Nor did I observe that she was lost, nor reflect with myself, till we were come to the rising Ground, and sacred Seat of ancient Ceres: Here, at length, when all were convened, she alone was wanting, and gave *sad* Disappointment to all our Retinue, especially to her Son and Husband. Frantic, *with Grief*, whom did I not

NOTES.

that he is clear of all Imputation of Vanity. He magnifies his Courage in one Situation, only to make the tender Fears of his Humanity and natural Affection the more conspicuous in another.

740. *Nec post oculis est reddita nostris.* This Episode of *Creüsa*'s Death is introduced not merely for the Importance of the Event, but, as it subserves several Purposes of the Poet. It gives him an Opportunity farther to illustrate *Æneas*'s Piety, by shewing him once more exposed to all the Dangers of the War in quest of his Wife; and, in consequence of that, leads us back with the Hero to visit *Troy* smoking in its Ruins, and brings us acquainted with several affecting Circumstances, without which the Narration would not have been complete. And then, which seems to be the chief Thing that *Virgil* had

Quem non incuſavi amens hominumque Deorumque!
Aut quid in everſâ vidi crudelius urbe!
Aſcanium, Anchiſenque patrem, Teucroſque Penates,
Commendo ſociis, et curvâ valle recondo.
Ipſe urbem repeto, et cingor fulgentibus armis.
Stat caſus renovare omnes, omnemque reverti
Per Trojam, et rurſus caput objectare periclis.
Principiò muros, obſcuraque limina portæ,
Qua greſſum extuleram, repeto; et veſtigia retro
Obſervata ſequor per noctem, et lumine luſtro.
Horror ubique animos, ſimul ipſa ſilentia terrent.
Inde domum, ſi forte pedem, ſi forte tuliſſet,
Me refero: irruerant Danai, et tectum omne tenebant.
Ilicet ignis edax ſumma ad faſtigia vento
Volvitur; exſuperant flammæ; furit æſtus ad auras.

Quem hominumque Deorumque non incuſavi amens! aut quid vidi crudelius in urbe everſâ! Commendo ſociis meis, et recondo in curvâ valle, Aſcanium, patremque Anchiſen, Teucroſque Penates. Ego ipſe repeto urbem, et cingor fulgentibus armis. Stat ſententia *renovare omnes caſus, revertique per omnem Trojam, et rurſus objectare* meum *caput periclis. Principiò repeto muros obſcuraque limina portæ, qua extuleram greſſum: et retro ſequor veſtigia obſervata per noctem, et luſtro ea lumine. Horror* eſt *ubique, ſimul ipſa ſilentia terrent animos* meos. *Inde refero* me *domum, ſi forte, ſi forte tuliſſet pedem* eo: *Danai irruerant, et tenebant omne tectum. Ilicet ignis edax volvitur vento ad ſumma faſtigia; flammæ exſuperant; æſtus furit ad auras.*

TRANSLATION.

accuſe of Gods or Men! Or of what more cruel *affecting* Scene was I Spectator in all the Deſolation of Troy! To my Friends I recommend Aſcanius, my Father Anchiſes, with the Gods of Troy, and lodge them ſecretly in a winding Valley. Myſelf repair back to the City, and brace on my ſhining Armour. I am reſolved to renew every Adventure, reviſit all the Quarters of the Town, and expoſe my Life once more to all Dangers. Firſt of all I return to the Walls, and the dark Entry of the Gate by which I had ſet out, and backward unravel *all* my *former* Steps with Care amidſt the Darkneſs, and run them over with my Eye. Horror ſtalks around; at the ſame Time the very Silence *of the Night* affrights my Soul. Thence homeward I bent my Way, if by Chance, by *any Chance*, ſhe had moved *thither:* The Greeks had now ruſhed in, and were Maſters of the whole Houſe. In a Moment the devouring Conflagration in Sheets is rolled up by the Wind to the lofty Roof; the Flames *ſoon* mount above; the fiery Whirlwind rages to the Skies. I advance to Priam's royal Seat, and reviſit

NOTES.

had in his Eye, it makes Way for the Appearance of *Creüſa*'s Ghoſt, who both affords ſeaſonable Comfort to *Æneas* in the Height of his Diſtreſs, by predicting his future Felicity, and relieves the Mind of the Reader from the Horrors of War and Bloodſhed, by turning him to the Proſpect of that Peace and Tranquillity which *Æneas* was to enjoy in *Italy*, and of that undiſturbed Reſt and happy Liberty whereof *Creüſa* herſelf was now poſſeſſed in the other World. See Verſe 775, &c.

750. *Stat. My Purpoſe is fixed, ſententia* being underſtood. While the Mind is in Doubt and Deliberation, it reels and varies from one Thing to another, *fluctuat, vacillat*; but, when it is determined and reſolved, then it ſtands ſtill, and is at reſt, *conſiſtit conſilium, ſtat ſententia.*

760. *Priami*

Procedo ad sedes Priami, revi seque arcem. Et jam Phœnix et dirus Ulysses, lecti custodes, asservabant prædam in vacuis porticibus, in asylo Junonis: Troïa gaza erepta incensis adytis, mensæque Deorum, crateresque solidi ex auro, captivaque: vestis congeritur huc undique: pueri et pavidæ matres stant circum in longa ordine: Quinetiam, ausus jactare voces per umbram, implevi vias meo clamore, mæstusque ingeminans Creüsam nequicquam vocavi eam iterum iterumque. Infelix simulacrum atque umbra ipsius Creüsæ, et imago major notâ visa est ante oculos mihi quærenti, et furenti in tectis urbis sine fine. Obstupui, comæque steterunt, et vox hæsit meis faucibus. Tum cœpit sic affari me, et demere meas curas his dictis:

Procedo ad Priami sedes, arcemque reviso.
Et jam porticibus vacuis, Junonis asylo,
Custodes lecti Phœnix et dirus Ulysses
Prædam asservabant: huc undique Troïa gaza
Incensis erepta adytis, mensæque Deorum,
Cratereſque auro solidi, captivaque vestis
Congeritur: pueri et pavidæ longo ordine matres
Stant circum.
Ausus quinetiam voces jactare per umbram,
Implevi clamore vias, mœstusque Creüsam
Nequicquam ingeminans, iterumque iterumque vocavi.
Quærenti, et tectis urbis sine fine furenti,
Infelix simulacrum, atque ipsius umbra Creüsæ
Visa mihi ante oculos, et notâ major imago.
Obstupui, steteruntque comæ, et vox faucibus hæsit.
Tum sic affari, et curas his demere dictis:

TRANSLATION.

the Citadel. And now in the desolate Cloisters, Juno's Sanctuary, Phœnix, and cursed Ulysses, a chosen Guard, were watching the Booty: Hither, from all Quarters, the precious Trojan Moveables, saved from the Conflagration of the Temples, the Tables of the Gods, the massy golden Goblets, and plundered Vestments, are amassed together: *Captive* Boys, and timorous Matrons, stand all around in a long Train. Nay, more, adventuring even to dart my Voice through the Shades, I filled the Streets with Outcry, and in the Anguish of my Soul, with vain Repetition, again and again invoked Creüsa. While I am in this *fruitless* Search, and with incessant Fury ranging through all Quarters of the Town, the mournful Ghost and Shade of my Creüsa's Self appeared before my Eyes, and her Figure larger than the Life. I stood aghast! my Hair rose on End, and my Voice clung to *my* Jaws. Then thus she bespeaks me, and relieves my Cares with these Words: My darling Spouse, what Pleasure have you thus

NOTES.

760. *Priami sedes—reviso.* *Creüsa* was *Priam's* Daughter, which is the Reason why *Æneas* goes to the Palace in quest of her.

764. *Mensæque Deorum.* The Tripods of the Gods, which served either for delivering the Oracles, or for bearing the sacred Vases.

765. *Captivaque vestis.* i. e. Either Pieces of Tapestry, or of fine Needle-work, in which the *Phrygian* Women excelled, and as the Word signifies, *Æn.* I. 645.

Arte laboratæ vestes, ostroque superbo.

772. *Infelix simulacrum.* Unhappy, not on her own Account, for she declares herself blessed and happy, Verse 785; but the Cause of so much Misery to *Æneas.*

773. *Et notâ major imago.* Spectres and Apparitions are commonly represented of an enormous Stature, Fear having Effect to swell Objects to the Imagination. Thus *Livy* informs us, that, when *Decius* devoted himself for his Country, he appeared to the Spectators more grand and august than ordinary: *Aliquanto augustior humano visu.*

782. *Lydius*

Quid tantum insano juvat indulgere dolori,
O dulcis conjux? non hæc sine numine Divûm
Eveniunt: nec te hinc comitem asportare Creüsam
Fas, aut ille sinit superi regnator Olympi.
Longa tibi exsilia, et vastum maris æquor arandum.
Ad terram Hesperiam venies, ubi Lydius arva
Inter opima virûm leni fluit agmine Tybris.
Illic res lætæ, regnumque, et regia conjux,
Parta tibi: lacrymas dilectæ pelle Creüsæ.
Non ego Myrmidonum sedes Dolopumve superbas
Aspiciam, aut Graiis servitum matribus ibo,
Dardanis, et Divæ Veneris nurus:
Sed me magna Deûm genetrix his detinet oris.
Jamque vale, et nati serva communis amorem.
Hæc ubi dicta dedit, lacrymantem et multa volentem
Dicere deseruit, tenuesque recessit in auras:

O d[illegible] [illegible] te [illegible] [illegible] Di[illegible] regnator superi Olympi [illegible], te asportare Creüsam [illegible]. Longa exsilia futura sunt tibi, et vastum æquor maris est arandum tibi. Venies ad Hesperiam terram, ubi Lydius Tybris fluit leni agmine inter arva opima virûm. Res lætæ partæ sunt, regnumque partum, et regia conjux parta est tibi illic: pelle lacrymas dilectæ Creüsæ. Ego non aspiciam superbas sedes Myrmidonum Dolopumve, aut ibo servitum Graiis matribus, ego quæ sum Dardanis, et nurus Divæ Veneris: Sed magna genetrix Deûm detinet me in his oris. Jamque vale, et serva amorem communis nati. Ubi dedit hæc dicta, deseruit me lacrymantem, et volentem dicere multa, recessitque in tenues auras.

TRANSLATION.

to indulge a Grief which is but Madness? These Events fall out not without the Will of the Gods. 'Tis not decreed you carry Creüsa hence to accompany you, nor is it permitted by the great Ruler of Heaven supreme. In long Banishment you must roam, and plough the vast Expansion of the Ocean: To the Land of Hesperia you shall come *at length*, where the Lydian Tyber, with his gentle Current, glides through a rich Land of Heroes. There prosperous Days, a Crown, and royal Spouse await you: Dry up your Tears for your beloved Creüsa, *who is now happy, and at rest*. I, of Dardanus's noble Line, and the Daughter-in-Law of divine Venus, shall not *be cursed to* see the proud Seats of the Myrmidons and Dolopes, nor go to serve the Grecian Dames; but the great Mother of the Gods detains me *in her Service* in these Coasts. Now, farewell, and preserve your Affection to our common Son.

With these Words she left me in Tears, and ready to say a thousand Things, and vanished into thin Air. There thrice I attempted to throw my Arms around

NOTES.

782. *Lydius Tybris.* The River *Tyber* divides the *Tuscans* from *Latium*, and is therefore denominated *Lydian*; for the *Tuscans* were a Colony from *Lydia*, planted in *Etruria* or *Tuscany*, by *Tyrrbenes* the Son of *Atys*, King of *Lydia*; which *Tyrrbenes* was sent out by his Father in Time of a Famine to seek a Settlement in some other Country, and after long Wanderings at length fixed his Residence, and planted a Colony in *Italy* upon the upper Banks of the *Tyber*, and called the *Tuscans* after his own Name. This is what *Virgil* himself tells us, *Æn.* VIII. 47[illegible].

——*Ubi Lydia quondam*
Gens bello præclara, jugis insedit Etruscis.

Ibi ter conatus ſum *circumdare brachia* mea illius *collo*; *imago fruſtra comprenſa ter effugit manus* meas, *par levibus ventis, ſimillimaque volucri ſomno. Nocte ſic conſumtâ, demum reviſo ſocios. Atque hìc admirans invenio ingentem numerum novorum comitum affluxiſſe*; *matreſque viroſque, pubem collectam exſilio, miſerabile vulgus!* hi *convenere undique, parati animis opibuſque* ſequi *in quaſcunque terras velim deducere* eos *pelago. Jamque Lucifer ſurgebat* in *jugis ſummæ Idæ, ducebatque diem*; *Danaique tenebant limina portarum obſeſſa, nec ulla ſpes opis dabatur* mihi. *Ceſſi, et petivi montem, genitore ſublato.*

Ter conatus ibi collo dare brachia circum;
Ter fruſtra comprenſa manus effugit imago,
Par levibus ventis, volucrique ſimillima ſomno.
Sic demum ſocios conſumtâ nocte reviſo.
Atque hìc ingentem comitum affluxiſſe novorum
Invenio, admirans, numerum; matreſque, viroſque,
Collectam exſilio pubem, miſerabile vulgus!
Undique convenere, animis opibuſque parati,
In quaſcunque velim pelago deducere terras.
Jamque jugis ſummæ ſurgebat Lucifer Idæ,
Ducebatque diem: Danaique obſeſſa tenebant
Limina portarum: nec ſpes opis ulla dabatur.
Ceſſi, et ſublato montem genitore petivi.

TRANSLATION.

her Neck; thrice the Phantom, graſped in vain, eſcaped my Hold, ſwift as the winged Winds, and reſembling moſt a fleeting Dream. Thus having ſpent the Night, I at length re-viſit my Aſſociates. And here, to my Surprize, I find a vaſt Confluence of new Companions had joined us; Matrons and Men, and Youths drawn together to *ſhare* our Exile, a piteous Throng! From all Hands they convened, reſolute *to follow me* with their Souls and Fortunes, into whatever Country I inclined to conduct them over Sea. By this Time, the bright Morning-ſtar was riſing on the craggy Tops of lofty Ida, and uſhered in the Day: The Greeks held the Entrance of the Gates blocked up, nor had we any Proſpect of Relief. I gave Way *to Fate*, and, bearing up my Father, made towards the Mountain.

NOTES.

796. *Ingentem affluxiſſe numerum.* It appears that this Multitude, either by this very Act of reſorting to *Æneas*, and putting themſelves under his Protection, or by ſome more explicit Declaration of their Mind, made Choice of him for their King; which Appellation is ſtill given him afterwards throughout the *Æneid.*

801. *Jugis ſurgebat Lucifer Idæ.* Becauſe Mount *Ida* lay on the Eaſt of *Troy*, and conſequently *Lucifer*, *Venus*, or the *Morning-ſtar*, the Forerunner of the Sun, appeared to thoſe at *Troy* to riſe as from Mount *Ida.*

804. *Ceſſi.* Dr. *Trapp* renders it, *I retired*; but it appears much more elegant to underſtand it, with others, as an Expreſſion of *Æneas*'s Piety and Reſignation, eſpecially conſidering what goes before, *nec ſpes opis ulla dabatur.*

P. VIR-

P. VIRGILII MARONIS
ÆNEIDOS
LIBER TERTIUS.

POstquam rês Asiæ Priamique evertere gentem
Immeritam visum Superis, ceciditque superbum

ORDO.

Postquam visum est Superis evertere res Asiæ, gentemque Priami immeritam, Iliumque superbum cecidit,

TRANSLATION.

AFTER it had seemed good to the Gods to overthrow the Power of Asia, and Priam's Race, not for any Fault of theirs, and stately Ilium fell, and Troy, *now* built by Neptune, smokes in Ruin; we are de-

NOTES.

This third Book of the Æneid contains more Matter than any of the rest: In it we have the Substance of the whole Odyssey, and the Annals of no less than seven Years; whereas none of the other Books, except the fourth, which includes the Events of that Summer *Æneas* spent at *Carthage*, extends beyond some few Days. *Virgil* has likewise given us here a Specimen of his Knowledge of Geography, and the Manners of People. The several Nations whom he makes his Hero visit, the Adventure of the *Harpies*, by whom we may understand either bad Women, or, according to others, the Stings of a guilty Conscience; the Story of the *Cyclops*, by whom are imaged men sunk into a brutal Nature by Cruelty and Intemperance, shew us how a wise Man ought to conduct himself amidst the various Snares and Temptations to which human Life is exposed. It is observed, however, that this Book, notwithstanding the Copiousness of the Subject, the Eloquence of the Style, and the many Sublime Passages it contains, which are as numerous in this as in any of the rest, is yet, of all others, the least read, which seems more to be owing to its Situation, than any other Reason; for the preceding second Book, which contains the History of the Sack of *Troy*, exhibits to us somewhat so grand, that in Comparison of it we think meanly of this. The fourth again has so many Charms from the Tenderness of the Subject, that we are impatient to get at it. Thus, it being sufficient for the Thread of the History to know that *Æneas*, after the Destruction of *Troy*, arrived at *Carthage*, Numbers of Readers either wholly overlook this third Book, or, having given it a superficial Reading, disdain to study it like the rest: Nevertheless we may say, that, next to the sixth, there is none of them from which more may be learned, whether with regard to the ancient Geography, in which it is so exact, or those several Portraitures that relate to civil Life; or, lastly, the fine Monuments of ancient Religion, which are hardly to be met with any where else.

2. *Immeritam.* Because their Ruin was owing to the Crimes of *Paris* and *Laomedon*, not their own Demerit:

——————sanguine nostro
Laomedonteæ luimus perjuria Trojæ.
Geor. I. 502.

————————Ilion, Ilion
Fatalis incestu que judex,
Et mulier peregrina vertit
In pulverem, ex quo destituit Deos
Mercede pacta Laomedon, mihi
Castæque damnatum Minervæ,
Cum populo et duce fraudulento.
Hor. III. Carm. III. 18.

 3. *Ilium*—

et Neptunia Troja omnis fumat humo; agimur auguriis Divûm quærere diversa exsilia, et desertas terras, molimurque classem sub ipsâ Antandro, et montibus Phrygiæ Idæ, contrahimusque viros incerti quò fata ferant nos, ubi detur nobis sistere. Prima æstas vix inceperat,

Ilium, et omnis humo fumat Neptunia Troja;
Diversa exsilia, et desertas quærere terras,
Auguriis agimur Divûm: classemque sub ipsâ
Antandro et Phrygiæ molimur montibus Idæ;
Incerti quò fata ferant, ubi sistere detur,
Contrahimusque viros. Vix prima inceperat æstas,

TRANSLATION.

termined, by Revelations from the Gods, to go in quest of distant Retreats in Exile, and unpeopled Lands: We fit out a Fleet just under the Walls of Antandros, and the Mountains of Phrygian Ida; and draw our Forces together, not knowing whither the Fates point our Way, where it shall be given us to settle. Scarce had the first Summer begun, when my Father Anchises gave Command to

NOTES.

1 *Ilium—Neptunia Troja.* *Ruæus* would have *Ilium* here to mean the Citadel, and *Troy* the whole Town, to save a Tautology. But every one may see that *omnis Troja fumat humo*, is much fuller and stronger than *Ilium cecidit*, and the Thought is quite different, as well as the Expression. *Virgil* uses *Ilium* only in the Neuter Gender; *Horace* has *Ilios*, and *Ovid Ilion* in the Feminine, like other Names of Cities.

3 *Fumat.* There is a much greater Force and Propriety in using the present Tense here, than if it had been the Preterite, which we have endeavoured to express in the Translation.

3. *Neptunia Troja.* The Mythologists make both *Neptune* and *Apollo* the Builders of the Walls of *Troy*; but *Homer* and *Virgil*, if I rightly remember, ascribe that Work to *Neptune* alone. See the Note on *Æneid* II. Verse 610.

4. *Diversa exsilia.* I take *diversa* here in the Sense of *Longinqua*, as it is used by *Ovid*:

Arva Phaon celebrat diversi Typhoëos Ætnæ.
Ep. st. Saph. to Phaon, Verse 11.

Though the *Trojans*, under several Leaders, as *Æneas*, *Helenus*, *Antenor*, settled in different Regions; the *diversa exsilia* here, it is plain, refers only to *Æneas* and his Followers, who were all appointed by the Gods to go in quest of one and the same Settlement. For the *agimur auguriis Divûm quærere diversa exsilia*, and *molimur classem sub Antandro*, must both belong to one and the same Nominative, *viz. I and my Followers.*

4 *Desertas terras.* By *desertas terras* we may either understand the Country which *Dardanus* had left; or rather, *Æneas* speaks the Language of his Heart at that Time. Having then the dismal Idea of the Destruction of his Country awakened fresh in his Mind, and the uncertain Prospect before him of a Settlement in some unknown Land, as it immediately follows, *incerti quo fata ferant, ubi sistere detur*, it was natural for him to have uncomfortable Apprehensions of the Country he was going to, to call it a Place of Banishment, a Land of Solitude and Desertion; especially if we add, that it was the Design of *Æneas* to move *Dido*'s Compassion, and therefore to paint every Circumstance of his Story in Colours of Suffering and Distress. There are some, however, who read *diversas terras*, instead of *desertas.*

5. *Auguriis Divûm.* This refers to all the prophetic Intimations he had given him of his future Fate by the Apparition of *Hector*, *Æn.* II. 295, by the lambent Flame that played about *Ascanius*'s Temples, Verse 681, by the Course of the falling Star, and the Thunder on the Left, Verse 694; and, lastly, by the Interview he had with *Creüsa*'s Ghost, Verse 781.

6. *Antandro.* *Antandros*, now *S. Dimitri*, was a City in the *Lesser Phrygia*, at the Foot of Mount *Ida*, where was Plenty of Trees for building a Navy, and at the same Time a convenient Bay, where the Ships could be concealed from the View of the *Greeks*.

7. *Incerti quò fata ferant.* *Æneas* had been plainly told by *Creüsa*'s Ghost that his Settlement was to be in *Italy*, and the Place had been so distinctly marked out, that one is surprized to find him in any Uncertainty about it. Perhaps he did not firmly believe that Vision, or the Impression was begun to wear off from his Mind; the Apprehension of the Danger, and Difficulty of the Voyage, concurring with the then dejected State of his Mind, filled him with anxious and distrustful Thoughts, notwithstanding all the Assurances he had given him of getting safe to *Italy* at length.

8. *Prima æstas.* *Scaliger* computes the Time in which *Troy* was taken to have been towards the

Et pater Anchises dare fatis vela jubebat.
Litora tum patriæ lacrymans portusque relinquo,
Et campos ubi Troja fuit: feror exsul in altum, 11
Cum sociis, natoque, Penatibus, et Magnis Dis.
Terra procul vastis colitur Mavortia campis,
Thraces arant, acri quondam regnata Lycurgo,

et pater Anchises jubebat nos dare vela fatis. Tum ego lacrymans relinquo litora patriæ, portusque, et campos ubi Troja fuit: exul feror in altum, cum sociis, natoque, Penatibus, et Magnis Diis.

Procul, terra Mavortia in vastis campis colitur (Thraces ararunt eam) quondam regnata ab acri Lycurgo,

TRANSLATION.

hoist the Sails, in pursuance of Heaven's Decree. Then, with Sorrow, I leave the Shores and Ports of my native Country, and the Plains where Troy *once* stood: An Exile *forlorn* I launch into the Deep with my Associates, my Son, my Household-gods, and the Great Gods *of my Country*. At a Distance lies a martial Land, *well* peopled throughout its wide extended Plains (the Thracians cultivate *the Soil*), over which in former Times fierce Lycurgus reigned, an ancient hospitable Re-

NOTES.

the End of the Spring, so that *Æneas* set out in the Beginning of the Summer immediately following. *Catrou*, however, insists that *Æneas* could not have got his Fleet ready in so short a Time, and therefore will have *prima æstas* to signify the Beginning of the Spring, *viz.* of the next Year; for he observes that the Ancients divided the Year only into two Seasons, Summer and Winter, which he confirms from Geor. III. 296.

——*Dum mox frondosa reducitur æstas,*

where it is agreed that *æstas* signifies the Spring of the Year. What makes this the more probable, continues he, is that this long Stay of *Æneas* at *Antandros* is taken from History. *Dionysius* of *Halicarnassus* informs us, that he drew together a new Army at that Place (he should have added, and fortified himself on Mount *Ida*), but, not thinking it prudent to engage his harassed Troops, he capitulated on honourable Terms; one of which was, that he should be allowed to depart from *Troas* with his Followers without Molestation, after a certain Time, which he employs in equipping a Fleet.

10. *Lacrymans.* It has been observed already, on the softer Part of *Æneas*'s Character, that the Shedding of Tears is a natural Indication of Humanity and Compassion; I may add, often involuntary and constitutional, and nowise unbecoming a Hero, nor inconsistent with true Fortitude and Greatness of Mind. But there is no Necessity of understanding this Word in its mere literal Sense, as if *Æneas* actually shed Tears upon every Occasion where this Word is applied to him; the Expression, I think, often implies no more than *lugens*, as *Ruæus* justly renders it in this Place; *Æneas* went away mourning, and with a sorrowful Heart, not for his own private and personal Sufferings, his Banishment into distant Climes, but because his Country was now in Ruin and Desolation; he sorrowed at bidding Farewel to those once delightful Plains where *Troy* had stood, but was now no more. *Et campos ubi Troja fuit.*

12. *Et Magnis Dis.* By the Great Gods, *Virgil* probably would have us understand the Images of the *Dii majorum gentium*, viz. *Jupiter*, *Pallas*, *Mercury*, *Apollo*, &c. whose Worship the *Roman* Historians and Poets allege to have been introduced by *Æneas* into *Latium*. Some, however, take the *Magni Dî* to be the same with the *Penates*, who, as *Macrobius* tells us, were denominated Θεοὶ μεγάλοι, *Dii Magni*, *the Great Gods.* See the Note above on Æn. II. 293.

13. *Procul.* It is observed that *procul* signifies sometimes *in View*, as it were *pro oculis*; as in the sixth Eclogue, Verse 16.

Serta procul tantum capiti delapsa jacebant.

And so it may be understood here, for *Thrace* was but at a small Distance from the Port whence *Æneas* set out, only on the other Side of the *Hellespont*. But, because *Æneas* is describing the Country to *Dido*, I am inclined to think that *procul* refers to *Carthage*, where he then was, and therefore to be understood in the common Acceptation.

14. *Lycurgo.* The Son of *Dryas*. This is that King of *Thrace*, who is fabled to have banished *Bacchus* and his Votaries out of his Kingdom;

fuit *antiquum hoſpitium Trojæ, Penateſque* ejus *ſocii* fuerunt noſtris, *dum fortuna fuit* nobis. *Feror huc, et loco prima mœnia* in *curvo litore, ingreſſus iniquis fatis: Fingoque Æneadas nomen de meo nomine. Ferebam ſacra Dionææ matri* meæ, *Diviſque auſpicibus cœptorum operum, mactabamque nitentem taurum in litore ſupero Regi Cœlicolûm. Tumulus forte fuit juxta,* in *quo ſummo erant virgulta cornea, et myrtus horrida denſis haſtilibus. Acceſſi, conatuſque convellere viridem ſylvam ab humo, ut tegerem aras frondentibus ramis, video monſtrum horrendum, et mirabile dictu. Nam guttæ* ex *atro ſanguine liquuntur huic* arbori, *quæ arbos prima vellitur* è *ſolo, radicibus* ejus *ruptis, et maculant terram tabo. Frigidus horror quaſi membra mihi,*

Hoſpitium antiquum Trojæ, ſociique Penates,
Dum fortuna fuit. Feror huc, et litore curvo
Mœnia prima loco, fatis ingreſſus iniquis;
Æneadaſque meo nomen de nomine fingo.
Sacra Dionææ matri, Diviſque, ferebam
Auſpicibus cœptorum operum; ſuperoque nitentem
Cœlicolûm regi mactabam in litore taurum.
Forte fuit juxta tumulus, quo cornea ſummo
Virgulta, et denſis haſtilibus horrida myrtus.
Acceſſi, viridemque ab humo convellere ſylvam
Conatus, ramis tegerem ut frondentibus aras,
Horrendum, et dictu video mirabile monſtrum.
Nam, quæ prima ſolo ruptis radicibus arbos
Vellitur, huic atro liquuntur ſanguine guttæ,
Et terram tabo maculant: mihi frigidus horror

TRANSLATION.

treat for Troy, and whoſe Gods were leagued with ours, while Fortune was with us. Hither I am carried, and found my firſt Walls along the winding Shore, entering *on that Enterprize* with Fates unkind, and from my own Name I call the Citizens Æneades. I was performing ſacred Rites to my Mother Venus, and the Gods, the Patrons of my Works begun, and to the exalted King of the Immortals I was ſacrificing a ſhining Bull on the Shore. * Hard by there chanced to be a riſing Ground, on whoſe Top young Cornel Trees ſhot up their *tender* Twigs, and a Myrtle rough and overgrown with thick Spear-like Branches. I came up to it, and attempting to tear from the Earth the verdant Wood, to cover the Altars with the leafy Boughs, I ſee a dreadful Prodigy, and wonderous to relate. For from that Tree which firſt is torn from the Soil, its rooted Fibres being burſt aſunder, Drops of black Blood diſtil, and ſtain the Ground with Gore:

NOTES.

dom; for which Impiety, the God revenged himſelf upon him, by depriving him of Sight, as it is in Iliad VI. Verſe 130.

15. *Hoſpitium antiquum.* That is to ſay, there had been a long continued League of Friendſhip and Hoſpitality between the two Nations, by virtue of which the *Thracians* gave hoſpitable Reception to all Strangers from *Troy*, and the *Trojans* in their Turn repaid the Kindneſs and Civilities to the *Thracians*. This Hoſpitality was ſometimes between whole Nations, ſometimes from one City to another, and ſometimes between particular Families.

15. *Sociique Penates.* There was ſo ſtrict an Alliance between the two Nations, that *Servius* tells us, *Polymneſtor*, King of *Thrace*, married *Ilione*, *Priam*'s Daughter.

18. *Æneadas.* The City is called *Ænos* by *Mela* and *Pliny*, and the latter tells us that the Tomb of *Polydore* is near that City.

19. *Dionææ matri.* *Venus*, ſo called from her Mother *Dione*.

21. *Taurum.* *Servius* and *Macrobius* will have it, that a Bull was one of thoſe Animals that were prohibited to be offered to *Jove* in Sacrifice, and that *Virgil* deſignedly makes *Æneas* to have offered here an unwarranted Sacrifice to *Jupiter*, to make way for the inauſpicious Omen that followed it. But *La Cerda* proves, from the beſt Authority, that nothing was more common than to ſacrifice Bulls to *Jupiter*, as well as to the other Gods.

23. *Haſtilibus.* The long tapering Branches of the Tree are properly termed *Haſtilia, Spears*; but

Membra quatit, gelidusque coit formidine ſanguis.
Rurſus et alterius lentum convellere vimen
Inſequor, et cauſas penitus tentare latentes:
Ater et alterius ſequitur de cortice ſanguis.
Multa movens animo, Nymphas venerabar agreſtes,
Gradivumque patrem, Geticis qui præſidet arvis;
Rite ſecundarent viſus, omenque levarent.
Tertia ſed poſtquam majore haſtilia niſu
Aggredior, genibuſque adverſæ obluctor arenæ;
(Eloquar, an ſileam?) gemitus lacrymabilis imo
Auditur tumulo, et vox reddita fertur ad aures:
Quid miſerum, Ænea, laceras? jam parce ſepulto,

gelidusque ſanguis coit præ formidine. Rurſus inſequor et convellere lentum vimen alterius, et penitus tentare cauſas latentes; et ater ſanguis ſequitur de cortice alterius. Ego movens multa in animo, venerabar Nymphas agreſtes, patremque Gradivum qui præſidet Geticis arvis, ut rite ſecundarent viſus, levarentque omen. Sed poſtquam aggredior tertia haſtilia majore niſu, genibuſque obluctor adverſæ arenæ (eloquar ne an ſileam?) lacrymabilis gemitus auditur ex imo tumulo, et vox reddita fertur ad meas *aures: O Ænea, quid laceras* me *miſerum? parce* mihi *jam ſepulto,*

TRANSLATION.

Shivering Horror ſhakes my Limbs, and my chill Blood is congealed with Fear. I again aſſay to tear off a limber Bough from another, and thoroughly explore the latent Cauſe: And from the Rind of that other the purple Blood deſcends. Raiſing in my mind many an anxious Thought, I with Reverence beſought the rural Nymphs, and Father Mars, who preſides over the Thracian Territories, to ſecond the Viſion in due Form, and give a favourable Tern to the Omen. But after that I attempt the Boughs a third Time with a more vigorous Effort, and on my Knees ſtruggle againſt the oppoſing Mold; ſhall I ſpeak, or ſhall I forbear? A piteous Groan is heard from the Bottom of the riſing Ground, and a Voice ſent forth reaches my Ears: Æneas, why doſt thou tear an unhappy Wretch?

NOTES.

but the Word has a peculiar Propriety here, as it alludes to the Spears and Darts with which *Polydore* had been transfixed, which grew up into thoſe Trees.

35. *Gradivum patrem.* *Gradivus*, we are told, is a Name that expreſſed *Mars* in Time of War, as *Quirinus* did in Time of Peace. Critics are not agreed as to the Derivation of the Word; ſome giving it a *Greek* Etymology, from κραδαινω, *to brandiſh*; while others bring it from the *Latin*, *gradus*, or *gradior*, *an advance*, *to advance*, or take the Field.

35. *Geticis arvis.* The *Getes* were a People inhabiting that Part of *Dacia* which is now called *Moldavia*; their Neighbourhood to *Thrace* is the Reaſon why that Country is here called *arva Getica*, *the Lands of the* Getes.

35. *Nymphas venerabar—Gradivumque patrem.* The reaſon, why *Æneas* addreſſed his Worſhip on this Occaſion to *Mars*, the Poet himſelf gives us, becauſe it was he *Geticis qui præſidet arvis*, who preſided over the Country: He was the God whom the *Thracians* and theſe other warlike Nations chiefly worſhipped in ancient Times. By the Nymphs again, whom he prays to in Conjunction with *Mars*, we are probably to underſtand the *Hamadryads*, a Sort of rural Goddeſſes, whoſe Deſtiny was connected with that of ſome particular Trees, with which they lived and died. So that *Æneas* might conſider this horrid Omen, as an Indication of their Diſpleaſure, for his offering to violate thoſe Pledges of their Exiſtence.

36. *Secundarent viſus.* In the ancient Rights of Divination, two Omens were required for Confirmation; and though the firſt had been unlucky, yet, if the ſecond was proſperous, it deſtroyed the firſt, and was termed *omen ſecundum*; if otherwiſe, *alterum*: And hence *ſecundus* came to ſignify *proſperous*, and *ſecundo*, *to proſper*.

41. *Jam parce ſepulto.* It was a Law of the twelve Tables, and, indeed, is the common

Voice

parce ſcelerare tuas pias manus: Troja tulit me, non externum tibi: hic cruor non manat de ſtipite. Heu fuge terras crudeles, fuge littus avarum. Nam ego ſum Polydorus; ferrea ſeges telorum texit me confixum hìc, et increvit acutis jaculis. Tum verò, preſſus quoad mentem ancipiti formidine, obſtupui, comæque ſteterunt, et vox hæſit faucibus. Quondam infelix Priamus furtim mandarat hunc Polydorum alendum Threicio Regi, cum magno pondere auri; cum jam diffideret armis Dardaniæ, videretque urbem cingi obſidione. Ille rex, at opes Teucrûm ſunt fractæ, et fortuna receſſit, ſecutus res Agamemnonias, armaque victricia, abrumpit omne fas, obtruncat Polydorum, et potitur auro vi.

Parce pias ſcelerare manus: non me tibi Troja
Externum tulit; aut cruor hic de ſtipite manat.
Heu fuge crudeles terras, fuge littus avarum:
Nam Polydorus ego: hic confixum ferrea texit
Telorum ſeges, et jaculis increvit acutis.
Tum verò, ancipiti mentem formidine preſſus,
Obſtupui; ſteteruntque comæ, et vox faucibus hæſit.
Hunc Polydorum auri quondam cum pondere magno
Infelix Priamus furtim mandârat alendum
Threïcio regi; cum jam diffideret armis
Dardaniæ, cingique urbem obſidione videret.
Ille, ut opes fractæ Teucrûm, et fortuna receſſit,
Res Agamemnonias, victriciaque arma ſecutus,
Fas omne abrumpit, Polydorum obtruncat, et auro

TRANSLATION.

Spare me now that I am in my Grave; forbear to pollute with Guilt thy pious Hands: Troy brought me forth no Stranger to you: Nor is it from the *dead* Trunk this Blood diſtils. Ah, fly this barbarous Land, fly the avaricious Shore! For *the unhappy* Polydorus am I: Here an Iron Crop of Darts hath overwhelmed me, transfixed, and over me ſhot up in pointed Javelins. Then, indeed, inly depreſſed with perplexing Fear, I was ſtunned, my Hair ſtood on End, and my Voice clung to my Jaws. This Polydorus unhappy Priam had formerly ſent in Secrecy with large Sums of Money to be brought up by the King of Thrace, what Time he began to be diffident of the Arms of Troy, and ſaw the City with cloſe Siege blocked up. He *(the King of Thrace)*, ſo ſoon as the Power of the Trojans was cruſhed, and their Fortune gone, eſpouſing Agamemnon's Intereſt and victorious Arms, breaks every ſacred Bond, aſſaſſinates Polydorus, and by

NOTES.

Voice of Humanity, *Defuncti injuria ne afficiantur, Let no Injury be offered to the Dead.* Therefore *Polydore*'s Ghoſt calls out to *Æneas, Parce jam ſepulto,* as if he had ſaid, *Let it ſuffice that I ſuffered ſo much while alive*; leave me now at leaſt to enjoy Reſt in my Grave.

42. *Non Troja externum tulit.* *Polydore* was the Son of *Priam*, and *Creüsa*'s Brother, and conſequently allied to *Æneas*, his Fellow-citizen, and not an Alien or Foreigner, which is the Meaning of *externus*. *Cicero* makes *Polydore* not *Priam*'s Son, but his Grandchild by his Daughter *Ilione*, who was married to *Polymneſtor*, King of *Thrace*.

54. *Agamemnonias.* *Agamemnon*, the Son of *Atreus*, King of *Mycenæ*, and Brother to *Menelaus*, was choſen General of the Confederate Troops of *Greece* in the *Trojan* Expedition. After the Deſtruction of *Troy* he returned to *Mycenæ* with his Captive *Caſſandra*, *Priam*'s Daughter, and was aſſaſſinated with her at a Banquet, by the Treachery of his wife *Clytemneſtra*, and his Nephew *Ægiſthus*, her adulterous Paramour.

55. *Fas omne abrumpit.* *Polymneſtor*, by murdering *Polydore*, broke through both the Ties of Conſanguinity and Hoſpitality, which were held ſo ſacred, that he who violated them, by putting his Gueſt to Death, was reckoned equally guilty with a Parricide.

Vi potitur. Quid non mortalia pectora cogis
Auri ſacra fames! poſtquam pavor oſſa reliquit,
Delectos populi ad proceres, primumque parentem,
Monſtra Deûm refero; et, quæ ſit ſententia, poſco.
Omnibus idem animus ſceleratâ excedere terrâ,
Linquere pollutum hoſpitium, et dare claſſibus Auſtros.
Ergo inſtauramus Polydoro funus, et ingens
Aggeritur tumulo tellus: ſtant Manibus aræ,
Cæruleis mœſtæ vittis atrâque cupreſſo;
Et circum Iliades crinem de more ſolutæ.
Inferimus tepido ſpumantia cymbia lacte,

O ſacra fames auri, quid non cogis mortalia pectora perpetrare! poſtquam pavor reliquit oſſa mihi, refero monſtra Deûm ad delectos proceres populi primumque ad parentem; et poſco quæ ſit eorum ſententia. Idem animus eſt omnibus excedere ſceleratâ terrâ, linquere pollutum hoſpitium, et dare Auſtros claſſibus. Ergo inſtauramus funus Polydoro, et ingens tellus aggeritur tumulo: aræ ſtant Manibus, mœſtæ cæruleis vittis atrâque cupreſſo; et Iliades ſolutæ quoad crinem, de more, ſtant circum. Inferimus ſpumantia cymbia è tepido lacte,

TRANSLATION.

Violence poſſeſſes his Money. Curſed Avarice, on what *deſperate Wickedneſs* thy Influence drives the Minds of Men! After my quaking Fear was gone, I report the portentous Signs of the Gods to our choſen Leaders, and chiefly to my Father, and demand what their Reſolution is. All are unanimous to quit that curſed Land, abandon the polluted Society, and ſpread the Sails to the Winds. Therefore we ſet about the Renewal of Polydorus's Funeral Obſequies, and raiſe a large Mound of Earth for the Tomb: An Altar is reared to his Manes, mournfully decked with leaden-coloured Wreaths, and black baleful Cypreſs; and round it the Trojan Matrons ſtand with Hair diſhevelled according to Cuſtom. We *next* offer the Sacrifices of the Dead, Bowls foaming with warm Milk, and Goblets of

NOTES.

57. *Sacra fames.* *Sacer* ſignifies either *ſacred* or *accurſed* as here. The Reaſon of which ſee in a former Note on Æn. I. 632.

57. *Quid non mortalia pectora cogis, auri ſacra fames!* The ſame Sentiment is more fully expreſſed by *Juvenal*, Satire XIV. Verſe 173.

Inde fere ſcelerum cauſæ, nec plura venena
Miſcuit, aut ferro graſſatur ſæpius ullum
Humanæ mentis vitium, quam ſæva cupido
Indomiti cenſus.

62. *Inſtauramus funus.* We renew his Funeral Obſequies, becauſe he had been buried before without the due Solemnities; the performing of which was reckoned ſo indiſpenſable a Duty, that they were therefore called by the *Romans Juſta*, and by the *Greeks* [illegible]. *Virgil* here gives a very particular and full Deſcription of the Funeral Rites performed by the *Romans* in the Interment of the Dead.

63. *Stant Manibus aræ.* It appears that two Altars were conſecrated to the Manes, and two to the Gods, as we learn from Verſe 305, where it is ſaid of *Andromache*,

Et geminas, cauſam lacrymis, ſacraverat aras.

She had conſecrated to *Hector*'s Shade two Altars. So Ecl. V. 66.

——— en quatuor aras;
Ecce duas tibi, Daphni, duoque altaria Phœbo.

64. *Cæruleis vittis.* Theſe Fillets were of a deep violet or purple Colour; a Colour between blue and black, which is that of *cæruleus*.

66. *Inferimus.* Among other Ceremonies, there were Sacrifices offered to the Dead, which were termed *Inferiæ*, from this very Word here uſed *infero, to pour into, or on the Grave.* The Liquors were Milk, and the Blood of the Victims, as here: And ſometimes Wine was added, as Æn. V. 77.

Hic duo rite mero libans carcheſia Baccho
Fundit humi, duo lacte novo, duo ſanguine ſacro.

et pateras ſacri ſanguinis, condimuſque animam ſepulcro, et ſupremùm ciemus magnâ voce.

Inde, ubi prima fides fuit pelago, ventique dant maria placata, et Auſter lenis crepitans vocat nos in altum, ſocii deducunt naves, et complent littora. Provehimur è portu, terræque urbeſque recedunt.

Gratiſſima tellus, ſacra matri Nereidum, et Ægæo Neptuno, colitur in medio mari, quam, errantem circum oras et littora, pius Arcitenens

Sanguinis et ſacri pateras; animamque ſepulcro
Condimus, et magnâ ſupremùm voce ciemus.
Inde, ubi prima fides pelago, placataque venti
Dant maria, et lenis crepitans vocat Auſter in altum,
Deducunt ſocii naves, et littora complent.
Provehimur portu, terræque urbeſque recedunt.
Sacra mari colitur medio gratiſſima tellus
Nereidum matri, et Neptuno Ægæo:
Quam pius Arcitenens, oras et littora circum

TRANSLATION.

the ſacred Blood *of the Victim: Thus* we give the Soul Repoſe in the Grave, and with loud Voice addreſs to him the laſt Farewel. This done, when firſt we durſt confide in the Main, when *the favouring* Winds indulge us with peaceful Seas, and the South-wind in ſoft whiſpering Gales invites us to the Deep, my Mates launch the Ships, and crowd the Shore. We are wafted from the Port, and the Lands and Citie *in Proſpect* retreat. Amidſt the Sea there lies a charming Spot of Land, ſacred to *Doris*, the Mother of the Nereids, and Ægean Neptune, which *once* unfixed, and floating about the Coaſts and Shores, the pious *God* who wields

NOTES.

67. *Animamque ſepulcro condimus.* Becauſe it was a prevailing Opinion among both *Greeks* and *Romans*, that the Soul could not reſt without Burial. For which Reaſon they were ſo anxious about Funeral Rites. Hence, by the bye, *conditorium* came to ſignify a *Burial-place*

68. *Magnâ ſupremùm voce ciemus.* Both to call the Soul to its Place of Reſt, and to take their laſt Farewel, by pronouncing *Vale* three Times aloud.

73. *Sacra mari, &c.* This is the Iſland of *Delos*, one of the *Cyclades*, concerning which it is fabled, that when *Juno*, enraged againſt *Jupiter* for loving *Latona*, ſwore that *Latona* ſhould not have a Spot on Earth to bring forth in; *Jupiter*, to ſecure to her ſome Place out of *Juno's* Reach, directed her to *Delos*, which was then a floating Iſland, till *Apollo* fixed it after his Mother's Delivery; and therefore its Name was changed from *Ortygia* to *Delos*, which in the *Greek* Language ſignifies *apparent*, or *revealed to View*, it having been hid before under the Waves; or, according to others, becauſe *Apollo* there gave forth Oracles plain and intelligible, but every where elſe in dark and obſcure Terms.

74. *Nereidum matri. Doris*, the Wife of *Nereus*, and Mother of the fifty *Nereids* or *Sea-nymphs*.

74. *Neptuno Ægæo.* Becauſe *Delos* is in the *Ægean* Sea, now the *Archipelago*, called the *Ægean* Sea, from *Ægeus*, the Father of *Theſeus*, who threw himſelf into it, haſtily preſuming that his Son, who had undertaken to combat the famous *Minotaur*, was ſlain. The Story is this: It was agreed between the Father and the Son, that, if *Theſeus* ſubdued that Monſter, he ſhould, at his Return, put up a white Flag or white Sails; but if he failed in his Attempt, and was ſlain, the Ship ſhould return with black Sails. But *Theſeus*, returning victorious, forgot to hang out the white Sails, through Grief, as it is ſaid, for the Loſs of his beloved *Ariadne*, whom *Bacchus* raviſhed from him. The Father, who was expecting him with Impatience from the Top of a high Rock, no ſooner ſaw the Ship all in Mourning, than he threw himſelf into the Sea, imagining his Son was dead.

75. *Quam pius Arcitenens. Apollo*, ſo ſoon as he was born, ſlew with his Arrows the Serpent *Python*, ſent by *Juno* to deſtroy *Latona*. Whence he is ſtiled *Pius Arcitenens, the pious God who wields the Bow.* Thoſe who are not pleaſed with this Senſe of the Epithet *pius*, as applied to *Apollo*, may read *prius*, to agree with *errantem*, which *Pierius* aſſures us is the Reading in ſome ancient Copies.

76. *Mycone*

Errantem, Mycone celsâ Gyaroque revinxit,
Immotamque coli dedit, et contemnere ventos.
Huc feror: hæc fessos tuto placidissima portu
Accipit: egressi veneramur Apollinis urbem.
Rex Anius, rex idem hominum, Phœbique sacerdos,
Vittis et sacrâ redimitus tempora lauro,
Occurrit: veterem Anchisen agnoscit amicum.
Jungimus hospitio dextras, et tecta subimus.
Templa Dei saxo venerabar structa vetusto:
Da propriam, Thymbræe, domum; da mœnia fessis,
Et genus, et mansuram urbem; serva altera Trojæ
Pergama relliquias Danaûm atque immitis Achillei.

revinxit celsâ Mycone Gyaroque, deditque coli immotam, et contemnere ventos. Huc feror: hæc placidissima accipit nos fessos in tuto portu: egressi veneramur urbem Apollinis. Rex Anius, idem rex hominum sacerdosque Phœbi, redimitus quoad tempora vittis et sacrâ lauro, occurrit nobis; agnoscit veterem suum amicum Anchisen. Jungimus dextras hospitio, et subimus tecta. Venerabar templa Dei structa ex vetusto saxo: O Thymbræe, da propriam domum, da mœnia nobis fessis, et genus, et urbem mansuram; serva altera Pergama Trojæ, relliquias Danaûm atque immitis Achillei.

TRANSLATION.

the Bow, fast bound with high Gyaros and Mycone, and fixed it so as to be habitable, and mock the *insulting* Winds. Hither I am led: This most peaceful Island receives us into a safe Port after our Fatigue. At *our first* Landing, we pay Veneration to the City of *Apollo*. King Anius, who was both King of Men and Priest of Phœbus, his Temples bound with Fillets and sacred Laurel, comes up, and presently recollects his old Friend Anchises. We join Right-hands in Amity, and come under his *hospitable* Roof. I venerated the Temple of the God, a Structure of ancient Stone, *and thus began:* Thymbræan *Apollo*, grant us, after all our Toils, some fixed Mansion; grant us Walls of Defence, *a happy* Offspring, and permanent City: Preserve these other Towers of Troy, a Remnant *escaped from* the Greeks and mercilefs Achilles. Whom are we to follow? Or whither

NOTES.

76. *Mycone celsâ Gyaroque revinxit. Mycone* and *Gyaros* are two of the *Cyclades* Islands on either Side of *Delos*, which hem it in, and seem, as it were, to bind it fast that it cannot move out of its Place; which Situation had given Rise to the Poetical Fiction. *Gyaros* is the little Island to which the *Romans* used to banish their Felons and greater Malefactors. Hence that Expression in *Juvenal*, Sat. I. 73.

Aude aliquid brevibus Gyaris aut carcere dignum.

77. *Contemnere ventos.* Because formerly it is said to have been often driven about by the Winds, and drowned beneath the Waves.

80. *Rex Anius.* According to the ancient Custom established in several Nations, whereby the Offices of King and Priest were invested in the same Person.

84. *Saxo vetusto.* Because, whatever Injuries the other Buildings of the Island had suffered, the Sanctity of the Temple still preserved it from Violation. Hence, says *Cicero*, in his Pleadings against *Verres*, to set forth the horrid Nature of his Sacrilege in rifling the Temple of *Delos*: *Tanta ejus auctoritas religionis et est, et semper fuit, ut ne Persæ quidem, cum bellum toti Græciæ, diis, hominibusque indixissent, et — classem ad Delum appulissent, quidquam conarentur aut violare aut attingere.* In Verr. 18.

84. *Venerabar.* It appears from ancient Monuments, that the Altar of *Apollo* at *Delos* was never stained with the Blood of Victims, but only honoured with Prayers, Flowers, and other simple Rites of ancient Worship. Therefore *Æneas* says only, *venerabar, I offered up Prayers.*

85. *Thymbræe.* We learn from *Strabo*, that in the Confines of *Troy* there was a Plain named *Thymbra* (from the vast Plenty of the Herb *Thymbra* or Savory, says *Servius*, which grew there),

Quem sequimur? quòve jubes nos ire? ubi jubes nos ponere sedes? O pater, da nobis augurium, atque illabere nostris animis. Vix fatus eram ea, omnia repente visa sunt tremere, liminaque, laurusque Dei; totusque mons circum visus est moveri, et cortina mugire, adytis reclusis. Nos *submissi petimus terram, et vox fertur ad aures* nostras: *O Dardanidæ duri, eadem tellus, quæ prima tulit vos à stirpe parentum, accipiet vos reduces læto ubere: exquirite* vestram *antiquam matrem. Hic domus Æneæ dominabitur cunctis oris, et nati* illius *natorum, et qui nascentur ab illis.*

Quem sequimur? quòve ire jubes? ubi ponere sedes?
Da, pater, augurium, atque animis illabere nostris.
Vix ea fatus eram, temere omnia visa repente,
Liminaque, laurusque Dei; totusque moveri
Mons circùm, et mugire adytis cortina reclusis.
Submissi petimus terram, et vox fertur ad aures:
Dardanidæ duri, quæ vos à stirpe parentum
Prima tulit tellus, eadem vos ubere læto
Accipiet reduces: antiquam exquirite matrem.
Hìc domus Æneæ cunctis dominabitur oris,
Et nati natorum, et qui nascentur ab illis.

TRANSLATION.

commandest thou us to go? Where to fix our Residence? *Holy* Father, grant us a prophetic Sign, and glide into our Minds. Scarce had I thus said, *when* suddenly all seemed to tremble, both the Temple itself, and Laurel of the God; the whole Mountain quaked around, and, the Sanctuary being exposed to View, the Place of the Oracle groaned. In humble Reverence we fall to the Ground, and a Voice reaches our Ears: Ye hardy Sons of Dardanus, that Land which first produced you from your Forefathers Stock, the same shall receive you in its fertile Bosom after all your Dangers past: Search out your ancient Mother. There the Family of Æneas shall rule over every Coast, and his Childrens Children, and who from them shall spring. Thus Phœbus. Vast emotions of Joy, with

NOTES.

there), where was a Temple to *Apollo*, thence stiled *Thymbræan*.

91. *Liminaque, laurusque Dei.* It was usual for the Gods to give Signs of their Approach, by making the Earth to quake. The *Laurel* was probably in the Temple itself, as it was at *Delphos*, whence the Oracle was sometimes delivered, according to that Verse of *Lucretius*, Lib. I. 740.

> *Pythia quæ tripode ex Phœbi, lauroque profatur.*

9[illegible]. *M[illegible]circùm.* The Mount here spoken of [illegible] *Cynthus*, whence *Apollo* and *Diana* were den[illegible]ted *Cynthius* and *Cynthia*.

92. *Cortina.* The Covering of the Tripod, where the Priestess delivered the Oracle, was called *Cortina*, it is here put for the Oracle itself.

92. *Adytis.* The *adyta* again is the Sanctuary or inner Part of the Temple, where was the Oracle.

94. *Dardanidæ.* *Servius* and *Macrobius* observe, that the *Trojans* might have understood from this the Meaning of the Oracle; for by calling them *Dardanidæ*, and not *Teucri*, they might have known that *Italy* was designed, whence their Ancestor *Dardanus* came, and not *Crete*, the Seat of *Teucer*'s Nativity.

97. *Hic domus Æneæ.* These two Verses are almost a literal Translation of *Neptune*'s Prophecy concerning *Æneas* in the Iliad, Lib. XX. Verse 307.

> Νυν δε δη Αινειαο βιη Τρωεσσιν αναξει,
> Και παιδες παιδων, τοι κεν μετοπισθε γενωνται.

> *On great Æneas shall devolve the Reign,*
> *And Sons, succeeding Sons, the lasting Line sustain.* Mr. Pope.

From which Passage of *Homer*, however, it is inferred, that *Æneas* came not into *Italy*, but remained in *Troas*, and succeeded to the Crown of *Troy* after *Priam*, it being here said, Τρωεσσιν αναξει, *he shall reign over the* Trojans; and consequently, that this whole Account of the Original of the *Roman* Empire is a Fiction, contrived to do Honour to the *Romans*, and particularly to flatter the Vanity of *Augustus*. *Dionysius*

Hæc Phœbus: miſtoque ingens exorta tumultu
Lætitia; et cuncti quæ ſint ea mœnia quærunt;
Quò Phœbus vocet errantes, jubeatque reverti.
Tum Genitor, veterum volvens monumenta virorum,
Audite, o proceres, ait, et ſpes diſcite veſtras:
Creta Jovis magni medio jacet inſula ponto,
Mons Idæus ubi, et gentis cunabula noſtræ:
Centum urbes habitant magnas, uberrima regna:
Maximus unde pater, ſi rite audita recordor,
Teucrus Rhœteas primùm eſt advectus in oras,

Phœbus fatus eſt hæc: ingenſque lætitia exorta eſt miſto tumultu; et cuncti quærunt quæ ſint ea mœnia, quo Phœbus voce errantes, jubeatque eos reverti. Tum Genitor meus, volvens monumenta veterum virorum, ait, O proceres audite, et diſcite veſtras ſpes: Creta inſula magni Jovis jacet in medio ponto, ubi eſt mons Idæus, et cunabula noſtræ gentis: Habitant centum magnas urbes, regna uberrima: Unde Teucrus maximus pater, ſi rite recorder audita, primùm eſt advectus in Rhœteas oras,

TRANSLATION.

mingled Tumult, aroſe, and all are anxious to know what City is deſigned; whither Phœbus calls a wandering Crew, and wills *them* to return. Then my Father, revolving the hiſtorical Records of the Ancients, ſays, Ye *Trojan* Leaders give Ear, and learn what you have to hope for: In the Middle of the Sea lies Crete, the Iſland of mighty Jove, where is Mount Ida, and the Nurſery of our Race. The Cretans inhabit an hundred mighty Cities, *all* moſt fertile Realms: whence our renowned Anceſtor Teucrus, if I right remember the Tradition, firſt arrived on the Rhœtean Coaſts, and *there* choſe the Seat of his Kingdom. No

NOTES.

ſius of Halicarnaſſus, indeed, propoſes a very ingenius Solution of the Difficulty, alleging the Prophecy to be fully accompliſhed in *Æneas*'s reigning over the *Trojans* in *Italy*; and in this he is followed by *Euſtathius*, in his Commentary on that Paſſage of the Iliad. But thoſe, who are curious to ſee this Queſtion fully examined, may conſult *Segrais*'s Preface to his Tranſlation of the Æneid, and *Bochart*'s Diſſertation in a Letter to him on that Subject, which is publiſhed at the End of *Segrais*'s Notes on the *Octavo* Edition. I ſhall only obſerve farther, that *Virgil*, inſtead of *Trojanis dominabitur*, anſwering to Τρωεσσιν ανάξει in *Homer*, renders it, *cunctis dominabitur oris*, which is probably the Reaſon why ſome have ſubſtituted in *Homer* παντεσσιν *omnibus*, inſtead of Τρωεσσιν *Trojanis*.

104. *Creta Jovis magni.* The Iſland of *Candia*, in the *Mediterranean*, denominated *Crete*, from *Cres*, who reigned there after *Jupiter*. It is ſituated between the *Archipelago* northward, and the *Libyan* Sea to the South. There *Jupiter* was brought up in a Cave of Mount *Dictys*:

Dictæo cœli regem pavere ſub antro.
Geor. IV. 152.

His Mother *Rhea* carried him thither from *Arcadia*, or *Phrygia*, to ſave him from his Father *Saturn*, who ſought to deſtroy him. In the ſame Iſland he died at the Age of eighty Years, according to *Suidas*. The *Cretans* ſhew his Tomb in the City of *Gnoſſus*.

104. *Medio Ponto.* Becauſe, as *Servius* and *Strabo* obſerve, it is ſituated between ſeveral Seas, the *Libyan*, the *Ægyptian*, the *Achaian*, and *Ionian*; that it is hard to ſay to which of them it belongs.

105. *Mons Idæus ubi.* All acknowledge a Mount *Ida* in *Crete*, particularly *Pliny*, Lib. IV. Cap. 12. *Montes, Cadiſtus, Idæus, Dictæus, Corycus.*

109. *Centum urbes habitant.* Hence *Homer*, in the Iliad, gives *Crete* the Appellation of ἑκατόμπολις, Il. IX. Verſe 649. And *Horace*, Lib. III. Ode 27.

Quæ ſimul centum tetigit potentem oppidis Creten.

As alſo in his Epod. Ode 10.

Cretam centum urbibus nobilem.

The chief of thoſe Cities were *Gnoſſus*, *Gortyna*, *Cydon*, and *Dictymna*.

106. *Uberrima regna.* Anſwering to *ubere læto*, another Circumſtance in the Prophecy, which fixed *Anchiſes*

108. *Teucrus Rhœteas.* *Teucrus*, the Son of

Scamander

optavitque locum regno: Ilium et arces Pergameæ nondum steterant, habitabant in imis vallibus. Hinc venit mater Cybele cultrix terræ, Corybantiaque æra, Idæumque nemus: hinc venere fida silentia in sacris, et hinc juncti leones subiere currum dominæ.

Optavitque locum regno: nondum Ilium, et arces
Pergameæ steterant; habitabant vallibus imis:
Hinc mater cultrix Cybele, Corybantiaque æra, 111
Idæumque nemus: hinc fida silentia sacris,
Et juncti currum dominæ subiere leones.

TRANSLATION.

Ilium then nor Towers of Pergamus were raised; in humble Vales they dwelt. Hence *came* Mother Cybele, our Patroness, and the brazen Cymbals of the Corybantes, and the Idæan Grove: Hence that faithful Secrecy *observed* in her sacred Rites, and *hence the Custom* of yoking harnessed Lions in the Chariot of the imperial *Goddess*. Come then, and, where the Commands of the Gods point

NOTES.

Scamander the *Cretan*, is said, in Time of a Famine, to have left the Island with one Third of the Inhabitants in quest of a new Settlement; and, being warned by an Oracle to fix his Residence where he should be attacked in the Night-time by an Earth-born Race, he came to *Phrygia* near *Rhœteum*, a Promontory of *Troas*, in the *Hellespont*, and there being pestered by Swarms of Mice, he took up his Settlement, and built a Temple to *Apollo Smintheus*, so called from σμινθος, which, in the *Phrygian* or *Cretan* Language, signifies *a Mouse*.

108. *Rhœteas.* *Rhœteum* was a City and Promontory of *Troas*, on the Coast of the *Hellespont*, where *Teucer* with his Colony arrived from *Crete*. He introduced thither the Worship of *Cybele*, the Mother of the Gods, and gave to the Mountains of *Phrygia* the Name of *Ida*, from Mount *Ida* in *Crete*, and changed the Name of the River *Xanthus* into that of *Scamander*, after the Name of his Father. Hence *Homer* says that River was called *Xanthus* by the Gods, but *Scamander* by Men. *i. e.* the former was its ancient and more venerable Name.

109. *Optavitque locum regno.* *Strabo* agrees with *Virgil* in making *Teucer* the first who reigned in *Troas*: Not long after him *Dardanus* arrived from *Italy*, married *Batea*, *Teucer*'s Daughter, and succeeded him in the Kingdom.

111. *Mater cultrix Cybele.* Some read *matris cultri Cybeles*, alluding to the Custom of making the Priests of *Cybele* Eunuchs. This Goddess, who is the same with *Ops* and *Rhea*, was called *Cybele*, probably from *Cybelus*, a Mountain in *Phrygia*, where she was particularly worshipped. Her Ministers were termed *Corybantes*, and, among other Circumstances practised in her Worship, used to beat brazen Cymbals; the Original of which Institution, they tell us, was to hinder *Saturn*, by their Noise, from hearing the Cries of the Infant *Jupiter*, when he lay concealed in the Caves of *Dictys* in *Crete*.

111. *Mater Cybele.* *Cybele*, according to *Strabo* and *Lucretius*, denotes the *Earth*, which is the common Mother of Men and Beasts:

Principio tellus habet in se corpora prima
Quare magna Deûm mater, materque ferarum,
Et nostri genitrix hæc dicta est corporis una.
Lucret. II. 589.

And *Macrobius* speaks of it as a Thing which no Body could call in Question:

Quis enim ambigat matrem Deûm terram haberi?
Sat. I. 21.

112. *Hinc fida silentia sacris.* The Mysteries of *Cybele*, as those of *Ceres*, were concealed with great Care from the Vulgar, to make them the more regarded.

113. *Et juncti, &c.* Her Chariot was drawn by Lions, to denote that maternal Affection, figured by *Cybele* or Mother *Earth*, triumphs over the most ferocious Natures, as *Lucretius* explains it:

Adjunxere feras, quod quamvis effera proles
Officiis debet molliri victa parentum.
Lib. II. 604.

And *Ovid*, 4 Fast.

———— cur huic genus acre leonum
Præbet insolitas ad juga curva jubas.
Nimirum feritas quoniam mollita per illam
Creditur: id curru testificata suo est.

113. *Dominæ.* This is an Epithet belongs to *Cybele*, as Mother of the Gods.

118. *Meritos*

Ergo agite, et Divûm, ducunt quà juſſa, ſequamur :
Placemus ventos, et Gnoſſia regna petamus :
Nec longo diſtant curſu ; modò Jupiter adſit,
Tertia lux claſſem Cretæis ſiſtet in oris.
Sic fatus, meritos aris mactavit honores,
Taurum Neptuno, taurum tibi, pulcher Apollo ;
Nigram Hiemi pecudem, Zephyris felicibus albam.
Fama volat, pulſum regnis ceſſiſſe paternis
Idomenea ducem, deſertaque littora Cretæ ;
Hoſte vacare domos, ſedeſque aſtare relictas.
Linquimus Ortygiæ portus, pelagoque volamus :
Bacchatamque jugis Naxon, viridemque Donyſam,
Olearon, niveamque Paron, ſparſaſque per æquor
Cycladas, et crebris legimus freta conſita terris.

Ergo agite, et ſequamur quà juſſa Divûm ducunt : Placemus ventos, et petamus Gnoſſia regna : Nec diſtant longo curſu ; ſi modò Jupiter adſit, tertia lux ſiſtet noſtram claſſem in Cretæis oris.

Sic fatus mactavit meritos honores aris, mactavit taurum Neptuno, taurum tibi, o pulcher Apollo ; nigram pecudem Hyemi, albam pecudem felicibus Zephyris. Fama volat Idomenea ducem pulſum ceſſiſſe paternis regnis, littoraque Cretæ eſſe deſerta, domos vacare hoſte, ſedeſque aſtare relictas. Linquimus portus Ortygiæ, volamuſque ſuper pelago : legimuſque Naxon bacchatam jugis, viridemque Donyſam, Olearon, niveamque Paron, Cycladaſque ſparſas per æquor, et freta conſita crebris terris.

TRANSLATION.

out our Way, let us follow : Let us appeaſe the Winds, and make for the Gnoſſian Realms. Nor lie they at the Diſtance of a long Voyage : Provided Jove be with us, the third Day will land our Fleet on the Cretan Coaſt. This ſaid, he offered the proper Sacrifices on the Altars, a Bull to Neptune, a Bull to thee, *O* graceful Apollo ; a black Sheep to the wintery Power, and a white one to the propitious Zephyrs. A Report flies abroad, that Idomeneus, the *Cretan* Leader, baniſhed *by his Subjects*, hath quitted his paternal Kingdom, and that the Shore of Crete is *now* naked of Defence ; its Manſions emptied of *our* Foe, and forſaken Palaces ſtand *open to receive us.* We leave the Port of Ortygia, and ſcud along the Sea : We cruize along Naxos, on whoſe Mountains the Bacchanals revel, green Donyſa, Olearos, ſnowy Paros, and the Cyclades ſcattered up and down the Main, and narrow Seas thick ſown with cluſtered Iſlands. With various

NOTES.

118. *Meritos mactavit honores. Honores* ſignifies *Sacrifices*, as has been obſerved in a former Note. See Æn. I. 636.

120. *Nigram hyemi.* By *hyems* here we are to underſtand the ſtormy Winds, as Æn. V. 772.

——————— *tempeſtatibus agnum*
Cædere deinde jubet.

They were worſhipped in order to avert their Fury, as the Zephyrs were to procure their auſpicious Influence.

122. *Idomenea. Idomeneus*, the Son of *Deucalion*, and Grandſon of *Minos* King of *Crete*, in his Return from the *Trojan* War, being overtaken with a Storm, made a Vow to the Gods, that, if they would ſave him in his extreme Danger, he would ſacrifice to them whatever Thing he firſt met : This happened to be his own Son, on whom the Father performed his Vow. Upon which a Plague having ariſen, his Subjects conſidered him as the Cauſe of that public Calamity, and baniſhed him from the Iſland. This is the Account which *Servius* gives.

124. *Ortygiæ. Delos* was anciently called *Ortygia*, from Ὄρτυξ, *a Quail*, thoſe Fowls having been very numerous in that Iſland.

125. *Viridemque Donyſam.* This Iſland was famous for producing green Marble, as *Paros* was for its pure white Marble, ſo much celebrated by Antiquity:

Urit me Glyceræ nitor
Splendentis Pario marmore purius.
Hor. I. Carm. Ode 19.

So *Seneca* in *Hipp.*

Lucebit Pario marmore clarius.

127. *Cycladas.* The *Cyclades* are ſo called from κύκλος, *circulus*, becauſe they were diſpoſed in a circular Form around *Delos.*

131. *Certam*

Nauticus clamor exoritur cum vario certamine: Socii hortantur, petamus Cretam proavosque. Ventus surgens à puppi prosequitur nos euntes, et tandem allabimur antiquis oris Curetum. Ergo avidus molior muros optatæ urbis, vocoque eam Pergameam; et hortor gentem lætam cognomine amare focos, attollereque arcem tectis. Jamque fere puppes subductæ sunt *in sicco littore; juventus operata* est *connubiis novisque arvis: dabam jura domosque, cum subito lues tabida miserandaque, tractu cœli corrupto, venit membris, arboribusque, satisque, et annus fit lethifer. Linquebant dulces animas, aut trahebant ægra corpora:*

Nauticus exoritur vario certamine clamor:
Hortantur socii, Cretam, proavosque petamus.
Prosequitur surgens à puppi ventus euntes;
Et tandem antiquis Curetum allabimur oris.
Ergo avidus muros optatæ molior urbis;
Pergameamque voco; et lætam cognomine gentem
Hortor amare focos, arcemque attollere tectis.
Jamque fere sicco subductæ littore puppes;
Connubiis arvisque novis operata juventus;
Jura domosque dabam: subito cum tabida membris,
Corrupto cœli tractu, miserandaque venit
Arboribusque, satisque lues, et lethifer annus.
Linquebant dulces animas, aut ægra trahebant

TRANSLATION.

Emulation the Seamens Shouts arise. The Crew *thus* animate one another, FOR CRETE AND OUR ANCESTORS LET US SPEED OUR COURSE. We sail full before the Wind, and at length skim along to the ancient Seats of the Curetes. Therefore with Eagerness, I raised the Walls of the so much wished-for City, call it the City of Pergamus, and I exhort my *new* Colony, pleased with their Name, to keep much at home, and raise Turrets of Defence on their Roofs. And now the Ships were mostly laid up on the dry Beach, the Youth had performed Sacrifice *for Success* on their Nuptials and new Settlements: I was begun to dispense Laws, and appropriate Houses, when suddenly, from the Infection of the Climate, a wasting and lamentable Plague seized on our Limbs, the Trees, and Corns, and the Year is pregnant with Death. *My Friends* left their sweet Lives, or dragged along their sickly Bodies: At the same Time the *raging* Dog-

NOTES.

131. *Curetum oris*, i. e. *Crete*, the Mansion of the *Curetes*, the Ministers of *Cybele*, thought to be the same with the *Corybantes* and *Idæi Dactyli*. *Strabo* derives their Name *Curetes* from κουρα, *tonsura*, because they had the Forepart of their Head shaved or shorn.

133. *Pergameamque*. *Pliny* mentions *Pergamus* among the Cities of *Crete*.

134. *Amare focos*. *Servius* thinks this implies a Recommendation of the Study of Religion and Sacrifices: *Ruæus* understands it of the Care of their Families. I offer a third Sense, and take the Meaning to be, that *Æneas* would have them keep much at Home, and not straggle abroad for some Time, till they should know what Sort of Reception the Inhabitants of the Island would give them, whether they were come among Friends or Foes. This both agrees with what follows, *arcemque attollere tectis*, their being ordered *to raise a Strength for their Defence in case of an Attack*; and was a proper Caution in their present Circumstances: Add to this, that the Word is used in this very Sense, Æn. V. 163. when *Gyas* would have his Pilot to steer close to the Shore, he says, *Littus ama*, *depart not from the Shore*, or, in the poetical Style, *court the Shore*.

136. *Operata*. It was customary to offer Sacrifice before they entered on Marriage, or any important Business of Life, and the Verb *operari* is used in this Sense, Geor. I. 339.

Lætus operatus in herbis.

And by Juvenal, Sat. XII. 92.

Et matutinis operatur festa lucernis.

140. *Linquebant dulces animas*. Dr. *Trapp* thinks this a very odd Expression, and would fain

Corpora: tum ſteriles exurere Sirius agros:
Arebant herbæ, et victum ſeges ægra negabat.
Rurſus ad oraculum Ortygiæ, Phœbumque, remenſo
Hortatur pater ire mari, veniamque precari;
Quem feſſis finem rebus ferat; unde laborum
Tentare auxilium jubeat; quò vertere curſus.
  Nox erat, et terris animalia ſomnus habebat.
Effigies ſacræ Divûm, Phrygiique Penates,
Quos mecum à Trojâ, mediiſque ex ignibus urbis,
Extuleram, viſi ante oculos aſtare jacentis
Inſomnis, multo manifeſti lumine, quà ſe
Plena per inſertas fundebat Luna feneſtras.
Tum ſic affari, et curas his demere dictis:
Quod tibi delato Ortygiam dicturus Apollo eſt,
Hìc canit, et tua nos en ultro ad limina mittit.
Nos te, Dardaniâ incenſâ, tuaque arma ſecuti;

tum Sirius cœpit exurere ſteriles agros: Herbæ arebant, et ægra ſeges negabat nobis victum. Rurſus pater hortatur ire ad oraculum Ortygiæ, Phœbumque, mari remenſo, precarique eum veniam; quærere quem finem ferat feſſis rebus, unde jubeat nos tentare auxilium laborum, quò vertere curſus.

Nox erat, et ſomnus habebat animalia ſuper terris. Sacræ effigies Divûm, Phrygiique Penates, quos extuleram mecum à Trojâ exque mediis ignibus urbis viſi ſunt aſtare ante oculos mei jacentis inſomnis, manifeſti multo lumine, quà plena Luna fundebat ſe per inſertas feneſtras. Tum ſic cœperunt affari, et demere curas mihi his dictis: Apollo canit tibi hìc idem quod dicturus eſt tibi delato Ortygiam, et, en, ultro mittit nos ad tua limina. Nos ſecuti ſumus te tuaque arma, Dardaniâ incenſâ;

TRANSLATION.

ſtar burnt up the barren Fields. The Herbs were parched, and the unwholeſome Grain denied us Suſtenance. My Father adviſes, that, meaſuring back the Sea, we again apply to the Oracle of Ortygia, and Apollo, and implore his Grace, *to know* when he will bring our Toils and Wanderings to a Period; whence he will bid us attempt a Redreſs of our Calamities, *or* whither turn our Courſe. It was Night, and Sleep reigned over all the animal World. The ſacred Images of the Gods, and the tutelar Deities of my Country, whom I had brought with me from Troy, and the Midſt of the Flames, were ſeen to ſtand before my Eyes as I lay awake, conſpicuous by a Glare of Light, where the Full-moon darted her Beams through the intervening Windows. Then they thus addreſſed me, and diſpelled my Cares with theſe Words: What *Apollo* would announce to you, were you waſted to Ortygia, he here reveals, and lo unaſked, he ſends us to your Dwelling. We, after Troy was conſumed, followed thee and *the Fortune of*

NOTES.

fain change *linquebant* to *reddebant*, and accordingly tranſlates it, *they render their ſweet Souls*: And, indeed, it muſt be owned, to ſay a Perſon *leaves his ſweet Soul*, ſounds odd enough, becauſe that is making the Body to be the Perſon. But, if we put *Lives* inſtead of *Souls*, *they left their ſweet Lives*, which is the true rendering of the Words, the Oddity of the Phraſe diſappears. The Expreſſion is equivalent to that in the Georgics:

Præcipites altâ vitam ſub nube relinquunt.
Geor. III. 547.

141. *Sirius* Alſo called *Canicula*, or *the Dog-ſtar*, a peſtilential Conſtellation, which riſes about the End of *July*, when the Heat of the Sun is moſt intenſe.

143. *Ortygiæ*. See the Note on Verſe 124.

151. *Inſomnis*. I chooſe to read *inſomnis* in one Word, *while I was awake*, becauſe it ſeems to agree beſt with the Circumſtances of this Apparition, particularly with what immediately follows,

————————————quà ſe
Plena per inſertas fundebat Luna feneſtras.

nos ſub te permenſi ſumus *tumidum æquor* in *claſſibus*; nos *iidem tollemus in aſtra* tuos *venturos nepotes, dabimuſque imperium urbi. Tu para magna mœnia magnis, neque linque longum laborem fugæ. Sedes* ſunt *mutandæ* tibi: *Delius Apollo non ſuaſit tibi hæc littora, aut juſſit* te *conſidere Cretæ. Locus eſt,* quem *Graii dicunt Heſperiam cognomine, antiqua terra, potens armis atque ubere glebæ: Oenotrii viri coluere* eam: *nunc fama* eſt *minores dixiſſe gentem Italiam, de nomine ducis. Hæ* erunt *nobis propriæ ſedes: hinc Dardanus* eſt *ortus, Iaſiuſque pater, à quo principe* Dardano eſt *genus noſtrum. Age, ſurge, et lætus refer longævo parenti hæc dicta haud dubitanda: Require Coritum, terraſque Auſonias:*

Nos tumidum ſub te permenſi claſſibus æquor;
Idem venturos tollemus in aſtra nepotes,
Imperiumque urbi dabimus. Tu mœnia magnis
Magna para, longumque fugæ ne linque laborem.
Mutandæ ſedes: non hæc tibi littora ſuaſit
Delius, aut Cretæ juſſit conſidere, Apollo.
Eſt locus, Heſperiam Graii cognomine dicunt,
Terra antiqua, potens armis atque ubere glebæ:
Oenotrii coluère viri: nunc fama, minores
Italiam dixiſſe, ducis de nomine, gentem:
Hæ nobis propriæ ſedes: hinc Dardanus ortus,
Iaſiuſque pater, genus à quo principe noſtrum.
Surge, age, et hæc lætus longævo dicta parenti
Haud dubitanda refer: Coritum, terraſque require

TRANSLATION.

Thy Arms; under thy Conduct we have croſſed the ſwelling Sea in Ships: We too will exalt thy future Race to Heaven, and crown thy City with imperial Power: Do thou prepare Walls mighty for the mighty *Inhabitants*, and flinch not from the long Labours of thy *wandering* Voyage. You muſt change your Place of Reſidence: Theſe are not the Shores that Delian Apollo adviſed you to *purſue*; nor was it in Crete he commanded you to ſettle. There is a Place, the Greeks call it Heſperia by Name; a Country of ancient Renown, powerful by its Arms, and the Fertility of the Soil: The Oenotrians peopled it *once*; now there is a Report, that their Deſcendants have called the Nation Italy from the Founder's Name. Theſe are our laſting Settlements; hence Dardanus ſprung, and Father Iaſius, from which Prince our Race is derived: Haſte *then*, ariſe, and with Joy report to thy aged Sire theſe Intimations of unqueſtionable Credibility: Search out the City Coritus, and the Auſonian Lands: Jupiter forbids *your Set-*

NOTES.

For what Occaſion was there for the Light of the Moon to let him ſee the Gods, if he was aſleep? Beſides, *Æneas* expreſsly tells us himſelf, Verſe 173. *Nec ſopor illud erat, nor was this a Dream, or the Effect of Sleep.*

163. *Eſt locus.* This and the three following Verſes are taken from Æn. I. 534. *Ilioneus* had recited them to *Dido* before, when he informed her of their diſaſtrous Voyage, and the Place for which they were bound. As they are the Words of the Oracle, it would have been diſreſpectful to alter them in the leaſt; beſides, *Dido* would be the more confirmed in the Truth of *Æneas*'s Relation, when ſhe found two Witneſſes delivering their Teſtimony preciſely in the ſame Terms.

197. *Dardanus Iaſiuſque pater.* *Dardanus* and *Iaſius* had both one Mother, *Electra*, the Daughter of *Atlas*, and Wife of *Coritus*, King of *Tuſcany*; but *Jupiter* is given for the Father of *Dardanus*. He, upon the Death of *Coritus*, killed his Brother *Iaſius*, and, being baniſhed *Tuſcany* on that Account, firſt fled into *Samothrace*, then into *Phrygia*, where he married *Teucer*'s Daughter, and built the City *Troy*, which he called *Dardania* after his own Name.

170. *Coritum.* *Coritus*, the Name of a Mountain and City in *Tuſcany*, ſo called from *Coritus*, the ſuppoſed Father of *Dardanus*.

171. *Auſonias,*

Ausonias: Dictæa negat tibi Jupiter arva.
Talibus attonitus visis ac voce Deorum,
(Nec sopor illud erat, sed coràm agnoscere vultus,
Velatasque comas, præsentiaque ora videbar;
Tum gelidus toto manabat corpore sudor)
Corripio è stratis corpus, tendoque supinas
Ad cœlum cum voce manus, et munera libo
Intemerata focis. Perfecto lætus honore
Anchisen facio certum, remque ordine pando.
Agnovit prolem ambiguam, geminosque parentes,
Seque novo veterum deceptum errore locorum.
Tum memorat: Nate Iliacis exercite fatis,
Sola mihi tales casus Cassandra canebat.
Nunc repeto hæc generi portendere debita nostro,
Et sæpe Hesperiam, sæpe Itala regna vocare:

Jupiter negat tibi Dictæa arva. Ego attonitus talibus visis ac voce Deorum, (nec illud erat sopor, sed videbar mihi agnoscere vultus coràm, comasque velatas, oraque præsentia; tum gelidus sudor manabat è toto corpore) corripio corpus è stratis, tendoque, ad cœlum manus supinas cum voce, et libo focis munera intemerata: honore perfecto, lætus facio Anchisen certum, pandoque rem ordine. Agnovit ambiguam prolem, geminosque parentes: seque deceptum esse novo errore veterum locorum. Tum memorat: Nate exercite Iliacis fatis, sola Cassandra canebat mihi tales casus. Nunc repeto eam portendere hæc fuisse debita nostro generi, et sæpe vocare Hesperiam, sæpe Itala regna.

TRANSLATION.

tlement in the Cretan Territories. Astonished by this Vision and Declaration of the Gods (nor was it *a* mere *Illusion* in Sleep, but methought I clearly discerned their Aspect before me, their filleted Hair, and their Forms full in my View; then a cold Sweat flowed over my whole Body), I fling me out of Bed, and lift up my Hands supine to Heaven with my Voice, and pour hallowed Offerings on the Fires. Having finished the Sacrifice, with Joy I certify Anchises, and disclose the Fact *to him* in Order. He owned the ambiguous Offspring, and the double Founders *of the Trojan Race*, and that he had been deceived by the modern equivocal Names given to ancient Countries. Then he thus bespeaks me: O my Son, tried and exercised in Woe by the Fates of Troy, Cassandra alone predicted to me that such was to be our Fortune. Now I recollect that she foretold this should be the Destiny of our Race, and that she often turned her Discourse on

NOTES.

171. *Ausonias.* *Italy* was denominated *Ausonia*, says *Servius*, from *Auson* or *Ausonius*, the Son of *Ulysses* and *Calypso*. If so, it must be by Anticipation that *Virgil* makes that Name known to *Æneas*, for *Calypso*'s Son was hardly born at that Time.

171. *Dictæa arva.* The *Cretan* Territories, called *Dictæan* from *Dicte*, a Mountain in *Crete*, where *Jove* is said to have been educated.

177. *Munera libo intemerata.* A private Offering of pure Wine and Incense, which used to be poured upon the Fire, in Honour of the *Lares* or *Household-gods*.

179. *Anchisen facio certum.* Perhaps we had been at a Loss to know whether this was good *Latin*, but for *Virgil*'s sacred Authority.

181. *Seque novo*, &c. Some Copies read *parentum* instead of *locorum*.

182. *Iliacis exercite fatis.* In the same Manner is he addressed by *Anchises*'s Ghost, Æn. V. 725. *Æneas* was thus harassed and afflicted, not for any personal Demerit, but because of his Connexion with *Troy*, the whole Race of the *Trojans* being the objects of *Juno*'s fatal Resentment, and destined to suffer grievous Misfortunes.

183. *Sola—Cassandra.* He says only *Cassandra*, because her Prophecies were always disregarded. See the Note on Æn. II. 246.

Sed quis crederet Teucros venturos ad littora Hesperiæ? Aut quem tum vates Cassandra moveret? Cedamus Phœbo, et moniti meliora sequamur. Sic ille ait; et cuncti ovantes paremus ejus dictis. Deserimus quoque hanc sedem, paucisque relictis, damus vela, currimusque vastum æquor cavâ trabe.

Postquam rates tenuere altum, nec ullæ terræ jam amplius apparent, undique apparet cœlum, et undique pontus; tum cæruleus imber astitit supra caput mihi, ferens noctem hyememque; et unda inhorruit tenebris. Continuò venti volvunt mare, magnoque æquora surgunt: nos dispersi jactamur in vasto gurgite: nimbi involvere diem, et humida nox abstulit nobis cœlum: ignes ingeminant, nubibus abruptis.

Sed quis ad Hesperiæ venturos littora Teucros
Crederet? aut quem tum vates Cassandra moveret?
Cedamus Phœbo, et moniti meliora sequamur.
Sic ait: et cuncti dictis paremus ovantes:
Hanc quoque deserimus sedem, paucisque relictis
Vela damus, vastumque cavâ trabe currimus æquor.
Postquam altum tenuere rates, nec jam amplius ullæ
Apparent terræ, cœlum undique, et undique pontus;
Tum mihi cœruleus supra caput astitit imber,
Noctem hyememque ferens; et inhorruit unda tenebris.
Continuò venti volvunt mare, magnaque surgunt
Æquora: dispersi jactamur gurgite vasto:
Involvere diem nimbi, et nox humida cœlum
Abstulit: ingeminant abruptis nubibus ignes.

TRANSLATION.

Hesperia, often on the Italian Realms. But who could believe the Trojans were to come to the Hesperian Shore? Or whom then did the prophetic Cassandra move? *But now* let us resign ourselves to Phœbus, and, since we are better advised, let us follow *the Gods*. He said, and exulting we all obey his Orders. This Realm we likewise quit, and, leaving a few behind, unfurl our Sails, and bound over the spacious Sea in our hollow vessel. After the Ships were got into the Deep, and now not any Land is longer in View, *only* Sky and Ocean all around: Then a blackening Cloud stood over my Head, bringing on Night and a wintry Storm; the Waves put on the Horrors of Darkness, the Winds overturn the Sea, and swelling Surges rise: We are tossed hither and thither on the expanded Face of the Deep: Clouds wrapped up the Day, and humid Night snatched the Heavens *from our View*; from the bursting Clouds Flashes of Lightning redouble. We

NOTES.

188. *Moniti meliora sequamur.* *Ruæus* and Dr. *Trapp* construe these Words thus, *Moniti sequamur meliora*; but it seems more elegant to keep to the Order in which they stand: *Now that we are better advised, let us follow or obey, viz. the Gods.*

194. *Cæruleus imber.* Clouds that threaten Rain, especially before Thunder and Lightning, are often tinctured with a deep Blue, intermingled with Black; and therefore we need not charge *Virgil* here with the Absurdity of putting *cæruleus* for *ater*, as some Interpreters would persuade us. *Cæruleus* is what we may call *leaden-coloured.*

199. *Ingeminant abruptis nubibus ignes.* Some ancient Copies and Manuscripts read *abrupti nubibus ignes*, which both sounds better, and seems to be confirmed by that Passage in *Lucretius*, which *Virgil* had probably here in his Eye:

Transversosque volare per imbres fulmina cernis:
Nunc hinc nunc illinc abrupti nubibus ignes
Concursant: cadit in terras vis flammea vulgo.
Lib. II. 213.

201. *Ipse*—

Excutimur curſu, et cæcis erramus in undis.
Ipſe diem noctemque negat diſcernere cœlo,
Nec meminiſſe viæ mediâ Palinurus in undâ.
Tres adeò incertos cæcâ caligine ſoles
Erramus pelago, totidem ſine ſidere noctes:
Quarto terra die primùm ſe attollere tandem
Viſa, aperire procul montes, ac volvere fumum.
Vela cadunt; remis inſurgimus: haud mora, nautæ
Adnixi torquent ſpumas, et cœrula verrunt.
Servatum ex undis Strophadum me littora primùm
Accipiunt. Strophades Graio ſtant nomine dictæ
Inſulæ Ionio in magno; quas dira Celæno
Harpyiæque colunt aliæ, Phineïa poſtquam
Clauſa domus, menſaſque metu liquere priores.

Excutimur curſu, et erramus in cæcis undis. Palinurus ipſe negat ſe diſcernere diem noctemque in cœlo, nec meminiſſe viæ in mediâ undâ. Adeò erramus pelago tres ſoles incertos cæcâ caligine, totidem noctes ſine ſidere. Tandem quarto die terra primùm viſa eſt ſe attollere, montes procul cœperunt aperire, ac volvere fumum. Vela noſtra *cadunt, inſurgimus remis: haud eſt mora, nautæ adnixi torquent ſpumas, et verrunt cœrula* maria.

Littora Strophadum primùm accipiunt me ſervatum ex undis. Inſulæ dictæ Strophades Graio nomine ſtant in magno Ionio mari; *quas* inſulas *dira Celæno aliæque Harpyiæ colunt, poſtquam Phineïa domus clauſa eſt* iis, *liquereque priores menſas metu.*

TRANSLATION.

are driven from our Courſe, and reel along the duſky Waves. Palinurus himſelf owns he is unable to diſtinguiſh Day from Night by the Sky, and that he has forgot his Courſe in the Mid-ſea. Thus for three Days that could hardly be diſtinguiſh *from Night* by *reaſon of* dark Clouds, *and* as many ſtarleſs Nights, we wander up and down the Ocean. At length, on the fourth Day, Land was firſt ſeen to riſe, the Mountains from afar open *to our View*, and roll up their Smoke: The Sails ſubſide, we * ply the labouring Oars; inſtant, the Seamen with exerted Vigour toſs up the Foam, and ſweep the azure *Deep.*¶ The Shores of the Strophades *Iſlands* firſt receive me reſcued from the Waves. The Strophades, ſo called by a Greek Name, are Iſlands ſituated in the great Ionian *Sea*; which direful Celæno and the other Harpies inhabit, from what Time they were expelled Phineus's Palace, and frighted from his Table, which they formerly haunted. No

* *Inſurgimus remis. We riſe on the Oars*, as the Rowers do when they row hard, and with great Keenneſs.

NOTES.

201. *Ipſe—Palinurus.* i. e. *Palinurus* himſelf, with all his Skill. He was the Pilot of *Æneas*'s Ship, of whom ſee more Æn. V. 883.

211. *Ionio in magno.* Not that Sea which waſhes *Ionia* in *Leſſer Aſia*, but that Part of the *Mediterranean* which flows between *Sicily* and *Greece*.

212. *Harpyiæ.* The *Harpies*, according to *Heſiod*, were the Daughters of *Thaumas* and *Electra*, but not ſaid to be one of the *Harpies*. The Word comes from ἁρπαζω, *rapio*, to denote their rapacious Nature. *Apollonius* calls them Διος κυνας, *the Hell-hounds of* Jove; and *Virgil*, *Furies*, Verſe 252, and *diræ*, *Fiends*, Verſe 262. Whence *Servius* concludes, that they were denominated *Harpies* on Earth, *Furies* in Hell, and *Diræ*, *Fiends* in Heaven, as one and the ſame Goddeſs was called *Diana* on Earth, *Luna, the Moon*, in Heaven, and *Proſerpine* in Hell.

212. *Phineïa.* *Phineus*, King of *Thrace*, having put out the Eyes of his two Sons, whom their Step-mother falſely accuſed of attempting a Rape upon her, was for his Cruelty ſtruck blind by *Jupiter* in his Turn, and delivered over to the direful Perſecution of the *Harpies*, till *Calais* and *Zetes*, two of the *Argonauts*, whom

Haud ullum *monstrum est tristius illis, nec ulla sævior pestis, et ira Deûm, extulit sese Stygiis undis. Vultus volucrum* sunt *virginei*, est iis *fœdissima proluvies ventris, manusque uncæ, et ora semper pallida fame. Ubi* nos *delati huc intravimus portus, ecce videmus læta armenta boum passim* in *campis, caprigenumque pecus errans per herbas, nullo custode. Irruimus ferro, et vocamus Divos ipsumque Jovem in prædam partemque: tunc extruimusque toros* in *curvo littore, epulamurque opimis dapibus. Et Harpyiæ subitæ adsunt horrifico lapsu de montibus, et quatiunt alas magnis clangoribus, diripiuntque dapes, fœdantque omnia immundo contactu: tum dira vox* erat iis *inter tetrum odorem. Rursum* nos *instruimus mensas, reponimusque ignem aris, in longo successu, sub cavatâ rupe, clausi circum arboribus atque horrentibus umbris.*

Tristius haud illis monstrum, nec sævior ulla
Pestis et ira Deûm Stygiis sese extulit undis.
Virginei volucrum vultus, fœdissima ventris
Proluvies, uncæque manus, et pallida semper
Ora fame.
Huc ubi delati portus intravimus, ecce
Læta boum passim campis armenta videmus,
Caprigenumque pecus, nullo custode, per herbas.
Irruimus ferro, et Divos ipsumque vocamus
In prædam partemque Jovem tunc littore curvo
Exstruimusque toros, dapibusque epulamur opimis.
At subitæ horrifico lapsu de montibus adsunt
Harpyiæ, et magnis quatiunt clangoribus alas;
Diripiuntque dapes, contactuque omnia fœdant
Immundo: tum vox tetrum dira inter odorem.
Rursum in secessu longo, sub rupe cavatâ,
Arboribus clausi circum atque horrentibus umbris,

TRANSLATION.

Monster more fell than they, no Plague and Scourge of the Gods more cruel *ever* issued from the Stygian Waves. They are Fowls with Virgin-faces, a most loathsome Flux of Entrails, Hands hooked, and Looks ever pale with Famine. Hither conveyed, so soon as we entered the Port, lo we see joyous Herds of Cattle up and down the Plains, and Flocks of Goats along the Meadows, without a Keeper. We rush upon them with our Swords, and invoke the Gods and Jove himself to share the Booty. Then along the winding Shore we raise the *banqueting* Couches, and feast on the rich Repast. When suddenly with dreadful darting Motion the Harpies are upon us from the Mountains, shake their Wings with loud rustling Din, prey upon our Banquet, and defile every Thing with their impure Touch; At the same Time, together with a rank, noisome Smell, they *emit* hideous Screams. Again we spread our Tables in a long Recess, underneath a shelving Rock, inclosed around with Trees and gloomy Shade, and once more we plant

NOTES.

whom he had hospitably entertained in their Way to *Colchis*, in quest of the Golden-fleece, relieved him from them in the Manner already mentioned.

223. *In prædam partemque.* For in *prædæ partem*, as, in the first Book, *molemque et montes*, for *molem montium*. The *Romans* had a Custom when they were going out to War, or to the Chace, to vow to consecrate to the Gods a great Part of the Spoil or Capture; whence *Jupiter* had a Temple at *Rome*, under the Title of *Jupiter Prædator*, *Jupiter who presided over lawful Plunder*. *In partem vocare*, is of the same Import with *participem facere*, *to make them Sharers with us of the Booty:* So the Phrase is used by *Cicero* for *Cecinna*, *Mulieres in partem vocatæ sunt.*

226. *Magnis—clangoribus.* Some ancient Copies read *plangoribus.*

232. *Ex*

Inſtruimus menſas, ariſque reponimus ignem.
Rurſum ex diverſo cœli, cæciſque latebris,
Turba ſonans prædam pedibus circumvolat uncis:
Polluit ore dapes. Sociis tunc arma capeſſant
Edico, et dirâ bellum cum gente gerendum.
Haud ſecus ac juſſi faciunt, tectoſque per herbam
Diſponunt enſes, et ſcuta latentia condunt.
Ergo, ubi delapſæ ſonitum per curva dedere
Littora, dat ſignum ſpeculâ Miſenus ab altâ
Ære cavo: invadunt ſocii, et nova prœlia tentant,
Obſcœnas pelagi ferro fœdare volucres.
Sed neque vim plumis ullam, nec vulnera tergo,
Accipiunt; celerique fugâ ſub ſidera lapſæ,
Semeſam prædam et veſtigia fœda relinquunt.

Rurſum ex diverſo tractu cœli, cæciſque latebris, turba ſonans circumvolat prædam uncis pedibus, et polluit dapes ore. Tunc edico ſociis ut capeſſant arma, et bellum eſſe gerendum cum dira gente. Illi faciunt haud ſecus ac ſunt juſſi, diſponuntque enſes tectos per herbam, et condunt latentia ſcuta. Ergo, ubi Harpyiæ delapſæ dedere ſonitum per curva littora, Miſenus dat ſignum cavo ære, ab altâ ſpeculâ; ſocii invadunt eas, et tentant nova prœlia, fœdare ferro obſcœnas volucres pelagi. Sed neque accipiunt ullam vim plumis, nec ulla vulnera tergo; lapſæque celeri fugâ ſub ſidera, relinquunt ſemeſam prædam et fœda veſtigia.

TRANSLATION.

Fire on the Altar. Again the noiſy Rout *ſhooting* from a different Quarter of the Sky, and obſcure Retreats, flutter around the Prey with hooky Claws, *and* taint our Viands with their Mouths. Then I enjoin my Companions to take Arms, and wage War with the accurſed Brood. My Orders they punctually obey, diſpoſe their Swords ſecretly among the Graſs, and conceal their Shields out of Sight. Therefore, ſo ſoon as darting down they raiſed their ſcreaming Voices along the bending Shores, Miſenus with his hollow *Trumpet of* Braſs gives the Signal from a lofty Watch-tower. My Friends ſet upon them, and engage in a new Kind of Fight, to employ the Sword in deſtroying obſcene Sea-fowls. But they neither receive any Impreſſion on their Plumes, nor Wounds in the Body; and, mounting up in the Air with rapid Flight, leave behind them their Prey half conſumed, and the ugly Prints of their Feet. ❙ Celæno alone took her Seat on the

NOTES.

232. *Ex diverſo cœli.* i. e. *ex diverſo cœli tractu*, for I ſee no Reaſon for making it a Kind of Adverb, ſignifying *overthwart*, as Mr. *Ainſworth* has done in his Dictionary. Though the Mythologiſts make the *Harpies* but three in Number, yet *Virgil* ſpeaks here, as if the whole Iſland had been crowded with them, calling them *turba*, and *gens*, ſo that they no ſooner left one Quarter of the Iſland, than they were peſtered with them in another. The Poets do not always reſtrict themſelves either to hiſtorical or fabulous Tradition, but only ſo far as it ſuits beſt with their Deſign; ſo that, however others confine the *Harpies* to three, it follows not that *Virgil* does ſo.

239. *Miſenus.* The Son of *Æolus*, Trumpeter to *Æneas*, Æn. VI. 164.

241. *Obſcœnas—volucres.* Either Birds of bad Omen, or impure, abominable, to be abhorred upon Account of their Naſtineſs, as above deſcribed.

241. *Pelagi volucres.* *Heſiod* makes them the Offspring of *Electra*, the Daughter of the *Ocean*.

241. *Fœdare ferro.* The primary Signification of the Word *fœdo* is *to mangle, cut in Pieces*, or *make Havock*, as appears from the more ancient Authors, particularly *Ennius* and *Plautus*, who uſe it in that Senſe, as

Ferro fœdati jacent, *Ennius apud Servium.*

And ſo *Plautus*, Amph Ac. I. Sc. I. 91.

Fœdant et proterunt hoſtium copias.

See Æn. II. 55, where this Verb is uſed in the ſame Senſe.

246. *Infelix*

Una Celæno, infelix vates, consedit in excelsâ rupe, rupitque hanc vocem è pectore: O Laomedontiadæ, paratisne inferre bellum, etiam bellum pro cæde nostrorum *boum, juvencisque stratis, et pellere insontes Harpyias è patrio regno? Ergo accipite, atque figite hæc mea dicta* in vestris *animis: Ego maxima Furiarum pando vobis quæ* Jupiter *pater omnipotens* prædixit *Phœbo, quæ Phœbus Apollo prædixit mihi. Petitis Italiam cursu ibitisque* in *Italiam, ventis vocatis, licebitque* vobis *intrare* ejus *portus. Sed non cingetis datam urbem mœnibus, antequam dira fames, injuriaque nostræ cædis subigat vos malis absumere ambesas* vestras *mensas.*

Una in præcelsâ consedit rupe Celæno,
Infelix vates, rupitque hanc pectore vocem:
Bellum etiam pro cæde boum, stratisque juvencis,
Laomedontiadæ, bellumne inferre paratis?
Et patrio insontes Harpyias pellere regno?
Accipite ergo animis atque hæc mea figite dicta:
Quæ Phœbo pater omnipotens, mihi Phœbus Apollo,
Prædixit, vobis furiarum ego maxima pando.
Italiam cursu petitis; ventisque vocatis
Ibitis Italiam, portusque intrare licebit:
Sed non ante datam cingetis mœnibus urbem,
Quàm vos dira fames, nostræque injuria cædis,
Ambesas subigat malis absumere mensas.

TRANSLATION.

Brow of a high Rock, a Prophetess of Plagues, and from her *heaving* Breast burst forth these Words: War too, ye Sons of Laomedon, is it your Purpose to make War *upon us as a Compensation* for our Oxen which you have slain *and fed upon*, for the Havoc you have made among our Bullocks, and *do you intend* to banish the innocent Harpies from their hereditary Kingdom? Lend then an Ear, and in your Minds fix these my Words: What Almighty Father Jove revealed to Phœbus, Phœbus Apollo to me, I the Chief of the Furies disclose to you. / To Italy you steer your Course, and Italy you shall reach after repeated Invocations to the *thwarting* Winds, and you shall be permitted *at length* to enter the Port: But you shall not inclose the given City with Walls, till cruel Famine and Disaster, for shedding our Blood, compel you first to gnaw and eat up your Trenchers

NOTES.

246. *Infelix vates.* As *felix* sometimes signifies *propitious*, *favourable*, so *infelix* here, and elsewhere, *unfriendly*, *inauspicious*, *ill-boding*; so that *infelix vates* answers to *Homer's* μαντις κακων.

248 *Laomedontiadæ.* In calling them Sons of *Laomedon*, she reproaches them, as being impious, unjust, and faithless, like that Prince who had falsified his Promise even to the Gods themselves.

249. *Patrio regno.* They were Daughters of a Sea-goddess, and the Isles were sacred to the Gods and Goddesses of the Sea, so that the *Strophades* was their proper Heritage by their Mother.

252. *Furiarum maxima.* She takes this Name to herself, as it would seem, only to inspire them with the greater Terror, though *Servius* and others, as has been said, infer from this Passage, that the *Harpies* and *Furies* were the same.

257 *Ambesas—absumere mensas.* The Sense of this Prediction is seen from its Accomplishment in the seventh Book, Verse 116. This is not merely poetical Invention, it was an historical Tradition, related by *Dionysius* and *Strabo*, that *Æneas* had received a Response from an Oracle, foretelling that, before he came to his Settlement in *Italy*, he should be reduced to the Necessity of eating his Trenchers. *Varro* says he got it from the Oracle of *Dodona*. *Virgil* puts this Prophecy in the Mouth of the *Harpies*, as being both suitable to their Nature, and more apt to raise Surprize when coming from them.

260. *Nec*

Dixit, et in ſylvam pennis ablata refugit.
At ſociis ſubitâ gelidus formidine ſanguis
Diriguit: cecidere animi: nec jam amplius armis,
Sed votis precibuſque, jubent expoſcere pacem;
Sive Deæ, ſeu ſint diræ obſcœnæque volucres.
At pater Anchiſes, paſſis de littore palmis,
Numina magna vocat, meritoſque indicit honores:
Dî, prohibite minas; Dî, talem avertite caſum,
Et placidi ſervate pios. Tum littore funem
Diripere, excuſſoſque jubet laxare rudentes.
Tendunt vela Noti: fugimus ſpumantibus undis,
Quà curſum ventuſque gubernatorque vocabant.
Jam medio apparet fluctu nemoroſa Zacynthos,
Dulichiumque, Sameque, et Neritos ardua ſaxis.

Dixit, et, ablata pennis, refugit in ſylvam. At ſanguis gelidus, præ ſubita formidine, diriguit ſociis: animi eorum cecidere: Nec jam amplius jubent expoſcere pacem armis, ſed votis precibuſque, ſive ſint Deæ, ſeu diræ obſcœnæque volucres. At pater Anchiſes, palmis paſſis de littore, vocat magna numina, indicitque meritos honores: Dî, probibite veſtras *minas; Dî, avertite talem caſum, et placidi ſervate pios. Tum jubet diripere funem è littore, laxareque excuſſos rudentes. Noti tendunt* noſtra *vela; fugimus* ſuper *undis ſpumantibus, qua ventuſque gubernatorque vocabant curſum. Jam nemoroſa Zacynthos apparet* in *medio fluctu, Dulichiumque, Sameque, et Neritos ardua ſaxis.*

TRANSLATION.

with *greedy* Jaws. She ſaid, and on her Wings upborne flew into the Wood. As for our Crew, their Blood, chilled with ſudden Fear, ſtagnated *in their Veins:* Their Minds were quite dejected: And now they are no longer for having Recourſe to Arms, but urge *me* to ſollicit Peace by Vows and Prayers, whether they be Goddeſſes, or curſed and inauſpicious Birds. My Father Anchiſes, with Hands ſpread forth from the Shore, invokes the great Gods, and enjoins due Honours to be paid them. Ye Gods, ward off *the Effect of* your Threatenings; ye Gods, avert ſo grievous a Calamity; and propitious ſave your pious Votaries. Then he orders to tear the Ropes from the Shore, looſe and diſengage the Cables. The South-winds ſtretch our *bellying* Sails: We fly over the foaming Waves, where the Wind and Pilots urged our Courſe. Now amidſt the Waves appear woody Zacynthos, Dulichium, Same, and Neritos with its ſteepy Rocks. We ſhun the

NOTES.

260. *Nec jam amplius armis, ſed votis expoſcere.* This is another Inſtance of *Virgil's* conciſe elliptical Stile. It is plain, that *expoſcere pacem* cannot agree, in Propriety of Language, both to *armis* and *votis*, or *precibus*, though it does ſo in the Conſtruction, for they are two quite contrary Ideas; ſo that *pugnare*, or ſome ſuch Word, muſt be underſtood to *armis:* But the Senſe, nevertheleſs, is as obvious, as if the Sentence were ever ſo full and compleat.

261. *Jubent.* This ſhews the Earneſtneſs and Importunity with which they urged *Æneas* to bring about a Peace with them.

264. *Meritoſque indicit honores.* See the Note on Book firſt, Verſe 636.

270. *Zacynthos.* The Iſland *Zante*, on the Weſt of the *Peloponneſus.*

271. *Dulichium.* Now *Dolicha*, one of the *Echinades* Iſlands; they go all under the common Name of *Curzulari.*

271. *Same.* Or *Samos*, the ſame with *Cephalenia*, now *Cephalonia.*

271. *Neritos.* A woody Mountain in the Iſland of *Ithaca*: *Homer* calls it Νηριτον εινοσιφυλλον.

Effugimus scopulos Ithacæ, regna Laërtia, et exsecramur terram altricem sævi Ulyssis. Mox et nimbosa cacumina montis Leucatæ, et Apollo formidatus nautis aperitur. Nos fessi petimus hunc, et succedimus parvæ urbi. Anchora jacitur de prora; puppes stant in littore. Ergo tandem potiti insperata tellure, lustramurque Jovi, incendimusque aras votis; celebramusque Actia littora Iliacis ludis. Socii nostri nudati exercent patrias palæstras oleo labente: juvat nos evasisse tot Argolicas urbes, tenuissique fugam per medios hostes.

Effugimus scopulos Ithacæ, Laërtia regna,
Et terram altricem sævi exsecramur Ulyssis.
Mox et Leucatæ nimbosa cacumina montis,
Et formidatus nautis aperitur Apollo.
Hunc petimus fessi, et parvæ succedimus urbi.
Anchora de prora jacitur; stant littore puppes.
Ergo insperatâ tandem tellure potiti,
Lustramurque Jovi, votisque incendimus aras;
Actiaque Iliacis celebramus littora ludis.
Exercent patrias oleo labente palæstras
Nudati socii: juvat evasisse tot urbes
Argolicas, mediosque fugam tenuisse per hostes.

TRANSLATION.

Clifts of Ithaca, Laertes's Realms, and curse the Land that bred the inhuman Ulysses. Soon after this the cloudy Tops of Mount Leucata, and *the Temple of* Apollo, the Dread of Seamen, opens to our Eye. Hither we steer our Course oppressed with Toil, and make up to the little City. The Anchor is thrown out from the Prow; the Ships are ranged on the Shore. Thus at length possessed of wished-for Land, we are purified *for offering Sacrifice* to Jupiter, and kindle *Fires on* the Altars in order to perform our Vows, and signalize the Promontory of Actium by celebrating the Trojan Games. Our Crew, having their naked Limbs besmeared with slippery Oil, exercise the Wrestling Matches of their Country: We reflect with Pleasure on having escaped so many Grecian Cities, and pursued our Voyage *without Interruption* through the Midst of our Enemies.

NOTES.

272. *Scopulos Ithacæ.* Ithaca, now, *Isola del compare*, or *Val di compare*, the Island between *Cephalenia* and *Dulichium*. *Ulysses*'s native Seat; it was very barren, rugged, and mountainous, and therefore he calls it *Scopulos Ithacæ*, and subjoins, by Way of Irony Contempt, *Laertia regna*, as, in the first Book, *Neptune* first calls *Æolus*'s Realms *Immania Saxa*: Then adds in a Strain of Derision,

——————*Illa se jactet in aula*
Æolus, et clauso ventorum carcere regnet.
Æn. I. 144.

274. *Leucatæ.* The Island *Leucas*, *Leucates*, or *Leucate*, now *S. Maura*, subject to the *Turks*, and the Seat of a Bashaw. It lies between the *Acroceraunian* Mountains and the *Peloponnesus*, so near to the Promontory of *Actium*, in the western Coast of *Epirus*, that it is said to have once adjoined to that Continent. It got the Name of *Leucate*, *the white Island*, from a famous white Rock adjoining to it, which *Strabo* calls το αλμα, *i. e. the Lover's Leap*; it being supposed to have Effect to cure despairing Lovers, who were wont to throw themselves down from thence into the Sea. Among those who are said to have tried the Experiment, is the celebrated Poetess *Sappho*.

275. *Formidatus nautis Apollo.* Strabo informs us, that on Mount *Leucate* was a Temple dedicated to *Apollo*, where a human Sacrifice was yearly offered up in Honour of that God; For this Reason, or on Account of the Ruggedness of the Coast where this Temple stood, *Virgil* calls it *Apollo formidatus nautis*; the Name of the God to whom the Temple was dedicated being put for the Temple itself.

276. *Parvæ succedimus urbi.* This City was *Ambracia*, at that Time very inconsiderable, but *Augustus* enlarged it afterwards under the Name of *Nicopolis*.

277. *Stant littore puppes.* May signify the *Sterns rest on the Shore*, as Dr. *Trapp* has it.

280. *Iliacis ludis.* He alludes to the Games which *Augustus* celebrated in Commemoration of his Victory over *Antony* at *Actium*. *Virgil*, to pay his Court to *Augustus*, supposed *Æneas* to have landed on that Coast, and to have instituted those very Games which he appointed to be cele-brated

Interea magnum Sol circumvolvitur annum,
Et glacialis hyems Aquilonibus asperat undas. 285
Ære cavo clypeum, magni gestamen Abantis,
Postibus adversis figo, et rem carmine signo:
Æneas hæc de Danais victoribus arma.
Linquere tum portus jubeo, et considere transtris.
Certatim socii feriunt mare, et æquora verrunt.
Protinus aërias Phæacum abscondimus arces, 291
Littoraque Epiri legimus, portuque subimus
Chaonio, et celsam Buthroti ascendimus urbem.
Hic incredibilis rerum fama occupat aures, 294
Priamiden Helenum Graias regnare per urbes,

Interea Sol circumvolvitur magnum annum, et glacialis hyems asperat undas Aquilonibus. Figo postibus adversis clypeum ex cavo ære, gestamen magni Abantis, et signo rem hoc carmine: Æneas posuit hæc arma relata de Danais victoribus. Tum jubeo eos linquere portus, et considere transtris. Socii feriunt mare certatim, et verrunt æquora. Protinus abscondimus aërias arces Phæacum, legimusque littora Epiri, subimusque Chaonio portu, et ascendimus celsam urbem Buthroti. Hic incredibilis fama rerum occupat nostras aures, Helenum Priamiden regnare per Graias urbes,

TRANSLATION.

Mean while the Sun finishes the Revolution of the great Year, and frosty Winter exasperates the Waves with the North-winds. On the fronting Door-posts *of the Temple* I set up a Buckler of hollow Brass, which mighty Abas wore, and notify the Action by *this* Verse: *These Arms Æneas* WON *from the victorious Greeks.* Then I order *our Crew* to leave the Port, and take their Seats on the Benches. They with emulous Ardour lash the Sea, and sweep the Waves. In a Trice we lose Sight of the airy Towers of the Phæacians, cruise along the Coasts of Epirus, and enter the Chaonian Port, and ascend the lofty City of Buthrotus. Here a Report of Facts scarce credible invades our Ears, that Helenus, Priam's Son, was reigning over Grecian Cities, possessed of the Spouse and

NOTES.

brated every fifth Year. Whence we may with some Probability conjecture, that four Years were now elapsed since *Æneas* left *Troy*, and that the following 284th Verse,

Interea magnum sol circumvolvitur annum,

refers to the Beginning of the fifth Year.

284. *Magnum annum.* A Year of twelve solar Months, to distinguish it from a lunar Year.

285. *Asperat undas.* It provokes or sharpens all their Keenness and Rage, makes them rough, boisterous, and nipping cold.

286. *Abantis.* This *Abas* was probably one of those *Greeks* who were in Company with *Androgeos*, whom *Æneas* and his Party slew, and stripped of their Armour, which they exchanged for their own. *Servius* tells us a long Fable about him, which is hardly worth the Pains to transcribe.

288. *Æneas hæc, &c. Detracta consecravit,* or the like, is understood, it being in the usual elliptical Stile of Inscriptions.

291. *Phæacum.* The Inhabitants of *Phæacia*, or *Corcyra*, now *Corfu*, an Island that lies to the West of the Promontory of *Actium*. It is celebrated by the Ancients for its fruitful Gardens and Orchards:

Proxima Phæacum felicibus obsita pomis
Rura petunt.

Ovid Met. XIII. 719.

——————*Illa jubebit*
Poma dari, quorum solo pascaris odore,
Qualia perpetuus Phæacum autumnus habebit.

Juven. Sat. V. 150.

Here it is that *Homer* places the famous Gardens of *Alcinous*, who was King of that Island.

292. *Epiri.* A Country in *Europe*, once a flourishing Kingdom; it is bounded by the *Ionian* Sea on the South and West, by *Achaia* and *Thessaly* to the East, and *Macedonia* to the North. It was divided into *Chaonia*, *Thesprotia*, *Acarnania*, and *Ætolia*.

294. *Incredibilis fama.* To be sure this was

potitum conjugio sceptrisque Pyrrhi Æacidæ, et Andromachen iterum cessisse patrio marito. Obstupui, pectusque est incensum miro amore compellare virum, et cognoscere tantos casus. Progredior è portu, linquens classes et littora. Tum forte Andromache libabat cineri Hectoris *solennes dapes et tristia dona, ante urbem, in luco, ad undam falsi Simoentis, vocabatque Manes ad Hectoreum tumulum, quem inanem sacraverat ex viridi cespite, et geminas aras causam lacrymis. Ut amens conspexit me venientem, et Troïa arma circum me, exterrita magnis* his *monstris, diriguit in visu medio, calor reliquit* ejus *ossa: labitur, et tandem vix fatur longo post tempore: O nate Deâ, affersne te mihi vera facies, verus nuncius? vivisne? aut, si alma lux recessit* tibi, *ubi est Hector? Dixit, effuditque lacrymas, et implevit omnem locum clamore.*

Conjugio Æacidæ Pyrrhi sceptrisque potitum,
Et patrio Andromachen iterum cessisse marito.
Obstupui, miroque incensum pectus amore
Compellare virum, et casus cognoscere tantos.
Progredior portu, classes et littora linquens.
Solennes tum forte dapes, et tristia dona, 301
Ante urbem, in luco, falsi Simoëntis ad undam,
Libabat cineri Andromache, manesque vocabat
Hectoreum ad tumulum, viridi quem cespite inanem, 304
Et geminas, causam lacrymis, sacraverat aras.
Ut me conspexit venientem, et Troïa circum
Arma amens vidit, magnis exterrita monstris,
Diriguit visu in medio; calor ossa reliquit:
Labitur, et longo vix tandem tempore fatur:
Verane te facies, verus mihi nuncius affers, 310
Nate Dea? vivisne? aut, si lux alma recessit,
Hector ubi est? Dixit, lacrymasque effudit, et omnem

TRANSLATION.

Scepter of Pyrrhus the Grandchild of Æacus, and that Andromache had again fallen to a Lord of her own Country. I was amazed, and my Bosom glowed with strange Desire to greet the Hero, and learn the History of so signal Revolutions of Fortune. I set forward from the Port, leaving the Fleet and Shore. Andromache, as it chanced, was then offering to *Hector's* Ashes her anniversary Feast and mournful Oblations before the City in a Grove, by the Streams of the fictitious Simois, and invoked the Manes at Hector's Tomb; an empty *Tomb* which she had consecrated of green Turf, and two Altars, Incentives to her Grief. So soon as she saw me coming up, and to her Amazement beheld the Trojan Arms around me, terrified with a Prodigy so great, she fainted away at the very Sight: Vital Warmth forsook her Limbs. She sinks down, and at length after a long Interval *thus* with faultring Accent speaks: Goddess-born, do you present yourself to me a real *substantial* Form, a real Messenger? Do you live? Or, if from you the auspicious Light is fled, *say* where *my* Hector is? She said, and shed a Flood of Tears, filling all the Place with *doleful Shrieks*. While she is in this

NOTES.

a very surprising Revolution of Fortune, that the Son of *Priam* was the King of *Epirus*, and possessed of the Throne of *Pyrrhus*, that very Son of *Achilles* who had put his Father and so many of his Relations to Death; and that he was now wedded to his Brother *Hector's* Widow, after she had been married to his most inveterate Enemy. Yet these Events are not the Poet's Invention. For *Justin* tells us, that *Pyrrhus* was reconciled to *Helenus*, shared with him his Kingdom, and gave him *Andromache* in Marriage, Lib. XVIII. 3.

297. *Patrio marito.* *Andromache* herself was a *Theban* Princess, but, by marrying *Hector*, *Troy* became her Country.

305. *Geminas aras.* Some will have it, that one

Implevit clamore locum. Vix pauca furenti
Subjicio, et raris turbatus vocibus hiſco:
Vivo equidem, vitamque extrema per omnia duco.
Ne dubita; nam vera vides.
Heu! quis te caſus dejectam conjuge tanto
Excipit? aut quæ digna ſatis fortuna reviſit?
Hectoris Andromache, Pyrrhin' connubia ſervas?
Dejecit vultum, et demiſſâ voce locuta eſt:
O felix una ante alias Priameïa virgo,

Vix ſubjicio pauca ei furenti, et turbatus hiſco raris vocibus: equidem vivo, ducoque vitam per omnia extrema. Ne dubita; nam vides vera. Heu! quis caſus excepit te dejectam tanto conjuge? aut quæ fortuna ſatis digna reviſit te? Andromache Hectoris, ſervaſne connubia Pyrrhi? Illa dejecit vultum, et ſic locuta eſt demiſſâ voce: O Priameïa virgo, una felix ante alias,

TRANSLATION.

Tranſport I with much ado briefly reply, and in great Perturbation open my Mouth in theſe few broken Words: I am alive indeed, and ſpin out Life through all Extremes. Entertain no Doubt, for all you ſee is real. Ah *ſay* what Accidents of Life have overtaken you, ſince you was thrown down from *the happy Poſſeſſion of* your illuſtrious Lord? Or what Fortune, ſome Way ſuited to your Merit, hath viſited you once more? Is then Hector's Andromache bound in Wedlock to Pyrrhus? Downward ſhe caſt her Eyes, and thus in humble Accents *ſpoke:* O happy, ſingularly happy the Fate of Priam's Virgin-daughter, who, compelled

NOTES.

one of theſe Altars was for *Hector*, and the other for his Son *Aſtyanax*, whom the *Greeks* had thrown headlong from the Tower of *Troy:* But others think they were both for *Hector*, it being cuſtomary to erect two Altars to the Manes, eſpecially to Heroes, who were conſidered as a Sort of Deities, and the infernal Deities delighted *in an even Number*. See the Note on Verſe 63.

319. *Hectoris Andromache.* Some read *Hectoris Andromachen*, to conſtrue with the preceding Verb *reviſit*. The Paraphraſe which *Ruæus* gives of the Paſſage is not accurate: *O Andromache, teneſne conjugium Hectoris, an Pyrrhi?* Now, whatever Senſe he may put upon the Words *teneſne conjugium*, when joined to *Hectoris*, in the firſt Part of the Sentence, they muſt, in Propriety of Writing, ſignify the ſame Thing, when joined to *Pyrrhi* in the laſt Part; ſo that, according to him, the Meaning of *Æneas*'s Queſtion will be, Say, *Andromache*, whether you are wedded to *Hector* or to *Pyrrhus?* Which every one ſees to be abſurd, eſpecially after *Æneas*'s having ſaid immediately before, *dejectam conjuge tanto*, that ſhe was brought low by the Loſs of that great Lord, meaning *Hector*. The Conſtruction therefore is, *Hectoris Andromache, ſervaſne connubia Pyrrhi?* And is *Hector*'s *Andromache* wedded to *Pyrrhus!* which is not ſo much a Queſtion, as an Exclamation of Surprize and Condolence. That *Hectoris Andromache* is to be conſtrued this Way, appears from *Juſtin*, who gives her the ſame honourable Deſignation, Lib. XVII. Cap. 3. *Atque ita Heleno, filio Priami regis—regnum Chaonum, et* Andromachen Hectoris—*uxorem (Pyrrhus) tradidit.*

321. *O felix una ante alias Priameïa virgo.* *Quintilian* quotes this as an Example of *Virgil*'s Talent in the *Pathetic:* In order to ſhew the Extremity of *Andromache*'s Miſery, he makes her even envy the Fate of *Polyxena*, which, in the Eyes of all the World beſides, was moſt wretched and deplorable: How wretched then muſt *Andromache*'s State have been, if, compared to her, even *Polyxena* was happy? *Quam miſer enim caſus Andromachæ, ſi comparata ei felix Polyxena?* Inſtit. Lib. VI. Cap. 3. See alſo *Macrob.* Saturn. Lib. XIV. Cap. 6.

321. *Priameïa virgo.* Polyxena, the Daughter of *Priam* and *Hecuba*, with whom *Achilles* fell in Love. She was the innocent Occaſion of *Achilles*'s Death; for *Priam* having invited that Hero to *Troy*, under Pretext of giving his Daughter in Marriage, while ſhe was in the Temple of *Apollo*, where the Marriage Rites were to have been performed; *Paris*, in the Time that *Deiphobus* was embracing *Achilles*, came

juſſa mori ad hoſtilem tumulum ſub altis mœnibus Trojæ; quæ non pertulit ullos ſortitus, nec captiva tetigit cubile victoris heri! nos vectæ per diverſa æquora, patriâ incenſâ, in ſervitio enixæ tulimus faſtus Achilleæ ſtirpis, ſuperbumque juvenem, qui, deinde ſecutus Ledæam Hermionen, Lacedæmoniosque Hymenæos, tranſmiſit me famulam habendam Heleno famuloque ipſi. Aſt Oreſtes, inflammatus magno amore ereptæ conjugis, et agitatus Furiis ſcelerum,

Hoſtilem ad tumulum Trojæ ſub mœnibus altis
Juſſa mori; quæ ſortitus non pertulit ullos,
Nec victoris heri tetigit captiva cubile!
Nos, patriâ incenſâ, diverſa per æquora vectæ,
Stirpis Achilleæ faſtus, juvenemque ſuperbum,
Servitio enixæ, tulimus; qui deinde ſecutus
Ledæam Hermionen, Lacedæmonioſque Hymenæos,
Me famulam famuloque Heleno tranſmiſit habendam:
Aſt illum, ereptæ magno inflammatus amore
Conjugis, et ſcelerum furiis agitatus, Oreſtes

TRANSLATION.

to die at the Enemy's Tomb under the lofty Walls of Troy, ſuffered not in having any Lots caſt for her, nor as a Captive ever touched the Bed of a victorious Lord! We, after the Deſolation of our Country, being tranſported over various Seas, have in Thraldom bore with a Mother's Throws the Inſolence of Achilles's Heir, and a haughty imperious Youth: Who afterwards, attaching himſelf to Hermione the Grand-daughter of Leda, and a Lacedemonian Match, delivered me over a Slave into the Poſſeſſion of Helenus, *likewiſe* a Slave. But Oreſtes, inflamed by the Violence of Love to his *betrothed* Spouſe *now* ſnatched from him, and hurried on by the Furies of his Crimes, ſurprizes him in an un-

NOTES.

came behind, and ſhot him to Death with an Arrow. *Achilles*, with his expiring Breath, enjoined *Pyrrhus* to revenge his Death upon *Priam*'s perfidious Family when *Troy* was taken, and particularly to ſacrifice *Polyxena* at his Tomb, which accordingly was put in Execution.

323. *Sortitus non pertulit ullos.* After the Conqueſt of *Troy*, the *Grecian* Princes drew Lots among themſelves for the Choice of the Captives. This is the Calamity from which *Andromache* pronounces *Polyxena* happy in being delivered by Death.

327. *Servitio enixæ.* *Enixa* ſignifies not only one who has ſuffered the Pains of Child-bearing, but alſo who has been harraſſed with ſore Toil and Labour in general; and ſo ſome of the beſt Expoſitors underſtand it here: And, indeed, one is naturally led to this Senſe, for there ſeems to be no Propriety in the Expreſſion, if we underſtand it of her having borne a Son to *Pyrrhus*.

328. *Ledæam Hermionen.* Hermione was the Daughter of *Menelaus*, King of *Sparta* or *Lacedæmon*, by *Helen*, the Daughter of *Jupiter* and *Leda*. She was betrothed by *Tyndareus*, *Leda*'s Huſband, in *Menelaus*'s Abſence, to her Couſin *Oreſtes*, the Son of *Agamemnon*; and again betrothed at *Troy* by *Menelaus*, to *Pyrrhus*, the Son of *Achilles*, who went to *Sparta*, and carried her off. *Oreſtes*, in Revenge, ſlew *Pyrrhus* at *Delphos*, whither he had gone to conſult the Oracle about his future Offspring by *Hermione*.

331. *Furiis agitatus Oreſtes.* Oreſtes, the Son of *Agamemnon* and *Clytemneſtra*, ſlew his Mother *Clytemneſtra*, who was acceſſary with *Ægiſthus* to the Murder of his Father. After this Action, he is ſaid to have been long haunted and tormented by the *Furies*, i. e. He was ſtung with grievous Remorſe for imbruing his Hands in his Mother's Blood. He was expiated at length, and received Abſolution from the Court of *Areopagus* at *Athens*, and having married *Hermione*, after he had put *Pyrrhus* to Death, united the Kingdom of *Sparta* to his own hereditary Dominions.

331. *Furiis agitatus.* The *Furies* were three in Number, *Alecto*, *Tiſiphone*, and *Megera*. *Cicero* has a remarkable Paſſage to explain what was meant by the *Furies*: *Nolite enim putare, quemadmodum in fabulis ſæpenumero videtis, eos, qui aliquid impie ſceleratèque commiſerint, agitari*

Excipit incautum, patriasque obtruncat ad aras.
Morte Neoptolemi, regnorum reddita cessit
Pars Heleno; qui Chaonios cognomine campos,
Chaoniamque omnem, Trojano à Chaone dixit;
Pergamaque, Iliacamque jugis hanc addidit arcem.
Sed tibi qui cursum venti, quæ fata, dedere?
Aut quis te ignarum nostris Deus appulit oris?
Quid puer Ascanius? superatne, et vescitur aurâ,
Quem tibi jam Troja——
Ecquæ jam puero est amissæ cura parentis?
Ecquid in antiquam virtutem, animosque viriles,
Et pater Æneas, et avunculus excitat Hector?

excipit illum incautum, obtruncatque ad patrias aras. Ex morte Neoptolemi, pars regnorum reddita cessit Heleno; qui dixit campos cognomine Chaonios, omnemque regionem Chaoniam à Chaone Trojano, addiditque Pergama, hancque Iliacam arcem jugis. Sed qui venti, quæ fata dedere cursum tibi? aut quis Deus appulit te ignarum nostris oris? quid puer Ascanius agit? superatne, et vescitur aura? quem Troja jam tibi—— ecquæ cura amissæ parentis jam est puero? ecquid et pater Æneas, et avunculus Hector excitat eum in antiquam virtutem animosque viriles?

TRANSLATION.

guarded Hour, and assassinates him at his Country's Altar. By the Death of Neoptolemus a Part of his Kingdom fell into the Hands of Helenus; who denominated the Plains Chaonian, and the whole Country Chaonia from Chaon the Trojan *his Brother*; and built on the Mountains *another* Pergamus and this Trojan Fort. But *say* what Winds, what Fates have guided your Course? Or what God hath landed you on our Coasts without your Knowledge? What is become of the Boy Ascanius? Lives he still, and breathes the *vital* Air? Whom, on your Care, when Troy was——Has the Boy now any Concern for the Loss of his Mother? Is he incited by *the Example of* both his Father Æneas and Uncle Hector to ancient Valour and manly Courage? Thus bathed in Tears she spoke, and

NOTES.

ri et perterreri Furiarum tædis ardentibus. *Sua quemque fraus, et suus terror maxime vexat; suum quemque scelus agitat, amentiaque afficit; suæ malæ cogitationes, conscientiæque animi terrent: hæ sunt impiis assiduæ, domesticæque Furiæ; quæ dies noctesque parentum pœnas à consceleratissimis filiis repetant.* Pro Roscio. 24. These Stings and galling Remorses were *Orestes's Furies*, which the Poet therefore calls *Furiæ scelerum, the Furies of his Crimes.* It is probable, however, that *Orestes* pictured to his own disturbed Imagination this Notion of his being haunted by the *Furies*, armed with all those Terrors in which they were drawn by the Poets; as *Suetonius* relates to have been the Case of *Nero. Sæpe confessus exagitari se materna specie, verberibus Furiarum, ac tædis ardentibus.*

332. *Patrias ad aras.* Pyrrhus was slain at the Altar of *Apollo* of *Delphos*, and his Father *Achilles*, at the Altar of *Thymbræan Apollo* at *Troy*. Interpreters therefore are puzzled to explain what is meant by *patrias aras*, some understand the Altars of *Apollo*, at whose Altar his Father was slain before; *Ruæus*, after *Turnebus*, explains it *the Altar of his Country*, because the Temple of *Delphos* was in the Center of *Greece*, *Pyrrhus*'s Country.

335. *Trojano à Chaone.* Chaon was one of *Priam*'s Sons, and the Brother of *Helenus*, who slew him unwittingly in Hunting, and, in Honour to his Memory, called his Kingdom after his Name.

340. *Quem tibi jam Troja.* This is a Proof that *Virgil* left the *Æneid* imperfect; for, however he might, for the Sake of Variety, designedly leave some Verses unfinished when the Sense was compleat, it cannot be imagined that he would chuse to leave an unfinished Sense. Some have absurdly filled up the Verse thus:

Quem tibi jam Troja peperit fumante Creusa,

not considering that *Ascanius*, at the Taking of *Troy*, was old enough to accompany his Father in his Flight. Others,

Quem tibi jam Trojâ obsessâ est enixa Creusa;

which, however it may be *Virgil*'s Sense, has nothing of his Poetical Spirit.

341. *[illegible]* A Question is here raised,

Illa *lacrymans fundebat talia, ciebatque longos fletus incassum; quum heros Helenus Priamides affert sese à mœnibus, multis eum comitantibus, agnoscitque suos, lætusque ducit eos ad limina; et multum fundit lacrymas inter singula verba. Procedo, et agnosco parvam Trojam, Pergamaque simulata magnis, et arentem rivum Xanthi cognomine* dictum, *amplectorque limina Scææ portæ. Necnon et Teucri simul fruuntur sociâ urbe. Rex accipiebat illos in amplis porticibus. In medio aulai libabant pocula Bacchi, dapibus impositis auro, tenebantque pateras.*

Jamque dies, alterque dies, processit, et auræ vocant vela, carbasusque inflatur tumido Austro. Aggredior vatem his dictis, ac quæso talia: O Trojugena, interpres Divûm, qui sentis numina Phœbi, qui sentis *Tripodas, lauros Clarii* Apollinis, *qui* sentis *sidera,*

Talia fundebat lacrymans, longosque ciebat
Incassum fletus; cum sese à mœnibus heros
Priamides multis Helenus comitantibus affert,
Agnoscitque suos, lætusque ad limina ducit;
Et multum lacrymas verba inter singula fundit.
Procedo, et parvam Trojam, simulataque magnis
Pergama, et arentem Xanthi cognomine rivum,
Agnosco; Scææque amplector limina portæ:
Necnon et Teucri sociâ simul urbe fruuntur:
Illos porticibus rex accipiebat in amplis.
Aulaï in medio libabant pocula Bacchi,
Impositis auro dapibus, paterasque tenebant.
Jamque dies, alterque dies, processit; et auræ
Vela vocant, tumidoque inflatur carbasus Austro.
His vatem aggredior dictis, ac talia quæso:
Trojugena, interpres Divûm, qui numina Phœbi,
Qui tripodas, Clarii lauros, qui sidera, sentis,

TRANSLATION.

heaved long unavailing Sobs; when the Hero Helenus, Priam's Son, advances from the City with a numerous Retinue, knows his Friends, with Joy conducts them to his Palace, and sheds Tears in Abundance between each Word. I set forward, and survey the little Troy, the *Castle of* Pergamus, that bore Resemblance to the great Original, a scanty Rivulet that bore Xanthus's Name, and I embrace the Threshold of the Scæan Gate. The Trojans too at the same Time enjoy the friendly City. The King entertained them in his spacious Galleries. In the Midst of the Court they quaffed Brimmers of Wine, while the Banquet was served in Gold, and each stood with a Goblet in his Hand. And now one Day, and a second passed on, when the Gales invite our Sails, and the Canvas bellies by the swelling South-wind. *Then* in these Words I accost the prophetic *Helenus*, and question him thus: Son of Troy, Interpreter of the Gods, who knowest the divine Will of Phœbus, *the Mysteries of* the Tripods, the Laurels

NOTES.

raised, how *Andromache* came to know that *Creüsa* was lost. But where was the Difficulty of her being apprized of this before she left the *Trojan* Coast, especially when *Æneas* himself returned to *Troy* in quest of her.

345. *Libabant pocula.* It was customary for them at Entertainments, after the first Service, to introduce a Drinking-bout, with a Libation to the Gods. See Book first, Verse 740.

360. *Tripodas.* The Tripod was a Kind of three footed Stool, whereon the Priestess of *Apollo* sat when she delivered the Oracles.

360. *Clarii lauros.* They had a Way of Divination, by burning a Branch of Laurel, the Crackling of which was a good Omen; but, if it consumed away without Noise, it was unlucky, as in *Tibullus*, Lib. II. 5. 81.

Ut succensa sacris crepitet bene laurea flammis,
Omine quo felix et sacer annus erat.

360. *Clarii.* Clarius was an Epithet given to *Apollo*, from *Claros*, a City in *Ionia*, near *Colophon*, where he had a famous Temple and Oracle.

361. *Volucrum*

Et volucrum linguas, et præpetis omina pennæ,
Fare, age; namque omnem cursum mihi prospera dixit
Relligio; et cuncti suaserunt numine Divi
Italiam petere, et terras tentare repostas:
Sola novum, dictuque nefas, Harpyia Celæno
Prodigium canit, et tristes denunciat iras,
Obscœnamque famem. Quæ prima pericula vito?
Quidve sequens tantos possim superare labores?
Hic Helenus, cæsis primum de more juvencis,
Exorat pacem Divûm, vittasque resolvit
Sacrati capitis, meque ad tua limina, Phœbe,
Ipse manu multo suspensum numine ducit;
Atque hæc deinde canit divino ex ore sacerdos:
Nate Deâ (nam te majoribus ire per altum

et linguas volucrum, et omina præpetis pennæ, age, fare; namque religio prospera mihi dixit omnem cursum, et cuncti Divi suaserunt mihi petere Italiam, et tentare repostas terras: Harpyia Celæno sola canit novum prodigium, nefasque dictu, et denunciat nobis *tristes iras obscœnamque famem. Quæ prima pericula vito? quidve sequens possum superare tantos labores? Hic Helenus, juvencis primum cæsis de more, exorat pacem Divûm, resolvitque vittas sacrati capitis, ipseque ducit me manu ad tua limina, O Phœbe! suspensum multo numine; atque sacerdos deinde canit hæc ex divino ore: O nate Deâ (nam manifesta fides est* mihi *te ire per altum* mare *majoribus auspiciis.*

TRANSLATION.

of the Clarian *God*; who knowest *the Science of* the Stars, the ominous Sounds of Birds, and the Prognostics of *every* Wing that swiftly flies. Come *then*, declare (for *hitherto the Omens of* Religion have pronounced my whole Voyage to be prosperous, and all the Gods, by Indications of their divine Will, have directed me to go in Pursuit of Italy, and attempt a Settlement in Lands remote: The Harpy Celæno alone predicts a Prodigy strange and horrible to relate, and denounces *against us* direful Vengeance, and foul unnatural Famine) what are the principal Dangers I am to shun? Or by the Pursuit of what Means may I surmount Toils so great? Upon this Helenus first solicits the Peace of the Gods by sacrificing Bullocks in due Form, then unbinds the Fillets of his consecrated Head, and himself leads me by the Hand to thy Temple, O Phœbus, anxious with great Awe of the God: Then the Priest, from his Lips divine, delivers these Predictions: Goddess-born (for that you steer through the Deep on some

NOTES.

361. *Volucrum linguas, et præpetis omina pennæ.* Some birds were subservient to Divination by the Sounds they uttered, and these were called *Oscines*: Of which Kind were the Crows, Ravens, *&c.* Hor. III. Carm. Ode XXVII. 2.

Oscinem corvum prece suscitabo
Solis ab ortu.

Others again answered the same End by their Manner of flying, and were called *Præpetes*.

370. *Vittasque resolvit.* The Priest, in performing Sacrifice, had his Head bound about with Fillets; but, now that he is going to prophesy, he assumes the loose Air of an Enthusiast, as is said of the *Sybil*, Æn. VI. 48.

Non comptæ mansere comæ.

372. *Multo suspensum numine.* Some read *suspensus*, which means, that *Helenus* was full of Anxiety and Perturbation from the Influence of the God. But it is much better applied to *Æneas*, who had good Reason to be in awful Suspense about his future Fortune.

375. *Auspiciis majoribus.* Among the various Omens and Prognostics whence they got Insight into Futurity, some were of a more important Nature, awakened greater Attention, shewed a more extraordinary Interposition of the Gods, and portended the Birth of some more glorious Events: Of this Kind were the heavenly Signs, Visions, and extraordinary Appearances, which had all along accompanied *Æneas* since he first set out from *Troy*.

rex Deûm sic sortitur fata, volvitque vices, is ordo vertitur) dictis expediam tibi pauca è multis, quo tu hospita tutior lustres æquora, et possis considere Ausonio portu; nam Parcæ prohibent te scire cætera, Junoque Saturnia vetat Helenum fari ea. Principio, longa via invia longis terris procul dividit Italiam à te, quam tu, ignare, jam rere esse propinquam, parasque invadere vicinos portus. Et remus lentandus est in Trinacriâ undâ, et æquor Ausonii salis lustrandum tuis navibus,

Auspiciis manifesta fides, sic fata Deûm rex
Sortitur, volvitque vices, is vertitur ordo)
Pauca tibi è multis, quo tutior hospita lustres
Æquora, et Ausonio possis considere portu,
Expediam dictis: prohibent nam cætera Parcæ
Scire, Helenum ferique vetat Saturnia Juno.
Principio, Italiam, quam tu jam rere propinquam,
Vicinosque ignare paras invadere portus,
Longa procul longis via dividit invia terris:
Ante et Trinacriâ lentandus remus in undâ,
Et salis Ausonii lustrandum navibus æquor,

TRANSLATION.

Enterprize of great Moment *to me* is unquestionably evident: So the Sovereign of the Gods dispenses his Decree, thus he fixes the Series of revolving Events; such the Scheme of Things is hastening to the Birth), that you may with the more Safety cross the Seas to which you are a Stranger, and settle *at last* in the Ionian Port, I will unfold to you a few Particulars of many; for the Destinies hinder you from knowing the rest, and Saturnian Juno forbids Helenus to reveal it. First of all a long intricate Voyage, with a Length of Lands, divides *you from* Italy, which you ignorantly deem already near, and whose Ports you are preparing to enter, as if they were just at hand. Before that happen, you shall both ply the bending Oar in the Trinacrian Wave, and visit with your Fleet the Plains of the

NOTES.

375. *Fata sortitur.* *Dispenses his Oracles by Lot*, alluding to the Manner of consulting the Oracle, which was sometimes by drawing Lots.

379. *Prohibent nam cætera scire.* Pierius observes, that in almost all the ancient Copies there is a full Stop at *scire*; and *Servius* chooses this Pointing for several Reasons, which I shall mention, and add some others. First then, if we make both Parts of the Sentence refer to *Helenus*, there will be an inconsistency between the first Part and the last: *Prohibent scire—farique vetat.* Would *Juno* forbid to declare or reveal to others what he did not know himself? Besides, he had said before, he would only inform him of a few Events of the many that were to befal him: *Pauca tibi è multis expediam*; which implies, that *Helenus* knew the rest, but was restrained by Heaven from communicating them to him: Some of these Events it was not proper for him to know, because the Accomplishment of them depended on his own Free-will: Others again *Juno* with-held *Helenus* from revealing to him, that he might be the more perplexed with Doubt and Anxiety, and the more surprized and unprovided against the Calamity: Of this Kind is the Interpretation of *Celæno*'s Prophecy, which *Helenus* appears to have understood, for he bids him not to be much concerned about it, since the Gods would extricate him from that Distress, Verse 394.

Nec tu mensarum morsus horresce futuros,
Fata viam invenient——

So also the Death of his Father, with respect to which *Æneas* questions not *Helenus*'s Foreknowledge, but only complains of him for not revealing it to him, Verse 712.

Nec vates Helenus, cum multa horrenda moneret,
Hos mihi prædixit luctus.——

384. *Trinacriâ.* *Sicily*, so called from its triangular Form, made by three Promontories of *Pelorus*, *Pachynus*, and *Lilybæum*, in which it terminates.

384. *Lentandus.* A descriptive Word, which denotes the bending Motion of the Oar, occasioned by the Resistance of the Waves; and therefore signifies that they were to struggle hard in rowing.

385. *Ausonii.* See above, the Note on Verse 171.

Infernique lacus, Ææxæque insula Circes;
Quàm tutâ possis urbem componere terrâ.
Signa tibi dicam: tu condita mente teneto.
Cum tibi sollicito, secreti ad fluminis undam,
Littoreis ingens inventa sub ilicibus sus
Triginta capitum fetus enixa jacebit,
Alba, solo recubans, albi circum ubera nati;
Is locus urbis erit; requies ea certa laborum.
Nec tu mensarum morsus horresce futuros:
Fata viam invenient, aderitque vocatus Apollo.
Has autem terras, Italique hanc littoris oram,
Proxima quæ nostri perfunditur æquoris æstu,
Effuge: cuncta malis habitantur mœnia Graiis.
Hìc et Narycii posuerunt mœnia Locri,

infernique lacus, insulaque Ææa Circes, antequam possis componere urbem in tuta terra. Dicam tibi signa: tu teneto ea condita mente. Cùm ingens sus inventa tibi sollicito, ad undam secreti fluminis sub littoreis ilicibus, jacebit enixa fœtus triginta capitum, alba, recubans solo, et albi nati circum ejus ubera, is erit locus urbis, ea erit certa requies tibi laborum. Nec tu horresce futuros morsus mensarum: Fata invenient tibi viam, Apolloque vocatus aderit. Effuge autem has terras, hancque oram Itali littoris, quæ proxima perfunditur æstu nostri æquoris: cuncta ista mœnia habitantur malis Graiis. Hìc et Narycii Locri posuerunt mœnia,

TRANSLATION.

Ausonian Sea, the infernal Lakes, and Ææan Circe's Isle, before it be in your Power to build a City in a quiet peaceful Land. The Signs I will declare to you, keep them treasured up in your Mind. When, thoughtfully musing by the Streams of the secret River, you shall find a large Sow that has brought forth a Litter of thirty Young, reclining on the Ground, under the Elms, that shade the Banks *of the River*, white *the Dam*, the Offspring white around her Dugs: That shall be the Station of the City: There is the Period fixed to *all* thy Labours: Nor be disturbed at the future Event of eating your Tables: The Fates will find out an Expedient, and Apollo invoked will befriend you. But shun those Coasts, and those nearest Limits of the Italian Shore, which are washed by the Tide of our Sea: All *those* Cities are inhabited by the mischievous Greeks. Here the Locrians of the City Narycium have raised their Walls, and Cretan Ido-

NOTES.

386 *Æææque insula Circes.* Circe was the Daughter of the *Sun* and the Nymph *Perse*; she is called *Ææan* from *Æa*, an Island and City belonging to the Kingdom of *Colchos*, about the Mouth of the River *Phasis*. She married the King of the *Sarmatians*, whom having poisoned, she fled to *Italy* to a Promontory, which from her was denominated *Circe's Mount*, now *Circello*; The Marshes surrounding it, which are now drained, gave it the Form of an Island.

387. *Tutâ terrâ.* He says *in a safe Land*, because he had been baffled in his former Attempts to build in *Thrace* and *Crete*.

390. *Littoreis ingens.* See the Accomplishment of this Prediction in the eighth Book, Verse 42. The Holms, that shade the Banks of the *Tyber*, are here called *littorea, along the Shore or Bank.*

393. *Is locus urbis erit.* Here *Alba* was built, which had its Name from this Omen of the white Sow and her white Pigs:

Et stetit Alba potens albæ suis omine dicta.
Propert. IV.

396. *Has autem terras.* The Lands of *Calabria* and *Apulia*, formerly called *Magna Græcia, Great Greece*, which *Helenus* points out to *Æneas*, their Distance from *Epirus* not being very considerable.

399. *Narycii Locri.* The *Locrians* originally were a People of *Phocis* in *Achaia*. They followed *Ajax Oileus* to the Siege of *Troy*, Iliad II. 527, and a Colony of them settled in *Magna Græcia*, either under the Conduct of the

same

et Lyctius Idomeneus obſedit Sallentinos campos milite: hic eſt illa parva Petilia ſubnixa muro Philoctetæ Melibœi ducis. Quin, ubi tuæ claſſes tranſmiſſæ trans æquora ſteterint, et jam ſolves vota, aris poſitis in littore, tu velare adopertus quoad comas purpureo amictu, ne qua hoſtilis facies occurrat tibi inter ſanctos ignes in honore Deorum, et turbet omina. Socii tenento *hunc morem ſacrorum, tu ipſe teneto hunc: caſti tui nepotes maneant in hac religione. Aſt ubi ventus admoverit te digreſſum* hinc *Siculæ oræ, et clauſtra anguſti Pelori rareſcent;*

Et Sallentinos obſedit milite campos
Lyctius Idomeneus: hic illa ducis Melibœi
Parva Philoctetæ ſubnixa Petilia muro.
Quin, ubi tranſmiſſæ ſteterint trans æquora claſſes,
Et poſitis aris jam vota in littore ſolves;
Purpureo velare comas adopertus amictu:
Ne qua inter ſanctos ignes in honore Deorum
Hoſtilis facies occurrat, et omina turbet.
Hunc ſocii morem ſacrorum, hunc ipſe teneto:
Hac caſti maneant in religione nepotes.
Aſt ubi digreſſum Siculæ te admoverit oræ
Ventus, et anguſti rareſcent clauſtra Pelori;

TRANSLATION.

menus with his Troops has poſſeſſed the Plains of Salentum: Here ſtands that little City Petilia defended by the Walls of Philoctetes the Melibœan Chief. Further, when your Fleet, having croſſed the Seas, ſhall come to a Station, and you ſhall pay your Vows at the Altars raiſed on the Shore, *be ſure to* cover your Head, muffling yourſelf up in a purple Veil; leſt the Face of an Enemy, amidſt the ſacred Fires in Honour of the Gods, appear, and diſturb the Omens. This Cuſtom, in Sacrifice, let your Friends, this yourſelf obſerve: To this religious Inſtitution, let your pious Deſcendants adhere. But when, after ſetting out, the Wind ſhall waft you to the Sicilian Coaſt, and the Streights of narrow Pelorus ſhall

NOTES.

ſame *Ajax Oileus*, or rather (he having died in his Return from *Troy*, ſee *Æn.* I. 44.) of *Evanthes*. There they built a City called *Narycia* or *Narycium*, probably after the Name of *Naryx*, *Ajax*'s native City.

400. *Sallentinos campos.* The *Sallentines* were a People in the eaſtern Part of *Italy*, whoſe Country ſtretched out into the Sea, like a Peninſula, over-againſt *Epirus*, now called *Terra d'Otranto*, formerly *Meſſapia* and *Japygia*. They derived their Name from the Promontory of *Sallentinum*, the ſame with *Japygium*, now the Cape of *Saint Mary*, which terminates that Part of *Italy*.

401. *Lyctius Idomeneus. Idomeneus* is ſo called from *Lyctus*, a City in *Crete*, whence he being expelled, for the Reaſon above mentioned, came into this Part of *Italy*, and there planted a Colony. See Verſe 104.

401. *Melibœi parva, &c. Philoctetes*, the Son of *Pœas* King of *Melibœa*, a City of *Theſſaly*, at the Foot of Mount *Oſſa*. He ſet Fire to *Hercules*'s Funeral-Pile at that Hero's Requeſt, and received a Preſent from him of his Bow and Arrows, that were dipped in the poiſonous Blood of the Hydra of *Lerna*. He ſet out for *Troy* with the other *Greeks*, but was ſhamefully abandoned by them in *Lemnos*, becauſe of an ulcerated Wound he had got by the Bite of a Serpent. But, it being fated that *Troy* could not be taken without thoſe Arrows of *Hercules* which were in his Poſſeſſion, they were forced to recal him. After *Troy* was taken, hearing that the *Melibœans* had made a Revolt, he repaired to *Calabria*, and there built *Petilia*, or, according to others, fortified it with Walls.

405. *Velare comas.* It was cuſtomary for the *Romans* to cover their Heads in Sacrifice, and other Acts of Worſhip, to moſt of their Gods, as we learn from many Paſſages of the *Roman* Authors:

Invocat Deos immortales, ut ſibi auxilium ferant
Manibus puris, capite operto——

ſays *Plautus*, Amphit. Ac. V. Sc. 1. Verſe 41. And this Cuſtom they derive from *Æneas*.

411. *Rareſcent clauſtra Pelori. Pelorus*, or *Pelorum*, now *Capo di Faro*, is a Promontory on the eaſtern Point of *Sicily*, ſo nigh to *Italy*, that is ſaid by ſeveral Authors to have been once contiguous, and torn aſunder from it by an Earthquake,

Læva tibi tellus, et longo læva petantur
Æquora circuitu: dextrum fuge littus, et undas.
Hæc loca vi quondam, et vastâ convulsa ruinâ
(Tantum ævi longinqua valet mutare vetustas)
Dissiluisse ferunt: cum protinus utraque tellus
Una foret, venit medio vi pontus, et undis 417
Hesperium Siculo latus abscidit; arvaque, et urbes
Littore diductas angusto interluit æstu.
Dextrum Scylla latus, lævum implacata Charybdis 420
Obsidet; atque imo barathri ter gurgite vastos
Sorbet in abruptum fluctus, rursusque sub auras
Erigit alternos, et sidera verberat undâ.
At Scyllam cæcis cohibet spelunca latebris, 424
Ora exsertantem, et naves in saxa trahentem:
Prima hominis facies, et pulchro pectore virgo,
Pube tenus; postrema immani corpore pristis,

læva tellus et læva æquora petantur tibi longo circuitu, fuge dextrum littus et dextras undas. Ferunt hæc loca, quondam convulsa vi et vastâ ruinâ, dissiluisse, cum protinus utraque tellus foret una, pontus vi venit medio, et undis abscidit Hesperium latus Siculo latere, *æstuque angusto interluit arva et urbes diductas* à sese invicem *littore. Scylla obsidet dextrum latus, implacata Charybdis obsidet lævum, atque imo gurgite barathri ter sorbet vastos fluctus in abruptum, rursusque erigit eos alternos sub auras, et verberat sidera undâ. At spelunca cohibet* in *cæcis latebris Scyllam exsertantem ora, et trahentem naves in saxa. Prima facies* est *hominis, et virgo* cum *pulchro pectore, tenus pube: postrema* est *Pristis immani corpore,*

TRANSLATION.

open wider to the Eye, veer to the Land on the Left, and to the Sea on the Left by a long Circuit: Fly the Right *both* Sea and Shore. These Lands, they say, once with Violence and vast Desolation convulsed (such Revolutions long Tract of Time is able to produce) burst asunder; when in Continuity both Lands were one, the Sea rushed impetuously between, and by its Waves tore the Italian Side from that of Sicily; and *now* with a narrow Frith runs between the Fields and Cities separated by *different* Shores. Scylla guards the right Side, implacable Charybdis the Left, and thrice with the deep Eddies of its *voracious* Gulph swallows up the vast Billows into the broken Abyss, and again spouts them out by Turns high into the Air, and lashes the Stars with the Waves. As to Scylla, a Cave confines her within its dark recesses, reaching forth her Jaws, and sucking in Vessels upon the Rocks. First she presents a human Form, a lovely Virgin down to the Middle: Her lower Parts are those of a hideous Pristis, with

NOTES.

Earthquake, as *Virgil* here relates, though it is more probable that this Circumstance is fabulous. See the Description of *Sicily* in the *Universal History*. The *Claustra Pelori* are the Streights of *Messina*, which naturally open to the View, and grow more wide, the nearer one approaches to them.

420. *Scylla.* *Scylla* is a Rock in *Calabria*, opposite to *Charybdis*, both of them very dangerous to Ships; hence they are represented by the Poets as hideous devouring Monsters. *Virgil* gives us here the fabulous Description of *Scylla*, Verse 424. She was the Daughter of *Phorcus*, whom *Circe* is said to have transformed into this Monster, because she was her Rival. *Charybdis* again is given out to have been a rapacious Whore, who, having taken away *Hercules's* Oxen, was thunderstruck by *Jupiter*, and thrown into the Sea, where she was transformed into a devouring Whirlpool.

427. *Pristis.* The *Pristis* is a Fish commonly reckoned of the Whale-kind, of a prodigious Length. *Pliny* mentions some of them in the *Indian* Sea to have been two hundred Cubits in Length,

commissa quoad *caudas delphinum utero luporum. Præstat te cessantem lustrare metas Trinacrii Pachyni, et circumflectere longos cursus, quàm semel vidisse informem Scyllam sub vasto antro, et saxa resonantia cæruleis canibus. Præterea, si qua prudentia est Heleno vati, si qua fides* est ei, *si Apollo implet ejus animum veris*, O *nate Deâ, prædicam tibi illud unum præque omnibus, et repetens iterum iterumque* hoc te *monebo; primùm prece adora numen magnæ Junonis; libens cane vota Junoni, superaque potentem dominam supplicibus donis: sic denique* tu *mittere victor* ad *Italos fines, Trinacriâ relictâ. Ubi* tu *delatus huc accesseris Cumæam urbem, divinosque lacus, et Averna sonantia in sylvis;*

Delphinum caudas utero commissa luporum.
Præstat Trinacrii metas lustrare Pachyni
Cessantem, longos et circumflectere cursus,
Quàm semel informem vasto vidisse sub antro
Scyllam, et cæruleis canibus resonantia saxa.
Præterea, si qua est Heleno prudentia, vati
Si qua fides, animum si veris implet Apollo;
Unum illud tibi, nate Deâ, præque omnibus unum
Prædicam, et repetens iterumque iterumque monebo:
Junonis magnæ primùm prece numen adora;
Junoni cane vota libens, dominamque potentem
Supplicibus supera donis: sic denique victor
Trinacriâ fines Italos mittere relictâ.
Huc ubi delatus Cumæam accesseris urbem,
Divinosque lacus, et Averna sonantia sylvis;

TRANSLATION.

Dolphins Tails joined to the Wombs of Wolves. It is better with Delay to circuit round the Extremities of *the* Sicilian *Promontory* Pachynus, and steer a long winding Course, than once to view the misshapen Scylla under her capacious Den, and those Rocks that roar with her Sea-green Dogs. Farther, if Helenus has any Skill, if any Credit is due to *him as* a Prophet, if Apollo stores his Mind with Truth, I will give you this one previous Admonition, this one, O Goddess-born, above all the rest, and I will inculcate it upon you again and again: Be sure you, in the first place, with Supplications worship great Juno's Divinity: To Juno cheerfully in Hymns address your Vows, and vanquish the powerful Empress *of the Skies* with humble Offerings; thus at length, leaving Trinacria, you shall be dismissed victorious to the Territories of Italy. When wafted thither, you shall reach the City Cumæ, the hallowed Lakes, and *the Floods of* Avernus resounding through the Woods; you shall see the raving Prophetess, who, be-

NOTES.

Length. It is likewise called *Pistrix* by *Cicero*.

Et sparsam subter caudam pistricis albæsit.

The Name is derived from πρίςης, *Sector*, because they cut the Waves with wonderful Agility.

429. *Pachyni. Pachynum* is the southern Promontory of *Sicily*, now *Capo Passaro*.

432. *Canibus resonantia.* This explains the Reason why *Scylla* was represented as terminating in the Figure of Wolves or Dogs, because, according as the lower Parts of the Rock were struck with the Waves, hoarse growling Sounds were heard, like the Baying of Dogs, or Howling of Wolves.

441. *Cumæam urbem. Cumæ* was a City in *Italy*, on the *Campanian* Coast.

442. *Divinosque lacus.* The Lakes of *Lucrinus* and *Avernus* in *Campania*, near *Cumæ*, termed divine from their Vicinity to the Grot of the inspired *Sibyl*.

442. *Averna sonantia silvis.* The Lake *Avernus* was formerly environed with thick Woods, whereby, the Air not having free Access to purge away the Exhalations that arose from

Insanam vatem aspicies; quæ rupe sub imâ
Fata canit, foliisque notas, et nomina mandat.
Quæcunque in foliis descripsit carmina virgo,
Digerit in numerum, atque antro seclusa relinquit:
Illa manent immota locis, neque ab ordine cedunt.
Verùm eadem, verso tenuis cum cardine ventus
Impulit, et teneras turbavit janua frondes;
Nunquam deinde cavo volitantia prendere saxo,
Nec revocare situs, aut jungere carmina curat:
Inconsulti abeunt, sedemque odere Sibyllæ.
Hic tibi ne qua moræ fuerint dispendia tanti,
(Quamvis increpitent socii, et vi cursus in altum
Vela vocet, possisque sinus implere secundos)
Quin adeas vatem, precibusque oracula poscas
Ipsa canat, vocemque volens, atque ora resolvat.
Illa tibi Italiæ populos, venturaque bella,

aspicies insanam vatem quæ canit fata sub imâ rupe, mandatque notas et nomina foliis. Virgo digerit in numerum, atque relinquit seclusa in antro, quæcunque carmina descripsit in foliis: illa manent immota in locis, neque cedunt ab ordine. Verùm cum tenuis ventus impulit ea, cardine verso, et janua turbavit teneras frondes; nunquam deinde curat prendere ea volitantia in cavo saxo, nec revocare situs, aut jungere carmina. Abeunt inconsulti, odereque sedem Sibyllæ. Hic, ne qua dispendia moræ fuerint tibi tanti (quamvis socii increpitent, et cursus vocet vela in altum, possisque implere sinus secundos) quin adeas vatem, precibusque poscas ut ipsa canat oracula, volensque resolvat vocem atque ora. Illa expediet tibi populos Italiæ, bellaque ventura,

TRANSLATION.

neath a deep Rock, reveals the Decrees *of Heaven*, and commits to the Leaves of Trees her Characters and Words. Whatever Verses the Virgin has inscribed on the Leaves, she ranges in harmonious Order, and leaves in the Cave inclosed by themselves. Uncovered they remain in their Position, nor recede from their Order. But when, upon turning the Hinge, a small Breath of Wind has blown upon them, and the Door, *by opening*, hath discomposed the tender Leaves, she never afterwards gives herself the Trouble to catch the Verses as they are fluttering in the hollow Cave, nor to recover their Situation, or join them together. *Thus her Votaries* depart without a Response, and detest the Sibyl's Grot. Let not the Loss of some Time there seem of such Consequence to you (though your Friends chide *your Delay, the Necessities of* your Voyage strongly invite your Sails into the Deep, and you may have an Opportunity to fill the bellying Canvas with a prosperous Gale) as to hinder you from visiting the Prophetess, and earnestly intreating her to deliver the Oracles herself, and vouchsafe to open her Lips in vocal Accents. She will declare to you the Italian Nations, your future

NOTES.

from it, they became so foul and unwholesome, that it is said no Bird could fly over that Lake without being suffocated. Hence it got the Name of *Avernus*, quasi *aornos*, *inaccessible to Birds*, and, from its pestilential Quality, was taken for the Mouth of Hell, Æn. VI. 126.

Facilis descensus Averni.

443. *Insanam vatem.* *Insana*, here, is not to be taken in a bad Sense, it signifies *inspired with a divine Fury, extatic, and transported out of her Senses.*

453 *Hic tibi*, &c. I here follow the Pointing that is in *H. Stephens's* Edition, which connects *tanti* with *quin adeas*, and shuts up the two Lines that intervene in a Parenthesis. This makes the Construction easy, and the Sense clear.

et quo modo fugiasque ferasque quemque laborem, venerataque dabit tibi secundos cursus. Hæc sunt quæ liceat te moneri nostrâ voce. Age, vade, et factis tuis fer ingentem Trojam ad æthera.

Quæ postquam vates sic locutus est amico ore, dehinc imperat dona gravia ex auro sectoque elephanto ferri ad naves; stipatque in carinis ingens argentum, Dodonæosque lebetas, loricam consertam hamis, trilicemque auro: et conum insignis galeæ, cristasque comantes, arma Neoptolemi: sua dona sunt et meo parenti. Addit equos, additque duces. Supplet remigium; simul instruit socios armis. Interea Anchises jubebat aptare classem velis, ne qua mora fieret vento ferenti nos.

Et quo quemque modo fugiasque ferasque laborem,
Expediet; cursusque dabit venerato secundos.
Hæc sunt quæ nostrâ liceat te voce moneri.
Vade, age, et ingentem factis fer ad æthera Trojam.
Quæ postquam vates sic ore affatus amico est,
Dona dehinc auro gravia, sectoque elephanto,
Imperat ad naves ferri; stipatque carinis
Ingens argentum, Dodonæosque lebetas,
Loricam consertam hamis, auroque trilicem,
Et conum insignis galeæ, cristasque comantes,
Arma Neoptolemi: sunt et sua dona parenti:
Addit equos, additque duces.
Remigium supplet; socios simul instruit armis.
Interea classem velis aptare jubebat
Anchises, fieret vento mora ne qua ferenti.

TRANSLATION.

Wars, and by what Means you may shun or sustain every Hardship; and, with Reverence addressed, will give you a successful Voyage. These are all the Instructions I am at Liberty to give you. Go then, and by your Atchievements raise mighty Troy to Heaven. Which *Words*, when the Prophet had thus with friendly Accent pronounced, he orders Presents next of great Value to be carried to the Ships, consisting of Gold and Ivory; and within the Sides of my Vessel stows a large Quantity of Silver-plate, and Caldrons of Dodonean Brass, a Mail thick set with Rings, and wrought in Gold of triple Tissue; together with the Cone and waving Crest of a shining Helmet; Arms which belonged to Neoptolemus. My Father too has proper Gifts conferred on him. He gives us Horses besides, he gives us Guides: he supplies us with Rowers, and at the same Time furnishes our Crew with Arms. Meanwhile Anchises gave Orders to equip our Fleet with Sails, that we might not lose the favouring Gale. Whom the Inter-

NOTES.

460. *Venerata.* The Ancients used the active Verb *venero*, as in *Plautus in Trucul. Date mihi huc Stacten, atque ignem in aram, ut venerem Lucinam meam.*

466. *Dodonæosque lebetas.* i. e. Kettles of fine Brass, like that of *Dodona*, a City in *Epirus*, where *Jupiter* had a famous Oracle of great Antiquity. The Maner of delivering that Oracle was, we are told, by a certain Number of brass Kettles or Basons, which were contrived to hang contiguous to one another, so that the Motion of one might be communicated to all the rest; and from the Sounds they emitted the Meaning of the Oracle was gathered.

467. *Loricam consertam hamis.* The *Lorica* was a Cuirass or Coat of Armour for covering the Body from the Neck down to the Waist. It was at first composed of Leathern thongs, whence it got the Name of *Lorica*, from *lorum*, *a Thong*. Afterwards it was wrought with Iron *laminæ*, or thin Plates of Iron, with Hooks or Rings linked together, sometimes single, sometimes two-fold, sometimes three-fold. The two last were termed *bilix*, *trilix*.

467. *Hamis auroque.* i. e. *Hamis aureis*, *with Rings or Hooks of Gold*, as in the Georgics, *maculis insignis et albo*, for *maculis albis insignis*, *distinguished by white Spots*, Geor. III. 56.

476. *Bis*

Quem Phœbi interpres multo compellat honore:
Conjugio Anchisa Veneris dignate superbo,
Cura Deûm, bis Pergameis erepte ruinis,
Ecce tibi Ausoniæ tellus; hanc arripe velis:
Et tamen hanc pelago præterlabare necesse est.
Ausoniæ pars illa procul, quam pandit Apollo.
Vade, ait, O felix nati pietate. Quid ultra
Provehor, et fando surgentes demoror Austros?
Nec minus Andromache, digressu mœsta supremo,
Fert picturatas auri subtemine vestes,
Et Phrygiam Ascanio chlamydem: nec cedit honori:
Textilibusque onerat donis, ac talia fatur:
Accipe et hæc, manuum tibi quæ monumenta mearum
Sint, puer, et longum Andromachæ testentur amorem,
Conjugis Hectoreæ. Cape dona extrema tuorum.

Quem interpres Phœbi compellat multo honore: Anchisa dignate superbo conjugio Veneris, cura Deûm, bis erepte Pergameis ruinis; ecce tellus Ausoniæ est tibi; arripe hanc velis: et tamen necesse est ut præterlabare hanc pelago. Illa pars Ausoniæ, quam Apollo pandit tibi, est procul. Vade, ait, O felix pietate nati: quid ego provehor ultra, et fando demoror surgentes Austros? Nec minus Andromache, mœsta supremo digressu, fert vestes picturatas subtemine auri, et Phrygiam chlamydem Ascanio, nec cedit suo honori: Oneratque eum textilibus donis, ac fatur talia: O puer, accipe et hæc, quæ sint monumenta tibi mearum manuum, et testentur longum amorem Andromachæ Hectoreæ conjugis: cape extrema dona tuorum.

TRANSLATION.

preter of Apollo accosts with high Respect: Anchises, honoured with Venus's illustrious Bed, the Object of Heaven's *peculiar* Care, twice saved from the Ruins of Troy, lo there the Coast of Ausonia lies before you; thither speed your Way with full Sail: And yet you must steer your Course beyond that *Coast:* That Part of Ausonia which Apollo opens *to your Hope* lies remote. Go, says he, happy in the pious Duty of your Son: Why do I farther insist, and by my Discourse retard *you from enjoying* the rising Gales? In like Manner Andromache, grieved at our final Departure, brings forth to Ascanius Vestments wrought in Figures of Gold, and a Phrygian Cloak; nor falls short of her Dignity; she loads *the Boy besides* with Presents of her *Labours* in the Loom, and thus addresses him: Take these too, my Child, which may be Memorials to you of my Handy-work, and testify the permanent Affection of Andromache, the Spouse of Hector: Accept the last Presents of thy Friends: O *the dear* Image, which is all that I have

NOTES.

476. *Bis Pergameis erepte ruinis.* First, when Troy was taken by *Hercules*, and a second Time, when it was burnt by the *Greeks*.

483. *Subtemine auri. Subtemen* is properly *the Woof*, as *stamen* is *the Warp*.

484. *Phrygiam chlamydem.* i. e. *Of Needle-work*, an Art of which the *Phrygians*, according to *Pliny*, were the Inventors. The *Chlamys*, properly, was a military Garment, a Kind of Cassock or upper Vestment, which the General wore over his Corslet.

494. *Nec cedit honori.* This is capable of three Senses, for it may either signify that *Andromache* confers Gifts on *Ascanius* suitable to his Dignity, or that she is nothing short of the Honour conferred on *Æneas* and his Followers by her Husband: Or, lastly, that the Gifts are worthy of the Giver, and becoming her Quality, which is the Sense given in the Translation.

485. *Textilibus donis.* As the other Presents were of Needle-work, so these here are the Works she had wove in the Loom, in which it was usual for the Ladies of that Age to employ

O imago mei Aſtyanactis, quæ ſola ſuper eſt mihi: ſic ille ferebat oculos, ſic manus, ſic ora; et nunc pubeſceret æquali ævo tecum. Ego digrediens affabar hos, lacrymis obortis: Vivite felices vos quibus ſua fortuna jam eſt peracta: nos vocamur in alia fata ex aliis. Quies eſt parta vobis, nullum æquor maris vobis *arandum. neque arva Auſoniæ ſemper cedentia retro* vobis *quærenda: videtis effigiem Xanthi, Trojamque quam veſtræ manus fecere; opto, melioribus auſpiciis, et quæ fuerit minus obvia Graiis. Si quando intraro Tybrim arvaque vicina Tybridis, cernamque mœnia data meæ genti; faciemus urbeſque olim cognatas, populoſque propinquos ex Epiro, ex Heſperiâ, quibus idem Dardanus* fuit *auctor, atque idem* fuit *caſus. faciemus,* inquam, *utramque Trojam unam animis. Ea cura maneat noſtros nepotes.*

O mihi ſola mei ſuper Aſtyanactis imago!
Sic oculos, ſic ille manus, ſic ora ferebat:
Et nunc æquali tecum pubeſceret ævo.
Hos ego digrediens lacrymis affabar obortis:
Vivite felices, quibus eſt fortuna peracta
Jam ſua: nos alia ex aliis in fata vocamur.
Vobis parta quies; nullum maris æquor arandum;
Arva neque Auſoniæ, ſemper cedentia retro,
Quærenda. Effigiem Xanthi, Trojamque videtis,
Quam veſtræ fecere manus; melioribus, opto,
Auſpiciis, et quæ fuerit minus obvia Graiis.
Si quando Tybrim, vicinaque Tybridis arva
Intraro, gentique meæ data mœnia cernam;
Cognatas urbes olim, populoſque propinquos,
Epiro, Heſperiâ, quibus idem Dardanus auctor,
Atque idem caſus, unam faciemus utramque
Trojam animis. Maneat noſtros ea cura nepotes.

TRANSLATION.

now left of my Aſtyanax! Juſt ſuch Eyes, ſuch Hands, ſuch Looks he ſhewed: And now of equal Age with you would have been blooming into Youth. I, with Tears in my Eyes, thus addreſſed them at Parting: Live in *Joy and* Felicity, ye whoſe Fortune is now accompliſhed: We are ſummoned from Fate to Fate: To you Tranquillity is ſecured; no Expanſe of Sea have you to plough; nor to purſue the Lands of Auſonia ſtill flying *from us.* You *are bleſſed to* ſee the Image of Xanthus and Troy which your own Hands have built. Heaven grant it be with happier Auſpices, and be leſs obnoxious to the Greeks. If ever I ſhall enter the Tyber, and the Lands that border on the Tyber, and view the Walls allotted to my Race, we will hereafter make of our kindred Cities, and allied People, *yours* in Epirus, *and mine* in Italy, who have both the ſame Founder Dardanus, and the ſame Fortune: *we will, I ſay, make of* both one Troy in *mutual* Affection *and Good-will:* Be this the future Care of our Poſterity.

NOTES.

themſelves, as is evident from the noted Story of *Penelope*'s Web.

489. *O mihi ſolo,* &c. I take the Conſtruction to be thus: *O Imago, ſola ſuper,* i. e. *ſuperans,* or *quæ ſupereſt mihi, mei Aſtyanactis:* As *Valerius* ſays, *Nec ſpes ulla ſuper,* i. e. *ſupereſt.*

419. *Aſtyanactis.* The Story of *Aſtyanax* is thus: When the *Greeks,* after the Deſtruction of *Troy,* were hindered from returning Home by contrary Winds, *Calchas, that Prophet of Plagues,* declared that they muſt make a Sacrifice of *Aſtyanax,* the Son of *Hector* and *Andromache,* in regard that, if he grew up, he would prove a greater Hero than his Father, and avenge his Country's Woes. *Ulyſſes,* therefore, finding him where he had been concealed by his Mother, threw him down from the Wall, upon which the *Greeks* ſet ſail.

505. *Utramque Trojam.* By this we are to underſtand

Provehimur pelago vicina Ceraunia juxta ;
Unde iter Italiam, cursusque brevissimus undis.
Sol ruit interea, et montes umbrantur opaci.
Sternimur optatæ gremio telluris, ad undam,
Sortiti remos, passimque in littore sicco
Corpora curamus : fessos sopor irrigat artus.
Necdum orbem medium nox horis acta subibat ;
Haud segnis strato surgit Palinurus, et omnes
Explorat ventos, atque auribus aëra captat.
Sidera cuncta notat tacito labentia cœlo,
Arcturum, pluviasque Hyadas, geminosque Triones,
Armatumque auro circumspexit Oriona.
Postquam cuncta videt cœlo constare sereno,
Dat clarum è puppi signum : nos castra movemus,
Tentamusque viam, et velorum pandimus alas,
Jamque rubescebat stellis Aurora fugatis,

Provehimur pelago juxta vicina Ceraunia, unde iter, cursusque est brevissimus undis, in Italiam. Interea sol ruit, et opaci montes umbrantur. Sternimur gremio optatæ telluris, ad undam, sortiti remos, passimque curamus corpora in sicco littore: sopor irrigat nostros fessos artus. Necdum nox acta horis subibat medium orbem; Palinurus haud segnis surgit strato, et explorat omnes ventos, atque captat aëra auribus. Notat cuncta sidera labentia tacito cœlo, Arcturum, pluviasque Hyadas, geminosque Triones, circumspicitque Oriona armatum auro. Postquam videt cuncta constare in sereno cœlo, dat clarum signum è puppi: nos movemus castra, tentamusque viam, et pandimus alas velorum. Jamque Aurora rubescebat, stellis fugatis,

TRANSLATION.

We pursue our Voyage near the adjacent Ceraunian Mountains; whence lies our Way, and shortest Course by Sea to Italy. Meanwhile the Sun goes down, and the opaque Mountains are wrapped up in Shade. On the Bosom of the wished-for Earth we lay us down by the Waves, having distributed the Oars by Lot, and all along the dry Beech indulge ourselves in soft Repose: Sleep diffuses its *balmy* Dews over our weary Limbs. Night, driven by the *winged* Hours, had not yet reached her mid-way Course, *when* Palinurus springs alert from his Bed, examines every Wind, and lends his Ears to catch the *coming* Breeze: He observes every gliding Star in the silent Sky, Arcturus, the rainy Hyades, and the two northern Bears, and throws his Eyes around Orion armed with Gold. After he sees all Appearances of settled Weather in the serene Sky, he gives the loud Signal from the Stern. We decamp, attempt our Voyage, and expand the Wings of our Sails. And now, the Stars being chaced away, blushing Aurora appeared,

NOTES.

understand *Buthrotus*, the City of *Helenus* in *Epirus*, which bore a Resemblance to *Troy*, and was inhabited by a *Trojan* Colony, and the City which *Æneas* designed to build in *Italy*, and call by the Name of *Troy*.

506. *Ceraunia*. The *Ceraunia*, or *Acroceraunia*, as they are also called, are exceeding high Mountains that bound *Epirus* on the North; they have their Name from κεραυνὸς, *Thunder*, to which, by their Height, they are much exposed.

507. *Cursusque brevissimus*. The Distance between *Epirus* and *Italy* is not reckoned above seven hundred Furlongs, or one and twenty Miles.

517. *Armatum auro*. Because the Belt and Sword of the Constellation *Orion* are formed of very bright Stars, as in *Lucian*,

Ensiferi nimium fulget latus Orionis.

cùm procul videmus colles obscuros, humilemque Italiam. Achates primus conclamat Italiam; socii salutant Italiam læto clamore. Tum pater Anchises induit magnum cratera coronâ, implevitque eum mero, stansque in celsâ puppi vocavit Divos: O Dî, potentes maris et terræ tempestatumque, ferte nobis facilem viam vento, et spirate secundi. Optatæ auræ crebrescunt, portusque patescit jam propior, templumque Minervæ apparet in arce. Socii legunt vela, et torquent proras ad littora. Portus curvatur in arcum ab Eoo fluctu, cautes objectæ spumant salsâ aspergine; ipse latet: turriti scopuli demittunt brachia gemino muro, templumque refugit à littore. Hìc vidi in gramine primum omen, nempe *quatuor equos candore nivali tondentes campum latè.*

Cum procul obscuros colles humilemque videmus
Italiam. Italiam primus conclamat Achates;
Italiam læto socii clamore salutant.
Tum pater Anchises magnum cratera coronâ
Induit, implevitque mero; Divosque vocavit,
Stans celsâ in puppi.
Dî, maris et terræ tempestatumque potentes,
Ferte viam vento facilem, et spirate secundi.
Crebrescunt optatæ auræ; portusque patescit
Jam proprior, templumque apparet in arce Minervæ.
Vela legunt socii, et proras ad littora torquent.
Portus ab Eoo fluctu curvatur in arcum,
Objectæ salsâ spumant aspergine cautes;
Ipse latet; gemino demittunt brachia muro
Turriti scopuli; refugitque à littore templum.
Quatuor hìc, primum omen, equos in gramine vidi
Tondentes campum latè, candore nivali.

TRANSLATION.

when far off we spy the Hills obscure, and lowly Plains of Italy. Italy Achates first calls aloud; Italy the Crew with joyous Acclamations hail. Then Father Anchises decked a capacious Bowl with a Garland, and filled it up with Wine; and invoked the Gods, standing on the lofty Stern. Ye Gods, who rule Sea and Land, and Storms, grant us a prosperous Voyage by *a favourable* Wind, and breathe propitious. The wished-for Gales begin to swell; and now the Port opens nearer to our View, and on the Promontory appears the Temple of Minerva. Our Crew furl the Sails, and turn about their Prows to the Shore. Where the Waves break from the East, the Port bends into an Arch, the jutting Cliffs foam with the sparkling Brine; *the Port* itself lies hid: Two Turret-like Rocks stretch out their Arms *on either Side* in a double Wall, and the Temple recedes from the Shore. Here, on the grassy Meadow, I saw, as our first Omen, four Snow-white Steeds grazing the Plain at large; and my Father Anchises *calls out:*

NOTES.

525. *Coronâ induit.* To crown the Bowl; *vina coronare* sometimes signifies no more but to fill the Cup brim-full, as Æn. I. 728; but here it is to be taken literally for adorning the Bowl with Flowers, according to the ancient Custom, otherwise *implevitque mero* would be mere Tautology.

531. *Templum in arce Minervæ. Strabo* mentions a Temple of *Minerva*, on the Promontory of *Iapygium*, which probably is here designed.

536. *Refugit à littore.* i. e. Though at some Distance it appears just in the Port, yet, when you come nearer, the intervening Space between the Port and it widens, and it seems gradually to retire from the Shore.

537. *Primum omen.* They used carefully to observe the first Objects that offered to them at Landing in any Country where they designed to settle, and from thence drew Prognostics of their future good or bad Fortune.

549. *Cornua,*

Et pater Anchiſes: Bellum, ô terra hoſpita, portas;
Bello armantur equi; bellum hæc armenta minantur:
Sed tamen iidem olim curru ſuccedere ſueti
Quadrupedes, et fræna jugo concordia ferre:
Spes eſt pacis, ait. Tum numina ſancta precamur
Palladis armiſonæ, quæ prima accepit ovantes;
Et capita ante aras Phrygio velamur amictu:
Præceptiſque Heleni, dederat quæ maxima, ritè
Junoni Argivæ juſſos adolemus honores.
Haud mora, continuò perfectis ordine votis,
Cornua velatarum obvertimus antennarum;
Grajugenûmque domos, ſuſpectaque linquimus arva.
Hinc ſinus Herculei, ſi vera eſt fama, Tarenti
Cernitur: attollit ſe Diva Lacinia contra,
Cauloniſque arces, et navifragum Scylacæum.

Et pater Anchiſes ait: ô terra hoſpita, portas bellum; equi armantur bello; hæc armenta minantur bellum. Sed tamen iidem quadrupedes olim ſueti ſunt ſuccedere curru, et in jugo ferre concordia fræna: eſt, ait, ſpes pacis. Tum precamur ſancta numina Palladis armiſonæ, quæ prima accepit nos ovantes. Et velamur quoad capita Phrygio amictu, ante aras: præceptiſque Heleni, quæ dederat maxima, ritè adolemus juſſos honores Argivæ Junoni. Haud eſt mora, continuò, votis perfectis ordine, obvertimus cornua velatarum antennarum, linquimuſque domos Grajugenûm, arvaque ſuſpecta. Hinc cernitur ſinus Tarenti Herculei, ſi fama eſt vera: Diva Lacinia attollit ſe contra, arceſque Caulonis, et Scylacæum navifragum.

TRANSLATION.

War, O foreign Land, thou bringeſt *us*; for War-Steeds are harneſſed; War theſe Cattle threaten. But yet the ſame Quadrupeds have long been uſed to ſubmit to the Chariot, and in the Yoke to bear the peaceful Reins; Hope, *therefore*, there is of Peace, he ſays. Then we addreſs our Prayers to the ſacred Majeſty of Pallas with claſhing Arms arrayed, who firſt received us elated with Joy; and before her Altars we draw over our Heads a Phrygian Veil: And according to the Inſtructions given us by Helenus, on which he laid the greateſt Streſs, in due Form we offer up to Argive Juno the Honours enjoined. Without Loſs of Time, ſo ſoon as we had orderly fulfilled our Vows, we turn about the Extremities of our Sail-yards, and quit the Abodes and ſuſpected Territories of the Sons of Greece. Next appears the Bay of Tarentum, ſacred to Hercules, if common Report be true: And *on the* oppoſite *Side of the Bay the Temple of* the Lacinian Goddeſs emerges, the Towers of Caulon, and Scyllacæum the Coaſt of Shipwrecks.

NOTES.

549. *Cornua*, &c. *Fulvius Urſinus* brings this as an Example of a rhiming Verſe in *Virgil*; but in this he was miſtaken, as Dr. *Clarke* juſtly obſerves: For, there being an Eliſion of the laſt Syllable in *velatarum*, the Verſe runs off very ſmoothly thus:

Cornua velatar' obvertimus antennarum.

551. *Herculei Tarenti.* *Tarentum*, a famous City and Port in *Calabria*, called *Herculean*, either becauſe it was founded by *Phalantus*, one of *Hercules*'s Deſcendants, or becauſe that whole Territory was ſacred to *Hercules*, and the City *Tarentum* founded by himſelf, where he is ſaid by *Strabo* to have had a Coloſſus of Braſs in that City, the Work of the celebrated *Lyſippus*, which *Fabius Maximus* tranſported to *Rome*, and ſet up in the Capitol.

552. *Diva Lacinia.* The Temple of *Juno Lacinia*, near *Croton*, another City on the ſame *Calabrian* Coaſt. She had the Epithet of *Lacinia*, from the Promontory *Lacinium*, on which her Temple ſtood.

561. *Rudentum.*

Tum procul è fluctu Trinacria cernitur Ætna;
Et gemitum ingentem pelagi, pulsataque saxa
Audimus longè, fractasque ad littora voces:
Exsultantque vada, atque æstu miscentur arenæ.
Et pater Anchises: Nimirum hæc illa Charybdis;
Hos Helenus scopulos, hæc saxa horrenda canebat:
Eripite, O socii, pariterque insurgite remis.
Haud minus ac jussi faciunt; primusque rudentem
Contorsit lævas proram Palinurus ad undas:
Lævam cuncta cohors remis, ventisque petivit.
Tollimur in cœlum curvato gurgite; et iidem
Subductâ ad Manes imos descendimus undâ.
Ter scopuli clamorem inter cava saxa dedere;
Ter spumam elisam et rorantia vidimus astra.
Interea fessos ventus cum sole reliquit;
Ignarique viæ, Cyclopum allabimur oris.

Tum Trinacria Ætna procul cernitur è fluctu; et longè audimus ingentem gemitum pelagi, saxaque pulsata, vocesque fractas ad littora: vadaque exsultant, atque arenæ miscentur æstu. Et pater Anchises ait: Nimirum hæc est illa Charybdis: Helenus canebat hos scopulos, hæc horrenda saxa, O socii, eripite vos, pariterque insurgite remis. Illi faciunt haud minus ac jussi, Palinurusque primus contorsit rudentem proram ad lævas undas: cuncta cohors petivit lævam remis ventisque. Tollimur in cælum curvato gurgite, et iidem descendimus ad imos Manes, undâ subductâ. Scopuli ter dedere clamorem inter cava saxa; ter vidimus spumam elisam, et astra rorantia.

Interea ventus, cum sole, reliquit nos fessos; ignarique viæ, allabimur oris Cyclopum.

TRANSLATION.

Then at a Distance from the Waves is seen Trinacrian Ætna; and from afar we hear the loud Growling of the Ocean, the beaten Rocks, and broken Murmurs *rolling* to the Shore: The Shallows exult, and Sands are mingled with the *whirling* Tide. And, *says* my Father Anchises: Doubtless, this is the famed Charybdis: These the Shelves, these the hideous Rocks Helenus foretold. Get ye hence, my Friends, and with equal Ardour rise on your Oars. Just as commanded they obey: And first Palinurus whirled about the creaking Prow to the Left. The whole Crew with Oars and Sails bore to the Left. We mount up to Heaven on the arched Gulph, and down again we sink to the Shades below, the Wave having slipped from under us. Thrice the Rocks bellowed amid their hollow Caverns: Thrice we saw the Foam dashed up *from the Rocks*, and the Stars drenched with its dewy Moisture. Meanwhile the Wind with the Sun forsook us spent with Toil; and, not knowing our Course, we run upon the Coasts of the

NOTES.

561. *Rudentem.* Others read *rudente*, by which they understand a Cable or Rope that was fastened to the Helm of the Ship, wherewith they turned it which Way they would.

567. *Rorantia vidimus astra.* *Catrou* thinks this Hyperbole too bold, and therefore explains *astra* to mean nothing else but the Brine that descended in dewy Drops, that sparkle like Stars or Gems when struck by the Sun-beams.

568. *Interea ventus cum sole reliquit.* These Circumstances have a happy Effect to prepare the Reader for the ensuing terrible Description of Mount *Ætna.* The Winds are hushed, to make the Bellowings of the Mountain more distinctly heard, and Night is brought on, that in the dusky Sky the sulphureous Flames may be more conspicuous.

569. *Cyclopum oris.* The *Cyclops* were the first Inhabitants of *Sicily*, especially about Mount *Ætna.* They are said to have been of a gigantic Make, and of a savage Nature, cruel and inhospitable. Hence the Poets took Occasion to paint them of a monstrous Form, with only one great Eye in their Foreheads, and a Sort of Cannibals,

Portus ab acceſſu ventorum immotus, et ingens
Ipſe; ſed horrificis juxta tonat Ætna ruinis:
Interdumque atram prorumpit ad æthera nubem,
Turbine fumantem piceo, et candente favillâ;
Attollitque globos flammarum, et ſidera lambit:
Interdum ſcopulos, avulſaque viſcera montis
Erigit eructans, liquefactaque ſaxa ſub auras
Cum gemitu glomerant; fundoque exæſtuat imo.
Fama eſt, Enceladi ſemuſtum fulmine corpus
Urgeri mole hac, ingentemque inſuper Ætnam
Impoſitam, ruptis flammam exſpirare caminis:
Et, feſſum quoties mutat latus, intremere omnem
Murmure Trinacriam; et cœlum ſubtexere fumo.
Noctem illam tecti ſylvis immania monſtra
Perferimus; nec, quæ ſonitum det cauſa, videmus.

Portus eſt immotus ab acceſſu ventorum, et ipſe ingens; ſed juxta Ætna tonat horrificis ruinis, interdumque prorumpit ad æthera atram nubem, fumantem piceo turbine et candente favillâ; attollitque globos flammarum, et lambit ſidera: interdum eructans erigit ſcopulos avulſaque viſcera montis, glomeratque liquefacta ſaxa ſub auras, cum gemitu, exæſtuatque imo fundo. Fama eſt corpus Enceladi, ſemuſtum fulmine, urgeri hac mole, ingentemque Ætnam inſuper impoſitam exſpirare flammam ruptis caminis: Et, quoties mutat feſſum latus, omnem Trinacriam intremere murmure, et ſubtexere cælum fumo. Per illam noctem, nos tecti ſylvis perferimus immania monſtra nec videmus quæ cauſa det ſonitum.

TRANSLATION.

Cyclops. The port itſelf is ample, and undiſturbed by the Approach of the Winds; but, hard by, Ætna thunders with horrible Ruins, and ſometimes burſts forth to the Skies a black Cloud, aſcending in a pitchy Whirlwind of Smoke, and glowing Embers; throws up Globes of Flame, and kiſſes the Stars: Sometimes belching, flings on high the Ribs and ſhattered Bowels of the Mountain, and with a rumbling Noiſe in wreathy Heaps convolves in Air molten Rocks, and boils up from the loweſt Bottom. It is ſaid, that the Body of Enceladus, half conſumed with Lightning, is preſſed down with this Pile, and that cumbrous Ætna, laid above him, *is therefore ſtill* ſpouting forth Flames from its burſt Furnaces: And that, as often as he ſhifts his weary Side, all Trinacria, with a *deep* Groan, inly trembles, and overſpreads the Heaven with Smoke. Lying that Night under the Covert of the Woods, we ſuffer from thoſe hideous Prodigies; nor ſee what Cauſe produced the *dreadful* Sound; for neither had we the Light of

NOTES.

who fed on human Fleſh. From their Vicinity to Mount *Ætna*, they were alſo given out to be employed by *Vulcan* in forging *Jupiter*'s Thunderbolts. This Port of the *Cyclops*, where *Æneas* landed, is about that Shore where the City *Catana* now ſtands at the Foot of Mount *Ætna*.

571. *Ætna*. Now called *Mount-Gibel*, a famous Volcano in *Sicily*, not far from the eaſtern Shore.

578. *Fama eſt Enceladi*. As Poetry delights in the marvellous, *Virgil* here gives the fabulous Account of the Origin of this burning Mountain; which imports, that, in the War of the Giants with the Gods, *Enceladus*, the moſt formidable of them, was thunderſtruck by *Jove*, and buried under Mount *Ætna*, and that the Convulſions and Eruptions of the Mountain were the Effect of his ſhifting his Situation, and turning himſelf from the one Side to the other. *Ovid*, after *Pindar*, aſſigns *Typhœus* to this State of Puniſhment, Met. V. 340.

585. *Æthrâ*

Nam neque erant ignes astrorum, nec polus lucidus in sidereâ æthrâ; sed nubila in obscuro cælo, et intempesta nox tenebat lunam in nimbo.

Jamque postera dies surgebat primo Eoo, Auroraque dimoverat humentem umbram polo, cum subito nova forma viri, confecta suprema macie, ignota, miserandaque cultu, procedit è sylvis, supplexque tendit manus ad littora. Respicimus: dira illuvies erat ei, *barbaque immissa*, et *tegmen consertum spinis; at* quoad *cætera Graius, et quondam missus ad Trojam in patriis armis. Isque, ubi procul vidit Dardanios habitus et Troïa arma, paulùm hæsit conterritus aspectu, continuitque gradum: mox præceps tulit sese ad littora cum fletu precibusque:* O *Teucri, testor* vos *per sidera, per superos, atque hoc spirabile lumen cæli,*

Nam neque erant astrorum ignes, nec lucidus æthrâ
Sidereâ polus; obscuro sed nubila cœlo;
Et Lunam in nimbo nox intempesta tenebat.
Postera jamque dies primo surgebat Eoo,
Humentemque Aurora polo dimoverat umbram;
Cum subitò è silvis, macie confecta supremâ,
Ignoti nova forma viri, miserandaque cultu
Procedit; supplexque manus ad littora tendit.
Respicimus: dira illuvies, immissaque barba;
Consertum tegmen spinis; at cætera Graius,
Et quondam patriis ad Trojam missus in armis.
Isque ubi Dardanios habitus et Troïa vidit
Arma procul; paulùm aspectu conterritus hæsit,
Continuitque gradum: mox sese ad littora præceps
Cum fletu precibusque tulit. Per sidera testor,
Per Superos, atque hoc cœli spirabile lumen,

TRANSLATION.

the Stars, nor was the Sky enlightened from the starry Firmament; but *settled* Gloom all over the dusky Sky, and a Night of reigning Darkness muffled up the Moon in Clouds.

And now the next Day with the first Dawn was rising, and Aurora had dissipated the humid Shades from the Sky; when suddenly there bolts forth from the Woods a strange Figure of a Person unknown to us, emaciated to the last Degree, and in lamentable Plight; and, with the Air of a Suppliant, stretches forth his Hands to the Shore. We look back: *A Spectacle* he was of horrid Filth, his Beard over-grown, his Garment tagged with Thorns; but, in all besides, he was a Greek, and had formerly been sent to Troy accompanying the Arms of his Country. So soon as he spied at some Distance our Trojan Dress and Arms, struck with Terror at the Sight, he paused a while, and stopped his Progress: *Then*, in a Trice, flung headlong to the Shore with Tears and Prayers. I obtest you, *says he*, by the Stars, by the Powers above, by this celestial Light of Life, ye

NOTES.

585. *Æthrâ sidereâ. Cicero* defines *æthra* or *æther*, to be what we call the Firmament, or highest Part of the Heavens, where the fixed Stars are supposed to be placed: *Quem complexa summa pars cæli, quæ æthra dicitur*——*In æthere autem astra volvuntur.* De Nat. Deor. Lib. II. 45

587. *Nox intempesta.* Properly signifies *Midnight*, or *the darkest and deadest Time of the Night*; but here, I think, it denotes the Quality of that Night in particular, that one Face of thick Darkness prevailed through the whole Night, like what is usual at the Midnight-hour.

594. *Cætera.* That is, his Gait, his Mien, Complexion and Voice, bespoke him a *Greek*.

600. *Hoc cæli spirabile lumen.* This Light of Heaven, by which we live and breathe.

Tollite me, Teucri; quaſcunque abducite terras:
Hoc ſat erit. Scio me Danais è claſſibus unum,
Et bello Iliacos fateor petiiſſe Penates:
Pro quo, ſi ſceleris tanta eſt injuria noſtri,
Spargite me in fluctus, vaſtoque immergite ponto.
Si pereo, manibus hominum periiſſe juvabit.
Dixerat; et genua amplexus, genibuſque volutans
Hærebat. Qui ſit, fari, quo ſanguine cretus,
Hortamur; quæ deinde agitet fortuna, fateri.
Ipſe pater dextram Anchiſes, haud multa moratus,
Dat juveni; atque animum præſenti pignore firmat.
Ille hæc, depoſitâ tandem formidine, fatur:
Sum patriâ ex Ithacâ, comes infelicis Ulyſſei,

Tollite me; abducite in quaſcunque terras: Hoc erit ſat. [illegible] *me eſſe unum è Danais claſſibus, et fateor me petiiſſe Iliacos Penates bello. Pro quo, ſi injuria noſtri ſceleris eſt tanta, ſpargite me in fluctus, immergiteque in vaſto ponto. Si pereo manibus hominum, juvabit me periiſſe. Dixerat, et amplexus genua noſtra, volutanſque genibus, hærebat. Hortamur* eum, *fari qui ſit, quo ſanguine cretus; deinde fateri quæ fortuna agitet* eum. *Pater Anchiſes ipſe, haud moratus multa, dat dextram juveni, atque firmat animum* ejus hoc *præſenti pignore. Ille fatur hæc, formidine tandem depoſita: Sum ex patriâ Ithacâ, comes infelicis Ulyſſei,*

TRANSLATION.

Trojans, ſnatch me *hence*; convey me to any Climes whatever, I ſhall be ſatisfied. It is true, I am one who belonged to the Grecian Fleet, and, I confeſs, I bore Arms againſt the Walls of Troy: For which, if the Demerit of my Crime be ſo heinous, ſcatter my Limbs on the Waves, and bury them in the vaſt Ocean. If I die, I ſhall have the Satisfaction to die by the Hands of Men. He ſaid, and claſping our Knees, and wallowing on the Ground, clung to us. We urge him to ſpeak who he is, of what Family born; and next, to declare what *hard* Fortune purſues him. My Father Anchiſes frankly gives the Youth his right Hand, and fortifies his Mind by that kindly Pledge. At length, all Fear removed, he thus begins: I am a Native of Ithaca, a Companion of the unfortunate Ulyſſes,

NOTES.

602. *Scio.* As if he had ſaid, I am conſcious I have no juſt Claim to your Favour. I muſt rank myſelf among your Enemies, and have nothing but my Wretchedneſs to recommend me to you.

603. *Iliacos Penates.* As the *Penates* ſignify *the Houſhold Gods, the Gods of the Country,* hence the Word is put for the Houſes and Country itſelf, and every Thing which Men hold dear and ſacred; as Æn. I. 527.

Non nos aut ferro Libycos populare Penates
Venimus.

607. *Genua amplexus. Servius* obſerves that the ſeveral Members of the Body were conſecrated to particular Deities; as the Ear to *Memory*: Whence *Virgil* ſays,

Cynthius aurem vellit, et admonuit, Ecl. VI.

The Right-hand to *Faith*, and the Knees to *Mercy*; whence Suppliants were wont to graſp and embrace thoſe Parts of the Body.

611. *Præſenti pignore. Præſens* ſignifies ſometimes *favourable*, for the ſame Reaſon that *adſum* ſignifies *to favour*, or *to be propitious*: Thus the Word is uſed by *Virgil* in other Places, as Ecl. I. 41.

——————————*licebat*
Nec tam præſentes alibi cognoſcere Divos.

And Geo. I. 10.

Et vos agreſtum præſentia numina Fauni.

The Right-hand has been reckoned a Pledge of Friendſhip amongſt moſt Nations. A memorable Example of which we have in *Darius*, whom *Q. Curtius* repreſents dying with theſe Words in his Mouth: *Alexandro hoc fidei regiæ unicum*

dextræ

nomen est mihi *Achæmenides: profectus* sum *Trojam, Adamasto genitore paupere (utinamque* illa *fortuna mansisset mibi). Hic immemores socii deseruere me in vasto antro Cyclopis, dum trepidi linquunt crudelia limina. Domus* ejus *repletur sanie cruentisque dapibus, intus opaca, ingens: ipse* est *arduus, pulsatque alta sidera (Dî avertite talem pestem terris) nec est facilis visu, nec affabilis dictu ulli: Vescitur visceribus miserorum, et atro sanguine. Egomet vidi, cum* ille *resupinus in medio antro frangeret ad saxum duo corpora de nostro numero prensa magnâ manu, liminaque aspersa sanie natarent: vidi cum manderet* eorum *membra fluentia atro tabo, et tepidi artus tremerent sub dentibus.*

Nomine Achæmenides, Trojam genitore Adamasto
Paupere (mansissetque utinam fortuna) profectus.
Hìc me, dum trepidi crudelia limina linquunt,
Immemores socii vasto Cyclopis in antro
Deseruere. Domus sanie dapibusque cruentis,
Intus opaca, ingens: ipse arduus, altaque pulsat
Sidera (Dî talem terris avertite pestem)
Nec visu facilis, nec dictu affabilis ulli:
Visceribus miserorum, et sanguine vescitur atro.
Vidi egomet, duo de numero cum corpora nostro,
Prensa manu magnâ, medio resupinus in antro,
Frangeret ad saxum, sanieque aspersa natarent
Limina; vidi, atro cum membra fluentia tabo
Manderet, et tepidi tremerent sub dentibus artus:

TRANSLATION.

Achæmenides my Name; I went to Troy, my Father Adamastus being poor, but would to God I had never changed my State of Life! Here was I deserted in the huge Den of the Cyclop by my Companions, while in Hurry and Consternation they fly from his cruel Abodes, unconcerned *for me*. The Cell, *horrid* with Gore and bloody Banquets, within is gloomy *and* vast: *The Cyclop* himself, of towering Height, beats the Stars on high (Ye Gods avert such a Pest from the Earth), of *terrible* forbidding Aspect, and inaccessible to every Mortal: He feeds on the Entrails and purple Blood of Wretches *whom he has slain*. I myself beheld, when having grasped in his capacious Hand two of our Number, as he lay stretched on his Back in the Middle of the Cave, he dashed them against the Stones, and the bespattered Pavement floated with their Blood: I beheld, when he ground their Members distilling black Gore, and their throbbing Limbs qui-

NOTES.

dextræ pignus pro me dabis. Hæc dicentem, acceptâ Polystrata manu, vita destituit. See also *Justin*, Lib. II. Cap. 15.

615. *Paupere.* He mentions his Poverty as an Excuse for his going to War, it being Necessity that drove him to it, not Choice. *Sinon* pleads the same Excuse, *Æn.* II. 87.

Pauper in arma pater primis huc misit ab annis.

617. *Cyclopis in antro.* See *Homer's* Odyssey, IX. 105.

621. *Nec visu facilis, &c. Cujus possit etiam aspectus vix e sustineri*, says *Servius*: And to the same Purpose *H. Stephens*, *Cujus ne aspectus quidem facile quis sustineat.* Instead of *nec dictu affabilis ulli*, *Servius* and *Stephens* read *affabilis*, according to some ancient Copies; and the former explains it, *Sermone non explicabilis, hideous beyond the Power of Words to express.* But *affabilis* seems to agree better with the former Part of the Sentence, and *Macrobius* says it is borrowed from an Expression in *Attius's Philoctetes*: *Quem tueri contra, neque adfari queas. Whom you cannot bear to look upon, nor to accost.*

632. *Immensus,*

Haud impune quidem, nec talia passus Ulysses,
Oblitusve sui est Ithacus discrimine tanto:
Nam simul expletus dapibus, vinoque sepultus,
Cervicem inflexam posuit, jacuitque per antrum
Immensus, saniem eructans, ac frusta cruento
Per somnum commista mero; nos, magna precati
Numina, sortitique vices, unà undique circum
Fundimur, et telo lumen terebramus acuto
Ingens, quod torvâ solum sub fronte latebat,
Argolici clypei, aut Phœbeæ lampadis instar:
Et tandem læti sociorum ulciscimur umbras.
Sed fugite, O miseri, fugite, atque ab littore funem
Rumpite.

Haud quidem fecit id impune; nec Ulysses passus est talia, Ithacusve est oblitus sui in tanto discrimine. Nam simul ac, expletus dapibus sepultusque vino, posuit inflexam cervicem, immensusque jacuit per antrum, eructans saniem, ac frusta commixta cruento mero per somnum; nos, precati magna numina, sortitique vices, unà fundimur circum eum undique, et acuto telo terebramus ingens lumen quod solum latebat sub torvâ fronte, instar Argolici clypei aut Phœbeæ lampadis; et tandem læti ulciscimur umbras sociorum. Sed fugite vos, O miseri, fugite, atque rumpite funem ab littore.

TRANSLATION.

vered under his Teeth. Not with Impunity, it is true; such Barbarity Ulysses suffered not *to pass unrevenged*, nor was the Prince of Ithaca wanting to himself in that critical Hour. For so soon as *the Monster*, glutted with *his inhuman* Food, and buried in Wine, reposed his reclined Neck to Rest, and lay at his enormous Length along the Cave, disgorging Blood in his Sleep, and Gobbets intermixed with gory Wine; we, having implored the great Gods, and distributed our several Parts by Lot, pour in upon him on all Hands at once, and with our pointed Javelins bore out the huge single Eye which was sunk under his lowring Front, like a Grecian Buckler, or the solar Orb; and *thus* at length we joyfully avenge the Manes of our Friends. But fly, ah Wretches! fly, and tear the Cables from

NOTES.

632. *Immensus*. Others read *immensum*, but the former is more elegant and harmonious.

635. *Terebramus*. *Donatus* thinks it should be read *tenebramus*, *we extinguish the Light of his Eye*; a Word which he thinks denotes the Quickness and Celerity of their Action. But *tenebramus* is one of *Virgil*'s Words; and *Homer*, whom he copies in this Description, expresly mentions the Circumstance of boring out the Monster's Eye, and compares the Action of *Ulysses* and his Companions, to that of a Carpenter boring a huge Beam with a Wimble.

636. *Latebat*. It was hid, because his Eye was shut in Sleep, as *Servius* justly observes; a sufficient Answer to those who object how it could possibly be concealed when it was as large as the Sun's Orb.

636. *Solum sub fronte*. Those who would see the Rise of this Fiction, may consult *Banier*'s *Mythology*, Vol. IV. P. 290, *&c.* of the *English*. Some allegorize this Circumstance of their having but one Eye; *Eustathius* particularly says, it figures that in Anger, or any other violent Passion, Men see but one single Object, as that Passion directs, or see but with one Eye; and that Passion transforms us into a Kind of Savages, and makes us brutal and sanguinary like this *Polypheme*: And he, that by Reason extinguishes such a Passion, may, like *Ulysses*, be said to put out that Eye. See Mr. *Pope*'s Notes on Odyssey IX. Verse 119. Others tell us, that *Polypheme* was a Man of uncommon Wisdom and Penetration, who is therefore represented having an Eye in his Forehead, near the Brain, to denote his superior Prudence and Sagacity; but that *Ulysses* outwitted him, and was said, for that Reason, to put out his Eye.

637. *Argolici clypei*. The Grecian Bucklers were large enough to cover the whole Body. Hence *Homer* gives them the Epithet ἀμφιβρότη, *that covers the whole Man*: And, as they were round, this Comparison denotes both the Figure and Magnitude of his Eye.

639. *Miseri*. He calls them miserable, in being exposed to such Danger.

Nam qualis quantusque Polyphemus claudit lanigeras pecudes in cavo antro, atque pressat ubera; centum alii tales infandi Cyclopes vulgo habitant ad hæc curva littora, et errant in *altis montibus. Tertia cornua lunæ jam complent se lumine, cum traho vitam in sylvis, inter deserta lustra domosque ferarum, prospicioque vastos Cyclopes ab rupe, tremiscoque sonitum pedum vocemque. Rami dant* mihi *victum infelicem,* nempe *baccas, lapidosaque corna, et herbæ pascunt me vulsis radicibus. Collustrans omnia, primùm conspexi hanc classem venientem ad littora; addixi me huic, quæcunque fuisset; satis est* mihi *effugisse nefandam gentem. Vos potius absumite hanc animam quocunque leto.*

Vix fatus erat ea, cum videmus in summo monte pastorem Polyphemum ipsum moventem se vastâ mole inter pecudes,

Nam qualis quantusque cavo Polyphemus in antro
Lanigeras claudit pecudes, atque ubera pressat;
Centum alii curva hæc habitant ad littora vulgo
Infandi Cyclopes, et altis montibus errant.
Tertia jam Lunæ se cornua lumine complent,
Cum vitam in silvis, inter deserta ferarum
Lustra domosque, traho, vastosque ab rupe Cyclopas
Prospicio, sonitumque pedum, vocemque tremisco.
Victum infelicem, baccas, lapidosaque corna
Dant rami, et vulsis pascunt radicibus herbæ.
Omnia collustrans, hanc primùm ad littora classem
Conspexi venientem; huic me, quæcunque fuisset,
Addixi: satis est gentem effugisse nefandam.
Vos animam hanc potius quocunque absumite letho.
Vix ea fatus erat, summo cum monte videmus
Ipsum inter pecudes vastâ se mole moventem

TRANSLATION.

the Shore. For such and so vast as Polyphemus pens in his hollow Cave the fleecy Flocks, and drains their Dugs, a hundred other direful Cyclops commonly haunt these winding Shores, and roam on the lofty Mountains. The horned Moon is now filling up her Orb for the third Time, while in these Woods, among the desert Dens and Holds of wild Beasts, I linger out my Life, and descry from the Rock the enormous Cyclops, and quake at *every* Sound of their Feet and Voice. The Berries and stony Cornels, which the Branches supply, is my wretched Sustenance, and the Herbs feed me with their plucked up Roots. Casting my Eyes around on every Object, this Fleet I spied first steering to the Shore: To it I was resolved to give up myself, whatever it had been: It suffices me, that I have escaped from that horrid Crew. Do ye destroy this Life by any Sort of Death, rather *than leave me to their Mercy.* Scarce had he spoke, when on the Summit of the Mountain we see the Shepherd Polyphemus himself, stalking

NOTES.

645. *Tertia jam Lunæ,* &c. Literally, *The Horns of the Moon are filling themselves up with Light for the third Time.*

653. *Addixi.* This Word strongly marks his State of Despair; it signifies that he made over himself to them as their Property, that they might dispose of him in whatever Manner they pleased; being one of the three Words pronounced by the *Roman* Prætor, when he determined a controverted Right, *do, dico, addico.*

659. *Trunca*

Paſtorem Polyphemum, et littora nota petentem :
Monſtrum horrendum, informe, ingens, cui lumen ademtum.
Trunca manum pinus regit, et veſtigia firmat :
Lanigeræ comitantur oves ; ea ſola voluptas,
Solamenque mali : *ac collo fiſtula pendet.*
Poſtquam altos tetigit fluctus, et ad æquora venit ;
Luminis effoſſi fluidum lavit inde cruorem,
Dentibus infrendens gemitu : graditurque per æquor
Jam medium, nec dum fluctus latera ardua tinxit.
Nos procul inde fugam trepidi celerare, recepto
Supplice, ſic merito ; tacitique incidere funem :
Verrimus et proni certantibus æquora remis.
Senſit, et ad ſonitum vocis veſtigia torſit.
Verùm ubi nulla datur dextram affectare poteſtas,
Nec potis Ionios fluctus æquare ſequendo ;

et petentem nota littora : monſtrum horrendum, informe, ingens, cui lumen eſt ademtum. Trunca pinus regit manum, et firmat ejus veſtigia : Lanigeræ oves comitantur eum, ea eſt ſola voluptas illi, ſolamenque mali : fiſtula pendet de collo ejus. Poſtquam tetigit altos fluctus, et venit ad æquora ; lavit inde fluidum cruorem effoſſi luminis, infrendens dentibus, cum gemitu ; jamque graditur per medium æquor, nec dum fluctus tinxit ejus *ardua latera. Nos trepidi* cœpimus *celerare fugam procul inde, ſupplice recepto, ſic merito* à nobis, *tacitique* cœpimus *incidere funem ; et proni verrimus æquora certantibus remis.* Polyphemus *ſenſit* hoc, *et torſit veſtigia ad ſonitum vocis : verùm ubi nulla poteſtas datur affectare dextram, nec potis* eſt *æquare Ionios fluctus ſequendo* nos,

TRANSLATION.

with his enormous Bulk among his Flocks, and making towards the Shore, his uſual Haunt : A horrible Monſter, misſhapen, vaſt, of Sight deprived. The Trunk of a Pine guides his Hand, and firms his Steps. His fleecy Sheep accompany him ; this his ſole Delight, and the Solace of his Diſtreſs ; *From his Neck his Whiſtle hangs.* After he touched the deep Floods, and arrived at the Sea, he therewith waſhes away the trickling Gore from his quenched Orb, gnaſhing his Teeth with a Groan : And now he ſtalks through the Midſt of the Sea, while the Waves have not yet wet his gigantic Sides. We, in hurrying Conſternation, haſten our Departure far from that Shore, having received our Suppliant, who thus merited our Favour : we ſilently cut the Cable, and, bending forward, ſweep the Sea with ſtruggling Oars. He perceived, and at the Sound turned his Steps. But when it is quite out of his Power to reach us with his eager Graſp, and himſelf unable in purſuing us to equal the Ionian Waves, he raiſes a prodigious Yell,

NOTES.

659. *Trunca manum pinus regit.* This is *Virgil*'s ingenious Way of giving us an Idea of *Polyphemus*'s gigantic Size. From the enormous Staff he wields in his Hand, we are left to imagine the Strength and Dimenſions of his Body : *Nam quod illud corpus mente concipiam,* ſays *Quintilian, cujus trunca manum pinus regit ?*

661. *De collo fiſtula pendet.* Theſe Words ſeem ſpurious ; *Donatus* rejects them ; they are not in *Heinſius*, and ſome other Editions, nor is there the leaſt Mention of this Circumſtance in *Homer.*

669. *Ad ſonitum vocis.* This may either refer to the Sound of their Voices ; for though it is ſaid they went off *taciti*, this can only mean with little Noiſe ; for it was impoſſible but ſome muſt ſpeak to give the neceſſary Orders ; or, in general, to the Noiſe of their Oars, &c. for *vox* ſometimes ſignifies any Sound whatever.

670. *Dextram affectare.* This is a very uncommon Phraſe ; *Servius* explains it, *anxia quadam aviditate manum ad navem injicere, eagerly to graſp at the Ship.* Some ancient Copies read *dextra attrectare*, in which there is no Difficulty.

[illegible]

tollit immensum clamorem, quo pontus et omnes undæ intremuere, tellusque Italiæ penitus est exterrita, Ætnaque immugiit curvis cavernis. At genus Cyclopum, excitum è silvis et altis montibus, ruit ad portus, et complent littora. Cernimus Ætnæos fratres astantes nequicquam torvo lumine, ferentes alta capita cœlo; horrendum concilium: tales quales cum aëriæ quercus, aut coniferæ cyparissi constiterunt celso vertice, alta silva Jovis, lucusve Dianæ. Acer metus agit socios præcipites excutere rudentes quocunque, et intendere vela secundis ventis. Contra, jussa Heleni monent, ni teneant cursus inter utramque viam, nempe *Scyllam atque Charybdim, parvo discrimine lethi:*

Clamorem immensum tollit, quo pontus, et omnes
Intremuere undæ, penitusque exterrita tellus
Italiæ, curvisque immugiit Ætna cavernis.
At genus è silvis Cyclopum et montibus altis
Excitum ruit ad portus, et littora complent.
Cernimus astantes nequicquam lumine torvo
Ætnæos fratres, cœlo capita alta ferentes;
Concilium horrendum: quales cum vertice celso
Aëriæ quercus, aut coniferæ cyparissi
Constiterunt, silva alta Jovis, lucusve Dianæ.
Præcipites metus acer agit quocunque rudentes
Excutere, et ventis intendere vela secundis.
Contra, jussa monent Heleni Scyllam atque Charybdim,
Inter utramque viam, lethi discrimine parvo,

TRANSLATION.

wherewith the Sea and every Wave deeply trembled, and Italy, to its inmost Bounds, was frighted, and Ætna bellowed through its winding Caverns. Meanwhile the Race of the Cyclops, roused from the Woods and lofty Mountains, rush to the Port, and crowd the Shore. We see the Ætnean Brothers, standing with their one Eye, louring *Terrors on us* in vain, [illegible]ing their Heads aloft to Heaven; a horrid Assembly: As when aerial Oaks, or Cone-bearing Cypresses, Jove's lofty Wood, or Diana's Grove, together rear their towering Tops. Violent Fear impels our Crew to tack about to any Quarter whatever, and spread their Sails to any Wind that would favour their Escape. On the other Hand, the Commands of Helenus warn them not to continue their Course between Scylla and Charybdis, a Path which borders on Death on either Hand: Our Resolution

NOTES.

680. *Coniferæ cyparissi.* The Fruit of the Pines and Cypresses is called *Cones*, because they grow in the Shape of a *Cone*.

681. *Constiterunt.* Some read *constiterant* for the sake of the Quantity; but there is no Need of that Alteration; for *Virgil* generally shortens the penult Syllable in those Tenses, as

Obstupui steteruntque comæ, &c.
Matri longa decem tulerunt fastidia menses.

683. *Ventis intendere vela secundis.* i. e. says *Donatus*, to sail wherever the Winds would carry them; for all Winds are favourable, if we follow their Impulse.

683. *Contra, &c.* I am inclined to think this whole Sentence is wrong pointed, and that it ought to be thus:

Contra, jussa monent Heleni Scyllam atque Charybdim:
Inter utramque viam, lethi discrimine parvo,
Ni teneant cursus, certum est dare lintea retro,

And then the Construction will be: *Contra jussa Heleni monent Scyllam atque Charybdim.* On the other Hand, *Helenus's* Instructions warn us to beware of *Scylla* and *Charybdis*: Therefore *ni teneant* (perhaps *teneam*, in the first Person, as *prætervehor*, Verse 688) *cursus inter utramque viam, parvo discrimine lethi, &c.* That we may not continue our Course so as to border on Death, or run the imminent Hazard of Destruction between both, *viz. Polyphemus* on the one Hand, and *Scylla* and *Charybdis* on the other, it is resolved to sail backward.

685. *Inter utramque viam.* See the former Note.

685. *Ni teneant cursus.* Some Copies have *ne*; however, *ni* often signifies the same with *ne*, particularly in *Plautus*, and the more ancient *Roman* Authors.

685. *Certum est dare lintea retro.* That is, they are resolved to steer a backward Course for *Italy*,

Ni teneant cursus: certum est dare lintea retro.
Ecce autem Boreas angustâ ab sede Pelori
Missus adest. Vivo prætervehor ostia saxo
Pantagiæ, Megarosque sinus, Tapsumque jacentem.
Talia monstrabat relegens errata retrorsum
Littora Achæmenides, comes infelicis Ulyssei.
Sicanio prætenta sinu jacet insula contra
Plemmyrium undosum; nomen dixere priores
Ortygiam. Alpheum fama est huc Elidis amnem
Occultas egisse vias subter mare; qui nunc
Ore, Arethusa, tuo Siculis confunditur undis.

certum est dare lintea retro.

Ecce autem Boreas missus ab angustâ sede Pelori adest: prætervehor ostia Pantagiæ e vivo saxo, Megarosque sinus, jacentemque Tapsum. Achæmenides, comes infelicis Ulyssei, monstrabat nobis talia, relegens littora retrorsum errata.

Insula jacet prætenta Sicanio sinu contra undosum Plemmyrium: priores dixere nomen ejus Ortygiam. Fama est Alpheum, amnem Elidis, egisse occultas vias huc subter mare; qui amnis nunc confunditur Siculis undis, tuo ore, O Arethusa.

TRANSLATION.

therefore is to sail backward. And lo the North-wind commissioned from the narrow Seat of Pelorus comes to our Aid. I am wafted beyond the Mouth of Pantagia *fringed* with living Rock, the Bay of Megara, and low-lying Tapsus. These Achæmenides, the Associate of accursed Ulysses, pointed out to us, as backward he cruized along those Coasts that were the Scene of his *former* Wanderings.

Before the Sicilian Bay outstretched lies an Island opposite to rough Plemmyrium: The Ancients called its Name Ortygia. 'Tis said, that Alpheus, a River of Elis, hath hither worked a secret Channel under the Sea: Which *River disembeguing* by thy Mouth, O Arethusa, is now blended with the Sicilian Waves.

NOTES.

Italy, by sailing round *Sicily*, according to *Helenus*'s Admonition.

Præstat Trinacrii metas lustrare Pachyni
Cessantem, longos et circumflectere cursus, &c.
Verse 429.

688. *Missus adest.* As they were resolved to sail backward, the North-wind favoured this their Design; and therefore *Æneas* speaks of *Boreas*, the North-wind, as a Person sent or commissioned from Heaven to befriend and assist him.

687. *Pelori. Pelorus*, now *Capo di Faro*, is a northern Promontory of *Sicily*, next to *Italy*: it is called *Angusta*, on account of the Streights that there divide *Sicily* from *Italy*, which are but about a Mile and a Half over.

689. *Pantagiæ. Pantagia*, or *Pantagias*, a River between *Catana* and *Syracuse*; the Mouth of it is inclosed on either Side with a steep Rock.

689. *Tapsumque jacentem. Tapsus* is a Peninsula in the Bay of *Megara*, which lies low, and almost level with the Waves.

690. *Relegens retrorsum.* We have a parallel Passage to this in *Horace*, Carm. Lib. I. Ode XXXIV. 3. where, according to Dr. *Bentley*'s ingenious Correction, *iterare* is joined with *cursus relectos*, as here we have *retrorsum relegens*:

—————— ——————nunc retrorsum
Vela dare, atque iterare *cursus*
Cogor relectos.

Instead of *relictos* in the common Editions.

690. *Errata retrorsum.* According to the Opinion of those who make *Ulysses* to have sailed from the Country of the *Lotophagi* in *Africa*, to Mount *Ætna*, and the Territory of the *Cyclops*, along the eastern Coast of *Sicily*.

691. *Infelicis Ulyssei. Infelix* here has the same Signification as Verse 246, on which see the Note.

693. *Plemmyrium.* A Promontory not far from *Syracuse*; between which City and the Promontory lay the Island here called *Ortygia*.

694. *Alpheum. Alpheus*, a celebrated River in the *Peloponnesus*, taking its Rise from Mount *Stymphalus*, and running through *Arcadia* and *Elis*.

696. *Arethusa.* A Fountain in the west Side of the Island *Ortygia*. The Poets feign, that

2 *Alpheus,*

Nos ut jussi veneramur magna numina loci: et inde exsupero præpingue solum stagnantis Helori. Hinc radimus altas cautes projectaque saxa Pachyni; et procul apparet Camarina nunquam concessa fatis moveri, campique Geloi, immanisque Gela, dicta cognomine fluvii: inde arduus Acragas, quondam generator magnanimûm equorum, longè ostentat maxima mœnia. Ventisque datis, linquo te, O palmosa Selinus: et lego Lilybeïa vada dura cæcis saxis. Hinc portus et illætabilis ora Drepani accipit me,

Jussi numina magna loci veneramur: et inde
Exsupero præpingue solum stagnantis Helori.
Hinc altas cautes projectaque saxa Pachyni
Radimus; et fatis nunquam concessa moveri
Apparet Camarina procul, campique Geloi,
Immanisque Gela, fluvii cognomine dicta.
Arduus inde Acragas ostentat maxima longè
Mœnia, magnanimûm quondam generator equorum.
Teque datis linquo ventis, palmosa Selinus;
Et vada dura lego saxis Lilybeïa cæcis.
Hinc Drepani me portus et illætabilis ora

TRANSLATION.

We venerate the great Divinities of the Place as commanded; and thence I pass the too luxuriant Soil of the overflowing Helorus. Hence we skim along the high Cliffs and prominent Rocks of Pachynus, and at a Distance appears *the Lake* Camarina, by Fate forbid to be ever removed, the Geloian Plains, and huge Gela, called by the Name of the River. Next towering Agragas shews from far its stately Walls, once the Breeder of generous Steeds, and thee, Selinus, fruitful in Palms, I leave, by Means of the given Winds; and I trace my Way through the Shallows of Lilybeum, dangerous by *reason of many* latent Rocks. Hence the Port and unjoyous Coast of Drepanum receives me: Here, alas!

NOTES.

Alpheus, the River God, being in Love with this Fountain-Nymph, rolled his Streams from *Elis* by a Passage under the Ground, and passed through the Sea, without intermixing, into *Sicily*, where he rose up with the Fountain *Arethusa*, and mingled his Streams with hers. What makes this Fable more absurd is, the Distance between the *Peloponnesus* and *Sicily*, which is at least 450 Miles.

698. *Stagnantis Helori. Helorus*, or *Elorus*, is a River in *Sicily*, that runs between *Syracuse* and the Promontory of *Pachynus*. It overflows all the Fields about at certain Seasons, like the *Nile*, to which the Fertility and Fatness of the Soil here mentioned was owing.

699. *Pachyni. Pachynus*, or *Pachynum*, is the southern Promontory of *Sicily*, now called *Capo Passero*, or *Passaro*, one of the three, whence it is denominated *Trinacria*.

701. *Camarina*. A Lake near a City of the same Name, built by the People of *Syracuse*. It is said, *fatis nunquam concessa moveri*, because, in Time of Plague, which was thought to arise from the pestilential Vapours of that Lake, the Inhabitants, being designed to drain it, consulted the Oracle of *Apollo*, who forbad them to move or disturb it; μη κινει Καμαριναν, ακινητος γαρ αμεινων. Notwithstanding which Prohibition, they drained the Lake, and had Cause to repent it afterwards; for the Enemy, entering by that Ground where the Lake had stood, made themselves Masters of their City.

704. *Magnanimûm generator equorum. Servius* quotes *Pindar* in Proof of the *Agrigentines* having been famous for sending Horses to the *Olympic* Games. Their City *Agrigentum*, or *Agragas*, was on the southern Coast of *Sicily*, at the Mouth of the River *Agragas*, formerly one of the largest Cities in the Island: It is called *Arduus*, because it was built on the Summit of a Mountain.

705. *Palmosa Selinus*. A City on the same Coast, whose Plains abounded with Palm-trees.

706. *Vada Lilybeïa. Lilybeum* was another of the three Promontories of *Sicily*, whence it had its Name *Trinacria*. It lies on the western Point of the Island; its Rocks run out into the Sea, to the Distance of three Miles, and are covered with the Waves; whence *Virgil* mentions its stony Shallows and hidden Rocks, *vada dura saxis cæcis*.

707. *Drepani. Drepanum*, now *Trepani*, a maritime Town in *Sicily*, that lies northward from

Accipit. Hìc, pelagi tot tempeſtatibus actus,
Heu! genitorem, omnis curæ caſuſque levamen,
Amitto Anchiſen. Hìc me, pater optime, feſſum
Deſeris, heu! tantis nequicquam erepte periclis.
Nec vates Helenus, cum multa horrenda moneret,
Hos mihi prædixit luctus; non dira Celæno.
Hìc labor extremus, longarum hæc meta viarum.
Hinc me digreſſum veſtris Deus appulit oris.
Sic pater Æneas, intentis omnibus, unus
Fata renarrabat Divûm, curſuſque docebat.
Conticuit tandem, factoque hìc fine quievit.

Hic, actus tot tempeſtatibus pelagi, heu! amitto Anchiſen genitorem, levamen omnis curæ caſuſque: hic, O optime pater! tu deſeris me feſſum, heu! erepte tantis periclis nequicquam. Nec vates Helenus, cum moneret me multa horrenda, prædixit mihi hos luctus; non dira Celæno prædixit. *Hic* eſt meus *labor extremus, hæc meta* mihi *longarum viarum. Deus appulit me veſtris oris digreſſum hinc.*

Sic pater Æneas, omnibus intentis, unus renarrabat fata Divûm, docebatque ſuos curſus: tandem conticuit, quievitque fine facto hic.

TRANSLATION.

after being toſſed by ſo many Storms at Sea, I loſe my Sire Anchiſes, my Solace in every Care and Suffering: Here thou, beſt of Fathers, whom in vain, alas! I ſaved from ſo great Dangers, *here thou* forſakeſt me ſpent with Toils. Neither prophetic Helenus, when he gave me many dreadful Intimations, nor execrable Celæno, foretold me of this mournful Stroke. This was my finiſhing Diſaſter, this the Termination of my long tedious Voyage. Parting hence, a God directed me to your Coaſts.

Thus Father Æneas, while all ſat attentive, he the only Speaker, recounted the Deſtiny allotted to him by the Gods, and gave a Hiſtory of his Voyage: He ceaſed at length, and here, having finiſhed his Relation, retired to Reſt.

NOTES.

from the Promontory of *Lilybæum*, at the Diſtance of about eighteen Miles. It is called *illætabilis ora, an unjoyous Coaſt*, becauſe here *Æneas* loſt his Father.

709. *Genitorem amitto.* In this *Virgil* differs from *Strabo*, who makes *Æneas* to have arrived at *Laurentum* with his Father *Anchiſes*, and his Son *Aſcanius*.

The End of the First Volume.

www.ingramcontent.com/pod-product-compliance
Lightning Source LLC
Chambersburg PA
CBHW021338110726
47900CB00005B/1520

* 9 7 8 3 3 3 7 3 6 7 9 9 2 *